THE
ARCHER'S HEART

THE
ARCHER'S HEART

BY
ASTRID AMARA

Blind Eye Books
blindeyebooks.com

The Archer's Heart
by Astrid Amara

Published by:
Blind Eye Books
1141 Grant Street
Bellingham, Washington 98225
blindeyebooks.com

Edited by Nicole Kimberling
Cover art, illustrations. and maps by Dawn Kimberling
Proofreading by Tenea D. Johnson

This book is a work of fiction and as such all characters and situations are fictional. Any resemblances to actual people, places or events are coincidental.

First edition September 2008
Copright © 2008 Astrid Amara
Printed in the United States of America

ISBN 978-0-9789861-3-1
Library of Congress Control Number: 2008922267

This book is dedicated to Angus.

MARHAVAD

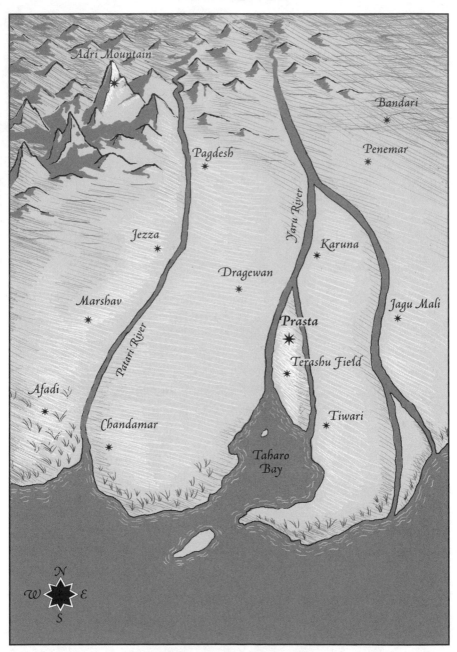

CONTENTS

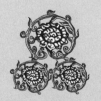

CHAPTER 1

AFTER FIVE YEARS IN EXILE, THE CITY OF PRASTA'S VIBRANCY overwhelmed Keshan Adaru's senses. The sweltering streets boomed with festival music. Craftsmen and dancers mingled with pickpockets and scam artists and animal herders as they all plied their trades in the tight crowds. As Keshan drew in a breath of the humid air, the aromas of cheese, curry and roasting chicken mingled with the scent of a thousand holy juniper wood fires to make the city smell, for that one afternoon, sacred. Yet the sheer noise of the festival transformed what was considered a pious city into a place where the hot monsoon hung low and damp with the weight of unbridled revelry.

The annual monsoon festival had swollen Prasta's already burgeoning population. City hostels overflowed and the wide streets teemed with men and animals. Draya pilgrims and priests moved in violet-robed streams and both Suya caste craftsmen and lowly Chaya servants moved aside for Keshan and his brother. Hiding themselves in the deepest shadows of alleys and midden, the untouchable Jegora kept well away. They didn't even dare to raise their eyes to meet Keshan's gaze.

Born to the lordly Triya caste, he and his brother Iyestar outranked even the Draya. Men hurried to drive their oxen aside and pilgrims bowed in reverence as Keshan's chariot rolled past.

Keshan's older brother, Iyestar, nodded to the palace walls up ahead. "Who do you think is going to win Suraya?"

Keshan shrugged. "I'm not sure. It's been years since I've been in the palace. I have no idea whose skills have developed since I was last here." Keshan gripped the central pole of the chariot as it bounced over the rutted streets near the market. "I suppose she grew up to be gorgeous?"

"She's the sexiest woman in Marhavad," Iyestar said. "Add to the fact that her father is lord of the wealthiest state in the kingdom, and you can pretty much count that everyone is going to be at the competition today."

"If either Yudar Paran or Darvad Uru win her, it will greatly improve their chances of being chosen as the next king, given Lord Nadaru's political influence."

"Nadaru favors Yudar," Iyestar told Keshan. "He is a traditionalist. He's always been supportive of Yudar's claim to the throne."

"Is Yudar any good at archery?" Keshan asked.

Iyestar laughed. "Are you kidding? I'd be surprised if he could string a bow. He's too busy reading his religious texts and passing judgment to spend any time with weapons."

Their chariot approached the western bridge across the Yaru River. The smells of fish and sewage washed over Keshan, quickly followed by the refreshing scent of jasmine, wafting from the palace gardens.

"Of course, marrying Lord Nadaru's daughter certainly wouldn't do our family any harm either." Iyestar looked wistful, then glanced to Keshan. "Do you think you might try for her?"

"No. Darvad can have her, if he can win her." Keshan shook his head. "I haven't returned to Prasta to find another wife. I'm looking for a man."

Iyestar's eye went wide.

"Not so loud, Keshan!" Iyestar hissed. His gaze darted over the crowed as if anyone could hear them over cries of street performers or the booms of pilgrims' drums.

"It's not what you think," Keshan assured his brother. "At least not yet." He couldn't help but tease a little. "The man I need is the one from my vision. I will find him here. I know that much."

"I have no doubt that you are right," Iyestar admitted. "But for your first day back from exile, could you at least try not to cause a scandal with talk of visions of the future and great uprisings against the Triya? The royal court is tense enough."

"Don't worry," Keshan replied. "I'll restrict myself to an evening of harmless flirting."

"With women?" Iyestar asked in a whisper.

"I told you, I'm not here for women," Keshan said, just to see his brother's reaction. He wasn't disappointed; Iyestar looked like he'd bitten into a lemon. Keshan laughed and Iyestar sighed heavily.

"I need a drink," Iyestar decided.

"Well, the palace seems as good as any place to have one." The vast red walls of the palace loomed up before them. The chariot rolled across the steep bridge and they passed through the ornate brass gates of the western entrance. The perfume of the royal gardens floated down to Keshan.

As soon as Keshan and his brother stepped from their chariot, Suya servants quickly led them through the halls and out to the verdant garden where Lord Nadaru Paria had chosen to stage the challenge for his daughter's hand in marriage.

An immense silk pavilion, festooned with pink ribbons and gold tassels, dominated the garden. Groups of Triya lords had already gathered under flowering shade trees.

Many wore heavy bejeweled diadems as well as glittering, ceremonial armor emblazoned with their crests. Keshan and his brother had both decided to forego the hot confines of breastplates and diadems, choosing instead to adorn themselves with strings of abalone shell and pearls from their home in Tiwari. Keshan knew very well that the lustrous beads suited his dark skin and only heightened the impact of his short, black hair and dark eyes.

Servants scurried between the crowds with refreshments and delicacies plucked from tables loaded down with sweet pastries, fresh cut oranges and fried cheeses with chutney.

Iyestar immediately found the drink he desired, and handed Keshan a glass of wine. Keshan searched through the groups of men around him, seeking some sign that one of them might be the champion from his visions. A few were handsome but none held his interest longer than a few moments.

Of the entire crowd, only two men stood out dramatically. Both were tall, with long black hair, and Keshan was certain from their features that they were brothers. The younger of the two was a muscle-bound giant; even his voice seemed too large as it boomed across the garden. The older brother was lean, almost delicate. An expression of regal disapproval seemed etched into his otherwise attractive face. Both wore the golden armor of royal princes.

"Our Paran cousins," Iyestar commented as he followed Keshan's gaze. "The big one is Baram Paran, the other is Yudar Paran."

Keshan knew of Yudar. The Prince's dedication to traditional law was unwavering. In his position as Royal Judge, Yudar's rulings were mercilessly devout.

Iyestar leaned close to Keshan. "Not the man of your future?" he whispered.

Keshan laughed, pleased that his brother could tease him, even here in the palace, where the holy laws were strictly enforced by both the Regent Mazar and the Royal Judge.

"Let's see if we can't find anyone more interesting to introduce you to inside the pavilion," Iyestar suggested.

In the center of Suraya's wedding canopy, dozens of red velvet chairs were placed around a pool of fragrant water. A glimmering gold bauble, cut in the shape of a fish, hung from silver wire above the pool. Even the slightest breeze caused the dangling fish to spin. Nearby, two soldiers guarded a table, upon which lay a heavy bow and a quiver of white arrows.

None of the guests had taken their seats yet. They remained at the far end of the pavilion, enjoying both the shade and the cool breezes that fluttered through the silk walls.

"There's Darvad," Iyestar said, pointing to a knot of brightly colored Triya warriors. It had been five years since Keshan had last seen Darvad Uru, one of the two men vying for the throne, and he hadn't changed at all. He was darkly handsome, with a square jaw and broad, muscled shoulders. His golden breastplate glinted in the late afternoon sun.

"He's been asking after you for weeks now," Iyestar said. He pulled on Keshan's arm. "Come on, let's say hello."

But Keshan hesitated. "Let's not. Firdaus is there, and I don't feel like having an argument without finishing my wine."

Iyestar frowned. "Darvad expects me to join him."

"Then go." Keshan smirked at his brother. "I won't get lost on my own, I assure you."

Iyestar raised an eyebrow. "I'm more worried you may lose your inhibitions and end up banished for another five years."

"I promise to behave." Keshan knew his smirk wasn't helping his argument.

But Iyestar relented. "Stay out of trouble." He left Keshan's side and joined Prince Darvad and Darvad's friends, leaving Keshan to stand against the garden wall and watch the congregation of warriors.

Keshan didn't have to worry about being left alone for long. Since entering the garden, he heard people whisper his name. He knew he had a reputation amongst the courtiers, and that the scandal of stealing Firdaus' wife, five years on, was still a hot topic amongst the gossip mongers at the palace. Now that Iyestar was gone, small clusters of Triya noblemen and courtiers ventured over, to introduce or reacquaint themselves.

The sound of a conch shell broke up the mingling, and everyone was instructed to take a seat.

Keshan turned to follow the crowd into the canopy, when suddenly he saw a young man racing for the pavilion. Unlike the other Triya, who were dressed in their finest, brightest silks and armor, this man wore the plain dark cotton of a soldier.

He vaulted over the flowering hedges, his short hair mussed, his skin flushed, and his vest open.

Keshan stared openly as the man paused to straighten his clothes. Only then did he seem to notice Keshan watching him. He glared back.

Keshan sucked in his breath in surprise. The man had bright blue eyes, a rarity in Marhavad. Along with his tall body and light brown skin, the man's eyes brought an instant surge of arousal through Keshan's body. It had been years since he had experienced such a sudden, overpowering attraction to anyone. The man continued to gaze at him intently.

"Jandu! Get over here!"

Prince Baram's voice bellowed over the crowd. The handsome young man spun around. He hastily ran a hand through his mussed hair and rushed to join Baram.

As soon as Keshan realized that this was Prince Jandu, Yudar's youngest brother and fourth in line for the throne, disappointment flooded him. The Parans represented everything that Keshan had returned to Prasta to change. But even knowing that, desire fluttered through him, and Keshan decided that a little harmless flirtation might be fun after all.

CHAPTER 2

JANDU SQUARED HIS SHOULDERS AND STRODE INTO THE PAVILION. It was a spectacle of shiny baubles and pearly saucers, pink ribbons and gold tassels. The scent of jasmine and freshly cut, ripe oranges filled the air—a heady assault after the dusty archery grounds that Jandu had only just left. He hadn't meant to be late or to arrive dressed like some Suya soldier, but he had lost track of time in the midst of battle practice.

Around him, Triya warriors decked in jewels and gleaming ceremonial armor watched him stride past with varying degrees of amusement, deference, and disdain. Every man he passed wore bright silk trousers or a long silk dejaru sarong. Absurdly bejeweled diadems sat atop their heads like flimsy helmets.

Annoyance flared through Jandu. What was the point of all their gilded armor if not to remind them that they were born to be warriors? They were hypocrites, dressed in their gaudy armor and sneering at him, for coming late with the dust of a battleground clinging to him.

Jandu held his head high, feeling proud of himself. Let them smirk. He could best every one of them on the battlefield and they all knew it. Jandu allowed himself a satisfied smile. Then he glimpsed his older brothers. Yudar regarded him with an icy glare and Baram looked furious.

Jandu's brothers rarely looked alike. Yudar was thin and fragile, with soft gentle eyes. Baram was enormous and pure muscle, with a face that was as broad as it was long and a fierce glower to his expression. But when they both disapproved of

Jandu, they immediately resembled each other, eyebrows scrunched in unison, noses turned distinctly upward.

Jandu bowed his head and quickly slunk to his seat beside Baram.

"You are late," Baram growled at him.

"But I'm here," Jandu replied.

Baram shook his head. Yudar's attention had already shifted to the man on his left. Sahdin Ori, one of Yudar's staunchest supporters, whispered to Yudar about the new tax laws.

Jandu scanned the crowd and watched the man he'd seen in the garden take the seat next to Iyestar Adaru. The two of them bowed their heads close as they talked. But then the man seemed to have felt Jandu's stare. He glanced back to Jandu, making eye contact and smiling widely.

Jandu leaned over to his brother Baram. "Who is that man?" he whispered.

Baram frowned. "That's Keshan Adaru. He's our first cousin."

"I thought he had been banished." Jandu stole another glance at him.

"His five years of penance are over," Baram whispered. "But I doubt he's learned his lesson."

The low thrum of a gong resounded through the room, silencing all conversation.

Lord Nadaru Paria stepped beside the archery target, his hands pressed together in the sign of peace. He was thin and bony, and had a neatly trimmed black beard and kind eyes. He smiled upon the congregation.

"It is an honor to see so many of my fellow Triya lords and warriors on this auspicious day," Nadaru began. "My daughter Suraya recently turned twenty four, and asked me to find a suitable husband for her."

Nadaru held out his hands and two servants opened the silk flaps of the pavilion. Suraya Paria entered, followed by her brother Rishak.

Rumor had it that Suraya had been made from fire, and it seemed to be true, the way her dark eyes smoldered, the way her skin was a deep, fire-burnt brown, her hair a dozen shades of mahogany, darkening to charcoal, lightening to yellow. She was beautiful, and the men around Jandu immediately reacted. Baram shifted in his seat, and even Yudar stared salaciously.

Suraya and Rishak stood at their father's side. Lord Nadaru turned his attention back to the assembled Triya.

"Suraya and I have chosen this challenge to test the intelligence, concentration, and skill of the greatest warriors across Marhavad. Whoever wins this competition shall have the honor of marrying my daughter."

The look of anticipation on the men's faces around the room amused Jandu. Half of them looked at Suraya wantonly, like she was already their wife. And half of them were twice her age. Suraya regarded her suitors with a bemused expression.

Nadaru went on. "Here you see a pool of water, reflecting a spinning target that has been mounted on the ceiling. Your goal will be to string the bow I've provided and shoot the spinning fish that his hanging from the disk in the eye. However, you cannot look at the fish. You have to look at the reflection of the fish in the pool to win."

The room erupted in noise as the men contested the plausibility of accomplishing such a task. Even Jandu questioned whether he could hit the fish in the eye, since the eye could not even be seen from this distance.

Baram leaned backwards in his chair and glared at Jandu. "You know this challenge had to be chosen with you in mind, don't you?"

"Probably." Jandu shrugged. "But I'm still not going to compete."

"Suraya might not get married at all now."

Jandu grinned. "Especially since I'm the only one who can hit that fish." He stretched his back and prepared to watch joyously as the others failed.

"Let the competition begin!" Nadaru called out. He handed his daughter an elaborate garland of orange marigolds for her to drape around the winner.

Jandu looked to his left once more, checking on his cousin Keshan. Keshan met his gaze with a knowing look as if the two of them were sharing a secret joke. His lips were a rich red and sensual. He had gold hoop earrings, barely visible under the curl of his short dark hair. He wore the finest of Triya clothing casually, lounging in dark yellow silk trousers and a gold embroidered vest. Jandu couldn't keep his eyes from dipping to the bright red sash, slung low across Keshan's lean hips.

Jandu suddenly didn't care about the competition anymore. Keshan Adaru was infamous throughout Marhavad, and not just because his mother came from the enchanted demon race of the Yashva. Keshan had defied Firdaus Trinat, the powerful lord of Chandamar, by stealing the man's bride-to-be and it was rumored that he had spent the five years of his exile in the demon kingdom.

But what made Keshan most unconventional was that, despite being the son of a lord, Keshan consorted with people of all castes and creeds, going so far as to declare the time-honored caste system criminal. He had an open disdain for many of the Shentari religious traditions that Marhavad was founded upon.

Keshan winked at Jandu. Jandu quickly looked away, forcing himself to focus his attention on the competition.

The first man to compete was the elderly lord of Penemar, who took several minutes to make it over to the table where the bow was laid out.

"Grandpa there wants some action," Jandu whispered into Baram's ear. Baram laughed loudly. Yudar and several of his supporters scowled at them both.

The lord of Penemar could barely lift the bow off the table, much less string it. He sat down quickly.

The routine was the same for all of the older gentleman who tried their hand at a young blushing bride who they didn't have to bribe into their beds. Jandu shook his head, hoping he never grew to be such a deluded old fool. He yawned.

The challenge only started to get interesting once Druv, the young lord of Pagdesh, had his turn. He was the first to actually lift the bow completely off the table and start stringing it. But the bow was designed not to be strung easily. He struggled for several minutes, breaking out into an embarrassed sweat and swearing, until he finally threw the bow down.

"This challenge is rigged!" he spat at Nadaru.

"He can't get it up," Jandu whispered to Baram. Baram snickered.

Next up was Darvad, Jandu's half-brother.

"Piss-drinking bastard," Baram hissed under his breath.

"Quiet. Respect our half-brother," Yudar whispered. He was always urging his two younger brothers to be more polite to Darvad. But Jandu had seen the hint of a smile on Yudar's lips a moment ago and he suspected that Yudar took a secret pleasure in their rude comments. After all, there was no love lost between Yudar and Darvad. Even as children the two of them had competed intensely.

Darvad bowed to Suraya, and she smiled coyly at him. He turned to the bow and placed his hands on it.

Jandu immediately smirked at Darvad's error. There was no excuse for it. Mazar had instructed Darvad in exactly the same battle lessons that he'd given to Yudar, Baram and Jandu himself.

They had played together, studied together, and fought together since they were all children. And yet a smile from a pretty girl was obviously all it took to wipe Mazar's instruction from Darvad's memory.

Darvad was the first person to successfully string the bow. Triya noblemen throughout the room broke out in applause. Jandu couldn't believe that so many of them could have failed to recognize Darvad's grave error.

Jandu snuck a quick glance at Keshan. Keshan watched Darvad intently. Suddenly Jandu found himself jealous of the way Keshan eyed Darvad so expectantly.

Darvad grabbed an arrow from the quiver and knelt beside the pool of water. He immediately looked up at the fish.

"You must shoot using the reflection," Lord Nadaru reminded him.

Darvad scowled. He looked down at the water's reflection and then tried to pull back the bowstring.

His arms twitched and his muscles trembled, but he couldn't pull the bowstring back. A number of Yudar's supporters snickered. Darvad stared at them as if he could kill them with the evil eye.

Darvad struggled with the bow a minute longer, and then put the bow down, breathing heavily.

"That's what you get for paying attention to the girl and not the bow, fucker," Jandu said under his breath. He loved this.

"Watch your language," Yudar whispered, but his expression was one of quiet satisfaction.

Darvad sat back down, flushed with humiliation. Jandu relished every second of it. Out of the corner of his eye he searched to see how the defeat had affected Keshan. To Jandu's annoyance, Keshan still watched Darvad and his cluster of close friends.

The herald read from his list of competitors. "Next to compete is Tarek Amia, lord of Dragewan."

Jandu didn't really know much about Tarek, other than he was of the lower Suya caste and excelled at archery. Since he kept Darvad's company, Jandu assumed that he was probably evil.

As Tarek approached the bow on the table, Jandu noticed that Keshan's interest again peaked. Jandu stared hard at his cousin, hoping to distract Keshan's attention. Someone as remarkable as Keshan didn't need to be so fascinated by a lowly Suya.

Tarek brought his hands together and prayed to the bow. Jandu had to give the Suya credit. That was what Darvad, and most of the men before him, had failed to do.

Tarek lifted the bow easily and strung it without difficulty. Jandu watched, fascinated by the balance in Tarek's movements.

Tarek was several years older than Jandu, but they both had dark, slightly curly black hair, and high cheekbones. Someone even once accused them of looking like brothers. At the time the comment had enraged Jandu, but now, as Tarek took a perfect stance and drew the bowstring back easily, Jandu could see the resemblance.

"No!" Suraya suddenly shouted. It was the first time she spoke. "I will not marry a charioteer's son."

Voices raising objections and support to Suraya's refusal flared through the room. Nadaru looked displeased and held up his hands, asking for quiet.

"He may be the only one who can win," Nadaru said softly to his daughter.

Suraya shook her head. "I don't care. I'd rather remain a maiden than marry below my caste."

Tarek looked momentarily crushed, but he regained his composure quickly. He unstrung the bow and put it back on the table, and then bowed before Nadaru.

"My apologies. I meant no offense." He sat back down, pale with the insult. Darvad patted his back and then pushed another of his friends forward to take the challenge.

Firdaus Trinat, the lord of Chandamar, swaggered to the table.

Jandu caught the immediate frown that appeared on his cousin Keshan's face. Firdaus and Keshan were said to have been enemies from the first moment they met and Jandu was sure that being banished on Firdaus' account hadn't warmed Keshan's disposition towards the man any.

Jandu watched Firdaus anxiously. The man was developing a slight gut, and his long black hair thinned at the roots. But his square jaw, massive forearms and thick chest lent him a formidable appearance. There was also something slightly ethereal to the way Firdaus moved. It was said that Firdaus had Yashva blood, like Keshan. Firdaus lifted the bow with ease, and managed to string it as well. Applause rang through the room. Without hesitating, Firdaus loosed his arrow. A loud crash echoed through the pavilion and the spinning fish plunged into the water.

Men all around the room jumped from their seats to get a closer look at the results. But Lord Nadaru scowled as he pulled the fish from the water. The arrow jutted up from the belly of the fish.

"You have missed the eye," he said.

"Your challenge is unrealistic," Firdaus said. His voice was low. "It is the best a man of this earth can do. I demand my prize!"

Nadaru looked to his daughter. Suraya offered the slightest shake of her head, clearly unenthused by the prospect of being the second wife of a man almost twice her age.

Nadaru pulled the arrow from the fish and then held out his arms for silence. "If no other man here can match your skill, Lord Firdaus, you may claim my Suraya."

The room erupted in chatter once more. Jandu felt bad for Suraya, who looked about to cry as she eyed her potential future husband. But it was not his problem. He was not here to rescue Suraya.

A few other young warriors tried, but none succeeded in even stringing the bow. A deathly hush settled over the attendees, realizing that they had exhausted the potential in the room and no one had even gotten close to Firdaus' accomplishment.

"Perhaps I made it too hard," Nadaru said.

Jandu anxiously looked to Keshan, wondering if he would compete as well. But Keshan, like himself, only watched the festivities. Then Keshan suddenly turned and stared straight at Jandu. He raised an eyebrow, and smiled almost lasciviously. It was an inviting smile—a beckoning smile.

Into the stillness of the room, Keshan spoke. "I thought I was going to get a demonstration of Jandu Paran's legendary skill today. But I suppose he feels too underdressed to compete."

All eyes turned to Jandu.

Jandu hid his shock by casually straightening out of his slouch. "Well, cousin, if you're going to ask me that way, how can I refuse?"

Baram laughed and slapped Jandu on the shoulder so hard that Jandu had to struggle not to topple over. Suraya smiled softly at him. Nadaru positively beamed. Dread snaked through Jandu's gut, but he was already standing and all eyes were upon him.

Jandu stepped to the bow, but before he began, he looked behind him, making sure that his cousin watched. Keshan stared at him intently, his expression expectant.

Jandu brought his palms together to pray to the bow. He had learned from his master Mazar that any weapon needed to be respected in order to be wielded properly. After doing so, he lifted the bow with ease.

Jandu's heart beat faster. He braced the base of the bow with his sandal as he reached down and pulled the bowstring up and around the top. He looked briefly at Keshan as he pulled an arrow from the quiver. Keshan stared at him with his mouth slightly open, his eyes wide. He looked like he was holding his breath. Ever so slightly, Jandu nodded to him. If his cousin wanted a display of his prowess Jandu would give him one.

Jandu knelt and gazed into the water. He cocked back the arrow and pointed it upwards, concentrating on the spinning reflection of the fish.

Just before released his arrow, he realized that the reflection was deceptive. The fish spun in the opposite direction, he could tell by the reflection of his own face in the water. He smiled to himself. He concentrated on the fish, until all he saw was the fish's eye.

He counted the spins to space the timing. And then he released his string.

The fish fell from the spinning disk with a loud snap and crashed into the water. Jandu stood as Nadaru and the surrounding men rushed to the pool. Nadaru reached his hand into the water and pulled out the golden fish, showing the rest of the room that Jandu had succeeded in shooting the arrow directly through the small eye. The room erupted in applause and cheers.

"Are you happy with my demonstration, cousin?" Jandu called out over the noise. Keshan rewarded him with a brilliant smile.

Jandu's stomach tightened at the beauty of Keshan's expression.

And as Suraya placed the marigold garland around his neck, Jandu realized, terribly, wonderfully, that he was, for the first time in his life, infatuated with someone other than himself.

CHAPTER 3

AS SERVANTS TIED BACK THE SILKEN WALLS OF THE PAVILION, a gust of monsoon wind rolled over Jandu, feeling like hot breath. All across the garden he could see tables strewn with succulent dishes and awaiting wedding guests. A Draya priest stood ready to perform the ceremony. Friends and strangers, dressed in their dazzling ceremonial armor, offered Jandu their congratulations.

Jandu thanked them in a daze.

He didn't know how he got into this mess and he had no idea how he would get out of it. Well, that wasn't entirely true. He got into it because he wanted to show off, as usual.

But now he was going to get married. The thought made Jandu distinctly uncomfortable. His mother had died shortly after his birth and Jandu had grown up in the sole company of other men. While he found women kind-natured and well-behaved as a rule, they confused him with their strange seriousness and lack of interest in archery.

"Congratulations, idiot!" Baram cheered lovingly. He crushed Jandu in a brotherly embrace that bordered on painful.

Yudar merely looked on, worry creasing his brow.

"I can't marry her," Jandu told them in a whisper. He didn't know how he could explain his reluctance. His unwavering belief in his own superiority? His lack of interest in women in general? His singular dedication to the warrior arts? He simply knew that this marriage was wrong for him.

"I know," Yudar said. He frowned. "It goes against the Book of Taivo."

Confused by his brother's agreement, Jandu searched his mind for the lesson on the precepts of Shentari faith, trying to recall what obscure, ancient law his brother referred to this time.

"If you were to father a son, he would be older than any child either I or Baram fathered. And since neither of us is consecrated as King, your son would have the right of primogeniture to challenge our children for the throne."

"What?" Baram looked as confused as Jandu felt.

"I have been thinking of the problem ever since the moment you pierced the fish eye," Yudar said, clearing his throat. His face had flushed almost guiltily. "I believe there is precedent to break the Shentari tradition in this case."

Jandu looked at Yudar, and suddenly, everything made sense. "You should marry her, Yudar." Jandu was certain that Nadaru would be delighted to wed his daughter to a future king.

Although Yudar flushed brighter at Jandu's suggestion, he shook his head. "I cannot. I did not compete. You did."

"I competed for you," Jandu suggested.

Baram narrowed his eyes. "No, you competed to show off. Call it like it is."

Jandu grinned. "All right. But that's all the more reason that I shouldn't marry Suraya. I didn't do it for her."

"It doesn't matter," Yudar replied. "You did not declare yourself to be competing in my stead, so legally I can't claim her. However—"

"Fellow Triya warriors! I must protest this marriage!" Firdaus pushed his way through the throng of well-wishers. He held himself tall. His friend and, no doubt, co-conspirator Darvad stood beside him as if urging him on.

"It is against our holy Book of Taivo for Jandu Paran to marry Suraya Paria. A younger prince must not wed before his elder brothers when a Regent holds the throne! It will lead the kingdom into chaos and war. So it is written."

A sudden, deathly pall stifled all conversation. Jandu felt a flicker of hope. He wouldn't have to marry Suraya now.

"What is this?" Lord Nadaru rushed to them. Suraya followed behind and stepped close to Jandu's side. Her face was pale, her eyes almost fearful. Jandu realized that if his claim to her became invalid then she would become Firdaus' second wife.

Yudar cleared his throat and stepped between Firdaus and Lord Nadaru. Though small compared to his brothers, Yudar had a royal presence that made him seem larger than he was. He held himself straight-backed with his chin tilted upwards, his dark brown eyes shining with inner wisdom.

"It is true that the Book of Taivo specifically states that under these conditions royal siblings must be married in order of age," Yudar said. "However, the laws established under the prophet Tarhandi allow for such a circumstance, assuming that all siblings marry the wife together."

The silence seemed to grow deeper and more disturbed, as everyone attempted to digest what Yudar said. Even Jandu, who had a lifetime of practice deciphering his brother's cryptic religious code, stumbled over the idea. When he finally understood Yudar's proposal, he almost choked.

He grabbed Yudar's shoulder. "What are you talking about?" he hissed.

Yudar smiled at him serenely. "With Lord Nadaru's permission, all three of us will marry Suraya."

The silence exploded in outrage. Even the baboons seemed to shriek louder in the nearby trees. It took several minutes for Nadaru to call the party to order.

Jandu wondered for an instant why they all cared so much. Why couldn't Suraya just choose some man—other than himself—and have done with it? And then he caught sight of his bride, dressed in her delicate red silk zahari dress, her eyes painted with kohl. She was absolutely gorgeous. Baram fidgeted nervously and stared at her.

Firdaus and Yudar looked as flushed and committed as men in sword combat. Head to head, they debated the issue with the kind of speed and precision that Jandu reserved for calling down a magical sharta.

"The Book of Taivo specifically prohibits this marriage!" Firdaus shouted.

"But the laws of the Prophet Tarhandi allow for polyandry should the bride choose to marry all siblings." Yudar was calm and had a little smile on his face, looking assured in the way that only scholars who knew the words of God by heart could be.

"That is an ancient law! It is hardly practiced any more. It has been over a century since a woman has had multiple husbands!" Firdaus looked genuinely scandalized by the idea.

Yudar merely raised an eyebrow. "The antiquity of the law does not negate it. The Prophet Tarhandi's precepts are well-established in the Shentari temple, and many laws dating from the same time period are used to hold up religious edicts today."

"Tarhandi's laws are about cattle thievery and agricultural disputes!" Firdaus' voice raised in anger.

Jandu just shook his head. Anyone in Prasta knew better than to challenge Yudar to a religious debate. Yudar had every single holy law memorized and an uncanny knack for knowing exactly what obscure text to cite to perfectly support his argument.

Yudar's smile widened. "The nature of Tarhandi's laws are irrefutable, as he was a prophet from God. His standards form the basis of judgments every day across this noble country. Based on this, his word is irrefutable."

Suraya's father watched the debate like an active child, jumping in place and trying vainly to butt in. Finally, he simply stepped forward.

"Prince Yudar is more than just knowledgeable about the Book of Taivo," Nadaru stated. "He is also the Royal Judge for the Regent. His decision stands."

"Unfair!" Darvad cried out, stepping forward. "He cannot serve as judge in this matter, as it affects him personally."

"But he is the Royal Judge for the State of Prasta. I will abide his decision," Lord Nadaru stated flatly.

Jandu cleared his throat. "Shouldn't we ask what Suraya wants to do?"

"Shut up!" Firdaus yelled at him. "Do not interrupt!"

Jandu's fingers itched for his sword.

But his words must have gotten through, for Nadaru held up his hands in the sign of peace and begged silence. "Please! Let me consult with my daughter. Suraya, what would you say in this matter?"

Suraya blushed, but she stood straighter. "It was prophesized upon my birth that I would marry three great men. I had not thought that I would wed them all at once but... this must be what the prophet intended."

All of them stared at Suraya silently.

Suraya still blushed furiously. "I will do this. I will fulfill the prophecy."

Jandu had some very strong opinions about prophecies. He didn't like them. He didn't believe in them. He rebelled against the idea that his destiny was not in his own hands.

Yudar nodded. "We shall all be married tonight then, it seems." He looked at Suraya, and Jandu could see how desire already clouded his brother's vision.

Jandu tried to imagine how it would feel to share a wife with his brothers. He'd never considered himself the marrying type anyway. He honestly couldn't conjure any feelings of jealousy, only embarrassment at their odd situation.

Jandu felt Suraya's hand clench around his arm. He looked to her and she faced him resolutely.

Jandu took a deep breath. "You're sure this is what you want?"

"I'm not sure of anything," she said. "But this morning, I could have been married to anybody." She swallowed as she looked at Firdaus, still fuming. "Besides, I think I'd rather die than be Lord Chandamar's second wife."

At this, Firdaus spat on the ground and turned and stormed away. Darvad followed him.

"I wouldn't want to marry him either," Jandu said.

Suraya looked at him oddly, then reached out and squeezed his hand. It felt strange and girlish and reassuring all at once. "It will be all right, Jandu."

Jandu nodded. "Well, let's get married then. Although, as Keshan Adaru pointed out, I'm not dressed for the occasion." Not for the first time Jandu glanced through the crowd, searching for Keshan, but he failed to find him.

"I don't care how you're dressed," Suraya assured him.

"Good," Jandu said. "Because I'm a lazy dresser, Baram looks ugly in everything, and Yudar has no sense of style."

Baram slapped Jandu in the back of the head, almost knocking him off his feet.

Suraya laughed. "Well, at least you're honest."

The wedding ceremony was brief and directly afterwards the wives, daughters, and sisters of the Triya nobles flooded the garden. Musicians followed, as did more servants who brought out further offerings of food and wine. The feast was a spectacle, with dishes formed in the shapes of fish and birds, cream custards and spicy butter sauces, tenderly roasted meats and fine cheeses. The opulence of Nadaru's food coupled with Jandu's dramatic triumph at the archery challenge and the resulting triple marriage were enough to guarantee that the wedding would be discussed for years to come.

For now though, the palaver dropped to a constant, steady murmuring which mingled with the clink of porcelain cups as celebratory wine began to infuse the party with true jollity.

To Jandu's dismay, his cousin Keshan was not invited to sit at the celebration table. But his half-brother Darvad joined them briefly, offering a toast. His cadre of companions—Firdaus, Tarek, Druv, and Iyestar—emulated him, though Firdaus looked unhappy. Then Darvad took his leave and his friends followed, to mingle and gossip at other, more welcoming tables.

The sun set and torches illuminated the night, flickering an eerie yellow glow over the guests. Perfumed smoke filled the air with the scent of sandalwood. A heavy wind blustered sweet summer warmth over the wedding party in dramatic gushes of sound and sensation.

Lord Nadaru showed a disheartening tendency towards the extravagant. Jandu forced himself not to yawn through numerous speeches and superfluous rituals, all repeated thrice as Yudar went through them, then Baram, and then at last himself. Drunken congratulations assailed Jandu from every angle.

He quickly wearied of the attention. When he at last caught sight of Keshan in the crowd of guests he desperately wanted to join him. But Jandu was a prisoner at the table of honor. He brushed his bangs from his forehead and watched his cousin Keshan mingle with the wedding guests, chatting with supporters of Yudar and Darvad alike. Jandu brooded, while his brothers ate and discussed the logistics of their new living arrangements.

"We should be husband for a year at a time," Yudar decided, smiling at his own wisdom. "For one year, you will be my wife, Suraya. And then it will be Baram's year, and then Jandu. That way you can get to know us each individually, and there will be no jealousy."

Suraya nodded. Jandu noted that she hit the wine early and often.

Far across the garden a group of young men burst into laughter as Keshan told some joke.

Jandu wished he could have heard Keshan's words. He had no doubt that they would have been intriguing, perhaps even scandalous, as everything about his cousin seemed to be. Keshan had fought a bloody battle with his uncle when he was only sixteen and after that he'd been central in relocating the

Tiwari capital city to the coast to avoid further conflict with his neighboring state. He was a famed musician and infamous seducer and, according to Yudar, the sponsor of several very dangerous amendments to the holy laws.

Jandu anxiously awaited Yudar's dismissal. It wasn't Jandu's night to be husband, after all. But Yudar was otherwise occupied. He held Suraya's hand, and an unusual glow of happiness colored his skin. He seemed bronzed by joy. It made Jandu pleased to see it. It wasn't easy to make Yudar forget his worries, but Suraya's beauty seemed to soothe his concerns, for the time being at least.

Nadaru had brought in dancers from across Marhavad, and as they began their show, Jandu was finally excused. He rushed from the table and made his way towards Keshan.

As Jandu approached, a knot formed in his stomach. Keshan watched him, a pleased smile on his face.

"Hi." Jandu spoke quickly. "I wanted to introduce myself."

"Jandu Paran." Keshan said his name slowly, like a sigh of relief.

Jandu blushed, and was horrified. He was acting like a girl.

Jandu reached down to touch Keshan's feet in respect at the same time that Keshan bent down to do the same. They bumped heads and both stood up, startled.

"Watch it!" Jandu cried out.

Keshan scowled, rubbing his head.

Jandu laughed. "Sorry! It's my fault. But you should let me touch your feet first. I'm younger than you."

"By what, six months?" Keshan asked. "Besides, you're a prince."

Keshan reached out and fingered Jandu's plain white vest. Jandu froze at the intimate touch. His body tingled where Keshan's hand brushed against him.

"This is not typical wedding attire," Keshan pointed out.

Jandu shrugged. "I'm not a proponent of Triya fanfare when it comes to clothing."

"I agree," Keshan said. "When I'm home alone I just walk around naked."

Jandu cocked his head. "Really?"

"No." Keshan grinned widely. "I just wanted to see your expression when I said that." Keshan grabbed Jandu's arm, and led him over to his table. "Come, sit down with me and Iyestar."

Iyestar didn't look anything like his younger brother Keshan. Where Keshan was svelte and elegant, Iyestar was thick-boned and muscular. He had an impressive neck and his facial features were broad and kind. Jandu wondered how they ever found diadems to fit the circumference of his skull.

Iyestar was distinguished for being a heavy drinker, and the wedding had not been an exception. With eyes half-closed in inebriation, he held an entire jug of wine carelessly, spilling aromatic purple liquid out the top with each dramatic hand gesture.

Jandu felt uncomfortable sitting there, beside one of Darvad's best friends while Yudar and Baram were left behind, laughing and celebrating with Suraya. It seemed almost treasonous. But then Iyestar reached out and pinched Jandu's cheeks affectionately. "Hello there, little cousin."

At six feet, Jandu rarely considered himself little. Acknowledging Iyestar's height, he let the comment slide.

"Are you enjoying the festivities?" Jandu asked.

Iyestar burped in response.

"You'll have to excuse my brother, he's an animal," Keshan said. "I don't believe he inherited any of our mother's grace."

"At least I'm not a witch like you," Iyestar commented.

Keshan rolled his eyes. He put his arm around Jandu's shoulders and pulled him closer to whisper. "My brother thinks that anyone who has any sort of education is enchanted and, therefore, a witch."

"You do have magical powers though, Keshan." Iyestar pointed ineffectively at them both. "Don't deny it."

"I'm not denying it," Keshan stated. "But I'm no witch."

Jandu had the distinct feeling that he was listening to some long-standing fraternal argument, and chose not to say anything. Iyestar clumsily leaned over and refilled Jandu's wine cup, splashing wine onto Jandu's hands in the process.

"Your performance today was amazing, cousin," Iyestar said. "You are a fantastic archer."

Jandu nodded. "Yes, I am."

Iyestar chuckled. "Oh, so that's true, then."

"What?"

"That you are also full of yourself."

Jandu looked to Keshan for support, but Keshan simply grinned, leaning back in his chair. Jandu checked to make sure his brothers were doing okay without him. They both stared at Suraya dotingly.

Keshan followed Jandu's gaze. "Do you want to join them?" he asked.

Jandu shrugged. "Four's a crowd."

Keshan seemed to watch him closely. "Are you angry that your brothers took your bride?"

"I don't mind," Jandu said.

"Really?" Keshan raised an eyebrow. "Surprising."

Iyestar filled up Keshan's cup from his jug of wine. "So what comes next? A honeymoon in the mountains?"

Jandu snorted. "Yudar won't leave the capital, especially not during the festival. There is too much politicking for him to miss out on a moment of it."

Iyestar nodded. "Darvad's the same way."

"And you?" Keshan asked. "What do you want to do, Jandu?"

"Honestly?" Jandu got the impression that Keshan was talking about something larger than his honeymoon. "Travel. Take on challenges worthy of my skills. Meet interesting new people. I've hardly gone anywhere. I can't even imagine what some of the states of Marhavad look like."

"Trust me, Prasta is the best city in the entire kingdom. You haven't missed anything," Iyestar mumbled.

But Keshan disagreed. "There are some beautiful places in this world, Jandu. Especially my capital, Tiwari. Perhaps I could take you there one day. We could walk the beaches together, and I could teach you how to fish."

"That would be fantastic." A warm, liquid happiness filled Jandu. He suspected the wine's influence.

"Let's plan on it then." Keshan leaned over and placed his warm palm on Jandu's shoulder. Something about Keshan's touches, about the way he looked at Jandu, subtly affected Jandu. Perhaps Keshan's half-Yashva blood had some magical effect? Jandu drew closer to Keshan, despite the fact that the feeling seemed dangerous.

"You aren't returning to Tiwari right away?" Jandu asked, suddenly panicked at the idea that Keshan would leave as soon as the festival ended.

"I'll be staying in Prasta for a while," Keshan replied. "We should spend some time together. I think we might find we have some tastes in common."

Again, Keshan seemed to be saying more than the sum of his words. Jandu tried but could not quite grasp the implication. Then Baram was calling him back to the table of honor and he grudgingly excused himself. Iyestar gave him a wine jug salute. Keshan only smiled.

Even though it seemed politically dangerous and almost disloyal, Jandu decided he couldn't wait to spend time with his scandalous cousin again.

CHAPTER 4

THE PALACE OF PRASTA ROSE LIKE AN ISLAND OF SOLID ROCK from the middle of the great Yaru River, its fortified red sandstone walls formed in the shape of an elongated spearhead. Inside, multiple courtyards and marble hallways connected the dozens of buildings, architecturally distinct from one another, creating a labyrinth of pathways. Over fifty separate gardens dotted the palace, each one blocked in by walls of rooms, some structures extending up several floors to form ornately carved stone balconies that peered over the gardens or the banks of the river.

The central throne room was the seat of power for the entire nation, overseen by the Regent Mazar. But the rest of the sprawling, circuitous palace was dotted with pockets of Yudar Paran and Darvad Uru's influences. In the decade since King Shandarvan's death neither group had managed to make a decisive claim on the throne. Darvad was the eldest son, born two months before Yudar, but Yudar's mother had been the king's first and more honored wife. Neither omens read by Draya priests nor the holy texts had offered a solution. In a year both Yudar and Darvad would be thirty and the Regent's allotted reign would end. Mazar would have to appoint one or the other of the princes to be King.

As Keshan ambled through the palace grounds, he noted an architectural shift, years of careful crafting under either Yudar's supporters or Darvad's, changing the very appearance of the buildings. Keshan wandered, not minding the fact that he was lost. He hadn't wandered the royal palace at Prasta since he was a little boy. Now that the outrageous Paran wedding festivities had finished, and most of the lords had returned to their own states, Prasta settled back into normalcy.

Keshan wound his way through the western part of the palace, where Darvad held court, admiring the sculptures and brightly painted murals showing erotic images. Darvad's world was sensual, full of images of wine and women, of peasant life and animals and great wars.

As Keshan moved east, the decoration sobered. The Paran quarters edged the eastern river bank, and stretched towards the southern gates that opened onto the vast royal forest. The Paran family artwork consisted of religious statues, and scenes from the holy Book of Taivo, displaying the multiple heads of God and the fiery shartic weapons of the Shentari prophets. The statues of prophets stared down at Keshan with what he interpreted as potent malevolence.

Several times, guards stopped Keshan, inquiring whether they could help him find his way. Some asked out of kindness. Others asked out of distrust, anxious to lead him away from more sensitive areas. In both cases, Keshan politely refused and moved on at his own pace. He liked the feeling of being lost here, here in the midst of such grandeur.

A gentle breeze blew through a carved marble hallway, which opened on both sides to stone gardens filled with fragrant orchids. Outside, another short but powerful monsoon downpour drenched the city. Safely sheltered under the marble hallway, Keshan felt the cool relief of the rain and smelled the sweet earthy scent of wet stone.

"Iyestar?" Keshan peered into one of the countless rooms. There were gold-leafed paintings of a forest scene on the plaster walls, and archery targets set up at even intervals. The targets suggested that archers would be found nearby. Following his instincts, he turned the corner down a long marble hall and nearly ran directly into Jandu Paran.

"Keshan!" Jandu dropped to the ground and touched Keshan's feet. Keshan quickly urged him upwards.

"Please don't do that. It makes me feel old."

Jandu blushed endearingly. "Sorry."

Keshan took a moment to just admire the beauty of his cousin. Jandu was Keshan's ideal of a warrior prince, both handsome and powerful. His light brown complexion glowed, and enhanced the startling brightness of his blue eyes. Even dressed plainly, in a long blood red dejaru sarong and a simple white cotton vest, Jandu appeared bold and regal. His body was tight and trim, the contours of his abdominal muscles clearly visible under his open vest. Keshan couldn't help the flutter of attraction he felt every time he looked upon Jandu's delicious body.

"What brings you to the palace?" Jandu asked.

"I'm looking for my brother," Keshan said. "He wanted to be informed when I finished unpacking."

"So you are here for good? In Prasta?" Jandu's voice betrayed his enthusiasm.

Keshan smiled at him. "For at least the next few months. Iyestar may have to return to Tiwari, but I am free to stay behind."

Jandu smiled back. "Come on, I'll take you to him. He's practicing archery in the stone garden, with Darvad and his gang of thugs."

Keshan laughed, but he didn't miss the obvious distaste in Jandu's comment. It would be awkward, befriending Jandu. Darvad would not like it. But Keshan had never been one to obey the whims of anyone else.

"So how is married life?" Keshan asked.

Jandu shrugged. "Not my turn for another two years, thank God. But it suits Yudar. He and Suraya were staring in each other's eyes all during breakfast."

The hallway terminated at a large courtyard, surrounded by a waist-high stone wall. The cobblestones were under a good inch of water as the monsoon storm continued to pour down around them.

"We can walk around this way," Jandu said, pointing to the left, "or we can take a short cut through the courtyard, which would be a lot more fun."

Keshan grinned. "I don't melt in water."

Jandu didn't hesitate. He vaulted the wall and dashed into the downpour, hooting as he did so, his long legs striding widely as he ran. Keshan's silk trousers were immediately drenched but he didn't care. The water felt luxurious after the morning's sweltering heat, and he laughed along with Jandu as they both scrambled over the wall and skidded to a halt in the cool stony corridor of another building.

Jandu shook his head, sending sprays of water droplets everywhere. Keshan ran his hand through his own, pushing back his damp locks.

Jandu smiled at him. "Your diadem is crooked." He straightened it, and then pulled back with a frown. Jandu turned and led them down another hallway, his sandals squeaking against the stone floor.

"I notice you don't wear one very often," Keshan said.

"I think they're showy," Jandu said.

"Like you can talk," Keshan said back.

Jandu laughed. "I don't know why I have such a reputation for being vain. The only thing I brag about is my archery and I have earned the right to be proud. I am the best archer in the kingdom and I know it. What's wrong with saying so?"

If the statement had come from anyone else, Keshan would probably have disliked him. But Jandu's self-assurance seemed charmingly honest and Keshan found it attractive. Jandu wasn't compensating for some failing or insecurity by bragging. He truly believed he was the best.

They walked in silence for short distance. Jandu fidgeted slightly. His eyes darted to Keshan.

"You realize that Firdaus Trinat is probably going to be with Darvad and your brother," Jandu said.

"So?"

There was another pause, as if Jandu gathered courage to continue. "Doesn't it bother you? Your brother is friends with the man who had you exiled?"

"I don't hate Firdaus. My exile was just and not hard to endure. Firdaus is no threat to me now," Keshan replied. "And Iyestar is friends with Darvad so meeting Firdaus is unavoidable. I would understand if you don't want to see him, though. He's bound to be angry with you."

Jandu didn't respond. He stared ahead, and Keshan could tell he debated saying something. After years of living with the Yashvas, who were so hard to read emotionally, it was a pleasant change to spend time with men, with their feelings so clearly displayed.

"Does it bother you that I'm Yudar's brother?"

Keshan thought of telling Jandu the truth, that it *did* bother him. Yudar represented everything that Keshan had spent the last ten years of his life fighting against. But this was harmless, Keshan told himself, this innocent flirtation. It wasn't Jandu's fault that his brother represented the traditionalists.

"I'm not interested in who your brothers are. I'm interested in you," Keshan said.

Jandu blushed, and moved forward once more, walking at a faster pace.

"Besides," Keshan added, "my political interests have nothing to do with who should be king. I am more concerned about the plight of the lower castes, and whomever can support me in improving the equality of this nation deserves my gratitude."

"Equality? Between the Triya and Suya?" Jandu grimaced in distaste.

"Between all the castes."

"All of them?"

Keshan sighed. "I know that is not your belief or the belief of your brother, who holds tradition above humanity." Keshan had the sinking feeling that his flirtation with Jandu might be nearing its unsatisfying end. It was too bad, since he'd been so sure Jandu was attracted to him.

"Why do you care so much about the lower castes?" Jandu asked. Keshan heard no malice in his question, only curiosity, so Keshan answered him truthfully.

"It reflects poorly on the ruling class when the people of this nation struggle under such tyranny. In a society where three-fourths of the people live burdened by religious law that prevents them from equality merely because of who their parents are, everyone suffers. Only in a truly egalitarian society can all of us achieve the greatness that the Shentari faith claims to strive for."

"But you are Triya," Jandu said.

"Only because my father was Triya, and his father before him. We need to change, to herald in a new era where a person is judged on his actions, not on his blood. It is what God wants for us."

Jandu scowled. "How can you be so certain?"

"I have seen it. In a vision."

Jandu stared at Keshan as though Keshan were slightly mad.

Keshan just smiled, accustomed to this reaction.

"Say that again?" Jandu said.

"I have visions of the future. Prophecies, some may call it, although where they come from or why I will never know. Maybe it's my Yashva blood. But my entire life, I've been able to see glimpses of the future. And the future I see is one where caste no longer dictates righteousness."

Jandu looked at him oddly. Keshan felt almost intimidated by the intensity of Jandu's stare. But then the corner of Jandu's mouth quirked up and he grinned.

"You are one weird guy," Jandu said. He continued to lead the way down the hallway. "Powers of prophecy? Were you the one who predicted Suraya would marry three warriors?"

Keshan fell in beside him once more. "No, I wish my power was that useful. I wish I could predict the weather or know what will be served at the royal dinner tomorrow."

"That's easy. It's always butter chicken on Wednesdays."

Keshan laughed.

"What do you see?" Jandu asked.

"Just images, really, and sometimes accompanying sounds or smells. Often faces are blurred, or other details that seem meaningless are crystal clear.

"Sometimes I see an entire scene, and then weeks later, it happens. Or I'll catch images of something, disjointed and unfocused, and then later on I'll recognize them from a past vision. There is no pattern, and I have no control over them."

"Can you change what you see?" Jandu asked. "If something breaks in your vision, can you intercede to stop it from breaking?"

Keshan shook his head. "Half the time I don't know what I'm seeing."

"But how can you be sure these visions are telling you that everyone should be equal?" Jandu asked.

Keshan didn't miss the disapproval in Jandu's tone. "I've had a vision of the future, and of a great battle where the Triya are defeated by peasants. God chooses against us."

Jandu stayed silent for a long while. Keshan assumed Jandu to be considering this, but then Jandu suddenly asked, "Have you had any visions of me?"

Keshan almost laughed. Here he tried to explain his destiny, a mission he had from God, and Jandu only wanted to know if he had a starring role.

"No. Can't say that I have, unfortunately. Visions of you sound very appealing."

Jandu blushed again.

Keshan wanted to explain more, but he realized that his words were probably wasted on Jandu. Jandu's interest in Keshan's prophecies extended only as far as they concerned him, so he wouldn't care to hear the more personal details about why they fuelled Keshan's mission.

But ever since he could remember, he had a recurring vision of himself, beside a man who declared the end of all castes. The two of them were armed, fighting for a new world. And although the details were hazy, and Keshan could never see the man's face, he was almost certain that man was Jandu's half-brother, Prince Darvad Uru.

Darvad Uru had openly befriended a lower caste man. In speeches, hc praised the workers of Marhavad, calling them the greatest strength of the nation. He asked that merit be based on deed rather than blood.

Keshan admired Darvad's will, his disregard of tradition, and his promise to make changes to the old ways of Marhavad once he became king. Iyestar had assured Keshan that Darvad's ambitious nature was fueled by the desire to see a new world replace the atrophied one that surrounded them.

In all likelihood, Jandu would become one of Keshan's political enemies. The Paran brothers had been raised in the pious shadow of their father, and their belief in Triya superiority was unlikely to change.

But Jandu was handsome. More than handsome. Gorgeous. It had been many years since Keshan had felt such reciprocal longing from another man. Clearly he trailed this young warrior through the palace not because of his mission to change society, or to propel his own political career forward, but for desire. His body took over, flirting with this brash young warrior, and it wasn't going to do anyone any good.

"Here we are." Jandu led him through a gate into the stone garden. The downpour had stopped, and now everything steamed, baking in the hot sun.

Darvad aimed at a target across the garden that had been affixed to a bail of hay. Sweat slicked back Darvad's hair as he worked in the intense humidity of the afternoon. Beside him stood Tarek, Druv, Firdaus, and Keshan's brother.

Darvad lowered his bow and smiled at Keshan, bringing his palms together in the traditional sign of peace. The other men followed, except for Iyestar, who just came over and hugged Keshan brusquely.

"What took you so long? Did you get lost?" Iyestar frowned slightly at Jandu.

"I was just chatting with Jandu," Keshan said, raising his hands to return the sign of peace.

Jandu bowed his head politely. "I should go…"

"Stay." Keshan touched his arm. "I still haven't found out how you shot the eye of Suraya's fish."

The other men seemed uncomfortable with Jandu's presence, but quickly turned back to their competition. Keshan sat down on an embroidered rug that had been laid out on the hot cobblestones and, with obvious hesitation, Jandu joined him.

"Once I realized that the pool was like a mirror, reversing everything, hitting the eye was just a matter of timing." Jandu described how he counted the rotations of the fish as it spun. Keshan barely watched the men practicing in front of him, his eyes focused intently on Jandu.

"I already knew I could do it, I just didn't have a reason until you called me out," Jandu said.

"I'm sorry I challenged you," Keshan said. "I couldn't help myself. I'm a troublemaker."

The two of them gossiped about other lords and some of the more exotic performances that had apparently caused a scandal during the festival. Talking to Jandu came easily, and Keshan had to admit that he enjoyed the respite from constant political and religious debate.

As they chatted, they watched Darvad and his companions challenge each other. Darvad, Tarek, Druv and Firdaus took turns shooting at the target. After each round, the men would recollect their arrows, using each warrior's unique markings on the shaft of the arrow to determine the winner. Iyestar's role seemed to be purely for encouragement, yelling at them while he lounged on the sidelines.

Keshan did not excel at archery. Nevertheless, he knew a good archer when he saw one. Tarek's movements were swift and seamless. Tarek always hit the bull's eye. He won every round. And when Darvad complained that it was impossible to beat Tarek at anything, Tarek volunteered to start shooting with his left hand.

"I'm surprised you aren't jumping up and joining in," Keshan said to Jandu, keeping his voice low.

Jandu stretched out and propped himself up on his elbows. He watched the competition with a bored expression.

"Well, I wouldn't want anyone to see that Tarek is actually better than me."

Keshan stared at him, shocked.

Jandu smiled. "Just kidding. But actually, I have a bad feeling it'd be close. And then I'd have to respect him. But it would be disloyal to my brother if I befriended Tarek."

Keshan started to explain that they too would have a similar problem if they remained friends. But then Jandu said, "Besides, Tarek is a Suya."

Keshan shut his mouth. What was he doing? Sitting here with a man so full of himself that he considered himself better than Tarek simply by birthright?

Keshan shouldn't have been surprised. After all, Jandu had grown up surrounded by Triya religious zealots, and the tenet they revered before all others was the Shentari hierarchy.

The Triya are God's chosen lords .The world is given to them to rule and to defend. They alone will hold the holy secrets of the Shartas.

The Draya are God's messengers. They will keep the temples and pray for their Triya lords.

The Suya are God's workers and will create in God's name.

The Chaya are God's servants and will serve the people of God and work God's land.

The Jegora are the outcaste, scourges in God's eyes and unworthy of God.

The belief that the Suya, Chaya and Jegora were lesser people, less entitled, was so woven in the very fabric of Marhavadi culture that even intelligent, well-meaning people like Jandu found themselves incapable of thinking otherwise.

"I've competed against Tarek before, you know, " Jandu said. "It was during the Mahri Competition. The challenge was open to all Triya, but usually only the sons of the wealthiest lords ever compete. And then Tarek showed up, wearing cotton, looking poor and," Jandu gave Keshan a sideways look, "—very underdressed."

"You will never forget that, will you?" Keshan asked.

Jandu smirked. "We all mocked Tarek, of course. But then he started shooting arrows with unparalleled accuracy. When he released the bowstring, he stood still as stone, his gaze unwavering. I had never seen anyone like him."

Keshan looked up to where Tarek took his turn at the target. Jandu was right; the man became statuesque, it looked as though he did not even breathe. A whirr sounded, and the arrow smashed through the wooden target to strike bull's eye once more.

"I remember being excited," Jandu continued. "My whole life, I have always been unrivaled in archery and here stood a man who could truly challenge me." Jandu looked almost wistful, a smile on his face, his eyes closed.

But then he sighed. "Then Yudar pointed out this old charioteer who had entered the arena, and announced that the man was Tarek's father. Tarek was Suya and he never intended to tell anyone."

"What happened then?" Keshan watched Tarek, feeling instantly sorry for what the man had probably gone through that day.

Jandu shrugged. "He was humiliated, of course, and thrown out of the competition. But then Darvad stood up and called him a great warrior."

Keshan nodded. That action alone fuelled his support of Darvad.

"Darvad gave Tarek the State of Dragewan then and there, swearing lifelong friendship... completely insane." Jandu sat back up, staring at the two men being discussed. "They're inseparable now."

Keshan spoke hesitantly. "Well, it would be within Darvad's power to raise Tarek to a Triya once he's king. Only the king can change God's castes."

"But he isn't king yet and he isn't going to be. Yudar is the rightful heir." Jandu frowned at Keshan. "I thought we weren't going to talk politics. I hate politics. I shouldn't even be here."

Jandu stood to leave, when suddenly Darvad called out to him. Jandu turned back to his half-brother, showing no dislike, but definitely no affection either.

"Go tell Mazar that I will be late to dinner this evening," Darvad said.

"Have a servant tell him," Jandu said.

"Mazar is in his private chambers. I need you to tell him for me."

Everyone else in the garden stopped what they were doing. A thick tension simmered, Keshan felt waves of animosity radiating off of Jandu. But Jandu was younger than Darvad, and the same traditions that dictated Jandu's disdain for Tarek also made it impossible for him to refuse a demand from an older relative.

"All right." Jandu turned and frowned at Keshan. "I'll see you later." Jandu bent down to take the dust from Keshan's feet.

Keshan reached down and stopped him. He held Jandu's arms.

"Don't do that," Keshan said quietly.

"You're my elder," Jandu said. He narrowed his eyes at Darvad. "I always respect my elders."

"I know. But don't." Keshan kept hold of Jandu's arms, feeling the sinewy muscles flexing beneath soft skin. "It doesn't suit us."

Jandu stared at Keshan for a moment longer, and then turned away. As he walked away, Keshan shook his head. What was he doing?

"Keshan!" Darvad called, "come shoot with us."

He took the bow Darvad offered, forcing the excitement of Jandu's touch from his mind. He had a mission to fulfill. And the person who was going to do that was Darvad, not Jandu.

CHAPTER 5

Tarek dreamed of the river.

He always dreamed of the river on nights when he had difficulty falling asleep, as if his mind returned to the source of everything.

In his dream, he was a young boy, crying for help. Other times he thrashed in the water, demanding that it stop. He was never at peace in the river. There was something timeless and unforgiving in its nature, the way it cut through everything indiscriminately, the way it never stopped to reason.

Tarek awoke in terror.

It took him a minute to get his bearings. After having spent thirty years of his life living in his parent's one-room shack beside the banks of the Yaru, it still surprised him to wake up in a broad bed with silk sheets, without the smell of the river overwhelming him. His eyes adjusted to the early morning light streaming into the room through two open balconies.

The stone sculpture of the prophet Harami in the corner of the room, the woodcarving above his bed, the garish pinks and greens of the furniture, overstuffed pillows, vases with peacock feathers—all of it had been here when he had acquired Dragewan's townhouse. Tarek suddenly felt disgusted by it all. Now that this ornate manor belonged to him, he would see the gaudy decor stripped.

"Attendant!" Tarek shouted. He was angry at himself for not knowing the man's name. Truthfully, he'd spent a month or two at most in this house since it was granted to him. Most of his time was occupied in the royal palace.

"Yes, my lord?" A squat, balding man stood with his head bowed, avoiding eye contact.

"Call the house steward. I want all the decorations in this room removed."

If the servant found the request strange, he said nothing. "Yes, my lord."

Tarek stretched and stepped out of bed. He realized the servant remained.

"You can go."

The servant hesitated. "My lord? What would you like the decorations replaced with?"

Tarek frowned. "Nothing. I want bare walls. One chair. That's it."

"Yes, my lord." The servant bowed deeply and fled the room.

Tarek watched him go. He should really be nicer. He wasn't comfortable with having servants, and so he didn't know how to treat them.

Tarek wasn't much more than a servant himself. He was the son of a charioteer, a servant of the wealthy Triya caste. His father now resided in a large manor in Dragewan, but his hands were arthritic claws, useless after years of tightly gripping reins. His health had failed, and even with the care of the best physicians, Tarek knew his father's death approached.

Still, Tarek had to be grateful. His father could spend the last of his days in comfort, being fed by servants of his own, enjoying the warm springs of the Dragewan palace grounds, luxuriating in the views of the perfect garden. What more could Tarek have wished for?

Well, he could have had his mother with him as well. She died two years earlier when fever had swept through their village. Tarek was not over it. He would never be over it. His parents had been his whole world.

Tarek dressed quickly, in light blue trousers and golden armor. He wore a gray harafa scarf over his chest, and put on the ruby and diamond rings that had been given to him since he had become lord of Dragewan a year ago. He still wore the plain gold earrings he had been given by his mother, the only trace of his life prior to his rise of power.

Tarek owned several diadems. Remembering his appointment with Darvad for breakfast, Tarek chose the heaviest of them all, a golden crown studded with sapphires that would match the rest of his outfit. Darvad liked to see him in all his finery.

As his charioteer prepared the horses, one of Dragewan's state ministers approached Tarek, requesting a review of some documents. Tarek looked them over briefly, and made a few recommendations, however he left most of the decisions up to them. He was not trained in governance, and he trusted his ministers with most of the important details of running the state. Dragewan was small and by no means wealthy, but it could keep its people fed with income from its copper mines. For that, Tarek was grateful. Darvad could have granted him territory with nothing, after all.

The chariot ride from his house to the palace was short, but the journey was slow this morning as workmen with rickety wagons congested the wide, shaded boulevards surrounding Tarek's townhouse.

Once inside the palace, a servant led Tarek to Darvad's private quarters. Tarek hoped to be the first one there, as he disliked sharing Darvad with other friends and advisors. Happily, Tarek arrived early enough to catch Darvad alone. Darvad smiled as Tarek entered the room and embraced him warmly.

Darvad was pure muscle, every part of his body toned, chiseled, and perfected. He had joyful brown eyes and brown hair that remained permanently restricted under the massive gold diadem that Darvad perpetually wore. Darvad also wore large earrings, shaped like maces, and had on bright golden armor inlaid with the image of the sun.

He looked beautiful to Tarek. And that was a problem.

Tarek had known his entire life that he found men attractive. It was simply a fact of nature. He kept his desires to himself, and other than a few discreet encounters, had left his sexuality to wander off by itself, starve, and die. He had no interest in endangering the reputation of his family or himself just for a quick fuck. He had enough of an active imagination to amuse himself.

But Darvad was the first man that Tarek had fallen in love with. And he knew that Darvad did not reciprocate his feelings, which made the situation worse.

Spending all his time with someone he loved who didn't love him back hurt like a physical pain. The torment worsened the more time Tarek spent with his friend. If he stayed away from Darvad, he could purge the desire from his mind. But he missed Darvad terribly. And when he saw Darvad, his gratitude at being with him subdued his inappropriate cravings, for a time. But they would eventually flare up again, demanding attention, and it drove Tarek mad simply standing in the same room as Darvad without proclaiming his affections.

"How are you today?" Tarek asked.

"I'm wonderful. Druv and I were discussing matters last night, and we've come up with a brilliant idea." Darvad sat at the low table once more, patting the cushion beside him. "Come, sit down. Eat something."

Tarek sat down and let servants fill his cup with sweet, milky tea. Steaming jasmine rice, eggs, and a bowl of fresh mangoes were placed before him.

As Tarek ate, he studied Darvad's handsome features, letting himself indulge momentarily.

They spoke of Tarek's father, and for a moment, happiness overwhelmed Tarek. The sweet taste of mango on his lips, the sight of his best friend by his side, discussing Tarek's family warmly, it felt as though no other problems existed.

But the illusion shattered as soon as Druv joined them.

Tarek liked Druv Majeo, the dashing young lord of Pagdesh.

He was a popular and well-connected man with excessive political savvy. He shared his ample wealth with his friends and allies, and reputedly maintained a vast and powerful network of spies throughout Marhavad that none could rival. Darvad regularly sought Druv's counsel, because Druv knew the happenings in every state, at any given time.

Druv and Darvad exchanged warm greetings and then Druv took his place at the breakfast table. Tarek asked after Druv's wife, who had just given birth to Druv's third child.

But the amiable talk ended immediately thereafter. And this was why Tarek's spirits always sank when Druv appeared. A politician above everything else, Druv could not stop talking business.

"Did Darvad tell you our new plan to win over the more traditional lords to Darvad's ascension?" Druv asked Tarek.

Tarek shook his head. "I haven't heard."

"Yudar's influence over the religious lords is powerful," Darvad said. "We have to find a way to guarantee that the traditionalist states give me their support."

"And that's where you come in, Tarek," Druv said, smiling devilishly. He shoveled rice into his mouth as he spoke. "You are going to be our greatest weapon against Yudar's ascension to the throne."

Weariness washed over Tarek. He did not want to be anyone's political puppet, not even Darvad's.

But then Darvad placed his hand tenderly on Tarek's arm. Tarek's heart surged towards Darvad, hungry for the attention.

Tarek nodded. "What do I have to do?"

"Fight them." Darvad grinned, his food forgotten, focused entirely on Tarek. "Sit down with them, eat with them. They will be so offended that a Suya has shared their food that they will challenge you to duel. You fight them, with the condition that if they surrender, they must support my claim to the throne over Yudar's."

Darvad and Druv both laughed. They seemed oblivious to the notion that Tarek might not want to offend and then fight other lords.

But, Tarek reminded himself, he had taken a holy oath to stand by Darvad's side. The day that Darvad had proclaimed eternal friendship to Tarek and granted him lordship, Tarek had sworn to protect Darvad with his life. He would not break his oath.

Soon Iyestar and his brother Keshan also joined them, followed, moments later, by Firdaus. As they ate, Darvad informed them of the new plan. Iyestar didn't like it.

"You will only make them hate Tarek," Iyestar cautioned. "Not love you."

"We only need them to agree to support me until Mazar makes his decision," Darvad said. "Once he sees that even the traditionalists are supporting my claim, Mazar will have no choice but to select me over Yudar."

It hurt Tarek's pride to have to remind them of this, but it had to be said. "There is another problem. Since I am Suya, by traditional challenging rules, they can use magical shartas. They'll slaughter me."

In truth, even if Tarek were allowed to use magical weapons, he didn't know any. Only the Triya knew shartas, and these were carefully passed down generations in sacred traditions. The shartas were enchanted, said to come from the Yashva demons. They were hard to wield and even harder to withdraw. And some of them were devastating, capable of destroying entire armies, burning men to ash with a single word.

"I can teach Tarek a sharta from my people. None of the other lords will recognize it," Firdaus said casually, wiping his mouth on the back of his hand. "It can be uttered before the challenge begins, and so you will be armed and ready to defend yourself."

"Brilliant!" Darvad cried. "What do you think, Tarek?"

Tarek just nodded. He would do it because of his vow, and because he loved Darvad. But that did not mean he liked the idea.

Darvad leaned over and scooped some of his food onto Tarek's plate. "I know you love the crunchy rice," Darvad whispered.

"I'll host a dinner next week," Druv announced. "I'll invite some of Yudar's supporters, and we can put the plan into action."

"What I don't understand is why you don't simply challenge Yudar yourself, Darvad," Firdaus said. "Yudar is a scholar and not a warrior. You would win easily."

"I wouldn't recommend it," Keshan said casually, nodding to Firdaus. "Jandu Paran would most likely fight in Yudar's place. "

"So you think Jandu is a better warrior than me?" Darvad asked.

Keshan cocked an eyebrow. "Are you willing to chance it?"

"No," Darvad admitted.

Keshan offered Darvad a warm smile. "It's a rare man who has the wisdom to know when he shouldn't fight."

Darvad obviously appreciated the turn of the conversation but Firdaus looked disgusted.

"I've suddenly lost my appetite," Firdaus said lowly. He shot Keshan a cold glare and then made his way to the door. He left the room without another word.

An awkward silence ensued as the four men watched the heavy door fall shut.

"Good," Iyestar said, as soon as Firdaus was out of earshot. "That man is trouble, Darvad."

Druv laughed. Darvad just shrugged. "I know, he is strange. But he is powerful, and we need him on our side. Besides, he is part-Yashva, and has many tricks in his mind."

"I'm part Yashva," Keshan pointed out. "And so is Iyestar."

"Yeah," Iyestar said. "It's not all it's made out to be."

Keshan helped himself to eggs. "Your chef is fantastic, Darvad. I could eat here every meal."

Darvad smiled back. "You are welcome to."

Tarek watched Keshan eat. Tarek considered Keshan attractive, but in a soft, pretty way, rather than in the way that Darvad was handsome, masculine and strong.

"That is a beautiful pendant you have there," Druv said, pointing to the large pearl around Keshan's neck.

Keshan glanced down at the pendant and smiled. "Do you think so? My favorite artisan in Tiwari made it for me. It has the words of the Jandaivo prayer engraved on the back."

Druv admired it for a moment longer, and then turned his attentions back to Darvad.

"So we're going through with this plan? Tarek?"

"Of course," Tarek agreed.

Darvad nodded. But he eyed Keshan carefully. "It's good to have you with us Keshan, but I can't imagine that you've come just to bask in my company. There's something you want, isn't there?"

"Your company is a delight," Keshan replied. "But yes, I have something to ask you to consider."

Keshan reached into his pouch and pulled out a long scroll. He unrolled it and placed it in front of Darvad.

"I have listed here some of the current laws I would recommend changing once you become king," Keshan said. "They are the primary laws responsible for the degradation of the lower classes. I would like them abolished."

Keshan stared at Darvad, as if challenging him to disagree.

Tarek did not know Keshan very well. But he knew Iyestar, and knew that the Adaru family was noble and loyal. The idea of someone from such proud lineage working to improve the lives of lower caste members touched Tarek.

Darvad seemed somewhat annoyed to have his breakfast ruined with law, but this did not stop Keshan. Keshan began reading the laws as they currently existed, reciting them by heart rather than reading off the scroll.

"According to the Book of Taivo, if a Chaya caste member harms or kills a Suya, the punishment shall be lashes. But if a Chaya caste members harms or kills a Triya, the punishment shall be death. If a Suya caste member harms or kills a Chaya, the punishment is only a fine, but if a Suya harms or kills a Triya outside of a formal challenge, the punishment is lashes and imprisonment."

"I know," Darvad interrupted. "It is unfair."

The list went on. Darvad politely read along with Keshan, but Tarek knew him well enough to see he only half-listened.

Keshan opened another scroll. "And these are the laws regarding the Jegora."

Darvad held out his hands. "Wait a moment, Keshan." Darvad shook his head and chuckled. "While I fully support your agenda, I think we need to take things one step at a time. Let us work with improving the legal status of the Suya and Chaya before we start working on the untouchables, shall we?"

Druv laughed. Even Iyestar seemed momentarily embarrassed by his brother's enthusiasm. But Keshan frowned.

"The Jegora have it worst of all," Keshan said. "If they injure any other caste, they are sentenced to death. They face execution anytime a member of another caste feels he's been defiled by one of them. That can take as little as letting their shadow fall on another caste member."

"Look," Darvad interrupted. "I know their lives are terrible. And I hope to rectify that, I truly do." He nodded. "I will help you, Keshan. But before I make additional promises, I need to know now—where does your allegiance lie?"

Keshan looked surprised by the question. "With you, of course."

Darvad stared intently. "You have been keeping company with Jandu Paran."

"I like Jandu," Keshan admitted. "But I do not agree with his brother's politics, and I do not support Yudar's claim to the throne. It is you I support, Darvad."

"Then you have my support in return," Darvad said. "However, announcing my intentions to enact such drastic changes as the ones you are suggesting before I have the crown would be political suicide. Mazar wouldn't even consider giving me the throne. But I promise to address these issues the moment I become king." Darvad patted Keshan's shoulder.

The conversation drifted, and Tarek found himself wearying of the company. His days always followed this course, his desperate desire to see Darvad, and then his realization that he would have to spend hours listening to idle chatter he had no interest in. What he really wanted was more time with Darvad alone.

He wished he could get Darvad to focus on something other than the throne and his competition with Yudar. It bordered on obsession.

Darvad put his hand back on Tarek's shoulder. "After breakfast, I want you all to join me in the dancing hall. I've commanded a dance troupe to do a show for us in private." Darvad winked. "These are the most beautiful women you will ever see!"

Tarek feigned enthusiasm. As the men left, Tarek made an excuse to Darvad, saying he needed to return to the townhouse for Dragewan business.

Darvad's smile vanished. "What? But I want you to be there. Nothing is as fun without you." He smiled brightly, and honestly, and Tarek could feel Darvad's smile warming him to his bones. At moments, like this one, when the true Darvad would shine through the veil of ambition, and stun him with beauty, Tarek could do nothing but concede.

"All right. I'm sure that the business back home can wait."

Darvad hugged him, and Tarek felt, once more, at peace.

CHAPTER 6

"Beware."

Jandu called out the formal warning to his opponent and pulled back his bowstring. He focused on the orchid motif of his master's shield.

Suddenly, Master Mazar dodged to the left. Jandu held his bowstring taut, following his master's erratic movements.

Mazar whispered a sharta.

Jandu heard the dark sound of magic words, the sensation like ice down his spine. As Jandu processed the words, he quickly recalled the counter-curse needed to stop the weapon. But Jandu finished too late. Mazar released his sharta with a last hiss of breath and the ground beneath Jandu's feet gave way. Jandu fell, sinking up to his waist as the ground parted like water under his weight. Dust exploded in a cloud and he choked.

"Damn it." Jandu dropped his bow to drag himself free of the dry soil, coughing and batting his hand through the air to dispel the dirt. The weight of the soil pressed against him, and it took a great deal of effort to extract himself.

Mazar approached his star pupil, grinning. "Too slow, Jandu."

"My apologies, Master."

"Would you like some help?" Mazar asked.

"No, I'm good." Jandu groaned as he wriggled his hips and then his legs free. His white shirt and dark blue trousers were coated in a layer of dust.

Mazar patted Jandu's shoulder, causing another cloud of dust to explode from Jandu's shirt. "You have to be faster."

"I know. Let me try again."

Mazar studied his pupil for a moment, and then nodded. "All right. Same positions."

Mazar was thin, his muscles sinewy, and his wrinkled skin and grey beard showed his years. He kept his white hair short, and so his large ears protruded significantly, displaying the divot where the tip of his left ear had been clipped by an arrow. An impressive scar sliced across his chin.

But despite his ragged appearance, Mazar still moved with grace. His unrivaled dedication to the study of combat, especially shartas, allowed him to wield magical weapons better than anyone in Marhavad.

All of Mazar's experience made him more than just Jandu's hero. He was Jandu's father figure, the man who had taught Jandu everything he knew about archery.

"Beware!" Master Mazar called from across the practice field. The sun blazed directly overhead, and Jandu wiped sweat from his eyes.

Jandu readied his stance and took aim at his master. "Beware!" he called back.

As Mazar moved, Jandu followed him with his readied arrow. And then came the words of the sharta, shivering through his consciousness like a sinister whisper. The shartas were not of this world, and as they became real words, living words, a split rifted the sky and the Yashva world poured through.

"Adarami andaraya epizanash ashubana darha mandria bedru mandria…" The words shivered down Jandu's spine. He kept his eyes trained on his master as he uttered the counter-curse quickly, needing to speak the words before his master finished the sentence.

"Mandria bedru mandria darja ashubana epizanash adaraya adarami…" Jandu spoke the sharta backwards, speeding up towards the end, reversing the damage. He finished speaking at the same time as Mazar, and when Mazar uttered the final *"Chedu!"* to fire the weapon, nothing happened.

Jandu released his arrow, and shot the center of Mazar's shield.

"Well done!" cried Mazar, approaching his student once more. Jandu unstrung his bow proudly. He spat blood on the ground. Uttering shartas always made his mouth bleed. He noticed that Mazar did not share this problem.

"How come I bleed when I use shartas and you don't?" Jandu asked.

"Using magical weapons takes its toll uniquely on different bodies," Mazar said. He sounded out of breath, and plopped to the dusty earth below Jandu. He stretched out, looking drawn. "For me, it merely exhausts. I feel like I have just run up a mountainside. Just count yourself lucky that you don't piss blood like Baram."

Jandu sat beside his master and stared out across the empty practice field. It had once been a large citrus grove but now, the soil torn and scarred by shartas, only weeds thrived.

Jandu leaned back on his elbows, content to sit in silence with his master for a moment. The two of them rarely found time to train together anymore. "Yudar is losing his supporters in the east," Mazar said suddenly. "The lords of Bandari and Penemar are turning toward Darvad."

Jandu kicked at a clump of dirt but said nothing.

"At last night's dice game, I heard Darvad promise the lord of Bandari substantial tax benefits if he became king," Mazar said.

"What did my brother say?" Jandu asked.

"Yudar wasn't there."

Jandu raised his eyebrows. "My brother missed a dice game?"

Mazar laughed. "I know. I think it must have been the first time he has missed an opportunity to play dice in ten years. That Suraya has surely worked a spell upon him."

Jandu snorted and laid back down. He thought it impossible to distract Yudar from gambling. This marriage was really turning out to be good for him.

"It's a shame he missed that particular game, however," Mazar continued. "A lot of discussion took place between the lords in attendance."

"I'll tell him." Why was it so hard for everyone to recognize the fact that he did not want to discuss politics all day? "But I'd rather not talk about it right now."

At this, Mazar sat upright and glared at him. "Don't be so childish, Jandu. You cannot pretend as though it does not matter. This is the most important decision since the formation of Marhavad!"

Jandu cast his eyes downward. "Yes, Master."

"What makes it even more difficult is that both Yudar and Darvad know the Pezarisharta!"

"I know the Pezarisharta too," Jandu commented, but Mazar continued regardless.

"Anyone who has the power of the Pezarisharta can destroy the world. The entire world, Jandu. This is no idle power. Whoever I choose as king must be the kind of man who will take that responsibility seriously."

"I know, I know." Jandu had been drilled, day in and day out, for nearly a year in order to learn the ultimate weapon. Just reciting it took ages, and each word had to be uttered perfectly, in precise order to complete the sharta.

The Pezarisharta set fire to every living creature. It burned earth, sky and water alike.

"I can't speak for Darvad," Jandu said, "but I know Yudar does not even think about the Pezarisharta anymore. He once told me he purposefully tried to forget it. He doesn't believe any man should have such power."

"He is right."

"And yet you taught it to all of us."

"It is your birth right, as princes." Mazar stared blankly out at the dusty field.

Jandu studied his teacher. Although Mazar moved swiftly and dangerously for a man his age, the years as Regent of

Marhavad had changed him, added lines to his dry face, creased his brow. Jandu's father had thrust so much responsibility on the man, trusting Mazar with both the education of his sons, and maintaining his kingdom.

"Are you thirsty?" Jandu suddenly asked. "Would you like me to fetch you something to drink?"

Mazar turned to gaze at Jandu fondly. "Jandu, if I need something to drink, I'll ask one of the servants. You do not have to fetch for me."

"I know." Jandu blushed. "But you are my teacher. It is my duty to respect you."

"You are very good at fulfilling your duty, Jandu. It is one of the traits I most admire in you."

"I thought you most admired my modesty."

Mazar shook his head and Jandu laughed.

"Come on, let us practice once more," Mazar said, standing. "This time, I want you to initiate a sharta. Remember to concentrate. Do not lose your focus, or I will out-speak you."

Jandu stood as well. "Which should I use?" He did not like practicing such weapons on his master. Most were fatal.

"You choose," Mazar said. "Just remember, the more powerful the sharta, the more it will take from your body. Choose wisely." And without another word, Mazar sprinted out of sight, dashing into the nearby citrus grove.

Jandu quickly restrung his bow and chased after his master. He caught a glimpse of Mazar's silver armor ahead, and charged towards him.

As soon as Jandu was within range, he began uttering the Alazsharta, the words cutting his tongue as he spoke them. He could feel, rather than hear, Mazar's counter-curse forming. As Jandu ran and spoke, he pulled an arrow from his quiver.

"*Chedu!*" Jandu spat with the last word onto his arrow. The arrow brightened in his hand, and then returned to its former state. It buzzed in his hand, vibrating with power. He aimed and loosed the arrow at Mazar's shield.

The arrow struck Mazar's shield, but the sharta did not follow through. Alazsharta supposedly put the victim to sleep. And yet Mazar stood tall and proud, panting heavily but definitely conscious.

"How did you do that?" Jandu asked. He spit more blood from his mouth.

Mazar gasped in a deep breath and then answered. "I don't know." He frowned. "I did not finish the counter-curse in time."

"I did."

Jandu swung around to face the intruder. He relaxed immediately upon seeing Keshan.

"Hello." Keshan walked up to both of them, smiling. Despite having just uttered a counter-curse, Keshan looked calm, not even a bead of sweat upon his brow.

"Greetings, Adaru," Mazar said, bringing his hands together in the sign of peace.

"And to you, Regent." Keshan bent low and took the dust from Mazar's feet. When he stood, he looked sheepish. "I apologize for intruding upon your training, but whenever I feel a sharta forming I habitually dissipate it. Sorry."

Jandu hid his surprise behind a smile. "I didn't realize you were so fast."

Keshan shrugged.

"It is a healthy habit to cultivate," Mazar said. "And I am impressed. You were far out of range to be able to work so efficiently."

"I can feel them more than most." Keshan turned to Jandu. "I was looking for you, actually. I have the evening free, and wanted to see if you cared to join me for the temple acrobatic performance this evening."

Pride flooded Jandu, and he almost stumbled over his words in his enthusiasm. "I would love to." He turned nervously to his master. "Assuming it is all right with you, Master?"

Mazar nodded. "I'm too old to exercise much longer anyway. You boys go ahead." He patted Jandu's shoulder. "Besides, I have duties of my own to attend to. But I always appreciate a respite, Jandu. Ask me to practice whenever you feel the need."

"Thank you, Master." Jandu bowed low. He then turned to Keshan and the two of them made their way back towards the gates of the palace.

The excitement of spending time with Keshan still had not faded. Jandu frequently sought him out, but it seemed that Keshan appealed to far more men than just himself. The second Keshan walked into any room, dozens of people gathered around him, vying for his attention. Keshan always appeared excited to see Jandu, but was also easily led away by other lords, leaving Jandu feeling uncomfortably jealous.

To make matters worse, the flirtatious, intimate way that Keshan spoke with Jandu seemed to be the way Keshan spoke with everyone. Just when Jandu thought he was growing closer to his cousin, he would watch Keshan slide up to charm a young woman, or another Triya warrior, his smile sly and infectious.

Jandu had to come to terms with the fact that he was no one special in Keshan's world. If anything, he was an outsider who did not share his views or have a part in his mission. Often Jandu had to wait for Keshan's attention and some days it seemed like Keshan had no time for him at all. The thought disturbed Jandu deeply.

Because whenever the two of them were together, Jandu was filled with a hungry need for more. He had never been so confused and fascinated by anyone. They sat around and made jokes, or talked about nothing, and yet it seemed like the most important discourse in the history of the world. Jandu loved everything about being with his cousin. Keshan had a wonderful, if slightly raunchy, sense of humor, and never hesitated to argue with Jandu, which lesser lords refused to do out of respect for Jandu's lineage. Jandu could be himself around Keshan, and it was rare to find such friends in the palace, especially now.

"I thought most of the performers left last week," Jandu said, walking casually beside Keshan.

"A few acts still linger in town. Mostly because they haven't earned enough money to get back to where they came from."

Jandu scratched his arm, and as he did so, he caught a whiff of his armpit and scowled. "God, I need a bath. I better clean up before I show my face in public."

"I like the way you smell," Keshan said with a wink.

Jandu swallowed his words, choking on what should have been a clever reply. He flustered so easily around Keshan.

"But I can wait while you wash and change," Keshan said. "Besides, I've never seen your rooms. I'm curious."

"They aren't impressive," Jandu said.

Keshan reached out and tucked a loose strand of hair behind Jandu's ear. The touch startled Jandu, but Keshan just smiled. "You look pretty disheveled."

"I did just come crawling out of a dirt pit, thanks to Mazar's sharta." Jandu hoped his blush wasn't obvious. Keshan always surprised him this way, touching him in a confident, familiar manner that left Jandu weak in the knees.

"I felt that one too."

"How could you?"

"I'm half-Yashva."

"What does that have to do with anything?" Jandu nodded to the guards as they passed through the gates of the outer palace wall.

Keshan gave Jandu a surprised glance. "Do you even know what a sharta is?"

"Of course I do," Jandu said. "It's a magical weapon."

"But what it is? What it is really?" Keshan shook his head. "Triya. All they care about is the destruction. They don't care that every time they fire their shartas, they are pulling Yashvas into this world and transforming them."

Jandu frowned. "Transforming a Yashva?"

"A sharta is a spell which opens a door between the Yashva and human worlds, and then summons one particular Yashva into the human world. Every Yashva has a unique shartic nature, which is how they manifest themselves on earth. So when you use a sharta, you are pulling some Yashva from their life in their own world and transforming them into tools."

"This way." Jandu cut the corner between the armory and the guard tower, taking a short cut to his own rooms. "How come we are never taught this?"

"No one here cares about the Yashvas, even though they formed the world. We are only thought of as spirits, nothing more."

"What happens after the sharta is expelled?" Jandu asked.

"The summoned Yashva reappears in the Yashva kingdom, exhausted and pissed off." Keshan smiled. "I saw it while I stayed with them during my exile."

Jandu wanted to ask Keshan more questions about his time in the Yashva kingdom, but Keshan's expression had closed. Jandu let it go.

Jandu's rooms were at the far end of one of the larger and newer buildings, overlooking a rose garden and pool that he shared with Baram. Keshan immediately wandered about, taking in the sparse decorations as Jandu excused himself and went to the bath. When he returned, refreshed and in a change of clothing, Keshan had an odd smirk on his face.

"I can't determine anything about you by your rooms," he said.

Jandu shrugged. "I don't spend much time here. If it were me, I'd just have targets on the wall."

"But who *are* you, Jandu Paran? Really?" Keshan smiled slyly.

Jandu laughed. "Just me. Handsome. Talented. Brilliant. You know the rest."

Keshan was staring at him strangely. "Do I? What else is there to know about you?"

Jandu could feel his face turning red. "There's nothing else to tell. I'm just me. I guess I should also say I'm the youngest Paran brother, fourth in line for the throne, Suraya's third husband, on and on. But that doesn't matter."

"It doesn't?"

"Not to me. All I want to do is shoot things, and have a good time." Jandu glanced over at Keshan, who regarded Jandu with almost a hungry expression.

"Well, then." Keshan cleared his throat. "Let's go show you a good time, shall we?"

They made their way to the eastern bridge, where one of the palace guards offered to prepare a chariot for them.

"I'd rather walk, if it's the same to you," Jandu said.

Keshan agreed, and they crossed the bridge and entered the heart of the bustling city of Prasta.

As Jandu walked, he relaxed. He had always been a constant mover. As a child, his family had made fun of him for his persistent fidgeting. He always drummed his hands on tables and squirmed in his chairs. In fact the only time Jandu was ever still was when he took aim. The moment he held a bow in his hands, the constant need to be in movement ceased, and he could focus all of that reckless energy into one goal, hitting his target.

As they passed through the central market, Jandu took comfort in the sights and smells of the city of his birth. Jandu loved Prasta, which sprawled lazily along both banks of the Yaru River. Stone walls stretched for miles around the city, carved white towers thrusting up from them like sentinels. Inside the walls, streets wound endlessly around each other from the meat market all the way to the temple district.

Down one street, Jandu smelled jasmine blossoms, only to be assaulted at the next alley by open sewage.

Jandu's presence as a Triya among the lower castes did not go undetected. As he and Keshan made their way through the crowds, most people stopped and bowed low. Jandu offered the sign of peace to onlookers, and often stopped walking altogether as some merchant or traveler bent to take the dust from his feet. Not for the first time, Jandu considered traveling incognito.

Keshan directed them into one of the poorer sections of town where Jandu rarely ventured. He felt out of place and uncomfortable, but Keshan's easy confidence and constant stream of amusing stories set Jandu's mind at ease. The streets narrowed. The mud and straw walls rose higher. Only the smells of cooking oil and the sight of washing hung on long lines across the streets proved that inhabitants dwelled within. Through the occasional open door, Jandu could peer in and see the small cobblestone courtyards where families gathered on mats, eating and fighting and cleaning and tending children as goats and chickens scuttled past.

Keshan guided him further than he'd gone before, to the very edge of Prasta. Here houses consisted of a single room, broken wooden doors, and small windows through which Jandu could glimpse dirty bedding. People drew away from them sharply, wary of such noble blood walking among them. A group of girls dressed in rags crossed the street as they saw Jandu and Keshan approach, fearful that their shadows would fall on them. Jandu rarely saw Jegora untouchables out and about, and his sense of discomfort grew.

"Where are you taking me?" Jandu demanded, interrupting Keshan's long-winded narrative of the time he stole pastries from some courtier's daughters. Jandu's fingers twitched against the hilt of his sword, causing the Jegora to cower away from him.

Keshan pointed to a simple mud temple up ahead. "An acrobatic troupe from Tiwari is performing there. Some of my friends back home recommended the show."

Jandu didn't have anything nice to say about the area they were in, so he kept his thoughts to himself. He knew Keshan liked the lower classes, but this was getting a bit too unconventional for him.

"Are you sure we will be welcome?" Jandu asked nervously.

"Are you kidding? They will be honored to have us." Keshan linked his arm casually in Jandu's and pulled him along.

The temple was very simple on the outside, mud bricks and shutterless windows. It was a Suya temple, and Jandu had never been inside one. If it had been Jegora, Jandu would have refused to enter, no matter how enchanted he was with Keshan's company.

Keshan didn't give him time to ponder the unhygienic implications further. He pulled Jandu inside. Jandu was relieved to see the images of God were the same as those that graced the most ornate of Shentari temples. The prophets gazed from the corners, and the tenets from the Book of Taivo were carved along the entrance wall, the letters painted in red, veiled by the countless streams of incense smoke.

As Keshan predicted, their appearance was greeted with disbelief, and then overbearing warmth. Temple attendants gathered pillows for Jandu and Keshan to sit upon, and a servant was sent to fetch Triya-caste purified tea for them.

Close to one hundred people already sat in the small courtyard of the temple, but an airy space was created in the center for Jandu and Keshan. At the front of the temple, near the offerings, the troupe performed their show. Five men and five women tumbled over the stone floor in dramatic twists and fanciful leaps, all to the steady rhythm of a flute and a rebo which looked to be missing several strings.

Jandu disliked the environment, but the moment the show started, he forgot his anxiety and simply enjoyed the performance. He had never seen anything like it. All throughout the piece, crude jokes were scattered, random positions spawning a series of lewd gestures, causing the audience around him to roar in delight and Jandu to blush horrifically. He never knew the lower castes reveled in obscenity.

Jandu stole glances to his side, watching Keshan's reactions. Keshan appeared captivated by the performance. He laughed and clapped and smiled constantly, his face lighting up every time a new number started. Jandu enjoyed his cousin's reactions as much as the show itself. Keshan shouted cheers and raunchy suggestions with the rest of the audience. Jandu was out of place here—but it was clear that Keshan felt comfortable.

The performance neared its finale. And then suddenly a loud scream and the sound of numerous horses thundered from outside the temple walls. For another minute, the acrobats continued their show. Then an explosion shook the ground, and no one could ignore what was happening outside.

The audience stood and streamed for the entry. Jandu jumped up as well, his hand on his sword, cursing the fact that he left his bow and quiver behind.

Keshan stood beside him, eyeing the frightened crowd.

"We can't let them go outside," Keshan said suddenly. He dashed for the entryway.

"Please! Everyone! Stay calm!" Keshan shouted, trying to bring order to the chaos. Jandu was momentarily terrified that Keshan would be trampled.

But the audience stopped at the door. Keshan guarded it with his body. "If you go outside, you will be harmed."

Something caught afire, right outside the temple, and now smoke drifted in the dusk and clouded even nearby people from Jandu's sight. He pressed his way through the crowd to stand beside Keshan.

"What is happening?" Jandu shouted in Keshan's ear, hoping to be heard above the panicked shouts.

"Robbers," Keshan said. "It happens in the poorer temples. Bandits block temple doors at events like this one, forcing payment from the people inside."

"What?" Jandu scanned the crowd. "These people don't have enough money to make it worthwhile!"

"The robbers pick on the poor temples because no one is going to defend them."

Lit torches were thrown over the temple walls, and the panic increased, people pushing each other out of the way to avoid the flames.

"Why isn't anyone sounding the alarm for the city guards?" Jandu cried.

Keshan glared at Jandu like he was insane. "This is a Suya temple." A loud thump shuddered against the door, causing the wood to bulge inwards. Keshan flew forward towards the fearful crowd.

"They're breaking the door!" someone cried.

"This is ridiculous," Jandu said. His bewilderment had cleared, and now he was just angry. "All I wanted to do was go and see a show, and now these bastards ruin it. Fuck this. Let's go get them."

Keshan narrowed his eyes. "There may be as many as twenty men out there, Jandu."

"I don't care," Jandu said. "I'm a fucking prince and I don't pay robbers. These bastards picked the wrong temple today."

Jandu wished he wore armor, and almost laughed at the thought. That would show him for making fun of Triya who dressed in helmets and breastplates just to attend festivities. He spotted an iron breastplate, which was part of the decorative armor of the Prophet Bandruban. He pushed his way through the crowd and untied the leather bands from the statue, grabbing the breastplate and the dull, decorative sword from the statue's hand. He returned to the door, which now pulsed and groaned with each ram from the outside. Smoke poured over the wall, choking the crowd trapped in the temple.

"Put this on," Jandu demanded, throwing Keshan the breastplate.

Keshan shook his head. "You wear it!"

"I'll be fine. Hurry."

Keshan glared at Jandu again, but quickly strapped on the breastplate. It was too large for him, and the metal was cheap, but it would be better than nothing. Jandu looked at the dull, ornamental sword. He gave Keshan his own sword instead, keeping the prophet's sword for himself.

Keshan in armor was a strange sight—such a slim body in such bulky attire. Jandu found his mind drawn to it. More fiery torches rained down over the temple wall. People scattered and screamed.

Jandu drew his sword. "You ready, Keshan?"

Keshan nodded. He turned to the crowd. "Stay back! Back away from the door! Everyone stay inside!" He placed his hands on the bolt.

"If I use a sharta, are you going to be angry?" Jandu asked suddenly.

"There is a time and place for magical weapons. And this is both of them."

Jandu closed his eyes and brought his hands together. He visualized the Barunazsharta in his mind, focusing all his thoughts on the poetry of the weapon.

And then he spoke. Quickly, quietly, he whispered the words he needed. He groped on the ground for a stone, which he spat the sharta onto, and then tossed the stone over the wall, into the midst of the robbers.

"Close your eyes," he told Keshan. He shut his own.

The world exploded into light.

Shouts of surprise filled the air as the blinding light blazed overhead. Jandu immediately opened the door and pushed himself into the cluster of robbers.

"Lock the door! Lock the door!" he cried to Keshan behind him.

The bandits were still blinded, rubbing at their eyes, groping for their weapons and stumbling towards Jandu.

Keshan rushed up beside Jandu, sword drawn.

Jandu's skin raised in goose bumps, and he heard the soft, silent uttering of a sharta. Keshan spat out the curse so quickly that Jandu had missed which one it was.

The men in front of them exploded backwards, propelled by a force of air. And then Keshan and Jandu charged.

Hand to hand combat was never Jandu's strongest skill. But he was energized this night, fuelled by the panic of the audience, by the outrage of having his evening ruined. He thrust the temple sword into the skull of one of his attackers. As the man fell, Jandu tore the sword from the man's lifeless grip. Another robber drove in with a short knife. Jandu parried his thrust with the temple sword and then stabbed his new blade deep into the man's chest. As the robber fell dead, Jandu saw fear kindle in the faces of his would be attackers. He threw himself upon them, slashing with both blades and driving them back. Bandits cried out and fell, bleeding. Their horses reared and fled. Oily smoke filled the air. Behind him, Jandu heard Keshan kill another man and then there were no more attackers left.

Jandu stood beside Keshan, watching the last remaining assailants flee for their lives. Almost twenty men lay in the street. Half of those had been destroyed by Keshan's sharta—their faces contorted by the force of the weapon's wind. Some lay bloody, staring upwards with blank, final stares, and a few groaned feebly, clutching at the dirt, unable to move but not yet gone.

The door to the temple opened tentatively, the wood creaking on its injured hinges. Slowly, the temple goers shuffled out, staring at the carnage in the street. Others came to witness, neighbors pouring from their homes, clutching children. When they saw one of the bandits still living they fell on him like animals, kicking him, spitting and cursing until he was dead. Even though Triya codes forbade this kind of dishonorable fight, these Suya needed their vengeance and Jandu let them take it. Who knew how many times these same robbers had attacked their temple? Jandu turned away.

A young woman with scorched hair bent down to touch Jandu's feet.

"Thank you," she mumbled. She looked up at him with a nervous smile. Jandu felt slightly better.

Jandu heard Keshan laugh, and turned to see him surrounded by Suya citizens, smiling as they closed around him, congratulating him with dramatic bows. Keshan slapped the men on their shoulders without regard to their lower caste.

And then the people moved to Jandu, bowing to him, touching his feet, offering him sticks of incense, desperate in their gratitude. Almost immediately, temple attendants dragged the bodies from the road, starting a huge pyre to burn the corpses.

Jandu cleaned his sword blade on a cloth and noticed his hands trembled with unspent aggression. Keshan was far more amiable with the survivors than he. He even hugged some of them. He listened with a sad face as they explained how these same men had terrorized them for more than a year.

Jandu excused himself, stepping down an alley and leaning against a cart. A goat tethered to the cart stared up at him placidly, chewing hay as though nothing had happened.

What the hell was he doing here?

Keshan found him before too long, approaching with a wide smile.

"You are fantastic in a fight," Keshan said. He stood very close to Jandu.

Jandu could smell Keshan's skin, coconut and sweat and wood smoke. Jandu suddenly longed to reach out and touch him, to transfer the smell to his own hands. Jandu turned away, embarrassed. Keshan quietly stepped behind Jandu and encircled Jandu's waist, his hands clasped around Jandu's stomach. Jandu's embarrassment turned to relief. He leaned back into his cousin, enjoying how Keshan's presence made his shoulder muscles relax.

Keshan turned Jandu around to face him. He didn't move his arms from around Jandu's waist. Keshan reached up and stroked the side of Jandu's face. It was such an intimate gesture that Jandu was shocked. But it felt too good to pull away.

The sun had set over an hour ago, but the street blazed in the light of the spontaneous funeral pyre. Dozens of people gathered around to discuss the attack on the temple.

What would those people think if they saw the two of them like this? Jandu shrugged Keshan's arms off. Keshan raised an eyebrow, but said nothing.

"Can we head back now?" Jandu asked. "I want to get away from here. I want to go somewhere clean."

Keshan offered Jandu his hand and said, "Shall we take a short cut?"

Jandu frowned. "From this neighborhood, there are no short cuts."

"You are very talented with shartas, so you should be able to do this."

"Do what?" Jandu's self-consciousness was slowly giving way to curiosity. He took Keshan's hand, relaxing further. It felt natural to have his hand linked with Keshan's.

"I'm going to show you a door. You already know the words. Now you have to craft them slightly so that they are less volatile." Keshan closed his eyes, and stretched out his arms, palms upwards towards the sky. He began reciting words, shartic words, but they were different than the weapons Jandu knew. They lilted at the end, trilled. Jandu mimicked Keshan's posture and repeated them, grateful that his mouth didn't bleed.

When the sharta finished, Jandu opened his eyes. He was still standing with Keshan in the dark narrow street. But he felt different. Something about the light shifted, shadows had appeared as if the sun still shone.

"What did you do?"

"Opened the door." Keshan grabbed his hand. "Looks the same, doesn't it? But now…"

Something blurry passed in front of Jandu, and he tensed. He grasped the hilt of his sword.

Another shadowy image rushed by. He could distinguish the shape of a body, but it was much taller than a human's, with shimmering blue skin, and the face was hazy, unformed.

"What was that?"

"A Yashva." Keshan squinted in concentration. "This way."

Keshan stepped into the air, pulling Jandu along behind. Jandu blinked—

—and they stood in a field. An empty field, as far as he could see. In the distance, far away, Jandu made out a strange mountain range, the hills jagged and piercing in every direction, like thorns on a rose. The air was thick here, fragrant with flowers and something indefinably sweet, like rotting blackberries and rich soil. Jandu felt bathed in warmth.

"Where are we?" Jandu whispered.

Keshan laughed. "Where do you think? In the Yashva kingdom."

Jandu gazed around him in amazement. "Really? But… how?"

"You've always known how, Jandu. Every time you use a sharta, you open the door between worlds. You just haven't ever stepped through that door." Keshan peered into the distance. "Come on."

The field, which had seemed endless, now moved in front of Jandu as if he were flying. Perception warped here, and he felt dizzy.

"I can't feel my feet touching the ground," Jandu admitted.

Keshan nodded. "That's because, technically, they aren't touching ground. This is all illusion."

"So how do you know where to go?"

"It's my illusion. Every Yashva has a different interpretation of this space." Keshan cocked his head as if thinking hard. "Think of it as your rooms back in the palace. An empty space for you to decorate how you will. You would prefer to have targets on the walls. Yudar, no doubt, has holy scrolls and paintings of the prophets. It is the same in the Yashva realm. Each Yashva has a different world, but we can interact here as well."

As the field flew by, Jandu caught sight of more Yashvas. They were taller than him, with lanky, thin bodies, shimmering blue skin, and dark, swirling eyes. They were beautiful, but strangely immobile, their faces like expressionless masks.

"Are they upset with me being here?" Jandu asked self-consciously.

Keshan shook his head. "No, merely curious. It says a lot about you, the fact that you are even here. You have a great deal of power. Most people cannot wield shartas, let alone summon the concentration required to enter a Yashva's home."

"It's beautiful." The field gave way to a flowing stream of rushing water, and on the other side, a collection of buildings, their exteriors pearly and turbulent in the soft, unnatural light. The fact that this was all Keshan's world, his mind, made the entire sight even more beautiful and intimate.

"Prasta's palace is right here," Keshan said, stomping the ground. The gesture produced no sound. Everything was muffled, echoed and distant. "We can go back, or we can have a drink here, where I stayed during my exile."

A giddy excitement filled Jandu. This was Keshan's private world. No one else had seen this but him.

"Let's stay. I want to see everything." Jandu let go of Keshan's hand and spun around, lifting his arms, breathing in the thick, fragrant air. His body tingled, every pore vibrating with the strange newness of the place.

"If you're going to dance, Jandu, dance with me," Keshan said.

"Offer me wine first," Jandu replied coyly. "That's how it's done."

"Oh, is that how it is?" Keshan's voice was low, almost syrupy smooth. His lids had lowered slightly, and he looked suddenly wanton and husky. "Well come on then, brave warrior. Let me get you a victory cup."

Keshan took Jandu's hand once more and gently pulled him towards the buildings. They zoomed into focus jaggedly, and Jandu struggled with his sense of perspective. Walls loomed at exaggerated angles as if the world had been sketched in watercolor.

The strange opalescent walls of Keshan's home glimmered and swirled in pastel colors as the eerie endless daylight played over their surfaces. The floors were laid with richly layered silk carpets in persimmon and royal blue, and dozens of silk pillows banked the walls.

A tall blue Yashva servant brought them drinks, her face blank and unreadable, her eyes blazing and seemingly shifting in her face. Jandu felt dizzy staring at the Yashva, and finally had to look away.

They drank. They shared a bottle of honey wine. Jandu couldn't tell if it the alcohol, or the sweet air which intoxicated him.

"Can I ask you a personal question?" Keshan asked.

"I guess," Jandu said.

Keshan sipped his wine. "Do you mind sharing Suraya?"

Jandu shrugged. "Not really."

"Many would find that unbelievable," Keshan said.

Jandu smiled. "I'm utterly righteous. That's how I can share my wife with my older brothers without issue."

Keshan laughed.

"I wonder if they feel the same way," Keshan mused.

Jandu finished his wine and stretched up, yawning as he did so. "We set firm rules after the wedding, and one was that we wouldn't talk about our romantic relationship with Suraya. And if anyone accidentally walks in on another brother when he is with Suraya, he has to go on a pilgrimage as penance."

Keshan whistled. "That seems harsh."

Jandu nodded. "It would be harsh enough just to catch Baram or Yudar screwing anyone."

"So you're not jealous at all, are you?" Keshan asked. Jandu could tell now, by the flush of Keshan's cheeks, that he was pretty drunk. Jandu himself was feeling heavy in the head.

He wanted to talk about things he knew he probably shouldn't talk about.

"The truth is, I think I'm in love with someone else." Jandu closed his eyes.

Keshan didn't reply. Jandu opened his eyes again, and saw Keshan staring at him sharply. He leaned in close to Jandu.

"Who are you in love with?"

Jandu smiled slowly. "I'm not telling."

Keshan kept a level gaze on him. Again Jandu felt that warm rush of blood whenever Keshan looked at him that way.

"Come on. You can tell me. We're friends," Keshan said.

"No."

Keshan stared at him a moment longer, and then broke eye contact. He stretched upwards, his hand brushing casually against Jandu's as he did so. Jandu felt electrified by his touch.

"Fine then, be that way," Keshan said, shrugging. "But does Suraya know?"

Jandu dismissed the question with a wave of his hand. "Who knows what women know? Maybe she'll find out when it's my year to be married to her. I don't have to deal with that for another two years."

Keshan raised his glass. "Good for you. Put off your problems till another day."

Jandu raised his empty glass, and clinked it against Keshan's. "I feel like I did my Triya duty today. I'm allowed a few failures of character in regard to my wife."

Keshan nodded. "Of course you are. You're perfect in every other way."

Jandu flushed. The fabric beneath him was warm and cocooning. He felt as though he could sink inside of it and sleep forever.

"I don't want to leave here," he suddenly admitted. He lay back. "I want to stay in here, with you, forever."

Jandu suddenly sat upright, panicked that he had said that aloud.

But Keshan did not chastise him. He watched Jandu with a strange, liquid expression.

Jandu cleared his throat. "We should probably get back to the palace, or Yudar will notice I'm gone and start to worry."

Keshan still stared. Stared hard at Jandu's mouth.

Jandu stood. His body resisted and he almost collapsed in the effort.

With a sigh, Keshan stood as well. "Fine then. I'll take you home."

Jandu suddenly wanted to touch him. Not knowing any other way to do so without being disrespectful, he reached down to touch Keshan's feet. Keshan stopped him halfway, as he had when they first met.

"How many times do I have to tell you not to do that?" Keshan said, his voice almost a whisper. He didn't pull his hands from Jandu's arms. "You're almost the same age as me."

"It's traditional," Jandu reminded him.

"It's too formal a gesture," Keshan said.

Jandu smiled. "All right." He brought Keshan in for an embrace. He would hug him like he hugged his brothers.

Keshan hugged back tightly. Jandu's heart beat faster. Their bodies drew even closer, and Jandu could feel Keshan pressed against him, could smell his hot skin. Their embrace went on several seconds too long. Suddenly embarrassed, Jandu let Keshan go, wanting to get as far away from the other man as possible before he made a fool of himself.

"Good night, Adaru," Jandu said.

Keshan looked at him with the sweetest grin.

"Sweet dreams." Keshan leaned forward, as if he would kiss Jandu on the forehead. Instead, he whispered strange words as he gently laid a hand on Jandu's chest and gave him a slight push.

Jandu fell but not far. He shook his head to clear it. Outside, it was dark, and the air stank of manure and sweat and rotting hay. He looked around, and realized that Keshan had just dumped him behind the palace stables.

CHAPTER 7

WORD OF JANDU AND KESHAN'S TRIUMPH OVER THE TEMPLE robbers spread quickly. By morning, lords, courtiers and their wives accosted Jandu, pressing him for details, desperate for gossip. Baram and Yudar congratulated Jandu on his bravery, and Suraya appeared quietly impressed.

Throughout the day, the tale of Jandu's defense of the temple grew in scope. Before noon, he had only killed twenty bandits, but by dusk, the ranks of defeated robbers had swelled to forty. And Jandu had killed them with his bare hands. Jandu corrected no one, choosing instead to bask in the sudden fame.

All day he waited for Keshan to appear and share the adulation, but Keshan remained absent that day and the next. Jandu even went so far as to casually find himself at Keshan's townhouse only to be told by the servants that the master had not been home. Had he stayed on in the Yashva lands? Why? How could he contact a man in another world? He could not remember the words to open the Yashva door.

Worse yet, could Keshan be with Darvad and his friends? Jandu imagined him talking about his mission while Darvad nodded in agreement, the Suya Tarek, like a dog, at his side and Druv smiling that knowing little smile of his—all of them sharing Keshan's vision of the future.

Yudar took advantage of Jandu's current popularity by asking him to entertain a party of influential gold and silversmiths, hoping that Jandu's new reputation as the defender of the people would smooth over the occasionally factious relations between Prasta's artisan guilds. Jandu agreed. He thought assisting Yudar would help him become a more well-rounded person like Keshan, a person who could not only fight but also make peace.

But the conversation of the artisans focused entirely on money and quickly bored Jandu. Money talk irritated him, and discussing how to form strategic alliances in order to make more of it, appealed to Jandu almost as much as chatting about methods of cleaning the latrines. He endured a joyless week of excruciating diplomacy before he finally faced facts. He would never be an effortless statesman like Keshan. After falling asleep in the middle of conclusive deliberations, Yudar politely asked Jandu to stop helping.

Although relieved to be spared more meetings, Jandu wished he could have proven himself to be more than just a warrior. And this thought, in itself, depressed him. A week ago, Jandu had been the proudest Triya in the nation. But now he was suddenly aware of all his shortcomings. He wanted to be more.

He realized it all had to do with Keshan.

Keshan was so perfect. He was funny and clever and compassionate, he was a fantastic statesman and a flirtatious guest, a skilled warrior and a musician. He knew the religious texts by heart, he remained current on all the local gossip, and he dressed to kill.

What could Jandu possibly offer such an admirable companion? Jandu could shoot a bow and look handsome doing it. That about summed him up.

Finally, seeking any diversion, he found himself sorting through storage chests from his childhood. He remembered some of his old fascinations. He found several scrolls full of sketches of falcons and eagles. He used to find birds of prey fascinating, and would draw them for hours. He found other scrolls covered in letters. He had practiced penmanship devoutly as a boy. He had loved wooden puzzles, piecing them together and even designing his own, which he would order one of the servants to build for him.

But he had given up all of these interests once he started formal weapons training at the age of ten. His artistic abilities, his interest in science, his curiosity had been abandoned in his single-minded pursuit of Triya weapons mastery. And now he realized with sudden disgust that he knew how to kill people. And that was all.

Jandu threw one of his puzzles back into his chest and kicked the entire box across the marble floor.

"Burn it," he told the servant. He slumped against the wall.

He wanted Keshan to think he was educated and talented and the kind of person Keshan would spend his spare time with. But Jandu could think of nothing to offer Keshan in return. It was an unequal friendship. And it made Jandu mad at himself for giving up all the childhood interest that could have made him a more attractive companion.

Until now, Jandu had rarely engaged in introspection. He had no experience even thinking about the kind of doubt that plagued him. So he tried to consider it in terms of something he did understand: archery.

Baram once asked Jandu how he could strike every target he aimed at. Jandu reminded his brother of the lesson they had all learned from Mazar, years ago when they were children.

Mazar had a stuffed sparrow placed on a tree branch, after which he turned to the four boys before him. Because Darvad was oldest, Mazar called on him first. He instructed Darvad to take aim, and then asked Darvad what he saw.

"I see the bird, and the branch, and the tree trunk. I see the sky behind the bird, and the grass at the base of the tree."

"Sit down," Mazar instructed. Darvad looked disappointed to have let down his master, but he took his seat.

Next came Yudar.

"What do you see?" Mazar asked again.

Yudar cleared his throat. He narrowed one eye. "I see the bird, and the tree trunk, and the tree. I see leaves blowing in the wind."

"Sit down," Mazar said once more.

Yudar bowed slightly. "Yes, master." He sat cross-legged beside Mazar.

Baram tried as well, and met with the same response.

"Jandu, your turn."

Jandu had stood and readied his stance. He pulled back the bowstring and took aim.

"What do you see?" Mazar repeated.

The world darkened. "I see the bird's eye," Jandu said. The eye was in the light. Nothing else mattered.

"What else do you see?" Mazar inquired.

"I see the bird's eye," Jandu repeated.

"Then loose your arrow."

Jandu released the string. It slapped painfully against his arm, but the arrow stayed true to the target. The bird tumbled to the earth. Mazar retrieved the target, and held it up for Jandu's brothers to examine.

"Learn from Jandu," Mazar told the others. "Learn that an archer sees nothing but his target. The rest of the world is lost in shadow."

Now when Jandu put his eye to a target and drew back his bowstring, the world contracted until only a pinprick of sight remained. His target. Fragments of sound, doubt, fear and desire: everything melted into the dark. Jandu would release the string, and claim his prize.

But for the first time, Jandu needed to direct his focus towards something other than archery. If he wanted to befriend Keshan, he would have to think of himself as a hunter stalking prey, rather than just a student aiming at a target. He must lure Keshan to him, take aim and fire. But he was at a loss as to what he could use to ensnare Keshan.

Jandu's family was far too busy to indulge his self-assessment. He got Baram alone for an afternoon and went on and on about how he would never be an intellectual. Baram responded by standing up, poking Jandu in the eye, and then walking out. Jandu then tried discussing his qualities as a human being with Yudar. Yudar listened, as he always did. He sat cross-legged in his chambers and smiled benignly at his brother, nodding as Jandu spoke as if Jandu were the center of the universe. But it seemed that Yudar had planned other activities. As Jandu described the different opportunities he had as a youth to better himself in the arts of medicine, he noticed Yudar frequently looking askance at Suraya, a blush forming across his face.

Jandu stopped talking when it was plain to see that Yudar had become aroused, trousers bulging, and it was probably not from Jandu's fourteen-year-old medical ambitions. Jandu slunk away, feeling worse when the door shut behind him and he heard Suraya giggle.

As a last effort, Jandu invited Master Mazar for a private lunch. He had servants bring tea and plied his teacher with sweets.

"I heard about your success in the temple," Mazar said. He was a glutton for sugar, and had his mouth filled with candied pastries before he completely sat down at the low table.

Jandu pushed his own plate towards his master. He himself had no interest in sweets.

"I am very proud of you," Mazar said. He smiled widely.

Jandu nodded. "Thank you."

"You are everything I have trained you to be," Mazar said.

"But I wonder—am I nothing but a warrior?"

Mazar scowled. "What?"

Jandu spoke quickly. "I just mean, shouldn't I have studied the finer arts as well? Like painting, or music?"

Mazar stared at Jandu as if he had just grown another head. "Don't be absurd," he spat. "You are the finest archer in the world. And you want more?"

Jandu shrugged.

"Do you think there is no art in using shartas?" Mazar said. "I have taught everything you know to your brothers as well.

And yet they cannot control the weapons like you can. None of them have your focus or concentration." Mazar grinned. "Remember the bird's eye?"

"I remember," Jandu said, sighing.

Mazar threw down his honey pastry with unnecessary force. His white eyebrows drew together. "Tell me what this is really all about."

Jandu flushed. He hated being so transparent.

"I just…" Jandu looked at his feet. "I want to befriend a person who has little interest in war and I don't have anything else to talk about." The silence hung between them. Jandu felt the gravity of his own words, and wanted to curl up in shame from it all. There could be nothing more embarrassing than this.

Mazar remained silent for so long, Jandu had to look up to make sure he hadn't simply left the room. Mazar stared at his pupil with a soppy smile.

"Oh, Jandu," Mazar said, shaking his head. "This girl you desire will love you even if you don't have anything smart to say to her."

Jandu frowned.

Mazar reached across the low table and touched Jandu's shoulder. "You have a great heart. And you shouldn't underestimate the appeal of a warrior to a woman."

Mazar smiled, and Jandu smiled back at him. Mazar didn't understand the situation, but it felt good to get the compliment nevertheless.

Mazar seemed satisfied with his own answer as well, and quickly swallowed the rest of Jandu's sweets.

That afternoon, Jandu decided he would go for a walk. The sun hung low over the banks of the lazy Yaru River, and Jandu wandered along the water's edge, singing to himself. He plucked at the bushy tops of high grasses as he walked, closing his eyes to the sun in his face.

"Jandu."

He turned quickly, surprised to be discovered so far from the palace. Keshan Adaru came up to him, his smile enchanting. Nervous excitement coursed through Jandu.

"What are you doing here?" Jandu asked.

Keshan pulled a blade of grass from beside him and started munching on the end. "I wanted to find you."

"Oh." Jandu hoped Keshan couldn't tell how fast his heart was beating.

"I was at the palace, discussing changes to the law with Darvad and Iyestar." Keshan noticed Jandu's wince, and grinned sheepishly. "Sorry, I forgot. No politics."

"I'm just tired of hearing about it all the time."

"Really?" Keshan said. "How relieving. That's why I sought you out. I need to rest my mind for an hour or so."

Jandu frowned. "So spending time with me is the equivalent of resting your mind? Am I an idiot or something?"

Keshan's left eyebrow quirked up. "Did I say that?" He munched on his blade of grass thoughtfully, then said, "I enjoy being with you. You are what you are, and I find that refreshing."

Jandu still felt slightly insulted, but he let the comment slide. "Surely you don't talk about politics with your brother all the time, do you?" Jandu asked.

"Iyestar and I don't really talk, we bicker." Keshan hooked his arm with Jandu's. "And you are far more pleasing to look at than my brother."

Jandu's pulse raced every time Keshan touched him. They walked together in silence until they rounded a bend in the river and approached the edge of the royal forest.

"There is a clear patch in the woods there where I used to practice archery as a boy," Jandu said, motioning with his hands to the nearby woods.

"Show me," Keshan said.

Jandu led the way through the tall grass, passing into the cool shade of the forest.

"Only Mazar knew about this spot," Jandu said. "Once he followed me here, assuming I was up to no good, sneaking off away from the others to lurk in the forest by myself. He was surprised to discover I just came out here and practiced."

"He probably expected to catch you jerking off." Keshan laughed.

Jandu looked at Keshan, startled. "What?"

Keshan shook his head. "You Parans. You've been raised in a tower of purity. You really need to travel more, get out in the world."

"I would love to see Tiwari one day," Jandu said. He led Keshan through a gap in the tree line and towards a glade.

Keshan stopped Jandu by putting his hand on Jandu's shoulder. Jandu's shoulder heated where Keshan's skin touched him.

"Promise me you'll come, then," Keshan said, staring deeply into Jandu's eyes. "I would love to show you the city."

Jandu felt his whole body stirring with the look Keshan gave him.

"I promise," Jandu said weakly.

Keshan smiled widely. Then he continued his way into the forest.

Jandu followed a step behind, blushing furiously. Being alone with Keshan almost felt shameful.

But why should he be ashamed? They were just men going for a stroll together, talking about visiting each other in the future. Jandu forced himself to calm down.

"Is this it?" Keshan asked, stopping in an oval clearing in the middle of the forest.

Jandu stood beside a scarred tree trunk, punctured over and over with weathered and broken arrow shafts. He grinned. "Yes. I haven't been here since I was seventeen."

Keshan came towards him. "I like it. There's a homey Jandu feel to the place. This is more personal than your rooms."

Jandu pointed up at an abandoned heron's nest. "I used to talk to the bird that lived here. She made a horrible racket every time I practiced, but she'd never leave. She became a companion of mine." Jandu smiled to himself. "I haven't thought of her all these years."

Keshan sat down on the forest floor and reached in his pocket. He pulled out a small silver case. He glanced up at Jandu, a mischievous expression on his face.

Jandu eyed Keshan suspiciously. "What are you doing?"

"Showing off," Keshan said. "Or getting ready to, anyway. This is my flute. You want to hear me play something? It'll only take a few minutes."

"Of course!" Jandu sat beside Keshan, so close their legs almost touched. "You play the flute?" Jandu asked.

Keshan raised an eyebrow. "Yes. I thought everyone knew that."

"Oh wait," Jandu held up a finger. "Actually, I remember hearing some story about how you lured women to you through music."

Keshan laughed as he pieced the parts of his flute together.

Jandu observed the instrument. "So is it an enchanted flute?"

"What?" Keshan looked at him.

"Are you going to lure me somewhere?"

Keshan's eyelids lowered slightly. "Only if you want me to."

Jandu blushed. He leaned against the tree and watched as Keshan began a soft, lilting song, and Jandu closed his eyes. He wrapped himself in the sounds, letting the music take him away from the tension of the afternoon. The song flirted along the scale; it tilted and lifted and trilled. It started sweet and slow and then sped to a furious pitch and pace, energizing him.

Keshan blew one long, final note, and then stopped, closing his eyes and leaning against the tree as well. He held his flute gently in his hands.

Jandu was too moved to say anything at first. And then, nervously, he reached over and squeezed Keshan's hand.

"That was beautiful," Jandu said, his voice thick with emotion.

Keshan opened his eyes slightly. "I came up with that song after we fought together at the temple. I've been working on it all week. I wanted to get it perfect before I saw you again." He laid his flute aside. "I call it Jandu's song. I hope you don't mind."

"Mind?" Jandu smiled crookedly. "I'm flattered."

"Good." Keshan stared deeply into Jandu's eyes.

Jandu frowned. "What?"

"Never mind."

"Tell me."

"I think you look beautiful right now," Keshan remarked.

Jandu's eyes widened. "What do you mean?"

Keshan shrugged. "I mean the way your hair is mussed from the wind, and the way the forest light plays across your eyes. Your cheekbones are so strong and your nose is slender and graceful. And your body—"

Jandu pulled back. "Stop it."

Keshan cocked his head. "What?"

"Stop talking like that."

Keshan leaned towards him again. "Like what? I'm just paying you a compliment, that's all."

"I know. Thank you. I mean…" Jandu looked away, hating the way he knew his cheeks burned with Keshan's words. What the hell was going on? He knew that Keshan had lascivious powers over women. The whole Prasta court retold tales of Keshan's exploits with servant girls in Tiwari. But Jandu had never heard of him using his magical powers on a man before.

What burned him more was that Keshan was succeeding. Jandu noted with horror that his body reacted to Keshan's nearness, growing more aroused than he had been his first night with a woman.

"You look worried." Keshan's low voice sent a shiver down Jandu's spine.

"I'm fine." Jandu tried to control his mounting panic.

"Are you?" Keshan moved closer. His heavy eyelids veiled his expression. He reached out and touched Jandu's chest with aching softness. "I'm not. There is something about you, Jandu Paran, that I cannot resist."

Jandu nearly admitted that something about Keshan seemed irresistible as well. But Keshan's proximity unnerved him. Keshan's eyes lidded, heavy with emotion.

Jandu filled with alarm. "What are you doing?"

Keshan leaned in and kissed Jandu. Shivers trembled down Jandu's spine at the sweet warmth of Keshan's lips. Keshan started the kiss chastely enough, it could have just been a kiss between friends. But then he gently pushed his tongue into Jandu's mouth.

Keshan's mouth tasted like coconut, sweet and earthy. All reason fled Jandu's mind, he closed his eyes, and leaned forward to feel more of the soft heat of Keshan's lips.

Keshan's hand dropped to Jandu's thigh, and Jandu felt fire ignite within him at the touch.

Jandu's eyes shot open. What the hell was he doing?

Jandu jerked away from Keshan's kiss, suddenly horrified by whatever magic spell Keshan's flute had worked on him. Was this some joke Keshan would share with Darvad and Tarek? Or a bet?

Keshan opened his eyes.

"Jandu…"

Jandu backhanded Keshan across the face. All the passion he had just felt drained away to be replaced with fury.

"Fuck you!" Jandu scrambled to his feet, backing away from Keshan. "How dare you kiss me!"

Keshan's hand rose to the spot where Jandu had slapped him. He glared at Jandu, shocked.

"I thought you liked it."

Jandu spat. He wiped his lips with the back of his hand to erase the memory. "You've enchanted me somehow!"

Jandu breathed deeply to control his anger. A Triya warrior never lost control. At least, that was what Mazar had once taught him.

He glowered at Keshan. "I don't know what kind of powers you have, but they won't work on me. Go back to screwing your servants and leave me alone, you fucking pervert!"

Jandu ran half the distance back to the river before he dared turn around. He saw Keshan staring at him, stock still in the gap between the trees, the side of his face red from where Jandu struck him. Jandu felt a momentary pang of guilt. But he realized that, too, was probably part of Keshan's spell, and turned back to the palace alone.

◆◆◆

That evening, Yudar summoned Jandu into the dice room.

Jandu disliked gambling, and he especially disliked the way the dice mesmerized his brother. Yudar, always so clear of mind and focused, lost his edge in the dice room as he obsessed over his next win.

Lords and courtiers filled the chamber, laughing and drinking and eating fruit as several games played out simultaneously. Jandu found his brother at the far end of the large room, throwing his dice and cheering at the results. But Yudar's smile disappeared as soon as Jandu appeared.

"What did you say to Keshan Adaru?" he demanded suddenly.

The guests around the dice board looked up at Jandu.

The question startled Jandu. "Nothing."

Yudar crossed his arms. "He is our cousin, and even though our views often differ, he is an honored guest in this palace. And now he has told Mazar that he will be leaving the palace grounds and will not return until invited back, saying it has something to do with you. So what happened?"

Jandu shrugged, hoping his face did no give away the sudden terror of being found out. "I have no idea."

Yudar stared at him coldly. But Jandu didn't give him any answers. Finally Yudar just waved him away, turning back to his dice game with a grimace. Jandu excused himself, feeling sick to his stomach.

That night, Jandu replayed the day over in his mind. He couldn't believe the audacity of a man like Keshan, who would dare march into a Triya's private wooded retreat and just go ahead and kiss him. Men kissing men! What kind of world did the Tiwari people live in? They were immoral, obviously.

But what bothered Jandu more than the disgust he had towards the wanton ways of the Tiwari tribe was his own immoral lust for it. That night, he couldn't sleep, haunted by the sweetness of that kiss. Everything about touching Keshan had felt right, especially when compared to the perfunctory nights he had spent with women.

Jandu swore to himself that the next day he would pray to all the prophets of the heavens to cure him of the terrible ailment that the infamous trickster Keshan Adaru had afflicted him with.

Jandu hoped he never saw his cousin again.

CHAPTER 8

Lord Sahdin of Jezza openly supported Yudar for the throne. If almost any of Darvad's friends had invited the staunch traditionalist to their house for a birthday celebration, the old lord would have refused on principle.

But the birthday invitation came from Druv Majeo, lord of Pagdesh, and so even the religiously devout Lord Sahdin had no choice but to accept. Outside of the palace itself, Druv's townhouse was the center of Prasta's political circle. It was the place to be seen, the place to stay informed, and the most popular destination in town for the up-and-coming Triya courtiers. Rejecting Druv's invitation was the equivalent of social suicide.

Darvad and Druv had schemed for weeks to prepare for Sahdin's fiftieth birthday party, inviting important Triya from both the traditionalist and modernist sides to witness the festivities. As Druv oiled his diplomatic machinery, Darvad and Firdaus drilled Tarek, preparing him to duel the old Triya lord.

On the night of the party, Tarek walked into the expansive guest hall of Druv's townhouse warily, half-expecting to be accosted for daring to enter. But his gold armor, his magnificent diadem, and his rich silk clothing allowed him to blend in with the impressive crowd of Triya warriors and their wives. He promptly helped himself to wine, desperate to steady his nerves. Social functions had discomforted him when he was a poor Suya in his home village. Now that he was masquerading as a lord and attending royal benefits of this scale, it was unbearable.

Druv's townhouse resembled a beehive, with alcoves and small sitting rooms forming intimate conversation nooks, connected by marble-laid walkways. It provided the illusion of privacy without any of the benefits. Clusters of people clumped together in comfortable heaps upon mountains of pillows, drinking excessively, eating too many pre-dinner pastries, watching each other hawkishly for news worthy of passing on to allies. As Tarek walked, heads turned, whispers buzzed from lips, and glances were exchanged. He felt self-conscious until he saw the same performance repeated for every guest who entered, each new person eliciting an instant wave of observation.

Just as he began to regret his decision to come, Tarek felt a squeeze on his shoulder. He turned to see Darvad's welcoming smile.

"How are you doing?" Darvad steered Tarek to an empty alcove and reclined upon the bank of pillows.

Tarek sat beside him and downed his wine. "I don't want to do this, Darvad."

"I know." Darvad touched Tarek's arm. "I know, and I appreciate that you will nevertheless."

"It's for your sake," Tarek reminded him.

"No, it's for *our* sake," Darvad corrected. "Once I am king, I will elevate you to Triya, and you will have as much say in the future of this country as any lord."

Darvad's kind words worked faster than the wine in easing Tarek's tension.

"Are you ready?" Darvad asked.

Tarek nodded.

"Then you better prepare. Use the Ajadusharta."

Tarek left the room. Almost all of the private spaces of the townhouse were currently occupied with chatting couples or trios. On the second level, however, Tarek discovered a vacant sitting room. He shut the door and breathed out deeply, working to focus his mind on the spell.

It had taken weeks for Tarek to command the Ajadusharta. Having never used shartas before, he had needed to learn in days what took most Triya boys years of training. Firdaus, who started as a gracious teacher, quickly became disenchanted with his pupil, threatening to give up entirely until Darvad soothed him into continuing.

It was embarrassing, but it was the truth. Tarek was no good at magic. Night after night, Tarek drilled the necessary words into his mind, speaking them over and over. The Ajadusharta leant the wielder a burst of superhuman strength, mighty enough to temporarily defend against the effects of other shartas. When Firdaus demonstrated the sharta in use, Tarek could feel power radiating off of his teacher.

But no matter how many times Tarek said the words, the subsequent rush of strength never followed. Tarek began to believe it was indeed a gift from God for only Triya warriors. What else could explain why he failed at this so miserably?

Again, it had been Darvad who encouraged him. Darvad, who abandoned parties with dancers, who left official dinners early, who gave up commitments in order to spend his evenings helping Tarek. Darvad's dedication made matters worse, because now Tarek could not fail.

And then, only a few nights before Lord Sahdin's birthday, Tarek had managed to clear his mind of all extraneous thoughts and worries, and actually *feel* the words. When he uttered the *"Chedu!"* ending the sharta, he gasped as a cold shudder ran through his body. The cold was immediately replaced with a growing heat, burning slowly and steadily through his veins, vibrating through his flesh. He had held out his arms, amazed that the tremendous force trembling through him was invisible to the eye.

At Druv's house, Tarek attempted the sharta several times, failing over and over again. The noise of the celebration downstairs, anxiety over the scheme, and fears of his own failings plagued his thoughts, now when it mattered most.

Tarek downed the last of his wine, put the glass down, and then stood, shaking the tension from his limbs. He closed his eyes and meditated, drawing his thoughts into himself. He whispered the Ajadusharta's complicated string of words once more, feeling them tumble over his tongue. When he finished, he was rewarded with a sudden, hot pulse through his body that made it hard to stand still.

The sharta burned in his bloodstream. He felt as though light shone from his eyes. He reached down for the empty wine glass and it shattered in his fingers.

Tarek watched blood leak from a cut below his thumb, stunned. He didn't even feel the wound.

Tarek hurried downstairs, eager to commence the plan before the sharta wore off. He knew from his last success that when the supernatural energy left him, he would be completely exhausted, barely strong enough to walk. He needed to challenge Lord Sahdin promptly.

Luckily, dinner was already underway by the time he returned to the guest hall. Seating had been arranged in advance, and Tarek found his place next to Lord Sahdin at the table of honor.

Sahdin frowned when Tarek took his place. Sahdin clearly disapproved of the arrangements. He quickly turned from Tarek to speak with the lord of Marshav instead.

Druv's elderly father-in-law sat to Tarek's right and provided kind, meaningless small talk during the meal. Tarek nodded his responses and said only what was necessary to maintain the illusion of a conversation. It was hard to focus on anything, even eating, while so much energy percolated in his body.

The meal was served on steaming platters, set strategically in the center of the low table in colorful presentations. Golden-red saffron rice, spicy grilled chicken, mint lamb, roasted eggplant, fried bananas and sesame seeds, spinach and cheese in a milk curry, shrimp with honey-glazed walnuts, one dish after another was laid before them until it became hard to see those sitting on the other side of the table.

During the meal, Sahdin remained turned away from Tarek. Sahdin picked at the large platters, choosing his food quickly and nibbling on his plate.

Tarek braced himself. He leaned across Sahdin to grab a pumpkin-stuffed pastry. Sahdin gritted his teeth but otherwise did not react.

The sharta pulsed in Tarek's blood stream, making him dizzy. Aggression roiled through him as well, a burning hunger to expel the energy with sheer force. He would have to act overtly.

Tarek reached over and took a chicken leg directly from Sahdin's plate.

Sahdin reacted instantaneously. He did not suppress a shudder of repulsion as he pushed back from the table and glared at Tarek in horror.

"You touched my food!" Sahdin gasped. "You filthy Suya!"

It did not matter how prepared he was for the insult, or how many times he heard it. Tarek's chest tightened with hurt and hatred.

"I am a welcome guest at this table," Tarek said. He kept his voice calm, but the sharta made his throat muscles tremble. "We are equals tonight."

Lord Sahdin stood. "We will never be equals, Suya! It is against the will of God to even utter such blasphemy!" He threw down his cup and pointed at Druv. "Your hospitality has insulted me, and all of Jezza!"

The others in the room fell silent. Druv stood and held out his hands in the sign of peace. "Lord Sahdin, forgive me! I mean no offense. Surely the actions of one of my guests cannot reflect poorly on me?"

"It is you who have insulted me," Tarek said, turning back to Sahdin. "I demand an apology."

"Apology?" Sahdin spat on the ground between them. "I challenge you, Suya filth! This insult cannot be carried away with words!"

Tarek bowed his head slightly. "I am not filth."

Sahdin spat again. "This Suya spouts endless bullshit."

Tarek changed his mind. He *was* going to kill Sahdin. "I accept your challenge."

Sahdin glared at Druv. "Call your priest!" Sahdin stormed out of the dining room.

A hush hung over the gathered crowd. And then everyone jumped up at once, the exquisite meal forgotten in the excitement of witnessing a traditional challenge. Even more exciting, this challenge would be between a Triya and a Suya. And on the Triya's birthday, no less. The guests poured out onto the large courtyard of Druv's townhouse, gathering along the edges to watch the duel.

Tarek lingered behind the press of the crowd. As he made his way outside, Darvad threw his arm around his shoulders and whispered in his ear. "Be careful, Tarek. I love you dearly—do not let that bastard harm you."

Darvad's words sent a tingle through Tarek's body, almost as powerful as the sharta in his blood. Druv patted Tarek's back and wished him luck as well.

Sahdin wasted no time. His charioteer had arrived and provided his master with leather gauntlets, Sahdin's battle helmet, a shield and sword. Tarek had no such armor available. But the sharta that coursed through him made him feel impervious.

A messenger had been sent to Druv's priest, and the man appeared only minutes later, out of breath and obviously fresh from his evening ablutions. His face was wet and he looked tired, but his purple robe was clean and he had his prayer beads firmly clenched in his hands.

The priest held out his hands for silence, and then ushered Sahdin and Tarek to the center of the courtyard. The dozens of guests formed a circle around them. Tarek could hear bets being placed, and partygoers rooting for Sahdin or Tarek. The challenge had taken on an air of a sports event, and the crowd seemed delighted.

Sahdin remained sober in his stance, however. Now dressed for battle, he looked more formidable than he had in his light yellow silks. Sahdin pulled out his sword and examined the blade.

"I ask God to consecrate this challenge, and know that if life be lost, it is lost in the name of God, and the prophets, and all of the tenets of our holy faith," the priest said. He mumbled the prayer for bravery and forgiveness, and then held his hands aloft once more for silence.

"I will now recite the holy rules of combat," the old priest said. Tarek almost rolled his eyes. When he got into fist fights back in the village, there were no long speeches. But Triya loved pomp and ceremony.

"These rules of war have been set by the Triya kings, and shall not be broken for fear of exile," the priest said. "Multiple warriors may not attack a single warrior. Two warriors may engage in personal combat only if they carry the same weapons and they are on the same mount. No warrior may kill or injure any warrior who has surrendered. Nor may a warrior kill or injure any other who is unarmed, unconscious, or whose back is turned away. No warrior may kill or injure a person or animal not taking part in the challenge."

At this point the priest turned and frowned at Tarek. "No Chaya warrior may lift a blade against a Suya or Triya. And no Suya can lift a blade against a Triya warrior."

Tarek knew the traditional rules, but the fact was, he had just been told to remain unarmed, and the outrage caused another burst of anger through him.

"Then how am I to compete in this challenge?" Tarek roared.

The priest looked surprised at the outburst. "You may defend yourself, Suya. That is all the law allows."

Lord Sahdin gave a snort of triumph and lifted his sword.

Darvad was at Tarek's side then, handing Tarek a shield. "Use mine. Let him see the crest of my house as you defeat him."

Darvad patted his back and then withdrew. Tarek stepped forward into the circle.

The priest lit incense and waved it over Sahdin's head, and then over Tarek. He made the sign of peace and then withdrew, leaving Tarek and Sahdin alone in the center of the courtyard.

Tarek could hear his heart beating. He held up his shield. He lifted his sword, although the scabbard remained over the blade.

Suddenly, Sahdin lunged. The tip of his sword thrust into Tarek's shield and the force of the blow sent Tarek stepping backwards. Again Sahdin advanced. He slashed at Tarek from an angle and Tarek blocked the sword with his own. Sahdin's blade cut deep into the leather scabbard and Tarek had to jerk his arm back to free it.

Sahdin slowly circled Tarek. Tarek parried each assault. His confidence increased. He was younger and stronger than Sahdin, and he could outlast his opponent if this was the worst he could give.

But then Sahdin, now breathing heavily, began to utter a sharta. Tarek could feel the energy of Sahdin's words, and a disturbing vibration shuddered over Tarek's skin.

Sahdin's eyes widened, seemed to almost bulge from his face, as he spat the sharta out towards Tarek.

"*Chedu!*" Sahdin cried, thrusting towards Tarek at the same moment.

A burst of fire blinded Tarek. He fell back, shielding his eyes and face. His body burned in instant pain, and then, with a sucking sound, the sensation pulled from him.

Tarek watched in horror as the fire ball that Sahdin summoned engulfed Sahdin himself. Sahdin emitted an unholy screech as his arms and the fabric of his dejaru caught afire.

Tarek's body ached and shuddered, but he forced it into action. He quickly dropped his sword and shield and ran to the entrance of the courtyard, grabbing the vase of a potted plant. He upturned the contents onto his burning opponent, covering Sahdin in water and damp soil.

Sahdin collapsed onto the ground, groaning. He dropped his sword and shield, his hands held out from his body, the skin blistered and broken.

Tarek knelt beside him and leaned in close. "Say that you will renounce your support of Yudar Paran, and I will spare your life." Killing the Triya lord was against the rules of combat but threatening him wasn't.

"Never," Sahdin hissed.

Tarek clamped a hand around Sahdin's throat. He didn't even have to squeeze. The old man's eyes bulged and tears streamed down his cheeks. The audience watched, rapt, but no one did anything to stop the duel.

Tarek released his grasp and Sahdin gasped for air.

"Say it!"

"I renounce my allegiance to Yudar Paran," Sahdin croaked.

"Say you will support Darvad Uru as the King of Marhavad," Tarek prompted.

"Darvad Uru has Jezza's support." Sahdin collapsed backward. All the fight had left him. Tarek stood, facing the onlookers.

"Help him!" Tarek ordered. Immediately, servants from the house rushed over and knelt by Sahdin's side, offering him water. Druv summoned his physician.

The focus of the crowd turned to Sahdin and his hideous burns. Tarek stiffly walked over to the edge of the courtyard. He sat on a stone step and tried to slow down his heartbeat. His arms and legs shook violently with the aftershocks of the Ajadusharta. His body felt drained.

Darvad rushed to him, carrying a glass of water and a cloth. "Are you all right?"

Tarek nodded. He took the water with shaking hands and drained the cup. Darvad started mopping his brow with the towel. Tarek took it from him.   Several servants helped Sahdin stand, in preparation to place him on a palanquin. Tarek stepped forward.

Sahdin turned to Tarek. His face was contorted in pain. But he bowed his head at Tarek.

"I don't know how you did that, Suya. But you have my apology. I concede the challenge."

Sahdin turned away and climbed into the palanquin.

Tarek left the party immediately after Sahdin's departure, went to his own townhouse and took a long bath. His body continued to shake, hours after the sharta had been expelled. He sank deeper in the water and forced himself to forget the shame of humiliating a Triya lord at his own birthday party. He had done it for Darvad. And the brightness of his friend's smile had been enough to burn away any regret.

CHAPTER 9

Every night, Jandu found it impossible to sleep.

His body felt heavy and hot with longing. Keshan had stirred something inside him, sensual and craven, and now he could not rid himself of the feeling. Everything seemed erotic. His mind crashed against carnal wishes on an hourly basis. The sight of workmen repairing a particular piece of furniture, the movement of a farmer against a plough, the arrival of pages carrying in his dinner—the strangest things made him flush with sexual desire. He felt sixteen again.

It was bad enough having to pretend like his mind wasn't completely focused on sex. Worse was how often he thought of Keshan. He thought of the smell of him. The way he moved, spoke, laughed. Jandu went to bed each night shaking with unspent desire, tortured by Keshan's spell.

Jandu had always been the most sexually reserved of all the Parans. While Baram slept with every servant girl in the palace, Jandu had always maintained his self-control. Even in his confusing teenage years, Jandu transferred all his energy to archery, rarely submitting to the passions flooding his system.

Sex hadn't obsessed him. It hadn't controlled him. And now he was being completely manipulated by his dick, unable to focus on even the simplest of chores. After he failed to accompany Yudar on a social call, his older brother formally summoned Jandu so that he could explain himself.

Yudar conducted most of his private business in a large, elegantly decorated room that opened out onto a magnificent rose garden. Unlike the palace's throne room, Yudar's greeting room had no chairs, and so guests would sit on pillows or piled silk rugs as they talked with him.

But Jandu chose to stand instead, taking his place beside the large mahogany desk in the corner. Scrolls and maps covered the desk. Parchments piled the floor, and more scrolls leaned against the walls.

Yudar stood with his back to his brother, intently reading a scroll. Jandu coughed. "You wanted to see me?"

Yudar turned and made a show of rolling the scroll he had been reviewing. He narrowed his dark eyes at Jandu. "You are not acting yourself."

Jandu froze. He hoped Yudar couldn't tell that Jandu had just been thinking about how much the paper weight on his desk looked like testicles. Jandu stared at his brother in mock innocence.

"I'm just distracted."

"By what?"

Jandu didn't answer. He stared at a map of the river on the desk.

Yudar sighed. "Fine. Don't tell me. But I can't have you sulking around the palace, ignoring my guests. Your irresponsibility is driving me insane, and I have too many problems right now to deal with you too."

Jandu straightened. "I don't need dealing with. Just give me something more to do, and I'll be fine."

"More to do? You didn't do what I asked you to do yesterday."

"Not true," Jandu protested. "I entertained those ambassadors from Bandari, just like you said."

"You called one of them a liar and then fell asleep during his daughter's flute recital!" Yudar slammed the scroll down on his desk. "And last night I asked you to accompany me on my visit to Lord Sahdin. You never showed up."

"I was caught up in an affair," Jandu said. He coughed. "I mean, I... I was involved in affairs of state."

"An affair?" Yudar said, almost to himself. He smirked. "She must be something, otherwise you wouldn't be turning so red."

"It's none of your concern!" Jandu turned to leave the room.

"I didn't excuse you." Yudar sounded more like a father every day. It used to please Jandu that Yudar treated him like a son. Now it drove him mad.

"Sorry, your highness," Jandu said, sarcasm thick in his voice.

Yudar sighed dramatically, and rubbed his eyes.

"Can I go?" Jandu asked Yudar urgently.

Yudar studied him a moment longer. "I wish you had come with me to visit Lord Sadhin. He seems strangely distant. I worry that something troubles him of late."

"Other than his burn scars?"

Yudar's expression darkened. "I'm glad to see that you find it funny to treat our fellow Triya's pain with such flippancy."

"I'm sorry," Jandu said. "Is there anything I can do now?"

"For Lord Sahdin? No. But I do have a task more suited to your skills, I think," Yudar said. "The gamekeepers have informed me that something strange is bothering the animals in the Ashari Forest. For the last few days, the wild boar and deer refuse to cross the clearing near the bend in the river. Even the birds seem to avoid the area. Go there and find out what's going on. Take as many of my men as you like."

"Why me?"

"Because if it is dangerous, I'm sure you can take care of yourself." Yudar smirked. "Besides, no one knows the forest as well as you do. You've been sneaking off there alone for years."

Jandu flushed. He immediately thought of the softness of Keshan's kiss.

"I'll see to it," Jandu promised and then he fled Yudar's chamber.

Jandu hurried through the long white corridors and darted through the sculpture garden to his own rooms. His thoughts kept flashing back to Keshan touching him in the woods. Once in his rooms, Jandu shooed his attendants away and spent ten minutes alone, taking care of pressing issues. When he re-emerged, he headed towards the palace stables.

Jandu ordered his gelding, Shedav, saddled. While he waited, he mulled over the idea of spending such a crisp and beautiful day with Yudar's soldiers in tow. He elected to go into the forest alone. He strapped on his quiver and bow, and rode Shedav away from town, down along the river towards the Ashari Forest.

As he traveled, he realized he would have to change his behavior. If Yudar, obsessed with his own ascension, noticed the change in Jandu, then others might, as well. Someone might figure it out. If they learned that Jandu lusted over a man, he thought he would die of shame.

On the other side of the river, Jandu saw travelers walking the wide road that led into the heart of Prasta. But on his side of the river, the land was the private property of the royal family and so he remained alone with his tormented thoughts.

The path eventually narrowed and Jandu had to cross a branch of the river to penetrate the Ashari forest. Shedav looked at the water warily, and disapproved of crossing until Jandu found a place where the river narrowed sufficiently enough that Shedav could jump across without getting his feet wet. Jandu dismounted.

The lush sounds of forest life filled the air. Birds, snakes, a hundred species of trees, they all congregated on this marshy curve of the river, huddling against each other for protection from the arid rolling plains to the north.

Jandu heard a branch snap behind him. Shedav spooked and bolted. Jandu swiveled and instinctively pulled an arrow from his quiver, nocking it.

There was no one there.

He relaxed, but searched the impenetrable green of the forest for movement. Something had startled Shedav. Jandu called out to him, but Shedav balked.

Swearing, Jandu walked slowly towards his horse. Shedav didn't run, but watched Jandu apprehensively.

"What's wrong?" Jandu asked him. He stroked Shedav's neck, and Shedav leaned into his hand. Suddenly Shedav whinnied and reared. Jandu stepped aside as he bolted, racing back down to the river's edge.

Jandu's skin crawled, but he saw nothing. He scanned the small clearing in the woods for signs of life, but other than a small bird up in the forest canopy he saw no one.

Something darted in the corner of his eye, and he spun once more.

He saw a blur and a glint of light. Jandu concentrated on the spot where he'd seen the first flashes. The hazy outlines of two men fighting furiously in sword combat became barely visible. Sparks bloomed around the combatants heads, and the air seemed to vibrate and shimmer, ripples coursing through it like it were the surface of a pond. Their shimmering blue skin and glossy black hair made the men appear as gods, towering above him in a blurry mirage of violence.

Yashvas. What were they doing here, in his world?

One of the Yashvas thrust. The other tried to parry but lost his balance and fell backwards into the undergrowth. But the bushes did not move. Jandu suddenly realized they weren't in his world. He was watching them in theirs. He couldn't see them if he looked directly at them. But by glancing away and concentrating, Jandu made out the bright colors exploding around the demons, made out their shimmering forms. Both of these creatures looked almost human. They wore armor and carried weapons like men. But their bluish skin tone and hazy, unfocused faces showed them for what they were.

The explosions above their heads increased in intensity. Jandu's heart beat faster. He was witnessing a great battle. The explosions had to be magical weapons of some sort. Suddenly a loud boom echoed across the forest. Jandu felt the air ripple and then burst. The noise of clashing swords crashed over him.

One of the Yashvas emitted a piercing scream, and then collapsed before Jandu and grabbed hold of his ankles.

"Please protect me!" The Yashva cried out, quivering at Jandu's feet.

Jandu gasped in shock. The Yashva had dropped his sword. Blood ran from numerous wounds all over his body.

As the Yashva looked up, Jandu gasped again. This was a woman. The surface of her long black hair swirled like an oil slick. Dark, purplish blood oozed from her lips and nose.

Jandu unsheathed his sword as the other Yashva strode towards him.

Jandu's honor would not allow him to ignore the pleas of a woman, particularly not one so badly wounded. But he had no idea how to fight a Yashva. They were the weapons that Triya used in battle against each other.

"Zandi!" the other Yashva yelled. "Let go of the mortal and come back here! This is none of his concern!"

Jandu stepped in front of the cowering demon. "She has asked for my protection and as a Triya it is my duty to provide it." He stood battle-ready, looking up at his towering opponent. "I am Jandu Paran! Prepare yourself!"

"I am your death," the Yashva said, smirking. "Prepare yourself, Jandu Paran!"

"Koraz," the Yashva at Jandu's feet moaned. "His name is Koraz."

Jandu knew the Yashva's name. The Korazsharta released an indestructible spear that could strike true for an extended distance.

Koraz lunged at Jandu, bringing his sword down with the strength of an elephant.

Jandu deflected the blade with his own sword. A tearing pain ripped through his shoulder. Koraz slashed at him again and this time Jandu's legs buckled beneath him as he blocked the powerful blow. He crumpled to his knees.

Koraz grinned maliciously. "You're strong," he said.

"I'm smart too." Jandu reached out and plucked a blade of grass. He pulled it to his lips and whispered the Korazsharta.

As soon as Jandu started speaking, the Yashva became enraged. Koraz struck at Jandu, forcing Jandu to roll away. He mumbled the words of the sharta, blood pooling in his mouth.

"Chedu!" Blood flew from Jandu's mouth as he shouted the final word.

Koraz screamed in rage and vanished. Jandu gripped the blade of grass. It shimmered and then grew into a long spear. It pulsed in his hand, the metal expanding and shrinking, hot to touch.

"God," Jandu whispered. He pulled himself upright, his arm aching at the shoulder. He gingerly held the spear away from his body.

Jandu felt someone touch the back of his calf and he spun around, spear ready.

Zandi instantly crouched, hands together in supplication.

"Please! I mean you no harm," she cried.

Jandu immediately lowered the spear. "Sorry."

"Thank you!" Zandi touched Jandu's feet. He leaned down to help her stand. When Zandi finally stood before him, Jandu could see that she was enormous. His head came only to her chest.

Zandi eyed the spear beside them warily. "You changed him into his shartic form."

Jandu nodded. "Luckily, I know the Korazsharta. When you said his name, I thought I would give it a try. My friend once told me…" Jandu clenched his jaw shut. He had been doing very well without thinking of Keshan.

"Your cleverness has saved my life," Zandi said, smiling despite the blood trickling from her nose.

Jandu bowed his head. "It was my pleasure." He studied the spear in his hand. "What happens if I throw this now?"

Zandi looked at the weapon with obvious fear. "You will dispel the sharta and Koraz will return to the Yashva kingdom."

"Will he come after you again?"

"Probably." Zandi shuddered. "We have fought for three days already."

Jandu wondered what she had done to earn such wrath. But it was not his concern. Getting involved in the business of the Yashvas seemed like a bad idea.

"I can't hold onto something this powerful forever," Jandu told her. "And I can't leave it laying around for someone else to find. If I give you a few days will you be able to escape from Koraz?"

Zandi shook her head. "It will be a hundred years before Koraz forgets my insult." Suddenly, Zandi reached out and grabbed Jandu's arm. "But you can hide me, beautiful Marhavadi!"

Zandi had grabbed the arm that Koraz had injured, and Jandu fought back an unmanly whimper. "How?"

"Change me into my shartic form! I will be your greatest ally," Zandi said. "I don't look it but I am a powerful weapon."

"What kind of weapon?"

"Whatever weapon you most desire." Zandi's eyes twinkled. "What form of combat do you most excel at?"

"Archery," Jandu said without hesitating.

"I will be your bow."

"But I don't know the Zandisharta."

"Do you know the Barunazsharta? It is like that, only softer." Zandi said, squeezing Jandu's arm tighter. Tears sprang to Jandu's eyes.

Jandu wondered how one uttered a sharta softly. He began speaking, changing the words of the sharta slightly, as he looked at Zandi. He wanted the sharta to fit her, feel like her, and the needed words came to him easily.

As soon as Jandu finished the sharta, Zandi began to melt. Her body softened. A shudder of revulsion shook Jandu as the flesh of Zandi's hand turned buttery and hot, and dribbled off his arm. It pooled on the forest floor and slithered together, a bluish ooze, forming a puddle that slowly began to shift and harden.

Then she took form, long and curved. Her color changed from dull blue to shimmering white gold, the surface forming patterns. Jandu crouched down and watched as delicate filigree curled over the surface of the exquisite weapon.

The forest grew silent. On the mossy ground lay the most beautiful bow he had ever seen. Long and sleek, its gold patterns moved in a slow river, the colors of its highlights and tints shifting depending on how he looked at it.

He had never seen such a gorgeous object in his life, and his heart swelled with pride that this was his. *She* was his.

"Can you hear me?" he whispered to Zandi. The gold lacquer warmed in his grip. Jandu's hands trembled with excitement as he quickly unstrung his old bow and transferred the string to Zandi. The bow bent in his hands, turning loose and liquid as he pulled the string taut. Once strung, the bow hardened again.

Jandu reached for an arrow from his quiver and took aim at a distant branch drooping with berries. When he loosed the arrow, it sang through the air. The berries exploded in the air and the branch fell to the ground.

Jandu laughed. He hugged the bow to his chest, feeling foolish, but no longer caring. He slung Zandi over his back and then reached down once more for the spear.

"Don't be such an asshole in the future," he scolded the spear. Then he threw it as hard as he could at a tree. The spear exploded into the wood, piercing through the entire trunk before disappearing out of sight. Jandu waited in the forest a moment longer, to see if Koraz would return, but he did not.

As Jandu stood in the soft forest light, a burning desire to share this story with Keshan overwhelmed him. It was Keshan's comment about the relationship of shartas and Yashvas that had saved Jandu's life, and given him this bow. Keshan would have been proud of him.

"Keshan is a pervert," Jandu said aloud, forcing himself not to think of the sensation of kissing Keshan, rubbing against his hot flesh. Keshan wasn't the only pervert. But rather than sully this victory with forbidden thoughts, Jandu cleared his mind of Keshan, and instead set out to follow Shedav's tracks and head home.

"My brothers are going to adore you, Zandi," Jandu whispered to his bow. And as Shedav caught sight of him and walked towards Jandu, Jandu thought he could even feel Zandi respond, a slight pulse at his back.

CHAPTER 9

TAREK WALKED QUICKLY ACROSS THE WIDE COURTYARD JUST inside the west gate of the palace. He was late. He was always late these days. He felt time struggle against him, squirming out of his grasp like an impatient child.

A sweet breeze rushed over him, fragrant with new blossoms. Even this failed to inspire joy in him. The breeze merely reminded him that it was already March, and he still hadn't visited his father back in Dragewan. Tarek had put off the visit for weeks now, kept away from his familial duties by Darvad's bid for ascension. Last year at this time, Tarek returned to his home village with his father to pay tribute on the anniversary of his mother's death. It had been an emotional week, filled with the smell of fish and incense and the sound of old women crying and the recitation of prayers and the constant, incessant, beating of wet clothes against the rocks of the river. A short year later, and Tarek had almost forgotten the anniversary. What sort of son was he that could forget his family so swiftly?

But this seemed to symbolize the life he had chosen now. He constantly let down the ones he loved. He prayed every morning for guidance to become a better person, and yet here he was, once again, rushing to Darvad's side for an evening of pleasure instead of making arrangements to return to Dragewan, to see his ailing father.

Tarek sprinted the last few steps to the small gaming room attached to Darvad's lavish suites. A blast of stale male air overwhelmed him. A haze of hookah tobacco and spilled wine and roasted meats and sweat hung over the room.

Tarek adjusted from the sweet freshness outside, sinking down onto the floor pillows silently. He sat next to Darvad, who looked up from the gaming board only to smile briefly.

"You're late," Darvad said.

"Did I miss anything?" Tarek asked.

Darvad snorted. "Firdaus and Druv have robbed Iyestar and I blind. The wily bastards are up to something, but I cannot see what. Watch them for me, will you?"

Iyestar and Darvad sat on one side of the large ivory board, and Druv and Firdaus shared pillows on the other side. Behind them, servants wafted large feather fans to encourage the spring air to filtrate the room, but all it did was press the smell of wine and smoke closer.

Tarek snapped his fingers, and a servant hastened over to hand him a goblet of wine. The way Firdaus' heavy eyelids drooped, and the way Iyestar's mouth seemed incapable of closing, told Tarek he was far behind on the drinking.

"Everything is in place for tomorrow night, by the way," Druv said casually. He nodded to Tarek.

Tarek's stomach tightened. Druv had invited another of Darvad's rivals over for a dinner party. Once again, Tarek would be forced to insult a lord into challenging him, with the prize being fealty to Darvad. This time it was Lord Kadal from the State of Marshav.

Tarek had not forgotten. He had just misplaced time once more. He thought the day would be in the distance, not upon him.

"I stake ten pieces of silver," Firdaus said. Tarek noted the slur in his voice.

Darvad nodded. "And I the same." Darvad threw down his elongated ivory dice.

The game involved moving a player's pieces from house to house across the board. A bet was placed each move, and the highest dice roll won that round's bet. However, if a player rolled a six, they were immediate winners and could roll again.

Darvad threw an unimpressive two. He scowled.

Firdaus blew on his own dice and threw them onto the board; a perfect six. He moved his pieces closer and then rolled again, achieving a four, the exact number he needed to land his first piece home.

"Damn you!" Iyestar shouted. "I tell you, Darvad, the snake has enchanted dice."

Firdaus held out his dice. "You may play with my dice and I'll play with yours. But know that I take such accusations very personally. If you play with my dice and still fail, I demand an apology."

Iyestar grabbed the dice from Firdaus' outstretched hands and shook them angrily. "I stake one shipment of Tiwari grain."

Firdaus drank deeply and then nodded. "And I stake ten cartloads of Chandamar coal." He gathered Iyestar's dice in his palm and flicked his wrist, throwing the dice down to get another perfect six.

Druv shook his head and laughed. "Amazing! This man has the luck of the prophets on his side!"

Iyestar's roll resulted in a measly three. Iyestar groaned, collapsing back on the pillows as Darvad sullenly moved their ebony piece three small steps.

The game continued like this, and Tarek quickly grew bored. He drank heavily, hoping to catch up to his friends, and refused food. When Firdaus and Druv won, Darvad challenged him to another round, which surprised Tarek. Darvad behaved strangely that night. He was curt and looked displeased. Tarek realized his friend was exhausted. Druv prattled on about local gossip, Firdaus cheated, and Iyestar drank. But Darvad just sat there, morosely throwing his dice and looking disenchanted with the world.

Everything changed, however, when a herald knocked and announced Keshan Adaru. Everyone immediately awoke from their trances.

"Sit down and join us, Keshan," Darvad offered, patting a spot between himself and Iyestar.

Keshan brought his hands together in the sign of peace and greeted everyone individually. When he bowed to Tarek, Tarek noted that the man smelled like cloves and cinnamon. His hair was wet as if he had just come from the bath.

"I'm surprised to see you here," Druv said, not even bothering to hide is obvious curiosity. "I heard a rumor that you were not setting foot in the palace until you received an apology from Jandu Paran."

For a moment, something dark and painful crossed Keshan's expression. But then it was gone, and Keshan's mouth slowly spread into a languid smile.

"I'm not here to see any Paran this evening. I've only come to have a word with Darvad, if I may." He sat next to his brother. A servant offered him a glass of wine, but Keshan refused.

"Congratulations on your recent challenge against Lord Sahdin," Keshan told Tarek.

Tarek bowed his head. "Thank you."

Keshan stared at him knowingly. "Quite an achievement, especially when so hobbled by the law."

"I had some help from my friends." Tarek nodded toward Firdaus.

Keshan smirked. "Still, an amazing triumph. I hope it sets a good example to everyone how unfair the laws are when it comes to Suyas fighting."

"I did not give him the Ajadusharta in order to help your ridiculous crusade," Firdaus snapped, glaring at Keshan. "I did so to help Darvad win supporters. Stop reading messages into actions that are not there."

Darvad sighed loudly. "Tarek's success has served many purposes. Let's leave it at that."

But Firdaus sneered. "I don't understand. Keshan claims to support our faction, yet he blatantly goaded Jandu Paran into winning Suraya and stealing the victory from me."

"Calm down, Firdaus." Keshan smiled slyly. "You make it sound as though there were a conspiracy against you."

"Don't you dare tell me to calm down!" Firdaus shouted, throwing his empty goblet down. He narrowed his dark eyes, his large eyebrows coming together in a thick line. "I have been insulted again and again by you."

"You are welcome to challenge me anytime, Firdaus," Keshan said smoothly. "And I have already paid a high price for my previous affront to your honor."

"Perhaps, but what of the Parans? They insult me everyday with their unnatural marriage arrangement. Suraya should not be disgraced in that manner," Firdaus spat. "I must have justice."

"Jandu won her legally," Druv said. "And she did agree to wed all three of them."

"They should not have been allowed to marry her!" Firdaus said. "A woman should not have more than one husband."

"You want to have two wives. Druv has three already," Keshan pointed out. "Why shouldn't Suraya have as many husbands as she likes? Or even wives for that matter?"

"Is there no end to your sick suggestions?" Firdaus said, an expression of revulsion on his face.

Darvad sighed again. "Keshan, please stop." Then, turning to Firdaus. "Once I am king, you will have your vengeance on the Parans. Until then, I cannot do anything."

"Cowards and fools!" Firdaus shook his head. "All of you! Darvad would win a challenge against Yudar, and yet you refuse to do the honorable thing."

Darvad shook his head. "We've been over this before."

"The law allows for a brother to carry the burden of a challenge. Jandu would fight in Yudar's place," Keshan said. "And Darvad would lose."

Darvad frowned. "Don't dismiss my abilities so quickly."

Keshan reached over and touched Darvad's shoulder. "I mean no offense, prince. And you know I am your ally. When I say that Jandu's shartic powers go beyond yours, it's not an insult, just a statement of fact."

"Was there a reason you came in, brother, or did you just want to rile everyone up as usual?" Iyestar slurred. He remained collapsed back on the pillows, his wine glass balanced on his stomach.

"I have come because Darvad asked me to discuss the legal changes I have requested some time this week," Keshan said. "I have been waiting for days, and have not heard from you, so I thought I would check in myself."

Darvad held his head. "For God's sake, give it a rest for just once, Adaru! We're in the middle of a game. Let me have an evening off, I beg of you."

Keshan's expression did not change. He bowed very stiffly, however. "My apologies, prince. I'll leave you then."

Darvad looked up sadly. "No. Wait, Keshan. You are welcome to join us."

Tarek felt a small kernel of jealously burst in his gut and radiate outwards. He had no reason to feel this way. Darvad had shown no overt interest in Keshan Adaru. But there was something unnaturally beautiful about Keshan, sensual, and Tarek worried that if the two of them became good friends, he would lose his place at Darvad's side.

To his relief, Keshan declined. "Perhaps it would be best if I took my brother home instead."

All of them looked to Iyestar, who had begun snoring loudly on the pillows.

Darvad laughed. "Poor Iyestar. Yes, that probably would be for the best, although he's left me to challenge Firdaus all alone."

"I'll be on your side," Tarek said suddenly, moving closer.

Darvad gave him a soul-wrenching smile. "Tarek. I can always trust you to save me."

Keshan struggled to wake his brother, resorting to slapping Iyestar across the face. Iyestar mumbled a growl and punched out his fist in response. Keshan deftly avoided the punch, and Tarek realized he must have had a lot of practice waking his inebriated brother up.

"Time to go home, Iyestar," Keshan said loudly and firmly, urging his brother into a sitting position.

"What?" Iyestar blinked. "But I don't want to go back to Tiwari right now."

"Not Tiwari, you fool, the townhouse." Keshan smiled apologetically to the group. "Come on, idiot."

"Fuck off, Keshan." Iyestar made to lie down again.

Keshan reached down and touched his brother's neck, just below his ear. Tarek did not see what happened, but Iyestar suddenly yelled out and shot upright.

"Fuck! I hate it when you do that!"

Keshan stood, offering his brother a hand up. A small fingerprint of ice melted off Iyestar's neck, and Tarek noted that Keshan's index finger was blue.

Keshan offered them a last bow before dragging his bigger brother out of the room. As soon as they left, Druv shook his head.

"They make quite a pair."

Darvad chuckled. "I can't tell if they hate each other or love each other. All I know is that they seem to be complete opposites."

"I'm surprised Keshan even showed up. I've heard Jandu refuses to speak to him," Druv said, the beady gleam of curiosity clear in his eyes.

Darvad shrugged. "I don't know what transpired. No one does. But Jandu has a temper that can rival Firdaus', and I'm sure Keshan just got in the way of it."

Firdaus rolled his dice. Another perfect six.

"You have got to be joking," Darvad said, shaking his head.

Firdaus did not looked pleased, however. He moved his piece, and then glared at Darvad.

"I don't trust Keshan."

"You don't trust anybody," Darvad said.

"I still think you're a fool for putting up with all of this nonsense. Be a man, Darvad! Challenge Yudar. Be done with it. Enough of Druv's excruciatingly slow political games."

Darvad raised an eyebrow. "And Jandu?"

For the first time that evening, Firdaus smiled. "Let me take care of Jandu for you. Consider it a gift."

"What do you mean?" Tarek asked.

Firdaus studied his dice, the smile still on his face. "I'll make sure he steals no future brides."

Druv frowned. "Any direct threat against the Parans will look bad, especially now, so close to the announcement of the throne."

"I don't like it either," Tarek said. He assumed Darvad would also disapprove.

But to his dismay, Darvad looked merely tired and frustrated. He pinched his eyes shut. "Fine. Do what you will, Firdaus. Now, please, can we just enjoy the rest of the game and stop discussing this? My head is throbbing."

"Of course, my prince," Firdaus said. "Your wish is my command." He threw down his dice. Another perfect six.

The game never really changed from there. Firdaus rapidly returned all of his pieces to home, and by the time they all stood from the board, stiff and drunk, Firdaus had won enough gifts and gold to buy Tarek's home village twenty times over. Even after a year of such life, Tarek could not get used to the kind of money these nobles bandied about as a pastime.

Losing exacerbated Darvad's foul mood. Drunk and bitter, he scowled as he said good night to his companions and stumbled towards his quarters. He leaned against the wall to support himself. Tarek rushed to his side. He threw his arm around Darvad's waist and helped him back to his bedroom.

"I'm sick of it, Tarek." Darvad tried to whisper, but his inebriated voice came out loud and echoed in the marble hallway. "I'm sick of all the in-fighting. I'm so exhausted..." Darvad leaned against Tarek. "What do you think I should do?"

Tarek swallowed. His entire body had filled with warm content at Darvad's touch. "I think you should stop thinking about it and go to bed."

Darvad smiled slightly. "You're right."

"You are a man, Darvad, not a god. Pray for guidance, and then go to sleep. Wake up refreshed."

"I swear, Tarek, you are the only true friend I have. Of course, you have your own motives as well, don't you?"

"Darvad, I don't care about my own wealth or position. I swore an oath of friendship to you, and that is all that matters to me. Even if I never get a penny from you, or respect from your brethren, I will be your friend."

Darvad leaned further into Tarek. "Then be a friend, and take my mind off all this bickering."

Tarek froze in the hallway. His heart stopped momentarily. And then he realized, no, he had just misinterpreted Darvad's wishes.

"I could tell you about the terrible scandal of the cow that ate the priest's ruby back in my village," Tarek offered.

Darvad looked up suddenly, an almost childish grin across his face. "Really? How does that story go?"

Tarek was a good storyteller. His village had been a hotbed of scandal— who was sleeping with who, who poisoned who's husband, what happened to the missing cow. Tarek told the story like a mystery, withholding critical details and only letting clues in here and there to who had impregnated the Draya priest's wife, and who had eventually vomited up the missing gem.

Darvad cried with laughter by the time they made it to his bedroom. Tarek wished they had farther to go together, so he could continue to make Darvad laugh. It was so good to see Darvad happy.

Darvad reached up and grabbed Tarek's hand. "Stay the night."

Wild panic and excitement rushed through Tarek once more. Darvad couldn't mean what he thought he did. Could he?

"It's too late to go home," Darvad slurred. "The blue room is ready for you next door. Have breakfast with me in the morning, and tell me more stories."

Tarek knew better than to feel crushed, but he couldn't help it. A hungry ache of longing filled him, and the bitterness of knowing he would never get to have Darvad the way he wanted. Looking at him now, so strong and dark and beautiful by candlelight, crawling into his bed, spreading his legs as he claimed his space, Tarek felt paralyzed with desire.

He had to breathe deeply to clear his mind of the sudden onslaught of unwelcome erotic imagery. "I should return home. My father's health is failing, and I need to make arrangements to bring him from Dragewan."

"All that can be accomplished tomorrow," Darvad said. He curled onto his side. His eyes closed. "I want to have breakfast with you tomorrow. And then maybe go hunting. Something away from all this infernal work, before you have to challenge Lord Kadal."

Tarek stood and silently watched his friend fall asleep. Then, despite his desire to return home, to make arrangements to visit his father, to be a better person, he simply stumbled into the adjacent blue room and collapsed. He knew he would wake up in the morning and do whatever it was that Darvad wished. If he wanted to go hunting, and eat together, and if he wanted Tarek to challenge more lords, Tarek would do it. Anything for those brief moments alone together, moments when, for just a fraction of time, Tarek could almost believe Darvad loved him.

CHAPTER 10

IN THE DAYS THAT FOLLOWED JANDU'S TRIUMPH OVER THE Yashva demon Yudar wouldn't stop hugging him, the distance between them gone, his earlier annoyance forgotten as Yudar bragged about Jandu and Zandi to anyone who would listen. Baram, who loved cooking, made Jandu spicy pastries and followed him around all day trying to feed him more. Jandu accepted as many as he could eat, but after fifteen, he tried to refuse.

"How can you expect to win another battle against a Yashva when you're so thin?" Baram cried, handing Jandu another plate of pastries. "Eat! They are made with my love!"

Shouting, Baram looked ferocious, like he could easily rip a tree from the earth. Jandu blanched and took the pastries. Nothing terrified Jandu more than having Baram screaming that he loved him.

Jandu occupied himself by helping Yudar arrange a celebration to honor their teacher, Mazar. The party was planned for the holy day of Asherwar. Of course, the celebration had political incentives as well, as it provided an opportunity for all of Yudar's allies to gather and lavish attentions on Mazar, just before Mazar made his decision between Yudar and Darvad for the kingdom.

Yudar sent invitations all over the kingdom. Those lords who had returned to their home states from the capital were urged back, and those in Prasta were asked to spend the auspicious day in the palace's grand banyan garden.

Jandu and Baram were sent to deliver personal invitations to those lords who remained in Prasta. Jandu knew it was busywork, better conducted by one of Yudar's dozens of ministers, but he enjoyed Baram's cheerful company, and it pleased him to be given something to take him away from the incessant politicking at the palace.

In the evenings, however, Jandu's mind was free to wander. And it always wandered to Keshan. Keshan, his body, his hair, his voice. Despite Jandu's ardent prayers to be rid of his passion for his cousin, he still awoke every morning with a burning need to touch Keshan again. He didn't know how long he would survive with this longing.

A few days before the ceremony, Yudar asked Jandu to dine with him and Baram to discuss an urgent matter. Although they had numerous chefs on staff, Baram insisted on cooking dinner for his brothers and wife himself. That night, they ate in Baram's private quarters. Baram glowed as his servants brought out the steaming plates of lemon rice, pheasant, and vegetables that he had so carefully prepared.

"You should see the kitchen designs I have planned once Yudar is king, Jandu!" Baram said. "I met with an engineer this morning. He can build small, enclosed containers for keeping vegetables and milk fresh, it has a pump inside for water… I've never seen anything like it. It will be the most impressive room in the palace."

"Let's hope the facilities improve your cooking," Jandu commented.

Baram threw a bread roll at him. Jandu caught it deftly and dipped the bread into one of Baram's delicious yogurt sauces.

Suraya looked radiant at the table. She wore a green zahari with silver beads. The gold of her earrings and nose ring gleamed in contrast to her dark mahogany hair. She smiled shyly at Jandu.

"Haven't seen you in a while," she said coyly.

Jandu flushed. "I've been busy."

"Hmm." She smiled knowingly. Jandu blanched. What if she *knew* that half the time he wasn't at dinner he was busy jerking off to the thought of Keshan? Maybe women had some magical powers of detection. Jandu made a mental note to ask someone about it. He had no idea who to ask, though.

"Jandu." Yudar turned his dark eyes on him.

"Yes?" Jandu poured more yogurt sauce over his rice. He noticed Baram grin proudly.

"Iyestar and Keshan Adaru will be staying in the palace for the ceremony. I've asked Keshan to bless the event for us."

Jandu froze, a handful of rice halfway between his plate and his mouth.

Yudar narrowed his eyes at him. "I don't know what happened between you two when he was last here, but you must apologize to him."

Jandu dropped his rice. "Apologize?" he sputtered. "You have no idea what he said to me!"

"It doesn't matter!" Yudar snapped. "He is more than just our first cousin, and more than brother to the Lord of Tiwari. It is crucial that Mazar sees harmony between us and that I am capable of extending my hospitality to those of differing views, and I will not have it known there is any distance between us."

"But!—"

"But nothing." Yudar pointed at Jandu. "When Keshan arrives, you will apologize. That is final!"

Jandu chewed on several things to say before abandoning the whole effort and just sighing. "Whatever."

Yudar glared at him. Jandu held out his hands.

"What? I will, I will!" Jandu cried.

Yudar smiled. "Thank you."

"I don't know what you two could possibly fight about," Baram said, digging into his own meal with fervor. He spoke with his mouth open. "You two seemed really happy together."

"I don't want to talk about Keshan," Jandu said.

"Fine," Baram said, shrugging.

"Fine," Yudar said.

Suraya shook her head, and drank more wine.

◆◆◆

Guests for the ceremony arrived the following morning. Those who did not have townhouses in the capital took up the offer to stay in the palace, and even some of those who had homes of their own availed themselves of the opportunity to lodge in the locus of action. Every guest room was filled with visitors.

Jandu and his family first attended the royal temple. They knelt on the rugs alongside Darvad and other lords in the city as the priest incanted songs to bless Asherwar as a holy day. Jandu submitted his forehead for a required smear of purple dye.

The palace was filled with purple lanterns, and everyone, even servants, smeared black kohl under their eyes and purple dye into their hair to celebrate God's gift of the world. Servants hung paper lanterns in each hallway of the palace to welcome God into every space. Small gold coins were scattered along the walkways to lead demons away from God and towards the ceremonial hell constructed in one of the smaller stone gardens.

The banyan garden received the greatest detail, where Mazar's celebration would occur. Opulent purple-dyed carpets covered the cobblestones, and long teak tables stretched from one end to the next to accommodate the hundreds of invited guests. Bright purple and red silk banners drooped from the second level balconies, and, in the wind, they waved over the trees like elegant fingers, beckoning the sky closer.

Mazar himself drifted around the palace, sweet as sugar cane, clearly flattered by the celebration in his honor. Jandu caught the look of annoyance in Darvad's eyes when their paths crossed. Darvad clearly disliked the fact that the dinner had not been his idea.

In the banyan garden, Jandu was supposed to await the beginning of the ceremony on the raised teak dais with Mazar,

Darvad, Yudar, and Baram, but after only fifteen minutes of his chair-rocking Yudar glared at him and Jandu decided to go stand by the entrance. Suraya handed out ceremonial garlands of lotus flowers as each guest entered the garden, and Jandu took it upon himself to bow and direct guests toward lavishly set tables.

Marhavad's finest noblemen gathered on seats around tables laden with food. A soft spring breeze wafted above them, shaking the branches of the four banyan trees that circled the enclosure and rippling the silk banners.

Jandu leaned against the brick garden wall and fiddled with his silver diadem. He knew Keshan was coming. His stomach knotted every time he thought of it. Despite himself, he'd taken a long bath that afternoon and searched for his finest clothes. He wore newly made white silk trousers with a red and gold sash, and he wore a plain white shirt, which fit his chest tightly, showing off his chiseled arms. For the first time he wished for showier colors in his wardrobe. He had adorned himself with silver bangles along with his father's silver necklace and matching loop earrings. He'd chosen his heaviest, most impressive diadem, but after wearing it for all of two hours, he had returned to his quarters and exchanged it for a smaller silver one. His hair spiked out from under it in a chaotic way, but at least it didn't feel like a stack of gold bricks on top of his head.

He still looked good enough to catch glances, and that's what mattered. As the lords and ministers and their wives poured into the garden, most looked at him, obviously fascinated by the contrast of his blue eyes and deeply tanned skin. Jandu smiled and bowed to all of the guests appropriately. Jandu had brought Zandi with him, and he left her clearly visible, leaning against the wall beside him like a trophy. The guests who knew about archery raised their eyebrows at the sight of the bow, and every time someone asked about it, Jandu unabashedly informed them that it was a Yashva protecting him in return for defeating another of her kind. Their looks of admiration somewhat ameliorated the tension of waiting for Keshan to arrive.

Jandu's stomach dropped every time the herald's horn trumpeted, announcing a new arrival. Any moment now, Keshan would walk in. Keshan would to walk in, and what would Jandu do?

He wanted to immediately pull Keshan into an alcove and beg him to kiss him again.

No. He wanted to hit him again to make sure the message was clear. And then apologize because his brother made him.

Or maybe just not look at him. Ever. That would probably be the best tactic.

And what if Keshan hated him now? What if he didn't care if Jandu refused to look at him? After all, Jandu has slapped him the last time they'd been together. What if Keshan hadn't even accepted Yudar's invitation? What if he stayed in Tiwari and snubbed them all?

The thought made Jandu break out into a sweat. If Keshan didn't come, then Yudar would never forgive him. And everything would be terrible, forever. Keshan had to come. He had to.

The announcer's trumpet blared. "His excellence, Lord Indarel of Afadi!"

Jandu sagged against the wall. He bowed politely, and motioned with his hand to an empty seat to the right.

The voices in the garden grew so loud, he could barely hear his own thoughts, which turned out to be a relief.

The trumpeter blasted another note, and Jandu straightened. "Lord Iyestar Adaru of Tiwari!"

As Keshan's brother entered the reception hall without Keshan, Jandu fought tears. Keshan wasn't going to come after all. Jandu had gotten his wish. He wouldn't see Keshan again.

An overwhelming crushing sensation filled him. Jandu couldn't remember ever feeling so heartbroken.

"The Honorable Keshan Adaru of Tiwari!"

Jandu jerked upright. He looked to the entrance and made eye contact with Keshan. He felt his face immediately flush red.

Keshan stared at him long and hard, as if trying to tell him something. But then more guests arrived, forcing Keshan forward and into the pressing crowd.

Jandu couldn't abandon his post now without it looking suspicious, and so he stood against the wall until the last of the guests arrived. It disheartened him to finally spot Keshan under one of the banyan trees, chatting amiably with Darvad's Suya, Tarek.

Jandu joined his family up on the dais. Keshan offered the blessings of Tiwari, Mazar's birthplace, and Yudar gave a touching speech praising Mazar's character and dedication to the kingdom. As he listened to Yudar's words and gazed at Mazar, Jandu felt pride and love well up in his breast. He was embarrassed at feeling so sentimental, though he was obviously not alone. By the time the speech ended, Mazar wept openly and the guests jumped to their feet, clapping and cheering the Regent. It seemed natural that Jandu would follow his brothers in bending low to touch Mazar's feet and ask for a blessing.

Mazar threw his arms around Jandu and held him tightly.

"Bless you, my favored son, bless you!" Mazar cried. He stroked Jandu's face.

Darvad, not to be outdone, clapped for attention before the guests were allowed to eat and gave an impromptu speech honoring Mazar as well, although everyone could see it for what it was, a desperate attempt to save face. Then, with a final toast to Mazar, Yudar invited his guests to eat.

The dinner feast was extravagant. Baram had overseen the kitchen preparations. He had themed the dishes after the four seasons, celebrating the natural change of the year and also the enduring permanence of Prasta.

ASTRID AMARA

Yudar's table of honor stood nearest the dais, and he sat with his brothers, wife, Suraya's father and brother, Mazar, and select lords and their wives. Darvad did not take up the invitation to sit at the main table, preferring a place between Tarek and Druv.

Jandu felt terribly flustered when he discovered that Keshan and Iyestar had been invited to sit at the table of honor. As Keshan walked across the garden, Jandu felt his blood thicken and warm as if drugged. He had gotten Keshan so wrong in his mind. He was far more beautiful in person than in Jandu's memory. Every step Keshan took, the small gestures of his hand, the way his voice lowered in pitch when he laughed, how he would absentmindedly fiddle with his waist sash when he listened to someone, how his eyes shined impossibly bright, the thickness of his hair, the pink hue of his lips. Jandu felt drunk with lust. He swallowed as Keshan approached their table. Jandu knew he had gone bright red again but that was the least of his problems. As long as he could control his voice. As long as he didn't allow his family to suspect his carnal thoughts.

Keshan studied Jandu with concern. Was Keshan worried Jandu would strike him again?

"Please, sit here," Yudar said, gesturing between himself and Baram. Keshan uttered a small prayer before engaging his meal.

"Keshan." Suraya said with the familiarity of a sister.

Keshan smiled at her. "You look beautiful today, Suraya."

"I hear your wife has come to Prasta with you," Suraya asked. "How is Ajani?"

Jandu froze. Wife?

Keshan nodded. "She said she couldn't wait to see you again, and would come whether I liked it or not." Keshan sipped his wine. "You two were friends as children, right?"

Suraya nodded. "Ajani and I studied religious texts together with my father's priest. I haven't seen her in years! But where is she?"

"She prefers to avoid the company of Lord Firdaus, but asked me to convey her regards and an invitation to call on her at the Adaru townhouse," Keshan said.

Jandu understood about half of every sentence.

Wife? What the hell was going on? He knew, abstractly, that Keshan had married. It had been the reason for his exile. Keshan abducted Firdaus' bride. But this fact never truly sank in to Jandu's awareness until now. A bitter ache filled him.

"Wife?" he blurted out. The rest of the table looked at him. Jandu turned crimson. "I didn't know you had a wife."

Yudar shook his head. "Of course you've heard of Ajani, don't you remember? Five years ago she was supposed to marry Firdaus, and didn't want to, so she wrote to Keshan and begged for his help."

"I'm sure you carried her off just for her own good," Suraya said with a smirk.

Keshan smiled back. "Only fulfilling my Triya duty."

"That's why Firdaus hates him," Baram tactlessly blurted out. He shrugged and then started on his third plate of food.

Jandu felt like vomiting. He glanced quickly at Keshan, who looked at him oddly, like he was trying to tell Jandu something telepathically.

It wasn't working. Unless Keshan was telepathically trying to make Jandu feel like he wanted to throw up, in which case it worked perfectly.

Jandu longed to flee the dinner, but it was too late now. Yudar looked at him often and fondly, and Jandu realized that Yudar needed him here, if only to symbolize the unity of the Paran household. So Jandu forced small bites of food down his throat, and followed the bites with vast quantities of red wine.

Keshan didn't say a word to Jandu, and Jandu didn't speak to him. After the dinner, the entertainment began. Musicians established themselves on the dais and accompanied a troupe of actors who replayed a scene from the Book of

Taivo. The breeze cooled as night fell, but the garden remained warm with so many bodies.

Several other guests approached Keshan and Iyestar during the meal, and finally they both made their excuses and left the table. Jandu watched Keshan's move through the garden carefully. Several times, he saw Keshan look directly at him and cock his head, as if motioning Jandu over. But Jandu remained rooted in his seat.

People began to dance, and soon only Jandu remained at the table of honor. Suraya and Yudar joined the festivities, and Baram laughed madly as he danced with Lord Kadal's ancient mother. Jandu sullenly drank his wine and poked at the remnants of his rice with his spoon.

He saw Keshan approach, a look of anxiety clear on his face.

"Jandu." Keshan's eyes darted around. "Can I speak with you for a moment?"

Jandu's tongue felt thick in his throat. He didn't know what to say.

"There you are, Adaru!" Druv Majeo slapped Keshan on the back and then threw his arm around him. "Come over here, I want you to meet my second wife." Keshan gave Jandu a strained looked and then let himself be led away.

Jandu tried to occupy himself by mingling with the crowd. He carried Zandi with him and explained to anyone and everyone who would stop long enough how he won her. He retold his short battle with Koraz in agonizing detail. He smiled often and laughed loudly, and secretly hoped each time he did that Keshan would hear him, and come closer.

Finally, his tactic seemed to work. Keshan maneuvered through the dancing crowd to Jandu's side. He raised an eyebrow at Zandi but said nothing about it. Instead he lowered his voice.

"I need to speak with you."

"I…" Jandu steadied his nerves. "I need to speak with you too. But not here. Come on." He led Keshan out of the crowd and through a set of ivory trellises. A spiraling staircase took them up to the second floor, where they could watch the festivities from the balcony.

They walked over thick layers of red carpets onto the stone balcony. Jandu rested Zandi against the wall and then leaned over the edge of the banister, staring down at the noisy revelry below. Keshan joined him on the balcony, leaning close.

"You need to be careful," Keshan whispered. He gazed intently at Jandu. "I think there may be a plan to assassinate you."

Jandu scowled. "What? That's what you wanted to say?"

Keshan frowned. "I am not sure who's really behind it, but—"

"Who cares about that? I have something more important to talk about."

Keshan scowled. "Like what, your Yashva bow? I already heard the story."

"I'm sorry," Jandu blurted out.

Keshan narrowed his eyes, but his voice went soft. "Pardon me?"

Jandu swallowed. He knew he was blushing, but he had to force himself through this. "I'm really sorry. About what I said that day in the forest."

Keshan raised an eyebrow. "Are you saying this because Yudar made you apologize, or because you really mean it?"

How could Keshan read him so well? "I mean it. I've been thinking about you incessantly." The second Jandu spoke the words he wanted them back. He closed his eyes and winced at his own stupidity.

"Jandu…"

"Look." Jandu grabbed Keshan's arm. He could smell the sweet coconut and salty scent of Keshan's skin. "I was cruel and I apologize. Please don't hold my actions against my brother or my family. Yudar wants your support and respects you. Please don't let my behavior change your feelings towards him."

Keshan's entire countenance softened.

"Jandu, any feelings I have towards you have nothing to do with your brother. I'm sorry too. I acted rashly that day in the forest, but I spoke the truth," Keshan said. "I couldn't lie about how you make me feel."

"Do you love Ajani?"

Keshan's eyes narrowed in annoyance. "What has that got to do with anything?"

"I just need to know," Jandu said.

"What do you want me to say? I care for Ajani. She's part of my family, and one of my friends." Keshan's lips were close to Jandu's face. Jandu could barely breathe. "But I don't want her in the way that I want you."

Jandu realized that he either just had to give in at this moment and kiss Keshan or turn away. He looked down at the party below him, at the couples drinking, laughing, and dancing. Then he noticed Yudar scowling up at him.

"I have to go." Jandu practically ran from the balcony.

"Jandu, wait!" Keshan's voice rose sharply behind him. "Stop!"

As he rushed to the door, Jandu felt a stranger's hand grip his shirt. He jerked away but not before he felt something hard and sharp slash across the side of his throat. His assailant grabbed at his hair and Jandu struck out, shoving the man back, but also tripping over the leg of a chair. As Jandu fell onto the soft red carpet, he felt the wet heat of his own blood pouring down his neck. He cupped his hand over the wound.

His assailant loomed over him, knife bright in the dim light. Then Keshan was there, grappling with the dark-clad man. Just as quickly the assassin slipped Keshan's grip. Jandu watched Keshan hit the wall with a heavy thud. Keshan slid down the wall. Jandu gained his feet in time to see the assassin jump from the balcony railing and land in the garden below. Jandu heard the shouts of surprise from the guests. Jandu rushed to the balcony, still holding his own throat, blood dripping down his arm. He caught sight of his brother, still seated at the dinner table.

"Yudar!" he bellowed down over the still-startled crowd. "Get a physician up here now!"

Jandu didn't wait for his brother's response. He rushed to Keshan. The assassin's blade was buried in Keshan's side, the tip breaking the skin through his back, just below his ribs.

Jandu gathered Keshan in his arms. He rested Keshan's head on Jandu's leg. Keshan was completely pale, but tried to smile weakly. "See? I knew I could get my head in your lap one day."

Tears welled in Jandu's eyes. He had been a fool to think he could just block out the way he felt about Keshan. And now it would be too late. He pressed his hands to Keshan's wound, hoping to staunch the flow of blood.

Jandu bowed over Keshan, his short dark hair hanging over his eyes.

"Don't die to save me," Jandu whispered. "I'll never get over it."

"I won't die today," Keshan said. He closed his eyes. "But God, it really does hurt a lot."

Jandu closed his eyes and tried to think of a sharta that would help heal his friend's wound. But the shartic words he knew only destroyed, they did not repair. Nothing in his warrior heritage granted him the power to heal wounds, only to inflict them. Keshan was so pale, the only color left was a deep purple in his lips. He looked dead. Jandu wept, his tears falling on Keshan's cheeks.

"Please, please, Keshan, stay alive for me!" Jandu felt the remorse that had been building since the moment he had repudiated Keshan. "Please forgive me for what I said to you that day in the forest. I didn't mean it."

"I know." Keshan smiled weakly. "I know you didn't mean it, and I know you didn't know that you didn't mean it."

Jandu frowned. "What?"

Keshan's eyes fell closed.

Jandu heard voices in the hallway and was relieved to see the royal physician rushing towards them, flanked by attendants.

The four men carefully lifted Keshan onto a stretcher and carried him toward the palace hospital, a set of quiet rooms tucked into the foreboding defense wall of the palace.

Jandu followed. As he ran, one of the royal doctors attempted to tend to Jandu's neck, but Jandu shoved him away. He already knew the wound wasn't deep; if it had been he wouldn't still be standing. He tried to follow Keshan into the surgery, but the royal physician firmly pushed him away, closing the doors in his face.

Yudar arrived, looking grim, followed by Suraya and Baram. Iyestar burst into the room and had to be prevented from entering the surgery, just as Jandu had. Soon onlookers crowded the hospital doorway, lords and courtiers and their wives. It seemed the entire party had moved from the banyan garden to the hospital. Finally, Mazar appeared, commanding all but Keshan's brother and Jandu back to the garden where they would not hinder the physicians in their work.

Hours passed in silence. Word came that the assassin had been caught and killed, though his identity remained unknown. Jandu allowed one of the assistant physicians to tend his wound. Iyestar sat across from him on a stool, looking sick and whispering something that sounded like a prayer.

Toward morning the royal physician summoned Iyestar and a few moments later, Iyestar returned to Jandu's side.

"How is he?" Jandu asked.

"If it doesn't get infected he should live," Iyestar said. "He wants to talk to you."

Jandu bowed and touched Iyestar's feet respectfully, and then entered the surgery. He slowly approached the bed where Keshan lay.

Keshan still lay on the marble operating table, the bloody remnants of his clothes wadded on the floor. Two assistants busied themselves bandaging Keshan's abdomen.

Jandu went straight up to Keshan and held his hand. His heart beat so quickly he wasn't sure he could slow it down long enough to get words out.

"Keshan," he said quietly.

Keshan opened his eyes. "Jandu."

Jandu's eyes burned from tears. He gripped Keshan's hand with all his strength. He could think of nothing that he could say in front of the physicians without arousing their suspicion, so he simply raised Keshan's hand to his lips.

The physicians looked at each other. One of them shrugged.

Keshan smiled so sweetly, Jandu thought his heart would break at the sight of it.

"I can't wait until I'm better," Keshan whispered, and then he winked.

CHAPTER 11

TAREK OPENED HIS EYES AND LOOKED AT THE DARK HAND on his shoulder.

He turned his head slowly, not wanting to wake the person in bed with him. His memory of the night before was foggy. One of the commanders of Dragewan's army slept soundly beside him. The man couldn't have been more than twenty, Tarek decided, studying his masculine features as he slept. He had curling black hair and thick black eyelashes. His lips pursed like a girls, but his face was already rough with dark stubble. He wore no clothing.

Tarek was immediately aroused, but also disturbed. Tarek rarely indulged in wild evenings and never woke up with strange men in his bed.

Along with a blinding headache, the truth smacked him in the temple. Of course. That was what happened last night. He got drunk with Darvad.

Depressed by the travesty of the attempted assassination against Jandu Paran, Tarek started drinking early. He obviously had too much. But then what?

God. Tarek sat up slowly, holding his head, regretting each new revelation. Did he really say those things to Darvad? He had told Darvad that he loved him. Darvad had responded by pulling Tarek into a drunken embrace and kissing him on the cheek.

And then—Tarek did the unthinkable. He kissed Darvad on the lips.

It was a friendly enough kiss, nothing sensual about it. And Darvad laughed it off, hiding his surprise with a chuckle.

But that kiss deeply affected Tarek. Because he wanted that kiss more than anything. Now he craved Darvad more than ever.

Burning with unspent sexual desire, Tarek had taken a chariot ride home. He called this commander up to his rooms late at night, and after he had offered the young man a few drinks, talked him into bed. Tarek could always detect which men would respond to his advances. And, from his sketchy memory, he recalled that this commander acted in ways to suggest that Tarek was far from being his first male lover.

Tarek stepped out of bed, careful not to wake the young commander. He pulled on his trousers and a golden vest that his servant had left out for him the evening before. As he dressed the man in the bed yawned and opened his eyes.

He looked around him in surprise. And then he spotted Tarek. His eyes widened.

"My lord!" The man stumbled out of bed, knocking his toe against the wood frame and causing him to buckle over in pain. Tarek admired the man's back side, and took a moment to look outside to see how late it was, and whether he could convince the commander to stay for a few more minutes.

"I'm late," the commander said. "I'm so sorry, my lord, I—" He stumbled as he gathered his clothes from the cold marble floor. "I slept later than usual."

"It's all right." Tarek yawned. "Take your time."

"The general expected me at dawn," the commander said.

Tarek raised an eyebrow at the sun. "Well, if there are any problems, tell the general you were with me."

The commander's eyebrows knotted. He clearly didn't understand.

Tarek sighed. "Tell the general I asked you to meet with me at dawn instead."

"Oh! Yes." The commander blushed. "I understand." He finished wrapping his pale blue dejaru and put on his shirt and armor. As he rushed towards the door Tarek handed the man his helmet.

The commander turned to Tarek and blushed. He wouldn't look him in the eye. "I… thank you… I mean…"

"You'll be even later if you stand here talking," Tarek said. "Go."

"Yes, my lord." The commander bowed low, and fled the room.

As soon as the man was gone, Tarek dropped to his bed and held his pounding head in his hands. What had he been thinking? He never slept with people he knew. That could prove to be a terrible mistake.

On the other hand, part of him didn't care. He was destroying his conscience for his best friend Darvad, why not destroy his reputation as well?

Tarek still couldn't remember all the details of the last evening, but he felt confident he hadn't performed his evening prayers. Tarek washed and then knelt down to pray.

As Tarek prayed, he begged for guidance. His life felt out of control. He loved his friend with such overwhelming obsession he knew he was blinded. But he also couldn't refuse it. He prayed harder.

His morning ablutions completed, Tarek finished dressing and then walked through the wide, airy corridors of his home to check on his father.

Tarek's father had arrived earlier the day before, and now Tarek's own physicians tended him. His father's proximity relieved some of his anxiety.

Tarek gave his father the largest of guest suites, with windows that opened to a spacious balcony and allowed breezes from the river to drift up and cool the air. But at this early hour, the heavy curtains shrouded the city from sight, and only a small candle provided illumination at his father's bedside.

Tarek approached quietly. His father still slept. A physician sat at his bedside, reading a religious scroll. The physician stood and bowed low to Tarek. Tarek put his finger to his lips.

His father's skin was thin and dry, and his breathing labored. He slept fitfully. Tarek reached down and squeezed his father's hand, but received no response.

Someone knocked on the doorway. Tarek scowled at the messenger, who bowed low in submission. Tarek left his father's side to whisper to the servant in the hall.

"What is it?" he asked curtly.

"An urgent message, my lord, from Prince Darvad." The messenger kept his head low. "He requests your presence immediately at the western gate of the royal palace."

"Damn it." Tarek looked back to his father. Couldn't he find just a few hours away from the palace for once? "Are you certain it is urgent?"

The messenger looked up nervously and then back at the floor. "Yes, my lord."

Tarek sighed. "Very well. Inform him I'll be there shortly."

◆◆◆

It took longer than usual to cross the bridge to the palace. Since the attempt on Jandu's life, palace security had been fortified and now every visitor was checked for weapons. Tarek's name was on a list of cleared guests who could approach the palace armed, but this took further clarification from one of the soldiers.

Hundreds of citizens thronged the palace gates. They were the poorest of people, dressed in the ragged cotton clothing of the Suya and Chaya castes. Tarek had no idea what the commotion was about. He pushed his way through the crowd, grateful for his heavy breastplate, which repelled the flailing hands and the press of bodies.

Tarek saw Darvad a moment later, standing within a circle of palace soldiers alongside Firdaus, Druv, Iyestar, and two ministers who Tarek did not recognize. Darvad laughed expressively as he flung small cotton bags of coin to the masses. Druv distributed bread, and Druv's young wife Mishari handed out bolts of white cloth to the gathered women.

Tarek finally pressed his way to the line of soldiers.

"Tarek! Let him through!" Darvad shouted, reaching through the wall of military bodies to yank Tarek within the circle. "We're celebrating the end of Asherwar in a new way!" Darvad laughed as more hands reached skyward, fingers waving to catch additional coins.

Tarek watched the proceeding chaos until Darvad handed him a heavy sack of coin bags.

"Here!" Darvad shouted above the crowd. "Tarek Amia, lord of Dragewan, is one of your own people, a Suya who has proven that skill and honor are more important than birth and blood! His generosity overflows to you all on this auspicious day!"

Darvad tossed more money into the air. The crowd surged towards Tarek, and he warily stepped back as the wall of soldiers flexed inwards. He reached into his sack and began to throw coins to the expectant crowd. He smiled as a young boy and his mother snatched a purple sack from the air and cried out his name in a blessing. A slow, tingling euphoria built within him as he breathed in the positive energy, the magnanimous happiness of everyone there. Darvad and his friends laughed and spoke with the people. The crowd cried out their gratitude and their names in devotion. Only the soldiers protecting the lords seemed somewhat disgruntled by Darvad's radical new tradition.

When the last of the gifts were gone, Darvad apologized to those left empty-handed, and promised a month of such gift-giving once he was king. The gathered crowd chanted his name and the prayer for his health and longevity.

Druv led the slow extrication back into the palace walls. They walked backwards, the soldiers protecting them from the grasping, thankful throngs until the palace gates could be shut. Even after the gates were closed, people continued to cry out Darvad's name and clasp the iron bars.

Darvad laughed, his face transformed by merriment. Tarek smiled back at him, love radiating through him. He was so proud of his friend, so honored to be part of Darvad's revolution.

"Whose idea was this?" Tarek asked.

Darvad smiled. "Mine. I thought that the Parans did a fine job honoring Asherwar in the traditional fashion. But if I am going to truly change the nature of this nation, I thought that Asherwar should come to represent something more. Something new. Yudar can honor the lords at a feast, but I will honor the people instead."

"It was brilliant," Tarek said. He looked at Darvad, and then hastily looked away, suddenly worried that the love he felt must be conspicuously obvious. Only last night Tarek had told Darvad he loved him. He would have to watch himself, or else Darvad might fully understand the terrible nature of that love.

"I hope you saved some of that bread for us," Firdaus told Darvad. "I'm starving."

"I have a celebratory feast awaiting us back in my suites," Darvad replied, slapping Firdaus on the back. "All of you, come with me."

They strolled along the labyrinthine palace walkways, speaking loudly. Inside the palace, Tarek could feel the heightened tension resulting from the attack on Jandu. Soldiers stood at every building, warily watching them pass. Their joy seemed insular, surrounded by sobriety.

As they passed by the central garden, Tarek caught sight of Jandu himself, speaking with his brother Baram. Both men looked up, startled, at the approach of Darvad's friends. Baram failed to hide his rage, lips curling in anger.

Jandu just watched them pass. Tarek saw the jagged cut below Jandu's jaw, the red flesh and black silk stitches standing out against Jandu's light brown skin. Tarek and Jandu made eye contact for a second. Jandu's expression was wary.

Darvad offered his half-brothers the sign of peace as he walked by. Jandu accepted the gesture with a slight bow, but he scowled at Firdaus. Everyone suspected who the culprit behind Jandu's attack was. And yet no one would come out and accuse Firdaus of the crime.

Jandu did briefly smile at Iyestar, who looked weary and sad. And then Tarek turned the corner, and the Parans, and all the turmoil outside the palace, were out of sight.

In Darvad's suite, Tarek enjoyed a meal of tea, fried cheese and vegetables, and roasted mango sandwiches. Druv's wife left them and the conversation turned back to politics. The attempt on Jandu's life along with the numerous challenges that Tarek had fought had alarmed Mazar and the regent had banned all further duels until the official announcement of the new king. Tarek expected Darvad to be angry with this. But this morning, he merely shrugged. "Mazar fears duels will exacerbate hostilities between traditionalists and moderates and could lead to open war. It's causing too much instability in the court."

Tarek couldn't help his sigh of relief. The challenges had left him feeling rotten.

Tarek noticed that Iyestar had said barely a word all morning. He had handed out gifts with the others, but now, in the tranquility of Darvad's rooms, he sat stiffly and barely touched his food. Tarek had seen Iyestar look poorly on many mornings, usually the result of wine. But this morning, Iyestar was particularly frosty, and he refused to even acknowledge Firdaus.

Firdaus seemed oblivious. He ate with both hands, his long gold necklace dangling precariously close to his plate of food.

"What do you propose to do now?" Tarek asked Darvad. "Will you wait for the announcement as planned?"

Darvad grinned. "I always like to have a contingency plan. Druv and Firdaus and I met earlier this morning to discuss what would happen if Mazar chooses Yudar over me."

A bolt of anger shot through Tarek at being excluded. Darvad frowned. "Don't be angry that you weren't there. You were too busy playing nursemaid to your father."

Tarek bristled. How could Darvad ask him to choose between himself and his father?

"It was a very boring meeting," Darvad assured him. "But we now have a strategy that will take care of all of Mazar's possible choices."

"Surely such gestures as the one today will win you support among the common people," Tarek said.

"The support of the common people doesn't mean shit to Mazar," Darvad replied. "He only cares about which lords will support me, and whether enough will do so to prevent a civil war."

"If Yudar takes the throne we all know the lower castes will revolt. Keshan has seen it happen." Druv poured everyone another round of sweet jasmine tea. "So we came up with a last challenge should Mazar make the wrong choice. It's amazingly simple, really."

"Simple because of my skill," Firdaus interrupted and Druv nodded in agreement.

"If Yudar becomes king, we offer a friendly celebratory game of dice," Druv said.

"And then we win the kingdom back from him." Firdaus smiled.

Darvad and his friends gloated in silence as Tarek absorbed the meaning of their words. They were going to cheat at dice. They were going to steal the kingdom from Yudar through gambling. The idea was so appalling that Tarek didn't even have a reaction.

But Iyestar did. Apparently this was the first he had heard of the plan as well, for he immediately stood.

"That's it." He threw his green harafa scarf over his shoulder and glared at the men. "I am leaving. I will have no further part in trickery."

Darvad instantly stood to console him. "Iyestar, old friend, don't—"

"No!" Iyestar stepped backward. "Your last foolish plan almost killed my brother! Death still hounds him. And for what? To ingratiate yourself to Firdaus so he can cheat for you?"

Firdaus stiffened. "Jandu threatened—"

"Enough." Iyestar made the sign of peace to Darvad. "Prince, you have my loyalty. And the generous acts you engage in prove to me that you will be a worthy king. But I will not take part in any more deception. You have my secrecy on this matter, but not my complicity."

Darvad seemed almost embarrassed. He reached out and touched Iyestar's shoulder. "I am doing this only to guarantee that changes we all want are undertaken. You know this is for our vision. For your brother's vision."

"I know." Iyestar nodded. "That is why you have my support. But do not involve me in these schemes any further."

"Of course. Do only what you feel is right, Iyestar."

Iyestar gave Tarek the sign of peace, and then departed. Tarek realized this was his opportunity to as well. To let Darvad know that being led by men like Firdaus and Druv would sully his reputation. To walk out as Iyestar did, still an ally and a friend, but not a conspirator.

But Tarek hesitated.

"My question is," Firdaus dropped a few grapes into his mouth, "what was Keshan Adaru doing with Jandu in the first place? I thought Keshan was your ally."

"Oh, give it a rest, Firdaus," Darvad snapped. He sat down glumly, all of his joy from the morning evaporated.

Firdaus merely shrugged. He moved onto another helping of fried vegetables, and ate with his mouth open. Tarek remembered his mother smacking him on the side of the head any time he'd displayed such poor manners. Maybe Firdaus just needed a good smack.

"Do not worry yourself, Darvad," Firdaus said loudly. "If Mazar chooses you, as he should, Iyestar will have no cause for concern. And if the dice game goes through, you will still end up looking like a hero."

"How is that possible?" Tarek asked, unable to keep the anger from his voice. "Anyone with eyes will be able to see it for what it is."

"But what kind of king would gamble his people away?" Druv asked. He raised his eyebrows. "We all know Yudar is addicted to dice. He will stop at nothing once he is on a losing streak. And with Firdaus on our side, he *will* lose. Once he has gambled the kingdom, it will be him that is shamed. People will not easily forgive a man who is so careless with his most valuable possessions."

"I doubt that Mazar will idly sit by and allow the son of King Shandarvan to live out his days a penniless beggar," Tarek said.

"Do you recall story of the Prophet Sadeshar?" Druv asked Tarek.

Tarek shook his head.

"He disgraced himself by distrusting the word of God. In the Book of Taivo, his followers send him into exile. If found within three years, his exile would begin again. But if he survived with no help from God or man in those three years, he would be considered sinless and free to reclaim his place at God's side."

"So the price of losing the dice game is exile?" Tarek asked.

Darvad nodded. "I must appear magnanimous, after all. Turn it into penance, and forgive all after three years."

"But will you?" Tarek asked. "Will you really give him the kingdom after his penance?"

Darvad smirked. "If I make sure he is found during his exile, I won't have to."

It was still a trick. Tarek stared down at his empty plate, debating what to do. The very idea of cheating at dice was so immoral, he should have walked out on principle, just as Iyestar had.

But then Darvad threw his arm around Tarek's shoulder, smiling in such a way that infused his very being. Darvad was so handsome when happy. And, after all, wasn't Darvad's vision of a new Marhavad worth sacrifices? Tarek himself tasted the joy of Darvad's vision that very morning. Wouldn't the end of the righteousness of the Triya caste be worth a liberal interpretation of the dice rules?

◆◆◆

Tarek returned to his house in darkness. He quickly scanned the faces of the soldiers outside his home, but gratefully did not find the commander amongst them. Perhaps he went back to Dragewan so that Tarek would be spared having to face him.

Inside, sweet beeswax candles lit the house. His father sat upright in bed with his eyes closed, but he opened them as soon as Tarek entered. His thin lips parted into a weak smile.

"My son. There you are."

Tarek dismissed the attendants, and sat in the chair beside his father's bed.

"Father," Tarek whispered, putting his mouth close to the dying man's ear. "I don't know what to do. I have sworn an oath to stand beside Darvad, but in order to keep that oath, I have to do things I don't believe in."

Tarek wasn't sure if his father heard him. His father closed his eyes and coughed loudly. But then he gathered his breath and spoke.

"An oath is a terrible burden," his father said. He weakly patted his son's thigh. "But you must keep your oath above all. The honor of a Suya is found in obedience to the lord to whom he is oath-bound. Do as your Triya lords command and you will never shame yourself nor your family."

Tarek nodded. He sat silently by his father's side until it appeared he had fallen asleep once more. Tarek leaned down and kissed his father's leathered cheek.

"I'm very proud of you, son," his father spoke so softly, Tarek could barely hear him.

Tarek squeezed his hand again and fled the room before his emotions overcame him.

CHAPTER 12

JANDU MET KESHAN'S WIFE, AJANI, FOR THE FIRST TIME THE day following the attack. After waking, Jandu practically ran to his friend's room, terrified that Keshan had died during the night.

Keshan slept soundly, but a plain-looking woman sat beside him and held his hand.

"Who are you?" Jandu asked.

The woman appeared affronted. "I'm Lord Adaru's wife!"

Jandu smiled charmingly to cover his mistake.

"My apologies," he said, bowing low to her. "I'm sorry to intrude. I'm—"

"—Prince Jandu Paran." Ajani's face was perfectly round, with large dark eyes and thick lashes. But her colorless lips lent no sensuality. Her hair was tightly pulled back into a nondescript bun. Jandu wondered how Keshan could marry her—he had his choice of any woman in Marhavad, and he had chosen this plain one?

She did have enormous breasts, he noted.

"It's a pleasure to meet you," Jandu said. "Keshan and I are cousins but only met recently—"

Ajani smiled thinly. "I know. All Keshan ever does is talk about you. Day in, day out. It's quite tiring."

Jandu decided he didn't like her.

"I can sit beside him while you have your breakfast, if you like," Jandu suggested. He raised his voice slightly, hoping Keshan would wake up enough to kick his wife out.

"No, I'm fine, thank you," Ajani said. She stared at Jandu pointedly. "I'll stay with him."

Jandu nodded. "All right." He took his leave of her.

Bitch. Jandu went off to sulk by himself.

He really shouldn't resent her, he thought. She was probably nice. She was an old friend of Suraya's. When he saw the two women laughing and walking the palace grounds together, he knew there had to be something appealing about Ajani. But he didn't see it at all.

Keshan recovered quickly. He claimed it was Baram's frequent gifts of turtle soup and hot buttered milk. But Jandu also caught Keshan mumbling strange prayers in the Yashva tongue. He watched letters of ice burst from Keshan's lips and disperse like mist over his wound, melting into his flesh. It was the first time Jandu had seen Yashva magic work to heal rather than to injure.

He wanted to sit by Keshan's side and ask him about this, and a thousand other things, but the one thing he wanted seemed impossible, because Keshan was never alone.

Every time Jandu attempted to sit with Keshan, Suraya was already in his room, or Baram arrived carrying another medicinal meal, or Darvad and his entourage were there to visit, or Yudar lay prostrating himself, thanking Keshan again for saving Jandu's life.

Someone always beat him to Keshan's side. He tried arriving early in the morning, before the sun rose. But Mazar was already there, discussing philosophy and ethics with Keshan. In the afternoon, Iyestar visited, reviewing Tiwari politics. And every evening, Keshan's world filled with women. Especially his wife. And it was soon very clear she didn't like Jandu any more than he liked her.

Thanks to Keshan's Yashva skills, he could walk by the end of the week, although he remained pale and moved cautiously. To celebrate he joined the Parans for breakfast on Yudar's balcony, which overlooked the river.

The wind stirred up the surface of the Yaru in frothy swoops, and gulls dove down at dangerous angles to seize spawning fish. Jasmine bloomed in pots scattered around the balcony, lending the air additional sweetness.

Jandu did not arrive fast enough to sit next to Keshan, so instead he picked at his food and glared at Ajani, who sat holding Keshan's hand the entire meal.

"He was so brave!" Ajani declared. Jandu tried to ignore Ajani retelling the epic tale of how she met Keshan. Again.

"We had only met once previously, at my sister's wedding competition," Ajani said. She smiled widely at Keshan. "But I sent him a letter anyway, praying to God that he would rescue me before I had to marry Firdaus."

Servants brought orange juice and lentil pancakes with sweet mango chutney. Jandu ate them without pleasure.

"Why didn't you tell your father you disapproved of the arrangement?" Yudar asked. He had won big at the previous night's dice game and now he brimmed with joy.

"You don't know my father. Firdaus' forests are more valuable to him than me." Ajani shook her head. "An alliance with the lord of Chandamar would have greatly helped my father, but I couldn't do it. I couldn't give up my heart to a man who has none."

Keshan said nothing as she spoke. He had his eyes half-closed as he always did when he tried to hide his emotions. But Jandu knew him well enough now to recognize the little smile on his face. Keshan wanted to say something and held back.

Keshan's eyes flickered briefly to Jandu. Jandu smiled at him, his whole body warmed with relief at even that little contact.

"So you wrote to Keshan," Suraya said, smiling at her friend. "And he came for you."

"Yes." Ajani grabbed Keshan's hand tightly, forcing him to relinquish his hold on his pancake. "I waited for him in the Prophet's temple. He rode in on his chariot and whisked me away. My father's entire army went after him for kidnapping, but

Keshan never faltered." Ajani leaned over and kissed Keshan on the cheek. Keshan gazed at her, and then pinched her nose.

Jandu pushed his breakfast away.

"So how does living by the ocean suit you?" Suraya asked Ajani. She rolled a pancake for Yudar and put it on his plate.

"Tiwari is magnificent, you must come and visit," Ajani said. She sipped at her orange juice and toyed with her long brown braid. "I was really nervous about it at first. It was during the great move, when half of Tiwari left the capital near Jagu Mali and started the new city from scratch. Moving was so unconventional, and yet Tiwari went with the decision, knowing Keshan would never let them down."

"That's not entirely true," Keshan said, the first time he spoke that morning. "Half of the ministers in Tiwari opposed the idea."

"But you convinced them," Ajani said.

Keshan shrugged. "No, they felt compelled to go since my brother agreed with me."

Yudar nodded. "It was a wise decision, Adaru. Unconventional, but wise."

Keshan laughed. "Iyestar was so angry at me! For weeks he said history would call us cowards for running from the skirmishes with the Jagu Malians. But I thought, who cares? Better history calls us cowards and there be a Tiwari people than to all die out as noble corpses. If war can be avoided, it should be, at all costs."

"It's just another example of how practically you see the world," Ajani said, patting her husband's shoulder. "You defied tradition and changed the rules. It is what we all love about you."

An uncomfortable silence hovered as Jandu and Baram looked to Yudar for a response. Yudar did not love Keshan's tradition-defying antics, and apparently everyone except Ajani knew it.

Keshan smoothed over the comment with a shrug. "Time will show whether or not it was a smart decision. Regardless, Tiwari now has a stunning new capital on the coast. It really is a sight to see." Keshan looked to Jandu pointedly.

The sun rose high across the river bank, and the full morning heat was upon them all. Jandu immediately began to sweat.

"Just because the Triya have rules for war does not mean that we should seek war," Yudar said. He nodded to Keshan. "And it is this that I admire about you, Adaru. Even the Prophet Bandruban recognized that war is an undertaking to be engaged in only at the closure of all other avenues of reason." Yudar had that tone that Jandu dreaded, the lecturing tone. Jandu rested his face against his palm and slowly shoved a ripe tomato into his mouth.

Yudar went on lecturing on the subject of war and bored the table senseless as he recited his favorite passages from the Book of Taivo. Suraya seemed to sense that the minds of her guests were wandering, and leaned over to whisper something in Yudar's ear.

Yudar's speech ended immediately.

"If you will excuse me," Yudar said, a pink tinge coloring his cheeks. He stepped away from the table. "I promised to look over some household expenses with Suraya." The two of them linked arms and fled the balcony with record haste.

Keshan smirked as they left. Baram didn't seem to notice, busy with his fourth helping of pancakes.

"It is hotter than fresh blood out here," Baram commented between bites of food.

"We should go swimming." Keshan looked directly at Jandu as he said it. Jandu's heartbeat quickened.

"That's a great idea," Jandu said. "I know just the spot."

"Oh, let's go, it will be fun!" Ajani cried.

Jandu speared his pancake with a knife.

"You can't, Ajani," Keshan said quietly. He rested his hand on the top of her hair. "Remember? You promised Suraya that you would accompany her to the cloth market. I overheard her discussing how much she is looking forward to it."

"Yes." Ajani frowned. "I suppose I did promise."

Keshan smiled. "Trust me, you are missing nothing. I'm sure I'll end up having to rescue Jandu anyway. What kind of swimmer can he be with such long legs?"

"Hey!" Jandu scowled. "I'm an incredible swimmer."

Baram burped. "You can't even dog-paddle Jandu."

"Shut up. Don't listen to him, Keshan. Let's leave him behind." Jandu stood. Hopefully, if they took their time getting to the water, Jandu would summon enough nerves to jump in.

Servants packed a lunch basket for them and prepared a chariot. They traveled along the northern path of the royal grounds towards the Ashari Forest. Now that Jandu finally had Keshan alone, he was nervous, and said little along the way. Keshan made small talk, discussing the different plants and animals they passed by. As they both gripped the central pole of the chariot car, Keshan's fingers accidentally brushed against Jandu's, and the sensation was strong enough to burn through the core of Jandu's body. The chariot bounced over the rutted dirt trail along the river, and Jandu found himself looking forward to the bumpier patches, places where he could reach for the pole and touch Keshan's hand instead.

Jandu stopped the charioteer near the location of his confrontation with Koraz. The charioteer laid out blankets. As soon as he finished unharnessing the team of horses, Jandu sent the charioteer home, promising that he and Keshan would take good care of the team and their car. The charioteer was new, obviously proud of his position, and appeared reticent in leaving the two Triyas alone with his prized responsibility while he walked the long distance in the midday heat.

By the time the charioteer finally left, the sun was at its zenith, and the air stopped moving altogether. It sat upon Jandu like a burning ember.

Keshan leaned back on the blankets by the water's edge and grabbed a cracker. "The Yaru always reminds me of my childhood. I grew up playing in this river."

"Then let's praise it by getting in it," Jandu said, throwing caution aside. The temptation of the cool water was greater than his fear of drowning. He stripped off his vest, took off his jewelry, and lastly, removed his dejaru.

Jandu slowly waded until the lazy current lapped at his waist. Turning, he saw Keshan running naked toward the water. Keshan dove in headfirst, plunging recklessly and hooting as he emerged for air. "It's so cold!" he cried, delighted.

Jandu waded up to his neck and then slowly swam with his head out of the water. Keshan came up behind him and placed his wet hands on Jandu's shoulders.

"Are you truly a bad swimmer?" Keshan asked.

"Let's just say I'm not the best swimmer." Jandu turned and smiled at him.

"So I shouldn't dunk you?"

"Not if you don't want me to hit you again." As soon as he said the words, he wanted them back. How could he have mentioned such a sore topic?

But Keshan just laughed, and ran his hand down Jandu's arm.

Jandu's heart raced. My God, was Keshan going to kiss him? Here? In the middle of the river?

Keshan brought his arm down on the water's surface, sending a sheet of water straight at Jandu's face. Then, grinning, he lunged backward, out of Jandu's reach. Jandu launched himself at Keshan, catching the other man around the waist and dragging him underwater. Suddenly aware that their naked bodies moved together, Jandu released him. Keshan gained his feet, sputtering, pushing wet hair back from his face.

"I was sure I could escape you," Keshan said. "I must still be feeling my injury."

Jandu shrugged. "No one is perfect, not even you."

Jandu climbed up the bank and collapsed back on the blankets. Now the sun felt marvelous, heating his cooled skin. He leaned back and closed his eyes.

"I think you are," Keshan said. "Well, other than being full of yourself and too conservative." He collapsed beside Jandu, wincing slightly as the movement pulled at his stitches.

Jandu snorted. "And you're too much of a troublemaker."

"I haven't even started making trouble yet." Keshan smirked. "And speaking of trouble, what's that Draya doing in your private forest? Does he belong to the royal household?"

Jandu looked to the direction of the palace. A man approached them, wearing the traditional purple robes and long unkempt hairstyle of a priest. But Jandu did not recognize him. His face seemed sunken and waxy.

"I don't think so." Jandu retied his dejaru and pulled on his vest and jewelry. The metal of his bangles burned in the bright heat, but he didn't want to appear unclothed before a priest.

Jandu furtively watched Keshan dress as well. Keshan's body was sleek and dark, and Jandu felt a deep, pleasant ache through his groin at the sight of him.

Keshan tied his trousers and pulled on his vest. As the Draya approached, Keshan's eyes suddenly narrowed. Jandu followed Keshan's gaze to the priest. For a flicker of a second, the image of the priest faltered. It shuddered in and out of Jandu's vision. He blinked as the priest grew blurry.

"I don't think this is a priest," Keshan said in a hushed tone. He took a step back.

"Blessings to you both." The priest's voice was jagged and harsh, and heavily accented. "Yashva Keshan, I need your service."

Keshan knelt. "My lord, how may we help you?"

Jandu stared at the priest, whose torso took on a bluish radiant tone. Blue flame burst out in a halo around his head.

"Kneel down," Keshan hissed. "This is Mendraz, King of the Yashvas."

Jandu dropped to his knees and bowed his head. His mind reeled. He had only met a few Yashvas before, and none had been on fire. The Yashva king radiated no heat, only light. Jandu chanced a glance up at Mendraz's face, and quickly looked back down at the dry soil. The king had yellow spiraling irises. Looking into them gave Jandu vertigo.

"I am sick, and need help," Mendraz said, his voice booming above Jandu like thunder. "I must consume the sacred Hedravan tree which grows in this forest. I sent Zandi to fetch it for me but she was unable to defeat Koraz."

Keshan lifted his head and brought his palms together in supplication. "I am sure Prince Jandu can get you whatever you need." Keshan stared pointedly at Jandu.

Jandu lifted his head. "Of course, your highness! You may take whatever you need."

"Every time I attempt to consume the Hedravan, Koraz extinguishes my blaze with rain."

"I could recite the Korazsharta," Jandu blurted. It worked before.

Mendraz's melting face seemed to almost smile. "Yes, I have heard of the mortal who outsmarted Koraz. You have become legendary amongst our people. But such trickery will not work a second time. Koraz has allies in the Yashva world that will protect the forest. I need you to help me as I feed."

"Of course, my lord. We are yours to command." Keshan bowed low once more.

Mendraz's fire curled forth in bulging rolls of pale blue flame. "Keep my fire burning. Do not let it go out."

"How exactly are we supposed to stop the rain from falling?" Jandu shouted above the roar of the flame. Already dark clouds formed over their heads and the summer air turned cold.

Beside him, Keshan broke out in a wicked grin. "Maybe you should just help King Mendraz start a bigger fire."

"What?"

"Koraz won't stop one tree from burning when the whole forest is on fire." Keshan overturned the picnic basket and extracted a jar of olive oil. "Give me an arrow!"

Jandu complied and Keshan dipped the tip of the arrow into the oil. Then with a word Keshan set the arrowhead alight.

"Fire at the grass," Keshan instructed.

"This is insane!" Jandu bellowed. "I can't burn down my own forest."

"Trust me! "

Jandu loosed the blazing arrow. Where it slammed into the undergrowth spires of white-hot flames shot up. Keshan ignited arrow after arrow and Jandu fired in a wide perimeter. Sparks and fire ignited the tinder-dry wood. Smoke rolled outwards in black clouds and the trees crackled as they were engulfed in shooting flames. Deer shot from the brush in panicked herds.

The sky opened up and rain pounded down on Jandu. In the distance he saw Mendraz's flame weaken. Jandu aimed an oil-soaked arrow at the tree and fired. The arrow pierced through the sky, whistling, then sank into the tree's trunk, igniting the bark.

Keshan handed him another arrow. The end of the shaft burned white-hot and steamed in the rain. Jandu shot another volley into the forest.

"We're running out of arrows," Jandu shouted, reaching into the nearly empty quiver on his back.

"Just keep shooting!" Keshan shouted back. The clouds intensified above them, swirling unnaturally, the rain falling as thick as a waterfall. The force of it drove Jandu to his knees.

Suddenly King Mendraz's blue flames shot high into the sky, piercing the dark clouds and searing them away to vapor. The rain instantly stopped, and steam hovered over the darkened landscape.

Jandu dragged in a deep breath and staggered to his feet. Keshan put his arm around him as they watched the forest burn. Mendraz's flames licked even higher. The forest was consumed. The world itself seemed to burn. Sparks danced in the air like mosquitoes, circling above Keshan and Jandu's heads.

Jandu and Keshan quickly dried in the heat of the nearby blaze.

"Step back from the fire, I'm afraid you'll get burned," Keshan told Jandu, motioning him further away. They departed the hot noise of the conflagration and made their way back down to the river's edge. They watched King Mendraz devour tree after tree. The sun set and the world became illuminated by eerie flickering light. Keshan checked on the horses and Jandu gathered their scattered belongings back into the car of the chariot. Jandu's arms ached, but he felt happier than he had his entire life. *This* was what he was meant to do. *This* was who he was. Fighting beside Keshan, with a magical bow, defending the king of the Yashvas. How much better could life be?

Jandu heard footsteps behind him and whirled at the intruder.

Mendraz stood before them, huge and magnificent.

Mendraz's face remained blurred. His body shimmered in and out of focus, dark brown one minute, and blue the next. His eyes were impossible to focus upon, spiraling inwards. He wore the fine gold and silver of any king, but like Zandi, this metal seemed to swim, it phosphoresced and shifted as if liquid.

Jandu and Keshan immediately knelt before him.

"In gratitude for your assistance, please accept a gift." Mendraz didn't move. But he whispered a series of words, too quickly for Jandu to understand. And before him there appeared a quiver of arrows.

Jandu continued to kneel, eyeing the quiver expectantly.

"It is inexhaustible," Mendraz explained. "So you will never again fear you've run out of arrows."

Jandu itched to reach out and grab the quiver. Instead he bowed his head. "Thank you, my lord."

"And for you, Keshan," Mendraz said. "I grant you use of my chariot. Repeat after me and you may summon the chariot at your will."

Mendraz recited a complex string of commands. Before Jandu and Keshan, a gold lacquered chariot coalesced from the air, opulent with precious gems, its thick iron wheels covered in Yashva symbols.

Keshan repeated the complicated string of Yashva sounds. Jandu looked up, admiring the golden glow of Keshan's skin in the flickering light of the forest embers. When Keshan finished the sharta, the chariot disappeared once more.

"I accept this gift with honor, my lord," Keshan said.

Mendraz's body radiated blue light. He offered them a peace sign, and then vanished from their sight.

The forest ruins smoldered. Only blackened roots and branches remained. A gust of wind shot hot sparks from the forest floor, filling the sky with dancing red lights.

Jandu looked at Keshan shyly. He lifted the inexhaustible quiver.

"I can't believe he gave me this." The pliant soft leather quiver was densely packed with arrows. He pulled one out, admiring their elegant fletching. To his surprise, his initials were already carved into each shaft.

"You deserve it," Keshan said. His voice had gotten husky. "You fought magnificently today."

"And you." Jandu put Zandi and the quiver down on a rock and turned to Keshan.

The winds died down, and ashes no longer blew everywhere. All the animals and demons had disappeared. It was finally just them—alone in the small fragment of forest left to the world.

Jandu could smell Keshan, his earthy, coconut smell, mixed with the sharp tang of burning wood. Keshan placed his hands on Jandu's arms, pulling Jandu closer.

Jandu's pulse beat faster. Keshan's touch brought a sleepy, rich fire throughout his body, like he had just downed several strong glasses of wine. Touching Keshan was inebriating.

The sky was completely dark. In the distance, Jandu heard a cockatoo calling its lover.

"When I look at you, I want you with such a longing that it drives all reason from my mind." Keshan's eyes were deep and languid. As Keshan pulled the two of their bodies together, a flare of pure longing burst through him.

"What are you doing?" Jandu whispered. Pleasure spread like warm oil from his hips where they made contact with Keshan's, down his legs, pooling in his groin.

Keshan leaned towards Jandu's face, and kissed him softly on the forehead.

"Expressing my love." Keshan kissed Jandu's left cheek, and then his right cheek. Jandu stood frozen, paralyzed between fear and desire.

Keshan leaned in and kissed Jandu on the lips. Jandu's eyes widened in surprise as Keshan pushed his lips harder against Jandu's, and then slipped his tongue into Jandu's mouth.

Keshan's tongue thrust deeper and Jandu moaned. He plunged his tongue inside, wanting to swallow Keshan whole. The feeling of pressing himself into Keshan's hot mouth sped the heady waves of liquid desire through his body.

This was not like kissing women. This was unlike any other kiss he ever experienced. It was like he was melting. He filled Keshan's soft mouth, feeling the hot explosion shake through him.

Keshan ground his hips against Jandu. Jandu's fear resurfaced. He worried what Keshan would think when he felt Jandu's erection. But then Jandu noticed Keshan's own hardness against his thigh, hot and thick, demanding attention.

"Don't worry," Keshan whispered, as if reading Jandu's mind. Keshan planted kisses along Jandu's chest, sliding down his torso, until he knelt before Jandu.

The wind picked up again, sending Keshan's jet black hair flying around his face. Keshan looked radiant and inhuman. Sparks danced through the air behind him.

Jandu's whole body shook as Keshan pressed his hands against Jandu's erection. Keshan undid Jandu's dejaru, pulled out his cock and wrapped his lips around Jandu. Shock flooded Jandu, and then embarrassment, and then all emotions but pleasure disappeared. Keshan teased the tip of Jandu's cock with his tongue, hot fingers gently massaging Jandu's testicles, each touch sending a thousand spasms of pleasure through Jandu's groin and up his spine. Jandu moaned aloud, unable to help himself.

Keshan opened his mouth impossibly wide and seemed to swallow Jandu whole. Jandu struggled to keep his legs locked. He rested his hands on top of Keshan's wild black hair.

"Keshan..." he gasped, afraid he would stop breathing at any moment.

This was the feeling he had been craving his entire life. Keshan upon him, pulling him inside. Jandu moaned again, feeling his knees buckle with the force of his ecstasy.

He longed to get Keshan out of his clothing. Jandu gently eased himself out of Keshan's mouth and knelt down.

"Let me touch you," Jandu said, surprised at the thickness of his own voice. He had never been so aroused he couldn't speak before.

Keshan smiled slowly, reaching up with his bangled hands and unbuttoning his vest. He undid the drawstring on his trousers and took them off carefully, each movement graceful and natural, like this was the most banal moment in his life, undressing for Jandu beside a smoldering forest.

Jandu's eyes feasted on Keshan's nudity. His body shone in the eerie moonlight like a pool of dark water. His skin seemed almost iridescent, and in the moonlight, appeared bluish. Jandu had never admired a man's body like this, with such carnal desire, but now the masculine scent of Keshan's flesh, the heavy width of his sex, the chiseled plains of his muscles, they seared into Jandu's mind, making him tremble with need. Jandu ran his lips and fingers along Keshan's smooth chest, down the cleft of his abdomen, watching Keshan's stomach rise and fall with his rapid breathing. Jandu nervously touched the tip of Keshan's cock.

Keshan shivered in pleasure.

"Jandu," he said his name like a mantra. "Jandu…"

Jandu didn't know what he was doing, so he let himself go by feel. He touched Keshan as he would touch himself, slowly stroking, and then brought his cock to Keshan's so they brushed together. The sensation sent shocks of electricity along Jandu's spine.

Jandu leaned down and put Keshan in his mouth. He had only imagined this, so he was unprepared for the sheer heat of Keshan's skin. The soft, velvety flesh, so hard and warm, felt better than Jandu could have ever imagined. He loved the taste of him, a mix of salt and cloves and musky skin, he loved the feel of Keshan growing impossibly large in his mouth.

Keshan's body tensed. He gripped Jandu's shoulders and then he came, Jandu swallowing the fullness of it, the taste alluringly salty.

Keshan sat up and pushed Jandu down on the grass. He brought his mouth back to Jandu to return the favor. Jandu looked up and saw the stars and sparks and Keshan's eyes, and then felt his groin shiver. Jandu exploded in Keshan's mouth, a moan escaping his lips, unable to hold it in any longer, having to give in to the feeling.

Jandu lay back, feeling dead.

His body shook with aftershocks of pleasure. The wind against his exposed genitals sent tingles down his spine. Keshan draped an arm over Jandu's bare chest.

"Keshan," Jandu whispered. "I love you."

Keshan responded by leaning over Jandu's face and kissing him so sweetly, Jandu wanted to die from it. He could taste himself in Keshan's mouth. As they dressed quietly, Jandu's mind raced again. What had they done? Surely it was wrong. Shame burned deeply inside him for what he did. He loved Keshan. Was that how he should have treated him? Allowed him to kneel and pleasure him?

Keshan appeared unconcerned. He had a deeply peaceful expression on his face. His lips looked slightly swollen from their encounter, and the sight only enflamed Jandu's passion further.

They harnessed their horses to the chariot and Keshan talked the entire way back, rambling on about his brother, about politics in Tiwari, and about his new school. He asked Jandu to come and teach archery there for a season.

Jandu could barely follow the conversation.

"So you will teach at the academy then?" Keshan asked. He had a slight smile on his face, as if he knew Jandu hadn't been paying attention.

"What? Sure." Jandu blushed furiously.

Keshan leaned towards Jandu, his lips right above his ear. "You'll have to stop blushing every time you look at me, Jandu."

Keshan surprised Jandu further by kissing him quickly and deeply. A moment later, their charioteer appeared on the road ahead, leading a search party. Jandu thought he could see Baram's armor among the gathered Triya and couldn't help closing his eyes in dread. They had obviously seen the fire from the palace and, knowing that Jandu and Keshan were out there, assumed the worst. First an attempted assassination, now a forest fire. Yudar wasn't going to want Jandu anywhere near Keshan now.

"I suppose I'm going to have to explain to Yudar what happened in the forest," Jandu remarked, thinking for the first time of what his brother might say of starting such a fire. "He won't be happy about it."

"Just focus on the gifts from Mendraz," Keshan suggested. He raised an eyebrow. "I wouldn't tell him about me sucking your cock though. I don't think he'd understand."

Jandu stopped on the road, reeling from the obscene impact of Keshan's words. He steadied himself, concentrated on not blushing, then followed Keshan forward to meet his brother.

CHAPTER 13

THE FEELING WAS LIKE A TREMOR, STARTING SMALL AND LOW, at the base of his spine, slowly building. It vibrated through his nervous system, expanding, the intensity increasing with each stroke of Jandu's fist, each hot, wet breath. Keshan threw his head back and hit it against the boards of the storage shed wall. His fingers twined into Jandu's hair and he pushed himself down Jandu's throat. Jandu moaned and the sound made Keshan come, biting his tongue to stop from crying out loud at the exquisite explosion of pleasure.

Keshan slid down the wall, coming to a crouch. Jandu steadied him. He panted heavily, his eyes shining bright, his mouth swollen, a small drop of Keshan's moisture evident on the corner of his lip.

Keshan pulled Jandu to him and kissed him, licking away the evidence.

An immediate surge of almost frightening ardor crossed over Jandu's expression. But then it faded.

"We better go," Jandu panted. "Yudar is looking for us. Well, for you in particular. He sent me to come find you."

"And come you did." Keshan smirked at his pun.

Jandu blushed. It amazed Keshan how, after all these weeks of illicit encounters behind outbuildings, in the woods, in storage sheds like this one, Jandu could still have enough innocence to be embarrassed.

Although naïve in the ways of love between two men, Jandu was a rapid, almost frenzied learner. There was an intensity to Jandu's passion that Keshan had never experienced, a piercing focus, as if the rest of the world melted away and only Keshan's body existed. Jandu fixated on Keshan's body like a target. His blue eyes took on a predatory sharpness, and then Jandu consumed him, a need to somehow improve and intensify dominating every moment they spent together. Jandu didn't seem to realize that making love was not a competition. But Keshan could not complain, because the fervor of Jandu's affections was staggeringly effective. Just seeing Jandu across a room was now enough to burn every nerve in Keshan's body with fiery arousal.

In the weeks following the encounter with King Mendraz, they hadn't been able to spend much time alone. Something had happened between Iyestar and Darvad, and so now Keshan spent his days relaying messages between them, talking with Darvad about his plan for changing the laws. And on top of that Ajani needed to be escorted to markets and to be entertained. That morning Jandu appeared, like an answered prayer innocently carrying message from Yudar.

That look had been there. That hungry, predatory look, and Keshan felt the blood rush to his groin, and within minutes he mumbled some excuse to his wife and followed Jandu into the nearest dark place, a shed near the stables.

Keshan warned Jandu that they needed to be cautious. Jandu merely blinked at him, as if unaware that their actions were not only considered immoral, but illegal, punishable by death. Keshan continued to urge caution, but then Jandu's long fingers snaked their way through his clothes and were gently stroking the underside of Keshan's testicles, and Keshan could feel his resolve weakening. Jandu kissed him, his tongue surging inside of him, both domineering and yet soft, and Keshan lost the thread of his argument entirely. There was no point in trying to discuss reason with Jandu when Jandu was pursuing him thus. Jandu was the most singularly focused individual Keshan had ever met, and now that Keshan was his preoccupation, little distracted him.

In the storage shed, Keshan stood and straightened his peacock blue dejaru. Ajani had purchased the fabric for him a week before and applied the golden trim herself. It was a gorgeous garment, and guilt flickered briefly in Keshan's mind as he ran his palms along the silk to press out the wrinkles.

"How do I look?" Keshan asked, straightening his diadem and pushing his hair back.

Jandu looked like he wanted to devour him. "Fucking fantastic." He leaned in to kiss Keshan once more. Keshan held him off, pressing his palm into Jandu's warm chest.

"You look like you've been screwing in a shed."

Jandu quickly straightened his own wrinkled clothing. They searched the dark shed for Jandu's diadem, which had tumbled off in their initial, frantic embrace.

"Here it is," Keshan called. He lifted the simple silver diadem and placed it on Jandu's head. Normally, Keshan didn't like silver, but on Jandu, the simplicity of the metal suited him. It emphasized the bright color of Jandu's eyes.

Jandu smiled at him. "Let's go." He took Keshan's hand and pulled him out of the shed, peering around surreptitiously for onlookers.

As they walked, Keshan concentrated on not gravitating towards Jandu's body. He forced a distance between them, exaggerating it as they bowed their heads and passed a group of Draya priests.

They circled the central garden and then passed through an open banquet, where Darvad entertained his ministers. As they walked by one of the tables, Jandu stole a butter pastry. He broke it into two, handing Keshan half.

"I'm famished," Jandu said.

"Me too. Fucking always makes me hungry." Keshan whispered it just to see the instant bloom of color across Jandu's cheeks. It was fun to taunt him this way. Jandu was uninhibited, even raunchy in closets, but in open spaces, the mere whisper of a lascivious word set his face ablaze.

The summer heat made certain rooms in the palace unbearable, and so Yudar held his court in a large room built into the wall of the palace, where the breezes from the river could drift in from the open balcony. The floor was covered in khaki and brown silk carpets, every furnishing tasteful, muted, and refined. Dozens of servants fanned the prince and his attendants with large feather fans, but this merely pushed the hot air around the room.

The herald at the door announced Jandu and Keshan.

Yudar's allies watched Keshan enter warily. They clustered around Yudar protectively.

Keshan bowed low to Yudar, touching his feet in a sign of respect.

"Prince Yudar," he said. "You have summoned me?"

"I summoned you half an hour ago," Yudar said, looking angrily at Jandu. Jandu stepped backwards into the crowd of ministers and messengers, and then disappeared from Keshan's sight completely. It was almost a relief when Jandu left the room. At least Keshan could concentrate on the task at hand.

"As the founder of the movement to refresh Marhavadi law, I thought I would turn to you for advice in choosing my successor as Royal Judge, should Regent Mazar select me as king."

Keshan's eyebrows shot up in surprise. He stared at Yudar in suspicion. He then noticed Mazar, watching the proceedings from the doorway. This was obviously a political move designed to show Yudar's ability to create consensus were he to be named king.

"I would be honored to assist you in this task, Prince," Keshan said. He kept his face carefully free of expression. He did not want Yudar to know that Darvad had already promised the position of Royal Judge to Keshan himself. "Although I admit I'm puzzled, since you must know that my legal views differ greatly from your own, and from the precedents you have set as Mazar's Royal Judge."

Yudar bowed his head. "This is true. But it is always preferable for those with opposing viewpoints to agree on a matter beforehand. Therefore I would like counsel. I have been considering my youngest brother Jandu for the position of Royal Judge. He is an apt learner and, under my tutelage, would provide a steady, reliable mediator for the people of our nation."

Keshan froze in shock. Jandu? As *judge*? Keshan's first reaction was to burst out laughing, but he stifled this quickly.

"I know you are friends with Jandu, and we continue to be grateful for the sacrifice you made in saving his life," Yudar said. "Without you, Adaru, this court would be plunged into grief."

Keshan bowed his head, mostly to give himself a chance to control his emotions. *My God.* He thought Jandu was an incredible lay, but could he ever seriously consider him in a role of power? The idea was terrifying. Brash and young, Jandu would be no more than a puppet for Yudar's outdated policies.

"Jandu is inexperienced in matters of governance, Prince," Keshan said, raising his head.

Yudar nodded. "I know. I would be surprised if he could recite even one passage from the Book of Taivo." Yudar smiled indulgently. "But he is intelligent, and if given a task, he can focus with dedication and drive that surpasses even the greatest of scholars."

Keshan knew very well how effectively Jandu could focus. A memory of Jandu, his eyes narrowed, concentrating on the tip of Keshan's shaft, as if he could pleasure Keshan just by looking at him, washed over Keshan, and he shuddered in remembered delight.

Keshan suddenly had an idea. What if *he* were to instruct Jandu on how to be Royal Judge? Couldn't he influence Jandu's decisions as effectively as Yudar? Perhaps Keshan could even make Jandu understand the plight of those who were not Triya noblemen. If he could instruct Jandu, lead him, then Jandu would be a better choice than any of the stodgier traditionalists Yudar could suggest.

"I do believe Jandu has great promise," Keshan said. "He has integrity and a good soul, and I would support such a nomination."

Yudar seemed surprised by Keshan's approval. His eyes widened, and then he clapped his hands together. "Excellent! This is wonderful news, Adaru. I am grateful for your blessing, and look forward to discussing such issues with you further."

Yudar dismissed Keshan, and Keshan left quickly. A giddy excitement coursed through him. If Mazar chose Darvad, then Keshan himself would be Royal Judge, and would be in charge of changing the society from the top down. But if Yudar was chosen, Keshan had little doubt that he would be able to influence Jandu.

Keshan wanted to begin work right away. He found Jandu in Suraya's garden, having lunch with Suraya and Ajani. Ajani rushed over to Keshan, hugging him affectionately. As always, Jandu quickly glanced away as Keshan returned her embrace.

"How have you been?" Keshan asked his wife.

"Wonderful! Join us for lunch. Suraya was just telling me about the priest who predicted she would be married to three men."

"Oh?" Keshan sat down next to Jandu, his knee brushing against Jandu's brazenly.

Ajani grabbed Keshan's hand. She had a habit of doing so, and it bothered him, but he smiled patiently. "Tell Suraya about your visions, Keshan! I'm sure she would understand."

Keshan spread a thick layer of creamy cheese onto a slice of bread. "I am going to eradicate the castes, starting with the Triya."

No one said anything. Once again, Keshan managed to bring all conversation to a halt. Keshan casually drank from his teacup. He was used to this sort of reception.

Jandu just shook his head. "The shit that comes out of your mouth…"

"It's true," Keshan said.

"But why?" Jandu frowned. "It doesn't make sense."

Keshan shrugged. "It's the only way to improve this society."

"And you are doing this because you saw it in a vision?" Suraya asked.

"I am doing so because it is right," Keshan said. He disliked discussing his visions because they were so personal and powerful, but at the same time he couldn't say if they were messages from God, telling him that he followed the correct path or just a side effect of his half-Yashva nature. Iyestar believed that they only granted him an ability to visualize the repercussions of his actions. Regardless, he knew that they were meant to be acted upon. But that wasn't the kind of statement that would convince a man like Jandu. Words alone seemed to have little impact on him. Keshan supposed that hours of listening to his brother Yudar's wearisome ruminations had made him immune to long speeches.

Experience informed Jandu's actions in a way lectures never would. One look at his friend told him that Jandu already tired of this conversation.

"And what makes you so sure this new world is going to be any better or any more righteous?" Jandu smirked.

"Don't speak to him like that!" Ajani snapped. She glared at Jandu.

Jandu frowned. "I'm just saying—"

"No, you are questioning Keshan! Can't you tell he is special? Different from the rest of us?" Ajani's voice rose.

Keshan moved to reassure her, but then Jandu grinned. "Different is definitely one thing to call Keshan."

Keshan burst out laughing. But Ajani was still not pleased.

"When Keshan was five years old," Ajani went on, "he defended a boy who was homeless on the street. An untouchable. Keshan sided with the untouchable against the son of a priest, a Draya. And the courts of Tiwari condemned Keshan to death for fouling himself with untouchable air, and for not protecting the Draya."

Suraya's eyes widened. "What happened?"

"I take it from his presence that the decision was over-ruled," Jandu said, smirking at Ajani.

Keshan laughed again which only further infuriated Ajani.

"Yes, the decision was overruled!" Ajani said, her voice rising. "And do you know why? Because he showed them all what true compassion is! It isn't some ancient code written in a book, it is a living, active decision that people make every day! And Keshan had the power to change these high courtier's opinions, at the age of five! Keshan is no ordinary person! Can't you see that?"

Jandu looked into Keshan's eyes. Keshan felt the stare through his entire body.

"I can." Jandu swallowed. "He is extraordinarily convincing when he wants to be."

Ajani looked at both men, which seemed to make her even more angry. "So apologize to him! How dare you question him!"

"Oh, Ajani, calm down," Suraya said, reaching over to pat her friend's shoulder. "Just ignore Jandu. He's always like this."

Jandu shrugged. "I'm always like this."

"He's obnoxious," Keshan added.

"And rude," Suraya said.

"And he argues about things he knows nothing about, because he has to be right about everything," Keshan said.

"Hey!" Jandu frowned.

Keshan reached forward to pour Jandu more tea as a peace offering, but found the teapot empty.

"Shall I order more?" Suraya asked, getting up to call a servant.

"No, don't bother," Keshan said. He stretched his arms, and looked meaningfully at Jandu. "I came to see if Jandu would run an errand with me."

"I can accompany you," Ajani said quickly.

"No." Keshan leaned over and kissed his wife on the cheek. "It is in a dangerous part of town, I would not dare take you there."

"I'm all yours," Jandu said, standing quickly. Anticipation already pinked Jandu's cheeks. "Shall we go?"

Keshan looked to him, and realized Jandu was going to be disappointed. He really did have an errand, one Keshan hoped would be enlightening for his new lover. But as Jandu moved to stand beside him, Keshan could almost smell the sex upon him, and Keshan's mind whirled.

Maybe a quick delay wasn't such a bad idea after all.

They beelined for the storage shed once more.

◆◆◆

"Not that I don't find your company charming, but where exactly are we going?"

Keshan strode alongside Jandu through the winding dusty streets of the leather market. Jandu was chatty enough in the chariot to the edge of the bazaar, but once they got out and started walking the narrow streets of the poorer neighborhoods on foot, Jandu's tension increased and he grew silent.

"I wanted to show you something," Keshan explained.

Untouchables of the Jegora caste huddled in doorways as Chaya caste merchants hawked leather shoes, bags, belts, and scabbards. The hot afternoon heat intensified the smell of freshly tanned hide and masked the stench of raw sewage. Wetted hay covered the dusty roads but did little to stop the persistent clouds of dirt that filled the air from so many bodies walking and pushing carts.

They passed by monkeys copulating and temple bells ringing and men sleeping in their carts, occasionally twitching to swat flies from their faces. In the distance, a squeaky stringed instrument called out to travelers, and a small boy was learning to play the pipe flute down the road.

At first, the crowd parted before them, dressed as they were in their silks and wearing their diadems, but then others began to converge and beg for money. Jandu went silent. Only when one holy man offered to lift fifty pounds of stones with his penis for a donation did Jandu laugh and make a contribution.

The streets narrowed further. They passed palm readers, cows, astrologers, statues of the prophets stained with purple dye. As they crossed through a crowded intersection, the noise of chimes and chants and cocks and children and hawkers accompanied their journey. Keshan smelled horrible things, glorious things.

They reached an open square. In the center of the circle stood a pillory. It looked almost innocent in the daylight, although close observation revealed nails and blood stains. Jandu frowned at it and asked what it was.

"It's a pillory," Keshan said. "Untouchables are forced into it and their ears are nailed to the boards while people hurl garbage and feces at them. It's lawful punishment if their shadow accidentally falls upon a Suya caste member."

Jandu grimaced. "How disgusting."

Keshan shrugged. "Better than if their shadow should fall on us. They could be executed."

"If I were Jegora I'd move out of the city," Jandu said. "Too many hazards walking around Prasta."

It was the first time Keshan ever heard Jandu speculate what it would be like to be lower class, and the thought offered him a little hope.

"Of course," Jandu continued, "I'd probably want to be as far away from other people as possible, if I looked as hideous as a Jegora."

Keshan's heart sank.

Jandu always did this. He would say something meaningful, considerate, and then immediately follow it up with some insult, almost like an afterthought. Keshan doubted Jandu even noticed it.

Jandu suddenly stopped Keshan, holding his arm. "You didn't take me all the way out here to teach me a lesson about untouchables, did you?"

"Maybe." He smiled, hoping Jandu's mood would lighten.

Jandu stepped in a pile of cow manure. He swore and kicked his sandal free. Now he definitely was in a foul mood.

"Well, make it quick," he grumbled. "This street is revolting."

"It's just poor."

"Poor, revolting, whatever you want to call it."

Keshan sighed. A woman approached them, eyes following her feet, and as soon as she looked up and saw them, she hastily crossed the street. Jandu stared at her branded hands, the symbol of the Jegora red and puffy, burned into her flesh.

"God," he whispered. "She's…"

"An outcaste," Keshan finished for him. "Once a Triya, now untouchable."

"I wonder what she did to deserve this kind of life." Jandu said. "It must have been horrible."

At a low, arched wooden door, Keshan knocked. The door promptly swung open, the hinges creaking loudly. "Lord Keshan! Come in! Come in!"

"Greetings, Tamarus!" Keshan called back. He turned and saw that Jandu watched the outcaste woman retreat down a narrow alley. His expression was grim. His frown only deepened when he looked at Tamarus.

"You cannot tell Yudar I came here," Jandu whispered.

"I'll add it to the list of things I'm never telling Yudar," Keshan said. He smiled warmly at Tamarus as he led Jandu into the courtyard.

Keshan's old friend Tamarus wore a magnificent white beard. The man was close to sixty, but his eyes still shone as bright and cheerful as they had when Keshan was a young boy.

Keshan entered the house and Tamarus immediately knelt at his feet, blessing Keshan.

"Welcome! Thank you for coming! Welcome!"

Jandu scowled as he stepped into the inner courtyard, which consisted of a shallow fire pit, densely packed soil, and half a dozen chickens, which aggressively flocked to Jandu's sandals and started clucking.

"Jandu, I want you to meet an old friend of mine, Tamarus Arundan. Tamarus, this is Prince Jandu Paran." Keshan smiled encouragingly at Jandu.

Jandu seemed at a loss as to what to do. It was against tradition for a Triya to have to bow to someone obviously of low upbringing. But he was a guest in Tamarus' home. Jandu fidgeted, and then gave a small, curt bow of his head. Keshan smiled wider. He had to give Jandu credit for trying.

Tamarus, at least, could be counted on to revel in his good fortune. He groveled at Jandu's feet, tears in his eyes, praising God for the honor of having one of God's chosen royals in his humble abode. This attracted a gaggle of children to the doorway, whose open stares only seemed to make Jandu more uncomfortable. Jandu looked to Keshan for help.

"We don't have much time," Keshan informed Tamarus. "Let me see her immediately."

"Of course! So sorry! So sorry!" Tamarus bounced off the ground, despite his age, and rushed ahead of them to the only other doorway in the courtyard. "She's in here."

"What are we *doing* here?" Jandu hissed in Keshan's ear.

"Tamarus is one of the Chaya's most beloved religious scholars. He once helped me craft some legislation in Tiwari. But now his wife is sick, and he asked me to come and see if my Yashva healing would assist her."

Jandu sighed. "Fine. Hurry. For God's sake."

Keshan stepped inside the small room, but Jandu did not follow.

"Are you coming?"

"I'll wait out here."

"I could teach you the sharta," Keshan said.

This got Jandu's interest. His scowl diminished slightly. "Oh?"

Tamarus knelt beside his wife's narrow cot. The low ceiling forced Keshan to kneel as well. The ground was clean and dry, but the walls were stained black with years of soot from cooking fires.

Jandu knelt beside Keshan on the floor.

Keshan reached out for Tamarus' wife's hand. He did not know the woman well, had only seen her a few times. But it was clear to see she was dying. Her face was ashen, her skin dull and unresponsive to the touch.

"How long has she been like this?" Keshan asked softly.

Tamarus reached out and stroked her hair. "Since Asherwar. The local healer removed a growth from her stomach, but she has been sickly ever since, and the wound has festered."

Keshan gently lowered the blanket and lifted the woman's thin cotton dress. The sight of the tumor was ghastly. Portions of the flesh had died and turned black.

Jandu gagged beside him. "God!" His face drained of color, but he did not turn away.

Keshan covered her up once more. He frowned at Tamarus.

"It may be too late for my help, friend."

"Anything you can do, Lord Adaru. Please!"

"Take her to a physician, for God's sake!" Jandu cried out.

"Physicians don't treat Chaya, Jandu. They have only their own priests and healers to help them." Keshan rubbed his palms together to warm them, and then placed them on either side of the woman's wound. He could feel Jandu tense beside him at the impure contact.

Keshan began speaking, chanting a low string of Yashva words, saying them slowly enough that Jandu would hear them and be able to repeat them. As he had hoped, Jandu rallied to the task.

Keshan repeated the words and then asked Jandu to chant with him. Jandu spoke lowly, saying the words with Keshan. He was an astonishingly fast learner. In three tries Jandu memorized the complex string of sounds, and Keshan could feel the power building behind them like wind, sucking from the Yashva kingdom and breaking the barriers of the worlds to surge through Jandu's mouth.

Keshan let go of the woman and held Jandu's hands. He tried placing them on the woman's side but Jandu immediately flinched and pulled back.

"What? No!" Jandu's hands curled into fists at his chest.

"The words won't work unless you touch her," Keshan said calmly, although the vehemence in Jandu's reaction had startled him.

Jandu hesitated, looking at the woman, and then back at Keshan. He shook his head. "No. I can't touch her. It's... it's wrong."

"Then leave," Keshan said in sudden anger. "You are no use to me here."

Jandu stood and left the room.

Keshan stifled his rage and placed his hands back on Tamarus' wife, uttering the sharta, fast and with concentration. Frost burnt his tongue and the words themselves drifted out of his mouth in icy mists. He blew them on her wound, where they melted and settled like dew.

Keshan instructed Tamarus on how to cleanse the wound, and what herbs to give his wife. He promised to return in a week to see if the spell had lessened the infection. He worried it was too late to do her any real good, but at least it would ease her pain, as all Yashva cures did.

When Keshan stepped back out into the courtyard, he saw that Jandu had fled. He could be such a close-minded, selfish bastard. Keshan had been wrong to hope Jandu could be taught to care.

As he walked home alone, Keshan finally faced facts.

This affair with Jandu had to end.

His hope of turning Jandu into a compassionate revolutionary was revealing itself to be a fantasy. What had he been thinking? Jandu was a Paran. Like his brothers, like his father.

He was descended from a long line of men who abhorred equality, and revered only the laws as laid down by their own ancestors, the crusty prophets of yore.

Keshan had worked for the last ten years of his life towards this moment, towards seeing a king enthroned who would abolish slavery to religious traditions. He did not need Jandu for any of that.

Was he really going to abandon all of this for a good lay? Absolutely not.

Over the following days, Keshan distanced himself from Jandu. He attended Darvad along with the other lords who supported the Uru claim to the throne.

Keshan pretended that his brother's absence was normal. He pretended that Jandu did not matter.

And yet, despite his resolve to end the affair, Keshan sought Jandu's face whenever he entered a crowded room. He plunged himself deeper into reviewing the new laws that Yudar had established in his tenure as Royal Judge, but the additional work did little to relieve the aching hunger in his body. He wanted to hear Jandu. Touch him. Smell him. He missed Jandu's sense of humor, his fascination with unimportant things. To his shame, he found himself even missing Jandu's bragging.

Keshan excused himself from one of Darvad's casual dinners that evening, hoping to cleanse his mind with meditation and fasting. He sent Iyestar in his stead, hoping that whatever rifted his brother and Darvad apart could be repaired over a good meal. But when Iyestar returned to their townhouse, his expression was dark and dangerous.

"We're leaving." Iyestar stated. He ordered the servants to start packing immediately.

They had spent so much time in the capital city, the Tiwari townhouse now felt like home. Keshan looked around the rooms he had lived in over the past few months, saddened to even consider leaving them.

"Dress. Now." Iyestar's voice slurred.

"You're drunk."

"Surprise." Iyestar faced Keshan. "Did you hear me?"

"Yes! But why? Why now?"

"I have made my decision." Iyestar moved to the side table and poured himself another glass of wine. "I don't have to explain myself to you."

"Yes you do." Keshan grabbed the wine cup from his brother's hand and slammed it on the table. "I have worked too hard over the last few months to let you randomly choose this moment to pull me out of the action!"

"We will not stay in this cursed city a moment longer."

Keshan bit back his angry response. It was just like his elder brother to make executive decisions without consulting Keshan first.

"What has happened?"

"Over dinner, Firdaus and I exchanged words. We're leaving." Iyestar grabbed his wine once more and finished it.

"Firdaus is nothing. No one."

"He has Darvad's ear," Iyestar said. "And he suspects you."

Keshan stiffened. "I have not changed my allegiance. I am still loyal to Darvad. What—"

"He suspects you and Jandu! Good God, did you think no one would notice? Your eyes practically glaze over when Jandu enters the room! Are you seriously going to dog that Paran prick around simply because he has a tight ass?"

Keshan froze, shocked. His brother had to have a lot to drink before he would ever openly discuss Keshan's sexual preferences. It was no secret between them, rather a sore topic reserved only for conflicts.

Keshan shook his head. "Iyestar, if you are certain that Darvad will win the throne, then it is even more important that we stay these last few weeks until the announcement. I should be here to be appointed Royal Judge. Think of what that would do for our family and for our people!"

"It's all too ugly," Iyestar mumbled, collapsing back onto Keshan's bed. He covered his eyes with his hands. "I'm sick and tired of Firdaus' taunts and insinuations. Sick of this palace. Sick of your flagrant flirtations."

"But—"

"No buts. We will be nowhere near the capital when Mazar makes his decision. We leave tonight, so say your goodbyes to whomever you wish." Iyestar looked at Keshan pointedly.

Jandu.

Despite his anger at the man, the idea of leaving Jandu without saying farewell coiled like pain in Keshan's stomach. He decided he must say good-bye. It was not a promise, or a compromise of Keshan's ideals. It was only polite.

By the time Keshan reached the palace, the Parans had already retired for the night. A guard accompanied Keshan to Jandu's suites, and stood by as Keshan knocked on Jandu's bedroom door and announced himself.

"Come in," Jandu said weakly, his voice low and broken from sleep.

Keshan gave one last nod to the guard and stepped inside Jandu's room, carefully locking the door behind him.

Jandu looked charming lying in his bed, his hair sticking up wildly, his eyes heavy with sleep. Jandu shaved almost religiously, but now the beginnings of stubble broke across his cheeks and chin, and he looked roguish, rough, his body dark and lean in the moonlight. He wore only a short maroon dejaru, knotted loosely at his side and barely reaching his knees.

Keshan smiled at him.

"Keshan?" Jandu whispered. "What are you doing here?"

"Iyestar and I are leaving Prasta tonight," Keshan answered. He sat beside Jandu on the bed. "We will be in Tiwari by tomorrow afternoon."

Jandu stared at him in shock. His clear distress warmed Keshan's heart.

"But why?" Jandu asked.

Keshan shrugged. "My brother has ordered it. I have to obey him."

"I thought you did as you pleased and didn't obey anyone." Jandu propped himself up on one elbow. Now that Jandu was fully awake, he seemed to recall that they'd parted badly. An edge of surliness crept into his tone. "Why come tell me?"

Keshan smiled seductively, reaching up to run his hand along Jandu's cheek. "I thought, if I couldn't stay, at least I could give you a proper farewell."

Jandu glanced to the door. "Did the guard notice you?"

"I'm not invisible."

"I know, but…" Jandu looked worried.

"Relax," Keshan said, flourishing a scroll. "I told him I needed to review some documents before I left in the morning."

Keshan tossed the scroll he'd brought to the floor and ran both hands through Jandu's hair. It felt magnificent between Keshan's fingers. He looked at his lover's body on the bed, and realized they had never done this, never made love somewhere comfortable. Keshan leaned forward and kissed Jandu softly. Jandu responded hungrily, pulling Keshan to him and immediately claiming Keshan's mouth.

Keshan had planned on taking his time, savoring this last sweetness. But Jandu's eyes lit with fierce greed, and suddenly Jandu gripped Keshan's shoulders and pressed him back against the bed. Jandu crouched above Keshan and devoured Keshan's body with kisses, lingering on each nipple, his hands deftly working loose the ties at Keshan's waist and pushing Keshan's trousers off.

Keshan had no choice but to lay back, stunned once more by the ravenous onslaught of Jandu's passion. Jandu was rough and soft all at once, tongue flicking gently as his fingers raked over Keshan's sensitive skin. His mouth lowered, sinking below Keshan's hip bone, laving the spot where Keshan's legs met his body. Jandu roughly spread Keshan's legs apart and pressed himself into Keshan's crotch, kissing until finally opening his mouth to swallow Keshan down his throat. Keshan moaned. Spasms of pleasure shot through his body like electrical arcs, he felt burned with sensation. He fought to not cry out, fearful of who in the palace might hear them.

Keshan forced Jandu away from him long enough to tear off Jandu's dejaru and expose him before Jandu intensified his actions.

"Jandu… you want to try something?" Keshan's voice was so thick with lust he could barely speak, the words broken and hushed.

Jandu didn't say anything, he just nodded. His tongue made lazy swipes along the insides of Keshan's thighs, along his shaft.

Keshan pulled away slowly, cursing himself for not thinking ahead. He quickly stood and searched Jandu's room until he found a jar of aloe oil.

Jandu watched him carefully, his eyes intense, his stare unbreakable.

"What are you doing?" Jandu asked.

Keshan scooped some oil onto his fingers and then reached behind him, preparing himself. Jandu grew very still, watching Keshan, his pupils dilating, his breathing growing ragged. Keshan didn't know if Jandu suspected what he was going to propose, but Jandu seemed very interested regardless.

"Let me do it," Jandu croaked, his voice breaking. He took position behind Keshan, and suddenly, Keshan could feel him, his long fingers gently stroking at the outside, not seeming to understand what he was meant to do. Keshan pushed back onto Jandu's fingers until one slipped inside. Jandu froze. And then he probed deeper, pushing in until Keshan gasped in pleasure.

Keshan arched his back and presented himself to Jandu.

Jandu hesitated. Keshan worried he might have moved too fast, expected too much. And then suddenly Jandu gripped Keshan's hips and hoisted him upwards into position. Jandu's look became focused, predatory once more. Keshan felt the heat and width of Jandu at his opening, a pause, waiting at the entrance.

And then slowly, carefully, Jandu plunged inside.

Keshan groaned. It had been so long since he had done this, felt this fullness, this heat, his body expanding to accommodate the width of Jandu. It didn't last long. Jandu trembled, his hands shaking as he grasped Keshan's hips, a delightful, inarticulate moan coming from his lips. Jandu reached around and took hold of Keshan's dripping member. Jandu's thrusts intensified with each pump of his fist. Keshan's world expanded and contracted around each penetration, his pleasure building until he felt the heavy heat of Jandu's scrotum slap against his own. That was all it took for him to shiver in a long spasm and come uncontrollably into Jandu's palm.

He clenched down, driving Jandu's orgasm from him as well. Jandu stayed buried deep inside of Keshan for a few minutes as they caught their breath, but eventually, Keshan felt him pull out. The loss left Keshan feeling empty, incomplete.

Keshan collapsed onto the bed, and Jandu fell beside him. Jandu kissed him. Keshan thought that now, at least, his passion could fade, but Jandu's kiss made him light-headed, he wanted more, he wanted it all the time, this taste, all of it, all over him.

"You all right?" Jandu asked breathlessly.

Keshan nodded. "I'll be back in a moment." He rose and padded barefoot through the side hall to Jandu's private bath, looking for a towel.

He was gone for only a few moments, and when he had left the room, Jandu had been smiling. But when he returned, he found Jandu with his hands covering his face, leaning against the bed, sitting on the floor.

Keshan rushed to Jandu's side. "What's wrong?"

To Keshan's further shock, Jandu had tears in his eyes. "I am so sorry I defiled you."

"What?" Keshan blinked at him in surprise, towel dangling limp in his hand. And then he laughed. He couldn't stop. He crouched down and pushed the hair back from Jandu's face to kiss his forehead. Of course Jandu would think that this was defilement. His strict religious upbringing wouldn't allow him to view it any other way. Compassion welled in Keshan.

"My God, Jandu, you can be such an idiot."

At these words some of Jandu's pride rekindled. He wiped his eyes. "No I'm not. I just—"

"I *liked* it, you fool. It's what I wanted you to do."

Jandu searched his face. "Truly?"

"Truly." Keshan laughed again. "And you didn't dishonor me. Quite the opposite, really."

Jandu leaned his head back against the bed and closed his eyes. "We could still be killed for what we just did. It is against all laws."

"It is, but it shouldn't be," Keshan said.

Jandu breathed a heavy sigh. "How can you expect me to believe that everything I have learned as right and wrong no longer applies?" Jandu ran his hand through his hair. "Not just now. The other day as well, at your friend's house. I know you expect more of me, but I just couldn't. I am not like you. I will never be like you."

Keshan smiled at the simplistic honesty of the statement. "I know. I shouldn't have pressed you. All I am asking you to do is judge your decisions by your own heart. That is all. Every day, ask yourself if you are acting on tradition or if you truly believe in what you are doing. When you do something, is it because it is how you have always done it, or because you feel it in your bones that it is the only choice you can morally make? That's how we all need to live our lives."

Jandu seemed calmer, but his eyebrows still came together, showing his frustration.

Keshan continued. "Do you think you are a bad person?"

"No."

"Do you think I am?"

"Perhaps. But I love you anyway," Jandu said vehemently. Keshan smiled at the conviction in his voice.

Keshan almost told Jandu he loved him as well. The words stuck in his throat. Did he really feel that way? Suddenly, Keshan was sick with the realization that he did. *My God*, it had happened, hadn't it? He had fallen in love with Jandu. What was supposed to be nothing more than a distraction, nothing but a quick fuck, had turned into a love affair.

Keshan stroked Jandu's face. "So why do you think it is wrong for us to love each other, in any way we like? Who are we hurting?"

Jandu hesitated. "It's just… God says it is wrong."

"In the Yashva kingdom, men may love men," Keshan told him. "Women may love women. And they are also the children of God. So why are we being held to different rules?"

"I don't know," Jandu sighed. "I don't know."

Keshan gently urged Jandu down onto the bed. He wrapped his arms around him, swinging his leg over Jandu's to pull their bodies closer. Jandu held him tightly. Keshan could feel his anxiety. Keshan had to remind himself that this was all new to Jandu. He was asking his lover to see the world differently, see himself differently.

"It's all right," Keshan said suddenly, knowing it was what Jandu needed to hear. Jandu nuzzled his head against Keshan's shoulder.

"So you aren't mad at me for what happened at your Chaya friend's house?" Jandu asked quietly.

Keshan shook his head. "I'm not mad."

Jandu smiled shyly. "And you enjoyed what we just did?"

Keshan pulled Jandu tighter. "I loved every second of it."

"So, maybe we should try it again?" Jandu's smile curled at the edges of his mouth.

"Oh, if only all religious debates could be won so easily." Keshan leaned in and kissed him. He knew this affair was dangerous. But now that he was in love, he had no choice but to accept it as he would have accepted one of his most beautiful and frightening visions.

CHAPTER 14

It had been a year since Suraya's marriage.

Rather than have any sort of ceremony, Yudar, Baram, Jandu and Suraya downplayed the year's change, attempting to make Suraya's shift from Yudar's wife to Baram's seem inconsequential. But Jandu could tell that Suraya was as nervous as Baram was excited.

After all, Suraya and Yudar had obviously grown to love each other. Suraya seemed to be able to read Yudar's mind, she glowed when he was around, and she acted like a proud, strong queen. Yudar was a calmer, happier man with her by his side. The marriage had been just what Yudar had needed to relax into the prospect of his rule.

Now that it was Baram's year with Suraya, she would not be giving up the title of queen, if Mazar chose Yudar for king—but she would be spending her nights in Baram's chambers. And though neither she nor Yudar said anything, Jandu knew them both well enough to see that the impending separation pained them. He understood that pain. Keshan had been gone for a little over a month and Jandu keenly felt a physical loneliness, which he'd never acknowledged before.

To distract himself, he sought out work. Once he was relieved of his role as regent, Mazar intended to establish a new academy for warriors in Prasta's temple district, and had requested Jandu's help with the school. He and Mazar spent hours developing the curriculum, and choosing the best young Triya warriors from around the nation to attend. The school would be a testament to the Triya people.

Keshan's words about ending the Triya caste returned to Jandu when he thought of Mazar's academy. But such thoughts hardened his resolve to improve the academy. Even if Keshan's premonitions were correct, to give in to Keshan's philosophy would be disloyal to both Mazar and Yudar. And Jandu was nothing if not loyal.

Jandu could successfully put Keshan's radical ideas out of his mind, but he failed when it came to Keshan himself. Jandu felt incomplete without Keshan. Yet there was nothing he could do about it. Yudar wouldn't even engage in a conversation about Jandu going to visit Tiwari. Since the assassination attempt, Yudar's naturally tight grip had become a stranglehold.

Unspoken tension suffused their family dinner the night that Suraya would leave Yudar's bed. Jandu hoped Yudar wasn't resentful, and hoped even more that Suraya didn't regret her decision. Their dinner conversation was uncomfortably stilted.

Before they turned in, Jandu decided to have a glass of wine on the balcony outside the dining room. He poured a second glass and held it out for Suraya, who joined him.

They stared over the balcony in silence, admiring the clear sky that revealed every star. Trees along the Yaru rustled as monkeys clambered their branches, and in the distance, they could hear cows crying out for their evening milking.

"Are you nervous?" Jandu asked finally.

Suraya didn't meet his gaze. She tugged at her heavy silver-threaded zahari as if it was uncomfortable.

"I'm scared out of my wits," she said finally. She looked to Jandu and smiled nervously.

Jandu brushed a loose hair from the side of her face. "That's normal. I'd be scared too, if I were you."

Suraya studied Jandu's expression. "You know, I wouldn't be this nervous if you were next. I don't know what it is about you, Jandu, but I feel very close to you. We have a different relationship than the one I have with Baram or with Yudar."

"I'm more lovable," Jandu said.

She shook her head. "No, you snot. It's not that. You look at me differently." She dropped her voice to a low whisper. "You treat me differently."

"I'm different," Jandu said, coughing to cover his embarrassment.

"Yes you are," Suraya said.

Jandu hugged her to him, a friendly hug. He didn't want Baram getting jealous now that it was his year. Jandu could see Baram pacing in the dining room, watching Jandu and Suraya in the starlight.

"You know what?" Jandu whispered in Suraya's ear.

"What?" Suraya had her eyes closed, her face close to Jandu's, close enough to kiss.

"Baram loves you so much he will treat you better than you've ever been treated before."

Suraya opened her eyes and stared at Jandu. For a moment, Jandu detected a flicker of disappointment. With horror he understood that Suraya had wanted him to kiss her.

"Baram will make a wonderful husband," Jandu continued.

"Yudar is a wonderful husband," Suraya said, sighing. She pulled from Jandu's embrace. "I just got used to being Yudar's wife, and now I have to learn all over again."

"Nothing big is changing, Suraya. Just the penis, really."

Suraya's jaw dropped. She stared at Jandu with wide eyes.

Jandu smiled. "And, having seen both Yudar's and Baram's dicks, I can assure you, they're pretty much the same."

Suraya turned completely red.

Jandu couldn't stop, though, now he verged on laughter. "Although I would caution that Baram has developed some unsightly back hair which you may want to address the first few weeks you're in bed with him."

Suraya reached out and smacked Jandu on the arm, and then started laughing hysterically.

"You're awful! I can't believe you! You're so disgusting!" Suraya had tears of laughter in her eyes now, and she hit Jandu weakly on the arm over and over. "What kind of person are you? Didn't you listen to the whole conversation we had about not comparing or talking about... *that*?"

Jandu shrugged. "When have I ever paid attention to Yudar's conversations anyway? Besides, I thought I'd put your mind at rest." He looked through the window at Baram's angry, towering figure and shook his head. "I don't want you to think that just because Baram is built like a monster the rest of his body is freakishly large as well."

Suraya wiped the tears in her eyes and laughed again. "Well, thanks for the warning."

"Yes, yes." Jandu swilled the last of his wine and then put his arm around Suraya and led her back to the dining room. "Now, we better go inside before Baram thinks I'm talking up my own dick a year too early."

That night Jandu slept fitfully, as he had since Keshan left. Palace life seemed meaningless without him. Dressing in the morning became a chore now that he didn't have to think about how Keshan might respond to his appearance. Even the hard week when Keshan avoided him had been less painful than this. At least then there had always been the chance that he would run into Keshan, or see him in some crowded hall. But now even that slim hope was gone.

They had exchanged letters, but other than some carefully disguised romantic innuendos, Jandu remained loveless since Keshan's departure. He practiced with Zandi daily. He spent hours with Mazar working on the academy, desperate to keep his mind occupied enough to not dwell on his heartbreak. But that night, as Baram finally conjugated his marriage, and Suraya explored a new man's body, Jandu was painfully aware of his separation from Keshan, and it tore at his gut like an ulcer.

In the morning, he anxiously awaited Suraya's presence for breakfast. When she finally showed up, she seemed pleased, although tired.

Before his brothers got there, Jandu went to her and kissed her on the top of her head.

"No sleep, it seems. Busy night?" He winked.

Suraya grinned slyly. "My God. I'm going to be dead of exhaustion by the end of this year."

Suraya's prediction came perilously close to the truth. The following week, every time Jandu tried to find Baram or Suraya, they were locked together in Baram's private chambers.

There had to be such a thing as too much sex. It was unnatural. But then again, if he had Keshan around, wouldn't he be screwing Keshan every moment he had?

"Jandu! There you are."

Jandu turned to see Yudar striding purposely towards him. Yudar dealt with his loneliness as he always dealt with problems, plunging deeper into work. He slept little and woke early every morning to serve out the last of his tenure as Royal Judge in the palace's courthouse.

"I want you to come with me today," Yudar said, fondly touching Jandu's shoulder. "It is about time that you see what transpires in the courthouse, and how a Royal Judge must act."

"Why?" Jandu noticed that his brother had been discussing the position with him often, even alluding to his wishes that Jandu would take a greater interest in the law. Jandu had a sinking suspicion that his brother hoped Jandu himself would sign up for the post. In Jandu's opinion, he couldn't think of a more horrible job. Sitting for hours on end, in day-long meetings, mediating disputes about cattle and wives and property? Even just thinking about it made him shudder.

"I told Mazar I would finalize the design of the new wrestling arena with Baram first, and then—"

"That can be done later. You are my guest today. I insist."

The courthouse was across the river from the palace, between the holy temple district and the public market. A white limestone courtyard dominated the entrance and was the location of all the executions in the capital. The original building burned a hundred years ago, and so the current structure was heavily influenced by the rich architectural designs of the eastern states. Engravings of the prophets glared down from dozens of stone alcoves, and detailed paintings of the laws adorned the plaster walls. Inside, the floor was bare marble, but the few spaces on the walls where the Book of Taivo was not written were covered in colorful tapestries depicting the great battles of the kings from a century prior.

Even at this early hour, a long line of plaintiffs and defendants snaked around the courthouse. One of Yudar's ministers sat at a table near the entrance, recording the names of those requesting mediation and the charges brought forth. Soldiers flanked the entrance, ensuring orderly conduct and to escort any convicted criminals to the bailiffs for transport to the jailhouse on the outskirts of Prasta.

Inside, citizens and ministers filled the available seats and lined the walls. Everyone stood and bowed respectfully as Jandu and his brother made their way to the front of the room. Jandu had originally hoped he could watch from the sidelines, but Yudar made it clear he wanted Jandu with him at the front of the room.

Jandu refused one of the three intimidating large velvet chairs, choosing as always to lean against the wall behind his brother. As soon as Yudar took his seat, the court session began. The first case was a man accusing his wife of adultery, but after the man failed to produce any evidence to support his claim, Yudar dismissed the case. At the second hearing, some Prastan merchants brought forward a thief caught stealing their goods. After them, Yudar was asked to determine compensation on the loss of a cow, accidentally poisoned when one farmer dumped refuse into another farmer's well.

Jandu's fingers tapped out a rhythm on his thigh in the hopes it would keep him awake. He couldn't remember ever being this bored before. He scanned the crowd for attractive men, and wondered which ones Keshan would find the most pleasing. He counted how many men in the crowd were balding. Then he counted how many sported facial hair. Then he guessed how many women dyed their hair with henna. And, eventually, he even began listening to the trials.

Yudar exhibited endless patience, his face sympathetically torn with grief at tales of loss, appropriately outraged at injustices, perfectly cold and determined when dictating punishment.

Yudar thrived here. He knew the laws and recited dozens of prior cases for any situation. If a man's chicken had been killed by another man's dog, Yudar quoted the exact paragraph in the Book of Taivo that applied, recited four examples of similar judgments made by the prophets, and then stated his decision. Yudar looked magnificent in the large chair, head held high, eyes blazing, hands pressed together as he concentrated.

Before the court now were two men, chained to guards with their heads bowed shamefully. They wore the dress of the Chaya caste, farmers who looked to have come from the west of Marhavad.

Another man, a horse trader, explained their crime to Yudar. Jandu wasn't really paying attention, busy as he was figuring out why his hair was so wild and unruly this morning and fiddling with his clothes, until he heard a word that drew his attention.

"….homosexual activity the likes of which I am morally opposed to describing," the trader said, sneering at the two men. "In the middle of the rice field! Where my children could have seen their depravity!"

Jandu's eyes widened. The horse trader brought out another witness, who confirmed that the two men had been copulating in a rice field at dusk.

Yudar looked appalled. He curled his lip in disgust as they told their story.

"Is this true?" Yudar asked the accused men. "Are you guilty?"

The two men looked at each other. One of them cried, his hands folded in supplication, but the other looked straight at Yudar with a stony expression.

"Yes," he said.

His companion hung his head and sobbed.

Jandu watched his brother's face. Yudar looked like he had been poisoned. He recoiled from the men as if he were somehow personally infected by their mere presence.

"Then by the laws of Marhavad, I hold you accountable for the unholy foulness you have engaged in," Yudar said to them. His lips set grimly. "I sentence you both to execution, and I hope you come to terms with God for the abominable crime you have committed."

Jandu stood against the wall until the criminals were led away. Yudar announced he would cease hearings to attend the immediate execution, as was his custom. Yudar believed in swift justice, and beckoned Jandu to join him.

Outside, Jandu asked Yudar to excuse him for a moment. He then politely bowed to the courtiers, left the courtyard, and ran around the corner where he vomited in the bushes. Memories of entering Keshan swarmed through his brain like a madness, making him shiver in horror at his own longings.

By the time Jandu rejoined Yudar in the courtyard, his hands had almost stopped shaking. Jandu folded his arms, hoping that Yudar would not notice his paleness.

Yudar's expression was grim. "I'm sorry you have to see an execution on your first day at court," he told Jandu. "But we must show the people that we fulfill sentences swiftly and efficiently."

There was no delay in carrying out Yudar's sentence. Citizens awaiting trial gathered around a large wooden platform to watch the execution. Most seemed eager for the diversion. Several women standing nearby already wept. Jandu guessed they were relatives of the condemned. One of the condemned men tried to wave to an older man who looked to be his father. A guard jerked the man's hand down and led him onto the platform.

Bailiffs brought Yudar and Jandu ornate chairs to sit on. This time, Jandu took up the offer, unsure if his legs would hold him up. Soldiers surrounded them, keeping the growing crowd at bay.

A bailiff blindfolded the men and then led to the platform where they were forced to kneel before the chopping block. In Yudar's Prasta, there was no grace period. The convicts had no chance to look at each other or say good-bye to their families. Such rights were revoked.

Jandu said nothing to his brother. He sat, still as stone, and stared at the two men, concentrating on not throwing up again. He said nothing as the crime of sodomy was publicly announced, along with their family names in order to disgrace their families throughout the kingdom.

His brother grimaced at the men and called them a "moral sickness."

The executioner swung back his large blade and lopped off the head of one man, followed by the other. The second required two strokes.

Jandu walked stiffly towards their chariot. Yudar followed, concern plain upon his face.

"Jandu, do you feel all right? You're completely pale." Yudar put his hand against Jandu's forehead, feeling for a temperature.

Jandu jerked his head away.

Jandu felt panic rise through his body like a fever, from his legs through to the tips of his fingers. He and Keshan could be executed like that, that quickly. Those men had families, loved ones who would never live long enough to escape the shame that the crime had brought upon them. That was him. Him and Keshan.

Jandu forced himself to speak. "I'm just sick, that's all."

"God, why didn't you tell me this morning?"

"I thought I'd be fine."

"I should never have taken you to the execution," Yudar said, shaking his head. "It always turns my stomach, even now."

"I'll be fine," Jandu said through gritted teeth. Though he knew that he wouldn't. He couldn't be. The call of sodomy above the crowd echoed in his ears. That was him. His brother would kill him, that easily. The circle of soldiers around him seemed sinister. The sound of the crowd cheering as the executioner held the two heads aloft, the screams of the old woman whose son lay dead, the impressions closed in around Jandu in a jumble of sick guilt.

"I've forgotten how shocking the executions are, especially when unprepared for one. I'll call you a doctor," Yudar said.

Jandu shook his head. "I just need to get out of this crowd, that's all. I'll return to the palace now, if it is all right with you."

"Of course." Yudar frowned. "I have to stay for the rest of the hearings, but I'll see you at dinner this evening." He watched Jandu with a look of pity.

Jandu numbly climbed into his chariot and told the charioteer to take him home. Prasta's wide royal avenue lay before him, but Jandu could barely focus on anything.

I have to calm down. Jandu tried to focus on what he wanted, what would make him feel better. Keshan came to his mind like a symbol of salvation.

I need him. Jandu closed his eyes and covered his face with his hands. How could he now, minutes after seeing two men die for their love, be thinking of Keshan?

But there was a bitter truth, Jandu realized. Like it or not, Jandu needed Keshan. There was no longer any question who he was. At least that had been determined the night Keshan left the palace. And part of being Jandu meant being in love with a man rather than a woman.

The image of the executioner's axe falling came again to his mind. Why had he just sat there and watched? Couldn't he have said something to Yudar, asked for leniency for them? Was he that much of a coward?

The second Jandu thought he had his emotions under control, the reality of who he was would smack him in the face again, and panic would rise through his body, making it difficult to breathe. He was suffocating on his own self-realization. Once home, he ordered the servants out of his rooms, and locked the door to his bedroom. He sat on his bed until his shaking subsided, and then he took some deep breaths.

"I have to see him," Jandu said aloud. He called one of his servants to ready a horse and bring a saddlebag.

Jandu changed into clothes better suited for riding. He put on a dark cotton dejaru and a blue embroidered sash. He combed his hair down and pushed aside his bangs, which were long enough now to fall into his eyes. He removed his silver diadem and looked at himself in the mirror. He looked like a terrified version of himself. Where was Jandu the brave archer now?

"Jandu fucks men," Jandu whispered to his reflection. He closed his eyes and fought back tears. He had to find Keshan. Keshan was the only one who could help him.

He slung Zandi and his quiver across his shoulders and packed clothing and gold coins into the saddlebag. Anxiety propelled him forward. He opened his door to leave and found Suraya standing there, hand raised as if to knock.

"The servants say you are ill." Suraya looked at the bow and saddlebag. She raised an eyebrow. "Is everything all right?"

"I have to get out of the city." Jandu shouldered his way past her and started down the hall.

"Where are you going?" Suraya chased after him, her sandals clacking on the marble floor. "Jandu—wait!"

"I will be back in time to hear Mazar's decision," Jandu said.

"Tell me where you are going!" Suraya demanded, her voice rising in anger that Jandu had never heard her express before. She darted in front of him, arms out to block his way. The silver threads in her zahari flashed in the mid-morning light.

Jandu's hold on his emotions was too tenuous to stay and chat. He tried to move past her but Suraya did not budge.

"Suraya, please." He teetered between anger and tears. "You can't help me."

Suraya's arms lowered. She searched his face, seeming to read for the first time his true emotion. "You're going to Tiwari, aren't you? To see Keshan."

To Jandu's horror, he felt his lip trembling. He didn't trust himself to speak so he nodded.

"And you'll be back before Mazar's announcement?" she asked.

Jandu nodded again.

"All right." Suraya sighed. "But if you aren't back in one week I'll personally drag you back to the palace myself. I am your wife, remember."

The idea of skinny-armed Suraya overpowering him was so absurd that Jandu broke into a laugh. Suraya smiled back at him. He knelt down to touch her feet and she told him to stop being so stupid, embraced him and let him go.

Jandu mounted Shedav and rode though the city. Life burgeoned around him, thriving and noisy, the air thick with the smells of the market, the fragrance of late summer jasmine, the stench of the sewers and burning milk, but none of it touched him. He would not rest until he saw Keshan.

Once through the white sentinel walls of the city, and surrounded by recently harvested fields, Jandu finally calmed. He continued along the main road leading out of the city until he reached the crossroads. To the north, the road followed the Yaru River to Karuna. To the east, it rolled through endless wheat and corn fields to Jagu Mali. Jandu took neither of these. He urged his horse toward the road leading south, through the forests and into Tiwari.

CHAPTER 15

Tiwari was a day's journey from Prasta, and so leaving as late as he had, Jandu had to pitch a tent halfway and wait until dawn to continue. After hours of nothing but dark, looming forestry, the main road hit the coastline and the world around Jandu exploded into lushness. The spiked yellow and scarlet clusters of sorrowless tree blooms blew across the roadway, mingling with purple silk blossoms and violet plums to turn the road into a spectacle of color, reds and whites and yellows, with the irresistible scent of roses mixing with the white stars of jasmine and wild vanilla.

The city of Tiwari was built high up on a bluff, whose jagged cliff edge dropped to a dangerous precipice and an even more dangerous shoreline, rugged with sharp rocks. At the entrance to the city, the sound of the crashing surf drowned out all other noises.

But a quieter sandy beach stretched to the south of the city, and beside it the city's main market and most of its population lived. Jandu jumped from his horse and cupped his hand to scoop up star-shaped petals and the fading pink blossoms of a nearby clematis.

Along the street, a sturdy row of white-barked trees spun their whorled leaves like tops in the ocean breeze, their slender tips striking each other to mimic the sound of rainfall. It was as if Jandu had entered a botanical paradise. The salt in the air mingled with the scent of dozens of fragrant bushes in the private gardens, the scent of someone baking fish in a clay oven, and a street vendor frying bananas. Beautiful, painted cows wandered the streets brazenly, their udders round and low.

Jandu led his horse down the street in a daze. The sun beat down on his spiky black hair, and bronzed his skin. It was early morning and people had just begun to venture out into the streets. The Tiwari people shared Keshan's light olive-colored skin, his slightly slanting eyes. There was a fierceness to their countenance that Jandu didn't recognize in his own royal blood. Something about the Tiwaris seemed almost combustible. And yet they were the nicest, most welcoming strangers he had ever met. As he made his way up the main boulevard, individuals ran out to offer him a cool glass of water or to bring grain for his horse. Jandu didn't know if it was just him, emanating a princely Triya demeanor with his fine horse and saddle, or if it was just the Tiwari way, but whatever it was, it made Keshan's capital a welcoming city.

As Jandu approached the Adaru palace, he started to worry about surprising Keshan.

What if he found Keshan with another lover? Keshan did, after all, have a reputation. Was Jandu really to believe that Keshan loved him and him alone? As Jandu made his way along the wide main boulevard, he saw more proof of how ridiculous such an idea was. This was an entire city built on the love of Keshan. These people had moved across their state to build their homes against this ragged cliff as a testament to that love. Keshan had to be shared with everyone.

And their time in Prasta—it had been a month ago. Forever in the highly malleable state of romance, Keshan could have moved on. Maybe Jandu's feelings were no longer reciprocated.

His stomach was in knots by the time he reached the palace entrance. Tiwari's seat of power was carved directly into the cliff's edge, with a long stone garden that doubled as a wall, stretching along the coast towards the center of the city. The palace jutted from the bluff like a challenge to the sea. Magnificent, lush flowers bloomed around the building softening its harsh red rocky face. Ivies intertwined across the vertical surface, covering every brick under a curtain of organic life. Giant palms shaded

Jandu from the sun's increasing heat, and coconut trees thick with fruit clustered at the main gate.

A soldier stopped him at the entrance, eyeing Zandi warily. "State your name and business."

Jandu hadn't bothered to wear his diadem. His head was sweaty and the cool salty breezes coming off the coast felt marvelous.

"I'm here to see Keshan Adaru. I'm his cousin," he said.

Apparently, that answer was not good enough, for the soldier signaled behind him and several other soldiers emerged from a guardhouse.

"What is your name?" the soldier asked.

"Jandu Paran, Prince of Marhavad."

The soldier frowned at Jandu's dirty sandals and his sun-tanned face.

"Lord Keshan is in the reception hall with Lord Iyestar, Prince," he said warily. "Follow me." The man nodded to another guard, who took the reins of Jandu's horse. After removing his saddlebag and throwing it over his shoulder, Jandu followed the soldier into the main house and down a long wooden hall lined with colorful portraits of animals.

Tiwari's main reception hall was a lot smaller than those in the Prasta palace, but it was opulent, with a gilded ceiling and glittering crystal along the sides, detailed murals painted on each wall, and a dramatic curving balcony that jutted from the side of the cliff and overlooked the frothing ocean below. Thick, overlapping carpets padded the floor. The room had two long rows of seats for visitors, leading up to the dais where Iyestar and his ministers sat. There were two petitioners in the room, talking quietly with a clerk in the corner.

Jandu peered behind the soldier and got his first good look at Keshan in a month. Keshan looked much more serious, he noticed. He leaned forward to speak with his brother, his hand resting on his hip, elbow thrust out in a domineering position. A golden yellow dejaru with embroidered trim clung to his long legs and a red sash emphasized his slim hips. Over his bare chest he wore a gold and red embroidered vest. Bands of beaten gold enclosed his tanned arms. Keshan's gold diadem was small, but dramatic, set with numerous rubies.

Keshan spoke intently with Iyestar; his eyes were nowhere near the entrance. Jandu stared at Keshan's face, at his dark hair, which had grown just past his ears, the beauty of his large brown eyes. As Keshan spoke, his lips moved slightly, full and round, and Jandu felt dizzy staring at him. His stomach somersaulted.

The soldier spoke to the attendant in the doorway in a voice so low Jandu couldn't hear him. He turned abruptly and returned to his post at the front gate.

The herald nodded at Jandu. "Prince Jandu Paran?" he checked.

"Yes."

The herald blared his trumpet, causing Keshan, Iyestar, the petitioners, and the ministers to turn and glance at the entrance in surprise. "Prince Jandu Paran!" the herald announced.

Jandu looked at Keshan anxiously.

All of Jandu's worries disappeared the moment he saw how Keshan's expression changed. It seemed like a weight lifted off of him, and a smile reached from ear to ear.

"Jandu!"

Keshan practically ran to Jandu. They met halfway along the hall. Keshan laughed. They embraced tightly, tears coming to Jandu's eyes.

"This is a wonderful, wonderful surprise!" Keshan cried, hugging him again, not caring about the spectacle that they made in the middle of the room.

Keshan put his hand on the saddlebag slung over Jandu's shoulder.

"Did you ride here alone?" he asked.

Jandu nodded.

"God, you must be tired." Keshan put his arm around Jandu and led him up to Iyestar.

Keshan beamed a magnificent smile. "Brother, look who has traveled all this way to visit us at last!"

Jandu knelt to take the dust from Iyestar's feet.

"Blessings to you, Lord Adaru," Jandu said ceremoniously.

Iyestar snorted. "I don't think you have to grovel to me, Jandu. You're a prince, even if you are in my city." Iyestar smiled. "Welcome. We are happy to have you."

Jandu doubted the sentiment, given Iyestar's close relations with Darvad, but he was too happy, touching Keshan, to care.

"Thank you for your hospitality."

"Iyestar, I'm afraid I must take my leave of you," Keshan said.

Iyestar nodded. "Once you're settled, please take dinner with our family this evening, Jandu."

"Thank you." Jandu bowed once more. Keshan took Jandu's arm and led him out of the room.

Outside of the reception hall, Keshan asked a servant to take Jandu's saddlebag to the guest room adjacent Keshan's own chambers. Then, without stopping, Keshan led Jandu through a long hallway, up a dramatic staircase, and along another corridor.

The view was phenomenal, overlooking the sea, the sound of the crashing waves shooting up the side of the cliff and straight into the room. Pelicans circled above Jandu's head.

"Come on." Keshan led Jandu up another flight of stairs that spiraled around a large statue of the Prophet Bandruban to the tower.

"Where are you taking me?" Jandu asked.

"To my room." Keshan looked over his shoulder at Jandu. "I have a present for you."

Jandu felt momentarily dizzy with that look.

"I think you'll like it." Keshan said.

"I've traveled all day to get here," Jandu said. "I need a bath and a bed."

"I've got the bed," Keshan said.

"A bath would be nice," Jandu smirked at Keshan.

"I'll give you one," Keshan whispered. They finally reached the top of the spiral staircase and Keshan pushed open the door.

Inside was the massive chamber that made up Keshan's quarters. It had balconies on three sides, overlooking the land and the sea. The walls were half-open, letting a gentle, warm breeze pass through the room.

Jandu took in the details of Keshan's private world. He saw Keshan's desk in the corner, crowded with scrolls and writing utensils. There was a map of Marhavad, and Jandu could make out the corner of the last letter he wrote to Keshan, hiding under a blotter.

Jandu smiled to himself. He unstrung Zandi and propped her up in the corner, and shrugged off his quiver. He walked around the room, admiring the inlaid wooden floor, the fine paintings of horses and cattle on the walls, and the massive canopied bed. It, like all the furniture in the room, was made of dark cypress and emitted a fragrant scent.

A small hallway led to Keshan's private bathroom, and across from that was a small rooftop garden he called his own, filled with lemon and juniper trees.

Jandu looked at the large marble bath and sighed contentedly.

"Shall I call servants to fill the bath for you?" Keshan asked.

Jandu smiled. "Well, now that I have you alone I want to—"

Keshan pushed Jandu against the wall and kissed him. Jandu savored the sweetness, the coconut earthy saltiness of Keshan's skin, the roughness of his cheeks, the softness of his lips. Keshan thrust his tongue deep into Jandu's mouth. Jandu kissed him back with equal fervor, and then pulled away and smiled.

"I guess you missed me, then," Jandu said.

Keshan laughed. "Missed you? All I think about is you. It's torture."

"Tell me about it," Jandu said.

"It's been the same for you?"

"No, tell me about it," Jandu said, grinning. "I love hearing about me."

Keshan shook his head. "You're the worst." He leaned in to nuzzle Jandu's neck. "I missed you so much that my dick got hard just reading that letter from you. I missed you so much that I wished I'd made a bronze mold of your cock so that I could—"

"—on second thought, talk later." Jandu grabbed Keshan's shoulders and pushed Keshan against the wall. He stifled Keshan's cry of surprise with a penetrating kiss. He didn't stop until he felt Keshan writhe against him, his hips involuntarily thrusting out for more contact.

Jandu didn't think when he kissed Keshan. He could only feel. And this was what he needed, after the terrible day before, full of self-awareness and introspection. Jandu needed to forget his brother, his own crime. He needed only this, a focus of his desires, and this realization made him grip Keshan even harder, slow and deepen his kiss, hoping to direct all his energy to Keshan's beautiful body.

When Jandu broke the kiss, Keshan stayed frozen, a delightful smile on his face, his eyes closed in pleasure. Jandu pulled down Keshan's dejaru. He knelt, staring for a moment at Keshan's cock, erect and pulsing with the need to be tended.

Jandu grasped Keshan's hardness, which was firm and warm in his hand, glistening at the tip. Jandu ran his tongue along its shaft, luxuriating in the musky taste of him. He tenderly bit the loose skin at the base of Keshan's scrotum and Keshan cried out loudly, shocking Jandu enough to make him freeze.

"Shouldn't we be quiet?" Jandu whispered.

"Not in my own house." Keshan pushed his hips closer to Jandu.

Jandu filled himself with Keshan. Keshan breathed out and closed his eyes once more, leaning his head back against the wall.

"Jandu…" Keshan tried to touch Jandu but Jandu pushed him back against the wall hard, forcing Keshan to stay where he was.

Keshan moaned in ecstasy. "Please…"

Jandu's mind blanked of everything but the feeling of Keshan in his throat, the taste of him on his lips. He kept his eyes open, working harder and faster until he could feel Keshan begin to shake, until he knew he was about to come. Then he let Keshan go. Keshan's eyes shot open in disappointment.

Jandu pulled Keshan to the bed. Keshan watched as Jandu removed his clothing and lay down.

Keshan straddled Jandu and kissed him deeply. That familiar feeling of drunken warmth coursed through Jandu's blood, causing every touch from Keshan to make him break out in a sweat of desire.

Keshan leaned down and licked at Jandu's nipples, playing with them using his teeth. Jandu sucked in air at the sweet pain of it.

"Keshan…" Jandu's body vibrated with pleasure.

Keshan spread Jandu's legs apart and laved Jandu's testicles with his hot tongue. Jandu lay speechless, stunned with the feeling, his body shivering.

Suddenly Keshan stopped his ministrations and reached over to pull a small glass jar from the bedside table.

"What is that?" Jandu asked.

"Rose oil. Use it." Keshan collapsed onto the bed, grinning proudly.

Jandu sank his fingers into the oil and let its coolness grease his fingers. He circled Keshan in his arms. He reached around and inserted one finger inside of Keshan, capturing Keshan's hiss of pleasure with another kiss. Keshan bit gently at Jandu's lower lip in response.

Jandu was so aroused his vision blurred. He prepared Keshan with two fingers now, slowly at first, and then slightly faster and deeper.

He touched Keshan in such a way that Keshan cried out, turning languid. Jandu wondered what it felt like, suddenly curious. He would have to find out later. But right now, with Keshan flush with desire, and his own needs screaming to be fulfilled, he could wait. Right now, he wanted to see Keshan make that face again.

"I want you inside me," Keshan whispered, his hot breath on Jandu's lips. He slipped his tongue inside of Jandu's mouth and ran it along his own tongue. "Please…"

Jandu enjoyed the control he had over Keshan at the moment.

"Not yet," he said. He turned Keshan over and instead worked him slowly with his fingers, all the while massaging his erection with his other hand.

"Jandu, please… I'm going to come."

Jandu tortured him like this for another minute, until he could feel Keshan about to climax. At that moment, he spread rose oil on his own member and thrust it deep inside of Keshan.

Keshan came almost immediately, groaning in pleasure. Jandu thrust only a few times before coming himself, loving the feeling of it, Keshan's flesh tight around him, vividly hot, the musky sweet smell of him, the sight of Keshan's gorgeous body prone, open, his for the taking.

Jandu still shook as he pulled out, tremors of pleasure coursing through his nervous system. Keshan rolled over and looked as content as a sleeping cat, his eyes closed and a soft smile on his face.

"I thought you'd like that oil," he said.

Jandu snuggled close and rested his head on Keshan's chest. "I do like it. Only it makes me wonder why you have a jar so readily available at your bedside."

Keshan laughed. Jandu loved the feel of that laughter, rumbling through his belly, raising Jandu's head with each muscle contraction.

Jandu smiled at Keshan. "Have you been practicing your skills on other boys?"

"I don't like boys, only men."

"Well then?" Jandu raised an eyebrow. "What man is the oil for?"

"It's for you." Keshan ran his fingers lazily through Jandu's hair. "I bought it as a present for you. It's been sitting here ever since I got home, waiting for just the right person to announce himself in our reception hall."

Jandu stretched alongside Keshan, kissing Keshan's neck as he nuzzled closer.

Keshan closed his eyes. "Not that it matters to me, but out of curiosity, why are you here? I thought Yudar would kill himself before he let you out of his sight."

Jandu's mood cooled as he recalled his departure from Prasta. "I didn't ask."

Keshan opened his eyes and studied Jandu's face carefully.

Jandu stared at the ceiling. "Yudar made me attend court with him yesterday morning. There were two men he sentenced to death."

"Oh." Keshan's unspoken question was obvious.

"They were lovers," Jandu told him.

"I'm sorry." Keshan continued stroking Jandu's head.

"I just sat there and watched," Jandu said. "I didn't even try to plead with Yudar for leniency. I was too afraid he would suspect me. I hated myself."

Keshan stared at Jandu but didn't say anything. He scooted down on the bed and brought his head to Jandu's, touching their foreheads together and throwing his arm around Jandu. They held each other for a long time, not speaking.

Finally, Keshan sat up. "If you want, we can stop this." He tried smiling, but Jandu could tell it was forced. "This romance is dangerous, I won't lie."

Jandu sat up as well. "I can no more stop this than I can stop my heart from beating."

Keshan sighed. "Poetic, but not very realistic."

"I don't know what to do." The panic Jandu felt back in Prasta swelled in his throat, made it hurt to swallow. "I came here hoping you would tell me."

"All we can do is be careful."

"And if we're caught?"

"I won't let your brother kill you." Keshan stated it firmly. "Not because of me. It won't happen. I love you. No matter what happens with your brother, with the kingdom, with your wife or my wife or the future of this country. I love you. Never doubt that."

Jandu smiled. Keshan's conviction gave him strength. "That's all I needed to hear."

"Well, good." Keshan plopped his head back down and grinned slyly. "Because I don't have anything better to say."

That evening, the Adarus held a feast in Jandu's honor. He sat at a low table on cushions, surrounded by Keshan's friends and family. Keshan's mother, Linaz, sat beside Keshan. Keshan's father had died several years prior, but his Uncle Inaud was there, a bizarre old man who sat next to Jandu and yelled in Jandu's ear the entire meal.

Keshan's mother was Yashva, and yet she looked almost human. Her skin was dark brown, but there was a bluish tint to it, and her eyes, while the right size and shape, still had that unnerving spinning effect that drew Jandu in, and made him feel like he was being hypnotized.

But what was most important was that Linaz had a good sense of humor and laughed at all of Jandu's jokes.

Dinner with Keshan's family was very different than eating with Jandu's own. Where even their private meals in Yudar or Baram's rooms were courteous and calm, Keshan's family shouted at each other and spilled wine and gestured emphatically with their arms, honored guest present or not. They were wild people, the Tiwari. He let Iyestar refill his wine glass over and over and tried to get into the spirit of things. When Iyestar leaned over and poked his finger in Jandu's chicken, yelling at him that he was a pussy for not trying the hot chutney, Jandu swallowed his extreme shock and just decided to kick Iyestar under the table. This started Iyestar laughing, great thunderous belches of happiness, making him spill his drink down his mother's zahari.

Jandu's Aunt Linaz didn't seem upset. She rolled her eyes, dabbed at the stain with a cloth, and continued to shout loudly into Ajani's ear.

Jandu looked around him and laughed. Now that the meal was over, six separate conversations competed for volume amongst the eight people at the table. It was madness. He smiled across the table at Keshan, who stopped shouting at Iyestar long enough to catch Jandu's eye and smile sweetly back.

"Did I tell you the story about the time I found a turtle?" Keshan's Uncle Inaud said suddenly, gripping Jandu's hand. Since Jandu had agreed to sit beside the old man, he had been subject to the random conversational whims of Keshan's obviously senile relative.

Although Inaud hadn't told Jandu the story, Jandu nodded anyway. "Yes. Yes, you did." He had to shout to be heard above Iyestar, who was roaring with laughter and shaking his fist at Keshan. "What a wonderful tale!"

Inaud smiled. "And all for the love of a coin!"

"Ah, yes."

"But who knew where the physician would take me next?"

"Who knew?" Jandu shrugged in an exaggerated manner, barely keeping back his laughter. Iyestar initiated yet another round of drinks, and competed with his brother and Jandu to see who could drink theirs the fastest. Keshan obviously practiced this game before, and spilled half his drink into another cup hidden under the table whenever Iyestar wasn't looking. Jandu shook his head at Keshan across the table. Keshan put a finger to his lips, urging Jandu into complicit silence.

Jandu wondered how Keshan could lie to his family and also be so honest with them at the same time. No one even raised an eyebrow at the blatant affection Keshan lavished on Jandu. They just accepted Keshan the way he was, and therefore, by association, Jandu as well. They may not have understood the kind of love the two of them shared, but they accepted Keshan's Jandu obsession casually.

Jandu thought he was close to his brothers, but now he saw true closeness—Iyestar and Keshan beating each other up at the table, both of them finishing each other's sentences, laughing like identical twins.

This was by far the best party Jandu had ever been to, and it amazed him that this was just an average family dinner for the Adaru's. He realized he was jealous. These were people that talked loudly, openly expressed their emotions, did not believe in prudishness, and had no real cares for the strictness of Shentari faith. And yet as well-trained Triya warriors they upheld the warrior code when they left the palace. Jandu fell in love with all of them by the end of dinner.

Jandu leaned back in his chair and rubbed his stomach, full from a delicious meal. Dancing girls appeared and a large troupe of musicians started a well-loved Tiwari tune, which everyone in the room sang along to. Jandu didn't know the words. Keshan's mother sat beside Jandu and whispered them in Jandu's ear, which only tickled and made Jandu laugh harder.

The lyrics were ridiculous, a long, corny ballad about the beauty and bounty of Tiwari's sea. At the chorus, the entire room, servants included, started shouting out the words as loud as they could.

"Tiwari! Oh, Tiwari! The homeland of my dreams!
May your plentiful shores feed us, may your blue skies oversee us!
Oh Tiwari, as long as I can see the sea,
I see who I'm supposed to be!"

"You're not singing!" Linaz scolded him.

"Sing! Sing!" A chorus broke out across the table. Jandu turned bright red. He couldn't sing at all. He barely mumbled prayers in public. But the chorus of would-be fans would not relent, and he was drunk enough to let Keshan's mother drag him upwards to stand on the table.

This alone would be worthy of a beating in the Paran house. Standing on the table? And yet here was Keshan's very own mother, kicking off her shoes and standing with him, wrapping her bony arms around Jandu's waist and dancing with him on the table as she repeated the lyrics. The musicians began again, and Jandu just decided to hell with it. He would sing.

"Oh, Tiwari, Tiwari, land of… lyrics screamed …" Jandu filled in. The audience rolled on the floor. "May your frightening shores feed me, may your rocks… not thrash me into smithereens as I try vainly to escape your horrendous undertow… As long as I can see the sea, I really need to pee…"

Even Iyestar cried tears of laughter by the time Jandu was done with his terrible rendition of their state anthem. Keshan kicked off his shoes, one of them flying out to hit one of the attendants in the shin. Keshan ran over and apologized to the woman, and then dragged her on the table with him, forcing her to dance.

As the tempo slowed, Keshan switched partners with his mother, so that he and Jandu could dance together and his mother danced with the servant. No one seemed to find this the least bit scandalous. Keshan pulled Jandu closer. Jandu wanted to kiss Keshan then and there, but didn't. This was enough. Enough to get arrested in Prasta. And enough to ease his self-doubt over his own inverted nature, make him feel better, feel alive.

By the time the music stopped, Jandu was so completely drunk he could barely stand. Keshan put his arm around him and weaved them up the grand staircase towards Jandu's room, which was directly below Keshan's quarters at the top of the tower.

They sang bawdy lyrics loudly until Ajani reappeared, blocking their way on the landing of the stair.

She seemed more beautiful than Jandu remembered. Maybe it was being in her own home. But Ajani had a relaxed, carefree look about her, her hair down loose around her round face. Her scowl, however, was the same scowl she had favored Jandu with every chance she got in Prasta.

She bowed to Jandu, and Jandu brought his hands together in the sign of peace.

"Ajani," Jandu said. "You look lovely tonight."

Ajani smirked coldly. "Thank you. I see you two have been falling for Iyestar's tricks."

Keshan waved his hand in every direction. "Oh, don't blame Iyestar, he was just happy to see Jandu too." Keshan pinched Jandu's cheek.

Ajani crossed her arms. "I've been waiting for you, in my chamber," she said quietly. She looked pointedly at Jandu. "Good night, Prince."

Jandu frowned. "But Keshan and I aren't done drinking yet." He laughed at the sound of his own voice, which cracked and wavered.

Keshan nodded. "It's true. I promised Jandu a night cap, and then I will come to you directly, sweet princess."

Ajani didn't move. "You—"

"—Shh." Keshan let go of Jandu and put his arms around Ajani. "When have I ever lied to you?" He whispered in her ear.

Ajani rolled her eyes. "Yesterday. And the day before. You lie to me every day, Keshan."

"But you still love me."

"Fool that I am." But Ajani softened at Keshan's words. Her coquettish expression sickened Jandu.

Keshan leaned towards Ajani's face, his lips just above her ear. "Let me make sure Jandu is settled for the night, and then I'll be there as soon as I can, all right?"

Ajani closed her eyes. "All right." She wandered off as if in a daze.

When she was gone Keshan grabbed Jandu's arm and practically ran up the stairs to Jandu's guest rooms. "Quick!" Keshan whispered. "Before she comes back!" He shut the door behind him and locked it, laughing.

Jandu laughed as well, but with guilt. "I'm stealing her husband. That makes me a bad person."

Keshan scoffed. "I would have fallen asleep as soon as I got into bed with her, that's what I always do." He moved towards Jandu seductively. "All my love is for you."

"Lucky me." Jandu looked around the guest chamber, marveling at its rich colors. Everything about the palace burst with vibrant patterns. The guest room was small, consisting of a bed and a few small cushions together on a carpet, with a small cypress table and chair in the corner. The balcony looked out to the sea, where the constant crash of the waves broke through the night and made even the blackness seem alive. Jandu had never slept with such a loud noise. He wasn't sure he would be able to.

Jandu sat tentatively on the guest bed, poking at the goose-feather mattress and shearling bedding. "This is nice."

Keshan didn't hesitate to sit beside him on the bed. Up close, Jandu could smell the wine on Keshan's breath, see the bleary effects of alcohol in his eyes. *Or maybe*, Jandu thought, *it's my sight that's gone blurry and he's just fine.*

"Listen to me," Keshan said. He grinned crookedly. "We're going to make it through everything, you and me. I can see the future, you know."

Jandu smirked. "What am I about to do?"

"Pinch my ass." Keshan laughed.

Jandu froze for a moment in surprise. He *was* going pinch Keshan on the ass, which was creepy. Instead he just flicked him on the arm.

"Wrong," Jandu said.

Keshan grinned. "Liar. I can see the future. And you know what I see?"

"What?" Jandu leaned closer to Keshan.

"I see you and me making love in a forest."

"We did that already."

"This is a different forest." Keshan slurred. "You have a burr digging into your shoulder blade."

"How sexy." Jandu's lips hovered beside Keshan's.

"Therefore I know we're going to make it," Keshan said emphatically. He shook Jandu's shoulders for effect. "Whatever happens with Mazar's announcement, with your brother, with me, never forget this: you and I are going to make love in a forest."

"With a burr in my back?"

"Yes." Keshan closed the distance and kissed Jandu. Like a wave, desire crashed over Jandu's body, drowning him in languid warmth.

"I'll remember," Jandu whispered.

And, for the rest of that week, Jandu held on to that thought. He spent his mornings teaching archery to his cousins, and in the afternoons he and Keshan walked the city, dining with Keshan's noisy family every night. Keshan and Iyestar taught Jandu how to swim without being pummeled to death by the waves, and Jandu learned how to fish. And, every night, there was the greatest escape of all, in Keshan's body, the taste and smell of him overwhelming Jandu's nights, making him burst with the joy of life. There was no need for fear, with Keshan in his future.

For the first time in his life, Jandu wanted to believe in destiny.

CHAPTER 16

THE NIGHT BEFORE MAZAR WAS TO ANNOUNCE WHO WOULD inherit the throne, most of the city of Prasta indulged in celebration. The night air filled with the sound of revelry and the cries of sheep being slaughtered for feasts. Music broke out in courtyards across the city, the notes of rebo chords and wind instruments wafting above the high clay and mud walls.

The impending announcement cast a heavy pall over the palace. Yudar spent the night in meditation. To respect the silence, Darvad celebrated elsewhere, at Druv's townhouse. By the time Tarek joined his friends, they were well into their festivities. Even Firdaus Trinat seemed drunk, and he rarely lost control.

Darvad lavished Tarek with praise and attention. They practiced archery in Druv's garden, and when it got too dark to see, they watched a dancing troupe inside. New food and wine flowed continuously. Darvad seemed in high spirits, although he admitted that he missed Iyestar and wished he had come.

"I am sure he means no offense by his absence," Tarek told him.

Darvad nodded. "I know that. It is the way with the Adaru family. They have their own traditions, they are not like us."

Despite the fact that his fate hinged on tomorrow's decision, Darvad glowed with optimism. It rubbed off on Tarek.

"You promised you would show me how to do the Salafani dance." Tarek was drunk, he knew it, and a part of his brain warned him that he could easily go too far in such a state, press his luck, press Darvad's friendship.

But Darvad was not offended by the request. He clapped Tarek on the shoulder and stood. "Of course! I did promise you, didn't I?" Darvad dashed to one of the female dancers. He grabbed her by the arm and swung her out into the middle of the room. The poor woman looked startled by Darvad's sudden grab.

"You dance Salafani-style?" Darvad asked her, smiling wickedly.

The woman nodded. "Of course."

"Then let's show my friend how it's done."

Tarek reclined on the pillows and watched, stifling his disappointment that Darvad had not volunteered to show him the moves personally. The dance started traditionally, with the two of them circling around each other, arms weaving in the air, legs deliberately strutting across the room. As the tempo increased, they drew closer together, each gyration in tandem, until they were nearly touching, their bodies pulsing and twisting in synchronicity. It was a very erotic dance. Tarek watched the movements of Darvad's body hungrily, the way his arms flexed, the careful placement of his feet. Darvad's eyes burned as they stared wantonly at the half-clad dancer, and Tarek imagined what it would be like to have such eyes turned on him.

"Let me try," Tarek said, standing up. He moved to Darvad, but the dancer quickly spun and grabbed his arm, misinterpreting him. Tarek struggled through the steps with her. She was patient. But Tarek's sexual frustrations only made his poor dancing skills worse, and he quickly tired of trying.

Darvad found another dancing girl, and stalked her like prey. Tarek didn't have the stomach to watch Darvad pursue a lover that evening. He slipped out of the room, wandering through Druv's house, his head spinning with wine.

Tarek decided to go for a walk and dispel the dizzying buzz. Druv's townhouse seemed too close; he needed air.

Sounds of merrymaking drifted from behind every wall. The wide, shady boulevard was home to a majority of Marhavad's lords and courtiers, and so each occupant anticipated either trepidation or celebration the following day. Tarek was not the only lord wandering the street in the darkness. He passed by carousing groups of young men, Triya warriors dressed in their finest, he passed musicians and merchants making late deliveries. Everyone offered him the sign of peace as he passed, and it touched him. On the eve of a decision that might spark a civil war, all parties were filled with hope, filled with something close to affection for each other. Anything seemed possible.

The street circled round a large park, and Tarek followed the curve of the road, strolling down a quieter side street. Here were the houses of the ministers of Prasta, wealthy Triya who were not soldiers, but professional politicians. While celebration could still be heard, the scene was more subdued, and Tarek embraced these moments of serenity as he sorted through his raging heartbreak.

Tarek passed by the red-painted gates of a temple and he decided to stop inside. The shrine itself was tucked back away from the street within a thick stand of coconut trees. The prophets gazed down at him, and the face of God, illustrated as a shining sun, wrought in pure gold, glittered from the ceiling of the incense-strewn temple.

Tarek lit a fresh stick of incense off a dying ember. He rubbed paste on his forehead and then knelt in prayer.

He lost himself in his mumbled words. Religion always comforted him, and now it served as a buoy, keeping him afloat in the tumultuous world of being the lord of Dragewan. He prayed for guidance. He prayed for strength.

Tarek heard voices and turned. Two priests walked together down the path. They paused when they saw him praying there, and turned aside to give Tarek privacy. They stopped within a three-walled wooden shelter near the gate, where Tarek had smelled buttery tea being heated.

Tarek continued his prayer, but the priests' presence intruded on his meditations. They no doubt assumed from his dress that Tarek was Triya, but if they found out a Suya was sullying their temple grounds, he could be punished. Darvad would defend him, as Darvad always did. But Tarek did not want to burden his friend with extra responsibilities, especially not on the eve of his ascension to the throne.

Tarek bowed his head low to God and then stood. His knees popped. He was getting out of shape, all this feasting and so little exercise.

In order to bypass the priests, Tarek walked a circuitous route back to the front gate, through the coconut grove, enjoying the perfumed warmth of the summer air.

Out of the corner of his eye, Tarek saw the flash of armor hidden behind the trees. He wasn't the only warrior hiding in the temple that night.

His first thought was that it was some reveler relieving himself against a tree, but then he heard the voices of two men. It was late for such congress, and Tarek approached warily, worried the men were up to no good. Temples had been desecrated over the last few months by young rabble-rousers.

Then he saw them.

Keshan Adaru and Jandu Paran stood whispering together. Keshan reclined against a tree casually, and Jandu stood close to him, his hand beside Keshan's head as he leaned on the tree for support. The two of them spoke in low voices, their armor and fresh clothes gleaming in the moonlight.

Tarek moved closer to hear what they were saying, keeping to the shadows, making no sound.

"…I can't." Keshan shook his head. He looked agitated.

"I want you there," Jandu pleaded. "I need you there. Please. Yudar won't mind. Hell, even Darvad would prefer you come to the ceremony. You've traveled all this way already."

Keshan shook his head. "No. I promised Iyestar I would accompany you to the city gates, no further. And look! I've already broken my promise."

"So break it all the way. Come with me to the palace."

"No. I'll spend the night in the Tiwari townhouse, but I must leave first thing in the morning."

The two of them stood awfully close together, Tarek thought.

"What does it matter?" Jandu asked. He ducked his head to look into Keshan's face, seeming to notice Keshan's obvious discomfort for the first time. "Are you all right?"

"Listen, I need you to do something for me," Keshan whispered.

"Anything," Jandu whispered back.

"Give me Zandi, just for a little while. You can get her in Tiwari after the ceremony."

The request clearly shocked Jandu, for he straightened, his hands leaving the tree. "Why do you want her?"

"A feeling."

"What feeling?"

Keshan sighed. He ran his hand through his hair. "I have a premonition that Zandi will be taken from you if I don't protect her."

"Keshan—"

"—Do you trust me?"

Jandu nodded. "Of course I do. Take her. Keep her as long as you wish." Jandu slid Zandi off his shoulder and rested her against the bark of the tree.

Keshan suddenly kissed Jandu.

Tarek stood, transfixed, mouth agape in shock.

Jandu thrust his tongue into Keshan's mouth. They drew closer together. Jandu pinned Keshan to the tree trunk, his hands on either side of Keshan's face.

Tarek never witnessed two men kissing before. Despite the fact that Tarek disliked Jandu, he couldn't deny that they were both exceptionally attractive men. The sight aroused him. Tarek watched them embrace, their breastplates grinding quietly together as they pressed closer, kissing slowly, lazily, as if they had all the time in the world, as if they had every right to be there, making love in the open.

When Tarek kissed men, it was always a furtive act, hasty and aggressive. He had never done this. The two of them made love with such gentle sweetness, their mouths caressing each other, their bodies trembling with a tremendous balance of strength and tenderness.

Watching them, Tarek awakened to the idea that love between two men could be something beautiful and pure, and not a desperate craving satisfied in darkness and in urgency.

Jandu whispered something to Keshan, and Keshan laughed, he let Jandu pin his body, hip to hip. Keshan licked at Jandu's lips, and Tarek suddenly felt a deep grief unlike anything he'd ever experienced. This was a sweet moment he would never know. There was a purity in this secret embrace, and now that he knew it existed, Tarek wanted to experience it more than anything else in his life.

A bone-deep sadness tore through him. He would never have this. Not with Darvad. It would forever be out of Tarek's reach, as long as he continued to love a man who could not—would not—love him back.

Tarek decided to leave the two lovers alone. His voyeurism, and his own arousal, disturbed him. This was a private moment, and Tarek ruined it by spying.

He heard a low voice from behind him, and realized that the priests approached. Despite his anger towards Jandu, Tarek determined that nothing should pollute this moment. He wanted Keshan and Jandu to have it, if he never could.

He leaned down and found a stone, and threw it close to the lovers. Jandu and Keshan broke apart immediately. They spoke again to each other, and then Jandu turned to leave. As they parted, their fingers touched briefly, and they walked in opposite directions, Zandi held in Keshan's arms.

Tarek waited a few seconds, and then continued through the trees towards the temple gate. He watched Jandu stealthily depart.

He still didn't like Jandu. Jandu gained admiration for his bloodline, rather than his talents. And while he was a good archer, Tarek was better. Yet Jandu would always receive more praise, and more credit, because of his lineage.

But, with this new revelation, a part of Tarek's heart softened toward Jandu. They had more in common than Tarek had originally supposed.

Keshan departed next, sneaking through the gate, Zandi bright on his shoulder. Not for the first time, Tarek wondered whose side Keshan was on. He clearly preferred Darvad's politics, and yet he had taken a lover from the opposite camp.

Once they were gone, Tarek made his own exit, abandoning Druv's party and deciding to walk the rest of the way home. He knew Darvad would miss him, but in all the wrong ways.

There was a peace there, in that temple, that could have washed away everything and left his heart healthy and whole.

But it was not meant for him.

CHAPTER 17

Jandu assumed Yudar would be angry with him for arriving back in Prasta at the last possible moment. Baram certainly had been. He'd almost punched Jandu for leaving, but Suraya restrained him, cautioning that a bruise would look bad at the formal ceremony.

Jandu got no chance to speak with Yudar the night he arrived home, as Yudar meditated in the palace temple. Therefore he sought Yudar the following morning, as his brother dressed into his formal wear alone.

"I'm glad you're here," was Yudar's only comment. His expression showed the anxiety that an entire night's meditation had not erased.

"Where are your servants?" Jandu asked.

"I sent them away. I wanted some quiet." Yudar looked over at Jandu and smiled almost ruefully. "You aren't the only one who occasionally requires solitude."

"Do you want me to leave?" Jandu asked.

"No. Stay." Yudar smiled at him. "I mean it, it's good to have you here. I feel like I'm missing something precious when you're not around."

"Flatterer." Jandu turned to Yudar's full-length mirror and adjusted his breastplate. He wore full armor this morning in honor of the importance of the ceremony. Jandu's heavy silver diadem already bothered him, and he'd only had it on for an hour.

"Did you have a pleasant journey?" Yudar struggled with the leather ties of his breastplate. He never developed the knack of tying knots out of sight.

"It was lovely," Jandu told him. "There are places in Marhavad where no one cares what happens today."

Yudar chuckled. "I wish I was there."

"Let me help you." Jandu took over tying Yudar's breastplate and back plate. They stood together in amiable silence.

"Hand me your gauntlets," Jandu said.

They were beautiful, gold and leather, with the Prasta crest of the sun emblazed across them, studded with a large black pearl. Jandu laced them tightly.

"Thank you, Jandu." Yudar reached out and hugged Jandu to him. Yudar shook slightly.

"Are you all right?"

"Just nervous," Yudar said.

"You'll be fantastic," Jandu told him, patting him on the shoulder. "You were born for this. You've been trained for this. No one could be a better king than you."

Yudar expelled a large breath of air. "Well, let us hope that Mazar feels the same way."

"Mazar is no fool." Jandu raised the massive, jewel-encrusted diadem from Yudar's table and placed it carefully on Yudar's head. "This is going to give you a headache."

Yudar smiled. "Some of us are used to wearing formal attire, Jandu." He looked at himself in the mirror. Gold adorned him, head to toe. His red silk trousers shimmered with gold thread, and his gem-encrusted sword hilt glittered magnificently. Even his shoes bore elegantly embroidered suns. He looked like a god.

"Let's go find out if I'm king."

"Good luck," Jandu said. He hugged his brother once more, and then followed him into the waiting entourage.

A procession of lords, ministers, messengers, soldiers, and relatives trailed Yudar as they made their way towards the large central garden. As Jandu walked, he tried to let the feeling of peace he acquired in Tiwari remain paramount.

But already, Jandu's week in Tiwari faded like a dream. That glorious warmth and confidence and sense of belonging suffered under the tension that strangled the palace. Jandu found it ironic that he felt more like himself there, in Tiwari, than he did here, in his own home. With lords and ministers and priests surrounding him, Jandu felt trapped. Real life anxieties chewed away at the thin edges of Jandu's memories.

Jandu's body sparkled in the sunlight as the morning rays hit his armor of burnished steel and silver, decorated with small golden suns, protecting his chest, back, and upper arms. He wore matching silver bands on his wrists and lower arms. The metal grew hot, but for once Jandu didn't care. Armor seemed like a wise decision on a day as tense as today.

Jandu had attended his share of formal announcements, but he had never seen anything like this. The garden was wall-to-wall bodies. Below, on the banks of the river, thousands upon thousands of citizens lined the roads and parks, looking up to see whether the Paran or Uru flag would be raised. Jandu took his place behind Yudar, alongside Baram and Suraya, at the front of the dais. Thousands of people stared at him, him and his family, and he brushed self-consciously at the curl of hair sticking out in front of his ear.

Baram matched Yudar in gorgeous gold armor. His diadem, too, shimmered with sapphires and pearls. And Suraya spared no detail, her diamond nose ring connected to her diamond earrings by a beautiful stretch of silver and pearls, her eyes darkened with kohl, henna on her hands, her dress luxuriant purple silk and silver embroidery.

"You look sexy," Jandu whispered in her ear.

Suraya smirked behind her painted hand. "Behave, Jandu."

On the other end of the dais stood Darvad Uru, resplendent in his own golden armor, alone. Nearby, his friends Tarek, Druv and Firdaus hovered, but on the dais, Darvad looked over-whelmed by the Paran's unity.

And between them, old and tired, was Regent Mazar.

"Today is an auspicious day, a day where God has granted me the wisdom to choose the best course of action for our beloved nation," Mazar began. "It is no easy task, because all the sons of King Shandarvan are fine men, noble men, with excellent hearts and strong arms, the Shentari faith within their souls. Choosing between Darvad Uru and Yudar Paran is like choosing between night and day, water and earth. Both are needed to bring balance and wholeness to our world, both are equally valuable to the people, and to my own heart."

Jandu stifled a groan. *Just say it already. Just get it over with. Everyone is waiting on one word.*

"I have had one long year to contemplate the repercussions of choosing one over the other, knowing that the wrong choice could lead to instability and war. Since the great battles of our forefathers, we have lived in relative peace under the banner of this palace, and I have no wish to darken the royal name or bring the wrath of God upon me by instigating a war. I have prayed for guidance, and this morning, God has taken me by the hand and shown me the path by which I must follow."

The silence hung over the entire city.

Mazar rubbed his eyes. And then he looked out at the crowd. "Because I cannot choose between night and day, between earth and water, or between my heart and my soul, I have determined that I *will not* choose."

Jandu's breath caught. *What the hell did that mean?*

"I will split Marhavad into two kingdoms," Mazar said. "And let both sons of Shandarvan share in the bounty, and grant us their wisdom."

There was a stunned silence. And then, instantly, chaos.

Darvad's face turned red and that vein in his forehead pulsed angrily. Even Yudar, who remained calm and controlled in public, seemed flustered by the announcement. He frowned and looked at his hands, as if God planted a message for him there.

"What total bullshit!" Baram exploded, fists raising. "If anything will cause civil war, this will do it!"

Luckily, Baram's exclamation was lost in the overwhelming drone of everyone else shouting at Mazar. Boos echoed across the garden. Lords shuffled and looked to Yudar or Darvad for support.

Jandu breathed heavily. He had no idea how to respond. He hadn't even considered this an option. No one had. He looked up and almost had to laugh as the flag raisers tried to raise both Paran and Uru flags on the pole at the same time.

Mazar cowered as the volume of verbal assault increased, as shouts filled the air.

"Please! Let us all calm down! We must have peace!" Yudar held his hand up over the crowd, begging for order, but no one could hear him above the roar of outrage. It took both him and Darvad together to finally still the masses, and even then, their eyes turned cold on Mazar for even contemplating dividing the nation into two.

Yudar bowed respectfully to Mazar and brought his hands together in the sign of peace. "We will abide your decision, Master Mazar, and beg God's blessings for this new chapter in the history of our beloved nation."

Darvad bowed as well, although the vein in his head still throbbed.

Darvad helped usher the tumultuous guests to the adjacent garden, where the celebratory feast was ready and waiting. Few seemed in the mood for food. But the wine was immediately opened and passed, and everyone eventually took their seats, rage crystallizing in the icy silence.

Small conversations took place, speculations, but the main table where the Parans and Darvad sat along with Mazar was about as far from the Adaru's reckless and delightful dining experiences as Jandu could get.

Jandu knew his old master well enough to recognize the strained grimace on Mazar's face. Once, when Jandu was just a boy, Mazar gave him a leather ball to play with. Jandu managed to toss it into the river less than half an hour later. Jandu tried to retrieve it and fell into the water instead, nearly drowning. Mazar discovered him and helped Jandu to shore, where he then beat Jandu mercilessly, shrieking at him for being so careless with his own life.

But what Jandu remembered most about the incident was the way Mazar looked about ten minutes after beating him. He'd worn a haunted expression of remorse and sick self-reproach.

The same sick apprehension enshrouded Mazar's expression now, as the uncomfortable official celebration slunk into its second hour. Mazar should have made a choice. And he didn't. Rather than alienating half of Marhavad, he had estranged everyone in one fell swoop.

The stilted conversations, whispers, and anxious glances between lords grew into an unbearable level of tension.

"I cannot bear this any longer," Darvad announced suddenly and loudly, standing up dramatically. He put his hand on Yudar's shoulder. "Yudar, you are my half-brother, and now my co-leader in this great nation. Let us put aside our differences and work together, in the spirit of cooperation."

Yudar returned Darvad's smile. "My feelings exactly, Darvad. I wish you no harm and look forward to working with you." Yudar stood and the two embraced. A nervous applause broke out.

"Come, let us celebrate the proper way. May I challenge you to a friendly game of dice, to show the good will between us?"

Yudar's eyes glinted. "Wonderful!" He clapped his hands.

"I don't want to play alone," Darvad told Yudar. "With your permission, I'd like to invite my friends to join me."

"Of course," Yudar said. He turned quickly to Jandu and Baram. "Both of you, come with me."

Jandu almost protested. Yudar knew how he felt about gambling. But Baram violently shoved Jandu in Yudar's direction. "Shut up and do what you're told, for once," Baram mumbled.

Outside, the spectators crowded around, following the two kings through the garden and into the gaming room at the edge of the courtyard. Those at the feast got up and practically ran to the gaming room as well.

Baram was still spitting in rage, but Jandu's anger had turned into a coil of apprehension, sitting cold and slick at the bottom of his stomach.

Servants prepared the room for the impromptu game. Someone fetched Yudar's own exquisite gaming board.

Jandu sat down cross-legged alongside his brothers on one side of the board. Yudar's pieces were carved of ivory, and Darvad's were made of ebony. A lone pair of dice lay on the board.

Jandu leaned forward to speak to Yudar from behind the great blocking girth of Baram.

"Yudar." He kept his voice low. "I have a bad feeling about this game."

Yudar sighed. He leaned forward to whisper into Jandu's ear. "I cannot refuse a challenge; you know that."

"But —" Jandu was interrupted by applause as Darvad himself entered the room. He quickly sat across from the Parans, flanked on either side by his friends Tarek, Druv and Firdaus. Darvad handed the long dice to Firdaus.

"Firdaus will roll for me," Darvad said. Just the presence of Firdaus made Jandu's skin crawl. Firdaus had overdone even his own usual opulence, wearing a garland of carnelians over his armor. Amber studded his diadem so thickly that the heron emblazoned across the gold surface was barely visible. A playful expression lit Firdaus' dark skin, and lifted his drooping moustache.

"And Jandu will roll my dice," Yudar said, already entranced by the sight of the board.

Jandu frowned. He didn't want to have anything to do with the game.

"Please take the first turn." Darvad offered Jandu the dice, then positioned his own ebony game piece. "I stake one hundred gold pieces from my share of the royal treasury."

Yudar nodded at Jandu as if to reassure him. "And I will stake the same."

Jandu felt the uncomfortable intensity of hundreds of eyes upon him. Lords and courtiers jostled each other to squeeze into the small gaming room. Already the warmth of their bodies coupled with the summer heat to make the space feel almost stifling. Jandu threw the dice.

"Five!" Yudar declared.

Firdaus scooped up the dice, rattled them in his hands, and then blew on them gently. He threw them down on the board.

The dice rolled a four.

Yudar's mouth was locked in a small, non-descript line. The intensity of his stare was the only evidence of his excitement. Whispered speculations rose through the crowd. Jandu could hear them placing their own wagers on the outcome of the game.

Still, the game went well for Yudar. Darvad's bets grew in size, but he continued to lose. He scowled when Yudar won his ruby collection, and Firdaus even had the decency to look embarrassed when he rolled a two, forfeiting Darvad's newest prized possession, a white stallion from the great stables of Chandamar.

Mazar joined the spectators, seating himself to Yudar's left. Anxiety still lined his face, but as the game progressed he seemed to relax slightly.

Baram laughed and taunted Darvad. Yudar sat stiff and still, but Jandu could see the thrill building in his eyes.

Every time Firdaus blew on the dice, Jandu thought he saw tiny flashes of light in the corner of his eye. Jandu looked around him, but no one else seemed to notice it. Jandu recalled that Firdaus was part-Yashva and his nervous tension grew.

Yudar only lost a few wagers toward the end, but he won the overall game. The spectators cheered him on. Jandu saw courtiers whose own fortunes hung in the balance of this new, precarious friendship watching the game closely. When Darvad asked Yudar for another round, and a chance to win back his horse and his rubies, Yudar agreed.

"Let's stop while we're ahead," Jandu whispered. He did not like Firdaus' flickering fingers, even if they hadn't helped Darvad win.

"We're just getting started," Yudar replied, smiling calmly. He put the dice in Jandu's hand. "May the prophets continue to bring good fortune to your hand!"

This second round, Yudar did worse. He soon lost his prizes from Darvad, as well as his own collection of precious onyx statues of the prophets. He lost their family's cloisonné pottery, their formal saddles, their silver and diamond-studded bridles, their chariots.

Each roll, Yudar did not hesitate to up the stakes. He won back the chariots and Darvad's mace, but he then began to lose again, losing more.

Yudar's expression did not change, whether he won or he lost. His eyes glazed over and he mumbled out stakes in a low voice.

As Darvad continued to win, Firdaus' expression grew euphoric. He grinned with every roll of six, and Darvad and Druv cried out happily, laughing at each new triumph. Only Tarek sat still, his grim face mirroring Jandu's own.

Firdaus rolled a six.

"The dice are loaded," Baram said. He glared at Firdaus.

"Such a claim is an insult to me," Firdaus stated loudly. "But if you feel so, we will switch to yours."

Baram grabbed the dice from Firdaus' hand and slammed them next to Jandu. He pushed Yudar's dice over to Darvad's side of the board.

The room grew hotter in the afternoon sun and the water in their glasses sweated profusely, but Yudar did not stop. By the time another hour had passed, Yudar had spent every penny he had.

Jandu had never seen Yudar like this. The stakes had risen so quickly, so quietly, that everyone seemed taken by surprise. It felt surreal, except that the room was too hot and the smells of sweating men too strong for it to be a dream. Yudar gambled all the time, but he rarely lost control like this.

"I stake all of my weapons and my armor," Yudar said quietly.

"Maybe you should stop," Baram told him.

Yudar refused. Jandu knew he would not stop because he understood how Yudar thought. His brother honestly believed he could win it all back, that all he needed was one lucky break. One bad throw of Firdaus', and then Yudar could use his skill to gain back his fortunes and more. Jandu suddenly realized that Yudar would not quit until he lost everything.

"We have to stop now." Jandu resolutely placed the dice on the board.

"No." Yudar's eyes never strayed from the board.

"I won't throw the dice anymore," Jandu hissed to Yudar.

"Fine, I'll roll myself." Yudar picked up the dice and cast them out on the board.

Yudar won, and relief swept through the room. Jandu swallowed to try and regain moisture in his throat. His body ached with tension. Darvad conceded all of his armor, and then staked some of Yudar's possessions back to him. When Yudar lost again, his confidence waned slightly. A sheen of sweat formed on Yudar's forehead.

Firdaus rolled a three, the exact number they needed to bring their piece home, and Yudar lost the game. Without pausing to think or have a drink of water, Yudar nodded frantically to Darvad. "Again. Let us play again."

"Are you sure?" Darvad asked. "I already own almost all of your possessions."

"You must at least give me a chance to win them back," Yudar said.

"That is enough," Baram told his brother. He put a large hand on Yudar's shoulder. "You've already gone too far."

"I know what I am doing," Yudar growled.

Baram frowned but relented.

Darvad and Yudar rolled to go first, and Yudar got the lead. But he soon lost the advantage as Firdaus miraculously threw sixes, fives, and the exact points he needed to reach each of the board's houses.

Jandu felt sick to his stomach.

Yudar licked his lips. "Baram's sword," he said quietly. "I stake that."

"No!" Baram shouted. "It's my sword, not yours! Gamble your own!"

"I'm your elder brother," Yudar snapped back, his voice rising. "What you own is mine."

Baram growled. "Yudar, stop now."

"Baram's sword," Yudar said again, nervously tapping the board. He looked anxiously at Firdaus. "Roll the dice."

Firdaus rolled a six.

Mazar moaned loudly and held his face in his hands. Jandu gaped as Baram, fuming, handed his sword to Darvad.

Yudar continued. He staked their gold, their jewels, their lands. He staked the finest breeding stallions and Jandu's horse, Shedav. He staked the crops they tithed, and he staked the last of their chariots. He went farther than he'd ever gone before, gambling away things that belonged to his brothers, his wife.

Finally, he said, "I stake Zandi, Jandu's bow."

Darvad grinned at Tarek.

A chill ran down Jandu's spine. "You cannot stake her," he told Yudar.

Yudar regarded Jandu blankly. "I will win her back for you, I promise."

"She isn't mine anymore. I gave her to Keshan." Jandu felt like throwing up. Did Keshan see this? Did he know this would happen?

Yudar ground his teeth. "Fine then. I stake my half of the kingdom of Marhavad."

"What?" Baram shouted.

"No, you cannot!" Mazar yelled at him. He crouched beside Yudar. "It is not yours to gamble away. It belongs to the people. It was given to you by God!"

"I am offering Darvad a chance to possess the throne in its entirely, the way our father intended it to be. I stake the kingdom." Yudar sweated profusely, and his eyes darted, but he still spoke calmly.

"No!" Jandu shouted. He couldn't take it any longer. "Yudar! Don't be so stupid!"

"How dare you speak to me like that!" Yudar hissed. His tense, calm façade shattered, replaced with rage. "I am your older brother, and your king!"

"Which is why I'm making you stop," Jandu said. He reached down to grab Yudar's arm, but Yudar pulled from his grasp. He stood in a flash and leaned in close to Jandu.

"I have it under control," Yudar whispered angrily into Jandu's ear. "You have to trust me! I know what I'm doing!"

Jandu stared at him. "You just bet our kingdom!"

"I'm going to get it all back, but I can't if I stop playing!" Yudar said, resuming his seat. He straightened his sash and stared at Darvad. "What do you stake?"

Darvad raised his eyebrow. "All your own possessions and all of mine."

"Fine," Yudar said. "Roll." He looked so calm, so assured that for a moment Jandu wondered if Yudar possessed some secret—knew some trick that would win everything back.

Firdaus rolled a three. The room gasped collectively. Even Firdaus looked stunned.

Jandu watched, holding his breath.

Yudar rolled the dice.

Two.

Shocked dismay echoed throughout the room. For the first time, Yudar began to look afraid.

Jandu rushed to his brother's side. "Get up, Yudar." He pulled on his arm. "Get up."

Yudar stared ahead of him, as if in shock. "I can't."

"You must!" Jandu cried.

Yudar shook his head. "I have no choice now. I have to keep playing. It's the only way I can get back the kingdom."

Jandu fought back the urge to punch his brother in the face.

"This is madness," Baram cried. He shook Yudar fiercely. "We have lost everything!"

"It is the only way!" Yudar started shaking. He looked at Firdaus and pointed at Firdaus' dice. "Roll again!"

"But you have nothing left to wager," Firdaus said.

"I stake my youngest brother, Jandu."

The room went silent. Darvad stopped smiling. He stared at Yudar in clear horror. Jandu felt his bones go cold, as if he were turning to ice. He couldn't believe Yudar's words. This couldn't be happening.

"Have you gone mad?" Baram shook with rage. "Yudar, think!"

Firdaus smiled. "You are willing to make Jandu a slave?"

Yudar clenched his fists. "Roll the dice!"

Jandu's throat had gone completely dry. He watched Yudar as if in a dream.

Firdaus rattled the dice in his hands, the sound deafening in the utter silence of the room. Then Darvad gently took the dice from Firdaus' hands.

"This stops now," he said.

"Darvad, let him gamble away his own flesh and blood if he wants to," Firdaus said.

"No," Darvad said. "Jandu is my half-brother. I will not see him enslaved."

"But we must continue!" Yudar was panicked now. He stood, his hands shaking. "The game must continue!"

"Yudar," Darvad said calmly. "You just staked your own brother."

"Enough!" Mazar stood. He looked furious. "This is one of the most despicable scenes I have ever had the displeasure to witness, and I thank God that your father is not alive to have seen it!"

As if suddenly awakened from a dream, Yudar snapped his attention up from the dice. His eyes went to Mazar and then Jandu.

"I didn't mean…" Yudar began, but didn't go on. Jandu could only stare at his brother, feeling betrayed. Then as if the shame had not been enough already, tears began to pour down Yudar's cheeks. He cupped his hand over his eyes. Baram leaned against the back wall, holding Suraya, who appeared to be on the verge of fainting.

"But what is to be done?" Druv asked.

"What can be done?" Firdaus shrugged. "Darvad is king now of all of Marhavad. The Parans have nothing left."

"I will not allow that!" Mazar's voice trembled with anger.

"But we cannot allow a man who would gamble his people and land away so carelessly to be king!" Druv gestured emphatically.

"I have a suggestion," Darvad said. "Perhaps Yudar may look to the example of the Prophet Sadeshar, and win back the favor of God and his people."

Jandu searched his memory for Prophet Sadeshar. He recalled something about an exile, but could dredge up no details.

Yudar obviously remembered. He went pale. "No! It's too much!"

"I don't think so," Darvad said smoothly. "Considering you've just given me control over the entire nation, I think it is very fair to ask you to serve penance for your recklessness. And, once the penance is served, I will grant you back your half of the kingdom, and we will be equals once more. I will not steal from you, Yudar."

Yudar glanced again to Jandu and all his pride seemed to crumple. He covered his face with his hands again. "Yes! By the grace of God, I will repent! I will follow the Prophet Sadeshar's actions!"

"Good!" Darvad cried. "You must go into exile and suffer three years of anonymity. No one may help you, or they will face the wrath of God and be banished from the Triya caste. And if you reveal yourselves, your penance begins again."

Jandu caught a satisfied look between Firdaus and Druv, and realized this was too perfect. They had this planned.

Jandu lunged at Darvad, grabbing him by the neck.

"You fucking prick! You set this up!"

"Guards!" Darvad choked. Suddenly hands were upon Jandu, yanking him backwards. He struggled to free himself. One of the guards punched him in the eye. Jandu's vision went black. He fell to his knees.

"Don't make this worse, Jandu!" Baram hissed in his ear. He pulled Jandu back towards the wall.

"The game was rigged!" Jandu cried.

"Enough! It is clear that we have all disgraced God on this day! But none more than Yudar Paran! I agree to the terms of Darvad's settlement." Mazar glared at Yudar. "Yudar. You and your family will go into exile. And, like the Prophet Sadeshar in the Book of Taivo, if you survive by the grace of God, you will emerge from your exile sinless, and prove yourself worthy of your noble birth once more."

"I will forgive everything after the exile," Darvad said, hand over his heart.

Yudar controlled his weeping long enough to look up and raise his palm to the sky. "I swear, to our beloved God, and on the Book of Taivo, that I accept this exile, and this punishment, for my sins." He looked to Darvad. "But please, do not punish my family as well." He knelt at Darvad's feet. "Let Suraya, Baram, and Jandu stay."

"You played this game as a family, and you have all lost as a family," Darvad spat. His voice rose above the crowd. "The Parans must go into exile this very day, or else they forever forfeit their right to this kingdom. They are to take only what they can carry. And anyone found helping the Parans in their exile will be disgraced and outcaste."

"So be it," Mazar said. He shook his head. "Make way for the Parans to leave us."

The room was a flurry of activity. People poured out of the gaming room to pass on the news.

Baram let go of Jandu. "You better get your things."

Jandu's vision was starry. He pushed his way through the crowd, heading for the chamber that was no longer his room.

Take only the things you can carry.

Jandu tried to move, to start packing. But his body would not obey. He was too shocked to do more than sit there on the edge of his bed, wondering how his world had tumbled to such a disastrous end, so quickly.

It seemed only moments later that Baram and Suraya found him. Together they hastily packed their belongings. He worked quickly to keep his mind off how angry he was with Yudar and of how frightened he was of the next three years.

Bailiffs came to escort them out of the palace.

Yudar said nothing as the four of them left the palace in stately procession. They wore white cotton trousers and shirts, the color of pilgrimage. Servants and allies and friends wept openly. They touched their feet and some rushed to offer them small tokens of their support. Jandu walked, eyes forward in a daze.

As they made their way to the city gates, a steady stream of grief-stricken nobles and wealthy Suya followed them. Many wailed as if at a wake. It was the most depressing sound Jandu had ever heard. The city wept for them. But there was nothing to be done. Yudar had sealed their fate.

At the outskirts of the city, a chariot pulled up alongside them. It stopped suddenly and Keshan jumped out. "I came as soon as I heard." He took one look at Jandu and his face darkened. "Who hit you?" he demanded.

"Did you know this would happen?" Jandu suddenly asked, rounding on Keshan. "Did you see this in your premonition?"

"No." Keshan's eyes were wide. "God, no. I knew Zandi was at risk. That is all."

Jandu felt immensely relieved. At least Keshan hadn't betrayed him.

Keshan glared at Yudar. "What kind of man are you?"

Yudar still said nothing to anyone. He cried silently, his face bowed. Baram and Suraya walked behind him, Baram's arm around Suraya as she too cried. Baram whispered to her but Jandu couldn't hear what he said. Jandu gazed forward, feeling perilously close to tears himself.

They had reached the crossroads. The procession behind them stopped, weeping and waving and throwing palm leaves toward them.

Keshan's charioteer kept his horses at a steady walk alongside the Parans. Keshan reached into the chariot and pulled out Jandu's bow.

"Take her back." He handed Zandi to him.

Jandu swallowed. Two days ago, he was happier than he had ever been in his life. The idea of running away from his family, here and now, suddenly flashed through his mind. He would go and live with Keshan in Tiwari. He could find happiness once more.

But then the stark reality hit him. Keshan, like the other lords of Marhavad, was forbidden to aid any of them. He risked worse than exile—becoming an outcaste if he defied Darvad.

"You should go," Jandu told him. "You cannot help us. You will be outcaste."

"I will talk with Darvad." Keshan said. "I will do all I can, Jandu, I promise."

Jandu turned and hugged Keshan tightly. He blinked back tears.

"I love you," he whispered into Keshan's ear.

"I'll find a way to help you, I swear to God." Keshan's fingers twined in Jandu's hair. And then he let go. He gave Suraya a brief hug, and Baram as well. Then he stepped back into the chariot. "Chezek, let's go."

Keshan's charioteer cracked the whip, and the horses broke into a startled canter.

Jandu watched Keshan go, and realized Keshan took his heart with him. But there was no turning back.

CHAPTER 18

THE THRONE ROOM GLITTERED WITH GOLD ARMOR AND SHONE with bright silky colors. Sunlight reflected off the dozens of bejeweled diadems, breastplates and gauntlets. Men with sword hilts encrusted with rubies and sapphires sashayed past platters of grapes and bowls of spiced chutney served with toasted breads. The sound of the lords of Marhavad rumbled like the grumbling of hungry bellies, all these Triya pressed together to form one shimmering image of incandescent power, gathered to submit to Darvad's oath-taking ceremony. Keshan felt sick inside, but gave no external evidence. He circuited the room, socializing, scandalizing, his smile bright, his sense of humor wicked. And silently he counted. Which lords and courtiers looked disgruntled, which ones whispered rumors. Some lords were noticeably missing from the ceremony entirely.

Keshan had assumed that Yudar's despicable behavior at the dice game would sway favor towards Darvad. But while most agreed Yudar went too far, others susurrated in discreet groups, questioning how someone as talented at dice as Yudar could have been beaten so soundly. Yudar's continued hold over the lords surprised Keshan.

Keshan flirted with the two unmarried daughters of the lord of Penemar until a trumpet blasted, urging the assembled to take their seats.

Keshan found his seat, next to his brother Iyestar's in the honored front row of the throne room. The throne itself sat high upon a gold-lacquered dais. Beneath it, one hundred velvet seats formed an oval that faced the dais. The seats were divided into four rows in which the guests seated according to rank, Shentari caste striation infiltrating every part of their culture.

After the dice game, Iyestar was happy to return to Prasta. But a new tension instilled Iyestar's personality, and even now Keshan could feel his brother's anxiety.

"Yudar's allies whisper that Darvad cheated at dice," Keshan said conversationally to his brother. Iyestar stiffened at his side, but said nothing. This told Keshan as much as words would have.

Keshan gave Iyestar a hard look. "Is that the reason we left Prasta?"

"I told you why we left Prasta," Iyestar said.

"Was this a contributing factor in our decision to leave Prasta?" Keshan kept at it.

"I was not at the game," Iyestar said carefully. "And I won't stoop to conjecture. Regardless of what Darvad may have done, it was Yudar who staked his kingdom and his brother. There is no excuse for it."

"No, but it may explain why there is more tension here than I expected." A clamorous chorus of trumpets interrupted their conversation and Darvad strode into the room, trailed by royal staff.

As he took his seat on the throne, Darvad looked splendid. He looked like a king. His expressive face showed kindness, but his hard-cut body illustrated the strength and power of will underlying that kindness. More than ten years had passed since anyone wore the crown, and now it sat resplendent on Darvad's brow. The crown was covered in diamonds, set in delicately engraved gold and silver, with the fur of a leopard forming a soft base.

Darvad brought his palms together in the sign of peace. Keshan and the others immediately fell from their seats and bowed low, heads on the floor, in supplication. When Keshan sat back, he made eye contact with Darvad, who smiled at him. Keshan winked back.

"Great lords of Marhavad," Darvad began, "today, I ask all of you to take a holy oath to defend this kingdom, and to serve as my loyal vassals. You swear by this oath to abide the laws of Marhavad, and to care for our people. You swear to uphold the law as established by my Royal Judge, and to act in your positions as lords with honor befitting the Triya race."

Darvad listed the traditional requirements of a lord of Marhavad in serving his royal master, and Keshan scanned the room. He still could not find the lord of Marshav. Lord Kadal was one of Yudar's most loyal supporters, and his absence was not going unnoticed. Keshan also could not find the lord of Jezza.

"You swear by this oath to fight alongside me should this kingdom face an enemy from the untamed territories." Darvad read from a scroll. He cleared his throat and looked to the audience. "And you swear by this oath not to aid nor assist the Parans during their three years of exile. Anyone caught helping the Parans during this period will be breaking a holy oath will be branded as a Jegora untouchable and outcaste from our Triya society."

Keshan tensed. It was the first inclusion of a new oath to the ceremony in decades. Of all the new ideas to bring about, why would Darvad choose this first?

"By this oath, you also swear to reconsider the status of the lower castes in your state, through proper security of their livelihood, safety in their neighborhoods, better sanitation, and better health care."

It was almost as though Darvad wrote that for Keshan alone, softening the blow of abandoning Jandu with a plea to help thousands of Suya, Chaya and even Jegora.

One by one, the lords of Marhavad stepped forward and bowed before Darvad, taking the oath to serve him in accordance with his specifications. Darvad's closest allies were the first in line; Tarek Amia, lord of Dragewan; Firdaus Trinat, lord of Chandamar; and Druv Majeo, lord of Pagdesh.

Keshan remained sitting, thinking. He was more than willing to take an oath and break it if need be. That was part of his character. He would not be pinned down by vows. But it bothered him that so many other men who he knew would die before breaking an oath stood and swore their obedience without hesitation.

The lords formed a queue. The room grew noisy once more. Iyestar stood and stretched. "Will you take the oath with me?" he asked Keshan.

"You are the lord of Tiwari, not me," Keshan said.

"I want Darvad to see your loyalty."

Keshan joined him in line. He hummed a small tune to himself as they waited. Each lord prostrated himself, took the oath, and was dubbed by Darvad's sword. The line moved slowly.

"You heard the oaths, didn't you?" Iyestar whispered.

"I have ears."

"And the one about helping the Parans."

Keshan shrugged.

Iyestar stealthily grabbed a hold of Keshan's arm and squeezed. "You must abide it. You—"

"—Don't worry. If you need me to take the oath with you, fine, I'll take the oath. But I will still do what is right, dictated by my heart, not by Darvad or by you or by anyone other than God."

Iyestar hissed into Keshan's ear. "This is serious, Keshan. I don't want you breaking this vow. In any case, I don't know why you would want to. Yudar gambled his people and his own brothers away."

"I have no interest in helping Yudar," Keshan whispered back. "You know very well I'd only help Jandu, and—"

"No." Iyestar jerked him out of line. Keshan let himself be dragged to the corner of the room. Iyestar glared down at him, his voice low and dangerous. "This is the end of your affair. Do you hear me? You will not interfere."

"It is not Jandu's fault that—"

"Listen to me, brother, and listen closely." Iyestar's voice barely controlled his anger. "I am taking the King's oath on behalf of all our people, you included. You will forget the Parans. They will endure their penance and return in three years, and then you can do whatever it is you wish with our cousin. But until then, you are not to see him. You are not to help him. You are not to even think about him, is that understood?"

"Iyestar, I am merely asking you to question—"

"My word is final!" Iyestar hissed through clenched teeth. "By God, do I have to find one of our cousins who has the power to curse to bring you in line? I will do it, I swear. Aunt Umia promised me that she would use her shartic curse on anyone if I asked her to."

"Will she curse me with the power to read minds?" Keshan asked, hoping levity would raise his brother from his rage.

Iyestar glared. "I'm serious. If I have to make her remove your ability to walk, or talk, or leave my sight, I will do so. Don't push me."

Keshan opened his mouth to reply but Iyestar was already gone, bristling as he stomped to join the line of lords once more.

He watched Iyestar bow low before Darvad. Iyestar spoke the oath clearly and carefully, and when it was over, he reached down and touched Darvad's feet. Darvad leaned down to help Iyestar stand, and then hugged him, his smile wide and honest.

"Iyestar, old friend, it is good to see you again." Darvad whispered something in Iyestar's ear, and the two laughed.

By the end of the oath-taking, it was clear which lords had not made it to the ceremony. Lord Kadal of Marshav sent a messenger begging the King's forgiveness and claiming illness. Lord Sahdin of Jezza sent a similar message.

Once the lords completed the oath-taking, they milled about the room, looking yearningly towards the garden where a feast awaited them. But Darvad held them back, begging their indulgence. He whispered something to an attendant, and a minute later, Royal Priest Onshu appeared, dressed in flowing violet-colored robes, his knotted hair thick with henna, his face marked with the tattoos of the Draya caste.

"My loyal lords," Darvad said, holding his hands out. He motioned for everyone to remain. "I would like to bring High Priest Onshu to the dais, along with my dearest friend." Darvad turned to Tarek and smiled. "Tarek? Come here please."

Tarek approached the dais with a self-conscious air.

"As God's representative here in our world," Darvad said, "I have the power to grant a rebirth to those souls worthy of blessing our noble Triya race. I have asked Draya Onshu to perform the rebirth ceremony for Tarek Amia, lord of Dragewan, to raise him to full Triya status."

Although many expected this, it still seemed to surprise some in the assembly. Tarek's eyes looked glassy with emotion as he stepped forward and bowed low before the priest.

Onshu prayed and washed Tarek's hair with holy water. He then rubbed sandalwood paste on Tarek's forehead. Tarek held out his hands and the priest lined them with henna markings. And then, in the boldest statement of all, Priest Onshu knelt before Tarek himself, hands on Tarek's feet.

"I grant you the power to protect my caste, o Triya, and trust you use the gift God has given you wisely."

Tarek could barely speak. "Thank you, Draya." The two made the sign of peace to each other, and then Onshu left.

Darvad had tears in his eyes. He and Tarek embraced, and the room broke out into applause. Keshan clapped along with them. He smiled, grateful that Darvad had chosen to do this. Of course he truly hoped that one day such gestures would be meaningless—that Suya or Triya, each man would be treated the same. But for the time being, it was as noble and equal gesture as the current laws allowed, and Keshan was proud of Darvad for it.

Darvad turned to face the lords once more, arm tight around Tarek's shoulder. "Let all men here know that Lord Tarek Amia of Dragewan is fully Triya, to be accorded all rights and honors as such. In addition, I now take this opportunity to appoint Tarek as Royal Judge for this throne, to bring justice to our kingdom, and to oversee my laws in the way only a man as noble and pure of heart as Tarek can."

Keshan felt momentarily winded. Shock flooded him, then anger. The position of Royal Judge was the most powerful in all the nation after the King, and Darvad had promised it to Keshan himself.

Keshan quickly concealed his anger. He clapped with the rest of the lords, who looked as stunned as he. Tarek was still a good choice, Keshan reassured himself. No one would be more sympathetic to the plight of the lower classes than a man who had suffered inequity himself. And Keshan hoped Tarek would be receptive to his ideas.

"I have kept you waiting long enough!" Darvad laughed. "Please join me for a feast to celebrate the occasion!" He gestured towards the garden, and immediately the men pushed their way towards the food and wine.

Keshan took his time leaving the throne room. Outside, the sun was setting, and the wind picked up. Keshan wrapped his harafa tighter around his torso, scanning for Tarek.

Even though it was Darvad's ceremony, Tarek was the man of the hour, and Keshan wasn't alone in his desire to speak with him. He made brief eye contact, and Tarek swiftly disengaged himself and came to Keshan's side.

They exchanged the sign of peace, and Keshan smiled.

"Congratulations, Lord Tarek."

"I hope you are not disappointed," Tarek said.

"Me? Upset?" Keshan smiled. "I'm delighted! I can't think of anyone who will be a fairer judge than you. And if you need any assistance from me, you know I will provide it." Keshan squeezed Tarek's shoulder. "You have to do all the hard work now—I get to simply pass you my recommendations."

"And I will treat them with the gravity they deserve," Tarek said solemnly.

And unlike any of the other sycophantic court Triya, Keshan believed him.

"We will change this world, Tarek. You, me, and Darvad."

Tarek nodded, and gave Keshan a proud smile.

"I look forward to it."

CHAPTER 19

YUDAR, ALONE, SHOULDERED THE BURDEN OF FINDING THEIR home. He believed he should be the one to suffer for their embarrassing exile. Jandu followed, asking no questions, offering no opinions. He was still too angry to speak to Yudar, too shocked by the turn of events.

Every step they took from Prasta further solidified the precariousness of their situation. In the back of Jandu's mind, the true gravity of their situation still hadn't set in. But as they hid from travelers and plunged deeper into the untamed countryside, the stark realties of exile became more and more apparent.

Yudar chose a spot far removed from civilization, in the foothills of the great northern Ekavi mountain range. Jandu, Baram and Suraya followed him up a trail tangled with vines past a small village. The trail was mostly used by pilgrims and ascetics to visit a remote holy retreat on the side of Mount Adri. The pilgrim's trail wound uphill for a day and a half before it reached the retreat and a large, placid lake that was frequented by cranes.

On the opposite end of the lake, they found a small, flat clearing in the thick of the forest, where ripe and bursting foliage drooped, thick-bowed and full of fruit, over the banks of the water. On one side of their new home, Jandu could see the smooth lake surface and the mountains beyond. On the other side was a steep drop down into a gorge cloaked by verdant palms. Trees clung to the cliffs with roots stretched across the rocks like talons. Merely looking down into the valley gave Jandu vertigo.

High above them in the dense canopy of trees, there came a constant rustle of monkeys, showing off daring feats of acrobatics.

With the monsoon hot and heavy upon them, their need for permanent shelter was dire. Their clothes and the few possessions they brought immediately began to mold. Even the leather of their shoes and belts turned green and stank with the moisture of the jungle.

Yudar took the task of building their house upon himself, speaking infrequently, working all day until his arms shook with exhaustion.

"I won't beg your forgiveness," he said, almost proudly, "because there can be none for the sin I have committed." He was in a mode of extreme self-flagellation, a look of serenity on his face as he tortured his body with the kind of hard labor a king was not raised to endure.

But Jandu and Baram did help him, because they were drowning in the monsoon. Their pitiful first attempts at shelters did little to keep them dry. None of them knew how to build so much as a hut, nor which materials held up best against the sultry, powerful winds. Their walls blew away or caved in during downpours, or rotted before their very eyes. It took months to finally construct two huts from bamboo and sandalwood that could bear the brunt of the oppressive, temperamental climate. They laid a roof with wood and thatched over this with wide leaves. They built the main hut large enough for two of them to sleep on the earth floor. An enclosed area to the side of the main hut formed their open-roofed kitchen. They crafted rough wooden boards into benches for sitting, and cleared an area against the back of the hut where they could view the calm waters of the lake while they ate.

The other hut was for the couple. It was smaller, just room enough for a bed and a small table constructed of sandalwood, and their small traveling chests. Baram and Suraya slept in there, while Jandu roughed it on the main hut's floor with Yudar.

Their new home was beautifully lonely. But even with a roof over his head, Jandu was painfully aware of his own degeneration. He was accustomed to servants taking care of menial tasks, and so now, on his own, he'd brought all the wrong things. He carried his armor and weapons up the mountain, but hadn't thought to bring a bucket. Picking banana leaves to use for plates was an all-day venture into the lush thicket. He struggled with sharpening his razors. His clothes never dried in the oppressive humidity, and when he tried to use fire to this purpose, his dejaru caught aflame.

The smell of hot, rotten feet was always around him.

Flies were everywhere, as were mosquitoes. Monkeys screamed through the trees and baboons stole their drying clothes. Worst for Jandu, the forest floor crawled with beetles. He hated beetles. And now he slept with them, worked with them, accidentally ate them. His nerves twitched with constant repulsion.

Baram made those first few months even worse. He could not bring himself to forgive Yudar for the crime of gambling away his throne and his brothers, and ceaselessly reminded Yudar of his offense. Yudar responded with a sullen calmness that he had affected shortly after the dice game, and his passivity further enraged Baram. Baram spent hours sitting beside the lake, skipping rocks, eyes raw and red with resentment.

Yudar seldom ate anything. He rarely said anything. He would just sit whispering that this wasn't Baram's fault, or Jandu's fault, or Suraya's. It was his. He had ruined them. And he was going to pay for it, he promised them.

But it was cold comfort to Jandu, who still loved his brother. Yudar's guilt brought Jandu no pleasure since he wanted to forget the dice game ever happened. Jandu knew Yudar was not himself when dice were in his hands. A trance consumed him, pushed logic and feeling from his mind, and he acted on some alien urge to gamble regardless of consequence. It was a sickness Jandu had witnessed prior to that game, but never thought could go so far.

With their need to remain hidden foremost in their minds, Jandu and his family minimized contact with other people. They did not befriend the Draya at the nearby retreat, and avoided speaking to pilgrims on the trail. The only contact they had was in the village, and on Jandu's first solo voyage to purchase necessities, he realized the true precariousness of even that. Every single villager stared openly at Jandu's blue eyes. Blue eyes were a rarity even among princes; here, in the remotest corner of Marhavad, they had never been seen before. All it would take is a rumor of a blue-eyed man with scars on his arms in a remote village to bring Darvad's henchmen.

Jandu found the costs of goods in the village appalling, especially salt, which had been commonplace in the palace but out in the wilds seemed more precious than gold. After counting the coins they brought, he realized their money would not last a season. He had to choose between an iron pot for heating water and a bag of millet. He chose the pot.

Other than the game Jandu hunted and the fruits Suraya gathered they relied on dried grain purchased in the village, and by the end of the third month, there was only a handful of rice left and no money to buy more. Jandu could do nothing but brood and watch his brothers grow thinner, soaking with sweat and rain in the monsoon heat, his proud armor tarnishing in the choking organics of the forest.

Yudar developed a cough that rattled deeply, distantly, like a faraway stranger. It kept Jandu up at night, along with the cries of baboons, the mating of tigers, the singing of peafowl, and the endless patter of insect feet.

Gradually, Jandu got better at surviving in the wild. Although he had never fetched his own meal from the palace kitchen, he could now weave his own platters in an evening. Jandu fortified and improved their hut, and they all crafted small household items for Suraya, trying to make life a little less wretched with every spoon they carved, every trap they constructed.

As always, Jandu was an impeccable hunter, although he never before had the distasteful experience of dressing a kill. Gutting a deer in the woods and carrying the bloody carcass over his shoulders for miles on end was an entirely new repugnance. Within minutes flies swarmed Jandu's entire body, the oppressive forest heat pushing the carcass limply onto his shoulder blades. Returning home, he would desperately want to change clothes after bathing in the lake, but he only had a few choices, and his other pair of trousers was already tearing at the cuffs and stained.

On one of Jandu's hunting trips, he found a small clearing in the forest, about fifteen minutes walk from the lake. Large camphor trees circled the clearing's edges, and cashew nut and horse flowers hedged the cool forest floor. A faceless, waist-high stone sculpture stood sentinel in the center of the clearing. Jandu had no idea who the statue was of or who built it, but it appeared very old, time having worn its surface smooth, decades of rain washing the finer carvings into nothing but soft lines in a vague human shape.

Jandu claimed this reclusive space in the jungle as his own, and went there daily, seeking a moment's respite from the constant haranguing of his depressed family, luxuriating in the cool shadows of the large trees. He leaned against the statue and stared up at the canopy and the thick clouds, pregnant with moisture, and succumbed to the only peace he'd felt since the dice game. Even the ever-present shrieks of forest life seemed quieter in this tranquil refuge.

But even these stolen moments of solitude did little to soothe Jandu's burning heart. Losing Keshan amplified Jandu's anger, turned it into pain. More than any other reason, his forced separation from his lover was the fuel that fired Jandu's craving for vengeance. Darvad's crooked game had pried Keshan from Jandu's arms. And for that alone, he would pay.

◆◆◆

One day after a successful hunt, Jandu returned home with a barking deer, large enough to feed them for several days, but not so big that its meat could go bad before they could eat it all. Baram skinned and cleaned the carcass, while Jandu washed in the lake. He chased off two baboons that tried to make off with his blue dejaru, and stepped on a fire ant as he gracelessly pulled on his once-white trousers. By the time he sat down with his family to eat, he was in a terrible mood. His head ached from the heat and heartache. Keshan's absence felt like a physical wound.

The rest of his family were in equal dispirits. Yudar's new religious stoicism prevented him from eating meat, and so he once again went hungry. And Baram spoke, for the hundredth time, of war.

"It isn't right for us to be sitting and rotting in a shack!" Baram cried, his fists shaking as he spoke. Suraya dodged his flailing arms as she ladled out broth and handed each of her husbands a banana leaf plate piled with roasted venison on top. Jandu noticed the rough callouses on her hands.

"We should declare war, Yudar." Baram pointed a finger at his older brother. "It is the Triya thing to do."

"We must serve out this penance," Yudar said calmly. He sipped at his broth, refusing the venison. "Only after we fulfill the agreed-upon conditions of the dice game can we ask for our half of the kingdom back. If Darvad refuses us, then we may discuss war."

"We have few allies now," Suraya commented.

Jandu didn't understand how Yudar could refuse the venison. He stuffed his mouth with the sweet, hot flesh, feeling his bones strengthen with the direly needed food. The meat sat rich and warm in his stomach, radiating energy through his limbs.

"I don't care," Baram sulked. "I'd rather lose a war that is justified than languish here in the wilderness."

Suraya sighed. "Your brother made a promise." Suraya had a habit now of not addressing Yudar directly. "We must honor that promise."

"The game was rigged." Baram repeated the sentence like a mantra. He said it every day, dozens of times a day, staring into space, feeding his own fury. "The game was rigged."

Jandu widened his eyes in mock-surprise. "The game was rigged? You don't say!"

"Don't, Jandu," Yudar said quietly.

"Tell me more, Baram! I had no idea." Jandu threw his banana leaf into the fire.

"We will get our vengeance, Baram," Yudar told Baram. "Just be patient."

"Patience!" Baram shook his head and stomped into the hut.

Jandu looked at Baram's half-finished plate, and reached over to steal some of his venison. Suraya slapped his hand away.

"Bad," she said. She smirked at him.

Jandu took a smaller piece, putting it on Yudar's plate.

"Yudar, you must eat something," Jandu said.

Yudar smiled sweetly. "I had broth. It was delicious, Suraya."

"You're skin and bones," Jandu said.

"Nonsense. I still walk for miles every day."

Jandu looked to Suraya for help, but she wasn't yet willing to forgive Yudar either. She barely acknowledged Yudar's presence. Now she sat down beside Jandu and started her own meal.

Jandu sighed, and then put the piece of venison back on Baram's plate. He knew Baram would be back later to eat what was left behind. Baram used to consume three or four meals for every one Jandu had. Baram's chronic hunger aggravated his surly disposition.

Jandu helped Suraya clear up after dinner. Afterwards, as Yudar read his holy scrolls in the fading light, Jandu searched for Baram.

He found his brother by the lakeside, skipping rocks. The sun set over the jungle, lending the air a magical pinkish glow. It reminded Jandu of Keshan's Yashva home.

Waves gently massaged the small circular pebbles of the bank with a quiet hiss. Jandu squatted beside his brother, chewing on a blade of grass like Keshan used to. Even that small gesture seemed to bring Keshan closer to him.

"Are you all right?" Jandu asked Baram.

Baram didn't look at him. He kept throwing stones. "You know I'm not mad at you."

"I know."

"I just… I can't let it go."

"Then don't," Jandu said. "But keep it to yourself." He sighed. "We have to be here for three years. Don't make every dinner a nightmare. Please, if only for Suraya's sake."

Baram dropped the stones in his left hand. "I won't pretend, Jandu. I won't act like everything is fine when it isn't. We're starving and poor and miserable."

"I know that!" Jandu swallowed to control his own anger.

"It's Yudar's fault for landing us here, and Darvad's fault for his trickery."

"Reminding him of it every five seconds will not change anything."

"I'm not going to pretend like this isn't the nightmare it is."

"Then stop sulking and do something with your anger," Jandu said. "Hunt. Build. Stab fish. Whatever. Just do something."

Baram suddenly whirled and threw a rock into the overgrowth behind them.

Jandu looked at Baram like he was insane. And then he heard a voice.

"Ouch!"

In an instant Jandu and Baram were up, charging the figure hidden in the bushes. Baram knocked him to the ground before he could speak and Jandu stood ready to punch him.

"My lords! It's me, Rishak! Rishak Paria!"

Jandu squinted at the man. He was dressed as a pilgrim, in plain white trousers and a white shirt. But nearby, Jandu saw a healthy, well-muscled horse, laden with goods.

Baram hauled Rishak up by his collar and glared at him.

"Suraya's brother! Rishak!" Rishak cried again, holding his hands together in the sign of peace.

Baram threw his arms around him and lifted him in the air, laughing. Jandu smiled as well, although Rishak's sudden presence made him nervous.

"Our apologies, we didn't recognize you!" Baram cried, finally letting Rishak free of his hug.

Rishak brushed leaves from his clothing. "I've been traveling in disguise."

"Rishak!"

Suraya ran from the direction of their hut and threw her arms around her brother's neck.

None of the brothers knew Rishak well. He was two years younger than Suraya, but renowned as an accomplished fighter despite his youth. He oversaw the State of Karuna's massive army, and personally led several battles against the barbarian lands to the west. He was lithe and tawny, but had Suraya's thick hair and tear-shaped eyes.

Rishak hugged his sister tightly and smiled at Baram and Jandu. Within a moment, Yudar came out as well, alerted by the commotion.

"How can you be here? How did you find us? Why are you here?" Suraya laughed and cried as she barraged him with questions.

Rishak kissed his sister's cheek. "Keshan Adaru found out where you were and sent me."

Jandu felt months of anger, frustration, and resentment evaporate.

"If he can find us, so can Darvad," Baram said, scowling. "We should leave."

Silence filled the evening air. Jandu couldn't bear the thought of leaving after it had taken them so long to build the tiny home that they had.

Suraya served her brother hot broth and offered him the wood bench in the hut. Illuminated by firelight, her face looked dark and beautiful.

Rishak sat with the other men and scoffed at their concerns. "Do you know how hard it was to find you? No one will be able to repeat what I have done. Besides, I had Keshan's help, and he was only able to locate you after he had a vision of Jandu at the priest's retreat on the other side of the lake."

As Rishak drank his broth, he told them of King Darvad's oath-taking ceremony, and the clause that required all lords to swear not to help the Parans or face becoming outcaste.

"Did no one protest?" Baram asked.

Rishak shrugged. "No one openly said anything. But trust me, there was plenty of grumbling. Most of your allies believed you were tricked, Yudar, and still support you in their hearts, even if they cannot with their words."

"Darvad is king for now," Yudar said, looking grave. "It would be foolish of them to disagree. How they act in three years, however, is another matter."

"Did you take the vow?" Suraya asked, refilling his cup.

"Father did," Rishak said. He kissed his sister's hand. Suraya glowed for the first time since the dice game. "Everyone did."

"Even Keshan?" Jandu couldn't help but ask.

"Iyestar took the oath on behalf of Tiwari," Rishak said. "So, yes, even Keshan has promised not to help." Rishak grinned. "But, in typical Keshan style, he immediately broke that promise by asking me to give you gifts from him, should I find you."

"Gifts?" Suraya smiled. "Did you bring soap?"

Rishak laughed. "Father said that would be the first thing you would ask for." He looked to Jandu. "Can you help me unload the horse?"

They had tied his horse to a nearby tree. Jandu and Rishak un-strapped the heavy saddle bags, and then unsaddled his horse. The last of the sun disappeared as the Parans gathered around Rishak's bags anxiously, like children awaiting sweets. Rishak first pulled out a thick roll of paper, which he handed to Jandu. "Keshan asked me to give this to you." Rishak looked at Jandu with curiosity. "And he sent a small chest for you."

Jandu only half-listened to Rishak's words. He was too busy staring at the letter Rishak brought to him from Keshan.

Rishak presented Suraya some new zaharis from their father and, as if reading her mind, a flagon of jasmine oil and several cakes of soap, along with spices and ghee for cooking.

Jandu opened Keshan's chest and tears came to his eyes. Keshan sent gold coins. Jandu wasn't sure if the tears were for shame at taking money from his friend or relief at not needing to starve any longer.

Despite the long journey, Rishak could only stay for a night, worried that his absence would be noted and someone alerted to the Paran's location. He let his sister serve him leftovers from their dinner. As he discussed politics with Yudar, Jandu made an excuse to depart and practically ran from his family into the dark forest.

It was harder for Jandu to find his secret forest clearing in the dark, but the large moon provided enough illumination to go by shadows, and he brought a torch along to read the letter. The sounds of night wildlife crept around him, but he no longer cared. He had a letter from Keshan. All threats seemed paltry.

Jandu propped his torch against the statue and then unrolled the scroll. Keshan's handwriting was smooth and curvy, sexual, and he wrote each letter with careful deliberation, the layout carefully planned, as if this were the third draft of a composition.

My beautiful, beloved Jandu—

I wake up and think about you, the smell of your skin, the taste of your lips, the way you walk, a tiger about to pounce, so graceful, so lithe in your movements, so confident, and yet so calm, lazy almost, a luxurious grace that defines what it means to be a prince.

Iyestar is yelling at me right now. I'm supposed to be sitting downstairs in the reception hall, working out a land agreement between the Sharnas and the Chafri. But my heart isn't in it. I want to be with you. The need weighs upon me like a wound, constantly reminding me of its presence, aching for attention.

There is not a moment of the day I don't feel your long fingers upon my flesh, your hot mouth upon me, taking me deep inside of you. Nights are a torment of heated memories. The gentleness of your caress, the roughness of your entry. My skin is on fire, imagining you kissing the places that are yours alone, your fullness penetrating both my body and my soul.

Jandu - I declare my absolute affection for you. I have become out of sorts in your absence, my desire for your touch driving me mad with need. I hope you have more restraint than I. My family is used to my lascivious ways, but you are living with a king who wishes he were a sage. I hope he never suspects what it is I burn to do to you.

I wish there were some way I could ease your terrible burden. I hope the gift I've enclosed provides some assistance to you, although I know nothing I can send will give you the relief you deserve. The fact that you are being punished for your brother's sins insults my sense of justice, and fuels my hunger for change. We have to hope for a different Marhavad, where a man is guilty of his crime alone, and that a family should not be forced into such torment because of the sins of one.

I would tell you of my successes in getting Darvad to acknowledge some of my legal changes, but I know exactly what you would do. You would roll your eyes and say, 'for God's sake, stop talking politics.' And then you would kiss me, and I would realize, yes, you are right, there is no need to focus solely on politics. There are other beautiful things in this world worth savoring. And one of them is you.

Yours, in this life and all others, Keshan.

Jandu laughed, eyes brimming with tears. Words that would have scandalized him a year ago now sent bolts of desire through him. He returned to the huts and used the last of their writing cloth and ink to quickly draft a return response to Keshan. As Rishak shared a wineskin with his sister and other brothers-in-law, Jandu sat by candlelight in the other hut, putting to words his hunger for Keshan's heart. He wrote briefly of their tormented three months in the forest, the agony of seclusion, of starvation. He thanked Keshan copiously for his generous gift, and then he made a request.

Jandu described in detail the location of the stone statue he had found in the dense forest. He even drew a map. He understood the risk; if anyone but Keshan received the letter, their location could be discovered and they would be undone. But Jandu's desperation for correspondence with Keshan was beyond reason. He didn't care about the risks.

Jandu asked Keshan to send a servant when he could, to pick up a letter from Jandu and to leave a letter in return. That way, they could stay in touch over the three years.

Jandu signed the letter and, as a last minute decision, drew a picture of himself trying to shave without a mirror and using his sword. Jandu had always been good at simple illustrations, and the picture was amusing enough that it left him grinning from ear to ear as he sealed the letter and brought it to Rishak.

In the morning, he begged Rishak to keep the letter secret and safe, and then stood with his brothers and Suraya to thank Rishak for his much-needed visit. As he disappeared from sight, and the rains started dumping as if on cue, only Jandu remained upbeat within their family. He was going to continue his relationship with Keshan, regardless of distance, vows, or logic.

CHAPTER 20

THE ROAD CONNECTING PRASTA WITH THE STATE OF MARSHAV
was wide and well maintained. Nevertheless, the season's
unusually strong monsoon pitted the soil and crumbled cobblestones. Two bridges washed out and Tarek's contingent was
forced to take alternate routes for long stretches, delaying him
further. Tarek's chariots crawled northwards, every rainstorm
the cause for another delay in another infernal village.

If Tarek traveled alone, he would not have minded. On
horseback, he was swift. He could have delivered King Darvad's
demands to the errant lord of Marshav as scheduled.

But as Royal Judge, Tarek now had an entourage to travel
with, including ministers from the royal palace, servants to
tend to their camps and food, and a detachment of Dragewan
soldiers for his protection. He traveled endlessly. In the two
months that he'd held the position, he'd been home less than
four days at a time.

And everywhere they went, people stopped him, demanding an immediate court where their cases could be heard.

After days of protracted travel and endless repairs to the
chariots, the rains finally ceased. Tarek hoped to make up for
lost time.

With a clear sky Tarek saw the countryside's bucolic
beauty. North of Prasta, Marhavad rolled in lush plains
between the Yaru and Patari rivers. Rice fields spanned the
horizon, and small, brightly-painted houses clustered along
the roadside in welcoming villages. They passed through the
small State of Shiadi and then cut across the fertile expanse of
Karuna. They passed fields of sugar cane, orchards ripe with

mangoes and oranges, and vineyards stretching to the river in long tunnels of vines.

Tarek had never been this far north. The people began to look different. Their skin was browner, less olive, and the sun bleached their black hair into shades of dark red and mahogany. Karuna mother-of-pearl decorated the doors of every house, and the women draped strings of bells around their waists and wrists, creating a music that jangled through the village. The men wore kohl paint under their eyes, and the Draya priests sported flamboyantly decorative tattoos on their foreheads and cheeks.

They stopped that evening at a larger settlement, a village near a lake, nestled within soft hills covered in green tea bushes. The air smelled fragrant, and a herd of cattle heralded their arrival.

The bright blue wooden structures of the village clustered around a mill beside the stream that fed the lake. Tarek waited in his chariot as servants saw to the best lodgings for their lord. If none could be found, he would be sleeping in his tent again.

This was not a hardship. Tarek almost laughed when Darvad first showed him what a Triya's tent could be like. Layers of animal skins covered the vast space, and the thick, brightly dyed wool kept out the wind and the elements. Large pieces of teak furniture stood amongst burning stands of fragrant sandalwood torches. It was more luxuriant than the nicest house in Tarek's old village.

"My lord." Tarek's servant, Laiu, bowed low at the foot of the chariot. "The innkeeper has a guest house worthy of Triya accommodation, and invites you to stay there."

"I accept." Tarek stepped from the chariot, stretching his arms as he did so. Long journeys on bumpy roads made his back ache. He rolled his shoulders.

Laiu noticed. "My lord, I will dispatch men to prepare your chambers for you. Would you like me to send a masseuse to you this evening as well?"

Tarek smiled. "Why not?" After all, he deserved it. He was running this errand for the King, he might as well get something out of it himself.

Tarek told Laiu to instruct the villagers that he would hear petitions before departing in the morning, and then he slunk off to his room for a bath and a rest.

As he sat, soaking in hot water scented with rose petals and rosemary, Tarek pondered Darvad's decision to make him Royal Judge.

Within the first week of his new post, Tarek strove to keep his promise to Keshan Adaru. He used Keshan's cleverly researched and worded documentation to propose sweeping changes to Darvad.

But Darvad urged caution instead. "Not yet, Tarek," he said. He smiled benevolently. "Be patient. Let us enact one law at a time, slowly, so as not to alienate anyone. Besides, I have a more pressing matter for the Royal Judge to attend to."

Darvad asked Tarek, as his first task in his new position, to go to the State of Marshav and demand an oath of fealty from Lord Kadal, who had not attended the oath-taking ceremony.

While this didn't seem like the most pressing matter for Tarek, it apparently ranked high enough on Darvad's list of unfinished business to justify the trip and expense. It was Darvad's first demand of his friend as King. At the same time, Darvad had demanded that Druv use his network of spies to find the Parans, and cautioned Tarek to keep an eye out for any clue, however small, on his journey north.

"Everything depends upon us finding the Parans in the next three years," Darvad said. "If you hear so much as a whisper that sounds intriguing, let me or Druv know. We will find them."

Tarek did not linger on the unpleasant obsession Darvad already had on maintaining a throne he had only just received. Instead, Tarek focused on the job at hand, convincing Lord Kadal that an oath of fealty was better than war.

Tarek thought the journey would be easy. He had no idea how popular the Royal Judge was, or how every villager would seek him out to be heard.

Now, in this quiet Karuna village, Tarek dreaded the idea of going outside and being thronged by those desperate for justice. He stayed in his bath until the water grew cold, and ate his dinner alone in his rooms. One of the servants massaged Tarek's tight shoulders into butter, and he luxuriated on the soft bed, the warm autumn breezes, thinking he could just stay there until dawn, and then dash out before anyone noticed him.

But he grew restless alone in the big house. Tarek finished his ablutions and read some of the documentation he hoped to memorize as Royal Judge, but his heart wasn't in it. He could hear the Dragewan soldiers singing outside his house. They set up tents in front of the home, and were now eating their dinner and playing music softly by a campfire. The sounds of men reveling downstairs plunged Tarek into loneliness. What was he doing here, in this house in the middle of nowhere, so far from Darvad, so far from his own family?

His soldiers raised a familiar tune from Tarek's childhood. It lured him outside, away from his solitude. A few men patrolled the camp, but most huddled around the campfire, sharing glasses of cheap rice wine and singing along with the beat one of them tapped out on a small drum.

When Tarek stepped out of the house, they stopped the music and stood to bow before him.

"Please, sit down, sit down," he said. "I just wanted to enjoy the music with you."

Tarek sat next to the young commander whom he had slept with several months before. As soon as Tarek made eye contact with the young commander, the commander blushed crimson.

Tarek was mad at himself for not remembering the man's name. But he could not tactfully ask any of the other soldiers without raising suspicion.

"Hello," he said to the commander.

The commander's face brightened further. He bowed low. "My lord. I trust my men have not kept your from your sleep."

"No, I wanted some fresh air and company," Tarek told the man. The commander looked years younger than the other soldiers, and yet he was in charge. He had to be quite a warrior to have advanced to his rank at such a young age.

"Your presence honors us," the commander said.

Tarek stared at the man's helmet. He had polished it to a gleaming gold. Tarek couldn't remember seeing anyone else with such a finely cared-for head piece. It made him smile. "I'm sorry—what is your name again?"

The man looked up at Tarek in surprise. "Anant."

Tarek smiled. "Right. Anant. I'm sorry." He touched the commander's shoulder briefly.

Nervously, the drummer began to play again. After a few drinks, the men ignored Tarek.

The commander sat beside him, looking at Tarek out of the corner of his eye. Tarek found it endearing.

"How old are you?" Tarek asked him in a low voice. He needn't have worried about his question carrying—several of the men who had been trying to sleep woke up from the loud singing, and now joined in, shouting with equal verve.

"I'm twenty one, my lord."

"You seem young to be a commander, Anant." Tarek liked how the name played off his tongue.

Anant smiled proudly. "My father was a commander in the Dragewan army before me. He taught me well. I advanced quickly."

"I see." Tarek turned to face him. Anant smiled back readily. Tarek couldn't remember how he had first flirted with this man, having blacked out most of that night, but now he realized that it couldn't have been hard. Anant was very receptive to flirtation.

"Are you happy in Dragewan's army?" Tarek asked. He was suddenly curious about what the common people said about him.

Anant nodded his head enthusiastically. "We have the finest army in Marhavad, considering our size." He grinned. "You are spoken of as a wise and strong leader."

Tarek studied Anant's features, thinking that maybe the young commander had been the one to start flirting with him that first night. Anant had thick black hair pulled back neatly in a knot, and dark, almond-shaped eyes with long lashes. Anant stretched his arms upwards. He wore an armored breastplate, but Tarek could still admire the tightness of his stomach as the armor slid upwards. Anant's skin was strongly masculine, covered evenly in dark hair, his face already darkened with stubble.

"Your defeat of the other lords who challenged you is a testament to both your own prowess as a warrior and to the State of Dragewan," Anant continued. "And the fact that you had to fight unfairly has inspired all of us in your army."

Tarek smiled. "It didn't feel inspiring at the time."

Anant lowered his eyes. "Of course, my lord. But I, for one, admire King Darvad for raising your caste and showing the world that true greatness is in the person, not the social standing."

Tarek swallowed. He really wanted to take this young man into the house. But mentioning Darvad's righteousness curbed Tarek's primal desires.

Tarek adjusted himself and then stood up. "I should turn in."

"Would you like me to accompany you?" Anant asked quietly.

Tarek liked the man's nervous honesty. "Not tonight. I'm on a holy mission for the King."

"Of course." Anant's face burned. He lowered his head. He stepped back from Tarek.

Tarek quickly put his hand on Anant's arm, and looked around to make sure no one paid them any attention. He leaned down to whisper in Anant's ear.

"But when we return to Dragewan, we will have to find some time to know one another better." He smiled, and with relief, saw Anant smile back.

"Good night, my lord," Anant said, bowing with his hands together.

"Good night, Anant." Tarek took one last lingering look at the young man, and then forced himself to turn around and return to the house.

◆◆◆

The remainder of their journey north passed swiftly, now that the rains ceased. Large Karuna fields gave way to smaller crops, separated by low stone walls. As they entered the State of Marshav, Tarek could feel the difference in the very air. People seemed more aggressive here, more on edge. Lord Kadal was renowned to be supported by the people but tyrannical in his rule, swiftly punishing those out of order. The straight lines of the Marshav fields bore testament to the vassal's deep sense of symmetry.

They made camp in an empty field beside the road that evening, and Tarek once more joined the soldiers around the fire. He got to know more about the young commander in his army. Although somewhat naïve and by no means sophisticated, Anant was both kind and enjoyable company. He came from an ancient Triya family that had much prestige in Dragewan but little money. Anant's honest, fierce loyalty to him despite his Suya birth gave Tarek a boost of confidence he had not known he needed.

Their approach to the city did not go unnoticed. A scout for Lord Kadal appeared on the horizon at dawn and then turned swiftly at a full gallop. The road congested as it met the Patari River and followed the water's edge into Marshav itself, an ancient walled city where the lord sat in a towering fortress at its center, surrounded by a garrison of the Marshav army.

Tarek strung his bow and had it ready in his chariot car. With the banner of the Royal Judge on his standard, Tarek attracted his usual attention. But here, people appeared wary, eyeing the soldiers with practiced caution.

At the heavy wooden gate to Lord Kadal's fortress, Tarek brought his entourage to a halt. The door opened automatically, and a steward appeared, groveling lowly before Tarek.

"Blessings upon you, Royal Judge!" the man cooed. He prostrated himself. "I have been asked by Lord Kadal to show you immediately to his reception hall. He is honored by your visit and offers you the best of Marshav hospitality."

Tarek and his ministers made their way inside the fortress as Anant and the soldiers guarded their chariots and watched over Tarek's servants. A heavy tension made the air thick. Tarek's hands twitched beside his sword hilt.

The fortress was sparsely decorated but vast in size, and Tarek's party walked a long corridor before coming to Lord Kadal's reception hall. Inside, Lord Kadal sat on his dais, fanned by servants and surrounded by his ministers. As soon as Tarek entered the room, Kadal rose from his seat and bowed low to Tarek.

"Blessings upon you, Royal Judge," Kadal said, bringing his hands together in the sign of peace. Kadal was older than Tarek, in his forties, but he was strong and fit. His eyes burned intensely.

"And to you, Lord Kadal." Tarek returned the gesture.

"I trust your journey was pleasant?"

"It was long, and delayed by the weather."

"I am sorry to hear that." Lord Kadal motioned to a servant off to the side. "See that Lord Tarek and his men have the finest housing and our hospitality for their stay." Kadal turned back to face Tarek. "May I inquire as to the nature of your visit? Your presence is an honor, but we were not informed of your journey."

"I had no time to send word ahead," Tarek said carefully. "I have come on behalf of our King, who has asked that I collect your oath of fealty."

Kadal did not react. Tarek assumed he must have known the reason for his appearance.

"Of course, my lord," Kadal said, smiling. "I did send a messenger to Prasta apologizing for my absence at the ceremony. Unfortunately, my health is a fickle thing, and I found myself too ill to leave for any extended journey during the oath-taking. However, I am more than happy to offer my fealty to you now."

Relief coursed through Tarek. He had not wanted a fight. But Kadal still had not read all of the terms of the oath. As Tarek handed Kadal the scroll with the oath, he watched Kadal closely. Kadal had been a staunch supporter of Yudar, and would not like the clause preventing any help to the Parans. But Kadal was a skilled diplomat. He showed no reaction to the document, merely nodding when he reached the end.

"I will abide the contract and welcome the new King as my leader," Kadal said.

"You read the clause stating that you will need to make changes to the way the Suya are treated? We will be initiating new laws regarding their status as land owners and their rights in the courts." Tarek could not help but ask the question. It might not have been pressing to Darvad, but it was to him.

"Naturally," Kadal said with a smooth smile. "I read the document entirely. I will abide your new laws as Royal Judge as I abided the laws of your predecessor."

For a moment, a giddy sense of excitement coursed through Tarek. Perhaps Keshan's changes would not be as difficult to press through as Darvad had feared. Perhaps Tarek could actually make changes that would improve the situation of a great number of people.

Kadal was a traditionalist, Yudar's ally, and a religious conservative. And if he was willing to make the changes in concurrence with the law, then anything was possible.

Tarek rose from his seat and offered Kadal the sign of peace.

"Then it is my great honor to stay with you this night, and return to Prasta in the morning to share the good news with the King."

"Tell King Darvad he has my blessing, and my loyalty," Kadal said, standing as well. The two bowed to each other. "Now, let me show you to your quarters."

"Thank you."

And as they walked the cold stone hallway, Lord Kadal—Shentari traditionalist, a man who would have barred Tarek from entering his chambers only a short month ago—reached out and touched Tarek's shoulder.

"I look forward to your changes with anticipation," Kadal said. He gave Tarek's shoulder a squeeze.

It felt like absolution.

CHAPTER 21

FOLLOWING RISHAK'S VISIT, JANDU TOOK SOME OF THE GOLD Keshan gave them and set off for the village. He returned with a cow, lentils, rice, and seeds to start their own garden.

He also returned with a small roll of parchment and ink.

The parchment cost dearly, but Jandu justified the secret expense as his only way to remain sane in the forest. The night he returned, he started a letter to Keshan. Baram and Suraya had retired for the night, and Yudar slept fitfully on his grass mat on the floor. The thin light of the butter lamp cast shadows everywhere. The rough parchment jarred his pen nib, and the ink blotched in parts and ran in others. But Jandu wrote anyway, desperate to confess his hidden feelings to somebody.

Jandu heard a stifled moan from his brother Baram in the other hut. He smirked. Even the deprivation of living impoverished in the forest hadn't cured Baram and Suraya of their sexual appetites.

Jandu wrote down the explicit things he wished Keshan could to do to him. A warm heaviness filled Jandu as he described the places he wanted to kiss on Keshan's body. He furtively glanced at Yudar's sleeping form, realizing that if he got caught with this letter, he was doomed.

Jandu signed the letter, flush with desire. In the spirit of his former letter, he also signed this one with a little stick figure drawing, showing Baram and Suraya screwing in one hut, Yudar sleeping next to him, and Jandu sitting on the floor by a candle writing. Again, the picture was so absurd he couldn't help but smile. He knew Keshan would love it.

He gently rolled the letter and placed it in a sandalwood box he had made that morning. He had originally planned on delivering the letter in the daylight, but he was too excited to sleep, and had grown used to walking to his secret statue in the darkness. He slipped out of the silent hut and plunged into the jungle darkness.

Jandu kept Zandi strung and his hand free to reach his quiver in case a wild animal approached. The other day he had been startled by a panther, which had looked at him oddly and then simply walked away. The panther had been far too beautiful to shoot, although Yudar chastised him later, saying the panther's skin could have been a luxuriant addition to their measly home.

It took twice as long for Jandu to find his statue than it did in the light, but once his eyes adjusted to the clearing, he spotted the smooth stone sculpture with ease. He put the letter box in an alcove at the statue's feet. It would take a person over a month to travel from Tiwari to this location. Jandu calculated that, in the best case scenario, it would be at least two months for Keshan to get back to him. After all, Rishak still had to travel all that way back.

But Jandu was willing to wait. After all, he had three years to fill—what were a few months?

◆◆◆

Life fell into a mundane routine of chores.

Yudar tended their cow, fished, and maintained their small garden plot. Baram cooked and crafted items for their house from what they could find in the forest. Suraya swept and cleaned their clothes, she sewed patches and washed cooking pots and tried her best to fight back the constant threat of being consumed by the jungle.

And Jandu spent most of his time hunting and foraging. He gathered firewood. He sharpened their weapons. He set traps throughout the woods and checked them daily. He worked with Baram to make constant improvements to their roof, which leaked over the monsoon and now, during the dry winter, kept blowing away in sudden gusts of wind. He slunk down to the village to watch the Jegora tan hides, and after learning their secrets, became adept at the process. Suraya's hut filled with furs. Baram accused him of trying to woo her before his year, but only jokingly, since he slept on the furs as well.

And he waited for news from Keshan.

Each day, he checked the clearing, only to find his box still there. He wrote more letters, one every few days, so that the box nearly burst with them, gathered at the base of the stone sculpture like an offering, each letter detailing the daily monotonies of his difficult new life, each letter sweetened with sex talk, each one accompanied by a clever line drawing at the signature, a small sketch of Jandu and his troubles in the forest.

Every time Jandu saw his own letters, his heart broke a little more. It had been over two months since Rishak's visit—Keshan had to have received his original request by now.

And then finally, one morning, Jandu stood, frozen, as he stared at the cream-colored scroll that lay on the forest floor, replacing Jandu's box of letters.

Jandu laughed out loud and fell upon the scroll like a starving cat on cream. The scroll wrapped around two beautiful silver dowels, and the cloth itself smelled perfumed. Incense and ocean water and Keshan's own unique coconut butter smell seemed to waft off the scroll, and it brought tears to Jandu's eyes. This letter had been touched by Keshan's own hands, making Jandu flush with longing. He ran his fingers over the text over and over again, rereading each word to see if he could extract more meaning. The letter began with Keshan admonishing Jandu for being so careless.

My sweet Jandu,

You are an idiot! What is wrong with you? I can't believe you were foolish enough to send me a map to your location. That may be the stupidest thing you've ever done, not to mention beginning this dangerous correspondence. This is very risky. I hope you understand what is at stake.

Having said that, I now solemnly swear to write you as many letters as I can. I will have my loyal servant Chezek make the journey north to your location as often as I can spare him. Write me constantly. Write me dozens of letters. I want Chezek to return with chests full of your words. I want to feel you through your letters.

I feel terrible for the burden you are going through (although I still think it's funny that none of you remembered to bring a bucket to the forest). It sounds as though you are suffering, and it makes me sick in my heart to think of you in such need.

Your drawing was fantastic. I love your artwork—you should do more illustrations, Jandu, you have true talent.

Now, let me tell you want I want you to draw a picture of. I want an image of you, your great body and fantastic cock, pinning me to the earth, pushing deep into me, your breath on the back of my neck as you fuck me senseless. I want you to make me feel it with your drawing, and as you draw, think of my fingers upon you, trailing up the insides of your thighs, stroking the irresistible softness of your scrotum, my fingers dancing upwards, pulling your shaft into my mouth—can you feel this ?— and I pull you to the back of my throat, the warmth and wetness of my lips upon you, milking you to a sweet, strangled release that echoes through that infernal forest.

I'll send Chezek back for a second round next month. Meanwhile, Iyestar is drunk as usual and I can hear him down the hall starting an argument with my mother.

Iyestar visited Darvad in Prasta a week ago. He says Mazar does poorly in your absence. Apparently, the great Mazar talks of nothing but you, Jandu, your bravery, your archery, and your nobility. Know that you and your brothers are missed dearly by those you left behind in Prasta.

Write me soon. My flute feels dead in my hands without you to inspire it.

With eternal love, your Keshan.

At the end of the letter, Keshan had been inspired by Jandu's line drawing to draw a small cartoon of his own. It was of Keshan, kneeling, hands together, promising not to help the Parans. Then, right next to it, it showed an extremely graphic image of the same Keshan stick figure sucking on Jandu's penis.

Jandu laughed out loud. He touched the letter over and over, moved beyond words. Jandu looked over his shoulder, terrified of detection. But he realized that no one in his family knew of the glade, and so he felt safe.

But keeping the letter was another issue.

The logical thing would be to burn it. But Jandu couldn't imagine doing such a thing. This letter gave him hope. It brought Keshan to him. Without it, he might as well just commit suicide, as he would never be happy again.

But he couldn't take it home. Even though Jandu kept a small chest of personal belongings in the hut, it was still available to anyone in his family. If Yudar found this letter, complete with a drawing of Keshan sucking Jandu's cock, it would be beyond horrible. Yudar would probably just kill him. The memory of the execution Jandu had seen in Prasta shuddered through Jandu.

There were moments, like this, when reason fled Jandu. A desire to run away from his family suddenly overwhelmed him. After all, it was Yudar's fault he was here. And if his brother knew anything about what dark secrets lurked in Jandu's heart, all of Jandu's fidelity would mean nothing. Yudar would banish him, at the least, and kill him at the worst.

I could leave them.

The thought flowered and then died in Jandu's heart. Escaping his family to go live with Keshan was a fantastic idea, but would never be more than a fantasy. Regardless of how Yudar would feel about Jandu's secret, Jandu still owed his older brother loyalty. It was the responsibility of family, and his duty as the youngest prince. And he would serve his brother first, and then see to his own needs afterwards.

Besides, even if Jandu left his family, he would still have to serve the rest of his exile before returning to Tiwari or risk making Keshan an outcaste. Better to be in exile with people he loved than completely alone.

With great emotion, Jandu slowly rolled up Keshan's letter. No, he wouldn't burn it. He wouldn't do that, even for Yudar. But he would hide it. He stashed the letter in a tree until he constructed two more sandalwood boxes—one to bury his beloved letters from Keshan in, and the other to hold the new set of letters Jandu couldn't wait to write.

These letters became more than just a correspondence with his friend. They were Jandu's life line, his connection with someone in the real world, away from the poverty of the forest, away from exile. The letters gave Jandu strength. And in this strength, Jandu's optimism returned.

◆◆◆

Over the next six months, Jandu received three letters from Keshan. Each word from his lover raised his spirits far above the damp and dreary places the forest dragged him into. Their food supply waned again, but Jandu didn't care. He traveled farther from home each day in order to find hunting grounds, but it didn't matter. His heart was full with Keshan's love. In his mind he repeated each sweet word over and over until his eyes shone with his inner happiness, and his joy radiated outwards, lighting his family as well, giving to them the strength and courage they needed to survive their terrible first year of privation.

One morning, he decided to write an entire letter to Keshan comprised entirely of drawings. He packed a satchel of his ink and some prepared birch bark, having run out of writing cloth several letters ago. On his way to his secret glade, he kissed his brother Baram's forehead, as Baram separated a pot of milk into curds and whey.

He whistled the tune he had learned in Tiwari and went down to the lake, where Suraya washed their clothes. Jandu snuck up behind her and tickled her under her arms. She screamed and threw a wet towel in his face.

Jandu pranced around the side of the hut, to the small clearing between the lush forest and their hut. Yudar tended their cow, speaking to her soothingly.

Jandu gave Yudar a slice of his rose apple, and smiled. Jandu had discovered that Yudar ate more if he were offered small snacks throughout the day. Yudar wouldn't sit down to a large bowl of soup. But he would greedily partake in small servings of curds, or fresh fruit, and several cups of broth, as long as they were brought to him in little increments. Suraya didn't have the patience to do it, but Jandu did.

"I'm off," he announced, waving to his family as he headed down the small muddy path that led to the pilgrim's trail. Yudar, Baram, and Suraya waved back, all of them smiling, Baram and Suraya looking at each other with the unspoken question as to why Jandu suddenly snapped into such high spirits.

Of course, none of them had idea why Jandu had sprung out of his depression. But Jandu returned to his old self, laughing all the time, telling jokes, and spontaneously singing and bragging about his magnificence. And once he stepped free of his melancholy, they all did. Jandu brought Suraya flowers every day, and she couldn't help but smile. Jandu agreed to practice the mace with Baram, and although Jandu ended up with a bruised rib and a nasty headache, Baram felt like a conqueror again. Even Yudar's cough finally disappeared.

Jandu wasn't sure exactly when he had let all the leftover anger at his brother go, but like the easing of a chronic pain, one day he just noticed it was gone and he was glad. It was hard to hate his family. He needed Yudar and Baram to be his allies, and when he was angry at Yudar, the world seemed darker to him.

Jandu deftly made his way through the thicket, following the pilgrim's trail north towards the retreat. Along the route, he passed by two groups of holy men, chanting prayers as they made their way to the religious retreat. Jandu bowed to them as they passed, keeping his head low and his eyes partially closed. He held his arms close to his body, hoping no one would notice his archery scars. He hid Zandi behind his back.

As soon as he could, he stepped off the main trail and pushed his way deeper into the jungle. In Prasta, the heart of winter would be cold and windy. Here, in the rain canopy of the mountains, even December brought an early morning heat that hovered over the earth like a hot breath. Jandu was sweating by the time he made his way to a small stream secluded in the brush. The water's edge teamed with birds—wood sandpipers and shelducks, yellownapes and barbets—singing uproariously as they splashed in the cool, thin trickle of mountain water that rushed over the rocks.

Jandu found a shady spot on a fallen log and took out his birch bark paper. He began a cartoon of his family, showing Yudar's bones protruding from his sides, Baram's eyes bugging out of his head from hunger, Suraya's hard and calloused hands chopping wood with their sharp edges. Jandu dwindled hours away, cracking himself up with his drawings. He drew one page of himself jerking off in the woods, and he realized that he was so far removed from the Jandu who had been raised by his strict and severely religious master, Mazar. The Jandu of a few years ago couldn't even contemplate the immorality of masturbation, let alone jokingly draw himself in the act, giggling as he added lurid flourishes. The sun beat on the back of his neck and he drew, heedless of time, but not entirely oblivious to the steady rhythm of forest life.

A gray junglefowl strutted by, waking Jandu up from his artistic trance. He swiftly pulled an arrow from his quiver and shot the bird from a few feet away.

"Sorry," Jandu told the bird. "But you are going to be a delicious dinner."

Jandu packed up his writing materials and made his way back home, breathing in the deep, mushroomy smell of the forest.

Baram was ecstatic about Jandu's kill, and set about preparing a grand feast, seasoning the rice they had left with cardamom pods and cloves, making a cream sauce for the bird, adding a touch of early season mango to sweeten it. They shared their dinner outside in the clearing between the hut and the lake, where they could enjoy the view of the water splashing against the base of the sharp peaked mountains, and listen to the calls of peacocks and quails in the forest.

They sat back after their meal contentedly, watching the color of the sky blush a brilliant pink, the humidity finally dropping to a warm balm. Jandu took out his sharpening stone and sharpened his sword, as Yudar unveiled the final pieces of the chess set he had spent the last ten months carving. Baram and Yudar huddled around the crudely drawn teak board as Suraya served warm milky tea and leaned against the hut wall, staring at her husbands.

"I'm pregnant."

No one moved. Even the air around them seemed shocked—the gentle breeze died as soon as the words were out. The night filled with silence.

Suraya smiled at Baram, then at Jandu and Yudar.

Jandu held his sword in the air, like he would stab the roof of the hut.

Baram went to her. "Are you sure?"

"Yes." Suraya grinned widely. "I wasn't sure until this week. But it's been two months since I've had my menses. Baram, we're going to have a child."

Baram cried out in joy and lifted Suraya into the air as the two of them laughed. Yudar, once he overcame his initial shock, stood up as well and offered his congratulations.

Jandu carefully put his sword back in its sheath and joined them in a group embrace. But he smiled for an entirely different reason. His year with Suraya just got a whole lot shorter.

Jandu had watched the approach of August and his nuptial night with growing anxiety. He loved Suraya dearly, but he didn't think of her in a sexual way. And while there were nights with the beetles on the hard floor of their hut that Jandu realized life could be better, in bed with Suraya, it seemed like a betrayal of Suraya's trust, to sleep with her because he had to. It seemed wrong to not want to have sex with her, and yet to do it anyway.

And, after all, Suraya was his brother's wife. Over the last year, through thick and thin, Suraya and Baram had suffered together. Suraya's feelings towards Yudar seemed to have waned, but her love for Baram was stronger than ever. Jandu didn't want to get in the way of that.

Suraya's pregnancy offered a way to get out of sleeping with Suraya entirely.

"This is such wonderful news!" Jandu cried. He pounded on Baram's shoulders affectionately. "Good going." Jandu patted Yudar's shoulder as well. "Better luck next time, champ."

Baram and Suraya burst out laughing, but Yudar gave Jandu an icy stare.

Jandu took a deep breath. "I have a suggestion."

Everyone turned to stare at him.

"I wonder… since she's pregnant with your baby, Baram… perhaps your year should extend?" Jandu spoke quickly, his hands stroking the sheath of his sword nervously. "After all, it seems strange for Suraya and I to be together when she's carrying your child."

Baram nodded, looking deep in thought, but Yudar didn't give it a moment's consideration.

"No." Yudar scowled. "No. We keep to the rules. It is the only way to maintain peace between us. Remember? We swore an oath when we married. It would be one year for each of us consecutively, regardless of circumstances."

"But we didn't address the issue of children…" Jandu started.

Yudar cut him off. "—Yes we did. We specifically talked about it. Weren't you listening?"

Jandu scratched his head, pretending to look at the lake.

Now that he remembered it, he was off flirting with Keshan when all of the big decisions were being made.

"We made rules," Yudar stressed. He looked upset. "We're living together in one shared hut, and we share a wife, for God's sake! We have to maintain the rules, or else we will fail as a family!"

"It should be up to Suraya," Baram said, his voice rising.

"I agree with Yudar," Suraya said shyly. She smiled at Jandu. "We will have our year together, and nothing will change." She blushed a furious red. "I mean, there will be some changes, but…"

Baram hugged Jandu tightly. Jandu groaned.

"Thanks for the thought, but it's not fair to you," Baram said. He had tears in his eyes, still glowing from the news of that he would be a father. "This will be our son, all of us together. "

"Or daughter," Suraya said quietly, but the brothers ignored her.

Jandu sighed. He couldn't slip out of this so easily, then.

"Fine," he said. "So it is." Suraya and Baram hugged again.

Yudar sat back down at the chess board, watching the two of them with a frown. "How are we going to feed a baby?"

Baram and Suraya let go of each other and stared at him.

Yudar gestured to the bones of the bird they just consumed. "Suraya, you barely get enough to eat now. If you're pregnant, you'll have to eat more. And when the baby is born…" Yudar looked around them, at the forest which had provided them so little.

"We'll move," Baram said. "After Suraya has the baby, we'll move to a city. Somewhere large where we can find work."

Jandu closed his eyes. The idea of living in a city again seemed like a distant dream. "We'll have to find somewhere we don't know anyone well. Darvad has spies all over the country."

"How do you know?" Suraya asked.

Jandu blushed. He knew this because Keshan had told him so in a letter. But none of his family knew of his correspondence.

He shrugged. "Druv Majeo is his friend; he has to have spies."

Yudar nodded. "Jandu is right. We have to find a place that is not allied with Darvad. And if we can get work in a palace, we may be able to find a place to provide for the child and Suraya."

Baram and Suraya were snuggling together, too in love to really participate in the conversation.

"Where do you suggest?" Jandu asked his brother.

"Afadi comes to mind," Yudar said. "When I visited Afadi as Royal Judge, I noticed that Lord Indarel had a large staff at his palace. We could say we used to work for the Parans in Prasta, and get work there."

"Brilliant," Baram said. He touched Yudar's head fondly.

"Afadi?" Suraya frowned. "It's so far south. And neighboring Chandamar is Firdaus' land."

"No one will expect us to go to such a small kingdom, where we have no connections," Yudar countered.

Suraya nodded. "It will be up to you. As long as we can provide what is best for the baby." She rubbed her belly fondly.

The next morning, Jandu woke early and went to his private retreat, and saw that Chezek had come during the night to replace his box of letters with another scroll from Keshan. Even in the early light, the silver dowel was warm to the touch.

Jandu unrolled the scroll on the forest floor. This time, Keshan had rolled two cloths in with his existing message, to provide Jandu with something to write back on. He obviously tired of deciphering Jandu's scrawl on birch bark.

Jandu no longer read the letter first. He scanned the end of the scroll to find the drawing. Both he and Keshan now devoutly drew each other small diagrams of what they were doing. Keshan couldn't stop talking in his letters about how talented he thought Jandu was, how Jandu should have been an artist.

Jandu could not say the same for Keshan's artwork, which was usually obscene and badly sketched with blotting ink. But it always made him laugh.

This time the large picture took up several rolls of the scroll. It showed a meeting in what appeared to be Tiwari's reception hall. The man with the extravagant diadem was obviously Keshan. He sat on a large pile of letters. Other than the exaggerated erection he drew himself with, there was nothing very sexy about this drawing.

Jandu read the letter and found out the reason why. Darvad's spies had heightened their efforts to find the Parans. Now that almost an entire year had passed and no sign of the Parans, Darvad increased the count of his bounty hunters and had infiltrated Tiwari with hundreds of spies. Darvad knew how fond Keshan was of Jandu. And he assumed that Jandu and his family would turn to Tiwari for aid.

Worse, Keshan informed him that even the Yashva kingdom was no longer safe. When Keshan tried to visit Jandu through the Yashva space, Firdaus' cousins had been there, following him.

The news sobered Jandu, and he buried the letter quickly. He walked home in a daze, pondering the warnings of Keshan's letter, and also the last lines, which Jandu assumed were meant to be romantic, and yet had somehow failed in their delivery: *Your heart will split this world into a thousand pieces.*

In his next letter, Jandu almost asked Keshan what he meant by the line. But then a sick feeling of self-doubt filled him. If it was another one of Keshan's prophecies, Jandu decided he didn't want to know.

CHAPTER 22

IN AUGUST, BARAM MOVED HIS SMALL COLLECTION OF POSSESSIONS out of the couple's hut. Suraya spent the morning cleaning the room and preparing it for her nuptial night with Jandu.

Jandu spent the day hunting.

He swore to himself as he searched the forest vainly for food. The religious sages in the retreat had stripped the forest of game. The Parans' food stores ran out the previous week, and now they were living off milk and whatever greens and fruit they could gather. Jandu realized they would have to start begging soon, if he didn't have better luck finding deer.

Hunting kept his mind off the upcoming evening, at least.

His family, hunkered down in panicked hunger, was desperate to make the rest of their communal living pleasant. Baram and Yudar never fought anymore, and all of them enthusiastically supported this previously agreed-upon switching of marital partners in an attempt to keep everyone else content. Even though Jandu knew Baram and Suraya were truly in love with each other, both of them were willing to sacrifice their mutual happiness in the name of harmony with the family.

But now, on the eve of consummating his marriage, Jandu decided they were all fools. It had been fun to think of how close they had all grown, living together and depending upon one another in the wilderness, but it was unreasonable to expect that harmony to continue purely based on some ideas they had the day they had met Suraya. What was it about Yudar and his damned devotion to rules?

Jandu was angry at himself for not being more adamant about abdicating his year with Suraya. Now, in the name of family peace, Baram would stifle his jealousy and be torn from the woman he loved. Suraya would have her third sexual partner in as many years. And Jandu would sleep with someone he didn't want to.

Jandu decided that he would not go through with it on the grounds that Suraya was pregnant with his niece or nephew. The mere thought left him chilly with horror. He had to make them understand.

But his courage faded as he returned home and ate dinner in silence. He didn't want his brothers to suspect the real reason he didn't want to sleep with Suraya. He didn't want anyone doubting his masculinity.

Baram had boiled down milk to thicken it and added roasted barley to make a porridge, seasoned with tamarind. They drank whey. They remained hungry after their plates were cleared.

Baram's attempts not to appear hurt or angry made dinner more uncomfortable. Jandu knew his brother too well. Baram kept skipping stones, a sure sign of his unhappiness. Yudar picked at his dinner. He looked sunken into himself, deep in thought.

Only Suraya seemed calm. She drifted between the backyard and the hut, gathering their leaf plates and throwing them into the fire, sweeping the inside of the hut, putting away the few food stores left. She showed no apprehension on her face, only a calm serenity. Jandu half-suspected she had secreted a bottle of wine somewhere and had drunk herself into a pleasant coma.

A bottle of wine was exactly what Jandu needed now. Anxiety washed over him in sweeping waves. He looked at Suraya's body, which had grown thinner but was still voluptuous and curvy, her large, round breasts threatening to burst through her zahari top, and tried to focus on how sexy she was. But he had known her too long in too fraternal a fashion to conjure any lust.

Suraya casually picked up Jandu's chest of personal belongings. She struggled with its weight.

"Jandu," she said softly. "Can you help me carry your things into the other room?"

Jandu felt his face redden. "Sure." He grabbed the chest from her, and followed her out of the hut into the other building.

He had spent little time in this separate room. Its coziness contrasted with the drafty hut he'd slept in for the past year. The sandalwood bed gave off a sweet scent. The mattress was small, made of cotton cloth stuffed with grass and leaves, and strewn with the furs Jandu tanned months ago. Suraya's zaharis hung around the small space, serving as decoration as well as storage. The room had a feminine touch, and smelled sweetly of camphor and butter.

"Where should I put it?" Jandu asked. Suraya pointed to a bare corner of the room. Baram's chest had lived there only a few hours ago. The thought brought a sheen of sweat to Jandu's forehead.

Suraya sat on the edge of the bed, and looked to Jandu coyly. Jandu put his chest down and then stiffly sat beside her.

"This is uncomfortable," he admitted.

Suraya laughed. She put her arm around him. "Remember how you once comforted me when I became Baram's wife?"

Jandu grinned down at her. "Yeah. You were scared out of your wits."

"I'm not scared now," Suraya whispered.

"No. But I am."

Suraya laughed again. She hugged Jandu to her tightly.

Jandu hugged back, hoping she didn't notice the tremor in his body. Their embrace felt nice. He always loved holding Suraya. If they could just do this, everything would be fine.

But Suraya slowly lowered Jandu's body on the bed. She stared down at him.

"You don't have to do this," Jandu said quietly.

"I want to," Suraya said.

"But Baram—"

Suraya broke his speech with a kiss.

Suraya had her eyes closed. Jandu stared at her. Keshan always stared back at Jandu when they made love.

Jandu quickly shut the thought out of his mind.

Suraya kept her lips on his, wanting more. Jandu's skin crawled with revulsion. He didn't want to stick his tongue in her mouth. But Suraya wasn't giving up. She prodded his lips with her tongue, seeking entry. Jandu realized he would just have to go with it. He closed his eyes and thought of Keshan.

As his hands explored her body, the differences were too stark to let his imagination wander. Where Keshan's muscles were firm, his arms tight, his flesh taut, Suraya was soft and curvy, smooth. Jandu preferred lying still, letting Suraya touch him, imagining her hands were Keshan's.

Suraya reached the hem of Jandu's trousers, and hesitated.

Jandu swallowed. He closed his eyes firmly, and then quickly undid the knot of his dejaru.

He turned quickly, crouching over Suraya. He kept his eyes closed, and blindly felt for the knot of her zahari. He untied it by feel. He opened his eyes and looked down at her face.

Suraya stared up at him, a look of fear on her face. Jandu realized he was going about this all wrong. He was rushing her, not taking his time, not kissing her or showing any affection at all. But he couldn't bring himself to do it. He would go through the motions, but he was incapable of pretending to feel something he didn't.

He reached down to open Suraya's legs, and with clumsy anxiety, entered her. Suraya sucked the breath back into her throat. Jandu looked at her long enough to make sure she wasn't crying, and then pushed inside of her, scrunching his eyes tight again, imagining the flesh was Keshan's flesh, imagining he tasted Keshan's skin, smelled his coconut clove scent, felt his muscles underneath his hands.

Jandu sped up his actions, and then, after intense concentration, he came quietly, stifling any moan he would normally make.

Jandu wasn't sure if he should continue his actions or not, but he didn't really think Suraya enjoyed this any more than he, so he stopped moving, pulling out of her quickly.

He rolled beside her and pulled up his dejaru quickly, retying the knot.

Suraya retied her zahari and stared up at the ceiling. She looked pale and horrified.

Jandu burned with shame. He knew this had been a bad idea. Now Suraya would hate him for being such a terrible lover.

"I'm sorry," he said quietly.

Suraya didn't answer. She continued to stare at the ceiling, as if in shock.

"I don't think this is a good idea." Jandu rolled over on his side.

"What do you want to do, Jandu?" Suraya asked. There was pain in her voice, accusation. "You find me so disgusting, you can't even look at me."

Jandu's eyes widened. "What? That's not it at all!"

"You are the one who won me."

"What's that supposed to mean?"

"Nothing." Suraya turned her back to him and curled up on herself, knees to her chest. "It just means that you're the one I chose, and yet you're the one who is most distant."

"I won you because I wanted to win. I wasn't trying to win you, especially."

"How romantic."

"I'm sorry," Jandu said, "but I'm being honest."

Suraya had tears in her eyes. She stared at him, heartbroken. "If it isn't me, then, what is it?"

Jandu sighed. He reached out and brushed a stray lock of hair from her face. "Suraya, for the last two years that I've known you, you have been my *sister*. I think of you as my sister.

You're pregnant with my brother's child. However depraved I may be, I am not a *sister fucker*."

Suraya's eyes grew wide at the expression.

Jandu swallowed. "The truth is, we've been friends for too long for me to think of you in any other way."

Suraya studied Jandu's face carefully. Color came back to her cheeks.

"I see."

"I'm sorry about all of this," Jandu said. "But it's better to be honest."

Suraya seemed to let out a thin breath she had been holding. She pulled the thin cotton sheet around her, and nodded. She tried smiling.

"Sister fucker, huh?" she said quietly.

Jandu laughed. "Yeah. That's what I feel like."

"I think I understand," Suraya said.

Jandu stroked her head. "I do love you, Suraya—as a sister."

Suraya reached out and stroked Jandu's shoulder. "All right."

Jandu smiled shyly. "You know, if you want to go back to Baram, I'm all for it."

Suraya studied Jandu's face. Her gaze was so intense, Jandu began to panic.

"What?" he asked nervously.

"Nothing." She smiled slightly. "You are just… surprising. That's all."

Jandu closed his eyes, luxuriating in the softness of the pillow beneath his head, the warmth of the shared sheet. "I'd prefer to pretend like we're man and wife, however, just so I can stay here in this comfy bed of yours."

Suraya rolled over and placed a soft kiss on Jandu's cheek. "It's all right by me if you stay. We can just keep each other company in the dark."

Jandu put his arm around her, and closed his eyes again. "That sounds perfect."

◆◆◆

Their marital life fell into an easy pattern. During the day, Jandu made sure his relationship with his wife was loving and enjoyable. He didn't want his brothers to suspect anything, and so he showered affection on Suraya every chance he had. He included Suraya in almost every activity, and the two of them walked the lake shore, collected interesting plants together, and made up stories about their enemies. Their favorite game was, "what disease does Darvad have?" where the two of them would sneak off by themselves for hours, drink milky tea and crack each other up with new, imagined ailments that pocked Darvad's skin and bloodied his sex life.

At night, the two of them settled comfortably together in the bed, curled around each other in the small space, and slept soundly. Jandu never tried to touch her after their wedding night. And Suraya never again made any advances either.

Life would have been pleasant, if they weren't desperately starving. By the time Suraya's pregnancy showed, they had no food stores left, no fresh meat, no fish, and only a thin supply of milk from their cow. Baram looked Jandu in the eye one morning, and then pointed his finger at him.

"You are going to have to beg," Baram told him. He pointed to the door. "So go. Beg."

Jandu scowled. "Why do I have to do it?"

"You want Suraya to beg?" Baram shouted.

"No!" Jandu glared. "I want *you* to beg! Or Yudar!"

Yudar held out his hands in the sign of peace. "I cannot take anything from pilgrims. I would rather starve then lead them to starvation."

"Starve, then," Baram spat at him. "But someone is going to have to feed the rest of us, and so it's up to you Jandu."

Jandu stood up and approached his brother. Even though Baram was several inches taller than Jandu, Jandu still looked angry enough to make Baram back up a step.

"Why don't *you* beg?"

Baram smiled. "You're the youngest. You do what I say."

"But—"

"Besides, I look intimidating. You look like an innocent, malnourished peasant in ripped clothing."

"No. You have to come with me. I'm not doing this alone!" Jandu grabbed an empty rice pot angrily, and stormed out of the hut.

Baram did come with Jandu the first few times, walking down the pilgrim's trail several miles from where Jandu sat, begging rice and grain off the travelers. But Baram was right, he looked too big for people to easily pity him. Alone, Jandu received twice as much. Soon Baram stopped accompanying him.

Jandu hated begging. The indignity devastated him. He had passed by beggars in the street back when he was a prince and despised their sad, pitiful eyes, detested the way they reeked of spoiled milk and soiled clothes, found their whole presence demeaning. Now here he was, the son of King Shandarvan, a fucking beggar. The shame was unbearable and yet it fed him and his family.

"Please help me," Jandu grumbled, holding out his begging bowl to the holy pilgrims, keeping his head down so that they couldn't see his blue eyes. No one would ever have guessed he once slept on feather beds. His clothes were stained and torn, his skin had darkened in the sun, and his hands had grown rough and calloused with chopping wood. The bones of his cheeks and ribs stuck out prominently.

"Help," Jandu mumbled. Occasionally someone would stop long enough to pour some rice from a sack into his bowl. It was considered bad luck to ignore the pleas of a beggar while on a holy pilgrimage. For once, their proximity to the retreat worked in their favor. But many pilgrims chose not to stop. There were too many hungry mouths, too many desperate people in these times to help every one of them.

When someone did give Jandu food, he fell to his knees and touched their feet, as was tradition. He had done so for several days before he realized that none of the pilgrims were Triya. He was touching the feet of Suya and Chaya caste men and women, soiling his purity.

Jandu tried to resurrect some of the old indignation he would have felt, dirtying himself with lower caste skin, but the truth was, a foot was a foot. The Parans might have been the only Triya on the mountain, but they were the ones that were starving. Suddenly, religious status seemed unimportant.

Jandu pushed the thought from his mind, but he couldn't help but notice that the clearly Chaya-caste pilgrims were more likely to give him something to eat than the better-off, Suya merchant caste. The poorer were more generous with the little they had. It made Jandu feel ashamed of the way he used to mock the Chaya. It also made Jandu miss Keshan even more, hearing Keshan's chiding voice in his mind.

Once, late one evening when Jandu had struck out with every pilgrim who wandered on the trail, Jandu followed a lone merchant making his way to the retreat to sell herbal medicines.

"Help me," Jandu pleaded, walking alongside the man with his bowl out.

The man was shorter than Jandu, and older. He eyed Jandu warily. "Leave me alone."

Jandu followed him. "Please. My wife is pregnant."

"Bugger off." The man quickened his steps. Jandu kept pace. The man watched the way Jandu strode up the hill and frowned. "You do not walk like a beggar."

"I don't?" Jandu looked at his feet.

"You walk like a thief."

Jandu narrowed his eyes. "What kind of fucking thief follows assholes like you up a mountain begging for a handful of some fucking rice?"

The man stopped and glared at Jandu. Jandu squared his shoulders and stared back.

"Fuck you," the man said finally. He spat in Jandu's face

and walked up the hill. Jandu's fists tensed, and he dropped his begging bowl.

Jandu's face clouded with rage and he took off after the man. He caught the older man easily, grabbed the man's shoulder and spun him around.

"If I wanted to take your money I'd have fucking well done it and left you dead on the side of the road. You want to know why I don't? Because I'm better than that, you prick." He let go of the man's shoulder, and watched him sprint up the trail in a panic. Jandu waited until he was out of sight, and then stooped down to pick up his begging bowl again.

He felt beaten.

But he continued to beg the rest of the winter. He thought the humiliation would wear off. He thought that spicing up his begging with telling jokes, or offering to read palms, would bring some joy into the situation. But there was a constant, sinking, understanding that Jandu was as low as he could get. It would have been easier if only he had gotten a letter from Keshan, but none came.

The winter months passed and as the air sweetened with blossoms and fruit finally hung throughout the forest, and the sky tumbled and rumbled with the threats of monsoon rain.

But still no new word from Keshan arrived.

Jandu's letters collected under the stone statue in his forest clearing like the leftovers of an abandoned library. He built a bigger box to store them all. Mice had gotten into the box and chewed on the pata cloth, ruining one of his better sketches. Three months without word from Keshan turned to four, and Jandu's optimism, the spark that had heated his family through the chilly first year and a half and brought a little light into their dark situation, faded from his heart completely.

On his way back from begging one evening, he checked the forest clearing to find that his box of letters had been knocked over by some wild animal, his precious words strewn around the forest floor like leaves. He let out a strangled cry and rushed through the glade, picking up his letters and putting them back in the box with trembling hands. When he returned the box in its place, with all letters accounted for, Jandu leaned against the statue and covered his face with his hands. Something broke in him. He could feel it, in his heart, a gentle snap, and he covered his face with his hands and wept. He lost his sense of righteousness, his sense of duty, his pride. And, worst of all, he had somehow lost Keshan too.

CHAPTER 23

Had Keshan found someone else? Someone who could touch Keshan in the ways that Jandu, hiding in the forest, could not?

Or, worse, had something happened to him? In Keshan's last letter he had mentioned the spies who swarmed through Tiwari, looking for signs of the Parans. Perhaps they caught Keshan and were torturing him now, trying to get information of the Paran's location. Maybe Keshan would break, and he would show them the map to their hiding spot. Jandu could be responsible for leading his family's enemies straight to them.

Not knowing drove his paranoia. Only the soothing continuity of Keshan's letters had given Jandu complacency. Now, without them, the bleakness of their situation became painfully obvious.

Jandu visited the statue daily on his way to beg on the pilgrim's trail, but his letters remained, with no word from Keshan. Jandu grew angry at being forgotten. And then depression set in.

Jandu wrote more letters, as if sheer volume would draw Keshan's servant. He wrote one every other day. They always started with deep affection, and then grew more and more hostile at Keshan's continuing silence.

And then, one morning, Jandu walked out to the clearing, and noticed all his letters were gone. His heart skipped a beat.

But nothing replaced them. Chezek had taken the letters but brought nothing in return. Jandu furiously searched the clearing but found nothing. Chezek had traveled for weeks to this point, and he didn't even bother to bring back a single sentence for Jandu?

His fury tumbled into fear as other, more horrible scenarios came to mind. Darvad's men captured Chezek, and their location had been discovered. His letters were found, and were making their way to Darvad this very moment. Or Chezek had been killed before he could drop off Keshan's scroll. Only terrible endings could explain such an odd occurrence.

Jandu couldn't sleep. He kept Suraya awake at night as he tossed and kicked off the cotton sheet, worry preventing him from even being able to enjoy dreams.

One night Suraya stared at Jandu as he rested his head on his hands and glared up at the ceiling of the hut, watching a trail of ants make their way from a hole in the thatch work along the ceiling and down the wall.

"What's wrong?" Suraya asked sleepily. She rubbed his shoulder gently.

"I can't sleep," Jandu said.

Suraya turned to face him as best as she could. Her large belly made the bed much smaller.

"Why not?" Suraya asked.

"I'm just worried." Jandu looked at her. Anxiety over Keshan's silence gnawed at him. He wanted to tell her so badly he almost blurted it out. And then, as always, he realized the insanity of his primary instinct. That would be the worst thing he could do. "You have to eat for two. You aren't getting enough for one."

Suraya watched his expression closely. "You need to stop worrying about me."

Jandu smiled falsely and kissed her forehead.

"Good night," he said, turning away from her.

"Sleep." She whispered it in his ear, as if a command. And for once, it seemed to work.

But Jandu awoke before everyone, before dawn. Unable to rest in bed any longer, he rose and wrote another letter to

Keshan. At dawn he left the letter under the statue, praying that Chezek had only been scared off and would be back any day to leave a note from Keshan.

But weeks went by without another word. Jandu's letters collected under the statue again, and then, as before, they disappeared one day, nothing left behind to suggest they were ever there.

Jandu swore, and searched the glade frantically. What the hell was going on? Why would Chezek come all the way from Tiwari to pick up his letters and yet leave nothing behind?

Unless something really had happened to Keshan. Jandu knelt suddenly on the damp forest floor and prayed for Keshan's safety.

With his eyes closed, he heard soft footsteps behind him. He stood and whirled around quickly, drawing his hunting knife.

Jandu's eyes widened. He lowered his knife.

Standing there, in the middle of the morning forest, was a woman.

She seemed ethereal. Her skin shimmered and swam, and Jandu instantly knew she was a Yashva. Her golden sheen, her flawless perfection, and her swirling eyes made her clearly inhuman.

She was beautiful, like an exaggerated effigy of a goddess. Her waist seemed impossibly thin between the voluptuous curves of her breasts and hips. She wore only a thin golden belt around her waist, barely covering her groin.

Her breasts were heavy and round, with large nipples pointed straight at him. Her thick black hair reached all the way to her lower back in a shiny straight curtain. Her eyes were almond shaped, spinning and flashing in a way that made Jandu dizzy.

He felt his cheeks grow hot with embarrassment at her nudity. Why did she stare at him?

"You must be Jandu," the Yashva whispered seductively. She stepped towards him. Jandu looked down and noticed she had no sandals. Her bare feet and hands were painted with henna patterns, and she wore gold anklets.

"Who are you?" Jandu asked. As she walked towards him, he backed up slightly.

"My name is Umia," the woman said, coyly blinking her eyes. "And I love you too."

Jandu froze. "Excuse me?"

Umia laughed quietly. She had a tinkling laugh that sounded like bells. "I love you too. I've received all your letters, sweet Jandu. I have shown myself to you to proclaim my equal affection."

Jandu felt the color drain from his face. "My... you read my letters?"

Umia nodded. She pointed to the statue in the middle of the clearing. "You left them at my effigy."

Jandu looked at the ancient, worn statue, and realized it was, indeed, of a woman. Age and rain had washed off her features, but the hips were now noticeably curvy.

"Umia, you are... a goddess?" Jandu asked, staring at her in awe.

Umia laughed again. She stood next to him, so close Jandu could smell vanilla in her hair.

"I am a Yashva," she whispered, "and one of Mendraz's consorts." She reached up and ran a hand along Jandu's bare chest. "And although I rarely have anything to do with humans, I can't resist you." She brought her lips close to his. "You are the most beautiful human being I've ever laid eyes on."

Jandu stared at her, feeling faint. *Oh God, now what?*

"Umia, I'm flattered." He backed up. The backs of his calves hit her statue. "But I'm afraid those letters, they weren't... I mean, I wrote them to someone else."

Umia smiled lasciviously. "Nonsense. I read them. Only I can inspire such lust in mankind." She raised an eyebrow. "You have quite an imagination. And you are very specific about what you'd like to do to me." Umia frowned. "Although some of it I didn't quite understand *how* I was supposed to—"

"—Umia," Jandu interrupted quickly. He knelt at her feet, bowing his head. "Please forgive me!"

Umia knelt as well, her breasts shaking as she did so. She held Jandu's face in her hands. "There's nothing to forgive. You love me, and I love you. I want you." She leaned closer. "Kiss me."

Jandu's mind raced on how he would get out of this situation. The last thing Jandu wanted to do was sleep with Mendraz's consort. Mendraz was his ally, the king of the Yashvas.

Umia kissed him. Jandu stiffened. After a moment, Umia pulled away, looking confused.

"Jandu," she said quietly, "are you not attracted to me?"

Jandu started to sweat. He didn't want to offend her. Who knew what power she had? But he also definitely didn't want to screw her either.

"Umia, you are the mother of all beauty. I see you as a mother, and worship you as one." Jandu brought his palms together and bowed low to her in respect.

Umia didn't say anything, but she stood quickly. When Jandu looked up at her, she shook with rage.

"How *dare* you insult me like this!" she spat. Her hands were in fists. "You compare me to your *mother*?"

Jandu held his hands in the sign of peace. "Please! I mean no offense! I just look at you as such a heavenly being, I would never propose to think of you in any way other than as something to be worshipped."

"Then worship me!" Umia glared down at him. "And make love to me, as I command! Be a man!"

Jandu's heart was in his throat. "I'm sorry, Umia. I... I cannot."

Umia's shock was plain. She obviously rarely had her requests denied.

"As you wish! Don't be a man." A soft blue tint surrounded her body. Her eyes glowed blue. Although Jandu had never seen it happen before, he had heard stories of demons with the power to curse. All the stories warned that demons turned blue first. Jandu blanched in horror.

She glared at Jandu. "If you are going to act like such a woman, I curse you to be one!"

"What!"

Umia pointed at him, the other hand on her curvy hip.

"I curse you, Jandu! You flirt with your words, and then scorn me with your body! Since you are so selfish with your manhood, you will lose it and be transformed into a woman!"

A gray mist of curse words formed around her head, and then exploded towards Jandu. Jandu covered his face with his arms as the shower of misty words fell on him, turning his skin cold, making him shiver to the marrow of his bones.

And without another word, Umia stormed out of the forest glade.

Jandu knelt there on the forest floor, too stunned to move.

"My God, my God!" He clenched his hands into fists. This was the worst thing that could ever have happened to him. "No!" He kicked the statue of Umia and ran back to his family, desperate for Yudar to think of some way out of this situation.

The whole way back, Jandu's mind raced. A curse was impossible to remove. And Yashva curses always came true. "God!" Jandu made a fist as he burst into the main hut and startled Yudar and Suraya, who were drinking tea and talking inside, away from the brutal afternoon sun.

Breathlessly, Jandu gave Yudar and Suraya an abbreviated version of what had just happened, skipping the part about the letters, and just stating that Mendraz's Yashva consort tried to seduce him, and when he refused, she cursed him. Suraya started laughing, but Yudar went pale.

"Holy beings have the power to curse," Yudar said. "It will come true, you realize."

Jandu kicked a wooden stool in frustration.

"Why didn't you just sleep with her?" Yudar demanded.

Jandu looked at him like he was crazy. "What are you talking about? She belongs to Mendraz," Jandu snapped. "And I want Mendraz to be our ally!"

"You should have done as she asked," Yudar said.

"Besides, I'm married to Suraya," Jandu protested. Suraya gave him a strange look, and Yudar did not appreciate Jandu's fidelity. Yudar paced the room, looking more worried about the situation than Jandu.

"This is bad, bad!" Yudar cried. "Jandu, you are a fool!"

Baram came in, having heard the shouting from outside. When they retold the story to him, he just shook his head at his younger brother.

"Why not just sleep with her?" he asked.

Jandu moaned and sank to his knees, covering his face. He felt a tickle on his chest and, in a total panic, rubbed his chest frantically to make sure he hadn't spontaneously developed large breasts.

"You need to pray," Yudar said. Jandu wasn't looking at him, so Yudar knelt down and shook Jandu by the shoulders. "Listen to me! You need to pray to Mendraz. Ask for help, Jandu. You helped him in the forest. Maybe he will help you now."

Jandu nodded. He stood shakily. "I'll try."

"Hurry," Yudar said.

Jandu didn't need the encouragement. He quickly made his way to the main path through the forest. He found an isolated spot and knelt down, closing his eyes and praying with all his heart to Mendraz.

Jandu brought his hands together, and called to Mendraz over and over. He had no idea if the Yashva could hear him, but Keshan once told him that Mendraz watched over the world, both the human one and the Yashva kingdom.

Jandu prayed for hours, long after the hot afternoon sun had set, after the sounds of the nocturnal animals filled the forest air, the loud croaking of frogs from the nearby stream, the hoot of owls, the constant rustle of undergrowth.

Jandu's knees ached as they pressed against the uneven stones and ground. He kept his palms glued together as he prayed, his eyes shut, focusing all his concentration on his one goal. Mazar had taught him that praying sincerely was a lot like shooting a bow accurately. It had to do with clearing one's mind of all extraneous thought, and meditating on one's only purpose. Jandu breathed deeply, calming his mind, focusing his energies.

Mendraz.

"I see you have angered another Yashva."

Jandu's eyes shot open in surprise. He saw nothing but the jungle around him.

And then, blurry, flittering through the jungle, Jandu could make out the towering blue figure of the King of the Yashvas. Mendraz stood before him, but was in the Yashva Kingdom. The King stepped forward, and brightened. Jandu shielded his eyes as the King stepped into the human world as if he were stepping over a fallen log.

"I'm impressed," Mendraz said, his accent thick, his voice booming. "You can see me even in the Yashva world. You have many impressive powers, mortal Jandu."

Jandu's eyes hurt with the brightness of light emanating from the demon. Jandu's heart beat wildly, and his throat seemed to close in fear. Even though he had seen Mendraz before, the sight still awed him. Mendraz's face and arms faded in an out of clarity, swimming through the air as if seen through warped glass, never fully in focus.

Jandu narrowed his eyes, to try and find Mendraz's face. "My Lord Mendraz!" Jandu prostrated himself low before the King.

"And one of your powers seems to be your uncanny ability to anger my people." Jandu thought he could detect amusement in his voice.

Jandu looked up. Mendraz appeared to be smiling, although his teeth vibrated, sharp and shining.

"I don't mean to cause any strife among the Yashva," Jandu said, bowing his head once more. "I cause enough problems in my own world."

Mendraz did laugh this time, a frightening sound that made Jandu think twice about being clever again.

"It is not surprising," Mendraz commented. "You are the first human in generations who is able to see into our world. You are bound to cause mixed feelings amongst my kind."

"My lord, I humbly request your assistance," Jandu begged. He spoke quickly, telling Mendraz of Umia's curse.

When he finished, Mendraz sighed. "Rise, Jandu. You're not a peasant."

Jandu stood up and looked expectantly at Lord Mendraz. "My apologies, lord! I didn't know what to do."

"Umia is very persistent when she sets her heart on something," Mendraz said. "I should congratulate you—of all the mortals Umia has fancied, you're the only one who refused her. Tell me though, if your letters were not meant to seduce Umia, who were they for?"

Jandu clenched his mouth shut. But Mendraz continued to stare, obviously willing to wait for an answer.

"They were—" Jandu flushed, closed his eyes, and prayed that Keshan had been telling him the truth about the freedom of the Yashva kingdom. "I wrote them for Keshan Adaru."

"I thought as much," King Mendraz said. "He has been praying for your safety every night for months. It's very wearying."

Jandu swallowed the burst of affection he instantly felt for Keshan. He folded his hands in supplication. "I am sorry. Can you help me, lord?"

Mendraz looked bemused. "Well, I cannot remove the curse entirely. It is her shartic power, that once her curse is uttered, it cannot be revoked. However, I can change it."

"Change it? How?"

"I can reduce the curse to one year. It will be any year of your choosing. Just pray to me, and I will let the year begin."

Jandu smiled weakly. "Thank you."

Mendraz looked like he was smirking. "I'm sure you will make a lovely woman."

"Thank you," Jandu said, his cheeks burning in shame.

Mendraz moved towards him quickly. Jandu braced himself. Mendraz reached down and put his hand on Jandu's head.

Nausea washed through Jandu as Mendraz touched him. He felt like his stomach was pulled up his throat. A rocking seasickness filled him, and then his mind pulsed as dozens of Yashva words shouted into his ear with shocking volume.

Jandu closed his eyes tightly. His head felt as though it would explode.

And then Mendraz lifted his hand off of him and disappeared.

"Be strong, ally of the Yashvas," Mendraz told him from the darkness.

Jandu steadied his balance, and shook his head to clear it. He had a pounding headache. And he couldn't see anything, his eyes still blinded by the brightness of the demon.

Jandu swallowed. Feeling slightly better, Jandu returned back to his family, and shared the news. Once the immediate disaster had been averted, his brothers chided him, first about not sleeping with a beautiful immortal, and secondly to guess what womanly attributes Jandu would develop. He shot nasty glances at them, and hit Baram in the head when Baram suggested that Jandu would be an adorable maiden.

The comments hurt Jandu's pride, and he groaned as they got worse, the rest of them laughing hysterically as they imagined a female Jandu. He almost snapped completely and told them all to fuck off.

But then he realized that, for the first night in ages, none of them complained about their hunger. And for the first time in what felt like a year, Jandu hadn't worried about Keshan. The rest of their lives were so miserable, a smaller tragedy lightened their mood.

So Jandu let them mock him, taking it diligently until he realized it would never end unless he hit Baram. This started a friendly brawl and ended with a broken bench and an angry wife, who demanded that they fix it.

It was sad when bad news was better than horrible news, but Jandu reveled in that one night, where he felt almost safe. Mendraz had helped him, and although he was not completely out of danger, at least the worst had been averted.

CHAPTER 24

NOT FOR THE FIRST TIME, KESHAN FOUND HIMSELF WAITING to see King Darvad.

Over the past year, Keshan had been treated warmly by Darvad. He and Iyestar enjoyed a place within Darvad's inner circle. Keshan split his time between Prasta and Tiwari, taking over pressing business at home when Iyestar was in the capital, and pushing his own agenda within the royal palace.

But recently, Darvad seemed hesitant to see him. Keshan suspected it was because he pressed his legal agenda every time he had a chance to meet with the king. Keshan knew he sounded repetitive, but it was the only way he could get his message through.

Tarek always took the time to listen to Keshan's concerns, and he kept his promise to push forward Keshan's legislation. When Tarek was in Prasta, he and Keshan built an easy friendship, based on a shared vision of the country's future. But now Tarek was away again, off on another errand for Darvad, subjugating the lords who balked at Darvad's rule.

Darvad's changes were not being accepted without challenge. In addition to Keshan's improvements, Darvad was also making sweeping revisions to the traditions of their culture. He lessened the control of the temple over the land. He reduced tithing to Shentari priests. He forced the Draya to pay more in taxes. And he required absolute fealty to his rule.

Each small outbreak of resentment was immediately answered by dispatching the Royal Judge. Tarek was a rare sight in the palace now, too busy traveling the country running Darvad's errands and forcing Darvad's heavy-handed rule amongst the lords.

Tarek's absence made Keshan's job harder. And now Darvad kept Keshan waiting for an audience, knowing full well why Keshan was there.

Keshan played his flute as he waited in a luxurious sitting room in the palace. At least he didn't have to wait for Darvad's attention in the reception hall, with the rest of the courtiers. Servants brought Keshan food and wine, and one of Darvad's stewards checked on him every half hour, begging forgiveness for the delay, assuring Keshan that he had not been forgotten.

But the wasted time rankled Keshan.

Finally, Keshan gave up waiting. He tucked his flute away and grabbed his scroll, and headed down the marble hallway in search of Darvad himself. He would interrupt the king if need be.

Keshan found Darvad in one of the palace gardens, talking quietly with Druv. The two of them sat around a chess board, but neither of them played. Blossoming orchids filled the garden. One of the palace cats sat on the low plaster wall, blinking lazily into the sunlight. The two men sat at a table on a bench with their backs facing Keshan.

"I have absolute confidence that they are not in Jagu Mali or Bandari," Druv said. "My reports from Marshav are not complete, but I have heard back from my scouts in two thirds of the state, and no one can report any sign of the Parans there either."

Darvad threw one of the chess pieces across the garden. The cat immediately leapt off the wall.

"Damn it, Druv! It does me no good to tell me where they *aren't*. I need to know where they are, and quickly! Half of their exile is over and there is still not a sign of them! You must try harder."

"I am using the full extent of my contacts, Darvad. But finding four people in the entire country, especially four people who are trying not to be found, isn't easy."

"How hard can it be? They stand out like demons! Three men and a woman, traveling together? One the size of a house, another with blue eyes? For God's sake, do I have to do this myself?"

"Darvad, I am trying. Have faith in me. We will find them in time." Druv suddenly looked back and saw Keshan. "It looks like we have a guest."

Darvad turned his head and glared at Keshan.

"Keshan!" Darvad's glare lessened slightly. "You surprised us. I didn't know you were waiting."

"I've been waiting for two hours," Keshan said. He smiled and made the sign of peace to both of them. "I decided I would come and find you myself before I grew old."

"Please, sit down and join us." Darvad gestured to the bench across from him and Druv at the table. "Were you given any refreshment?"

"Yes, I have had plenty of time to eat, thank you."

Druv stood. "I'm sorry, I have to concede the game to you, Darvad. Besides, you threw my queen across the courtyard."

"I would have beaten you anyway," Darvad said.

"Perhaps." Druv bowed to Keshan. "Excuse me, but I must leave you both. I must follow up on some errands."

An uncomfortable silence followed as Darvad accompanied Druv out of the garden, and then turned back to Keshan. His face darkened.

"I'm sorry to keep you waiting, Keshan, but I have been very busy."

Keshan raised an eyebrow. "Yes, I heard a little of what is occupying your time. I also heard that Tarek is leading a confrontation in Jagu Mali. How does it go?"

"It isn't much of a confrontation. Tarek is simply ensuring that Lord Bir is collecting the appropriate levels of taxes from his citizens. You should be pleased. Apparently Bir did not like the new laws lessening the punishments against the Chaya. Tarek is making sure he sees the light."

Keshan nodded. "I am glad to hear it."

"I have not forgotten your requests," Darvad said.

"I know. And I am grateful." Keshan passed over his scroll. "But there is so much more to be done. We still need to establish funding for schools for the Chaya."

"We have already made great strides with the Chaya."

"You are watering down my changes until they are meaningless!" Keshan realized his voice was rising, and took a deep breath. "We have only begun our work. What about getting priests to bless the Chaya temples without unreasonable payoffs?"

"It is next on my list of things to do," Darvad said wearily.

"And the changes to the status of the Jegora?"

Darvad rubbed his eyes. He was silent for a long moment. And then he stared at Keshan wearily.

"Keshan. Listen to me. We have to do this carefully. We cannot rush into anything."

"I hardly think it is rushing," Keshan said.

"These radical changes take time. The Jegora are despised by God. To embrace them in our culture is the equivalent of telling the priests that we shun the word of God. It is one thing to help the Suya and Chaya; they are God's children. But the untouchables? No one wants to include them, Keshan. Not even my most radical allies."

"But they have it worst of all," Keshan urged. "Even if we make small changes, we can improve their lot. Today, the untouchables are only allowed to wear the clothes of the dead. What if we remove that law? How does that harm anybody?"

"That isn't the point," Darvad said. "The Jegora wear clothing from the dead because it is in the Book of Taivo. The Shentari faith is based on the precepts in the Book, and if we ignore one of the precepts, then we are opening ourselves up to change them all."

"Yes."

Darvad sighed. "I cannot commit to that. Every law we have enacted still allows the Shentari faith to keep its precepts.

Once we start picking and choosing which of the holy tenets we abide, we may start a war. The Draya won't like it. The faithful won't like it. And I can't afford to lose everyone just to change the wardrobe of ten percent of the population."

Keshan stifled his bitter response. It would do no good to fight Darvad on this. Darvad was king, and Keshan would lose. He would have to try a different tactic.

"What about making changes that do not go against the Book of Taivo? Nowhere does it state that God encourages the beating of the Jegora, and yet this happens all the time. If we passed a law saying that harming the Jegora will result in punishment, we have not broken any religious belief, and we have made an immediate improvement to the lives of thousands of men and women across this country. Darvad, we live in a country where a Jegora woman may be dragged from her house and raped and there is no punishment or shame cast upon her attacker. They have no rights."

"They are untouchables. They have never had rights. I know this is hard for you to accept, but we cannot fight their battle just yet. Let us improve the plight of the Suya and Chaya for now. Please?"

Darvad looked sincere. And suddenly, Keshan felt sickened by the whole thing. Darvad *was* sincere. He wanted change. He embodied Keshan's hopes for a new world. And yet even he could not imagine a world where a Jegora was treated as a full human being. The idea was as foreign as it was to ask a cow for permission to milk her. The cow was there to serve human beings. And the Jegora were there to take care of dead bodies and clean up the sewers. Keshan suddenly felt like giving up. Weariness passed from Darvad into him. So many months of working so hard. So many trivial annoyances that he let go of. The dozens of spies which followed him daily, hoping that he would lead Darvad to the Parans; the madness of trying to communicate legal changes to a Royal Judge who was never there; and the more personal troubles. Iyestar and

ASTRID AMARA

he fought constantly now. Ajani's frustration with him grew
to new heights. And his inability to communicate with Jandu,
all of this mounted into a moment of crippling frustration.

"Thank you for your time," Keshan said brusquely. He left
the scroll with Darvad and made his way to the gate.

"Don't be angry with me," Darvad asked. He followed
Keshan to the gate and touched his shoulder. "I cannot bear
it. Too many people hate me already. I need you. I need you
on my side."

Keshan smiled weakly. "I am not angry. I am frustrated,
yes. But not angry."

Darvad smiled back. "Good. Then you know how I feel."
He embraced Keshan briefly. "Thank you for coming. I will
make sure you do not wait so long the next time."

Keshan turned and left the palace. As he suspected, the
moment he got into his chariot, a rider on horseback mounted
and trailed him. Druv's spies were obvious. Keshan wondered
if it wasn't deliberate, a way to keep Keshan in line.

The thought fuelled his anger. Because of them, he hadn't
heard a word from Jandu in months. Druv's spies had caught
Chezek the last time he had returned from the mountains.
And while they did not hurt Chezek, and although Chezek
managed to keep Jandu's letters safe out of their hands, the
risk was just too great.

But the months of silence gnawed at him constantly. For
all he knew, Jandu was dead. Frustration coiled within him,
made him reckless.

"I'll just visit him myself." As soon as he mumbled the
words, Keshan realized that he would break all the rules and
actually do it. He no longer cared about the repercussions. His
brother could be angry. Darvad could suspect him. It didn't
matter now. He needed to alleviate the worry in his mind, or
else he could not concentrate on anything else. He needed a
break from the palace, and from politics. And no one was as
good at making Keshan forget his troubles than Jandu.

As his chariot wound through the dusty streets of Prasta, a giddy excitement built in him. Once he had made his decision, he thought himself a fool for waiting so long. He could not be gone indefinitely, but at least he could have something to refresh him, rejuvenate him, after months of stagnant frustration.

That evening, he met with his loyal servant Chezek in private. Chezek had been Keshan's charioteer since he was a teenager, and he trusted the gruff man with his life. Only Chezek held the secret of Keshan's relationship with Jandu, and he never questioned it. Chezek's loyalty was unwavering, and so it was with him alone that Keshan plotted.

The following day, Chezek left the palace on the premise that he had an urgent message to deliver for Keshan. He returned, anxious, and urged Keshan that his good friend in Pagdesh was ill, begging Keshan to tend to him.

Keshan made the excuse to Iyestar, who eyed Chezek and Keshan both with an air of suspicion.

"I had no idea that you were so close to Gerevan Handari," Iyestar said, looking at the parchment Chezek had delivered.

"We have maintained a steady correspondence since he visited us in Tiwari," Keshan said calmly. "I owe him my attendance if he requests it."

Iyestar ground his teeth. He handed the letter back to Keshan. "Fine, go then. But no longer than a week. I need you here."

Keshan bowed to his older brother, and hid his smile of triumph until he was safely out of Iyestar's quarters. Immediately, he packed his belongings and sent Chezek to the market to purchase additional items, gifts for Handari's extensive family.

All of his preparations were watched carefully. It irked Keshan that even in his own townhouse in Prasta, Druv's spies monitored him. Servants Keshan once thought of as honest suddenly appeared in his chambers, looked through his documents. Keshan fought the urge to fire them, realizing they would only be replaced with other spies.

Men followed his chariot out of the city, and when they reached the open roads to the east, crossing the thin branch of the Yaru River that separated Prasta from the State of Karuna, new men arrived, tradesmen with an eerie sense of pacing who managed to change their route in accordance with Keshan's own.

They were followed through Karuna. By the time they reached the border, a group of men traveling as religious ascetics on pilgrimage were suspiciously close behind them.

Again Keshan wished he could just go through the Yashva kingdom, but human spies, no matter how tenacious, could not match the tracking ability of Firdaus' Yashva cousins. They had a better chance of success in the human world.

Keshan and Chezek detoured off the main route to Pagdesh, instead heading northeast along the narrow, winding roads of the State of Marshav. As soon as they were convinced that they had temporarily lost their trackers, Keshan sold the chariot and purchased two horses instead. He and Chezek loaded them down with the goods for the Parans and left before sunrise. The rest of their journey seemed free of spies, but they still took extra precautions once they reached the mountainous state of Pagdesh.

It had been years since Keshan had traveled this far north, and while he wished he had time to take in the sights, to see the towns and people he had only heard about, he had no time to spare. They crossed through herds of brightly painted cattle and flocks of sheep that scattered at their horse's canter. They didn't sleep in towns, resting past nightfall in secluded fields far from the sight of the road.

Once they reached the village at the base of Mount Adri, Keshan donned Chezek's heavy black turban, the trait of the Marshavi people, and put on his heavy long black tunic and baggy trousers. Delicate silver embroidery decorated the cuffs and front buttons. Chezek put on Keshan's own clothing, his bright yellow silks and bangles, even wearing Keshan's diadem.

Anyone looking closely at either man would know the deception immediately. Chezek was too old and grizzled to ever be mistaken for his master. But from a distance, they wore their parts well.

Keshan had never seen his servant in anything other than black, so seeing him now in gold embroidery and a tight yellow vest made him smile.

"Don't laugh," Chezek grumbled, straightening his diadem. "You'll need your energy for the mountain."

The two day trek up the mountain to Jandu's rendezvous point proved to be physically draining, but mentally soothing. The rhythm of steps leading endlessly upwards, and the steady beat of his horse's hooves, became a form of meditation, each footfall taking him further from the trials of his life, closer to Jandu.

As a young boy, Keshan spent months like he was now, in the middle of nowhere, alone with nature. He had loved it. He had learned how to detect weather changes from the slightest breeze, predict oncoming storms from the shapes of clouds, he had deciphered dozens of bird calls, discovered hundreds of plants, befriended wild animals, and spent lazy afternoons with cows.

All of that seemed a lifetime ago. He couldn't remember the last time he had taken a stroll even in his own garden in Tiwari. Even his daily swims in the ocean with Iyestar had become infused with unspoken tension.

Keshan rolled his shoulders back and closed his eyes as he walked, his horse's lead rope loose in his hand. Thick humid air engulfed his body like a warm bath and he let the calls of nature overwrite the quarrels and debates of court in his head, embracing the noisy silence of the forest.

When the sun went down beneath the mountains and darkness made it impossible to continue, he found a spot along the pilgrim's trail that looked amenable for a camp fire, and settled down for the night. He fed his horse and lit a small fire, noticing signs of previous campers. He wondered if Jandu had slept there. The thought filled Keshan with wanting. He was almost there.

In the morning, he left at first light and walked quickly. He hoped that Jandu would visit the glade that he had described in his first letter. Neither Chezek nor Keshan knew the exact location of the Parans' house, although Keshan figured it had to be nearby.

Keshan finally stumbled into the clearing in the forest that Jandu and Chezek had described a little past noon. He saw the statue first—stone blackened with age and worn smooth, the shapely curves of a woman's body barely detectable. But there were no letters beside it. Keshan grew alarmed.

He heard a rustle in the trees, and froze in fear. What if he had been followed? It seemed unlikely; there were parts of the pilgrim's trail where he could see down the mountainside for nearly a mile, and no one had been behind him.

But caution flooded him. He tied his horse in the thicket and hunkered down against a large tree. He closed Chezek's long-sleeved coat tighter around him and pulled the end of the black turban down, wrapping his face and obscuring all but his eyes. Crouched beside the tree, Keshan's had an unobstructed view of the clearing, but he was well-hidden behind a flowering bush. The rustle of someone approaching grew louder. His heart beat faster as he crunched his body tighter.

Jandu appeared in the glade, scowling.

It had been a year and a half since Keshan had seen him, and the changes startled him. Jandu seemed taller. His arms had developed lean and clearly defined muscles. But he was shockingly thin. The high cheekbones in his face were very prominent, his eyes seemed slightly sunken with hunger, and his stomach was as flat as a board. His thick black hair had grown longer and, unrestrained without a diadem or crown, seemed wild and unruly. His bangs fell into his eyes. Jandu pushed the hair back from his face angrily.

His dark blue cotton dejaru was stained and ragged. His old blue sash had faded nearly to white. The harafa he wore on his upper body was woven from rough cotton, and was also badly stained. Jandu draped it partially over his head like a beggar would.

Jandu's expression seemed fiercer to Keshan as well. His blue eyes burned with an intensity that startled Keshan. He looked angry at the world, which didn't surprise Keshan. The world had shat upon him, and now he was fumbling through a dense and unfriendly forest, looking desperately for news of his lover.

This thought constricted Keshan's throat with emotion. He knew he had missed Jandu, but now seeing him, scowling at bushes and furiously swiping at mosquitoes, he realized how much his own life had suffered without this temperamental man by his side.

Keshan shifted, and a branch cracked under his sandal.

Jandu narrowed his eyes in Keshan's direction. He stalked towards Keshan with startling speed.

"What do you want?" Jandu roared, suddenly grabbing Keshan by the throat and pulling him from his crouched position. He slammed Keshan against the tree trunk, holding him up by his neck.

As soon as they made eye contact, Jandu's eyes widened. He immediately let go of Keshan's throat.

"Keshan!"

"Hello. I—"

Jandu grabbed Keshan by the collar and jerked him forward, kissing him with almost painful force.

Keshan gave up trying to speak. He wrapped his arms around Jandu. Jandu pressed him back against the trunk of the tree and pinned Keshan there, grinding his hips into Keshan as he thrust his tongue deeply into Keshan's mouth.

A year and a half of desire rushed through Keshan's system, making him respond to every touch from Jandu's hands.

They felt different, calloused. But they touched Keshan's flesh with a familiarity that sped Keshan's heart.

Keshan tried to pull his mouth away from Jandu to speak, but Jandu's lips wouldn't let him go. Jandu bit Keshan's lip gently, forcing the contact. Jandu kissed him as if his life depended upon it.

Finally, breathless, Jandu pulled his lips away and stared down at Keshan.

"You fucker!" he said. There were tears in his eyes. "Why didn't you write me?"

"It was too risky," Keshan said. "Druv's spies caught Chezek."

Jandu's eyed widened. "Is he all right?"

"Yes, and they didn't find the letters. But we couldn't risk coming back."

Jandu studied Keshan's expression. "Then why are you here now?"

Keshan swallowed. "I needed to see you."

Jandu kissed him again. Keshan let his knees relax and he slid down the trunk of the tree, Jandu crouching down with him, never breaking contact with his lips. Keshan lay back upon the forest floor and Jandu crouched above him. He could feel Jandu's erection pushing against his thigh.

"I thought you were dead. Or tortured." Jandu's words were whispered between frantic kisses. "You have no idea how I've worried..."

"Well don't worry any longer. The only torture I've endured is of sexual deprivation."

For the first time, Jandu's mouth broke into a hesitant smile. He rolled off of Keshan and lay on his side beside him. Jandu reached out and pushed Keshan's turban off his head. He ran his hand through Keshan's hair, closing his eyes. "God, I missed doing this." He left his fingers entangled in Keshan's locks. "Turbans don't suit you."

"Well, neither does that harafa over your head," Keshan said, laughing. "You look like a Bandari street beggar."

Jandu pulled his hand back as if burned.

Keshan felt a fool.

"God, Jandu, I'm sorry. I didn't mean—"

"—That's all right. I *am* a fucking beggar. It's appropriate that I look the part."

"I didn't mean that. I was trying to..." Trying to what? Keshan suddenly realized that the way he used to speak with Jandu would no longer work. Jandu didn't have the same sense of humor he used to. Nothing about his current situation was particularly funny, after all. "I'm sorry."

Jandu ground his teeth. He looked as though he were about to speak, and then suddenly changed his mind.

"Talk later." Jandu pulled Keshan on top of him and kissed his mouth, a tremor of anxiety still coursing through his body. Even in the midst of all the political turmoil of Prasta, Keshan had never felt Jandu so on edge. The Jandu he knew was mellow, self-assured. This man was jumpy as a jack rabbit and his pride easily injured.

But Keshan's worries faded as the intensity of their embrace increased. Jandu's eyes slanted as his mouth ravished Keshan. Keshan savored the erotic roughness to his cheeks, the unbearable softness of his pink lips. Keshan ran his hands along Jandu's neck, feeling each bone, running his hands along his sternum. He gently circled Jandu's nipples with his fingers, listening for Jandu's telltale gasp that he enjoyed this. Jandu always made strange, inarticulate noises when they made love. It was one of his more endearing traits.

Keshan leaned down and flicked at Jandu's right nipple with the tip of his tongue. Jandu let out a small, peculiar groan, and a smile broke across Keshan's face.

Touching Jandu after all this time was an erotic mixture of familiarity and strangeness. He knew the smell of Jandu's body, the taste of it, his color and texture, and what spots on his body made him shout out in desire. But his body had changed. His ribs were prominent, declaring themselves across his chest. He had more hair on his chest than before, but it was dark and small, huddled in shy curls. Jandu's hips seemed narrower, due to the fact that his thighs had grown in size with all his walking.

"Keshan," Jandu moaned.

Keshan's own hardness urgently pressed against his tightly wrapped dejaru. He ignored it, instead sitting up to slowly, patiently, undo the sash across Jandu's waist.

Jandu watched him from beneath lowered lashes.

Keshan untied the knot of Jandu's dejaru slowly, drawing out the effort. He felt like he was unwrapping a present. The anticipation of seeing him naked made his own body shiver with desire.

He slowly pulled down the fabric wrapped around Jandu's waist, revealing his thick, slightly curved cock.

Keshan didn't touch it. He instead placed kisses around it, listening to Jandu's small noises as he squirmed to get Keshan's mouth closer to the tip. Keshan gently licked the salty skin of Jandu's inner thighs, loving the scent of maleness about him. Jandu was so masculine here, where small hairs darkened the soft sweet flesh of his legs, where his scrotum hung heavily and loose, the skin soft and salty to the tongue.

Keshan took his time with Jandu, not wanting to rush this. He had only a week at most to be with him, and he didn't know how much time alone they would be able to find.

And this was Suraya's flesh now, Keshan realized. He wondered absent-mindedly if she had ever done this to him— pulled his testicles into her mouth, her fingers playing close to his entrance, her breath hot on the sensitive base of his cock.

Keshan smiled to himself. Somehow, he knew this was his space here. This was his closeness to Jandu, their secret spot. When Keshan closed his lips onto Jandu, and Jandu hissed in pleasure, Keshan knew that this was a pleasure he alone in the world had. He let Jandu raise his hips up, let him thrust into the back of Keshan's throat, searching for the deepest place, the moment when he knew that Keshan had swallowed him whole.

But Jandu was Jandu. He rarely took his pleasure without seeing to Keshan's needs first. He had a boyish smile on his face, his eyes sparkling. "Come here," he said huskily. He sat up. His hands shook as he helped Keshan out of his trousers. Keshan knelt and let his cock touch Jandu's, loving the way that slight movement made Jandu's entire body go rigid with pleasure.

Jandu's naked body was so firm and masculine, so defined, but the way it trembled with anticipation was almost feminine. Until he met Jandu, Keshan hadn't realized his sexual desire could be whipped into such a frenzy.

After all, sex was fun with anyone. But sex with Jandu was so erotic, it made everything else seem limp and empty, it made everything else just fucking. But Jandu was a living, pulsing, definition of sex to Keshan—the noble yet languid way Jandu moved, the taste of him, from the salty flesh of his testicles to the sun-burnt sweetness of his neck, the rigid firmness of his stomach muscles and his strong arms, the infinite softness of his lips and inner thighs, the strong musky scent of his flesh—it was as if he were born simply to bring Keshan to his knees with craving.

Jandu grasped Keshan's member in his hot hands and pressed it against his own. He wrapped his hands around them both, stroking them together, his movements lubricated with Keshan's saliva.

Pleasure rocked through Keshan's entire body. Jandu nudged Keshan's legs wider with his knee, spreading Keshan open, speeding his pumping. With his other hand he gently stroked Keshan's testicles, his finger gently brushing backwards until he pressed into Keshan.

Keshan moaned. He leaned forward and kissed Jandu deeply, his hands gripping Jandu's shoulders. Jandu's blue eyes locked on Keshan's own. Jandu was the only lover Keshan had ever had who watched Keshan while making love. Keshan pushed back against Jandu's finger, pressing him deeper inside.

The feeling caused Keshan to come in one long explosion, his mind reeling by the force of it. How had he gone so long without this feeling?

Keshan reached down to help stroke Jandu to completion as well, their fingers intertwining around his swollen flesh, their palms wet with Keshan's cum.

Jandu let out a strangled moan and released in a long arc onto his own chest. Jandu collapsed backwards onto the forest floor, pulling Keshan down beside him. Keshan kissed him once more. Love fluttered in his breast as Jandu kissed back lazily and sweetly, his tongue making long strokes along his lips.

Keshan threw his leg over Jandu, suddenly exhausted. "You taste like berries and deer."

Jandu laughed.

Keshan retied his dejaru. Jandu looked reluctant as he did the same.

They lay there together, on the forest floor, holding hands and staring at the canopy of trees as Jandu caught Keshan up on everything that had happened since their last correspondence. Keshan wanted to lay in the warm glade forever. Moments stolen with Jandu felt like moments of escape. And he needed to escape his stressful life of politics in Tiwari as much as Jandu needed to escape the poverty and humiliation of exile.

"I hope you have dozens of letters for me," Keshan said.

Jandu sighed. "They're gone."

Keshan frowned. "What do you mean?"

"I had all those drawings... they've been collecting for months beneath that statue." He glared at the statue angrily. "And then *she* came and took them all."

"She? Who?" Keshan's eyes widened. "Suraya?"

"God, no!" Jandu looked just as horrified at the idea. "No, Mendraz's bitch of a consort, Umia! It's her statue. She thought I wrote the letters to her, and took them."

Keshan blinked at Jandu for a few moments, and then burst out laughing. Umia was his aunt. He grew up with stories of her human conquests.

"What did you do? I assume she wanted you to fuck her."

Jandu closed his eyes. "Yes. She wanted me to, but I didn't. So she cursed me."

Keshan froze. Umia's curses had been the scourge of their family for generations. He had never thought she would harm anyone he cared about. He quickly glanced over Jandu's body, looking for abnormalities.

"What curse?"

"I'm going to turn into a woman," Jandu said between gritted teeth. "I begged Mendraz to help, and he reduced the curse to one year of my choosing."

Keshan simply stared. The expression on Jandu's face warned Keshan against making light of the matter.

"I'm sorry." It seemed like such an empty, useless thing to say.

Jandu sighed, and squeezed Keshan's hand. "It's the least of our worries, honestly. Suraya's pregnant, and she isn't getting enough to eat here."

Jealousy flooded Keshan, but he forced himself to smile. "Congratulations."

Jandu quirked an eyebrow at him. "It isn't mine. It's Baram's child."

"But this is your year with her, right?"

"Yes. She was pregnant before me."

"Are you sure?"

Jandu smirked. "I know how to count." He leaned back and smiled at the sky. "Besides, I'm too in love with you to pretend with anyone else."

Keshan stroked Jandu's hair. "What are you going to do?"

"Yudar wants to go to Afadi and hide as servants. I don't particularly care where we go, as long as there is food and I don't have to beg anymore."

Keshan could feel Jandu's shudder. He leaned over and kissed Jandu sweetly.

But Keshan's stomach grumbled, announcing the late hour in the day. Jandu smiled shyly. "Are you hungry? We could go back to the house and see what Baram made for dinner. It probably won't be much, but it usually tastes good. He's mastered the art of making stale rice exciting and flavorful."

Keshan lowered his lips to kiss Jandu's neck. He was loath to give up this moment, the two of them, alone in the world. But Jandu had apparently made up his mind to feed his guest. He sat up and brushed the leaves and sticks from his clothing.

"I've brought some food as well," Keshan said. Keshan saw Jandu's eyes brighten, and then watched him try and hide his enthusiasm. Everything Jandu did right now was perfect. Keshan grabbed his hand again and kissed him.

"I love you," Keshan whispered.

Jandu smiled crookedly. "I love you too."

Keshan rested his forehead gently on Jandu's for a moment, sighing, and then the two of them left the forest glade.

CHAPTER 25

One look at the Paran's home in the forest confirmed Keshan's worst fears: he had not brought enough to help them. They were going to die of deprivation.

His heart ached as he realized he hadn't done enough. And yet they still welcomed Keshan into their home with the enthusiasm of puppies, all of them bounding around Keshan and touching him and laughing, sweeping the floor under his feet and offering him seats, handing him water and what little food they had. Even Yudar seemed honestly pleased to see Keshan, despite their differences.

But there was no comfort to be had in this bleak place. Jandu's letters had lied, hiding the level of their desperation.

Keshan saw they had sold everything they had of value, other than the chest in the corner that held their weapons and armor. Their clothes were in tatters, their sandals worn and held together with rawhide string. The hut leaked and it stank of mold. They had one pot and the few jars they had for food stores were cracked and stained. Their cow looked sickly, her coat patched with bites and her ribs prominent.

Yudar had changed most of all. Where he had once been the symbol of a healthy, strong Triya king, he now resembled an ascetic walking the last steps of his life. He had grown a beard, and his long hair was loose, oily and turning gray. His stomach and eyes sunk with hunger, and his arms had lost the muscles of a warrior. His ribs shot out in an angry display of malnutrition.

Baram was still intimidating, even starving, but his hair had thinned dramatically and his skin was riddled with cuts and bruises, thorns angrily eating at his flesh, a heat rash on his ankles, his body rejecting the humidity of the jungle. Suraya was hugely pregnant. Her hair was still fiery and beautiful, and her eyes had their liquid, smoldering sensuality, but dark circles had formed under them and her skin had taken on a yellowish tone.

"It looks like an outhouse, doesn't it?" Jandu asked Keshan softly.

Keshan tried to smile. "A cozy outhouse. With a nice smell."

"That would be all the sandalwood." Jandu helped Keshan move his saddlebags inside as Baram took care of Keshan's horse. Yudar offered Keshan a grass mat to sit by the water's edge. Their location was stunning—great green-covered mountain peaks jutted from a lake so calm the surface seemed like crystal. Keshan sat with the Parans and caught them up on world events, knowing they were desperate for news, hungry for a new face around the fire.

Keshan didn't disappoint. He was a fantastic, florid story-teller, his eyes growing wide and expressive, his hands moving in jarring, exaggerated gestures, as he mimicked the king and his lords, recounted disputes and whispered gossip. As he spoke, he could feel Jandu's eyes upon him, watching his gold bangles jangle with each flick of his wrist.

Yudar ate up the news of the kingdom hungrily, his eyes shining brightly. His expression remained rapt and focused, only clouding over when Keshan mentioned the numerous small skirmishes being led by the new Royal Judge, Tarek.

Yudar seemed poised to ask a question, but then thought better of it. He shook his head and smiled. "I never thought I would miss the position of Royal Judge as much as I do."

"I thought you were in line for the position, Keshan," Baram stated. He sat down beside Keshan and offered him another glass of water.

Keshan shrugged. "I think my politics are too radical for even Darvad. But Tarek is a good man, and I believe he will do what is right for Marhavad."

There was an uncomfortable silence. Jandu poked at the dirt with a stick, clearly bored by the discussion already. The idea made Keshan smile. At least one part of Jandu's personality had not changed.

"I have some small gifts for you," Keshan told them, retrieving his saddle bags.

"Adaru, your presence is a great enough gift for all of us," Yudar said, bringing his hands together in the sign of peace.

Keshan dug through the bags and handed out gifts. He offered Baram a bag of aromatic basmati rice from the south, salt and palm oil. He opened a cask of wine and shared it with his cousins, and while Baram and Yudar weren't looking, pressed into Jandu's hands a small leather purse of gold coins. He gave perfume and a new zahari for Suraya, as well as a bolt of white cotton cloth. While she admired the zahari, Keshan inquired after her baby.

Suraya rubbed her belly fondly and smiled. "I think it will be three more months." She shook her head. "That's all I can take, too. This child is heavy."

"He's Baram's child, what do you expect?"

After their meal, Yudar and Baram made Keshan a bed on the floor of the main hut by piling their grass mats and their blankets together for him. Keshan protested when he saw that this meant they would sleep on the packed-earth floor, uncovered, but they insisted. Jandu rested his hand on Keshan's head for a long, sweet moment, and then reached down to take the dust from Keshan's feet before he turned in for the night. It was such a formal gesture, and one that Keshan had always hated. Now though, in front of Jandu's family, Jandu made the gesture seem almost erotic, the emotions behind the touch true and overpowering, Jandu's hands resting on Keshan's feet a second longer than tradition, as if holding him to make sure he were real, as if transferring to him his love and hope. Then, with a sad smile, Jandu left to sleep with Suraya.

◆◆◆

As soon as the sun rose the following morning, Baram left for the village, taking some of the gold Keshan brought. After drinking tea with Suraya and Yudar, Jandu begged Keshan to hunt with him. They walked down the main pilgrim's trail until Jandu jerked to a halt, tilting his head to hear something. He quickly pulled Keshan into the dense forest and the two hid behind bushes until a group of holy men passed by.

Keshan hadn't thought much about what it must be like to hide from every passerby. Now he watched the tension harden Jandu's muscles, his shoulders pull in, watched the way Jandu's eyes darted up and down the trail for other witnesses. Keshan wearied of the anxiety in minutes. He couldn't imagine living this way for over a year.

"Come on." As soon as the trail was clear, Jandu led him back along the path until they cut once more into the woods. They walked together in companionable silence, and Keshan relaxed alongside him, enjoying the way Jandu's body moved through the forest like a predator, on edge yet assured.

After felling two junglefowl, Jandu settled down in a mossy clearing to rest.

"Play me a song," Jandu said. He grinned at Keshan, pointing at the velvet pouch on Keshan's belt that always held his flute. "Play that Jandu song you wrote. It's your best song."

Keshan smirked. "Of course you'd think so. But I better not play. I think I better teach."

Jandu frowned. "What do you mean?"

Keshan took out his flute and used it to point at Jandu.

"You are going to spend the last year of your exile hiding in Afadi, right?"

Jandu nodded.

"And you will be looking for work with Lord Indarel?"

"That's the plan." Jandu leaned against a log and stretched his long legs on the mossy ground.

"Is that when you will be hiding as a woman?"

Jandu looked away. "I haven't thought about it."

"It seems like as good of a year as any. No one will suspect you in such a disguise. Darvad's spies are looking for a man with blue eyes, not a woman. And if you do go to Lord Indarel as a female servant, you will need to have a skill. Archery and combat training will not get you work if you are wearing a zahari and have your hair up in ribbons." Keshan blew a solitary note on his instrument. Several birds above them took off in surprise.

Jandu narrowed his eyes. "What are you getting at?"

"Become a music teacher," Keshan said. "That's a respectable profession for a young woman, and one that is always needed in noble palaces. Indarel has teenaged children. I'm sure he would love a tutor for them."

Jandu shook his head. "I don't know anything about music. "

"Exactly. So I'm going to teach you now." Keshan blew a long, trilling note. "Besides, it could help your begging. People always prefer to get something for their donation."

Jandu snorted. "Keshan, you may be a good teacher, and I have a brilliant mind. But I doubt we have enough time for me to master the flute."

"You're a quick learner." He handed Jandu the flute.

Jandu looked down at the instrument. "I don't know about this."

"It's easy." Keshan leaned forward so his breath fell on Jandu's neck. "Just put your lips upon the tip and blow."

A soft pink tint colored Jandu's cheeks. He raised an eyebrow. "Is that all?"

Keshan smiled coyly. "Put your fingers along the shaft. Like this." He helped position Jandu's fingers on the flute. Their fingers moved together along the smooth silver. Keshan could hear Jandu's breathing change.

"Good." Keshan gently guided the flute to Jandu's lips. "Blow."

Jandu produced a sour note that once again set the white-throats to complaint. He shook his head and handed the instrument back to Keshan. He put his hand on Keshan's leg again.

"I'd rather blow something else."

"Later," Keshan said, although he was sorely tempted. "You have to work at this. Now practice."

"This isn't going to work. I don't even have a flute."

"You could borrow mine," Keshan offered, although the idea of being parted from his beloved instrument hurt.

Jandu shook his head. "Absolutely not. That would be like taking my bow away from me. Maybe I could be the first woman archery teacher in Marhavad..."

Keshan suddenly had an idea. "Zandi!"

"What?"

Keshan put his own flute down and reached around Jandu, grabbing his magnificent bow. Keshan placed Zandi on the ground before them and whispered a sharta.

They watched silently as Zandi slowly compressed and turned into a pool of liquid metal. The pool shrank further, coalescing into a long flute, the metal shimmering and shifting in the light, swirls of burnished color dancing between the valves.

Keshan laughed. He gently lifted Zandi. "Just ask her to change when you need her." Keshan stroked the instrument. The metal was still warm, and the valves seem to anticipate his touch, depressing effortlessly. "It's almost a shame to waste such a beautiful instrument on you."

Jandu gaped in horror. "What have you done? Turn her back!"

Keshan whispered to Zandi, stroking her as he gave a simple Yashva spell for change. The flute vibrated in his hand, and metamorphosed into the bow once more. The second the bow returned, Jandu pulled it away from Keshan.

"Stop playing with my things."

Keshan raised an eyebrow. "Glad to see you haven't become completely humble in your exile."

Jandu slumped against the log once more, stroking Zandi protectively. "I'm going to be emasculated enough when I turn into a woman. Did you think I would look forward to you taking my weapon from me as well?"

Keshan stretched his legs alongside Jandu's. "I'm not taking it away, I'm just transforming it. This way Zandi can remain by your side."

Jandu snorted. "You can't defend a kingdom with a flute."

"And you can't defend a kingdom if you're in permanent exile either," Keshan pointed out.

Jandu conceded that this was true. "And it is a clever way to keep Zandi with me all the time," he added. He looked at Zandi affectionately, and then nodded. "All right. Teach me how to change her."

Keshan taught Jandu how to transform Zandi, and then forced him through scales on the flute. He taught Jandu how unique colorations could be conjured for each individual note. Keshan didn't realize how much he enjoyed teaching flute, but he grew warm and content as he watched Jandu struggle through the lessons, his mind working on all the new information, his fingers adjusting to the feel of the instrument. Learning came easily to Jandu, aided by Zandi's magical nature. It was almost as though Zandi was playing herself.

But, like any good teacher, Keshan had to know when enough was enough. After an hour Jandu's eyes began to glaze over.

"Enough for today," he stated. He took Zandi from Jandu and whispered to convert her back into a bow. As soon as she changed, Jandu immediately strung her and slung her over his back.

Jandu stretched, his arms long and sleek, a golden brown in the forest. Keshan noted that he wore no jewelry anymore. And how could he? Yudar had lost everything of value to Darvad.

Impulsively, Keshan reached up and unclasped the pearl and gold pendant he always wore. The metal was warm in Keshan's hands, and slightly sticky with his sweat.

"Here." Keshan smiled. "I want you to have this." He pressed the necklace into Jandu's palm.

Jandu held it far from his body, as if it were volatile. "I can't take it. It's worth too much. It's too expensive."

"It's only a pearl," Keshan said. "You used to have dozens of them."

"I had no idea what a pearl was worth. Now that I know, I'm sure I can't accept such a gift," Jandu said. "Besides, look at me! People will think I stole it."

"Then just keep it in your pocket," Keshan urged. He pressed his hands around Jandu's, closing Jandu's hand into a fist around the necklace. "Just wear it secretly, close to your body."

Jandu's eyes welled with tears. He finally nodded and carefully put the pendant in his pouch. He wrapped his arms around Keshan's shoulders.

"You know, I never got my reward for being a good student," Jandu whispered.

"A pearl isn't enough? What sort of reward were you thinking of?"

Jandu peeled Keshan's vest from his shoulders and dropped it to the ground.

Keshan reached down and ran his hand slowly along Jandu's broad chest, down to the knot in Jandu's dejaru. He slipped his hand inside and within a moment had Jandu gasping for relief. Jandu leaned back against the forest floor and winced. He sat back up, pulling a burr from his shoulder.

Keshan watched Jandu for a reaction. He had seen this moment before, ages ago. Jandu studied the burr between his fingers, and then smirked at Keshan. "Hmm."

Keshan flicked the burr from Jandu's fingers and pushed Jandu back against the forest floor.

Keshan kissed Jandu with exquisite softness, his tongue gently probing Jandu's mouth, as light as a feather. He reached down into Jandu's trousers again and Jandu's member sprung loose. Keshan placed Jandu into his mouth, the same, excruciatingly slow and gentle teasing of his tongue now along Jandu's shaft, the flirtation of wetness and warmth. Jandu raked the soil with his hands.

"Jandu?"

Jandu and Keshan jerked apart as they heard Suraya call out. Jandu had barely enough time to stuff himself back in his trousers before Suraya pushed her large body through the bushes, coming across the two of them on the ground.

Even with Jandu's dejaru closed, Keshan realized they had been caught. There was no way to explain why they were doing so close together on the ground. Keshan felt a tremor of horror shake down his throat but composed himself. While Suraya's attention was on Jandu, he ran his fingers through his hair to straighten it and unclasped his earring, tossing it aside.

Keshan made a show of feeling through the leaves around him. "You haven't seen my earring, have you?"

"Wh—what?" she stammered.

"My earring." He pointed to his left earlobe, now bare. "I think I lost it around here."

"Earring?" Suraya repeated Keshan's word as if he was speaking a foreign language.

"It has great sentimental value," Keshan explained. "My mother gave them to me on my sixteenth birthday."

Jandu looked away from both of them. Keshan could see that his face was a brilliant scarlet.

Keshan watched Suraya's gaze lingering on Keshan's discarded vest.

"Can you help us search for it?" Keshan asked her sweetly.

"...Sure." Suraya frowned. She started pacing the area, seeming relieved to look at nothing but the forest floor.

Jandu stood frozen, his back to both of them.

"Come on Jandu, help me," Keshan said, searching the underbrush with energy. Keshan and Jandu made brief eye contact.

"It's over here!" Suraya cried.

Suraya bent over with great difficulty, and triumphantly lifted the small golden ring from the forest floor.

"Thank God for your sharp eyes!" Keshan cried, running up to her.

Suraya handed Keshan his earring and looked at him sharply. "I came to tell you that Baram is making dinner."

"Thank you," Keshan said.

The two of them stared at each other silently for what seemed to be a full minute before Suraya said, "You should be more careful."

Keshan finally broke eye contact and nodded. "I will be."

"You could lose something much more precious than gold," Suraya said.

"I know." All the mirth left Keshan's heart. In its place was a heavy, dank fear.

After Jandu's wife and brothers went to bed that evening, Jandu and Keshan sat by the glowing embers of the evening fire, poking at the charcoal with sticks, talking about foolish things that neither would ever waste paper in their letters to talk about. And in the night, with the company of the low, grumbling hoots of fish owls and the distant rustle of insects, Keshan found that peace that came with Jandu beside him. They didn't touch, what with their close encounter that afternoon and with Yudar and Baram sleeping on the other side of the hut wall. But they sat next to each other contentedly until the last of the embers died, and they were simply shadows to each other in the humid darkness.

"When I'm with you," Jandu whispered, "I feel like my heart has been broken open and music has burst into the silence." Jandu sighed. "I don't know how those around me can't see what you've done to me."

Keshan didn't say anything for a long time. He reached out and placed his hand on Jandu's chest, and held it there, pulsing heat and love through his fingers, his touch sending a message far more powerful than any words.

Finally, Keshan spoke, overcome with emotion.

"There is nothing that can ever explain, ever show, ever contain the strength of the love I have for you, Jandu."

Jandu cradled Keshan's face in his hands, and kissed him once, a slow, lingering kiss that had the fire of all the feelings that thundered through Keshan's body.

And then Jandu got up slowly and made his way in the darkness back to Suraya. He turned at the hut entrance and waved, and Keshan watched his shadow retreat, drawn in by the curtains of the darkness, his silhouette powerful, proud, perfect.

The next morning Keshan departed for Tiwari.

CHAPTER 26

As their second year of exile drew to a close Jandu took Keshan's advice and played Zandi while begging. Although it did not increase the generosity of many pilgrims, it made those who gave him something happier.

One morning, Jandu came across a magnificent black buck grazing, his twisted, striped horns and black and white body so beautiful, Jandu hesitated killing him. But he thought of Suraya, about to give birth, and how much he could sell the horns and hide for in town. Jandu reached for an arrow.

Zandi's splendor looked out of place in the lush greens of the forest. Her shimmering gold danced in the rays of light as Jandu silently strung his bow, watching the buck carefully, his hands deft and knowledgeable upon the brace. He drew back the string to its full release and let loose the arrow, the high-pitched whistle his only warning to the deer. Jandu shot him straight in the eye, and the buck collapsed immediately, twitching for several seconds.

Jandu sighed. He unstrung his bow again and hooked it behind his quiver, and pulled out his belt knife. Jandu gutted the deer, and then grunted as he slung the heavy animal over his shoulders. In seconds, the flies found him. He made his way home, filthy, distracted by insects, and inexplicably saddened by the death of the buck.

He left the skinning and cleaning of the animal to Baram, and plunged himself into the lake to bathe. When he went into Suraya's hut to change clothes, he noticed that she still lay in bed, unmoved since Jandu left early that morning.

"Suraya?" Jandu shook her shoulder. Her face was white. Cold fear gripped his heart.

"Jandu…" She reached beneath their thin sheet and pulled her hands back out, smeared with blood. "Something's wrong."

"Baram!" Jandu bellowed at the top of his voice. Jandu searched the room for something, anything to help her, but realized he had nothing. He knew nothing.

Baram and Yudar both barged through the door, dusty hands caked in earth.

Baram rushed to her side, falling to his knees. He took her hand as she started to cry.

"She needs a midwife," Yudar said, hovering in the doorway.

"I'll go to the village!" Jandu ran for the pilgrim's trail.

Jandu sped as fast as he could down the path, brushing past pilgrims without stopping to pay respects. Even running as hard as he could, it was nearly dark by the time he reached the village. The muddy main road through the center of the congregation of homes was nearly vacant, and only a few merchants still tended their booths at the market. Jandu asked one of them where the midwife lived. When he reached the midwife's house, her husband answered the door, a stout, elderly man who glared at the intrusion.

"Please!" Jandu was out of breath, and leaned his hands against his knees. "I need the midwife. My wife… there's a problem with her pregnancy. She's bleeding."

The man nodded, and shut the front door on Jandu. Jandu heard voices inside, and a moment later, the man returned with his small wife by his side.

"Where do you live?" the woman asked. She was older than Jandu imagined, and overweight. It would take her two days to get up the mountain.

"By the religious retreat," Jandu said. He took a breath to steady his voice. "Please. You must hurry!"

The midwife looked at her husband, and then shook her head. "There is no way I can leave now. It is already dark."

"But she could die!" Jandu's frustration overflowed. He punched the side of their mud wall with force. The midwife backed into the house and her husband stepped forward.

"She can't help you," he said crossly. "Now go home."

Jandu shook with anger. "She will help me. I order her to come help me!"

The man looked at Jandu's clothes, took in his disheveled appearance, the rents in his dejaru, the fierce burn of Jandu's eyes. He snarled coldly.

"You *order* her? Who the fuck do you think you are?"

It hit Jandu like a slap in the face. He was not a prince anymore. He couldn't order anyone to do anything no matter how dire the circumstances.

"Please," he said, lowering his voice to sound less frantic. "I'll pay you in work. I'll do anything for you. Please. My wife is bleeding, and she could die."

The midwife reemerged from behind her husband, sticking her head from behind his large girth.

"I can leave in the morning," she said quietly.

Jandu ran his hands through his hair. "Is there anything I can do? What should I do?"

"She needs vasaka leaves to coagulate the blood," the midwife told him. "Do you have any malabar trees that high in the mountains?"

Jandu searched his memory of the forest, but couldn't recall seeing any. He moaned in frustration.

"You may be able to buy some from Yarain, if he is still in the market," the midwife said. As she spoke, her husband glared down at Jandu. "You need to make a tea from the leaves. You can also give her cinnamon for her nausea, and if she starts having contractions early, give her lodhra."

"Lodhra…cinnamon…vasaka…" Jandu struggled to remember everything in his panicked state.

"I'm sorry I can't do anything more," the midwife said. She smiled sympathetically as her husband shut the door on Jandu.

THE ARCHER'S HEART

Jandu kicked the door in fury, and then sprinted to the end of the village road to the market.

Almost everyone had gone home. Jandu grabbed a man walking through the empty stalls and asked him where he could find Yarain. The man pointed to the end of the row.

The herbalist had already packed his wares into leather skins and was walking away from his stall.

"Wait!" Jandu chased Yarain down.

"I'll be back tomorrow," Yarain said. He took in Jandu's disheveled clothes and sneered.

"I need vasaka," Jandu said. "I need lodhra, and cinnamon. Please, my wife is bleeding."

Yarain put his leather skins down on an empty wooden table. "Vasaka flowers in the winter. I have only a few left, from the south."

"I'll take them," Jandu said.

"They are very expensive," Yarain said, raising his eyebrow at Jandu's clothes.

Jandu froze. He didn't have any money. What had he been thinking? He looked up at the mountain in desperation.

Suraya is dying as I stand here.

A tremor of horror shook through Jandu's bones. He had never been so helpless, so powerless. He looked at the man, and considered just taking his bags, but he wouldn't know which herb was what.

"Wait! I have this!" Jandu pulled out the pearl pendant Keshan had given him.

Yarain took the pendant and studied it closely. His mouth gaped when he realized it was pure gold, with a pearl worth more than all the buildings in the entire village.

"Give me all that I need," Jandu ordered.

Yarain scratched the gold with a dirty fingertip. "Is this real?"

Jandu slammed his fist against the wooden table so hard he splintered the end of it. "Damn it! Of course it is!"

Yarain narrowed his eyes. "You stole this."

"It was a gift," Jandu said, choking on his frustration. "Please hurry!"

With a dramatic sigh that obviously disguised the tremble of excitement in his hands, the merchant quickly pocketed the gem and opened up his leather skins. He took his time, sorting through endless bundles of dried and fresh leaves and roots, until he removed a small-leafed branch from a bush, dotted with small white flowers.

"This is the vasaka," Yarain told Jandu. He handed Jandu a box of cinnamon, dried into curled sticks. "Here is the cinnamon." He finally found the lodhra, and gave the whole lot of it to Jandu. He even wrapped up all of Jandu's purchases in one of his small leather skins.

"A bonus," Yarain said, smiling toothlessly, "for a good customer."

Jandu grabbed the bundle and raced back up the mountain, knowing that he had another day of running ahead of him.

He reached Suraya and his brothers the following afternoon only to discover that Suraya's bleeding had stopped on its own. Jandu collapsed on the floor of the hut in exhaustion, limply pointing to the herbs and explaining to Baram what the midwife had told him to do.

Suraya tried to put a pleasant face on for Jandu, saying she was fine, that she wasn't in any pain, but Jandu knew her too well now to believe her. There was a sick sheen to her face, a pale undertone that didn't go away regardless of how much she ate or slept. Her eyes developed heavy purple bags under them, and during the day she would pause, standing stock still and her eyes would clench shut as she held in whatever pain racked her body.

A week later, Suraya told Jandu that a midwife she once met recommended black horehound mint for nausea and bleeding. Suraya didn't say she was nauseous, or still bleeding, but the hairs on Jandu's arms stood erect as she asked him to try and find some in the forest.

Baram, Yudar and Jandu all volunteered to scour the forest to find mint for her. It was ridiculous, Jandu thought to himself, this desperate need to forage—but he saw how it soothed them all, to replace uselessness with action.

It was nearly dusk by the time Jandu finally found a patch of the herb. He hurried back home along the pilgrim's trail. Just as he was about to leave the road, he heard someone approaching on horseback. Riders rarely journeyed this far up the mountain. He stared down the hill warily.

The horse trotted up the slope at tremendous speed. Before Jandu could react, the rider was upon him, stopping his horse right in front of Jandu and dismounting.

Jandu took in the rider's golden armor, his pink silk trousers, his arm bands and bejeweled diadem. He then looked into the man's face.

"Jandu Paran." Druv Majeo, lord of Pagdesh, and Darvad's closest ally, smirked at Jandu with steely eyes. "Look at you! If it weren't for your demonic blue eyes I would have thought you were a shit cleaner."

Jandu glanced past Druv, looking for more riders. Druv had apparently come alone, which meant that he had not been completely sure of finding the Parans on the mountain. A tremor vibrated under Jandu's skin. He reached for Zandi on his back.

"God, how careless can you be?" Druv reached into his pocket and pulled out the pearl that Keshan had given Jandu. "Selling Keshan's pendant in such a backwater?" He put the pendant back in his pocket. "Looks like your three years of exile are going to begin again. Not to mention this little trinket is incontrovertible evidence that Adaru has helped you. You may be the world's best archer, but you are dead stupid."

Rage filled Jandu. All the humiliation, all the powerlessness of the last two years, it coalesced into something cold and sharp in his heart. He didn't think. Jandu swung Zandi around and nocked an arrow.

"Beware," Jandu hissed, the traditional Triya battle cry.

Druv stopped grinning. He backed up a step.

Jandu loosed the arrow. Druv choked as he fell back, the arrow lodged deeply in his throat. His hands groped at the shaft. Then he ceased to move.

Jandu had to move fast. He had just killed a lord, and Darvad's closest friend and ally. He reshouldered Zandi and unstrapped the horse's saddle bags. He unbridled the horse quickly and then slapped him on the rear, sending him whinnying back down the mountain in fright.

Jandu retrieved Keshan's pendant from Druv's pocket, and then reached down to Druv's belt and removed his coin purse. There was enough gold inside to finance their move to Afadi at the very least. Jandu attached the purse to his own belt, and threw the saddlebags and Druv's diadem on Druv's stomach.

He dragged Druv's heavy body for what felt like an hour, sweat blurring his vision. He finally reached the edge of a large gulley, filled with date palms and too steep to enter. With a grunt, he shoved Druv off the cliff. He watched the body tumble downward, breaking saplings and thumping on rocks, until it was out of sight.

Jandu stopped at the stream on his way back to his family and washed his face and hands of sweat and Druv's blood. His mind was numb, but his hands shook uncontrollably. It was nearly sunset by the time Jandu made it home. Yudar, Baram, and Suraya were drinking tea inside the hut, and all looked up when Jandu entered. He imagined what their expressions would be when he told them what had happened. And he couldn't do it.

"We have to leave now!"

Yudar would be furious and humiliated if he discovered that Jandu had broken the rules of their exile and murdered Druv. But Jandu also knew Yudar was too rigid to do the truly honorable thing, which was to keep them safe. It was the pragmatism of poverty. His own honor was less important than the safety of Suraya, Baram, and Yudar. It would be Jandu's sin, this lie, but it wouldn't matter because he knew he had done the right thing for them all.

"I ran into a soldier on the pilgrim's trail, loyal to Yudar," Jandu said. "He informed me that Lord Druv of Pagdesh and a contingent of his men are on their way here, right now, up the pilgrim's trail. He gave us some money and begged us to flee immediately."

The reaction couldn't have been greater if Jandu had set himself on fire.

All three of them jumped up in panic. Baram immediately drenched his cooking fire. Yudar opened the fence to let their cow wander free. They threw their belongings into two traveling chests. Baram carried the heavier chest himself, and Jandu and Yudar shared the burden of carrying the other.

"We can't risk the pilgrim's trail," Jandu repeated. The loose horse would summon Druv's entourage, but hopefully nightfall would slow them.

"We can try the valley," Yudar said. They all walked to the precipice that had formed the farthest limit of their property for two years. It was a sheer drop down over a hundred feet into the valley.

"No way," Baram said, shaking his head.

"There may be an easier route further south," Yudar said.

They walked along the ridge until they came across a less treacherous decline into the valley. But it was still steep and Jandu and Yudar stumbled frequently as they struggled with the chest.

"We have enough money to buy a horse and cart when we get to the village on the other side," Jandu said.

"If we survive this short cut," Baram grumbled. He slipped on the loose rocks but regained his balance, and then shouldered the chest and held out his hand for Suraya.

The path grew steeper towards the bottom of the valley, the palms and champak trees so thick along the slopes that they could barely make out their direction.

Suraya, breathless, flushed with exertion, hurried ahead. And then suddenly she tripped on an exposed root. She flew in the air, crashing on her face and extended belly, sliding down the hill headfirst until a large root stopped her slide.

"Suraya!" Baram dropped their chest of armor and ran to her side.

Suraya didn't get up. Yudar and Jandu dropped their chest as well, running to her aid.

Suraya moaned. They turned her over to see what seemed like an impossible amount of blood coming from between her legs. She was completely white.

"No!" Baram began to cry as he stroked her face. Suraya writhed and convulsed. The last of the sun slipped behind the thickening clouds, and soon they were engulfed in shadow, the cries of the macaques reaching a hysterical screech.

Suraya cried out to her mother for help. Jandu helplessly groped in the darkness, feeling nothing but blood, until his hands suddenly closed on the deathly still body that emerged from between Suraya's legs.

CHAPTER 27

TAREK'S TRIUMPHANT RETURN TO PRASTA WAS HERALDED with a celebration in the streets held in his honor, followed by a grand feast in the palace.

But all of this paled in comparison to the joy and love Tarek saw in Darvad's eyes. Darvad greeted Tarek at the gates of the city himself, leaping from his chariot to hug Tarek.

"Don't," Tarek cautioned, although he wanted nothing more than to hold his friend closer. "I'm filthy with travel and I smell terrible."

"I don't mind," Darvad said with a smile. He patted dust off of Tarek's breastplate. "You look like victory."

Darvad tailed Tarek through the palace and into Tarek's private suites as Tarek bathed and shaved, desperate for every detail of Tarek's most recent campaign.

Tarek had just led another show of force, this time in the small, feisty state of Bandari, where a group of Triya noblemen unfairly taxed the merchants and farmers well beyond the limitations established by King Darvad. Unlike previous confrontations, this one amounted to an exchange of forces. Darvad's own men, fighting alongside Dragewan's army, quickly quashed Bandari's rebellion.

After Tarek cleaned up, he wanted nothing more than to lie in his bed and sleep for a straight day. Months of travel and endless hours in chariots racked his body with aches and made him yearn for the comfort of the palace.

But Darvad had other plans. As Tarek wiped his face of soap and prepared to change, Darvad gripped Tarek's arm affectionately. There was a mischievous glint in Darvad's eyes.

"Wait a moment. Don't change into your nice clothes yet."

"Why?"

"Let's do something fun."

Tarek swallowed. "What?"

"I want to enjoy myself in Prasta."

"Doing what?"

"You'll see." Tarek saw laughter lines on Darvad's face that he hadn't noticed before. Darvad's demeanor had changed in the Parans' absence. Without the need to compete for superiority or attention, Darvad was a kinder, happier man. His spirit lifted in their absence; he seemed younger, lighter, and there was a spring in his step as he left Tarek's rooms and returned with an armful of plain cotton clothes.

"Put these on," Darvad said. He had his own bundle of cotton garments that he plopped on the bed. He undid the jewelry on his arms.

Tarek narrowed his eyes. "What are we doing?"

Darvad grinned. "We're pretending to be merchants."

"Oh?"

Darvad took off his necklace. "We're going to anonymously explore the city and see what trouble we can find."

Tarek's lips twitched into a smile. He studied the cheap cotton cloth in his hands. "You know, pretending to be lower caste isn't as thrilling to me as it probably is to you."

Darvad laughed. "That's true. But do it for me anyway. It will be fun. We can hand out money and be anonymous saviors to the people."

"Anonymous saviors would never wear these clothes," Tarek grumbled under his breath. Nevertheless, he put on the loose cotton blue vest that Darvad had given him.

Tarek tried not to stare as Darvad removed his fine white silk trousers. Tarek worked hard to cleanse his mind of unnatural, lustful thoughts. But they all came back as Darvad stood naked before him. Tarek had never seen his best friend without trousers on, and now that he saw the tightness of his back side, the firmness of his muscles, and how his legs tapered to his dark pubic hair, Tarek's skin prickled with desire.

Darvad tied on a black dejaru. Tarek quickly pulled on his borrowed dark trousers, worried that Darvad might catch a glimpse of Tarek's arousal.

Darvad giggled like a school boy as they completed their outfits with old shoes and dusty turbans. Tarek felt dirty and exhilarated. Dressing down was fun with Darvad by his side. They left the palace through the servant's corridor. Darvad smelled nice. Even in dark cotton, he looked powerful and attractive.

Tarek had spent most of his life walking through squalor in cheap clothes, anonymous, and unnoticed. But Darvad hadn't. His smile beamed as they made their way past fruit vendors and the meat market, and through the temple district, attracting no more attention than any other pair of raggedly dressed men in the streets.

But unlike the rest of the men wandering that sunny afternoon, Darvad and Tarek were on a mercy mission. Every time they came across a beggar, Darvad's smile widened and he reached into his hidden purse to present the man or woman with gold coins. The looks on the recipient's faces lifted Tarek from any lingering exhaustion from his seemingly endless crusade. Life was beautiful when people were made that happy. Men and women would bow before Darvad, hold his hand, hug him. And he ate it up. Darvad seemed to glow from within, and the same generosity that Darvad had showed to Tarek the day they first met now melted Tarek's heart, made him remember why he had taken his vow to stand by this man's side forever, why he loved Darvad so intensely.

Darvad tossed money into the streets, he pretended to read people's palms, he bought food from street vendors and gave it out to children. That which he didn't give away he splurged on Tarek and himself. They stuffed themselves with the grubby riches of street dining, the food tantalizing with its spicy smells and hot sauces.

Tarek took pity on an ancient man vending large jugs of wine who looked as though his back was broken from years of hard labor. Tarek bought two jugs, one for Darvad and one for himself, and then gave the man ten times the asking price. The old man cried, telling Tarek that his generosity would save his family from starvation for the rest of the year.

Tarek and Darvad found a shady tree outside one of Prasta's smaller Shentari temples and they drank wine from the bottle, making up stories of the lives of each of the passersby.

By the time the two of them stumbled back to the palace, they were drunk and giddy with all the good wishes they had been blessed with. They noisily navigated the palace corridors, arms around each other as they sang a lewd song the street kids of Prasta had taught them that afternoon. The servants and guards of the palace eyed them suspiciously, but Tarek didn't care. He didn't care what anyone in the palace thought of them, sloppily wasted in each other's arms. It was as close to a dream coming true as Tarek ever had.

When they turned the corner from the servants' hall to the royal suites, they literally ran into Mazar, who nearly fell to the floor. He glared at them as they started laughing. Mazar took in their clothing and shook his head, disapprovingly.

"What are you two doing?" Mazar asked, disgust clear on his face.

Tarek shrugged. "Singing."

"Your clothes are stained," Mazar pointed out.

Darvad clucked his tongue. "Can't get anything past this guy, can we Tarek?"

Mazar shook his head again. "That is no way to speak to your teacher."

"You haven't taught me anything in ages," Darvad pointed out. His finger wavered in the air as he pointed, his eyes lidded with inebriation.

Mazar straightened. "Years after he completed his training, Jandu used to announce himself as 'Mazar's pupil, Jandu Paran' at every engagement he attended."

Darvad's joy seemed to be sucked from his body. He went rigid with insult. "Jandu better not be announcing himself anywhere right now." His expression turned cold. "He could find it leading to three more years of banishment."

"Nevertheless, the respect he shows for me as his former teacher has never waned, and yet yours has disappeared completely," Mazar complained. He shook his head at his former pupil. "Your manners are deplorable."

"I respect people who help me now," Darvad said. He smiled at Tarek. "Tarek's loyalty to me has never wavered. You, on the other hand, can't sit through a meal at my table without mentioning those traitors to my face." Darvad's lip curled up, ugly and threatening. "You need a lesson in manners as much as I."

Mazar looked poised to speak further, but Darvad grabbed Tarek's hand and dragged him forward. "Let's go." Tarek allowed Darvad to lead him to his own suites.

That evening, Darvad held a private dinner for Tarek and invited his close allies within the palace. Tarek did not know these men; these were new friends of the king, people who Tarek had only been introduced to once or twice in the past. Druv was in Pagdesh, personally investigating a rumor of the Parans' location, Firdaus was home in Chandamar, and Iyestar attended another function that evening. And while Tarek never really enjoyed sharing Darvad's company with the other lords, at least he knew them and what to expect. This was an uncomfortable gathering, brash young diplomats who praised Darvad lavishly and pandered to his sense of humor. Tarek wondered how Darvad could not see through their slick ruse of false companionship. Then he realized that, even if he did see, Darvad had few choices.

Darvad summoned dancing girls once servants had cleared the food. Tarek sat beside him, his jealousy hidden. Darvad's new friends were brash men weary of tradition, men who loved drinking and women as much as Darvad did. There were some things that Tarek could not share with his best friend, and, like so often with Darvad, Tarek felt lonely abandonment. He was a fool for loving a man who could never love him the same way in return.

Darvad laughed uproariously at the rude jokes his companions made, and they drank sweet grape wine as the musicians started another set and the scantily clad women dancers began their act.

Tarek drank. He watched the women undress more with each dance and he drank more. Darvad's expression glazed over as the women stripped, and he and his friends hooted loudly as the girls shook their wares provocatively in the front of the room. Tarek wished he had gone to sleep after their afternoon together. He didn't want to be sitting here, watching Darvad inelegantly lunge after the women who came within reaching distance.

It was deep into the night when the musicians finished playing. Darvad invited a few of them back to his private chambers for more drinks. Tarek knew he shouldn't go but did so anyway, too drunk to stop drinking, to lonely to be away from Darvad's side. In Darvad's rooms, Tarek sat with the other men and drank until his mind blanked of feeling, until everything around him swam, blurry and distorted.

The last of the other guests left and it was just Tarek and Darvad, and two of the dancing girls. One of them sat on Darvad's lap and kissed him. Tarek watched Darvad's long finger snake along the girl's collar bone, inching closer to her breast. The other girl sat next to Tarek, trying to strike up a conversation.

Tarek ignored her. He kept his eyes on Darvad, who deepened his kiss with the dancer. He wore no shirt and so Tarek could see all the muscles in Darvad's stomach and back shift and tighten as he brought the girl into his embrace. He watched Darvad's hips moved towards her, watched his eyes glaze with arousal, watched him fondle her breasts.

"I'm going to bed," Tarek announced to no one in particular. Darvad and his girl didn't notice. Tarek stumbled as he stood, his body spinning with drunkenness. The girl beside him offered to accompany him to his room, but he refused.

"I prefer sleeping alone," he said to her. She looked hurt, but Tarek didn't care. He took one last look at Darvad kissing the dancer, and then headed down the hall to his guest chambers for the night.

Tarek's body raged with unspent desire. He felt like an arrow nocked into place—a breath of wind would set him loose, send him in a destructive path, flying with speed and anger. Tarek quivered with frustration as he made his way towards his rooms.

He heard footsteps coming around the corner and tensed. It was far too late for any of the older courtiers to be up, and the hallway only served Darvad's personal chambers and the guest chambers that Tarek stayed in when in Prasta. That meant the person could be coming to see him, and he was in no mood to talk to anyone.

Tarek rounded the corner and saw Anant.

The young commander bowed respectfully and held out a scroll. He breathed heavily, apparently having rushed through the palace to pass on the urgent message. Tarek recognized the scroll seal as that of his chief minister. He stared at the seal with vague curiosity.

But he was more interested in the pink blush that washed over the commander's face as he stood before Tarek.

Tarek reached out and grabbed Anant by his armor. He dragged him into his bedroom. Anant cried out in surprise. Tarek shut the door and locked it.

Anant stuttered. "My lord, I…"

Tarek pushed Anant against the wall with all his strength and kissed him, hard. All the heated lust, the jealousy, it poured from Tarek's mouth into Anant's. His tongue darted inside Anant's hot mouth, to the back of his throat, to the soft, hot space deep within him.

Anant went very still.

Tarek, blind with sexual hunger, let his hands run over Anant's body. He breathed quickly and deeply, taking in Anant's strong masculine scent, a musky sweetness mixed with dirt and sweat. Tarek fumbled with Anant's waist sash.

Tarek was afraid to look at Anant's face, because he didn't want to ask permission to do this. He had to fuck someone, right now, and if he saw fear or rejection in Anant's eyes, he wasn't sure he could stop himself from continuing. At last, however, he looked up and his gaze met with Anant's. Tarek couldn't read the expression in Anant's glare. Was it fear?

Tarek froze. What would Anant do? Run? Punch him? Tarek suddenly wished he would. He wanted Anant to understand how he was being used, a replacement for another, and he wanted Anant to beat him senseless.

But Anant leaned forward and kissed Tarek instead. Tarek responded with strength. He undid Anant's dejaru as they kissed, running his fingers over Anant's thighs, reaching between them to the warm, musky center of him.

Tarek closed his eyes. He thought of Darvad, the way his chest flexed and moved as he held the dancing girl. He visualized Darvad's light flesh, the intensity of his brown eyes, his rich brown hair.

Tarek grabbed Anant's shoulders and turned him around, pushing him against the wall. He brusquely kneed Anant's legs apart, holding him pinned.

Anant's breathing was quick and irregular. A tremor ran through Anant's shoulders and legs. He put his palms against the wall to support himself.

Tarek untied his dejaru and spat on his hand, rubbing himself before pushing into Anant. Tarek made love to him with closed eyes, hearing Darvad laugh huskily in the other room, visualizing Darvad's large hands. Tarek imagined his own hands resting on Darvad's hips, imagined that the pliant flesh he pushed into was Darvad's flesh, the cries Darvad's cries.

Tarek shuddered and came quietly, gritting his teeth against the carnal yell in his throat. He pulled from Anant and realized, guiltily, that Anant had no part to play in Tarek's thoughts. Anant faced the wall, panting heavily, unmoving.

Flush with guilt and sexual release, Tarek spun Anant around and then knelt. He brought Anant to climax with his mouth, quickly and uncontrollably, a quiet moan of surprise escaping Anant's lips, as if this was his first time, as if he never knew this could be done to his body. Anant pushed himself deeper and then came hotly down Tarek's throat.

Tarek stood and dressed himself. He forced himself to look Anant in the eye. "Thank you."

Anant seemed unable to speak, unable to breathe.

Tarek finished tying his dejaru and stepped towards the door.

Anant followed Tarek with his eyes but made no move to follow.

"You should dress now," Tarek said.

Anant's neck and face flushed bright red. He nervously retied his dejaru, his eyes firmly locked on the carpet.

"I'm sorry, my lord." Anant couldn't tie his sash. His hands shook. "I'm sorry."

Tarek watched the young man fumble nervously in front of him, and again guilt flooded his mind. He fucked Anant and thought of Darvad. It was wrong. Compassion inspired Tarek to walk over and tie Anant's sash for him.

"There." He straightened Anant's sash, and when Tarek looked up, he saw infatuation in Anant's eyes. A slick horror crept through Tarek's senses. Anant stared at Tarek like he would jump in front of a chariot for him.

Tarek backed away. "You have something for me?"

Anant frowned, not understanding.

"The scroll?"

"Oh!" Anant nervously reached down to retrieve the scroll from where he had dropped it. He handed it to Tarek. "I'm sorry, my lord."

Tarek took the scroll and walked away. One of his ministers who oversaw a network of legal informants reported that Lord Kadal had broken the new laws, executing commoners for minor infractions. The news filled Tarek with anger. Kadal had smiled when he promised he would respect Tarek as Royal Judge. He had patted Tarek on the shoulder. And less than a year later, he had broken his oath and gone back on his promises.

Tarek felt revived as if someone had splashed ice water into his face. The troubles of his heart could be set aside. He had more important matters to address right now.

Tarek looked up, surprised to see Anant still standing there, sheepishly staring at the floor.

"What?" Tarek barked, colder than he intended.

Anant swallowed. "The minister asked me to wait for a reply." He sounded deflated.

Tarek rubbed his temple. The way Anant looked at him was why Tarek had long ago made a rule never to screw people he knew. Things got complicated. He could already see the brewing storm of emotions in Anant's eyes, the love, hurt, and hope flashing like lightening. It made Tarek sick to his stomach to realize he was the cause.

Tarek shook his head. He didn't have time to worry about Anant's feelings right now. He handed the scroll back to the commander.

"Tell the minister and my general to prepare the army. I will be there shortly."

Anant bowed. "Yes, my lord."

Tarek watched Anant hesitate at the door. He was so transparent, this man. He stood waiting for a kind word, some confirmation of feelings, some hope of a reprieve.

"Go now," Tarek commanded. He couldn't coddle warriors.

Anant flushed again and bowed lower. "Yes, my lord." He hurried from the room.

Tarek stretched, crackled his knuckles, and then marched back down the hall to Darvad's chamber. He knocked on the door loudly.

"What?" Darvad sounded irritated. Tarek heard the dancing girl giggle quietly.

Tarek cleared his throat. "It's me."

Tarek listened as Darvad whispered something to the girl and padded across the room. The door opened slightly. Darvad popped his head out, his bright green dejaru held closed around his waist.

"What's happened?" Darvad asked.

Tarek stared at Darvad's partial nudity, took in the smell of sex on him. He felt his body stir. "War," he told Darvad. "I need you."

Darvad stepped out into the hall and shut the door behind him. A slow smile spread across his face, lighting him up from within, his face glowing, truthful, beautiful.

"You have me." Darvad put his arm around Tarek's shoulder.

Tarek filled him in.

CHAPTER 28

THEIR FIRST MEAL AFTER CREMATING THE BABY WAS THE MOST depressing Jandu had ever experienced. His family stared at the flames of their camp fire in silence. The last fire they had lit had burned the tiny body of Suraya's dead child.

Jandu pushed his food aside. He had no hunger, just a vague sickness, and a disbelief that he could feel any lower.

"Does anyone want more tea?"

Suraya spoke quietly, as if nervous about disturbing the silence. No one answered her. They sat together around the fire, although the heat was sweltering and the clammy sky pushed their sweat-soaked clothes against their skin. A roar of thunder echoed overhead. The sky brimmed with moisture.

But the darkness disturbed him, and Jandu turned to the fire gratefully. His body ached from their desperate scurry down the mountain. He and Yudar had carried Suraya most of the way, on a makeshift palanquin of branches and a zahari, until they reached a small farming community where they traded Jandu's stolen gold for a horse and cart. Grief accompanied them down the mountain like a physical presence, breathing on their necks, tearing at their hearts.

"I'll have more tea then," Suraya said under her breath, as if to herself. Jandu looked at his siblings, saw that no one had touched their dinner.

Baram hadn't said a word since his son was born dead. All day Baram had walked ahead of the rest of them, slashing at undergrowth that grew overnight to block the worn pathways south. Now he stared into the flames blindly, his shoulders tense.

He had scratches on the backs of his hands and blisters on his palms. He seemed bent on destroying the forest root by root to express his anguish.

Suraya looked terrible—her skin pale with dark circles under her eyes. She could only stand for a couple minutes at a time. She held her breasts and winced in pain as her milk dried up.

But as they had moved out of the mountain jungle and reached the plains of Pagdesh, Suraya pushed them all forward, assuring them she was fine, her eyes unwavering towards Afadi.

In silence, they extinguished their fire and made camp near a rocky outcropping that had a series of natural shelters, protected from the elements by a tremendous jut of stone. Baram and Yudar found places to sleep under the rock, and Jandu huddled with Suraya in a smaller cave-like shelter that had a soft bed of moss. It wasn't large, but it was dry.

"Are you all right?" Jandu whispered.

"I will be." Suraya leaned her head against Jandu's shoulder. She was quiet for a moment, and then spoke softly. "The baby was part of our years on the mountain. I need to leave him, and all that darkness, behind."

Jandu kissed the top of Suraya's head. "You are very brave," he said. "Braver than me even."

"I don't have much of a choice, do I? What I've lost..." Suraya squeezed Jandu's arm. "No. I'm not going to talk about it anymore. What's happened has happened. There was nothing to be done for it."

Jandu watched the rain fall in sheets, the water reflecting the half moon to make thousands of glinting droplets in the sultry darkness. "I failed you."

Suraya stared at Jandu. "What are you talking about?"

Jandu swallowed. "I wish I could have protected you." He turned and gripped Suraya's shoulders. "Will you forgive me?"

Suraya leaned in and kissed Jandu on the lips. Jandu stiffened, but he realized it was meant to be friendly.

"You did everything you could to help me," Suraya said with force. "So let's look forward."

"To Afadi," Jandu said, smiling.

Suraya smiled back. "Afadi."

Jandu hesitated. "And Baram?"

Suraya watched the brilliant flicker of rain. "I have no idea what I can say to make him feel better. I think he blames me."

"He blames himself."

Suraya sighed.

"Just talk to him," Jandu said.

"And say what?"

Jandu shrugged. "I don't know. If I were you, I'd just hit him about the face for a while and call him a fool, and when he finally starts crying like a baby, then you can forgive him and pull out your womanly charms."

"Oh?" Suraya laughed. "So hit him in the face, then pull out my charms."

Jandu flashed her a grin. "That's my girl."

Suraya shook her head. "I don't think it will work."

"If you want, I can hit him for a while. When we were kids, I used to smack him under the chin and make him bite his tongue. Even though he was bigger and stronger than me, I could make him cry. He hated it, but he would fall for it *every* time." Jandu laughed quietly, remembering. "Those were good times," he mused to himself.

"There will be more good times ahead," Suraya whispered back. She closed her eyes and leaned against Jandu to sleep.

"Yes, there will be." Jandu stroked her head. "I promise."

But not for me, Jandu thought to himself, realizing that his year as a woman would have to begin.

As Suraya fell asleep against him, Jandu's arm around her shoulder, he looked at her body and steadied his resolve. He could do this. It was only for a year. A woman's body wouldn't be that bad. He looked at her breasts, her hips, the way her bones protruded below her neck, the smallness of her feet. He had no choice.

Jandu slowly extricated himself from Suraya's sleepy grasp and found himself a secluded spot in the tall grass to give his penis five minutes of a fond farewell.

"Take care, fella," he told it. He knelt down in the rain and prayed to Mendraz as the Yashva king had instructed, and asked for his year of Umia's curse to begin. Then he went back to his camp and fell asleep. Jandu had hoped that, as soon as he made the request for the curse to kick in, he would wake up that morning and find he was a woman.

He was wrong.

"Of course," he said to himself, scowling under his blanket at his still-present penis. "That would be too easy."

Instead, as they made their way towards Afadi, Jandu had to watch as he gradually shifted gender.

This was not the only change. Every step they took away from the mountains exorcised a little more of the grief that haunted them. Baram no longer walked by himself, instead staying by Suraya's side. Suraya regained her health—Druv's gold ensured them enough food now—and Yudar took pride in leading their cart and horse. Baram spoke gruffly at first, demanding help or asking someone where something was. There was a shadow across his eyes, a grief that Jandu realized he would never be rid of. But Baram was Baram, and he rallied along with the rest of them. He and Suraya sat together, sharing quiet words, and Jandu wondered to himself what had happened between them to make them so comfortable together again.

As they traveled, Zandi got heavier. And then one morning, Jandu couldn't string her. He looked at his arms as if for the first time, and realized they were much thinner. The change over the week had been so gradual he hadn't noticed. But now he saw his biceps were as thin as Suraya's, and his arms had svelte, tiny wrists. The scars on his arms from the bowstring were still visible, but they were thin and faint, barely detectible under strangely soft skin.

Jandu burned with the bitterness of not being able to shoot her anymore. When he whispered the words to change her into a flute, he felt emasculated.

And he was shrinking, too. He kept tripping over his own feet, which changed shape in the night. He lost eight inches. The world grew around him.

Jandu's transmogrification was just the kind of thing the rest of his family needed to take their minds off Suraya's miscarriage. Baram needled Jandu, providing daily commentary on his appearance. He gleefully measured Jandu's shrinking torso against his own, and laughed for the first time since they left the mountain when he realized Jandu only came up to his chest. It seemed the only way Jandu's family could cope with the long, tiring journey through the rain was through mockery. And they were relentless.

Jandu's changes accelerated, growing more painful each day. His body ached constantly, and his muscles shook from exertion, even after he had been sleeping. Everything about him was sore, as if fevered—his jaw, his fingers, his pelvis. He had let his hair grow out ever since Druv discovered them, but now it lengthened faster, furiously making up time, until it hung down past his shoulders, forming shining, straight locks. His eyelashes grew. The hairs on his arms thinned, and his chest hair fell out. And, more painfully, his bones changed as his hips protruded, his shoulders thinned, his jaw line shifted.

And if this wasn't bad enough, the worse changes were yet to come. Jandu followed his family through forests and along rivers and down muddy streets, and tried not to complain, but there were terribly uncomfortable sensations pulsing from his groin, and with horror he realized his chest hurt like hell because he was developing breasts.

On the outskirts of the State of Karuna, they stopped a mile or so off the main trail for the evening. Baram immediately started a fire and Yudar went with Suraya to gather water from

a nearby stream to start dinner. Jandu sullenly went off to care
for the horse. He tied her to a tree and brushed her down, giving
her water and hay for the night.

Around the fire, he ate rice and curds in silent fatigue.
Jandu hadn't spoken a single word all day. His body ached
so badly he wanted to lay down and die. There was a sharp,
chronic throb at his groin, but he didn't dare look to see what
was going on down there. He sipped weak tea and crossed
his arms over his soft, bulging nipples, hoping no one would
notice his latest development.

But of course Baram never missed anything. He was oiling
the horse's harness at the fire, when he saw Jandu sulking. He
smirked.

"Lift your arms up, Jandu," Baram said.

"No." Jandu curled his arms tighter around himself. He
blushed as Suraya smiled at him. Her spirits had lifted since
Baram started talking again.

"Oh come on, Jandu, don't be shy," Suraya teased.

"I hate you all." The second Jandu said the words, his eyes
grew wide and he covered his mouth.

All three of them burst out laughing. His voice had
changed. It had risen suddenly, gotten high and girly. It wasn't
him at all.

"Fuck!" he cried out, sounding like a sixteen year-old girl.

Yudar had tears in his eyes. "No wonder you haven't said
a word all day!"

"It would have been easier to have just screwed that demon,
you know," Baram said. He slapped Jandu on the back.

Jandu flew forward, almost falling in the fire. He glared
at Baram, thinking he had been unusually harsh. Then Jandu
realized he himself was just unusually weak. He couldn't sit
through Baram's affectionate swings anymore.

Jandu promptly walked away from his family. He found a
secluded spot behind some bushes and urinated. He had purposely avoided looking at his penis during this transformation,

but now, in the fading evening light, he saw that his penis was almost gone. It looked pitiful and childlike. His testicles had shrunk as well, dwarfed by his thighs. It was the worst thing that could happen to him. He bit back a cry of horror, but he couldn't stop tears forming at the corners of his eyes.

Jandu looked around to make sure none of his family was around, and then he hastily touched himself, hoping the shrinkage was an illusion, maybe he could coax his cock back to its former grandeur. But this was worse. Fully erect, it remained a stub of what he once had. He measured it against his palm. Panic flooded his mind.

Jandu quickly retied his dejaru and sank to his knees, breathing heavily. He was ashamed, both of his body and of his own behavior. How could he be reacting so badly to something that was, in many ways, insignificant? Suraya had lost a child, and she acted stronger than he. But Jandu's whole body shook with anxiety. What if his penis never came back? What if he remained a woman forever?

Jandu tried to calm himself by noting that at least Keshan could still love him. After all, Keshan claimed to love both men and women. Maybe he wouldn't mind Jandu's strange new body. But this was cold comfort to a man who was staunchly proud of being a man, who had loved his body, and the bodies of other men. Losing his penis was like losing his mind. Worse even.

"What's wrong with you?"

Jandu jerked his head up and saw Baram looking down at him. Jandu was on his knees, his face in his hands.

"Are you all right?" Baram asked, more quietly.

Jandu accepted Baram's outstretched hand and stood up. He brushed the soil from the knees of his trousers and looked away. He knew his face burned red with his embarrassment, but he didn't want to talk about it with anyone.

Baram tried to lighten the mood by running his hand along Jandu's long black hair. "Hey, at least you're turning into a beauty."

"God!" Jandu buried his face in his hands and began sobbing.

Baram's smile disappeared. "Oh, shit. Jandu, I'm sorry."

"Fuck off!" Jandu walked away, wiping his eyes, desperate to hide.

But there was nowhere to go. Darkness sank down from the sky and the world seemed sinister. Jandu sat by himself in the darkness, letting his grief mingle with the aches in his body, until he grew cold.

His brothers and Suraya were very quiet when he returned to the camp fire. Jandu despised the pity he saw in their eyes. He wanted nothing more than to go through this horrible transformation alone, but here they all were, constant witnesses to his humiliation. Suraya silently handed him a cup of tea, and Jandu curled in on himself, his eyes downcast. He worried he'd start crying again.

"So how are we going to disguise ourselves once we're in Lord Indarel's palace?" Suraya asked. She stretched upwards as she yawned, trying to act casual as she directed attention away from Jandu.

"We should make up new identities," Yudar said. "Now is your chance to be that someone you've always wanted to be."

"I'm going to call myself Azari," Suraya said. She smiled. "I've always loved that name."

Yudar smiled at her. "Oh? And what will you tell the lord?"

"I shall tell him that I was a handmaiden to Princess Suraya, back in Prasta."

"You're too pretty to be a handmaiden," Yudar said.

"I had pretty handmaidens in Prasta," Suraya said. "Remember Ami? And Kera? She was gorgeous."

"I never saw them," Yudar said. He looked into Suraya's eyes. "Every other woman seemed plain to me once I met you."

Baram poked at the fire with a stick.

"What about you, Yudar?" Suraya asked. "What will your name be?"

Yudar shrugged. "I'll go by the name Esalas."

"Esalas?" Baram raised an eyebrow. "Wasn't he the kid that used to come around and sell us toys in Prasta?"

Yudar nodded.

"I remember him," Baram said. "He once sold you a set of dice that were painted, not carved. Remember? The numbers rubbed off the first week you had them."

Yudar smiled. "He was smart."

"He was a con," Baram said.

"I liked him," Yudar said. "So I'll name myself Esalas. Maybe I can offer my services as a dice instructor."

Jandu's stomach churned, but he didn't say anything. He hated the idea of Yudar near dice. But he had to remind himself that Yudar played dice his entire life and had never gotten them in trouble until the match with Darvad. And he wouldn't make the same mistake twice.

Yudar's voice was very soft as he spoke. "Since Jandu will be a woman, then perhaps you should be my wife, Suraya. Your year with Jandu is almost over anyway."

Jandu watched Baram for a reaction. Baram shredded his banana leaf plate silently.

"Who will you be, Baram?" Suraya asked. Jandu saw her pleading with him.

"I don't know," he snapped.

"Maybe you could cook?" Suraya suggested. "It's something you enjoy doing."

"And you're good at it," Yudar added.

They all were trying so hard, Jandu realized. It was pitiful.

Baram sighed. "Okay, then I'll be Bodan, the cook."

"Can't get beyond 'B', huh?" Jandu said. He winced at the high pitch of his voice. He looked around the fire, daring his family to comment, but Yudar only asked what name Jandu preferred to use.

"Who cares?" Jandu took out his knife and worked on smoothing an arrow shaft.

Baram smirked. "Your name will be Janali."

Jandu shook his head. "That's an ugly name."

"Well, you're going to be an ugly girl," Baram said. "Janali sounds like a girl version of Jandu."

"So do a lot of names," Jandu said.

"Janali sounds exotic." Baram touched Jandu's shoulder softly. "I could love a woman named Janali."

Jandu shrugged off Baram's hand and his laughter. He stabbed the sharpened end of the stick he just whittled into the earth over and over, as if this would somehow prove his manliness. He realized this was just the beginning of the humiliation yet to come.

"God," he said, impaling soil, "I'm really, really going to hate Afadi."

◆◆◆

By morning, Jandu realized he could not get out from under his blanket without causing a ruckus. He wrapped his harafa around him tightly and quietly shook Suraya awake. He whispered in her ear that he needed to borrow a zahari, or at least a zahari top.

And by the end of the week, his penis was gone, replaced by strange folds of skin that looked alien to him, scary and unfamiliar. By the time they crossed the Patari River and entered the State of Afadi, it was all over. Jandu was a woman. He looked, smelled, and talked like a tiny young lady, with large blue eyes and curling black lashes.

Afadi was drier than Jandu had imagined, and as they made their way towards the city, Jandu noticed that the surrounding pastureland seemed desiccated, even in the midst of the monsoon season. The older parts of town nestled closely with the tiled domes of the palace inside the thick white walls of the city, but newer residences popped from the earth like brown mushrooms along the river banks.

The rest of the state was filled with hundreds of herds of prized Afadi cattle. The cows were beautifully adorned, their horns painted red, bells and tassels hung around their necks. The cattle were the state's greatest wealth, coveted throughout Marhavad as the finest dairy-producing stock and sought after for their hardy natures. Jandu and his brothers made their way through endless herds of cattle, winding their way along well-trod paths towards the trailing line of the city.

At the river's edge, there was a large gated mansion, and a small cemetery down the road. Yudar stopped their horse and unfolded the large deerskin he had been saving for this moment.

"We should hide our weapons here."

Baram and Yudar took off their swords and placed them in the deerskin along with their armor, shields, spears, knives, and other weapons. Jandu reluctantly contributed his inexhaustible quiver after Yudar informed him that he could not just pretend it was a lady's handbag. At least he was able to keep Zandi with him. Still, anxiety tore at Jandu when Suraya sewed the deerskin shut.

In the ancient Afadi tradition, someone had hung a corpse on one of the Sami trees surrounding the cemetery. The smell was unbelievably foul. Baram grimaced as he hefted the heavy leather bag over his shoulder and climbed the tree. He placed the bag between two strong branches that wouldn't break, and made sure it was sheltered enough so that rain would not penetrate it.

"If someone can get past that stench to get my armor, they deserve to keep it," Baram cried.

At the city gates, Baram and Jandu waited with the horse and cart while Suraya and Yudar made their way to Lord Indarel Lokesh's palace. After the lord accepted their offers of service as a hand-maiden and dice teacher, Yudar sent a messenger to his "sister" Janali and "cousin" Bodan, and Jandu and Baram entered the palace a day later.

Jandu hooked his arm in his towering older brother's, and took a deep breath to steady his resolve.

"Let's hope Keshan taught me enough on the flute to be passable as a music teacher," Jandu said.

Baram reached down and pinched Jandu's cheek fondly. "I'm sure they'll hire you, even if you can't play a note. You're so cute, Indarel will want to eat you."

Jandu narrowed his eyes.

Baram led the way through the gate. "But you are still my little sister, so I'll be there to protect you."

"You're enjoying this too much," Jandu mumbled.

"I'm just trying to make light of a dark situation," Baram said.

"Yeah, well, I get my muscles back in one year, fucker. Don't forget it."

CHAPTER 29

TAREK SURVEYED THE CARNAGE OF THE BATTLEFIELD.

Corpses lay scattered across the barren Marshav plain like giant leaves, their bodies puffing in the monsoon heat, the smell overpowering the sweetness from the blooming camphor.

Over five hundred men from Marshav died after their failed attempt to rebel against King Darvad. Darvad and Tarek had arrived two days earlier, heavily armed and accompanied by both Dragewan and royal soldiers. The battle had been bloody and quick, Marshav's unskilled army no match for Dragewan's well-trained military. Tarek and Darvad fought in chariots along with Darvad's general and three other commanders, cutting large swathes of dead as they galloped the muddy fields surrounding the city. Tarek's arrows rarely missed. Inspired by his performance, Dragewan's archers led the attack, killing half of the insurgents before the foot soldiers even had a chance to enter the melee.

Tarek's blood sang with the battle.

The only disappointment came in the fact that they had not captured Lord Kadal himself, since Kadal had fled once the battle turned to favor the King. Darvad's spies reported seeing him flee to the State of Jezza, where Lord Sahdin was a close ally.

Tarek had never before fought beside Darvad, and the experience was glorious. If Tarek ever had any doubt about who he was, what he was made for, it was gone now. He was meant to fight, beside Darvad. The two of them worked like an expert team of horses, understanding each other's intent as they led charges against the rebels. Darvad's general oversaw the dirty task of cleaning up the mess, allowing Tarek time to relax and revel in his high spirits.

Tarek and Darvad were now bound together by friendship and by war. They retold their triumphs, vibrating with pride, each thrust and fired arrow recounted in grand detail.

Drunk with victory, Darvad quickly decided to lead the victorious army north into Jezza itself. They would hunt down Kadal, and punish Jezza for harboring a traitor to the throne. Tarek eagerly embraced the idea, looking forward to another opportunity to trounce Lord Sahdin for his insults years ago.

That evening, Tarek and Darvad played dice and drank wine in Darvad's tent. A gentle hum radiated through Tarek's bones. He realized it was pure, unadulterated happiness. They sat around the board, moving game pieces and reliving their recent exploits, when Darvad grew unusually quiet.

"What are you thinking about?" Tarek asked. He sipped his wine slowly, not wanting to get too drunk too fast. He realized he enjoyed the pleasures of wine too much these days.

"There's another reason I think this invasion is a good idea," Darvad said.

"Oh?" Tarek didn't need any more reasons. Fighting beside Darvad was enough.

Darvad's eyes had a wet sheen. "Do you remember Sahdin's daughter Aisa?"

Tarek frowned. "I don't think so. Have I met her?"

"She came to Mazar's birthday party with her father." Darvad's expression turned dreamy. "Tarek, you have not seen beauty until you have seen Aisa. She is like liquid fire. Her skin glows, she has large doe eyes, and her bosom…" Darvad sucked air through his teeth.

Tarek rolled his dice. He moved his piece across the board.

"I want her," Darvad stated. "I want her as my prize."

"The women should not be harmed in the invasion," Tarek said stiffly. "I don't want that kind of war."

Darvad threw down his dice. "I'm not going to just rape her," he spat. "Good lord, Tarek. This girl means a lot to me. I've fantasized about her for years." Darvad studied his dice, and growled as he threw them back in his cup with disgust.

"Are you going to marry her?" Tarek asked incredulously.

Darvad shrugged. "Why not? It is the traditional Triya way to find a bride. Invade and carry her off." He poured them both more wine. "It will honor her. She will be Queen of Marhavad. It is a position all women of Marhavad crave."

Tarek studied the palms of his hands to cool his furious heart. Jealousy, white hot and piercing, twisted in his throat and lungs. It wasn't as though Tarek never imagined his love would be tried like this some day. But he didn't want to deal with it now. Not now. Not when his own happiness seemed so fragile.

"So," Darvad said, obviously noticing Tarek's icy silence, "can I rely on your help to keep the men away from her until I can claim her?"

"I will do what I can," Tarek said. He threw down his dice, and won the game. Darvad shook his head in disgust, but Tarek felt no victory that evening.

◆◆◆

The following morning, as Darvad prepared to move the army, Tarek made rounds among his men, speaking with the commanders of each unit. Tarek felt the power he held as lord as if for the first time. To these men, he was no longer just a ruler forced upon them by the will of mighty Prasta, or the Royal Judge. He was a hero. They watched him walk through their ranks and they bowed low, pride burning in their eyes, their stances assured.

Tarek spoke quietly with his commanders, inquiring about the health of his men, their families. He never vented his anger or seemed anything other than assured in the company of his commanders. It was something he learned from his father, a master horseman who believed that quiet strength was more impressive and effective than rowdy bravado.

Tarek caught Anant's eye towards the end of the formation. Anant looked away hastily, and then ordered his men together to form a tighter rank. Tarek had only seen a glimpse of Anant's battle techniques in Marshav, but what he had seen was impressive. What Anant lacked in experience he made up for in sheer courage. Anant drove into the enemy as if heaven awaited him on the other side.

"Anant."

Tarek called him by his first name. This was not how he addressed his other commanders, but the strength in Anant's arms, the proud way he assembled his men, something about it made Tarek soft and amiable. He didn't smile at Anant, but he did bring his hands together in the sign of peace.

"Are your men ready?"

Anant nodded. "Of course, my lord. However I regret to report that we lost several spears in the battle. The men will replenish our supply, but it will take time."

Tarek smiled slightly. It was endearing, Anant's care for trifling things. A trait that both Tarek and Anant shared, having once lived with very little.

Tarek put his hand on Anant's shoulder. "You did very well. I'm proud of you."

Anant swallowed and looked down at his feet. Tarek watched, amused, as bright pink crept up Anant's neck.

"Tarek!"

Darvad strode towards him. The ranks of soldiers bowed low to their king, but Darvad didn't spare them a glance. He looked ready to murder someone.

"Bad news," Darvad said.

"What?"

Darvad looked down at Anant, who still stood rigid by Tarek's side. Darvad dismissed him without a second glance.

"A messenger has just arrived from Pagdesh. Druv is missing, presumed dead."

Tarek never really liked Druv, but the news came as a surprise. "What happened?"

The vein in Darvad's forehead pulsed with his anger. "It is unclear. The last he was heard from, he had strong evidence of the Parans' location and went to investigate himself. He had a pendant that had been brought to his attention and purchased from a poor herbalist in the rural mountain jungle. The pendant was worth a fortune, and had been crafted in Tiwari."

Tarek narrowed his eyes.

"He recognized it as Keshan Adaru's," Darvad continued, "and assumed that Keshan gave it to the Parans before their exile. He had direct evidence of their location. And now he is missing. Doesn't that sound suspicious?"

Tarek swallowed. "That is a leap of logic. The pendant could have been stolen, Darvad. It could have been a ruse. Yudar is not that stupid."

"Druv heard that a family moved to the mountain two years ago," Darvad said. "Three men and one woman. One of the men had blue eyes."

Tarek cursed under his breath. Why did the Parans have to appear now, when everything was going so well? Tarek could already see the glint of anger in Darvad's expression. Darvad's obsession over his half-brothers would always come between them.

"Send a messenger to Pagdesh," Tarek suggested. "Confirm these reports. There are so many suspicious rumors these days."

"No. I must go myself, and see if it's true. Not only to find the Parans, but to validate whether or not Druv is dead. He is one of my closest allies, and if he has been murdered then I promise to string up and hang whoever is responsible."

Disappointment flooded Tarek. "But we are on the verge of war, Darvad."

Darvad took off his diadem angrily and ran his hand through his hair. "I know. I know! But you must understand how important this is to me." Darvad replaced his diadem crookedly. Tarek fought the urge to straighten it for him.

"Look," Darvad said, "If I lose to the Parans, I lose my entire kingdom. I must find them!"

"You lose half the kingdom," Tarek corrected. "Remember, the kingdom will be split once the exile is over. You will still be a king."

"No!" Darvad shouted. "Mazar never should have divided it. It is all mine!"

"What do you want me to do?" Tarek looked around him— at the chaos created under Darvad. Courtiers and soldiers and servants rushed around as last minute preparations were made to invade Jezza. "You want me to tell everyone to go home, come back later, we'll attack Jezza when the King's schedule clears up?" Tarek couldn't hide the antagonism from his voice. "This is a bloody war! I can't just stop it for a moment while you rush up the mountains to sniff out a rumor."

Darvad looked shocked by Tarek's words.

"I'm not asking you to postpone the war," Darvad said. "Just to let me take care of this."

Tarek pursed his lips. "So you will not join me."

Darvad frowned. "No."

"You will go chase after Druv's dead body instead."

"It could lead me to the Parans," Darvad urged. "And he was too good of a friend to leave rotting without an investigation."

"Fine. Go." Tarek turned away from him.

"Tarek…" Darvad started.

"Leave," Tarek said, his voice low. "You have made your priorities clear. Defending your new laws, your 'New Marhavad', is less important than tormenting the Parans." And with that, he stormed to his tent.

Alone, Tarek realized his foolishness in speaking so brashly. Darvad was king, after all. Tarek had led several skirmishes on his own, without Darvad's support, and had succeeded admirably. He did not need Darvad by his side. And he should have been pleased to see Darvad's personal attention to the possible death of one of his allies.

But these thoughts didn't make him feel better. Fighting beside Darvad had been the pinnacle of his existence, the very definition of who he was. He had looked forward to it, and once again, the prospect of hunting the Parans had dashed his hopes.

"My lord!"

"What is it?" Tarek growled. He looked up to see his personal servant Laiu. He held a scroll in his hand.

"A message from your household in Dragewan, my lord," Laiu said. "Your attendants have asked that I wait for a return message."

Tarek rubbed his eyes. He couldn't handle any pressing matters in his own state right now. He grabbed the scroll with unnecessary force. As he read the message, he felt the blood drain from his face and his knees go weak in shock.

His father was dead.

All these months on the road, all these precious hours wasted running around the kingdom, and Tarek had all but abandoned his sick father back in Dragewan. Now his father had died, all alone, in a strange city with no one by his bedside.

"God." Tarek knelt down. "God!" He brought his hands together to pray. Grief flooded him.

Laiu waited beside him silently.

Tarek had to pull himself together. He wiped his eyes and stood again, although he still felt weak in the legs.

"Tell them..." Tarek swallowed. Tell them what? His father was gone. He couldn't pass on any messages to the one who wanted them most. And now, with the war, he would not even be able to attend his father's funeral pyre. "Tell them to cremate him in the honorable Triya tradition."

Laiu frowned. "But my lord... your father was not a Triya, and they may protest—"

"—Tell them to do it!" Tarek shrieked, too upset to control himself. "Tell them to do it, and if they don't, I will see them executed!"

"Yes, my lord!" Laiu fled the tent.

Tarek covered his face with his hands. He needed to be there. He needed to be with his father now, at least, in death.

"Tarek?"

"Oh for God's sake, what now?" Tarek yelled.

Darvad walked in, eyes wide in surprise. "I'm sorry. Am I intruding?"

Tarek closed his eyes. "I'm sorry, Darvad. I didn't realize it was you."

"My chariot is ready to leave. I wanted to apologize, and…" Darvad narrowed his eyes. "Are you crying?"

Tarek looked at him wearily. "My father has died."

"My God! I am so sorry!" Darvad reached out to touch Tarek's shoulder, and then hesitated. "Tarek, what can I do?"

"Nothing. It's all right. I'll be fine." Tarek sat down on his bed.

Darvad sat beside him. "What are you going to do?"

"What can I do?" Tarek snapped. "I'm going to war this very day. It's a week's journey to Dragewan."

Darvad touched Tarek's knee. "I will tend your father's funeral pyre."

Tarek blinked. "You will?"

Darvad nodded. "Of course. I am heading back to Prasta, to gather supplies before I go to Pagdesh. Before I leave, I will see your father put to rest."

All of Tarek's anger faded. He let his body go limp against Darvad's. The two of them sat there in silence.

"Thank you," Tarek said finally.

"He will have all royal honors," Darvad promised.

"And I will find Kadal and Sahdin for you," Tarek responded.

Darvad smiled weakly. "I wish I could be in both places at once."

"Me too." Tarek sighed.

"You will be magnificent on the battlefield, Tarek," Darvad said. "Your father will be proud of you in heaven."

Tarek's heart melted slightly.

"Remember to bring Aisa to me," Darvad asked.

Tarek's heart hardened again. "I'll try my best," he said, lying.

Darvad put his arm around Tarek's shoulder. "What a great joy it would be, to return having found the Parans, forcing them into three more years of exile, and to celebrate the memory of your father with a victory in Jezza and my marriage to the prettiest girl in Marhavad!"

"Yes," Tarek croaked, "how joyful."

Darvad let go of Tarek and left the tent. Tarck followed him outside to watch him jump into his chariot. The horses whinnied in protest. Darvad tapped his charioteer on the shoulder and they left.

Tarek turned to see his general. They bowed at each other.

"We're ready, my lord," the general said.

Tarek watched Darvad's chariot disappear around a dusty bend. His family was dead. His only loyalty now was to the man driving from he battlefield. Tarek took a deep breath, steadied his resolve, and turned back to his general.

"Let's go."

CHAPTER 30

JANDU STRUGGLED WITH HIS HAIR.

He fussed in front of his mirror for almost an hour, but he still couldn't force it into an attractive braid.

In frustration, he threw the ivory brush against the wall of his room, imagining the force would shatter the handle in two. Instead it limply smacked the white plaster wall and tumbled, unscathed, to the carpet. It didn't even mark the wall.

"Fucking pitiful," Jandu growled at his reflection. He examined his arms in the mirror for the hundredth time, both amazed and repulsed by their thinness, the frailty of his wrists, his tiny fingers.

He sighed and got up to retrieve his brush.

Jandu sat back down at the dressing table. His room was furnished with two small beds, two camphor chests, and several bright green sitting pillows on a plush green floor. He shared the room with another female servant, a young girl named Rani who had so many hair ribbons, brushes and accoutrements they poured out of the dresser's meager drawer and littered the surface of the table. Jandu pushed aside her cheap jewelry, her pink ribbons, her brushes, and set to his own hair again, determined to get it into a braid.

It had taken only one experience crossing Afadi palace's courtyard without one for Jandu to realize how many intricacies there were to being a woman. When he first strolled through the large palace courtyard, Jandu had been the instant fascination of every man in sight. For a fleeting moment, he had sweated horror—they all somehow *knew* he preferred men. The lust in their eyes was unbridled.

But then he had realized that the men stared because he was masquerading as an unmarried woman and walking around with loose hair and with a zahari top that was far too small.

This would be the only time in Jandu's life that he could openly look at men around him. But Jandu didn't have to be a woman long to understand the implications of his actions. Looking back at men expressed interest. And with his hair loose and his expression brazen, he was taking an unnecessary risk.

Jandu stared at his reflection as he inexpertly twisted his hair back. He had to admit he had turned into quite a catch. His body was petite and curvy. His breasts weren't large but they were taut and perky, bursting from the borrowed zahari top in an attempt to proclaim their existence to the world. His face was thin, his hair framing his skin like ebony surrounding a pearl.

In fact, the only part of Jandu's body that still showed the warrior inside was his eyes. They were the same intense, cold blue they had always been.

But he wasn't a warrior any more, he reminded himself. He was a music teacher—a music teacher who had been summoned to meet Lord Indarel, his wife Shali, and the child who Jandu would tutor. And if he was going to have a royal audience, his hair had to be in order.

"Fuck this," Jandu grumbled. He took a strap of leather and tied his long locks back like a soldier would.

A soft knock rattled his door, and Suraya peeped her head around the corner.

"Hello?" She smiled at Jandu.

Jandu dropped his brush and rushed to Suraya, pulling her in the room and slamming the door behind her. He yanked her into a forceful hug. It had been two days since he had seen her or any of his family. All of them had been dispersed to separate quarters throughout the palace.

"Jandu!" Suraya gasped, laughing.

"God, I've missed you," Jandu said. He used to kiss the top of Suraya's head when he felt affectionate. Now that he was shorter than her, he made do with pecking her on the cheek.

"How are you?" Suraya asked.

Jandu just grinned. He hadn't realized how much he missed his family until this moment. He originally thought that solitude would be a welcome relief after the years of having his family constantly around him. But he missed Suraya and Baram like a physical pain. He even missed Yudar's religious lectures. It was that bad.

"I'm trying very hard to keep a low profile. I'm worried someone will detect I'm an imposter," Jandu said.

Suraya shook her head. "Not by the looks of you. No one will guess you are a man, Jandu. They may think you are strange, but you'll be a strange woman. So don't worry." Suraya looked around his room. "Your room is nice. Ours is off the courtyard, it's noisy."

"It's all right," Jandu lied. Compared to the last two years, his room was luxury incarnated. Even as a servant, Jandu was entitled to quarters in the single women's quarters of the palace, light and cheery, with white walls, a plaster ceiling, and large, open windows high on the wall to let sunlight in.

"Do you share this room?" Suraya asked, noting the extra bed and chest, and the plethora of brushes and hair ribbons on the dressing table.

Jandu nodded. "Her name is Rani. She's one of the lady's maids and spends most of her time in the laundry. She seems nice."

Suraya frowned. "With a roommate to watch your every move, you are going to have to be careful."

"It makes everything more difficult. I have to pretend all the time."

Suraya narrowed her eyes at Jandu, suddenly taking in his appearance. "You are not going to meet Lord Indarel looking like that, are you?" She sighed. "Jandu, you have to put some effort into this."

"I'm trying!" Jandu scowled. He looked down at his plain yellow zahari. "But what can I do? Your zaharis are too big, this one is too small, and I can't make a pleat for shit."

Suraya tried to hide her laughter. This just made Jandu angrier.

"Don't laugh!" he yelled.

"I told Lady Shali your chest of belongings was stolen on the way here," Suraya said. "She will send her tailor to have a few zahari tops made for you."

"Thank God." Jandu squeezed his breasts. "I think they're going to pop out any moment."

Suraya blushed. "It's the style these days, dummy."

"Yeah, well, it's gross."

"We should go," Suraya said. "I'll give you a quick tour before we go to the reception hall."

Jandu hesitated. "Oh… Suraya?"

"Hmm?" She paused at the door.

Jandu stared at the floor. "Can you show me how to…"

Suraya waited while Jandu remained silent.

"Uh…" Jandu blushed.

"Jandu, are you menstruating?" Suraya's eyes grew wide.

"Ew! No!" Jandu scowled.

"So, what?" Suraya smiled coyly. "Having difficulty peeing?"

"Well, yeah, but that's not what I was going to ask you."

"What?"

"Can you show me how to braid my hair?" Jandu's voice was a girly whisper.

Suraya laughed. "Good lord. You can't even do that?"

"I'm a warrior!" Jandu made two fists. The henna on his hands made his fingers look even more delicate.

"Oh, *so* tough," Suraya mused. She came behind him and ran her hands through Jandu's hair. "Sit on the chair, warrior, in front of the mirror."

Jandu sat back and let Suraya run her hands through his thick hair as she stood behind him.

"Your hair is so pretty," she said. "I wish you would keep it long once you switch back."

"Long hair gets in the way when fighting," Jandu said. He closed his eyes and leaned back into Suraya's hands. Her fingers on his scalp felt wonderful.

"It doesn't bother Baram," Suraya said. She let go of Jandu's hair and reached up to undo her own braid.

"Baram fights with a mace like an animal," Jandu said. He watched Suraya in the mirror. "I fight like a god, with a bow. Hair is distracting."

Suraya snorted. "I don't know any animals that fight with blunt objects."

"Baboons."

"You're calling your older brother a baboon?"

"Among other things."

Suraya laughed. She positioned herself next to Jandu, and showed him how to braid her hair, and then his own. The sweet smell of the champak blossoms outside his room, and the soft ray of sunshine mellowed him to the point that his muscles felt like warm butter.

When Jandu's hair was finally in a tidy braid, Suraya led him out of his room and through an open walkway to the main courtyard.

Like Prasta, Afadi's palace consisted of numerous separate buildings, clustered around a large paved courtyard with a fountain in the center. The lord's suites were in a sculpted marble building on the east side of the courtyard. Stone buildings to the north and west housed the palace staff, one for married couples and the other for all of Lady Shali's endless young female servants. Jandu's building and the lord's suites were protected by quiet Afadi guards who huddled in the shadows of stone awnings to avoid the sunshine.

The fourth building around the courtyard, to the south, was the public reception hall. It was the only structure built directly into the great white walls of the palace grounds, allowing access to the city outside.

Suraya shook her head as she watched Jandu. "You need to work on your walk. You move like you're stalking something."

Jandu shrugged. "I've been walking like this my whole life. I can't change now." But he slowed down his pace, and tried to mimic Suraya's body movements.

"Well, try to be more lady-like." Suraya pointed to a smaller building behind the main servant's quarters. "Those are the kitchens. That's where Baram is."

"Have you seen him?" Jandu asked.

Suraya nodded. "I saw him preparing lunch when the lady asked me to bring her some lemon water."

"Does he look happy?" Jandu frowned at two men who watched his and Suraya's passage through the courtyard with wanton interest.

Suraya shrugged. "Not really. I think he works really hard."

"And you?"

Suraya smiled. "I'm working like hell, but I don't mind. It's still better than washing your blood-stained clothes in that freezing lake with no soap."

Jandu smiled and put his arm through Suraya's. "Sorry."

"Well, don't be," Suraya said. "Besides, I think you have your own work cut out for you."

"Why?"

"Wait until you meet Lord Indarel's children."

Jandu halted. "What? Are they horrible?"

Suraya grinned mischievously and led him into the public chambers.

Jandu entered the reception room and bowed low, along with Suraya. He looked up to study his new masters.

Lord Indarel was older than Jandu expected him to be. He had a neatly trimmed gray beard and thinning hair tucked behind a small but ornate diadem, complete with gold-encrusted images of the Shentari prophets.

Beside him sat Lady Shali, many years younger than him. She was not pretty, but she was elegant, with a refined nose and piercing brown eyes. She held her head high, her chin jutting out in challenge. Jandu wondered how such a small neck could support all her hair, rife with jewels pinned in every lock.

"Come closer," Lord Indarel commanded, beckoning Jandu towards him.

"Azari recommended Janali, her sister-in-law, to teach music to the children," Shali said.

"She taught children in Prasta," Suraya explained. "She is a wonderful tutor."

Indarel studied Jandu carefully. Jandu felt himself flushing under the scrutiny. He looked at the floor, worried his indignation at being examined like a piece of meat would show in his eyes.

"Look at me," Indarel ordered.

Jandu looked up. Indarel caught the smolder in Jandu's eyes, and he frowned.

"Do you *want* to work here?" Indarel asked.

"Yes, my lord," Jandu said. He looked down at his hennaed feet.

"What will you teach them?" Shali asked.

"Flute, my lady," Jandu said.

Shali smiled. "Lovely! I've always thought flute refined a person." She settled back into her chair. "Let's hear you play something."

"Yes, my lady." Jandu steadied his breathing as he reached down to the pouch on his belt and pulled out Zandi. The metal warmed in his fingers, as if Zandi expected his caress.

Jandu closed his eyes, and concentrated on the song Keshan taught him on their last day together. It had been the most complicated of all the songs Keshan taught, and it captured a variety of emotions through its sweeping notes. Jandu played the song well, letting his mind toy with the sounds as he thought of Keshan, the smell of his hair, the taste of his skin, the deep, red softness of his lips.

"That was beautiful."

Jandu opened his eyes, and saw that Indarel and Shali were both smiling down at him, their enthusiasm clear.

"You should teach our daughter, Vaisha," Indarel said.

"No." Shali shook her head. "Vaisha has no interest in music. But Abiyar does. Perhaps she can teach him?"

Lord Indarel did not seem pleased with the idea of his youngest son learning flute. But he also appeared to be completely under the power of his wife. "As you wish," he said to her.

Shali smiled in triumph. "Good! Then you will instruct Abiyar. Please stay with us and tutor him."

"Of course, my lady." Jandu bowed. "Thank you."

Suraya led Jandu out of the reception hall, and then took him to the servant in charge of Indarel's three sons as well as his young daughter, Vaisha.

Jandu met his student later that afternoon in one of the palace sitting rooms, a small room stark of color but lavishly furnished with plush couches and pillows.

His student, Abiyar, was fifteen years-old and strutted in as if he were King of Marhavad. He dressed like a noble hero, but his bravado contrasted dramatically with his scrawny, teenaged frame. His body was thin with lanky arms jutting out from under his armor like stalks. There was a fire in Abiyar's eyes, a soft burning, that showed both his intensity and his ultimate sincerity. His slightly slanted black eyes, long black hair, and excessive jewelry made him seem almost feminine in his young male beauty.

After introductions were made, the servant in charge of Lord Indarel's children excused himself and left Jandu alone with Abiyar and a guard. Abiyar's demeanor changed slightly. He nervously drew himself in and sat down shyly.

Jandu smiled at him. "Have you played any instrument before?"

Abiyar shook his head.

"The lord said you enjoy music," Jandu said. He took out his flute.

"I like music," Abiyar said quietly. His voice was soft. "But I've never learned to play any. My father says that men should learn the art of war, not music. Music is for girls."

"Not true," Jandu said. He pointed to the boy with his flute. "I know a Triya prince who has conquered at many battles, and is braver than any warrior I know. And he is very adept at playing the flute." Jandu held out the instrument.

Abiyar took it warily. He looked at the guard standing silent against the wall, and blushed.

"I should learn weapons," Abiyar said, forcing anger into his voice.

Jandu smirked. "Of course you should. But that doesn't mean you can't learn flute as well, my lord. After all, you seem to be an intelligent young man."

Abiyar frowned down at the flute. "This will take time away from my military training."

Jandu raised an eyebrow. "Did you have practice scheduled right now?"

Abiyar scowled. "No."

"So there's no problem then." Jandu nodded to the flute. "Put it to your lips."

"I don't want to."

"Well, your parents want you to. And so you have to. Do it."

Abiyar put his lips to the flute and blew. His angle was off, and so no sound emerged. Jandu reached up and adjusted the angle of the flute, and as he did so, a powerful blush spread across the boy's cheeks. Jandu scooted back immediately.

"Try it again," Jandu said.

Abiyar blew. A weak, trembling note came from the flute. He looked at Jandu and smiled widely.

Jandu smiled back. Abiyar curled in on himself in an embarrassed jumble of long limbs, his emotions undisguised behind an honest face.

"Shall I show you the notes?" Jandu asked.

Abiyar nodded. Jandu went through the basic scale with his student, noting that he seemed thrilled every time he succeeded at something, and became closed and withdrawn when he failed.

Although their initial lesson was only an hour long, Jandu felt completely exhausted by the end of it. He never realized how mentally straining teaching someone could be. It didn't help that Abiyar seemed disturbed by the whole lesson. Half of the time, Abiyar paid close attention to Jandu, listening to his notes, trying to mimic the sounds, memorizing the positions of the fingers. The other half of the time he stared at the guard by the door, watching him for a reaction, as if expecting the guard to drop his spear and start pointing and laughing at him.

When Jandu finally returned to his room, he was startled to see his roommate there. They had done a good job of avoiding each other for the last two days, but now Jandu realized that he would have to learn to live with her there.

"Hello," he said, smiling shyly and slipping past her to grab a towel from his traveling chest.

Rani was barely eighteen, and rather ugly. She had pretty black eyes but her skin was pocked and rough, and her hair was dry and a dull black in color. She smiled when Jandu walked in.

"Janali! How was your meeting with the lord? Will you be staying?"

Jandu nodded. "I think so. I gave Abiyar his first flute lesson today."

"Wonderful!" Rani nodded to Jandu's towel. "Are you going to wash up? Have you been to the bathhouse yet? It's beautiful. Come, I'll show you where it is!"

Jandu smiled politely. He wanted to be alone, have five minutes of not pretending. But Rani hooked her arm in his and led him down the hallway to the bathhouse.

As they walked, arm in arm, it suddenly hit Jandu that Rani was a Suya servant. Jandu was about to bathe in the same water as a lower caste servant girl. He tried to muster some sense of indignity, but he realized there was no point. He didn't feel it, not after his two years on the mountain.

Jandu learned that Lady Shali had an obsession with hygiene, and this was apparent in the design of the women's bathhouse. In her love of ornament, she spared no expense in granting her female servants the same luxury as she herself had, providing a roomy stone bathroom complete with constantly hot water, pumped in from a hot spring.

Jandu had heard of hot springs before but had never seen one in his life. The bathhouse enclosed the spring's waters with floors of tile and marble counters. A large, slatted dome let sunlight drift down into the room in striped patterns across the floor.

Rani raved about the bath house, how it was the finest in Marhavad, how lucky they were to have it, who frequented it, when it was busiest, when not to go, which soap to use, on and on she talked, she barely came up for air. But Jandu only half-listened. He was too distracted by the sudden, amazing sight of a room full of naked women.

He could feel himself blushing from his toes to the roots of his hair, but there was nothing to be done about it. In front of him were half a dozen women, chatting amiably with one another in varying states of undress. They washed their hair, dried, and changed clothes, the chatter constant and upbeat, whispers echoing through the stone chamber loud enough for everyone to hear.

Jandu had seen very few naked women in his life. Now he was stunned by the variety of women's bodies, the different shades and shapes. Men's bodies were beautiful to him, but women seemed strange and alien, the darkness of their nipples, the weird dimples and marks on their skin. He hastily looked away, following Rani's lead as she put her towel down on one of the marble benches and started to undress.

He took off his clothes quickly, nervous about showing off his own body. He practically ran for the bath water. Once submerged, he relaxed somewhat, leaning against the white marble and casually watching Rani beside him as she went about her daily ablutions, her mouth never shutting for longer than a few seconds at a time.

Five minutes in the bath, and Jandu was a convert. Hot springs were the best thing on earth. The fact that he was sharing bath water with the lower caste entered his mind and left with no sense of outrage, only a mild curiosity. If the Shentari faith had gotten the distinctions of caste so wrong, how else had the religion been misinforming him? His skin would not peel off in rejection of Rani's presence. The only thing that seemed in danger was his hearing, as Rani listed the grooms in order of handsomeness, as she warned which guards were mean and which were kind, and described in detail the latest scandal between a kitchen maid and one of the gardeners.

"So tell me about the lord's son," Jandu asked casually, picking up on the fact that Rani loved to gossip about everyone around her, especially her masters.

"Which one?" Rani asked. She took a deep breath and dunked her head under water, washing the soap from her hair. Jandu lathered his head and did the same.

"The young one. Abiyar," Jandu said.

Two of the women in the bath with them turned and joined Jandu's conversation uninvited.

"Well, he isn't much use, is he?" one of them said.

The other woman nodded. "I've heard that Lord Indarel is thinking of sending him to Chandamar as an ambassador. But it's mostly because he figures Abiyar can't do anything else."

The women laughed, and Rani scooted closer to Jandu. The heat in the air and the water soothed Jandu to the bones. He sunk lower, letting the soft, meaningless conversation wash over him like a balm.

"The lord loves his sons," Rani said, nodding to herself. "But he definitely has preferences. Everyone loves Ramad, the eldest son. You should see him, Janali! He is beautiful. And

Parik, Indarel's second son, will be one of the most respected astrologers in Marhavad. All of the lord's advisors say Parik has a gift. He can read the stars better than the Draya."

Jandu closed his eyes and nodded. "And Abiyar?"

"Well…" Rani splashed water on her face. "No one really says much about him. He's quiet, and bad with weapons, I hear. He isn't very smart."

"Oh." Jandu understood a little better why Abiyar was so nervous about appearing to enjoy flute lessons in front of the palace guard.

"But he's nice," Rani added. "Unlike Ramad. He's a stuck up snob and he torments his younger brother."

Jandu smiled to himself. Being the youngest of three royal sons, Jandu had a pretty fair idea of what it meant to be third in line for the seat of power, and the most exposed to the taunts and torments of older brothers. But Yudar and Baram, relentless as their insults might be, loved Jandu fiercely, and he knew it. Their comments were always in jest, and never meant to really harm him. Perhaps Rani simply misunderstood the nature of brothers chiding each other.

Or, judging by the insecure way Abiyar held himself, maybe he really was insulted. It wouldn't be the first time that brothers were honestly mean to each other.

By the time Jandu and Rani emerged from the water, their flesh was pruned and bright red from the heat. Stepping from the steamy bathhouse into the cooling evening air was one of the most energizing feelings Jandu had ever experienced, and for a fleeting moment, he allowed himself to feel content with his situation. He was a woman, true, and in hiding, yes, but at least he now lived in a beautiful place, with what seemed to be nice people. Rani chatted loudly with him all the way back to their room, and then she did her hair quickly and left for the night, working as one of Shali's evening attendants.

That night, Jandu was startled from sleep when the door of his chamber opened. He saw the shadow of the person entering the room, and realized immediately that this person was far too big to be Rani. Jandu shot out of bed, and grabbed Zandi. Then he realized that, even if he did change her back into a bow, he had no, arrows. He clenched his fists, hoping the few muscles he had been left with could fend off an intruder.

Baram shut the door behind him. He looked down at Jandu and smiled sheepishly.

"Did I wake you?"

Jandu scowled at him. "What are you doing here?"

Baram smirked. "I've snuck past the guards into the single women's quarters, what do you think I'm doing?"

He laughed as Jandu sneered at him. Jandu crawled back into bed.

"How are you doing?" Baram lowered his voice. He grabbed the two green pillows from the floor and made himself comfortable on the floor.

"All right." Jandu turned on his side so he could see his brother.

"Have you been in the women's bathhouse? I hear it's beautiful."

"You'd love it," Jandu said. "At any given time, there are about ten naked women in it."

"God." Baram sighed contentedly.

"Sometimes they wash each other."

"God!" Baram stretched. "You lucky, lucky bastard."

"Good thing I don't have anything to get up anymore," Jandu said, yawning. "The charade would be over in no time."

"How come you get to spend your days surrounded by naked, soapy women?" Baram whispered angrily. "I have to cook with this nasty old man from some western fishing village. He thinks the only way to prepare anything is by boiling it in water and then throwing handfuls of curry powder on it."

"You could improve upon that technique," Jandu said, and he meant it. The food he had eaten in Afadi had been bland

and unsatisfying. "I tried to find you this afternoon, but you must have been out."

"Really?" Baram smiled. "I would have liked to see you. I miss you guys."

"Me too." It was the most heart felt conversation Jandu could ever remember having with his brother, and it made him instantly suspicious his mind was turning into a woman's as well. He immediately switched topics. "So when will you improve the menu?"

"I would if I could get the old bastard to trust me. He doesn't like the looks of me," Baram said. "He says I'm too strong to be a cook. He says I'm going to kill him in his sleep."

"It's a fair fear," Jandu said. He closed his eyes. "You're big, mean, and ugly. I wouldn't trust you as far as I could throw you."

"You can't throw a jug of water any more," Baram said.

Jandu sighed.

"At least Yudar seems to be having a good time," Baram added.

"You've seen him?" Jandu asked. Suraya had informed him that Yudar was often by the lord's side, the two of them playing dice until late in the evening, but Jandu still hadn't seen a glimpse of his brother.

Baram nodded. "He looked very content. It's unfair. While I'm busting my ass, he sits in palatial suites and plays dice all day. And you get to sit around with naked chicks."

"I have also apparently become babysitter to the palace loser," Jandu said. "Its not all leisure for me."

"How's Suraya?" Baram asked.

Jandu shrugged. "All right. I think she's happy to be in a palace again, although she works very hard. Shali is a bossy bitch. She has Suraya running all over the place, gathering her clothes, bringing her refreshments, fetching one of the dozens of other servants in the household."

Baram said nothing, and so Jandu cracked open an eye to look at him. Baram looked furious.

"Baram?" Jandu whispered.

Baram shook his head. "She should never have to be a servant. She is a queen." He punched the pillow. "I hate this."

Jandu sat up. "Do you think I like it?" He pointed to his chest. "Look, you fucker! I've got fucking tits!"

"I'm trying not to look," Baram said. "It's been over a year since I've screwed anyone, you know. I'll be traumatized if I have even a fleeting erection inspired by my baby brother."

They both started laughing.

Jandu laid back in the bed, and Baram stretched out on the floor, yawning.

"I think Suraya is better though," Jandu added at last. He wasn't sure how to talk about what had happened to her in the forest. But he thought Baram should know, and they had spent so little time alone together since their desperate escape. "But if you see her, I mean—you really should talk to her. I know she misses you."

"Why me?" Baram spat. "I'm not her husband anymore."

"Because she loves you more than Yudar or me," Jandu said plainly.

Baram sat up. "Jandu..."

"...Look." Jandu sighed. "I don't want to get into a long discussion on this, but I just want you to know the truth." He looked at his brother. "She's yours. She wants you. She loves you. I'm not going to get in the way of that. "

Baram had tears in his eyes. He stared up at the wooden ceiling, his mouth working wordlessly, as if he were forming and rejecting sentences.

Jandu closed his eyes again. "So are you going to spend the night here and ruin my reputation, labeling me an incestuous slut, or are you going to find some other young maiden to sleep with tonight?"

Baram laughed weakly. Jandu hear him sniffling in the darkness.

"Although if you stay, I still get the bed," Jandu said softly.

"I'm a girl now. I've got tender skin."

Baram snorted. Jandu heard him wipe his nose, heard him pull himself back together.

"Okay," Baram said at last. "I'll leave you and your reputation alone. I'll go sleep in the kitchen, where I'm supposed to."

CHAPTER 31

THE FULL NOTE OF TAREK'S CONCH SHELL BLEW OVER THE CITY of Jezza.

Outside the brown brick walls of the city, Tarek's army waited for the Jezzan lord to show himself. The Jezzan army remained out of sight, tucked inside the city's fortifications. Tarek surveyed the walls and saw they had been designed for defense but not offense. There were no raised platforms from which archers could mount an attack.

Tarek stood in his chariot, just outside the city gate. Behind him, fanned out, were his commanders. Beside him, in his own chariot, was Regent Mazar.

Mazar had joined Tarek only the evening prior, bringing along a contingent of Prasta soldiers. Tarek was surprised that the grizzly old warrior would journey so far from the palace after all these years of peace, but Mazar explained that he felt it his duty. He, too, had taken a vow to serve the king of Marhavad.

Tarek had only known Mazar as Regent, had only seen him in silk robes. Now, donned from head to toe in ancient-looking armor, the old man appeared fierce. His silver breastplate and helmet glinted in the unforgiving sunlight.

"If King Darvad cannot be with you," Mazar had told him, "then I consider it an honor to fight in his stead."

Tarek bowed. "Your skills and experience will be a great asset, and the honor is mine."

Now eight units of foot soldiers and archers stood behind Mazar, Tarek, and Darvad's general. Tarek was proud of the order of his men, the clean lines of their ranks, the fierceness of their appearance. The colored banners held beside the unit commanders flapped furiously in the hot, dry wind of the plain. Over two thousand men stood ready to follow Tarek into these walls.

Tarek looked back at the barred gate.

"I challenge Lord Sahdin to bring forth the traitor, Lord Kadal, and to surrender!" Tarek bellowed, hoping his voice carried deep into the city. "Tell your lord to show himself!"

Tarek's heart beat wildly. He prayed Sahdin would be brave enough to face Tarek alone. It would save lives. But as the silence stretched into minutes, he realized that there was little chance that the lord would willingly give up Kadal, or the safety of his palace.

One arrow, ignited, flew over the city wall, falling short of Tarek. Its message was clear. If Tarek wanted Kadal, he would have to take him.

Tarek signaled to his commanders and then Tarek sounded his conch shell one more time.

Mazar and the other Triya in chariots blew their horns as well, and the sound of the notes rising brought the hairs on Tarek's arms up on end and sent a thrill of expectation through his veins. Adrenalin flooded his system.

"I can break the wall," Mazar shouted at Tarek.

"Then do it," Tarek said.

He watched as Mazar pulled an arrow from his quiver, notched it, and then aimed at the wall. Mazar closed his eyes and whispered a sharta over the weapon, the words strange and dangerous, beyond Tarek's comprehension.

Mazar loosed his string and the arrow whistled as it flew.

The arrow hit the wall. Stones exploded in a shower of dirt and flame. Dust burst upon the army and the echo of the detonation pealed over Tarek in a roar. Jezzan soldiers screamed as shrapnel bombarded them. The force of the impact carved a basin in the dry soil.

Before the Jezzan troops inside could react, Tarek charged into the gap. A roar went up from his troops as chariots filed in behind him, with his foot soldiers following suit.

Tarek's horses trampled over the explosion's crater and took off at a gallop towards the center of town. He raced for the palace. Once he killed Sahdin and Kadal the war would be won.

Dust blinded the Jezzan soldiers. Many stood, too shocked from the force of the sharta to react. As Tarek's soldiers poured through the hole, they took advantage of the Jezzan's surprise, cutting them down like sheep. Tarek had ordered two units to stay and safeguard their exit. The rest of his soldiers fought through the Jezzan defensive line.

Tarek only witnessed the beginning of the melee, as his view was quickly swallowed by the high walls and winding streets of the city. His charioteer rounded a corner and he briefly glimpsed the chaos left in his wake. Arrows clanged against helmets and breastplates. Screams rang through as the points found limbs and faces. Hand to hand combat broke out in a flurry of individual battles around the wall, down the narrow streets. There was no escape for the Jezzans, no ground to retreat to, and as his own soldiers continued to pour through the hole in the wall, the Jezzans, outnumbered, began to die in great numbers, struck down by spears, maces, and swords. The assault was monstrous and fast. Dragewan soldiers charged forward towards the Jezzan Palace, slashing a way through the remaining terrified Jezzan troops and following their lord into the streets of the city.

Jezza's streets were filthy gray, its buildings coated in decades of dust. Tarek's charioteer negotiated the tight corners and precarious angles of the stone buildings. Tarek ordered his charioteer up the main avenue while Mazar and the other charioteers split up through the other streets, each of them charging towards the palace. Two units followed Tarek. The yellow banners showed that one of the units was under Anant's command.

The road opened to a wider thoroughfare. Tarek spotted an enemy chariot racing towards him. Tarek notched an arrow and aimed at one of the two horses pulling the chariot. He loosed the arrow and the horse fell with a scream. As the horse fell, the other steed screeched in panic as the chariot bounded over the dead animal and flipped over on itself. A second chariot behind this swerved to miss the wreckage and charged Tarek. The Jezzan warrior inside shot a flurry of arrows but most flew wide.

Tarek didn't bother with his shield. He returned his own volley of arrows. The chariot flew past him and then circled around, seconds later coming back to attack Tarek from behind. Tarek took careful aim, bringing down first the archer and then the charioteer.

As Tarek raced to the palace, more chariots charged, but their forces split as they turned down different roads to challenge Tarek and Mazar separately. Chariots flew toward Tarek, but he dispatched one with another volley of arrows. The other chariot was taken down by Tarek's foot soldiers, who stabbed the horses with spears.

Tarek rushed to the palace gates.

Mazar arrived a moment later, rounding the corner of the other road. He recited over another arrow and shot this at the palace gate, and once again the masonry shattered in a discharge of mud and stone. Tarek's horses whinnied in fear but continued forward.

Tarek's chariot was overtaken by Anant's men, who pushed themselves at a sprint towards the enemy, butchering Jezzans to open a passage for Tarek.

Tarek abandoned his chariot. There were too many bodies, too much chaos to navigate a wheeled car. He slung his bow over his shoulder and grabbed his sword and shield, and jumped to the ground, pushing through the crowd of his men to make his way into the palace. Immediately his own men closed in behind him, shielding him from attack.

The palace courtyard was bricked in and small, with a pool and a statue of Prophet Tarhandi looming in the center.

Skirmishes blossomed across the courtyard, as man fought against man, soldiers falling, clubbed to death. Execution took mere seconds once the soldier was on the ground.

Given the hopeless situation, Tarek expected the Jezzans to run. But now that his forces had penetrated the palace, there was no place for the troops inside the palace to go. So they battled on, hand to hand combat bringing the men together in couples, a gory dance of blades and maces. The walls of the palace closed in the sound of the battle, creating a roaring echo which shook the ground as men screamed, as metal clanged metal, as bodies fell upon the hard stone. The dead lay in piles, especially around their broken entrance, where Tarek's men killed the Jezzans trying to flee.

Someone grabbed his arm and Tarek spun fiercely, sword raised.

Mazar panted beside him, his armor stained with the blood of his victims.

"Be careful!" Mazar said. " Sahdin knows the Pezarisharta. If he releases it, he could kill every living creature within the city!"

A Jezzan soldier charged at Mazar. Tarek and Mazar both attacked, cutting down the man in mere moments. Mazar dashed into a nearby melee.

Tarek climbed onto the base of Tarhandi's statue in the center of the courtyard. He slung his shield behind him and used his bow to cut down men from his vantage point.

To his right, he saw Anant hewing his way through a crowd of men. Two men attacked Anant at once. He dodged and managed to slice the back of the knee of one of them while evading the other. Disabled, the Jezzan fell, and Anant thrust his sword through the other soldier's neck. Blood sprayed for a dozen feet, covering Anant's armor in red. Anant wiped his eyes and surged on.

Tarek leapt down from the statue and blew his conch. Anant and his men immediately flanked Tarek.

"I need to get to Sahdin," Tarek commanded. At once Anant and his cadre of soldiers surrounded him and hacked their way into the palace. Men, both Jezzan and Dragewan, fell. But soon Tarek reached the entrance of the great hall. Few of his bodyguard remained and they spread out, wary of the dim spaces in the hall.

Suddenly a man called out.

"Judge!"

Tarek turned just as a wild-eyed Jezzan soldier, a commander, swung his mace. Tarek had no time to react.

Out of nowhere, Anant sprang between them. The mace smashed into the side of Anant's head. He crumpled to the ground. Tarek lunged forward, driving his sword into his assailant's belly.

Tarek heard Anant groan on the marble floor. Tarek knelt beside him.

"Anant!" he shouted. A shrill buzzing filled Tarek's ears.

"My lord! It's Sahdin!" someone called. Tarek swiveled to see Sahdin emerge from his throne room. His eyes burned in fury. He was fitted in his armor, his sword in his hand.

"Suya whore!" Sahdin hissed. He raised his sword.

Tarek raised his own. Unlike that evening at Druv's house in Prasta, Tarek could now fight fairly, on equal terms. Tarek blocked Sahdin's blows easily. The moment he saw Sahdin's mouth contort to form a sharta, Tarek swung with all his strength and sliced off Sahdin's head in one, clean stroke.

Only moments later, Kadal himself emerged. He wore armor as well, but it looked too small for him. He was clearly terrified.

"Royal Judge!" Kadal stuttered.

Tarek thrust his sword into Kadal's side, in between the plates of his armor. Kadal fell to his knees with a cry. Tarek grabbed his hair and exposed his neck, and then sliced his blade through.

A wail emerged from Sahdin's nearby attendants. The cry was taken up immediately by the soldiers around them, the sound rumbling into a dark roar, throughout the palace, as the Jezzan soldiers dropped their weapons and bowed to their conqueror.

The buzzing in Tarek's ears didn't stop.

Tarek called his general to give the order not to attack the unarmed Jezzan soldiers, and to take them as prisoners instead. But many of Tarek's men were blinded with blood lust, and it was several hours before the last of the skirmishes abated. Tarek meanwhile removed Sahdin's diadem and had one of his men hang it on the shattered palace gate, a reminder of what happens to traitors of the king.

In the evening, Tarek ordered torches lit and his soldiers worked to stack the bodies of the fallen Jezzans for cremation the following day. The bodies of Sahdin and Kadal were anointed and prepared for a funeral pyre that evening. Tarek allowed the lord's attendants to complete all formal respects for their former liege, who had fallen honorably in battle.

As final preparations were being made to light the pyre, Tarek addressed the mourning throngs. Tarek appointed one of his generals to oversee the safety of Jezza until King Darvad chose a new lord. He assured the people that so long as they were obedient to Darvad, no further harm would come to them.

Then a shriek, piercing and pitiful, came from a young woman, who rushed to Sahdin's funeral pyre and threw herself upon it, sobbing. One look at her bosom told Tarek that this was Sahdin's daughter, the luscious Aisa, Darvad's desired wife.

Aisa's attendants pulled her from her father's body as the pyre was lit. She sobbed loudly, uncontrollably, and her grief stirred the people around them. Jezzan citizens turned cold eyes towards Tarek.

"Get her out of here," Tarek ordered one of his commanders.

"Where should I take her, my lord?" The commander asked.

A cold, dank feeling crept through Tarek's bones. He looked at the weeping girl. This was his chance to save her for Darvad.

"Take her where you want," Tarek snapped. "It is not my concern."

The commander's eyes glinted briefly, and then he ordered his men to drag Aisa away. People stirred angrily. The situation was growing hostile.

Mazar, who had watched the proceedings by Tarek's side, stepped forward.

"On behalf of King Darvad, I offer those Jezzan citizens loyal to our beloved king the riches deserved of such fealty." He motioned to his waiting soldiers. They began to distribute coins—gold, jewels, the coffers of Jezza's lord. The crowd's atmosphere changed dramatically. Now a stampede formed, people vying for their share of the booty.

Tarek smiled coldly. "I trust you have saved enough of the coffers to pay the troops."

"Of course," Mazar snorted. He smiled at Tarek. "I may be old and weary, but I am no fool."

"You were magnificent," Tarek told Mazar, and he meant it. He wasn't sure how he would have breached the fortifications in the first place if it hadn't been for Mazar's shartas. Tarek realized that having Mazar by his side was, in many respects, more of an advantage than Darvad himself.

After the funeral, Tarek discussed securing their position with his general. He then dragged his exhausted body out to the back courtyard of the palace, where his army's tents were erected. He drank water like a dying man once he got there, and then inspected the casualties. Two hundred of his soldiers had died, with another three hundred wounded. Tarek walked past men with severed limbs, with slashed faces, with shattered bones. Tarek steadied himself, telling himself it was an acceptable level of casualties for a battle.

As he made his rounds, Tarek toughened his resolve against reacting to injury. Each consecutive solider made it easier. Until he saw Anant.

"Oh, God!" Tarek had forgotten. Selfish, conceited idiot, he had *forgotten* that Anant had saved his life. He rushed to Anant's side.

Anant was unconscious. His helmet had taken the brunt of the mace swing, but the left side of his face was in terrible shape. His cheek was swollen, his left eye was misshapen, and it seemed as if the distance between his eyes had widened.

The air caught in Tarek's throat.

The physician overseeing the injuries caught Tarek's reaction and tried to reassure him.

"He'll survive," the physician said. "He's very lucky—I think he'll keep his eye."

"Will he... be disfigured?" Tarek thought of Anant's deep, masculine handsomeness, so alluring when coupled with his shy blushes.

The physician sighed. "He'll live. That's all I can promise you right now."

Tarek nodded. "Do whatever you can. Help him." He stared at the physician. "He is a friend of mine."

"Oh!" The physician seemed flustered. "Shall I take him into the palace then? The other commanders who sustained injuries are there. The accommodations are better."

Tarek narrowed his eyes. "Anant is a commander. Why isn't he with them?"

"He said he wanted to stay with his men."

Tarek stared at Anant a long time before answering. "Bring him to the palace. Do everything you can." And he left the courtyard to finish his inspection.

CHAPTER 32

WITHIN A MONTH OF BEGINNING THEIR FLUTE LESSONS JANDU realized how he could improve Abiyar's concentration. Jandu had been initially confused by the boy's strange split-personality when it came to practicing music. On the one hand, he always seemed interested, and he enthusiastically attempted every challenge Jandu presented him.

On the other hand, he often scoffed at the instrument, calling it a "stupid girl's toy" and "beneath him." He glanced nervously at the guard who was assigned to him, and every time the guard looked back, Abiyar straightened, pushing out his chest, tightening his facial features as if annoyed.

Finally, Jandu just excused the guard by asking him sweetly to step outside. At moments like this, Jandu's feminine body served him well. He fluttered his eyelashes.

The guard didn't even bother to hide the fact that he stared at Jandu's breasts. "I am not allowed to leave him alone." But he looked tempted. For a month, he had stood through Abiyar's lessons with a bored, pained expression on his face.

"He isn't alone," Jandu said. "He's with me."

"It's all right," Abiyar said. He stood and narrowed his eyes at the guard. "Wait for me outside."

"As you wish, my lord." The guard ogled Jandu one last time, and then stepped from the room.

Jandu's mouth curled into a smile. "Right. Let's see how practice goes without an audience today."

Jandu made himself comfortable on the sitting room settee. Abiyar sat beside him, folding his thin legs nervously. His awkward body, his desire to please, and his brash bravado appealed to Jandu.

Since meeting Abiyar, Jandu had heard most of the palace rumors that circulated about the boy. People considered Abiyar girlish and weak. His brothers disliked him. Jandu had even heard several of the women in the bath house accuse the boy of being a faggot.

Which, of course, only made Jandu feel more protective of his young protégé. From the way Abiyar nervously glanced at Jandu's breasts and blushed with any close contact, Jandu truly doubted Abiyar was a homosexual. But his reputation was in dire straits. Jandu wanted to help resurrect it.

"Show me what we learned yesterday," Jandu said, handing the flute to Abiyar.

Without the guard, Abiyar's playing improved greatly. Even he seemed shocked by his own performance. Jandu realized that at this rate it wouldn't be long before Abiyar's natural musical abilities would surpass Jandu's own limited skill.

Halfway through the day's scales, a servant girl knocked quietly at the door and delivered a plate of food for lunch. Abiyar dove into the bread and cheese hastily.

Jandu shook out the flute and cleaned it with a cloth. "You're very good, Abiyar," he said. He froze, realizing his error in calling the lord's son by his first name.

But Abiyar didn't seem to mind. He smiled sweetly, too grateful for the rare compliment to be concerned with decorum.

"I told you I like music," Abiyar said. "And you are a good teacher, Janali."

Jandu smiled. "Tell me about some of your other teachers. Who is your weapons master?"

"Master Devdan," Abiyar said, mouth full of bread and cheese. "He is the most renowned Triya warrior in all of Afadi!"

"Then you are in good hands."

"Of course." Abiyar fiddled with his diadem. "I only have the best."

A warm, balmy breeze smelling of roses wafted in from the window, and Jandu leaned back, enjoying the feel of the air on his skin. His midriff was bare, and the air tickled his naval.

"Has Master Devdan started training you with shartas?" Jandu asked.

Abiyar's eyes widened. "Magical weapons? What do you think he is, a prophet?"

Jandu laughed. "Regular humans can use them too."

"No they can't," Abiyar said. "That is a myth."

"They can," Jandu insisted. "You just have to concentrate. There are two skills needed in learning a sharta. You must first learn how to summon it, and then learn the counter-curse, to withdraw it. Some are more difficult to recall than others."

This piqued Abiyar's interest. He turned to Jandu enthusiastically. "How do you know this?"

Jandu burned with a desire to show off in front of Abiyar. His mind was filled with so many magical weapons, it would startle even his own family. The years of training with Mazar formed an arsenal the likes of which most armies in Marhavad had never seen.

But if there was any one thing Jandu could do to completely blow his cover, it would be to unleash a magical weapon. He leaned his head back against his hands and sighed.

"I know a lot of things." He left it at that.

◆◆◆

In December, Abiyar began an intensive course of archery with his weapon's master in preparations for the upcoming New Year's festival. Jandu drilled Abiyar for details about his training, but Abiyar seemed almost shy about his master. Jandu would have given anything to meet this Devdan and to see some sparring. As it was, he was always stuck indoors, with a flute, or in his rooms, listening to Rani talk endlessly. And while Rani was good at giving Jandu the inside scoop on the scandals of palace life and rumors from around Marhavad, Jandu truly missed his old life, talking strategy and weapons and being around horses and swords and other men. Even Keshan, who eschewed violence and was more refined than other warriors, still sparred and shot targets in his free time. This passive life wearied Jandu.

One morning it was too brilliant outside for Jandu to sit indoors any longer. He left a message with Abiyar's servant, Bir, that he wanted to meet Abiyar outside for a change, and Bir reported back that the boy had archery practice that morning in his private courtyard. Jandu could instruct him there.

Jandu went to meet Abiyar at the scheduled time, but Abiyar was late. Abiyar's target of hay and cloth stood at the end of the courtyard. There were stone steps that led to Abiyar's rooms, and on the edge of the stone balcony Jandu found Abiyar's bow, carelessly abandoned like an unwanted toy.

Jandu lifted the bow to examine it. It was a heavy compound bow with a deep curve, and made of wood, sinew and bone, lacquered in a beautiful black diamond pattern. Pleasure rushed through Jandu's arms just holding it. Since the age of ten, there hadn't been a single day that Jandu hadn't shot an arrow. Now it had been months. Jandu twanged the string automatically.

He looked around, but no one was in sight. He promptly loosened the bowstring and adjusted its length. As he heard footsteps coming around the corner of the balcony, he quickly restrung the bow and put it on the steps.

Abiyar emerged, a large chunk of bread in his hands.

Jandu sat on the steps and pulled out his flute. "You're late."

"I was hungry." Abiyar stuffed the rest of the bread in his mouth and then reached down to pick up his bow.

Abiyar twanged the bow. Both of them reacted to the change in tone. Jandu smiled.

Abiyar studied his bow, then Jandu. "Did you do something to it?"

"I adjusted your brace height, that's all," Jandu said. "Your string was too short."

With newfound trust, Abiyar sat next to Jandu on the brick ledge, careful not to sit on Jandu's long red zahari. He held his bow out before him proudly.

"It looks different," Abiyar said.

"The lower brace height will push the arrow longer and faster. And the tauter string will result in less slap and a smoother release."

Abiyar studied Jandu's face. "Where did you learn this?"

Jandu watched Abiyar from the corner of his eye. "I was once a charioteer for Prince Jandu Paran in Prasta."

Abiyar's eyes grew wide. "You? A woman?"

"Why not? I've always been good with horses and weaponry, woman or not."

Abiyar's expression turned dreamy. "I hear Jandu is the best archer in all of Marhavad."

Jandu grinned. "He is."

"What's he like?"

"He's incredible."

"Is it true that he can hit a target from 300 yards?" Abiyar asked.

Jandu nodded. "Once I saw him hit a target 350 yards away."

"Wow." Abiyar shook his head. "I'd love to meet him."

"Maybe you will some day."

Abiyar looked at Jandu with sudden intensity. "Did Jandu teach you any other tricks? Archery tricks, I mean? I'm not so good at hitting small targets."

Jandu took a deep breath to calm his heart down. "I may be able to remember a few things."

Abiyar handed Jandu his bow. "Show me something."

The urge to show off was overwhelming, but Jandu resisted.

"Why don't you shoot at the target instead," Jandu put the bow back in Abiyar's hand, "and I'll tell you what I see."

Abiyar enthusiastically scooted off the ledge of the courtyard and took aim. He hadn't pulled the string back before Jandu was on him, standing behind him to gently correct his posture.

"Look, you're shooting in a wind, so open your stance," Jandu said. He moved Abiyar's body an inch to the left. "Keep your feet placed shoulder-width apart and your toes slightly outward, otherwise you'll lose your balance when you shoot."

Abiyar pulled his arms back, to show him his stance. Jandu frowned, realizing that Abiyar had way too much bow for a boy his age. It might have been appropriate for a grown man, or one of his stronger older brothers, but for Abiyar, it was too powerful. His arm shook as he pulled back the string.

"Do you have another bow?" he asked.

"Only this one. My father gave it to me."

Jandu understood that he would only insult Abiyar if he suggested a lighter one. "Well, your accuracy is ruined partially because your arm is lifting on release. Pull the string straight back until it touches your lips."

Abiyar clumsily pulled an arrow from the quiver on the ground and, with much fiddling, notched it into place. He shakily pulled back the string as Jandu had showed him, and fired the arrow just right of the target's center.

Jandu beamed a bright smile. "You see?"

"Wow! That's amazing!" Abiyar jumped up in joy.

"And if you always draw the string back the same way, you should have no problem repeating that shot."

Abiyar fumbled for another arrow, but this one he shot too low.

Jandu shook his head. "You're not paying attention to your body. Your chest is collapsing when you shoot, so you're losing all your back tension and not getting a fully developed draw."

Abiyar adjusted his position.

"No!" Jandu shook his head. "Look, give it to me…" Jandu took the bow and quickly drew back the string.

"Janali!"

Jandu loosed the string, and the arrow shot directly through the previous arrow Abiyar had shot.

Jandu turned to see Suraya scowling at him. "Yes?" he said sheepishly.

"What the hell are you doing?"

Jandu handed the bow to Abiyar, who stared at the arrow Jandu had just shot, awestruck.

"Nothing." Jandu gave Suraya a big, lying smile.

"What?"

"Just helping Abiyar."

Suraya crossed her arms. "Come here, little sister."

"But—"

"—Come here."

Suraya grabbed Jandu by the ear and led him around the corner of the building. She pushed him against the wall angrily.

Suraya narrowed her eyes. "You're a woman now, Jandu. Act like one!"

"I'm trying." Jandu sighed. "It's hard."

"You're a music teacher, not an archer," Suraya told him.

"But he had his string all fucked up—" Jandu started.

"Who cares?" Suraya snapped.

Jandu straightened. "I care. I don't want him to be unprepared. He's a Triya, Suraya, and the son of a lord. Some day he is going to be in a battle. If he went out like he was today, he would be killed."

Suraya sighed loudly. "Be that as it may, I don't think you should be teaching him anything but music. Anyone could have walked by right then, not just me. You act strangely enough in the women's quarters as it is, we don't need any more attention drawn your way."

"I know." Jandu looked away, realizing she was right. Practicing archery with Abiyar had been the most fun he'd had since arriving in Afadi. Jandu scowled, and then returned to Abiyar's courtyard.

"Change of plans," he said glumly. He sat on the stone steps and pulled out his flute. "Time for music."

Abiyar's shoulders sank in disappointment. "But you could teach me—"

"—I can't teach you anything," Jandu snapped. He sighed. "Your weapon's master is the one to instruct you. What do I know? I'm just a music teacher."

Abiyar was young and brash and often wrong, but he wasn't a fool. He stared at Jandu a long time, and then said, "You got in trouble didn't you?" Abiyar smiled. "So teach me another song. And don't make it a love song, please. If you teach me another one of those I'm going to puke."

◆◆◆

In January, as part of the New Year's festival, Lord Indarel held an annual archery competition outside the city gates in the large open expanse between the city walls and the old cemetery.

On Rani's insistence, Jandu dressed up for the occasion. Jandu's roommate loaned Jandu one of her nicest zaharis, a purple cloth with an intricate pattern of peacocks along the fringes. The peacocks reminded Jandu of Keshan's Tiwari standard, and so he loved it. He even gave in to Rani's constant nagging and let her do his hair, tying his long black mane into an intricate braid and attaching a band of small silver jewels throughout it.

Because it was a special occasion, Jandu decided to also wear Keshan's pendant. He had hidden the pendant long ago when he took it off Druv's dead body, but now he wore it with secret pride, letting the light dance over the pearl and his pale skin, warming with the dark colors of his gown.

The youngest age allowed in the competition was sixteen, so this was the first year that Abiyar would participate. The entire city came out for the event, and a makeshift arena was set up in the middle of the field, complete with bamboo risers for the audience to stand and better view the action.

It was also the first time Jandu had been out of the palace walls since arriving in Afadi. He walked through the city and towards the competition with Suraya and Yudar and Baram, together as a family for the first time in almost half a year.

Jandu brimmed with excitement. He had shared no more than a few words with Yudar since arriving, and now the two of them clung to each other and shared stories as they walked slowly with the long, snaking crowd through the gates of the city to the open field. Musicians filled the air with songs and the smell of roasting meat wafted over the crowd as droves of vendors sold food from carts. Hundreds of people stopped and greeted each other and shopped and laughed as the celebration for the end of winter began.

"To think you didn't even know how to braid your hair six months ago." Suraya shook her head in amazement, then she leaned a little closer. "You look gorgeous and that's a lovely pendant. Did Rani lend that to you as well?"

"No." Jandu blushed.

Suraya's eyebrow lifted. "Who then?"

Jandu didn't answer, and was relieved when Yudar pulled Suraya away to show her some tapestries that local women had woven for the celebration.

Jandu and his family planned to sit up in the risers and watch the show with the rest of Afadi's citizens, but upon seeing Yudar, Lord Indarel himself held out his hand and ushered the Parans to stand at the sidelines with the lord's attendants. Lord Indarel and Yudar had become very close over the last few months, and now they seemed almost inseparable.

Jandu scanned the Triyas in the arena, looking for Abiyar, but he couldn't see him.

And then, beside him, he heard someone whisper. "Janali."

Jandu turned slightly, and saw Abiyar. He too was decked out in his finest jewels, his golden armor polished to a fine gleam.

Neither of them looked at each other, they stared at the competition arena and the current archer. Abiyar held his bow up slightly.

"Does this look okay?" Abiyar whispered to Jandu.

Jandu looked briefly at the string and then back at the competitors. "Your string should have at least six twists in it, Abi," he whispered back. "That will round it better."

Abiyar twisted his string as he stood beside Jandu. Jandu looked around the field. But no one was paying attention to them. Indarel fawned over his two older sons, Ramad and Parik, admiring their weapons and giving them hugs. He completely ignored Abiyar, about to compete for the first time. It was as though Indarel assumed Abiyar would fail. A fierce, protective anger flooded Jandu. He put his arm around Abiyar, angry that no one helped him in his first competition, that Abiyar's master was nowhere in sight, and that the boy's father wouldn't bother to take the time to ensure his son's bow was correctly strung.

"Remember to relax your fingers when you shoot, so your hand can act independently of your wrist," Jandu whispered.

"All right." Abiyar looked nervous.

Jandu smiled down at him, and touched his ornate diadem fondly. "I'm proud of you, Abi. You're going to be great."

"Sure I will," Abiyar said. But the tremor in his voice gave away his nerves.

Abiyar's time to appear was at the end of the archery competition, since he was the son of the lord. This meant he endured watching dozens of other Triya sons hit their targets. Some fared better than others. Jandu lingered towards the front of the crowd of guests, watching each shot carefully, judging each archer on their stance, the way they drew their strings, their focus.

Lord Indarel's party at the event grew during the course of the competition, and now dozens of honored guests lingered in the area reserved for Indarel and Shali, who sat in thrones, watching the event unfold with vague interest. Lord Indarel was constantly distracted by his guests, coming to discuss politics or business as the competition proceeded. His daughter Vaisha stood beside her mother, both of them greeting the guests formally, dressed in their finest attire.

As Jandu moved closer to the edge of the box to watch a small Triya man take aim, he felt someone touch his arm beside him. He looked up and was surprised to see it was not a member of his family.

"Fascinating, isn't it?" The man, a Triya, spoke to Jandu with a glint in his eye.

Jandu immediately moved away from the man. "Yes." He pretended to yawn. "But archery is so dull." He hoped he hadn't been watching the competition too enthusiastically.

The Triya beside him laughed. "I don't believe you. I've been watching you. You look at the archers as though you wish you were with them."

Jandu narrowed his eyes. "What an absurd idea."

The man laughed again, his eyes hungrily raking down Jandu's body. "You are as witty as you are adorable." He brought his hands together and bowed low. "I am Hanu, ambassador for my brother, Lord Firdaus of Chandamar."

The very mention of Firdaus' name made Jandu flush with anger. He studied Hanu, and realized he looked like a younger, healthier version of Darvad's friend. He was tall and had large shoulders, and also carried a noticeable belly. Triya warrior he might be, but Jandu immediately dismissed him as a threat.

His dark brown eyes locked on Jandu's waist. Jandu took another step away from him. He looked around for his brothers.

"Nice to meet you," Jandu mumbled.

"And you are?"

"Janali." Jandu didn't smile. "I tutor Lord Indarel's son Abiyar."

"Ah, yes," Hanu smiled. "I heard there was a pretty young woman who managed to win Abiyar's heart. You are the younger sister of Esalas, the lord's dice partner, are you not?"

"Yes." Jandu looked away. "Excuse me. I need to find my family." He darted off to find Suraya and the others.

Jandu spotted Yudar and Baram just as the lord's sons entered the arena to compete. When Ramad, Afadi's heir apparent, stepped into the arena, a roar came from the crowd, and they chanted his name in pride.

Ramad was heavily adorned in gold armor and a full rainbow of colored silk, yellows and peaches and greens, his thick long hair tied back with leather, his diadem almost as large as his father's. He turned and bowed to the crowd dramatically, and the cheers rose. Lord Indarel looked beside himself with joy. Ramad strutted to the center of the arena and flexed his muscles unnecessarily as he took aim.

"Asshole," Jandu whispered under his breath. Of course, he had to remind himself that he did pretty much the same thing at his own archery competition back in Prasta. But he was a different Jandu back then.

Ramad shot a tight cluster of arrows at the center of the target. The crowd roared in joy. Jandu understood now that Abiyar did not have the same weapons master as his older brother did. There was no way these two boys were learning from the same teacher.

Ramad took his time. He had himself blindfolded and shot another volley of arrows. Many missed the bull's eye, but they still hit the target itself, which was close enough to please the crowd. Although Jandu had once gloried in this kind of grandstanding himself, he now thought it tacky, and strategically pointless.

Watching his older brother, Abiyar gripped his bow tightly, sweat breaking out across his forehead. His second brother Parik whispered something to Abiyar and Abiyar flushed in embarrassment.

Jandu gritted his teeth. These boys had no right to taunt Abiyar just for being the youngest. He tried to imagine growing up in a household where Yudar and Baram persecuted him. He couldn't imagine it. Through thick and thin, he and his brothers had always been inseparable. Since the death of their father, Yudar and Baram had protected him.

After Ramad, Parik's demonstration had less fanfare, but it was still warmly greeted by the crowds. They cheered the boy and flowers fell from the risers to his feet. Parik was not as good as Ramad, but he was adequate. His arrow groupings were accurate, although his stance needed work.

Abiyar, too, received cheers when it was his turn to compete, but many in the crowd watched him with more curiosity than reverence. This was the first time Abiyar would have to show his skills in front of his citizens. He strutted out to the middle of the arena, and from a distance, he seemed confident. But Jandu knew him well enough to see the tremor in his step. Jandu closed his eyes and prayed for his strength and courage.

Abiyar did not do as well as some of the other boys his age in the competition, and he paled in comparison to his brothers, although his performance was far from a failure. Lord Indarel barely noticed. Jandu still hadn't seen any sign of Abiyar's archery master and his anger grew when Abiyar returned to the royal grounds, and Lord Indarel did nothing to acknowledge his son.

Abiyar's personal attendants rushed to take his bow and offer him drinks. Jandu's view of his student was blocked by the sheer number of honored guests, but he caught a glimpse of Abiyar, and could see the disappointment on his face.

"I have to talk to Abiyar," Jandu told his family. He followed Abiyar's servants around the stands to a tent that had been set up for the lord's family. Jandu hesitated at the tent flap, worried it would look suspicious if he went in uninvited. But there was no one under the risers, and he felt safe.

"Abi?" He peeped his head in.

Abiyar's servant was stripping off the boy's armor. Abiyar looked devastated. He glared at Jandu. "Go away."

Jandu sighed. "Can I talk for a—"

"Go!"

Jandu swallowed, and left the tent. He bumped directly into a man's chest.

Hanu stared down at him. Jandu could see the tremble of excitement in the ambassador's hands.

"Janali! What a surprise." He reached out to touch Jandu's arm, and Jandu backed away.

"Come, don't toy with me," Hanu cooed. "I just want to walk with you."

"I can't." Jandu backed away further. "I'm busy."

"You are a servant of Lord Indarel," Hanu said. "And I am an honored ambassador. I am sure the lord could see fit to order you to accompany me."

Jandu didn't answer. He started back towards his family.

Hanu followed him doggedly. "I know you are not married. And I am a very generous man—"

"—Fuck off," Jandu spat. He walked faster. Rani's fine zahari impeded his movements. It was wrapped so tight around his legs that he could only take tiny steps.

Hanu lunged and grabbed Jandu's arm. He looked furious.

"How *dare* you—"

Jandu drove his fist into Hanu's mouth. When Hanu cried out in pain, Jandu stomped on his foot and then dashed as fast as he could back to the arena.

His heart pounded furiously by the time he got back to his family.

He could be severely punished for punching an ambassador. Especially the Chandamar ambassador. The peace between Afadi and Chandamar had been on a knife's edge for the last few years, and Jandu knew it wouldn't take much to slice through the ruse of amicability.

"What happened?" Suraya grabbed his hand, noticing the blood on it.

"Firdaus' brother just tried to molest me. I cut my knuckle on his tooth."

Yudar and Baram instantly glared at him.

"What?" Yudar said.

Jandu took deep breaths to steady himself. "The bastard! What did he think, I would just obey him?"

Yudar fiddled with his turban. "Oh no. This is not good."

"It's bad enough being a woman," Jandu snapped. "Now I must endure this?"

"Firdaus' brother? Hanu, the Ambassador?" Suraya asked.

Jandu put his fist to his mouth and sucked on his knuckle. "Yes. What are we going to do?"

"You are going to stay out of sight, that's what you are going to do," Yudar said. "Chandamar and Afadi are on the brink of war. This kind of insult could ruin the peace Indarel has spent years developing." He shook his head. "Everything is always difficult with you."

"Me?" Jandu asked angrily. "Why is this *my* fault?"

"Couldn't you just have politely said no?" Yudar asked.

"I did. He didn't accept it."

Baram hadn't said a word. Jandu looked at him and now saw the rage in his face.

"If he lays a hand on you, I swear I'll cut his throat," Baram growled.

Jandu had the absurd desire to laugh. It was so surreal, the whole situation. Baram having to defend *him* against another man. Jandu had never feared anyone, other than Keshan, but that was for an entirely different reason.

Yudar took a deep breath and looked at Baram. "You'll both do as I tell you. Jandu, remain in the women's quarters, and go out as little as possible. If Hanu doesn't see you, then you'll be fine. Hopefully he won't ask Lord Indarel for your dismissal."

"And if he does?" Jandu let Suraya take his hand and wrap it with a cloth.

Yudar sighed. "We'll deal with that situation if we come to it."

CHAPTER 33

Following Yudar's advice, Jandu remained in the women's quarters.

If Hanu told anyone what had happened between him and Jandu, no one had heard of it. Jandu asked his most effusive source of palace gossip, Rani, but she confirmed that Hanu wasn't saying anything about Janali or being punched.

Rani was wide-eyed and thrilled with Jandu's story, however. After the competition, she sat on Jandu's bed with him and begged for a blow-by-blow of the attack and defense. And after that she asked Jandu to show her how it was done. They spent a cathartic evening punching pillows and stomping on imaginary feet. Rani's expression when she practiced the moves Jandu taught her was so violent that Jandu wondered how many times she'd been in the same position but without his skill or training.

Jandu indulged her, having grown fond of her companionship. Recently, Rani had found herself a lover, one of the grooms in the stable, and so she was gone much of the time, leaving Jandu alone and bored in his own quarters.

Lady Shali, upon hearing that Jandu had sequestered himself, ordered a soldier to escort Jandu to and from his daily music lessons so that Abiyar could continue his studies. When Jandu heard about this, he felt he'd reached a whole new level of emasculation. He sought an audience with Shali to beg her not to go to such extremes for him.

"But I have to, don't you see?" Shali was having her hair done, and smiled coyly at Jandu as he stood in her doorway, awaiting her commands. "I don't know what you have done to him, Janali, but Abiyar is absolutely enchanted with you. You are the only tutor Abiyar has ever had that he speaks of with reverence. He begged me to see to continuing his flute lessons with you."

The knowledge that Abiyar wanted to see him sent a warm rush of happiness through Jandu. He hadn't spoken to him since the competition, and he worried that Abiyar was angry at him for some reason. Now Jandu bowed low and thanked Shali for her assistance in securing his safety.

◆◆◆

Back in the music room, Abiyar had a strange grin on his face.

"I'd forgotten how tiny you are," Abiyar said.

Jandu rolled his eyes. "It's been a week, Abi."

"Such a sweet week," Abiyar mused.

Jandu smirked back. "I'd forgotten how rotten you are." The two of them had taken to insulting each other lightly. Jandu briefly worried that his behavior might be construed as flirtation, but he always kept his distance from Abiyar, and just prayed the boy didn't harbor any romantic intentions.

Jandu patiently sat through a full flute lesson with Abiyar. Abiyar truly had a gift for music, unlike Jandu, and it was becoming painfully clear to both of them that the student's abilities outstripped the tutor's. Jandu remembered his own archery training under Mazar, and the day both he and his master realized he had surpassed Mazar. Jandu had felt a rush of pure pleasure, but also guilt that he'd hurt his teacher's feelings. But Mazar had shown nothing but pride at his pupil's abilities, congratulating Jandu on his achievements.

Jandu thought of that now, as he listened to Abiyar play in a way that he never could. Jandu's trills were flat and unenthusiastic. Abiyar manipulated the notes like they were puffs of air, blowing them in every direction, changing them, curving them around the rhythm. When Abiyar completed his song, Jandu clapped his hands.

"Brilliant! Abi, that was fucking brilliant!" Jandu clenched his mouth shut. Cursing was definitely not lady-like. But once again, Abiyar ignored Jandu's social transgressions.

"I'm almost as good as you," Abiyar said.

"Don't be modest," Jandu scoffed. "You're better than me."

Abiyar sat beside him, blushing nervously. "No. Janali, I meant…"

"…It's okay," Jandu said. He put his hand on Abiyar's shoulder. "I'm very proud of you. The truth is, my musical skills are limited. At the end of this year, I shall ask your mother and father to find you a more advanced music instructor who can take your training further than I can." He smiled. "You truly have a gift, Abi."

Abiyar, who had turned slightly pink when Jandu touched him, now blushed bright red and fidgeted with his trousers. Jandu pulled his hand back as if scalded. He recognized the boyish enthusiasm on Abiyar's young, shy face as he stared into Jandu's eyes. Abiyar *did* have a crush on him.

Jandu immediately changed the subject.

"Has your weapons master, Devdan, returned to continue your weapons training?"

Abiyar frowned. "He will be gone for another extended period of time. Until my father can find a replacement, I will be without an instructor."

Jandu shook his head. "For God's sake, why isn't your father getting you better training? What are you going to do if there's ever a war in Afadi?"

"I can handle it," Abiyar boasted. But they both knew it was a lie.

"It doesn't make sense," Jandu said.

Abiyar shrugged. "Sure it does. My father doesn't care if I die or not."

Jandu's expression softened. "That can't be true."

Abiyar looked resigned. "It is."

"Well I care," Jandu said quietly. "You may be your father's youngest son but that doesn't mean you should get less training or be treated unequally. In war, you will be expected to defend your state and this kingdom as skillfully as your older brothers. You don't have to be the heir apparent to love and protect your country."

"Of course I'll defend Afadi," Abiyar said. "But it doesn't matter to my father if I die in the process."

Jandu hesitated. "You know how I told you I once worked in Prasta, for the Parans?"

"Yes."

"Well, Jandu Paran is like you. The youngest of three sons. But even as the youngest, he was given equal amounts of training by their weapons master, Mazar. Even though he was the third son, and fourth in line for the throne, it didn't mean he was worth less than the others."

"That was Mazar," Abiyar said. "This is Indarel. My father. If it isn't about Ramad or Parik, he doesn't care." Abiyar smiled sadly. "I'm not saying that to make you feel bad for me, Janali. I'm just stating a fact. Everyone knows it. Why pretend it isn't true?"

Jandu looked at the floor, trying to come up with something positive to say. He didn't notice Abiyar get up, but when he heard the boy cough, he looked up, surprised to see Abiyar holding his bow.

Jandu narrowed his eyes. "What's this?"

Abiyar smiled. "Well, I think it's about time I take matters into my own hands. Until my father finds me another weapons master, perhaps you could teach me some lessons. You have admitted, after all, that my musical abilities have surpassed yours. But your archery skills still exceed mine."

Jandu frowned. "Abi, if anyone finds out, I could get in a lot of trouble."

"It will be our secret," Abiyar promised. He walked over and locked the door.

Jandu sighed. "And what are we going to shoot at? The wall?" He shook his head. "It will never work."

"We won't shoot," Abiyar's expression was almost pleading. "You can just help me with my stance and draw, that's all."

Jandu looked to the door. "There are guards outside. Don't you think they are listening?"

Abiyar's diadem came askew and tilted on his head. Frustrated with it, he took it off and tossed it onto the settee. His hair looked rumpled and shiny.

"Who cares what they think? My brother Ramad says the guards are ignorant Suya caste who have nothing to offer the world."

"Your brother should shut his mouth about things he knows nothing about," Jandu said. Not for the first time, he recognized the rage he felt over a lower caste insult, and realized how much he himself had changed from the days he had been a young brash prince living in a grand palace. There were times when Jandu used to tattle on sleeping guards to get them flogged. Now he went out of his way to make sure the guards in Afadi's palace didn't get into trouble. His whole perception of caste had changed through poverty and insult.

"Look, stupid, smart, whatever—the guards are going to hear us talk," Jandu said, lowering his voice. "And they are going to wonder why there is no music."

Abiyar smiled. "So we'll take turns playing the flute while you help me with my stance."

A thrill of excitement rushed through Jandu.

"Well?" Abiyar grinned at him, his bow held out. "I can't do much worse than I did at the competition. How about helping me improve?"

Jandu looked at the door, Abiyar, and the bow. A slow, dazzling grin spread across his face.

"Okay. But you do everything I say."

"I will."

They began their practice.

◆◆◆

It was another season before Lord Indarel finally chose another weapons master for Abiyar. During their lessons together, Jandu had perfected Abiyar's stance and the way he held his bow. But he knew his assistance was limited without being able to see Abiyar shoot. When Abiyar's new instructor Eshau arrived, a specialist in swordplay and archery and former general from the State of Jagu Mali, Jandu optimistically hoped Abiyar would at last receive the instruction he needed.

What he hadn't counted on was how seriously Master Eshau took his job. The first day he met with Abiyar, Eshau informed the boy they would practice several hours every day, and that this time was to be strictly limited to weapons training.

Abiyar missed several flute lessons before Jandu was finally irritated enough to hunt Abiyar down, intending to have a word with him about responsibility. Of course, he was also dying to meet this new weapons master, and see Abiyar shoot.

As Jandu came around the corner of Abiyar's private courtyard, he spied Eshau, a fierce-looking man, assessing Abiyar's archery skills.

Abiyar's aim had vastly improved in the months since the New Year's festival, and he struck the target close to the bull's eye, pride radiating from his lanky body in almost visible waves. Jandu smiled, allowing himself a moment of simple happiness, seeing this boy, whom he had grown to love like a little brother, perfect the basics of Jandu's favorite sport.

When Abiyar saw Jandu, his face broke into a boyish smile. "Janali!" He motioned to Jandu. "Come watch me shoot."

Master Eshau swiveled, and glared at Jandu. Jandu stuck his chin out, straightening under Eshau's withering gaze. Jandu might have been wearing pink, he might have horrid, glittery flowers embroidered on his zahari top and a white ribbon in his hair, but he still had some small shred of pride. He returned the truculent man's challenging glare.

Master Eshau shooed Jandu out of the courtyard. "No, no, no! We are training. No distractions!" He pushed Jandu toward the gate.

Jandu wanted very badly to hurt him. "Get your hands off me."

"Janali is all right," Abiyar said quickly. "She used to be Jandu Paran's charioteer."

Jandu cringed internally. Of all the excuses Abiyar could have made, this was the worst.

Eshau burst out laughing. "What lies have you been telling, little girl? I *know* Jandu Paran, and he would *never* have you for his charioteer."

Jandu studied Eshau's face, but he did not recognize him. "How do you know him?"

"Get out of here," Eshau said. "Abiyar, it is bad luck to practice archery in front of women."

Jandu looked at the man like he was insane. "What? Where did you get that bullshit? I've never heard anything more preposterous—"

"—Out!" Eshau shoved Jandu all the way through the gate, and slammed shut the iron metal door.

Jandu glared at him a moment longer before swearing and walking away.

"He doesn't know the first *thing* about Jandu Paran," he mumbled under his breath. "Name dropper. Asshole." He was so focused on his anger he didn't see Hanu crossing the courtyard at the same time.

Jandu froze, but then realized that Hanu would never assault him in front of so many witnesses. Not that Hanu didn't look like he would like to try. He watched Jandu's cautious movement back to his quarters with malice and lust.

Right before Jandu slipped into his building, he lifted his foot slightly in Hanu's direction, showing him the sole of his sandal. It was a childish insult, insinuating that Hanu was worse than excrement that Jandu would scrape from his foot.

The effect of the insult was instantaneous. Hanu ran towards him. But Jandu was safely back in the women's quarters before Hanu could get to him.

◆◆◆

The next morning, Abiyar met Jandu at their regularly scheduled time, but rather than carrying his flute case, Abiyar came with a bright, slightly lop-sided bouquet of pink cassias. After anxiously handing Jandu the flowers and pacing the room several times, he told Jandu that Master Eshau had officially cancelled Abiyar's music lessons.

Jandu could not hide his disappointment and this caused Abiyar to pace more furiously, running his hands through his hair, looking like he was about to cry. "I tried to tell him these lessons were important to me, but he won't have it, Janali! He says that flute is for girls and if I am to be a true Triya warrior, I should dedicate all my spare time to weapons, and nothing else."

Jandu gripped the flowers tightly and took a deep breath. His role in the palace had just been made irrelevant. Abiyar went on, stating that he was sure his new weapon's master would allow Abiyar time to take up flute with Jandu again, once he had improved his fighting skills.

Jandu sat on the couch and watched Abiyar work himself into a frenzy of guilt about ending their lessons. He felt a distant sense of loss. He had been passing on his knowledge of archery for months, and took tremendous pride in Abiyar's achievements. Now, suddenly, he had been replaced, and no one would ever acknowledge the work he had done.

Abiyar sat next to Jandu nervously, and looked into his eyes.

"Are you angry with me?" Abiyar asked.

Jandu sighed. "No. I am angry with Eshau, but I understand." He tried to smile. "It is for the best. You have to improve your battle skills. "

Abiyar was very still. He stared at Jandu strangely.

"And, if your father allows it, I will stay here in the palace until you need me again," Jandu said. He hoped Lord Indarel wouldn't kick him out. Less than two months of their exile remained.

"Of course he will!" Abiyar said. "If he doesn't I'll—I'll—"

"It's all right, Abi. Thank you."

Abiyar suddenly leaned over and clumsily, awkwardly, kissed Jandu.

Jandu jerked away. *Oh no.*

A sinking, hot liquid dread filled Jandu's gut. Embarrassment burned through him.

"I'm sorry." Abiyar covered his face in his hands. "I'm sorry."

Jandu swallowed, feeling sick. "Look. Abiyar. You're a great kid. But…"

Abiyar stood, looking both ashamed and desperate. "I must go, but I swear you will always have a place here."

The boy rushed from the room before Jandu could even reply.

Jandu let the flowers tumble from his feeble grasp. It hit him all at once, a debilitating low that broke Jandu's spirit. The starving. The begging. Suraya's miscarriage, losing Keshan, losing his manhood, running and hiding from Hanu, being kicked out of archery practice for being a woman. All of it was unbearable. And now, breaking a young boy's heart.

Jandu left the music room laden down with melancholy. The guard who escorted Jandu back to the women's quarters looked at him oddly but didn't comment.

When he returned to his rooms, he was surprised to see Suraya and Rani sitting together on the carpet, propped up by pillows, giggling over what appeared to be an absurdly large crock of wine. Jandu didn't even have enough vigor to scowl at them.

Seeing his face, Rani pursed her lips, her hands forming fists at her hips. "You look terrible."

"And I was feeling so great before you said that." Jandu collapsed on his bed. His tight zahari top restricted his breathing. He adjusted it, frustrated and sick of this whole despicable charade.

"You need a drink," Rani said.

Jandu moaned. "Rani, I'm in no mood for—"

"Drink!" Rani ordered. "Azari agrees with me, don't you, Azari?"

Suraya nodded and handed Jandu a cup, then leaned over and lit a new stick of incense with one that was burning down. The fragrance of sandalwood and pine smoke fluttered across the room and out the open window like a streamer.

Jandu sat down cross-legged with the women and allowed them to pour him cup after cup of wine. He hadn't eaten much that day so the wine worked quickly. He was lulled into complacency as Suraya and Rani gossiped about other women in the palace, and talked about the state of affairs outside Afadi's gates.

It had been a while since Jandu had had so much to drink, and he over-estimated what his small body could handle. He noticed with detached interest that his toes felt incredibly far away, and tingled coldly despite the heat of the afternoon.

Rani leaned over Suraya's relaxed body and retrieved one of her endless sewing projects. Suraya had brought sewing work with her as well, and within minutes the two of them were drunkenly giggling and embroidering, their voices lilting and mingling in a high-pitched, constant chatter about the various downfalls of men.

The conversation shifted to men and women, and Rani filled Suraya in on her ongoing, tumultuous romance with the groom.

"I just don't understand his behavior sometimes," Rani confessed, refilling all three of their cups. Jandu noted that her cheeks were very flushed. Even Suraya looked under the influence, her eyes drooping heavy and low, a gentle, soft smile on her face.

"One minute, he treats me like a goddess," Rani explained. "And the next he acts like I am scum! Like the only reason he ever tolerated me in the first place was for sex."

Jandu drained his wine cup. "That's probably true."

"Janali!" Suraya warned him with a glare. "Don't say that."

Rani looked appalled.

Jandu shrugged listlessly. "It's the truth. Men mostly think about fucking, killing, and eating. Trust me."

Suraya burst into laughter. "That's so funny, coming from you."

"Why?" Jandu smiled crookedly.

Suraya shook her head. "You know why."

"Why?" Rani asked.

Suraya laughed. "Janali used to have a very high opinion about men. She used to think they could do no wrong."

"That's not true," Jandu slurred, holding out his cup for a refill. "I've always thought there were shitty men out there. Just not me."

Rani furrowed her eyebrows. "What?"

Suraya's glared at Jandu. "Janali is very drunk. She makes no sense when she's like this."

Jandu was too gone to care about anything anymore. He watched an ant crawl across their floor in silent fascination. Its legs were so *small*.

"So, have you had a lover before, Janali?" Rani reclined against several of their pillows, her needle bright against the orange fabric.

"That's none of your business," Jandu said.

"Come on, tell me," Rani goaded.

Jandu looked at Suraya. She wouldn't make eye contact, but she wore a knowing grin.

Other than the constant, quiet puncture of fabric, both of the women fell silent. "I fell in love with someone once," Jandu finally admitted.

Rani smiled. "Was he a servant?"

"No. A lord."

"What was he like?"

"He's tall," Jandu said. "Strong, but he has a lithe body. Luscious lips. Gorgeous black hair. And he can make you believe anything."

Jandu blushed furiously. He had no idea why he just said that. The wine made his body tingle sickly. He felt Suraya's gaze, and had to concentrate to focus on her face. She no longer smiled. Her mouth formed a grim line.

Rani wanted more. "Well? What happened?"

"Nothing," Jandu said. "He is a Triya warrior. I'm a servant. End of story."

"But you had sex with him?"

Jandu's eyes grew wide. "Rani! Dirty little mind. Not everyone is a slut like you."

Rani laughed. 'Well, did you?'

Suraya's mouth twitched slightly. "Yeah, did you?"

Jandu felt like his face was on fire. "I'm not answering that."

"She did! She did!" Rani cried, laughing and clapping her hands. "You wouldn't avoid the question if you hadn't. What did his dick look like?"

"Enough! You perverts are more depraved than a room of drunken soldiers." Exhaustion and drunken nausea washed through Jandu, and this party wasn't much fun anymore. It had barely kept off the darkness he felt that morning. Now all of his earlier depression came flaring back, along with a strong desire to puke. Jandu's body handled alcohol differently than it used to. Jandu was never a heavy drinker, but he at least could hold his booze. Now the room spun around him.

Luckily, Rani seemed to have reached her evening quota at the same time as well. Without as much as a 'good night,' she leaned back against the pillows, closed her eyes, and promptly passed out.

Once they were both sure she was really out cold, Jandu and Suraya cleaned up the mess they made and draped a light blanket over Rani, gingerly pulling the embroidery from her hands.

"I guess she'll miss her appointment with her lover tonight," Jandu said.

Suraya looked down at her and nodded. "I should probably go as well. Yudar will wonder where I am."

"I'll walk you through the courtyard," Jandu said, thinking a walk might do him good. However, he had second thoughts about moving as soon as he stood. He lurched and leaned against the wall for support.

"You okay?" Suraya watched him with a strange, calculating glint in her eyes.

"Yes." He lowered his voice. "I'm just not used to that much wine in this small body." As he closed his door behind them, his stomach somersaulted.

As they passed a small alcove in the wall with a statue of the Prophet Bandruban, Suraya pushed Jandu into the shadows.

Jandu frowned. "What?"

"I need to ask you something." She spoke in a tense whisper. She stared down at Jandu, her arms crossed. She didn't look angry, but she wasn't pleased either.

"Maybe we should talk about this later." Jandu thought the statue of Bandruban looked particularly sinister.

"No. I don't know when we'll have a chance to talk alone again." She glanced down the hallway, and then looked back at Jandu. "I deserve the truth." Suraya's voice was a whisper, but it was strong with emotion.

Nausea swelled and receded through Jandu's body like waves. "All right."

Suraya took a deep breath. Her eyes never left his face. "You were never worried about being a 'sister fucker,' were you?"

"We are *not* having this conversation." He tried to push past her, out of the alcove.

Suraya grabbed his arm and held him there. "Jandu, you owe me the truth. This masquerade as a woman fits your true self better than any of us originally supposed, doesn't it?"

Jandu's fists clenched. "No! I am a man, Suraya!"

"Who loves men," she said.

"Who loves *a* man," Jandu spat. He backed away from her, his stomach churning. Oh God, did he just say that? His back rested against the base of the statue.

Suraya took another deep breath, and then crossed her arms. "So. How long have you been Keshan's lover?"

Jandu leaned over and threw up. He held out his hand against the wall to steady himself. His entire body began to shake in fear.

And then Suraya was beside him suddenly, holding back his braid and gently rubbing his back as he retched on the ground.

"Oh, Jandu!" Suraya's face was stricken with remorse. "I'm sorry! I didn't mean to frighten you!"

Jandu groaned and leaned back on his heels. He wiped his mouth with a shaky hand.

Suraya put her arm around his shoulders.

"I'm sorry! I just wanted the truth, that's all. That's all."

Jandu closed his eyes, willing his stomach to calm down. "I'm okay," he lied. This was turning out to be one of the worst days of his life.

She held him tightly. "You must know, Jandu. I will love you no matter what."

"Are you going to tell my brothers?" Jandu asked, throat scratchy and raw.

Suraya's eyes widened. "God, no! Yudar would never forgive you."

Jandu swallowed. "I'm sorry."

"Me too. I just wanted the truth." She smiled weakly. "Can you walk? I'll take you back to your room."

"Of course I can walk! I'm a warrior," Jandu said, but he did need her help walking. They turned back towards his room. His head reeled, his throat felt like it was on fire. He kept his mind focused on his door. He just had to get there.

Twenty steps at most. His goal was not to be sick again until he was alone.

As they walked, she tentatively whispered to him.

"You didn't answer my question." Suraya smiled at him shyly. "How long have you two been in love?"

Jandu studied her face carefully, trying to determine if she really wanted him to answer that question or not. Finally, he just shrugged. "Since your archery competition."

Suraya snorted. "How flattering. You fell in love with someone else on our wedding day."

Jandu laughed weakly. "I wasn't intending anything, really. It's all Keshan's fault. He's a vixen."

"So I've heard."

"I tried punching him once, but it didn't make things better."

"What?"

"Never mind." Jandu leaned on her as they walked.

"Are you happy together?" Suraya asked.

Jandu saw the hope, the acceptance, the nervousness in her eyes. He felt the warmth of her love. She knew him so well. And now, with growing excitement, he realized there was at least one person in the world from which he no longer had to hide.

"Yes," Jandu said. "We love each other."

"That's all I care about." Suraya stopped at the door, and stroked Jandu's braid. "I just want you to be happy, that's all."

"Thank you," he whispered into her ear. And then he dashed into his room, slammed the door, and was violently sick in the empty chamber pot.

CHAPTER 34

IF ONLY HE COULD KILL HIMSELF.

No. Tarek shook his head. Suicide was the greatest form of cowardice.

Tarek prayed harder. Since the army's triumphant return to Prasta, Tarek had been plagued by his bruised conscience. Now he bathed and begged forgiveness from God, knowing even as he did so that there could be no redemption from the evils he had committed.

Instead of tending his sick father, he had been swooning over his best friend. He did not even attend his own father's funeral pyre. Out of jealousy, he let Aisa slip out of his hands and commit suicide. He didn't bother to check on his lover who had risked his life to save him. And these evils, they were not something he could blame on Darvad's temper, or his low caste, or any other person. They were his sins. Tarek's soul was cracking, great, black rents, fissures of self-loathing.

Tarek dressed and then made his way through the courtyards and gardens of the palace towards the soldier's quarters to check on Anant. After the battle, Tarek requested that Anant be brought back to the palace to recuperate under the care of Prasta's finest physicians. He deserved it, having fought so bravely, and Mazar never questioned Tarek's request.

Tarek and Anant rarely exchanged more than a few words, Tarek checking on Anant's progress unemotionally, hoping somehow the soft cotton sheets and the leopard skin blankets would make up for the fact that Tarek had forgotten Anant's sacrifice on the battlefield. But with Anant it was impossible to tell. The man usually expressed himself in facial gestures, but now his face was so swollen that Tarek could no longer read his commander's emotions.

That morning, Anant remained sleeping. Tarek stood in the doorway, looking in. Anant's attending physician rushed to Tarek's side.

"He is much better," the physician whispered. "The King's Astrologer predicts he will recover completely in time."

Tarek nodded. He heard a commotion starting in the garden outside, and so he excused himself and checked to see what was happening. He recognized some of Darvad's personal attendants, carrying in the King's belongings. So Darvad had finally returned from Pagdesh.

Tarek had no news from Darvad since he had left to find Druv. He and Mazar awaited Darvad's return in the palace for a week, Mazar hungry to share news of their triumph, Tarek desperate to beg his friend's forgiveness for losing Aisa.

Tarek followed the commotion out towards the palace gate, only to discover that Darvad had arrived earlier in the morning and had not bothered to send word to him. This was not a good sign. Tarek was usually the first person Darvad sought out when he returned home. With a sense of foreboding, Tarek made his way through the palace until he found Darvad in one of the gardens, practicing mace with Iyestar Adaru.

Tarek entered the garden just as Darvad and Iyestar began to spar in earnest. They swung at each other with finely carved maces. These sparring maces were more ceremonial than effective, but they still landed blows with tremendous force. The clanging metal echoed through the high-walled yard and rang through Tarek's bones.

Tarek coughed to announce himself. "I'm sorry to disturb you," he lied. It seemed like truth constantly slipped further away.

Darvad dropped his mace, panting. He grabbed a cotton cloth from the table and wiped his face of sweat. He then went up to Tarek and hugged him, as was his custom. But there was no warmth in his eyes.

"Well?" Darvad asked.

Tarek looked at him, startled. "Haven't you heard? We won Jezza."

"Congratulations." Darvad didn't smile.

"I heard your victory was impressively quick," Iyestar said. He followed Darvad's example and wiped his face on a towel. He then immediately poured himself a goblet of wine. Tarek wanted one as well.

"How was your search?" Tarek asked. "Did you find Druv?"

"Druv is dead." Darvad went to the table and pulled an arrow from his bag. He handed it to Tarek. "This was in his throat. Recognize it?"

Tarek turned the arrow in his hands. At the base of the fletching, he saw the band of blue that marked the arrow as Jandu Paran's.

"You found them?" he asked.

"They were gone by the time I arrived." Darvad smiled coldly. "But it doesn't matter now. This arrow proves that the Parans broke the rules of the dice game. They were discovered, but instead of submitting themselves they murdered Druv. They will have to go into exile for another three years."

Tarek watched Iyestar out of the corner of his eye for reaction, wondering if Iyestar knew just how involved his brother Keshan was with Jandu.

Iyestar drank deeply from his glass. He bowed to Tarek, and then to Darvad. "I'm going to wash up," he said. "I'll see you at dinner."

Darvad nodded at Iyestar, but he then turned his cold stare back to Tarek. As soon as Iyestar was out of sight, Darvad sneered.

"How *could* you?"

"How could I what?" Tarek tried acting innocent.

"Aisa is dead!"

"She killed herself, Darvad. There was nothing I could do."

"You should have prevented her," Darvad said. He used the rag to wipe the sweat from his hair.

"If I had to watch her twenty four hours a day to make sure she didn't kill herself, do you really think she would have been happy carried off to be your bride?" Tarek stepped closer. "There are other women, Darvad."

Darvad angrily shook his head. "I don't want other women. I wanted her. She was special."

"I'm sorry." Tarek lowered his head, feeling the weight of his words. Darvad would never know how deeply sorry he was.

Darvad sighed, and then threw his rag on the ground. His expression lightened briefly. "Well. How did the battle go?"

"It was fast and brutal," Tarek said. "Mazar was amazing."

Darvad flashed a smile. Tarek felt his blood warm with that gaze. He was accepted again.

"Mazar should be the most feared Triya in all of Marhavad," Darvad said. "He knows shartas which would turn your hair white if you knew!"

"I'm not sure we would have won so soundly if it hadn't been for his shartas."

"I'm glad to hear it. I saw him early this morning when I arrived. He looked ten years younger. Old warriors need battle to remind them of their youth." Darvad slung his arm around Tarek's shoulder. He stank of sweat, but Tarek did not mind. The mere presence of Darvad always brought a flush of love and desire that stunned Tarek by its strength. Nothing he had ever felt could rival the strength of emotions he had for this man beside him.

"I'm sorry about Aisa," Tarek said again.

Darvad sighed. "What a waste. She was so beautiful."

Tarek tried to find comforting words, but he couldn't. He had done enough lying for one day.

Darvad didn't seem to need words, however. He released Tarek and stopped at the door of his private rooms. "Join Iyestar and I for dinner."

"Of course." And just like that, everything was all right between them. If only the other parts of his life could be resolved so easily.

◆◆◆

To Tarek's relief, dinner was a small affair. Darvad entertained Iyestar, Tarek, and Mazar in his own chambers, the men growing drunk and laughing together as Tarek and Mazar recounted their triumph.

Tarek spoke about Jezza proudly, but there was a sourness to the battle now. Even though he took great pride in his victory, and the thrill of battle sang in his soul, he had allowed terrible things to happen.

Darvad laughed. "I am so proud of you both! And jealous. I know my father taught us to love peace above all other things, but my body cries out for war. I want to fight again. I wish someone would openly challenge Prasta."

Iyestar was very drunk. He slurred as he spoke. "No one is going to challenge Prasta, Darvad. It is too powerful."

"Do you have any enemies you'd like me to dispose of?" Darvad asked him.

They all laughed. Iyestar shook his head. "If we did, Keshan would simply sweet talk them into forgiving us. My brother is the greatest weapon we have. Just put him in a room with a tyrant, and by the end of the hour, the man is Keshan's best friend." Iyestar closed his eyes and smiled. "Why fight when you have Keshan on your side?"

Darvad nodded politely. But Tarek saw the doubt in Darvad's eyes.

"Has Keshan heard from the Parans?" Darvad asked.

Iyestar's eyes shot open. "Why would you ask me that, Darvad?" He sounded hurt. "I don't want to be in the middle of this. Leave me out of your family affairs."

"I'm sorry." Darvad touched Iyestar's leg affectionately and Tarek felt an absurd sting of jealousy. "I know it is unfair of me to ask these things. But I worry about it relentlessly."

"I took an oath on behalf of all of Tiwari not to help the Parans," Iyestar reminded him. "That includes Keshan."

"Your brother has a tendency to break rules when he feels like it," Darvad pointed out.

Iyestar sighed. "True. But he knows the honor of our people is at stake. Above all, Keshan is extremely loyal to those he loves."

Tarek wondered if Iyestar knew what kind of love was shared between Keshan and Jandu. To him, it had seemed blatantly apparent. But he was more inclined than others to detect such feelings between men.

Iyestar's large head bobbed on his shoulders, and then snapped upwards as he started to pass out. He stood up slowly. Automatically, everyone else did as well.

"I should go to bed," Iyestar said, yawning. "It is a long trip back to Tiwari."

"Thank you for coming," Darvad said. The two men embraced, and then Iyestar bowed respectfully to Mazar and Tarek as he left the room. Mazar made his exit as well. When Tarek turned to follow suit, Darvad stopped him, resting his hand on Tarek's back.

"Wait a moment," Darvad whispered. He shut and locked his door.

Excitement flushed through Tarek's body.

Darvad turned to Tarek, a sheepish grin on his face. "I have a present for you."

Darvad swayed slightly as he approached Tarek. Tarek realized Darvad was drunker than he let on. He was always good at holding his liquor.

Darvad stood so close to Tarek, Tarek could smell the wine on his breath. Every part of Tarek's mind screamed for him to reach out and forcefully kiss Darvad with all his strength. He would push Darvad to the floor and drive his tongue into his mouth. Tarek was bigger and stronger than Darvad. He could have him if he chose to.

"When I was on my way to Pagdesh, I performed sacrifices at all the temples along the way to try and earn a boon," Darvad said. His voice was low, quivering with excitement. His hair shimmered in the flickering lights of the lamps, it glowed almost golden brown. "I was hoping to win the Gods' favor and to successfully catch the Parans in hiding, but they did not grant this to me." Darvad stepped even closer. Their bodies were mere inches apart. Tarek felt his throat closing with the strength of his desire.

"But one of the Draya priests at a temple near the Pagdesh border was moved by my devotion and gave me something else," Darvad whispered. His eyes shone, bright and happy. He held out his hand, and then closed his eyes. His lips worked silently as he whispered a sharta under his breath. There was a noise—off in the distance, a sound like a thunderstorm cracking far away—and then out of thin air a small, golden spear appeared in Darvad's hand.

Both the men stared at the weapon, awestruck. It was an unusual spear, only three feet in length, and thin, barely an inch in diameter. The metal shimmered and wavered as if it were liquid, as if the weapon itself were alive. The tip was so sharp and fine it seemed as if it tapered down into nothingness. Hundreds of ancient letters spiraled across the surface of the metal. Tarek had never seen anything so beautiful.

Tarek had to concentrate in order to speak. "What is it?" he whispered.

Darvad's smile stretched from ear to ear. "It is a weapon of the Yashva demons, the Korazsharta. This spear is crafted with a Yashva curse, to fatally hit its target, every time." Darvad used his free hand to grab Tarek's own. Tarek felt like he had been shocked. The contact was so warm, so sensual. Darvad uncurled Tarek's fist, opened his palm. He transferred the spear to Tarek's hand.

"I want you to have it," Darvad said.

Tarek's hand trembled with excitement. Even though his hand twitched, the spear he held didn't seem to move.

Watching the irregular steadiness of the weapon hurt his eyes. Although the gold looked heavy, it weighed almost nothing.

"Darvad..." he began.

"...Take it," Darvad urged. He squeezed Tarek's other hand. Electricity seemed to pass between them. "I want you to have it, to defeat Jandu."

Tarek swallowed. "You should keep it. I don't deserve it."

"Yes you do."

"No. Darvad..." Where could Tarek's confession begin? Anant's broken face? Aisa's terrified eyes? His father's empty bedroom? His own, disgusting urges?

"You are my best friend. Only you are worthy of such a weapon. I thought of you the moment I saw it." Darvad smiled.

Tarek gripped the spear. "Thank you," he said, choking with emotion. "I wish I could have... brought you something as well."

They were both silent, both aware of the regret and disappointment of Aisa. Darvad took a deep breath and exhaled loudly. "I want your friendship more than anything else."

Tarek weighed the spear in his hand, testing its balance. "You will always have it. You know that."

"I do." Darvad smiled again, large and bright, and he laughed. "Isn't it fantastic! I can't wait to see Jandu's face when you toss this at him!"

Tarek smiled as well. He looked at the spear. "How do I conjure it?"

"To get rid of it, simply drop it. It is a celestial weapon, so it will not fall to the ground."

Tarek turned his hand over and let go of the spear. It disappeared before it hit the ground. He shook his head in amazement.

"Incredible."

"To conjure it again, you must recite the sharta I learned from the priest."

Emboldened by Darvad's kindness, Tarek reached out and put his hand on Darvad's armor. He let his hand rest there, on Darvad's chest. He didn't push, but the contact was there, and it made Darvad raise his eyebrows.

"Teach me," Tarek said.

CHAPTER 35

"You eat it." Keshan pushed the last pastry on the plate towards Ajani.

"No, you eat it." She pushed it back towards him.

Keshan lifted an eyebrow at Iyestar, who sat beside him with his eyes closed. "You want it?"

Iyestar belched. The three of them sat in Keshan's private courtyard for lunch, catching up on Iyestar's visit to Prasta. There was a storm brewing out at sea and large, menacing waves crashed upon the rocks below.

"Come on, Ajani," Keshan urged. He grinned. "You need to get fatter."

"Why, so you can make up more excuses to sleep around?" Ajani asked, smirking.

Iyestar cracked an eye open. "Hello. I'm here."

"I see you," Ajani chided.

"I thought I'd remind you." Iyestar closed his eye again.

Keshan shook his head. "Fine, fine, I'll eat it." His loose hair blew into his eyes, and Keshan brushed his bangs out of his face. All three of them were dressed casually, enjoying a rare respite from governing for the day. Keshan reveled in the feeling of the wind rustling through his hair. He reached for the last pastry.

"You don't have to eat it," Ajani said. "I can call a servant to take it away."

"No, I feel bad for it." Keshan put the pastry on his plate. "It's lonely, all by itself on a big empty plate. We ate all its family members. He wants to join them. He is sad."

Iyestar shook his head. "You are insane, Keshan." He stood up slowly, stretching his long arms as he did so. "Are we going to practice or not?"

Keshan bit into the spicy pastry, closing his eyes as he did so. It was no longer piping hot as the first few had been, but it was still delicious.

Keshan looked to his brother. "I thought you would be tired of practicing mace after dueling Darvad all week."

"I'm not talking about maces," Iyestar said. "I want to practice swords, remember? We discussed this last night."

"I wasn't paying attention to you." Keshan winked at Ajani, who laughed.

Iyestar sighed. "Some day I'm going to prove to the world how evil you really are. Just wait."

"We shouldn't exercise right after eating," Keshan said.

Iyestar closed his eyes once more and tilted his face up to catch the hot July sun. At times like this, Keshan's older brother resembled a big cat.

"I'll carry you if you get a cramp," Iyestar said.

Keshan smiled. He picked up the last bite of pastry in his hand and popped it into his mouth.

Suddenly, his vision went blank.

Jandu cried out. A man's fist smashed into Jandu's face. With a dull crack, Jandu's nose broke, spurting blood across the bed.

Keshan spat out his food. The blood drained from his face.

Ajani noticed. "Keshan? What's wrong?"

He tried to smile. "Nothing."

Jandu choked as a man gripped his throat with both hands and strangled him.

Keshan stood so quickly that his chair fell backwards. Iyestar reached out and touched Keshan's shoulder. "Are you all right?"

Keshan looked at Iyestar, trying to control his panic.

It always happened like this.

Whenever Keshan had visions, at first they made no sense, consisting of nothing but a jumble of images and sounds. Keshan needed to meditate in order to clarify the order of events, understand what would happen.

"I need to rest a bit," Keshan lied. He saw the understanding on his brother's face and the confusion in Ajani's.

"Go then," Iyestar told him.

As Keshan made his way to his room, he heard his wife following him, so he locked his door. He sat on the floor and tried to calm down as he sat in lotus position.

A shadow fell over Jandu's face. He looked terrified. Jandu shut his eyes as someone jerked his head back by his long hair.

Keshan had to reach farther back in time. He had to see what had happened before.

The pink blossoms of a cherry tree blew loose across a white courtyard. Men walked past guards, led by a thin man in a turban.

Dice rolled. Someone begged forgiveness. Others laughed.

Keshan scrunched his eyes closed, concentrating on the images he saw, the sounds he heard. The vision shifted.

There was a stark but finely crafted room, with a marble floor and white down pillows. A man in a dark yellow turban set up a dice board. Three other men entered the room. One of them studied the man in the turban curiously.

"You are Esalas?" he asked.

The man in the turban nodded. "Lord Indarel is on a hunting trip with his eldest son, and his wife has asked me to entertain you until his return. Would you like to play a game of dice?"

The guest smiled. "Of course."

Keshan recognized the man immediately as Firdaus Trinat, lord of Chandamar. It had been years since Keshan last saw him at the palace, and Firdaus gained weight. His black hair now hung in a long ponytail down his back, his face rough with a beard.

Keshan also recognized one of Firdaus' companions. Hanu was the lord's younger brother, ambassador to Afadi. The fact that the two men appeared in a vision where Jandu was hurt did not surprise Keshan as much as he thought it would.

But the servant in the turban also looked familiar. Keshan closed his eyes and focused. He could feel like he was there if he concentrated hard enough. He relaxed his body into a trance-like state, until he could no longer feel his limbs, hear the sound of the ocean through his windows, or smell the incense of his own room. He concentrated on the white room in his vision, and on the man in the center of it.

He was thin and had a dark beard, but his eyes shone clearly with intelligence. Under the turban, it was hard to see the details of the man's face, but it was Yudar Paran, much changed from his years in exile, but still recognizable if one knew what to look for.

Firdaus asked Yudar what they would gamble. Yudar protested that he had nothing of value, and would play without staking anything. In response, Hanu opened a large chest of jewels, offering these to the dice teacher.

"I have nothing to offer in return," Yudar protested.

"Yes you do." Firdaus smiled. "I hear from my brother than you have a beautiful sister."

Yudar stiffened. He backed away from the dice board.

Firdaus smiled thinly. "My brother has not stopped talking about Janali since he first laid eyes on her."

"What are you suggesting?" Yudar whispered.

Firdaus shrugged. "Wager her. Just for one night. Me, Hanu, and my friend would like the comfort someone like her can provide."

Yudar blanched. "Impossible."

Firdaus said nothing. He and his friends watched Yudar expectantly.

"Are you mad?" Yudar looked like he was about to be sick. "Do you think I would let my sister sleep with you?"

"I mean no offense, Esalas. I just want to play dice, and I know you have nothing else to your name. And in return, I offer a great amount of wealth and jewels, which would honor your own wife."

Yudar stared at the dice board. He was calculating, considering the odds. In his mind, he could not lose. And so he risked nothing.

"We play by Prasta rules," Yudar stated firmly.

Firdaus laughed, and pulled out a set of ivory dice from his pocket. "Excellent!" Firdaus, Hanu, and their companion sat around the dice board.

Yudar looked at the men, and then steadied his resolve. He grabbed his dice. "I'm first."

Keshan's rage distorted the vision and in a moment it was gone.

He paced his room, letting the salty breezes of the ocean wash over his bare arms and chest. He angrily ran his hands through his hair. He stared at his bed for a moment, remembering the nights he had made love to Jandu under those sheets. Jandu had been so proud then, so full of life, strong and witty and brave. He thought of Jandu's brother, a man who was supposed to protect his younger siblings, gambling Jandu away like he were silver. Keshan wanted to kill Yudar. Keshan stuck his head out the window, watching his emotions reflected in the angry sea below, churning relentlessly in the storm, crashing upon the city's cliff like a purposeful assault.

If Keshan was going to see the rest of the vision, he had to calm down.

Keshan breathed deeply, slowly. He lit more incense, and sat on his bed, cross-legged. He listened to the waves, to the sound of his own household, the laughter of someone in a room below his, the clanking of plates, the distant whinnying of horses, and let the familiar and comforting atmosphere of Tiwari rock him into a lull, let him forget anger and fear, until he found his center of concentration again.

He closed his eyes, and imagined Yudar. The vision came flooding back to him, jagged and piecemeal. They were like images from a new memory.

Yudar held the dice.

The smell of lotus filled the air, and sweat from the men.

The sun streamed in from a high window.

Keshan focused.

Yudar was losing. Firdaus' pawns moved across the board, weakening Yudar's position. Firdaus rolled a six and the game ended.

Yudar's face was void of color. He stared at the dice board in shock, looking like a man who has been shot through the heart.

"It was a lucky throw," Firdaus said with a frown.

"No..." Yudar covered his face with his hands.

"That's the problem with dice," Firdaus said, stretching. "You can have all the skill in the world, but it means nothing if you run out of luck."

"No." Yudar's entire body began to tremble. "Please," Yudar croaked. "Forgive me! I can't bear it. Janali, she's—she's very special to me."

Firdaus' friend smirked. "You should have thought of that before you wagered her."

Yudar glared at him. "Shut your mouth, servant!"

"What are you, a Triya?" The man shot back. "Go ahead and retract your promise—we'll see what Lord Indarel has to say about it."

Yudar moaned, curling in on himself as if he were going to be sick.

Firdaus stood and stretched once more. "We'll be decent about this, Esalas. We won't tell anyone. There will be no shame on her, or on you." He put on his shoes at the door, and his companions followed him. "Will you show us to Janali's room?"

Yudar looked like he was choking, terrible retching sounds coming from his throat.

"Esalas?"

Yudar stared at the floor.

"Esalas?" Firdaus raised an eyebrow. "That is your name, isn't it?"

Yudar looked up. "Yes. Of course. Follow me."

The men emerged into the blazing afternoon sunlight of the southern coast. They crossed through a large white courtyard, past a blooming cherry tree, past guards who were stationed there to protect the women inside. Yudar spoke with the guards and they warily let the men pass.

Once again Keshan's fury engulfed the vision. He jumped from his bed and grabbed his sword. If the cherry tree was blooming in his vision, then he had no time. What was going to happen would happen any day, if not right this moment. Keshan strapped on his armor.

He whispered a sharta and stepped into the Yashva world, Firdaus' cousins be damned.

CHAPTER 36

JANDU LOUNGED ON THE PILLOWS OF HIS ROOM, DRAWING A picture of Keshan.

Ennui pulled at him like barbs, but this act of patiently recreating his lover gave him a pleasurable contentment that soothed his boredom. Soft afternoon light filtered in from the windows above. He used a flat wooden board to protect the carpet from his ink. Every angle of Keshan's face, every curl of his hair, could be conjured from memory, and Jandu lulled himself into pleasant memories as he drew.

Someone knocked on his door.

"Who is it?" Jandu called out. He sat up.

When Yudar entered, Jandu smiled. He hadn't seen much of his brother in the past few weeks. Jandu rose and hugged his brother. Tonight Yudar looked terrible, his skin white as clay and beaded with sweat.

"Oh God, Jandu," Yudar whispered. He shut the door gently, his hand trembling.

"What's wrong?" Jandu asked.

Yudar swallowed. Tears welled in his eyes.

Jandu frowned at his brother. "What's happened?"

Then Jandu heard the sound of men laughing in the corridor outside his door. He didn't understand why there were men in the women's quarters.

"I've done something very wrong," Yudar choked.

"What?" Jandu's heart beat faster. He had only ever seen Yudar this upset one time before. The thought of that night made him sick and nervous.

"I…" There was another knock on the door, and the voices outside rose. Yudar looked at his brother once more, tears now pouring down his face. "I'm so sorry."

Yudar fled the room, leaving the door ajar.

Jandu started after him, but was stopped at the door when three men entered the room. One of them he had never met before. But he immediately recognized Firdaus Trinat, and his brother Hanu. The other man locked the door behind him.

Jandu brushed his braid over his shoulder. "How dare you enter my room without permission!"

"I heard of your beauty from my brother Hanu," Firdaus said, leering lewdly. "Now that I see you, I think he did you no justice. You're the sweetest thing this side of the Patari."

Jandu glared. Firdaus looked older and fatter than when Jandu had last seen him at the dice game, but his sinister smile looked just as foul as it had then.

"What are you doing here?" Jandu demanded, crossing his arms over his chest protectively.

"Your brother gave us to you for the night."

Jandu felt as if he had been punched. "No. He wouldn't."

Hanu smiled thinly. "He lost you in a friendly dice game. He's not very good at gambling, you know. I have no idea how he convinced Indarel to be his teacher."

Jandu's ears rang, and he felt in his gut the raw agony of the truth. Yudar had staked him, just as he had before. Only now he wasn't a prince, he was just a small, unarmed servant girl.

"I have a say in the matter," Jandu said sharply, backing away. "I do not comply with my brother's wishes."

"You must pay your brother's debt," Hanu said smoothly.

"Where's your Triya honor?" Jandu yelled. "Do you think I'm—"

Firdaus slapped Jandu across the face so hard that Jandu crumpled to the floor. He was shocked by his own weakness. He had been hit by maces harder than that and remained standing.

"I owe no honor to a Suya like you, girl," Firdaus growled.

Jandu fingered the spot where Firdaus hit him. He stood up, glaring.

"You bastard," he hissed, hating the way his voice shook, his soft feminine tone. "You'll die for that."

Hanu laughed and lunged towards him.

Jandu turned to run away, but was caught by Firdaus' friend, who held him as Firdaus and Hanu approached.

Jandu kicked at the men. Firdaus grabbed his legs and held him. Jandu was humiliated by his lack of strength. Muscles that had long been allies failed him. The men dragged him over to the bed and forced him down.

Firdaus quickly climbed on top of him.

"You want her first, Hanu?" Firdaus asked calmly.

Hanu yanked Jandu's arm down onto the bed, pulling hard. "No, you go first, brother."

"What are you doing!" Jandu gasped.

Firdaus ripped open his zahari blouse.

Jandu only then really understood what was about to happen. It had seemed so inconceivable, unthinkable. But the second Firdaus' large hands painfully groped at his breasts, and the look of lust in his eyes became apparent, Jandu realized that the impossible was about to happen. He struggled harder against the hands holding him down.

"How could you?" he whispered, thinking of Yudar. It would have been kinder for his brother to kill him.

There was no forgiveness for this. Ever.

The other two men grabbed his legs and held him open as Firdaus squirmed and licked Jandu's skin. He took his time untying the knot in Jandu's skirt until Jandu lay naked before him.

Hanu took off his harafa scarf and brutally stuffed the cloth in Jandu's mouth. It tasted like sweat. Jandu gagged for air as his body was crushed by Firdaus' weight. Jandu told himself that this was not his body. This was just a disguise that he wore. He had to stay focused and look for his chance to escape.

"Lovely," Firdaus whispered, grinning.

Firdaus untied his dejaru while the other men watched lasciviously. Jandu could see their erections growing in their trousers.

Jandu managed to break one leg free and kicked as hard as he could, sending Firdaus off of him. Hanu brought his fist down hard on Jandu's nose, breaking it instantly. The pain was staggering. Blood exploded across Jandu's face and the bed. Jandu's vision blurred. He couldn't breathe. The cloth in his throat and the blood in his nose choked him, and he thrashed like a wild animal, desperate for air. He breathed fast and shallow, sucking through the thin cotton of the harafa in his mouth.

Firdaus climbed back on top of Jandu, his hands digging into Jandu's flesh to restrain him. Jandu twisted to throw him off, but Firdaus put his hands around Jandu's throat and choked him, painfully grinding his body against Jandu.

The other men held his legs open, wrenched his arms above his head. Jandu jerked violently, his eyes white and rolling, panic flushing through his system as he tried to find a way out of this assault.

Jandu tried to think of anything other than what was happening to his body. What was Yudar doing right now? When this was over, Jandu would kill him. He would relish killing him.

It was the only vindication he could look forward to, killing his brother for allowing Firdaus to fuck him.

CHAPTER 37

A JOURNEY THAT WOULD HAVE TAKEN KESHAN TWO WEEKS passed by in one day. The Yashva kingdom blurred past Keshan as he ran. Each step allowed him to traverse entire towns, fields, and mountains, warping in his consciousness as he strove towards Afadi.

His fury burned away his exhaustion. He plunged through the Yashva world recklessly, ignoring the startled faces of other Yashva. He didn't care if Firdaus' cousins saw him now. All that mattered was reaching Jandu in time.

At the palace, Keshan slowed his pace, focusing on the hazy outlines of the human world. He passed the cherry tree he saw in the vision, and looked to the building that was guarded. The women's quarters. Jandu was in there.

Keshan broke into a sprint, bursting through the barrier between Yashva and human worlds. The smells and sounds of humanity engulfed him in abrasive noise and humidity. Keshan listened for some sound to direct him to Jandu's room.

He heard the low laughter of a man's voice.

Keshan charged the door. He brought his palms together and closed his eyes, summoning a sharta. The wooden door shattered inwards. Keshan unsheathed his sword. He stared at the scene before him, and realized he was almost too late.

Firdaus lay between Jandu's legs, groping him obscenely. Firdaus' brother Hanu and another man crouched on either side, holding Jandu's legs open.

Hanu turned as Keshan appeared in the room. Hanu's face was red with anger. His trousers were around his knees, a vulgar display of the crime he was about to commit.

"He is mine," Keshan hissed, his voice dark and terrible.

"He?" Hanu asked. He didn't get a chance to say anything further. Keshan slashed his sword across Hanu's throat. Hanu collapsed, a bubbly croak seeping from his mouth as he died.

Keshan wasted no time. He slammed a knife into the other man's chest and twisted, spitting a Yashva curse as he did so. The man's body flew backward and hit the far wall with a sickly spatter. A strange pressure convulsed the air and almost at the same moment he heard the words of another sharta being spoken. Firdaus glared at him, his dejaru pooled on the floor, lips moving to form a curse. Keshan started the counter-curse, but he was too late.

Firdaus' words sank into Keshan's skin like icy syrup soaking through to his bones. The Yashva world grew distant, as if the door between them was closing, and then Keshan felt it, a solid thump, and then his entire awareness of the Yashva disappeared. Firdaus had bound him to the human world in preparation to unleash a curse upon him. Keshan lunged forward, swinging his sword.

"Wait, Adaru!" Firdaus gasped. He held one hand up in the sign of peace while the other gathered up his dejaru. "Peace! I didn't know she belonged to you." Firdaus gestured to Jandu, who scrambled backward, trying to cover himself. Firdaus continued his plea. "If you kill me, who will revoke the curse? The Yashva won't forgive you for killing me over a human!"

Keshan plunged his sword deep into Firdaus' guts. He pulled the blade upwards, cutting a wide slit in Firdaus' belly. Blood sprayed out and intestines tumbled out around Keshan's hands.

"I curse you!" Firdaus was so close Keshan could smell his breath.

"I don't care." Keshan shoved Firdaus away from him. Firdaus flopped backwards, dead.

Keshan wiped a spray of blood from his face, and then rushed to Jandu's side.

"Are you all right?" Keshan knelt beside Jandu, who crouched in the corner, coving his body with ripped zahari fabric. "I saw the dice game in a vision and I came."

Jandu didn't speak. His entire body shuddered as Keshan covered him with his own harafa. Jandu looked overwhelmed, his nose bleeding, his eyes wide as saucers.

Keshan reached for Jandu. Jandu recoiled from Keshan's hands and turned his head away, a look of absolute fear on his face.

Keshan sat beside Jandu, afraid to touch him. When Jandu tentatively reached a hand out, Keshan took it gently.

Jandu's hand trembled violently. Keshan tried to wipe the blood off of Jandu's face with his zahari, but Jandu pulled away, it obviously hurt his nose too much.

"I have to get you a doctor," Keshan said.

"No!" Jandu said hoarsely. "Just get me some water to clean up."

A woman gasped as she came upon the shattered door. Then she screamed. Instantly other women rushed from their chambers and crowded into the hallway. As the spectators took in the blood on the walls, the corpses, Keshan stood and blocked Jandu from view.

"Someone needs to bring the lord's physician," he said, his voice breaking with unspent anger.

None of the women moved. They stared in shocked silence.

"Now!"

A young girl curtsied and rushed away.

At that moment, Suraya pushed her way into the room. She looked different in servant's garb and with her long hair tightly tucked into a bun, but no other woman had eyes as large and expressive as hers.

"My God! My God!" Suraya screamed as she saw Jandu's bloody face, and the wreckage in the room.

Guards carrying heavy lances appeared and pushed their way through the women.

Keshan caught Suraya's arm. "Stay with him," he whispered in her ear. "Don't let anyone touch him."

"Keshan!" Suraya shook her head, uncomprehending. "What has happened?" She asked, her expression bewildered.

Keshan didn't have time to tell her anything more. The guards were almost upon him.

"These men attempted to defile my wife," Keshan said, half to Suraya and half to the guards. "Take me to Lord Indarel. I demand to be compensated."

The guards looked momentarily bewildered, as if having come to arrest the Triya, then being ordered to do exactly as they had planned, was too much to comprehend.

"Take me to Lord Indarel now!" Keshan bellowed. The guards backed away. One even bowed.

"This way, my lord," he said.

Keshan stepped over Firdaus' corpse, but stopped when he spotted something that had fallen from Firdaus' pocket. Keshan reached down and picked up a pair of dice. They glowed blue for a moment, and then faded. Keshan clenched them in his hand, his lip curling in anger.

"Enchanted." Firdaus cheated at this dice game, and no doubt at the one all those years ago in Prasta.

Keshan pocketed the evidence, and then left with the guards.

CHAPTER 38

BY NIGHTFALL, RUMORS OF KESHAN'S RAMPAGE HAD ALREADY left the boundaries of Afadi, on their way eastward. The entire city reverberated with the shock of it. The fact that Indarel's dice teacher and friend Esalas had gambled his sister away for sexual favors was big news. But even more dramatic was Janali's rescue. No one even knew that Keshan Adaru had left Tiwari. And yet he had appeared in Afadi out of nowhere, kicking through a door to save a servant. It was all too mysterious, too exciting not to be discussed at every table. There was nothing Keshan could do to stop it.

Indarel welcomed Keshan to his reception hall, grim-faced and sober with the fact that the lord of a neighboring state had been murdered in his house.

"We will have to reinforce our border," Indarel said. He eyed Keshan darkly. "We have been on the cusp of war for years, Adaru. This will no doubt bring a retaliation from Chandamar."

Keshan's eyes smoldered. Inwardly, he dared Indarel to challenge him, to blame him. He wanted to destroy Chandamar. And Afadi while he was at it. He had never felt such an all-encompassing desire to condemn an entire people to death before. It was not like him, and he had to breathe deeply to cool the flush of fury that burned his heart and made his fingers itch to unleash ungodly weapons of mass destruction.

"You have my support," Keshan stated.

"I expect it," Indarel said.

Keshan bowed his head.

"I also expect an explanation," Indarel said coldly. "While we have always been allies with Tiwari, you have endangered our entire state with your actions. If the rumors are true, if Esalas truly staked his sister legitimately in this dice game, then it is not our place to challenge it, as foul as Esalas' act might have been."

"I do have a claim to challenge it," Keshan said. "Janali is my wife."

Indarel stared at Keshan in stunned silence. Keshan schooled his expression into one of calm fortitude. The secret to a good lie was all in the face.

"Janali and I were married in Prasta," Keshan continued. "Her older brother Esalas took her away against my wishes. As her husband, it is my duty to protect her and to seek vengeance against her assailants. Esalas had no right to stake her, as she is mine."

Indarel was stunned. "You... you married a lower-caste servant?" he finally managed to say.

Keshan bristled. "Who I chose to marry isn't your concern. What is your concern is the impending retaliation from Chandamar. Once I am assured that my wife is safe, I will do everything within my power to guarantee Afadi's safety."

Indarel nodded stiffly. "Good. We do not have a quarrel with you, Adaru."

"Nor do I have any quarrel with Afadi. What will you do with Esalas?" Keshan asked. He hoped Indarel would execute him.

"I will confront Esalas later," Indarel said sadly. "I do not have time to deal with such matters now."

Keshan nodded. "And Janali?"

"My son Abiyar is escorting her to my wife's summer manor. She will be in good hands. I will write you a letter to grant you permission to stay with her."

"Thank you."

Indarel gave Keshan a weak smile. "Please rest tonight, and we will discuss our actions in the morning."

Keshan bowed respectfully, and then left to find Jandu.

◆◆◆

The summer manor was built along the river, surrounded by bucolic pastures and an old cemetery, about five miles from the city gates. The large, airy house surrounded a central garden and was protected by high stone walls. Along with numerous staff, several of Lady Shali's friends resided there during the hottest months of the year, as well as Lord Indarel's own mother. The only man Keshan saw was an elderly guard who treated Keshan warily. He read Indarel's letter over twice, and escorted Keshan the entire way through the manor.

Keshan saw a handful of other women relaxing in the garden or sheltering from the heat indoors in a large marbled sitting room. The guard kicked at the roaming peacocks as he directed Keshan to Jandu's room.

Keshan knocked at the door. A moment later, Suraya appeared.

She looked tired. "Hello, Keshan." She nodded to the guard. "It's all right. He can come in."

Keshan thanked the guard and then followed Suraya inside. Jandu's room was large and airy, with white cotton curtains billowing in the sweet smelling afternoon breeze. The teak floor was covered in richly embroidered rugs. A set of teak wooden doors led out to a private rose garden.

Jandu slept fitfully, curled in a clenched ball under the muted red cotton sheets of his bed.

"How is he?" Keshan whispered.

Suraya stood beside Keshan, frowning at Jandu. "The physicians sedated him with herbs to help him sleep." She swallowed and looked up at Keshan. "Is it true? Did Yudar really stake him to Firdaus?"

"Yes."

Suraya closed her eyes. Tears appeared but she wiped them away hastily. "I don't know how Yudar will live with himself after this."

"I don't care how he lives," Keshan hissed. "I only care about how Jandu will live with this."

"You saved him, though. You got to him before…" Suraya closed her eyes again, then seemed to recover. She smiled and laid a hand on Keshan's arm. "Go to him now. I'll leave you two alone. Just let him know… let him know how much we love him."

Keshan stared at her. She smiled shyly.

"I've told the guards to let you in and out. Feel free to sleep here as long as you are in Afadi. Lady Shali gave me a room down the hall so you two can have your privacy."

Keshan's eyes widened. She knew.

"Suraya, I hope you don't think…"

Suraya rose up on her toes and kissed Keshan's cheek. "Please take care of him for me."

As soon as she left, Keshan sat down on a wooden chair in the corner, watching his friend's fitful sleep.

Just the act of sitting flooded Keshan with exhaustion. He hadn't rested since his frantic run from Tiwari, and now his body ached with weariness.

Keshan worked the leather straps of his armor quietly, moving slowly as he untied his breastplate and arm bands. Free of the heavy armor, he stretched back against the uncomfortable wooden chair and closed his eyes.

But as the reality of what he had done sunk in, sleep became impossible. Bone-weary as he was, he couldn't escape the realization that he had just forfeited his own life as a Triya warrior.

As soon as it was discovered that the Parans had spent their third year of hiding in Afadi, it would be revealed that Janali was Jandu. And that Keshan had saved Jandu, breaking Keshan's vow to not help the Parans during their exile. Keshan would be stripped of his caste, no longer allowed in the palaces of the country, unable to make decisions for his family. He would not be able to fight in any war, or claim Triya justice. He had forfeited his identity and his entire social standing.

Iyestar was going to be furious at him.

The thought of his brother made Keshan momentarily smile, but the smile faded as soon as he realized how sad Iyestar would be. Keshan breaking a vow was not only Keshan's dishonor. His action would dishonor the entire Tiwari tribe. Keshan had sacrificed everything.

He tried to comfort himself, knowing that, if given the choice, he would do it again. Jandu had become more important to him than honor, than caste, even more important that his own family. It seemed fitting that the sacrifice Keshan had to pay to save Jandu from a violation so great would be heavy indeed.

But this was cold comfort. Keshan had been able to at least stop the worst of Jandu's violation. But it wasn't enough. He hadn't done enough. Since the beginning of Jandu's exile, Keshan had always provided just enough help to ease his conscience, but not enough to actually do Jandu any good. He brought money to keep Jandu from dying, but it wasn't enough to stop his hunger. He had killed Jandu's attackers, but only after they had beaten him. And despite the fact that Keshan was never one to harbor useless, accusatory thoughts, he couldn't shake the feeling that this was somehow his fault, that if he had just been a little faster, a little more attentive to his visions, he could have changed all this.

Keshan had often questioned his powers in the past, but had never felt so angry about them as he did now. They were there when he needed them, but they weren't powerful enough to truly save those close to him from harm. If he had done a better job of understanding his own capabilities, he might have been able to preempt Jandu's assault.

Keshan breathed deeply, and closed his eyes. Unbidden, the vision he had seen since a little boy came back to him, broken but unchanged. He sat with a warrior, firing his weapon in a great war, and changing the fate of Marhavad. But how could that vision be true now, after everything he had done?

Jandu suddenly started and sat up. He blinked, and when he saw Keshan sitting in the chair, he immediately tensed and leapt into a defensive crouch.

"It's okay, Jandu," Keshan said softly. "It's only me."

Keshan got up and sat on the edge of the bed. There was such suffering in Jandu's eyes. Keshan never imagined someone as proud, as fierce and as beautiful as Jandu could be reduced to such grief.

Jandu said nothing.

Keshan studied the changes in Jandu's body. Jandu as a woman was a lovely sight, only now he was marred with a broken nose and bruised face. He looked so dramatically different—small and petite, with curvy hips and breasts, his fingers long and thin, his face so tiny and pale. But there was still no question that it was Jandu. His eyes were so distinctive, as was the way he held himself, and even though his body had completely metamorphosed, Jandu's soul was plain to see. Keshan looked down at his hands, usually so still and assured. They trembled slightly now, with exhaustion and anger.

"Is there anything I can get you?" Keshan asked. "I've told Indarel that I married you back in Prasta, so now I can come and go as I please. Would you like me to bring you something? Tea?"

Jandu shook his head, looking away. "I can't bear you looking at me." His voice sounded strained.

"Jandu." Keshan reached out hesitantly to touch Jandu's hand. He paused when he saw the dark ring of bruises around Jandu's wrist.

"I look revolting," Jandu said.

"No, you don't," Keshan said. "Come here." He patted the bed and Jandu sat beside him, propped against the headboard. Jandu leaned into Keshan, his body so much smaller than it was before, his head barely reaching Keshan's shoulder.

"You are going to be all right," Keshan told him.

Jandu's lip trembled. "This is not a sword or an arrow wound. There is nothing honorable in these bruises." Jandu dragged his hand across his face, wiping his eyes in the most unladylike fashion Keshan had ever seen.

"What I don't understand," Jandu whispered, "is how he could have done that to me."

"Firdaus was vermin," Keshan said.

"Not Firdaus. Yudar." Jandu's shoulders began to shake with silent sobs.

Keshan let Jandu cry. He sat on the bed and let Jandu tire himself out. And finally, exhausted, Jandu slumped down into an uneasy slumber.

Keshan curled himself around Jandu's small body. As he drifted off to sleep, he realized he could kill Firdaus over and over, but it would never make a difference. It had been Yudar who hurt Jandu the most, and there was nothing Keshan could do to avenge the damage. Jandu had been betrayed by someone he loved, and even murdering Yudar would bring Jandu little peace. The damage was already done.

CHAPTER 39

THE DARKNESS OF THE NIGHT MINGLED WITH THE WINE IN Tarek's cup. He considered saying his evening prayers and then going to sleep. But the monsoon was back, hot and heavy outside, and even in his cool rooms in the palace, sleep in such heat would be difficult.

It felt wrong to pray and then sin, and so Tarek delayed his evening ablutions, simply washing his face in the basin before making his way through Prasta's palace to the soldier's quarters.

Tarek knocked on Anant's door. When he entered, he dismissed the servant and shut the door. He slowly approached Anant's bed. Anant sleepily stood to bow.

"Sit down, Anant, for God's sake," Tarek said. Anant sat down.

Anant's face had almost completely healed. The skin around his left eye was still discolored. But his sight was fine.

The physician had told Tarek that there were likely bone fractures behind Anant's eyes, causing his face to look slightly irregular. However the swelling in his cheek and jaw was gone and Tarek still found him handsome.

Tarek crouched beside the bed, leaning on the balls of his feet so that he was eye-level with Anant.

"How are you feeling?" Tarek asked.

Anant nodded. "Fine. Thank you, my lord."

Tarek studied the man in front of him in silence.

"My lord?" Anant asked quietly.

Tarek frowned. "You saved me."

Anant looked confused for a moment. "Of course I did."

"Why?" Tarek reached out and touched the tender, fresh scar across Anant's jaw.

Anant swallowed. "You are my lord."

"That's not good enough," Tarek said.

"I have other reasons," Anant said, his voice lowering.

Tarek stared at him so intently, Anant looked away.

"No, look at me," Tarek ordered.

Anant looked back at him and stuck his chin out defiantly. His eyes searched Tarek's face for understanding.

"What do you want from me?" Tarek asked softly. "Love? Sex? Power? I don't know what I can offer you, Anant. I don't know if I have any of those things in me."

Anant's eyes softened. "I don't want anything from you. I enjoy being with you. That's all."

"That's all," Tarek repeated. Anant nodded.

Tarek rubbed a hand over his face, suddenly tired. He stood, his knees cracking. He gave Anant a long look, and then held out his hand to him. "Then come to bed with me."

Tarek led him back to his own room.

◆◆◆

Tarek's slumber was disturbed by the dramatic sound of someone banging on his door.

Tarek blinked at the early morning darkness and cursed himself for being so careless. Anant lay sprawled naked beside him, sleeping soundly despite the noise outside. There was something endearing about Anant's ability to doze through anything. His dark body lay above the sheets, unashamed, his legs spread wide, one arm thrown over his eyes, the other on his chest, his hand gently rising and dropping with his breathing. Tarek wanted to lean down and smell his body, run his hands over Anant's dark flesh, touch his cock where it lay slumbering on a thick bed of pubic hair. Instead, Tarek gently shook Anant's shoulder.

Anant awoke sleepily, blinking as he got his bearings. He looked over at Tarek and smiled shyly.

"Good morning, my lord."

"You have to go back to your rooms through the window," Tarek whispered. He got out of bed and started dressing. "Someone is at the door."

Anant quickly pulled himself together. He hastily dressed, throwing his clothes on with a soldier's efficiency. Tarek caught his arm before he slipped out of the window.

"Wait," Tarek said softly.

Anant looked at him, expectant, hopeful, his eyes wide with anticipation.

"Come to me tonight," Tarek said. "Wait for me in my room. After the servants have gone to sleep."

A slow, dazzling grin spread across Anant's face. He bowed again. "Yes, my lord." He checked the courtyard for witnesses, and then dashed into the darkness.

Tarek watched him flee, and then shut his window to finish his own dressing. The room smelled of semen and sweat. It stank of Anant. It was both pleasing and terribly incriminating. He lit a stick of incense.

The person at his door grew impatient and knocked harder.

"Tarek!"

It was Darvad. Tarek quickly pulled on his vest.

"Hold on." He brushed his hair back from his face, and then opened the door.

Darvad looked pissed.

"I was asleep," Tarek started to explain, but Darvad scowled and waved the remark aside.

"Of course you were. It's two in the morning."

"What has happened?"

Darvad sat down on the bed without asking permission. Tarek felt his cheeks grow hot. It wasn't the first time that Darvad had been in his private rooms—they often spent many hours alone together in their own chambers, gambling and talking and drinking. But Darvad was sitting on stained sheets. Tarek felt exposed. He turned to his wash basin and grabbed his razor.

"Firdaus has been murdered."

Tarek froze, razor suspended in the air. "What!"

"Keshan Adaru killed him."

Tarek frowned. "But why? Why now, after all these years?"

"I received a request from Ishad Trinat, Firdaus' son. He has asked that I send you down to Afadi to investigate the circumstances. As Royal Judge, I need you to determine who is at fault and bring justice."

"And if it is Keshan?" Tarek asked.

Darvad sighed. "It is a tricky situation. You have to find out what happened. Firdaus' son claims it was an unprovoked attack, but I have heard rumors that Keshan defended a servant girl who was being gang-raped by Firdaus and his friends."

"What was Keshan doing in Afadi?" Tarek asked.

Darvad shrugged. "Another mystery. I've sent a message to Iyestar, and he will hopefully clarify issues for us. But you need to leave for Afadi."

"Right now?" Tarek looked at the darkness outside.

"Tomorrow at the latest." Darvad stood. He hesitated for a moment, and then touched Tarek's shoulder. "Other than you and Iyestar, all of my closest allies are dead."

"And Iyestar will not be pleased with either of us if we punish his brother," Tarek said. He had no desire to harm Keshan.

"If he has broken a law, then it is your duty to do just that," Darvad said sternly.

And as suddenly as he appeared, Darvad got up to leave. "Keep me informed. Bring messenger pigeons. Let me know what really happened to Firdaus." Darvad hugged Tarek quickly, and left.

Tarek looked out the window. It was too late in the morning to go back to bed. He spent the day preparing for the four day journey to Afadi, on the coast of Marhavad. He called for wine early in the morning, and drank steadily throughout the day, overseeing the selection of Dragewan soldiers to join him and retrieving his favorite bow from where it was being tuned. His charioteer had to be called back from Dragewan. Despite Darvad's urgency, Tarek refused to leave without the young charioteer, feeling a strong kinship with the man who had driven him into battle at Jezza.

Frustration coiled around him. Once again, he was off, leaving Darvad behind for God knew how long.

That evening Tarek blew into his bedroom like a storm. He threw his sandals off and poured himself another cup of wine. Then he turned and saw Anant standing in the corner.

Shit. He'd forgotten he'd invited him earlier.

"I'm in a terrible mood, Anant. I'm sorry. You should go." He swilled the wine.

Anant moved closer. In the darkness, his face looked almost perfect again.

"I can make you feel better," Anant said quietly.

Tarek snorted cruelly. "Doubt it." He poured himself another glass of wine and drank it down.

Anant stood a few inches away. Tarek could smell anise on Anant's breath. He frowned. "What?"

Anant's hands shook. But that didn't stop him from reaching uninvited to Tarek's waist sash and untying the knot. He pulled down Tarek's dejaru.

Tarek's breath left him, heavy.

"Anant..." He didn't know what he wanted to stay. He wanted to stop him. But he didn't. He let Anant nervously kneel, put his hands upon him, guide Tarek into his mouth. Tarek leaned his head back and moaned.

Anant felt so good. His mouth was so hot, so persistent, it swirled around him and pulled him deep into his throat. Tarek had to remember to breathe. He reached down and put his hands on Anant's hair, guiding him into a rhythm, pulling him closer, until the shadows in the room divided and brightness shone through Tarek's body. Pleasure shot from him in gasping arcs.

Anant didn't rise. He knelt, breathless, staring up at Tarek with love and admiration shining from his eyes.

"Anant," Tarek said again, sadly. He placed a hand back on Anant's head. "I am heartless."

Anant's gaze didn't waver. "I'll love you anyway."

"I know," Tarek said. He let go of Anant and pulled up his dejaru. "That's the problem."

Anant continued to kneel. His glance flickered to Tarek's packed trunk. "You're leaving?"

"I must go to Afadi. The lord of Chandamar has been murdered."

Anant swallowed. "Am I staying behind?"

Tarek was about to say 'yes.' But the look in Anant's eyes softened Tarek's mood. His anger, his frustration with everything, it ebbed slightly in Anant's presence. He wasn't Darvad, and this wasn't love. Tarek would not lie to himself. But it was comforting nevertheless.

"Come with me," Tarek said before he could change his mind.

Anant stood. He bowed low before Tarek. When he looked up, he appeared more confident and handsomer than Tarek remembered. Anant's mouth curved into a small smile.

"It will be my honor, my lord."

CHAPTER 40

Jandu could live with the constant throb in his nose, the bruises on his body, the ache of movement.

He even thought he could learn to live with the revulsion of his attack, the humiliation. Images of the attackers' faces remained branded in his mind, their sick grins leering down at him every time he closed his eyes. But Jandu could bear this. Eventually, he would learn to live with the repulsive memory of Firdaus' body grinding against his flesh.

But the way Yudar had betrayed him—this pain was unbearable. Hanu and Firdaus—their crime, while foul, was understandable. They were greedy and violent. But Yudar's treachery wounded Jandu deeper than any blade could penetrate. Jandu would have died a thousand deaths defending any one of his family members against such a crime. So how could his brother, the staunch supporter of truth and religious righteousness, not only allow such a thing to happen, but facilitate it? He led the men to Jandu's door. The guards of the women's quarters would never have permitted three strange men to enter Jandu's building if Yudar hadn't convinced them to do so.

Every time Jandu thought about it, he shook with fury. His brother had sold him as a whore. For the first time in his life, Jandu honestly and truly wanted to kill Yudar.

That was his mantra during his week of healing. He stared at the rose garden outside his new room and watched the bruises on his body turn from purple to yellow, and he fantasized about murdering his brother, and then ending his own life. He would slit his own throat. It was the honorable way out of this torment.

Keshan tended Jandu as if he were a sick child. Jandu's self-loathing made Keshan's presence insufferable. He couldn't stand the fact that Keshan had seen him so vulnerable and weak. It was terrible to go through this with the one person whose opinion Jandu cared about most of all.

Yet Keshan didn't seem to mind. He prattled on about trivial things, and kept Jandu posted on Afadi's preparations for war. Ishad, Firdaus' son and the new lord of Chandamar, had asked the King to send the Royal Judge as mediator. Now Indarel pulled all of his Afadi soldiers into the capital city, in advance of the arrival of the Chandamar negotiating party. The threat of war shuttered houses up and sold out bakeries, as the city prepared for a siege.

Secluded in his room, miles away from the chaos, Jandu saw little of the panic his attack had instigated. He heard activity in the courtyard as more Triya noble women moved into the retreat to escape the stressed city. But other than Suraya and Keshan, Jandu saw no one. After a week of such isolation, Lady Shali herself paid Jandu a visit, begging his forgiveness for suffering such injustice under her roof.

"Because of me, there will be trouble here," Jandu said, trying to appear the gracious, proper Suya girl.

"If we can't protect one woman alone in our own household, we deserve the trouble." Shali's voice shook with anger. "You are very special to Abiyar. I wish you a speedy recovery."

"Thank you, my lady." Jandu worked at politeness. But he was grateful when she finally left him alone.

Keshan was absent for most of the day, helping Indarel prepare for the arrival of Tarek Amia, the Royal Judge. Jandu took the opportunity to sit in his private rose garden. It was his first time outside since the assault, and the fresh air felt like a cool balm, soothing his weary spirit.

When Keshan returned, he whistled so as not to surprise Jandu. Jandu turned around and watched Keshan walk through the wooden doors into the rose garden. Keshan's movements were tense, angry.

"Keshan," he said. He smiled.

"Hi." Keshan pulled up an extra chair beside Jandu. They sat contentedly together as a strong breeze blew the fragrant red roses in a twisted circle.

"This garden is beautiful," Jandu said. Jandu caught himself absent-mindedly rubbing the bruises on his throat. He dropped his hands into his lap.

Keshan nodded. "It reminds me of my mother's garden when I was young. She used to hide sugared candies from me by hanging them above one of her rose bushes so I would be stuck with thorns if I tried to get to them."

"Did it work?" Jandu asked.

Keshan smiled. "No. I would get stuck full of thorns and eat the candies anyway. Then she'd punish me twice—once for stealing the sweets, and once again for having to clean up all my scrapes."

"I wish I knew you then," Jandu said softly.

"You'd make an excellent Tiwari maiden."

"You like the way I look right now?" Jandu asked.

Keshan nodded. "I wish I could touch you."

"I hate it," Jandu said. "I can't wait for this year to be over. I hate the weakness in my flesh. I just can't believe…" he frowned, absentmindedly covering the bruises on his face. He closed his eyes. "I can't bear the fact that you've seen me like this." Jandu turned his head.

"Don't look away," Keshan said sharply. "Don't you dare be ashamed."

Jandu was silent for a long moment. Then he forced himself to stare at Keshan. "I don't know what else to be."

"Be Jandu," Keshan said. "Be yourself."

Jandu shook his head angrily. "You have always said you have known our fates. Did you know this would happen? Was this part of some great plan?" He took a deep breath to steady his voice. "Why did this have to happen to me now?"

Keshan's eyes became soft and liquid, and Jandu momentarily feared that Keshan would cry. But Keshan just reached up and gingerly held Jandu's hand.

"I don't know why this happened. I wish I did. I've been trying to understand what this all means. But I don't have the answers. I only know what is shown to me." Keshan sighed.

Jandu swallowed. "I just—I just never expected this. Especially after meeting you. You've filled my head with such a sense of purpose. You've made me believe I could have a great destiny." Jandu stared at Keshan. "But now this—this changes everything. How can I be the greatest archer of Marhavad, how can I help make this world any better, when I can't even protect myself? When I am so *pitiful*?"

"Look at me." Keshan spoke in a low voice. He cradled Jandu's bruised face. "Nothing is changed about your future."

"I am useless," Jandu said.

"No you aren't." Keshan leaned close. "How do you think I recognized you? You look completely different, but you are still Jandu under it all. Through the years in the forest, through the servitude, through even this, you remain Jandu Paran, the same, fierce, proud, beautiful warrior I fell in love with all those years ago. He is safe inside of you, you just have to find him again."

Jandu swallowed. "I feel like Jandu Paran is dead."

"No!" Keshan gritted his teeth. "You've been through hell, but that's it! It's just been a shitty couple of years! And you are going to get through this, because I love you and I need you!"

The corner of Jandu's mouth twitched slightly. He pushed a stray lock of Keshan's hair out of his face. "You are always so fucking melodramatic, Keshan."

Keshan laughed and leaned forward to kiss Jandu's forehead. "Well, you bring it out of me. I wouldn't have to be so histrionic if you stopped getting into such precarious situations."

Jandu smiled and Keshan's face washed with relief, his body seeming to thaw suddenly, growing loose and relaxed like it used to be. He sat down in the chair again. "Are you feeling better?"

Jandu sighed. "Yes. I suppose I'll have to face the rest of the world again. Though God knows what I will do when I see Baram."

Keshan hesitated. "And Yudar?"

Jandu looked out over the roses. "I have nothing to say to him right now. If I see him, I'm going to kill him."

Keshan leaned over his chair, and hugged Jandu to him. A week ago, Jandu wouldn't have been able to stand it. But now, in the sweet river breezes of the summer house, safe and alone with Keshan, he allowed Keshan's embrace.

"I would kill them a thousand times for you, if I could," Keshan whispered.

Keshan tentatively pulled Jandu into his lap. Jandu wrapped his arms around Keshan, momentarily grateful that he was smaller than Keshan now, able to curl into Keshan's strong, protective body. Jandu sank into the heat of Keshan's chest, letting his warmth heal the bruised and broken spots Jandu couldn't wait to be rid of.

They were finally disturbed by a knock at the door. Jandu's throat went dry.

Keshan untangled himself from Jandu's arms and stood. "I'll get it."

"Give me one of your knives," Jandu said.

Keshan's expression darkened, but he diligently pulled one of his throwing knives from his belt and handed it to Jandu.

"Wait here," Keshan said. He went to the door. Jandu waited with Keshan's knife clutched tightly in his hand. He knew it was irrational to be afraid of every knock on the door, but he couldn't help himself.

Keshan returned to the courtyard and leaned against the door, a bemused expression on his face.

"There is a young man to see you," Keshan said.

Jandu narrowed his eyes. "Who?"

"Indarel's son, Abiyar. He begged an opportunity to talk to you."

Jandu sighed. Although it had been Abiyar who personally drove the chariot to the summer retreat a week ago, Jandu hadn't exchanged any words with him since that ill-fated kiss in the music room. Jandu was in no mood to deal with a teenage boy's crush. But he realized he couldn't hide in his room forever. Eventually he was going to have to see people other than Keshan and Suraya. And Abiyar was as good of a person to start with as any.

"I'll see him," Jandu said. He followed Keshan back into his rooms, tucking Keshan's knife under the blankets of his bed. He knew Keshan watched him, but he didn't say anything.

"He's got flowers," Keshan whispered. Jandu thought he detected a flicker of amusement on Keshan's face.

Abiyar stood in the doorway, his face already pink with embarrassment, his oversized armor hampering his movements as he held out a bouquet of flowers.

"I picked these myself," Abiyar stuttered. He eyed Keshan nervously.

Jandu accepted the flowers. "Thank you, Abi. They're beautiful." Jandu decided not to comment on the dirty fuzz above Abiyar's lip, the mustache an obvious attempt to appear more manly.

Abiyar nervously made eye contact. "Janali, I… I just wanted to say I'm sorry. You should have been safe in the palace. This crime is a stain on all good people of Afadi. I should have been there to defend you."

Jandu smiled. "You and your family have always treated me well. I am grateful for everything."

Jandu could feel Keshan's presence looming behind him, and he turned to see Keshan observing the young boy, his arms crossed over his chest.

"Abiyar, I want you to meet Lord Keshan Adaru of Tiwari." Jandu nodded to Keshan. "He is the Triya I told you about who is a master of the flute."

"Is he your husband?" Abiyar asked nervously.

"Yes, I am." Keshan answered, and Abiyar seemed to shrink.

Jandu smiled. "Keshan, you should hear Abiyar play. He's much better than I am. He has real musical talent. I'm sure you'd be impressed."

Keshan frowned at Abiyar and raised an eyebrow.

Abiyar looked like he wanted to curl up and die. "Well… if you need anything, let me know. I'm staying here to defend you and the other women here if there is any trouble."

The idea of little Abiyar defending the three dozen women in the retreat amused Jandu.

"Thank you, Abi. I have faith in you." He glanced down at the bouquet and added, "Thanks again for the flowers." But by then Abiyar had fled down the hallway.

Jandu shut the door and turned to Keshan. "That wasn't very nice of you."

"He's in love with you." Keshan said. "Can't I be a little jealous?"

"Last time I saw him, he kissed me," Jandu said.

Keshan raised an eyebrow. "Did you like it?"

"No. He's not my type." Jandu set the flowers aside. "And I don't think I'm his type either."

"He's in for a surprise," Keshan said.

Jandu nodded. And then they both started laughing.

"Poor, deluded kid," Keshan said.

"Everyone here thinks he's gay."

"Maybe he is." Keshan kissed the side of Jandu's face that was uninjured. "Maybe he can tell you're a man underneath this woman's body. I can." Keshan hugged Jandu.

Jandu shook his head. "I don't think so."

They held each other for a moment longer, but Jandu could feel Keshan tensing again.

"I have to go, Jandu. I need to be with Indarel when Tarek arrives."

Jandu let go of him. He had wanted Keshan to be as far away from him as possible all week. But now that Keshan was leaving, a dank, oily fear filled Jandu's stomach. "You have to promise to come back to me."

Keshan looked surprised. He kissed the top of Jandu's head. "I will. I'll see you soon, I promise."

Keshan stood stiffly in the doorway. Jandu could see the pain in his eyes, and suddenly realized what it must have cost Keshan to spend this week with him. It was probably as unbearable as it was for Jandu himself. He went to Keshan and hugged him once again, the two of them gripping each other fiercely, as if they would never see each other again.

"I love you," Keshan whispered. He kissed Jandu's forehead. And then he left Jandu alone.

◆◆◆

That night, Jandu could feel it.

There was a lengthening in his bones. His muscles shook as they transformed, pulling upon tendons as they grew.

He couldn't sleep through the pain, but he welcomed it regardless. He was changing back into a man. His final year of exile was over.

In the morning, Jandu felt a thrill of excitement and relief as he saw the changes that had already occurred. In one night, he had grown. Power surged through his arms and legs again.

This transformation was faster than it had been when he had turned into a woman. Jandu was grateful, but it was excruciating as well. By evening, he took to his bed once more, moaning as his bones shifted and his skin stretched, agonizing pulses radiating from his groin, every part of him sore and pounding. If he concentrated, he could actually see his toes lengthen.

What made it worse was the knowledge that his transformation had come a week too late. If he had even this much muscle a week ago, he might have been able to fight off the men who attacked him.

Jandu focused on the pain, and on the changes, and decided he could no longer think about his assault. He had to look forward. Their three years of hiding were up and he would be a prince again, and once he was, he would take his retribution.

CHAPTER 41

Two days after Keshan's departure, Jandu awoke in the morning to the sound of the alarm ringing through the summer manor.

Jandu rose to find out what the turmoil was, but the second he moved in his bed, he was distracted by his own torments. Bolts of pain shot through his groin. Parts were sealing, parts were protruding—it was an excruciating mess of nerves.

Suraya came to him moments later, as she had done every morning. They had used the excuse of his assault to justify his seclusion, and Suraya had brought him his meals and fresh linen. By now, his dramatic changes would cause a stir.

"Jandu!" Suraya walked in quickly and locked the door behind her.

Jandu moved slowly to meet her. Each step he took was sheer agony. Hot flashes of pain shot up his legs.

"Tell me what has happened," Jandu demanded, his voice breaking as it dropped nearly an octave. It was puberty all over again.

"A messenger reported that a battalion of Chandamar cavalrymen are on the other side of the river. It looks like they're on their way here." Suraya handed him a cup of tea.

Jandu stared at Suraya in shock. "What?"

Suraya shook her head. " Indarel stationed all of Afadi's army at the city gates. And now only the oldest men and youngest boys are left to defend us."

"Fool!" Jandu said, wincing. Even his mouth was changing, and his teeth felt strange and loose in his mouth. "How many soldiers are protecting this house?"

A flicker of fear crossed Suraya's eyes. "Ten guards. And Abiyar."

Jandu dropped his tea. "That's it? We're virtually undefended?"

Suraya shook her head. "I'm sure that Lady Shali's messengers will get to Indarel in time. He will send reinforcements."

"This place will be overrun by then." Jandu sat down on his bed. He shuddered. "We can't let them in here." He watched, almost distantly, as his hands began to shake. It was still too soon after his own attack to contemplate a horde of soldiers falling upon the defenseless women in the summer house. "We have to stop them."

"Abiyar volunteered to fight them alone," Suraya said. "His mother is in hysterics, but I thought you would be proud of him."

Jandu stood. He tried putting on his sandals but his feet had grown too large. He would have to go barefoot. He grabbed a loose cotton shawl to pull over his face to hide his mannish features.

Suraya watched his burst of movement warily. "What are you doing?"

"I'm going to help him." Jandu pocketed Keshan's knife. "I'll be his charioteer," Jandu said. "Or he can be mine."

Suraya's eyes grew wide. "Are you serious?"

"Of course." Jandu quickly tied his hair back with a leather strap.

"But Jandu…" Suraya lowered her voice.

"What other choice to we have? Let a sixteen-year-old boy face an army by himself?"

"You could get killed!" Suraya cried.

Jandu put his hands on Suraya's shoulders. "Fighting a battle does not frighten me, Suraya. But sitting here, helpless?" Jandu swallowed his revulsion. "No. I'd rather die fighting."

Suraya pursed her lips, making Jandu smile. She only did that when she was about to give in to something she disagreed with.

Jandu's large hands fumbled for the pouch in which he kept Zandi. He stroked his flute appreciatively, and then whispered the words Keshan had taught him.

The flute vibrated in his hands. The metal melted and dribbled from his hands, pooling on the floor. Suraya watched, awestruck, as Zandi reformed herself into his bow, the metal swirling, shimmering impossibly bright.

Jandu tried stringing her, but his arms shook and he could not bend Zandi enough to complete the task. Suraya shot him a look of concern, but Jandu ignored it. He carried Zandi in his hand. He'd try again later, or have Abiyar help him. Between the two of them it would be easy.

Servants rushed from room to room closing shutters and barricading the outside doors. Jandu covered his face with a harafa as he walked beside Suraya towards the gates.

"Talk to Lady Shali," Jandu whispered to Suraya. His voice grumbled low and deep in his throat. "Tell her to arm the servant girls with helmets and swords, whatever they can find. Have them stand along the wall."

"Why?"

"From a distance, they'll look like soldiers," Jandu said. "Maybe we can fool the raiders."

Suraya nodded, and then squeezed Jandu's arm. "Good luck."

Jandu leaned down and kissed the top of her forehead. They both smiled at each other as they realized it was the first time Jandu could do such a thing in a year.

As soon as Suraya left for Shali's suites, Jandu pulled his head scarf tighter and walked to the summer house guard.

He was an old man, half-blind and overweight. He looked agitated.

"I need to leave the grounds," Jandu told him, using his best falsetto voice. It sounded fake, and he winced at his own ruse.

But the guard seemed too distressed by the imminent attack to wonder at the size and sound of the woman who stood before him. "It's not safe. There is an invasion force on its way—"

"—I know. I will be back directly."

"Hurry." The man groaned as he opened the large wooden gate, and Jandu dashed outside.

Even though his bones ached, Jandu forced himself into a run. He darted across the eerily empty street. The two times that Jandu had been on the main thoroughfare to Afadi, it had teemed with people and noise and smells. Now it was deserted. Other than the lowing of cattle, the pastures surrounding the city walls were silent. No one traveled along the dusty road up to the river or towards Chandamar.

Jandu's body straightened and his muscles stopped shaking by the time he reached the cemetery across from the summer house. Jandu swore under his breath as he climbed the tree. The corpse that had been hung near their weapons was now a pile of bones on the ground, the noose dangling emptily from a branch studded with summer flowers. Jandu dropped the bag of weapons, and then scurried down the tree to check the contents for damage.

Baram's breastplate had taken the brunt of the impact, and was slightly dented, but everything else looked as beautiful and sharp as when they had hidden their weapons over a year ago. Jandu's eyes feasted upon his inexhaustible quiver, his own symbol clearly visible below the fletching of the enchanted arrows. He quickly retied the bag and, testing his strength, lifted it up onto his shoulders.

Every step he took, he felt stronger, and the bag felt a little lighter. Jandu pushed his body and himself. He walked faster, and then he ran, feeling the last of his pain fade to a dull ache, and then disappear. Exhilarating strength rolled through him. As Jandu approached the guard of the summer house, he realized he had grown almost an inch since he left less than an hour before. He passed the old guard at a sprint. He was out of sight before the old man hauled the gate closed.

Jandu raced to the stable. He arrived just as Abiyar took his seat in a small war chariot. He looked tiny in his armor and his expression was far away. Abiyar urged his two chestnut stallions forward without seeming to notice Jandu.

"Shit." Jandu jogged alongside the chariot. He threw the weapons inside and then jumped in, clutching the central pole for balance as the horses moved from a trot to a canter and out through the gate.

"What the...!" Abiyar glared around at Jandu. "What are you doing?" The horses cantered along the deserted street. Abiyar pulled the horses to a halt. He stood and glared at Jandu. "What do you think you're doing!"

"I'm coming with you," Jandu said, no longer hiding his masculine voice. Jandu untied the deerskin bag and quickly put on his armor. He tied on his breastplate, leather on one side and beautiful embossed silver on the other, in the shape of two elephants. Jandu unwrapped his head scarf and reached down for his helmet.

"Who are you?"

"Janali, you fool," Jandu said. "Who else would come out here to fight with you?"

"*Janali?*" Abiyar's shock was apparent. He stared openly at Jandu, his eyes widening. He looked over Jandu's body, taking in the differences. He grimaced. "What the hell has happened to you?"

Jandu opened the deerskin wider and stepped back, admiring the gleam of their weapons. Jandu strapped on his sword.

"Just get us across the river," Jandu ordered. "I'll take care of the rest."

Faces appeared over the summer house wall, as the women inside watched for invaders. Abiyar took no notice. His eyes were locked on Zandi, in Jandu's hand.

"Whose weapons are these?" Abiyar asked again, his voice barely above a whisper.

Jandu pointed to the large sword. "That belongs to Yudar Paran. The mace and sword there are Baram Paran's."

Jandu held out Zandi. "And this bow is mine."

Abiyar stared at him, slack-jawed.

"But..."

"I'm Jandu Paran," Jandu said.

"What?" Abiyar stammered.

"Hadn't you heard the story? We had to live in hiding."

"I heard you all died of privation!"

Jandu pulled on his helmet and tied the deerskin closed. "Well, you heard wrong. We were living with you. Yudar is Esalas, the dice teacher. And Baram is Bodan, the cook."

"Azari must be Suraya," Abiyar said to himself.

Jandu nodded to the reins. "If you want my advice, young lord, I suggest we hurry. We should meet the invaders as far from the summer house as possible, where we can see them clearly."

Abiyar stared at him. A slow, furious blush covered his face. "But you... you have *breasts*."

Jandu stopped smiling. "It's my disguise. Come on, Abi, focus on driving the horses."

With bold new confidence, Abiyar grabbed the reins and whipped the horses into motion across the river. Jandu took off his bangles and pulled on his leather archer's gloves. He flexed his hands in the leather, refreshing his body to the feel of them.

They reached the river. The monsoons were late this year, and the soil was parched for moisture. The horses' hooves brought up clouds of dust, and soon Abiyar and Jandu were coated in dirt.

As the chariot raced across the stone bridge, Jandu knelt and prayed. "Please, God, give me back the strength I need."

Abiyar stopped the chariot. Jandu stood and watched a distant cloud of dust emerging from the main road to Chandamar. In the dead stillness of the morning air, he could even hear the sound of hooves upon the earth. Abiyar adjusted his own helmet nervously.

"I'm scared." Abiyar gripped the reins, his fingers bone white.

"It's all right to be frightened," Jandu said calmly. "But to run when faced with danger is the definition of cowardice. You are many things, Abiyar, and coward is not one of them."

The cavalrymen suddenly appeared around the bend of the hill. They charged forward at a full-on gallop. The sun glinted off their swords. There was a distant roar, a battle cry, as they kicked their horses faster towards the summer manor. They raced towards Jandu and Abiyar, the column stretching back as far as Jandu could see. There were at least fifty of them.

"God." Abiyar's face was a deathly green. "God!"

"Focus on controlling the chariot," Jandu said. "I'll take care of the men." Jandu now could see the riders clearly. The earth seemed to shake from their furious gallop. Jandu reached down to string Zandi, praying that he now had the strength he needed to do so. It took more effort than it used to, but Jandu was able to string her. He smiled, and twanged the string, sending out its unique ring across the battlefield. In response, he saw the men straighten.

"This is going to cure all my ills," he told himself. He took aim.

Unshaven and poorly dressed, the cavalry looked like Chaya caste thieves. But the way they tightened into even rows of horses, five abreast, ten rows deep, was decidedly military. The men were armed with lances, maces, and swords. And although this gave Jandu a slight advantage, as none of the men had bows, it was still alarming.

These were clearly Triya soldiers in disguise. They galloped in formation, yelling as they charged towards Jandu and Abiyar's lone chariot.

"Abi, listen to me," Jandu said. "I'm going to use a sharta. Don't be alarmed. Don't move forward until I tell you, understood?"

"Yes." Abiyar's teeth chattered.

"I'm going to kill as many of them as I can before we have to move from the river."

"All right."

"Be ready." Jandu knelt in the chariot and closed his eyes. He brought his hands together in supplication and prayed, summoning the Manarisharta, one of the all-powerful, devastating weapons he had learned from Mazar. As he spoke the words under his breath, vomit rose in his throat. He could taste blood. His whole body began to tremble. A light emanated from his pores, but he clenched his eyes shut and finished the terrible curse.

All the hair on his body stood on end. There was a deep, all-encompassing silence, like a gap between waves.

Then the air crackled, on fire.

Electricity burst from Jandu's chariot and shot out towards the first line of riders. The arc of lightning shot forth and caught the riders ablaze, wind whistling and crackling around them, the stench of burning flesh washing over them.

The cavalry who'd been behind the blast scattered, veering away from the initial bolt, but reformed quickly, clearly trained to deal with shartic weapons.

Jandu leaned over the chariot and threw up a stream of blood. Jandu wiped his face with the back of his hand. His shook in aftershocks from the sharta.

The cavalry broke into three columns, two groups making their way around the left and right flanks of the dead bodies, another charging straight through the debris.

Jandu nocked an arrow and whispered the Rajiwasharta. He could already feel the drain of the first sharta through his body. He aimed the arrow at the right flank of men. As he spat the last words of the curse, blood trickled from between his lips. He loosed his string. The arrow hit the ground in front of the lead riders and split the earth. The soil collapsed, plunging horses and riders into the sinkhole. Jandu heard screams and breaking bones as the right flank was swallowed by the earth.

The other soldiers were now upon them. "Left!" Jandu shouted at Abiyar. "Swerve past the left flank!" Abiyar's frantic whipping got the horses off to a furious gallop. Their chariot wheels thundered along the ground. As they came within striking distance of the cavalry, Jandu closed his eyes and whispered another sharta, shooting the arrow deep into the ground and causing an explosion of dust to blind the soldiers and block the chariot from view.

Too exhausted to conjure any more shartas, Jandu took a deep breath and began to shoot arrow after arrow. His muscle memory returned, and he worked relentlessly, releasing a cloud of shafts into the dusty confusion. He heard screams and knew he had pierced the men even in the darkened chaos of the dust cloud.

The remaining cavalry circled to follow the chariot. Jandu turned to shoot behind him, aiming at the eyes of horses and the throats of men.

An explosion of pain blossomed in Jandu's groin. He clenched his teeth to stop from crying out, and looked down, expecting an arrow wound. Instead, he saw that he was uninjured. He kept shooting, pain shivering through his body in agonizing waves, and he watched as his arms enlarged before his very eyes, his height changed.

Nausea washed through Jandu as the world shrank around him. "Straight ahead!" he yelled to Abiyar.

Every time Jandu fired his bow, his arms grew stronger. Zandi lightened in his hands. The armor slid loosely on his chest as his breasts receded. He realized that, by the end of this battle, if he survived, he would be a man again. He fired faster, exuberant in the battle.

By now the remaining men galloped alongside the rushing chariot. A lance sliced Abiyar across the hands. Abiyar cried out, but he retained the reins, jerking the horses to the right to find a gap amongst the cavalrymen.

One of the men punctured their chestnut stallion in the shoulder. The horse screamed in protest but continued to run, fuelled by fear, tied to his companion.

Abiyar brought the chariot back around, and as he did, they were assailed from all sides by the last half a dozen men left alive, who beat at Abiyar's horses with maces and struck towards them with lances. One of the horses stumbled but they continued forward. The smell of blood filled the air.

A stabbing pain spasmed in Jandu's shoulder, and he looked to see he had been cut. Jandu roared, and then spit out a curse word that he didn't even remember he knew. Men all around him burst into ash. Only two cavalrymen remained.

Suddenly the rider to Jandu's left leapt from his mount into Jandu's chariot. Jandu was so surprised he let down his guard long enough for the man to push Jandu against the chariot's central pole, his sword ready to plunge.

Abiyar swerved, and the two men tumbled to the floor of the chariot. The man fell on top of Jandu, his hot body lying heavy upon Jandu's own, and Jandu reacted with total, absolute panic. He reached up and twisted the attacker's head with all his strength, breaking his neck. Jandu scrambled from under the dead body, loathing crawling like bugs on his flesh.

"Are you okay? Janali!" Abiyar was screaming.

Jandu focused on the last rider, who was almost out of range and galloping towards the hills. Jandu's rage would not let the man live. Pulling together the last of his strength, he clutched an arrow to his chest as he whispered a long string of Yashva words. Nausea swirled through his mind as he spoke them. His hand hurt as the shaft expanded within his grasp, and he watched, amazed, as the tip of the shaft changed to a crescent moon, glittering with a liquid metal similar to that of Zandi.

Jandu shot his arrow at the fleeing rider. The arrow emitted a high-pitched shriek as it flew from the bowstring, and sighed as it hit its target. The crescent tip severed the man's head.

"Stop the horses!" Jandu bellowed. It took almost a minute to get the frightened team to halt. Jandu was sick again, throwing up blood over the edge of the chariot, his stomach churning from so many magical weapons. He wiped his mouth with the back of his hand.

Abiyar looked back at Jandu, his face a mask of dirt, gray and frozen in fear. "Janal—I mean, Prince Jandu?"

Jandu looked at the back of his hands. They were man's hands. His body was that of a man. He ran his fingers over his face, feeling the familiar contours of his high cheekbones, his chin, his wide lips. He turned from Abiyar and touched the front of his zahari. He felt his penis there, and testicles, and he almost wept with relief.

He turned back and smiled at Abiyar. "Are you hurt?"

Abiyar swallowed. His voice was scratchy and hoarse. "I couldn't see when you took up your arrows, when you fixed them on the bow string, and when you let them off. I couldn't see you move. You were so fast." He brought his hands together in the sign of peace.

"You saved Afadi." Abiyar started crying.

"And you were the finest charioteer I have ever seen," Jandu said. He felt choked with emotion. His body shook with the leftovers of adrenalin and the intense usage of new muscles. But he didn't have a chance to relax. The Royal Judge would be in the city now, negotiating a peace. They needed to know that Chandamar had broken their treaty and invaded. He had to inform Lord Indarel of Chandamar's treachery.

"Abi, we need fresh horses. I have to tell your father Chandamar has attacked."

Abiyar turned the horses back towards the retreat. The stallions breathed heavily, their coats white with frothy sweat.

"Let me come with you," Abiyar shouted above the noise of the chariot. They rode back over the scorched ground, the wheels creating parallel lines of blood and gore across the parched soil.

"It will be dangerous," Jandu said. He leaned against the chariot's central pole, his body shaking with exhaustion. "We could step into a war."

Abiyar turned to face Jandu, his eyes misted over. "What do I have to fear with you beside me?" He turned to whip the horses. Jandu stared down at Abiyar, his heart flooded with affection. It made him sad to realize that their time together would be over soon. But Abiyar was better trained than when Jandu first met him. Jandu took great pride in Abiyar's achievements. He reached down and touched Abiyar's shoulder.

"All right." Jandu smiled. "But stop calling me lord."

Abiyar turned and beamed Jandu a smile.

As soon as they were close enough to see the gates of the summer house, Jandu heard the cheers from the women inside. They had watched the battle from the walls. Abiyar slowed the chariot at the gates. He turned nervously to Jandu, speaking in a low whisper. "Lord Jandu?"

"Jandu's just fine," Jandu told him.

"You aren't… you aren't going to tell anyone that I kissed you, are you?"

"No. Of course not."

"Because I really thought you were a girl," Abiyar said quickly. "I am not a faggot or anything."

The insult shot an icy tremor up Jandu's spine, but he covered up quickly with a weak smile. "I *was* a girl when it happened. But no, I won't tell anyone."

Abiyar looked relieved. He turned back to urge the horses through the summer house gate.

Inside, women assailed them from all sides, throwing flowers and offering water. Lady Shali rushed towards them and fiercely pulled her son into her arms. Suraya embraced Jandu, looking him over proudly.

"Look at you! You are back to your old self!" She walked with him back to his room. "I'll see if I can borrow a set of men's clothing from Lord Indarel's wardrobe, while you wash off that blood and dirt. "

"We won't be staying," Jandu said. "Abi and I will ride for the capital as soon as we change horses."

"I'll just get the clothes then," Suraya said, nodding.

Jandu caught her arm. "Fetch one more thing," he said.

Suraya raised an eyebrow. "What?"

Jandu held out his pony tail. "A pair of scissors."

CHAPTER 42

THE LATE MONSOON RAINS LEFT THE CITY OF AFADI SHROUDED beneath a mushroom of dust. Tarek had never been to the city before, but he saw glimpses of white washed walls and realized that, normally, the city was beautiful and bright.

But today, as Tarek made his way past thousands of garrisoned soldiers, both the buildings and the atmosphere of Afadi were tense and ugly. In the palace itself, more soldiers stood in formation, eyeing Tarek's banner and his contingent of soldiers warily.

Lord Indarel Lokesh greeted Tarek at the gate and ushered him into the reception hall personally.

"We are honored to have you with us, Royal Judge. This whole business has been very sad indeed, and we look forward to a rapid resolution of this crisis."

Within the marble reception hall, Tarek saw Afadi soldiers lined along one wall. On the other side of the room, the black crane banner of Chandamar and dark red uniforms of the Chandamar soldiers stood guard around their new young lord, Ishad Trinat, son of Firdaus.

Ishad looked like a healthier, more vibrant version of his father. He had Firdaus' piercing black eyes and broad shoulders, but his black hair was kept slick and short, and his body was fit and trim. Ishad stepped forward to greet Tarek, and Tarek offered Ishad the sign of peace.

"Blessings upon you, Lord of Chandamar," Tarek said.

"And upon you, Royal Judge," Ishad said.

"My condolences for your loss," Tarek said. "I knew your father well."

Ishad bowed. "Thank you."

Indarel ushered Tarek to a seat at the front of the room, in a semicircle with Ishad and Indarel. Courtiers, servants, and Indarel's son Ramad stood around them at a polite distance. Only when seated did Tarek notice someone was missing.

"Where is Keshan Adaru?" Tarek asked, searching the faces in the room.

"I am here, Royal Judge."

Keshan stepped out of the shadows, smiling at Tarek. Keshan bowed before Tarek. Tarek smiled at his friend and hugged him in return.

"How was your journey?" Keshan asked politely.

"Long and dusty." Tarek smiled at Keshan. "How is your health?"

"Good, thank you."

Ishad glared at both of them angrily. Tarek motioned to a servant. "Bring another chair for Lord Adaru. I believe he had an important part to play in what happened."

Keshan raised his eyebrow at Tarek, but other than that small gesture, Tarek could read nothing of Keshan's complicity on his face. Keshan looked tired, Tarek realized, his eyelids drooping, but otherwise, he appeared as nonchalant as always.

Ishad glared with open hostility as Keshan took his seat.

"Now," Tarek began, looking at the men around him. "What happened?"

"Keshan Adaru murdered my father and uncle whilst they stayed in Afadi under Lord Indarel's protection!" Ishad exclaimed.

Tarek held out his hand to silence the boy. He turned to Indarel. "Is this true?"

Indarel looked nervously to Ishad. "It is true that Keshan killed Firdaus and Hanu Trinat, as well as another companion." Indarel's expression darkened. "But it was his right to do so, Judge. He was defending a woman, one of my servants, who was being dishonored by these men! To assault her within my own house is a grievous insult against me and the State of Afadi!"

Tarek turned to Keshan. "Is that what happened?"

Keshan's finger beat out a nervous staccato rhythm against his thigh with his fingertips, but otherwise, he looked composed. "They beat her. She was screaming for help. It was the right thing to do."

Tarek felt sick even discussing it. He knew Firdaus, knew he was guilty. It sounded like something he would do. And it was too unlike Keshan to simply murder another lord, even a lifelong enemy, on a whim.

"Your father committed a crime," Tarek told Ishad.

Ishad stood angrily. "No! It was my father's right to claim her! He won the servant in a dice match!"

Tarek frowned. "How do you know this?"

"Indarel's dice teacher admitted it!" Ishad pointed to a thin, frail looking man in the corner.

"Come forward," Tarek demanded.

The man who stepped forward was nicely attired in clean cotton, with a yellow turban on his head. His beard was trim and tinged with gray. But he had a nasty-looking black eye and a split lip, and his expression was filled with remorse.

"Greetings, Royal Judge," the man said.

Tarek froze. He knew this voice. He looked into Esalas' eyes. How could no one else see who this was?

At that moment, Tarek understood why Keshan Adaru was here. He had just found Yudar Paran. Darvad would be thrilled. Regardless of what happened between Afadi and Chandamar, Tarek would triumph.

But then Tarek looked to the giant man beside Esalas, saw it was none other than Baram, and realized it had to have been Suraya who Firdaus had tried to rape.

"None of this has anything to do with Afadi," Indarel stated. "This is a matter between Keshan and Firdaus. We had no part in this, and we beg the judge to see Afadi is blameless."

Indarel pleaded with Tarek. "Keshan defended his wife! It is his own private affair, not ours!"

Tarek narrowed his eyes at Keshan. That, at the very least, was a lie. "*Your* wife?"

Keshan stared back at Tarek unflinchingly. "Yes. Esalas had no right to claim her."

"Why did you not make a formal protest? Inform Lord Firdaus that he was molesting your property?"

"I had no time. And I think we both know how unlikely it is that Firdaus would have stopped just for me."

"Lord Adaru is right, I had no claim to Janali," Yudar said, falling to his knees. He held out his hands in supplication. "Please, Judge, spare Lord Adaru. If anyone is to blame for what happened, it is me. Blame me. I am the one who endangered her."

Keshan stared down at Yudar with a look of pure loathing.

This was getting complicated. Tarek rubbed his hand over his face. "What is the date?"

No one said anything and the silence hung over the large hall. Tarek looked to Yudar. "What is the date?" he asked again, but in his mind, he already calculated the months.

Yudar frowned. "I'm not sure, Judge. It is close to the monsoon season."

"The monsoon season has already begun," Tarek said. "Your three years are over."

The silence stretched.

Yudar stood.

"I don't know what you mean—"

"Prince Yudar," Tarek said tersely, "perhaps you would like to explain truthfully what happened so I can make a fair judgment."

Yudar pulled off his turban. Men in the room gasped loudly. Indarel looked about to faint.

"Esalas… Esalas is Yudar Paran?"

Baram moved to stand beside his brother.

"Why don't you tell me who Janali is," Tarek said, already knowing the answer.

"Janali is my youngest brother, Jandu," Yudar said.

The room exploded with noise as men spoke simultaneously. Tarek's mind reeled. This was not what he expected.

Keshan remained sitting quietly, staring at Tarek expectantly.

"The Parans!" Ishad pointed at Indarel. "You have harbored the Parans under your care, against King Darvad's wishes!"

"I did not know!" Indarel stood as well. "I did not know they were the Parans! They were in hiding! And how was I to know that Jandu was a woman?"

"Lord Indarel has broken no oath," Yudar said. With each word, his voice gained confidence. "We fulfilled our exile in all accordance with the rules of the dice game. Indarel thought he hired servants, nothing more."

"Jandu is a woman?" Indarel's eldest son, Ramad, who stood beside his father, shook his head. "I don't understand."

"Jandu used a Yashva curse to transform himself for one year," Baram said. His voice boomed through the audience.

Ishad turned to Keshan. "You claimed that Janali was your wife."

Keshan's calm expression did not change. "Yes."

"But that is a lie."

"I could not tell the truth, or else I would have endangered Indarel's oath not to protect the Parans."

"But *you* knowingly helped them," Indarel stated carefully. Keshan said nothing.

"Then Keshan has broken the King's oath!" Ishad crossed his arms.

"No!" Baram bellowed. "It was your father who acted dishonorably toward my brother!"

"Regardless, Keshan Adaru broke his oath and should be branded an outcaste and disgraced," Ishad shouted. "If King Darvad expects Chandamar's continued support, he must stand by his own laws!"

Tarek's throat felt tight. He looked to Keshan, who seemed less assured than he was a few moments ago.

Was Tarek really going to brand Iyestar's brother an untouchable? Cast him from the noble Triya heritage that Tarek had only just gained himself? Tarek knew first hand what humiliation and poverty faced Keshan. And being an untouchable was ten times worse than being Suya. Keshan would no longer be able to suggest laws, make changes, even enter any Triya household. Tarek would be destroying one of his closest allies, one of the few men he respected and admired.

Tarek believed in Keshan's vision of a new world. How could he, in good conscience, destroy it all because the man had defended his lover?

Tarek looked behind him, to the tight unit of Dragewan soldiers that stood along the wall. Anant was there, staring blankly forward, but he made eye contact and Anant's mouth curved up in a slight smile.

What if someone had raped Anant? Wouldn't Tarek forego all oaths to protect the man? What if it was Darvad, instead of Anant? Without a second's thought, Tarek would have broken all the laws of the world to save him, and pay any consequences later.

Keshan loved Jandu, and now he was going to pay for it. Sickness welled inside of Tarek. He didn't want to do this.

"It sounds as though the course is clear," Indarel said softly. He would not look at Keshan. "I hope that if the Judge takes action against Keshan, then Afadi will remain blameless in the eyes of both Chandamar and Prasta."

"You want me to do this?" Tarek asked him.

Indarel looked embarrassed. "If it will save Afadi from war."

"Will this please Chandamar, and will they cease all threats against Afadi's boundaries if this happens?" Tarek asked.

Ishad sat back down. "We will consider it just retribution for what happened. And we will continue to stand by our King proudly."

Tarek looked to Yudar. The man seemed on the verge of tears.

"Do you have anything to say, Prince Yudar?"

"It is not Keshan's fault. It is mine," Yudar said quietly. "Punish me, Tarek."

But, as much as it would have pleased Tarek to do so, he had no legal grounds. "You fulfilled the terms of the exile," Tarek said. "Keshan did not." Tarek turned to the man in question. "Keshan?"

Keshan was now quite pale, but he smiled. "Yes, Judge?"

"Do you understand what this means?"

Keshan nodded.

"And do you acknowledge your guilt?"

Keshan's stare pierced through Tarek. "I would do it again if I had to."

"Look what you have done now!" Baram growled at Yudar. "You have ruined two lives!" Yudar flinched.

Tarek stood, his knees cracking with fatigue. "We will reconvene in the courtyard in one hour." He hesitated, but then turned to Indarel. "Bring a branding iron."

"Yes, Royal Judge," Indarel bowed low.

Tarek took three steps towards the exit, then turned back and signaled to Anant. "Come with me, commander."

Anant inclined his head. "Yes, sir."

The two of them made their way through the reception hall and out into the palace's courtyard. Afadi servants had set up a room for him in the guest quarters of the palace. Tarek immediately excused them, and then shut the door so that he was alone with Anant.

Anant relaxed, his broad shoulders loosening as soon as they were alone. He put his helmet down on a desk. "My lord?"

Tarek looked at him. What kind of person was Anant? He knew what Darvad would do in this circumstance. Despite being friends and allies, Darvad would have Keshan branded in a heartbeat. Darvad's hatred of the Parans made all other interests, even those of reform, those of friendship, secondary.

"I don't want to do this," Tarek said.

"No one wants to see their friends outcaste," Anant said.

"Do you want to know a secret?"

"If you'd like to tell me, my lord." Anant appeared worried.

Tarek ran his hand through his hair. He leaned forward to whisper. "Keshan Adaru and Jandu Paran are lovers."

Anant's eyes widened as he understood the implications. "Are they? Then Adaru really was defending his wife, so to speak."

"And now I am to punish a good man for defending his lover," Tarek said. "I want to tell Keshan to run."

"What would happen if you did that?"

It was an interesting question. "Chandamar would likely attack Afadi, and declare Darvad unfit as King. Darvad would be angry, possibly relieving me of my position. He would pursue Keshan. And the Parans would still represent a threat to Darvad's rule."

"Would Lord Keshan run if you told him to?"

"I don't know," Tarek said. "But I would let him if he did."

Anant moved closer. He smelled warm and salty, like sunburned skin. He touched Tarek's shoulder. "I think you should listen to your heart. What you do today will ruin a friend of yours. Stripping his caste can only be reversed by a king, and it sounds as though King Darvad will not do so."

Tarek turned from Anant. "You think I have a heart. But I don't. I'm going to do it. I promised Darvad I would serve him, and this is what he would want me to do."

"What has he done to deserve such unwavering loyalty?" Anant asked.

Tarek whirled on Anant. He was out of line.

But then Tarek realized it wasn't an unreasonable question. Tarek looked at Anant, and saw that he *was* a better person. Better than Darvad. Better than Tarek himself. Anant lived true to his own conscience, was not ashamed of who he was, or afraid of his own feelings.

Tarek shook his head. "I'm not like you. I took a vow. Even if my actions go against my conscience, I must stand by Darvad."

"Regardless of the cost to your soul?" Anant asked.

"Yes." Tarek sighed shakily. "I'm sorry. But I'm a horrible person."

Tarek expected Anant to look disgusted, or walk out, or reject him. He should have. Tarek deserved no sympathy. He was a man who was about to destroy his friend to follow the unkind desires of his liege.

Anant approached hesitantly. He wrapped his arms around Tarek, his breastplate rubbing against Tarek's.

"What are you thinking?" Tarek asked, awed that Anant would show affection, even after everything Tarek had done.

Anant smiled. "Honestly? I'm simply grateful that you admit to having a soul, after all."

Tarek laughed. He kissed Anant deeply, feeling the trust, the affection, radiate off of the young soldier.

This wasn't love, he reminded himself. This was nothing like what he felt for Darvad. But for now, as he made the decision to once again go against his own wishes to help Darvad, it was enough.

◆◆◆

As the afternoon sun lowered, long shadows stretched across the sandstone of the Afadi palace courtyard. Hundreds of people filled the space, forming a circle around the ceremonial fire. All of Indarel's advisors, commanders, and Triya vassals were there, as well as the Chandamar party, and Tarek's own soldiers and ministers. The soldiers of lesser castes watched the ceremony from the outside of the circle, looking on as Indarel's priests ladled butter into the fire and chanted prayers to God.

Indarel approached, holding a long branding iron in the shape of an X. The brand was immediately placed into the fire. The crowd gathered closer, pulling in from the long shadows to watch this unprecedented scene.

Keshan grew very quiet as the preparations began. He kept his distance from everyone, only smiling once when Baram came over and hugged him brusquely. Tarek again prayed that Keshan would just run away, call on some Yashva magic to transport himself to safety and spare Tarek's already battered conscience. But as the brand heated in the flames, and the priests' invocations ceased, Tarek realized his prayers would go unanswered.

Tarek called the Triya caste members together, and recited the passage from the Book of Taivo on the virtue of oaths and the honor of the Triya. After declaring Keshan's sins, Tarek summoned him forward.

All Tarek could read from Keshan's expression was resolve. He walked into the ceremonial circle and approached Tarek dutifully.

"Having broken a sacred vow, you are to be formally expelled from the caste of your birth." Tarek's voice was low and carried across the hushed courtyard. Tarek nodded to two servants, who carried a large teak table to the fireside. "Place your hands on the surface," he ordered.

Keshan put his hands on the table, palms down, fingers splayed.

"No!" Baram bellowed, watching and weeping from the side.

Keshan glanced to Baram and gave him a brief, pale-lipped smile. Two Afadi soldiers held Keshan's arms in place.

Tarek removed the iron from the fire. He hesitated for a moment, the heat of the brand overpowering, even at a distance. There was a flicker of fright in Keshan's eyes.

"I'm sorry," Tarek whispered. He lifted the long handle of the brand and pushed down with force against the back of Keshan's right hand.

Keshan's arm jerked in the soldier's grasp as he reflexively tried to pull away. He groaned and seemed about to collapse, but the soldiers held him up by his arms. Tarek pressed the iron against Keshan's skin for what seemed to be an age, making sure it burnt clean. He handed the brand to a servant, who returned it to the fire for the second strike. The smell of burning flesh sickened Tarek.

When the brand glowed yellow, Tarek raised it again and branded Keshan's left hand with the same mark. After he lifted the iron away, the two soldiers released Keshan and he swayed as if he would fall. But he didn't. His lips and fingernails looked bluish, and he breathed shallowly.

"He is casteless, and disgraced," Tarek announced. He reached forward and pulled Keshan's diadem from his head.

"He is casteless, and disgraced," answered the men around him. The Triya nearby reached forward and ripped Keshan's fine clothing from him. Ishad pushed his way forward, grinning malevolently as he violently jerked the jewels from Keshan's arms. Within seconds Keshan stood naked before them all, trying to cover his genitals with his injured hands.

All the Triya ceremonially turned their backs to Keshan. Tarek did so as well. In the subsequent silence, he heard the sound of Keshan's bare feet padding across the courtyard, and out of the palace, where he would never be welcomed again.

CHAPTER 43

THE SUN HAD NEARLY SET WHEN JANDU AND ABIYAR REACHED Lord Indarel's palace. Despite the late hour, a vast number of noblemen congregated in the courtyard. Jandu quickly dismounted and pushed through the crowds of courtiers. A large fire in the center of the courtyard filled the air with buttery smoke, which wafted over the fading daylight in dark spirals. Tarek Amia stood nearby, looking at his feet.

"Chandamar just attacked Afadi!" Abiyar yelled, rushing toward his father. "Chandamar attacked the summer retreat! They have attacked!" Jandu quickened his pace, protecting Abiyar as they cut through the throng of startled Triya nobles and ministers.

Lord Indarel turned towards them. "What are you talking about, boy?"

Abiyar was out of breath, and in his excitement, his voice raised pitch. "Cavalry charged the summer retreat! We had no defense!"

Indarel immediately paled. "My God. My God!" He reeled on a young man dressed in Triya garb. "You son of a bitch!"

Jandu studied the young man's face. From his resemblance to Firdaus, he had to be Ishad, Firdaus' son. A slick coil of loathing crept up Jandu's throat.

"Jandu Paran saved us!" Abiyar cried out. "He killed fifty men single-handedly! He saved us, father!"

Indarel spun back to stare at Jandu.

Jandu straightened. "Not single-handedly," he said. "Abiyar fought bravely beside me. The victory is as much his as it is mine."

"Jandu!" Jandu was immediately crushed in one of Baram's massive hugs.

"Let go!" Jandu gasped. His nose felt like it was breaking again.

"I will *not* let go! I *love* you!" Baram cried out. Those around them stared openly.

"You're making a scene!" Jandu whispered.

"I don't care!" Baram proclaimed, not whispering.

"You're... crushing... me!" Jandu cried.

Baram let go of him immediately. He put his hands around Jandu's face.

Baram looked like he had been crying all week. His eyes were red and swollen. "If Keshan hadn't been there, I wouldn't have just killed those fuckers. I would have tortured them first."

Jandu searched the crowd. "Where's Yudar?"

"Over by the fire. He looks bad. I beat the shit out of him."

Jandu touched Baram's shoulder.

"This is an outrage!" Indarel turned back to Ishad. "You call for a mediator, and attack us while we are negotiating a peace?"

Tarek stepped between the two men. He looked ready to murder Ishad as well. "You mean to tell me that after what I've just done, you have been duplicitous?"

"We have the right to defend our state," Ishad declared, squaring with Tarek. "And what you did is the King's will, not just ours. Keshan got what he deserved."

Jandu grew deaf to the sounds around him. He could feel his heart exploding in his chest.

"Keshan?" Jandu turned from Baram. "What did Ishad mean—he got what he deserved?"

The deep shadows of twilight made hollows of Baram's eyes.

"He's gone," Baram said, grabbing Jandu's arm. "He's outcaste, Jandu. He just left the palace grounds."

Jandu shook off Baram's arm.

"No!" He barged into the circle beside the fire and shoved Tarek. "What did you do, you bastard? What did you do!"

Tarek's expression was drawn. "I'm sorry, Jandu. I had no choice."

"Looks like you're going to have to find a new husband to defend you, Janali," Ishad sneered.

"You motherfucker!" Jandu lunged at Firdaus' son.

Jandu felt Tarek grasp him, pulling him backwards, and panic surged through him. He elbowed Tarek with all of his strength. Tarek gasped, releasing his grip. Jandu broke free, drew his sword and charged Firdaus' son.

Guards closed ranks around Ishad and the movement caused the entire crowd to cry out in fear. Baram caught Jandu brusquely and knocked his sword from his hands.

"No, Jandu! Stop it!" Baram shouted in his ear. "Don't!"

Jandu struggled out of his brother's grasp.

"Calm down! Everyone just calm down!" Indarel cried, raising his hands up, urging the soldiers back from each other. "Please, Prince Jandu! Calm down!"

Jandu could barely hear him, the blood pumped so loudly in his ears.

Indarel suddenly bowed before him. "Please! I beg your forgiveness, Lord Jandu, and give you my utmost gratitude and respect for saving our city from treachery!" Indarel had tears in his eyes.

Yudar stepped forward. Jandu could see evidence of Baram's fist all over his eldest brother's face. It brought no tinge of sympathy, however. Just looking at Yudar made Jandu flex against Baram's hold, desperate once more for his sword.

"Royal Judge, we have fulfilled the terms of our exile honorably and truthfully. Now that my brother is with us, I demand that you escort us to Prasta." Yudar spoke proudly. His glance flicked to Jandu, his eyes begging forgiveness.

"Let go of me!" Jandu hissed. He broke free of Baram's arms and picked up his sword. Everyone watched him.

"I will escort you to Prasta," Tarek said, coughing as he recovered from Jandu's strike. He looked to Jandu. "This can be resolved with the King."

Jandu stared at the men around him. Greedy, maneuvering, cowardly bastards, one and all. He sheathed his sword and pushed his way out of the crowded courtyard to find Keshan.

Long shadows filled the open streets. Jandu squinted in the darkness for some sign of Keshan. He had no idea where the untouchables of Afadi even resided.

A few blocks from the palace gates, hiding within the darkness of an alleyway, Jandu saw a group of them, their clothes in tattered, filthy rags. As Jandu approached they backed away, leaving Keshan standing there, half-naked, trying to tie on a blood-stained dejaru that one of the other outcastes must have given him.

"Keshan!" Jandu rushed to him. The Jegora lingered deep in the shadows, watching. Jandu didn't care. He reached out to embrace Keshan but Keshan took a very deliberate step back into the alley.

"Don't touch me." Keshan's voice sounded strained. "I'm Jegora now."

Jandu closed the distance between them and pulled Keshan into his arms. Keshan let out a sob of relief and clutched Jandu desperately. Jandu could feel tremors through Keshan's body. His skin felt cold and clammy. He held his hands away from their embrace.

Jandu pulled back and brushed sweaty hair off of Keshan's forehead. "You're sick. You need a doctor."

"No physician will treat me," Keshan said softly. As he drew back, his dejaru came loose. He caught it with a jerk of his terribly burned hands. The sight of them made Jandu almost sick. He couldn't imagine how much pain Keshan was in.

"Stop that for a minute." Jandu carefully placed his palms against Keshan's and whispered the words of the healing sharta Keshan taught him back in Tamarus' home. The words flowed through him, the rhythm clear, pushing the sounds out of his mouth to settle like mist over Keshan's angry wounds. Keshan's hands ceased to tremble, and though the brands did not completely heal, the red edges of the burns seemed less angry.

Jandu reached down and tied Keshan's dejaru for him. He grimaced. "This smells."

"At least I'm not completely naked."

Jandu reached to his side and untied his breastplate.

"What are you doing?" Keshan's voice was weak.

"Giving you my vest," Jandu told him.

Keshan shook his head. "I can't take it. If someone sees me wearing silk I will be stoned."

Jandu paused, looking down at Keshan. What were they going to do now? He retied his armor. He had to come up with a plan.

Keshan moved deeper into the alleyway and sat on an upended urn. Jandu sat beside him, and put his arm around him. Keshan leaned over slowly, and rested his head on Jandu's shoulder. From the shadows he could feel eyes on him. He wondered what the other Jegora made of this scene.

One by one, the implications of life as a Jegora hit Jandu. Keshan could never return to his beautiful palace in Tiwari. He could never ride a horse again, or wear any of his clothes again, or eat with any family member. He was banned from temples and from courts of law, from all academies and hospitals. The only work he would find would be as someone who cleaned the outhouses and latrines, or dressed the dead bodies, or cleaned up the funeral pyres. From this point forward, his only contact with animals would be disposing of carcasses and skinning dead cows.

"You could go to the Yashva kingdom," Jandu said, although the idea of being separated knifed through him.

"I can't. Firdaus locked me out before I killed him."

Jandu felt vomit rise in his throat at the very mention of Firdaus' name. Rage filled him, but there was nowhere to vent it and slowly, Jandu let it go. He didn't need anger now. He needed to help Keshan.

Keshan's skin was still clammy and pale. Jandu wrapped his arms around him, holding him tightly.

"You're an idiot," Jandu told him. "The second you realized what they were going to do, you should have kicked their asses."

Keshan snorted, but he kept his eyes closed. "If the King declares me untouchable, then I will become untouchable. It is inevitable, Jandu." Keshan swallowed painfully, and licked at his lips.

"Hold on a moment. I'll be right back." Jandu left Keshan in the alley and ran towards the gates. He returned a few minutes later with a gourd full of water. He helped Keshan drink from it so he didn't have to use his hands. Jandu sat down beside him again and Keshan leaned his head against Jandu's shoulder once more.

"Thanks."

"How do your hands feel?" Jandu asked.

"Like someone just burned them with a branding iron." Keshan closed his eyes.

"If I had gotten here only a few minutes earlier…"

"…You would have been killed for interfering," Keshan said. "And all of this would be for nothing."

Jandu brushed Keshan's bangs off of his forehead, and blew on Keshan's skin. Keshan closed his eyes again. "That feels nice."

They sat there in silence for a while, Jandu blowing on Keshan's forehead, and methodically brushing Keshan's bangs with his fingers. He heard the popping screech of a Malabar Hornbill in the distance, the lazy lowing of cattle, the rustle of vermin in the alley. Jandu looked down at Keshan's face. Color finally returned to his cheeks and lips, but he appeared sound asleep.

"I can't believe everything you've given up for me." Jandu said quietly. "I am unworthy of such loyalty."

Keshan opened one eye. "Have you been disloyal?"

"That's not what I mean." Jandu rubbed Keshan's back.

"What have you and Abiyar been up to these last few days?" Keshan tried smiling.

Jandu gently slapped Keshan's back. "Nothing, thank you very much. I'm as faithful as ever. You, on the other hand, are the one with the reputation."

"I doubt I'll get much play now. It's one thrill to fuck a Triya lord. It's another circumstance entirely to screw a branded casteless untouchable."

Jandu looked around, but no one was there, so he ran his hand along the inside of Keshan's thigh. He could feel the tension quivering in Keshan's muscles. "You're still sexy as hell. I'll screw you, Jegora or not."

Keshan laughed quietly. "Thank God."

"Do you want me to fetch a wet cloth for your hands?"

"No, I'll be fine."

"It's beginning to turn nasty colors."

"It's a burn, Jandu. It's going to look awful for a while."

"I'm so sorry." Jandu rested his head against Keshan's. "I'm sorry."

"Don't be," Keshan said. "I would have given up more than just my caste to protect you." Keshan looked at Jandu, eyes wet with emotion. "It's so good to see you back in your body. I'd almost forgotten how handsome you are."

Jandu heard men approaching, so he reluctantly untangled his arm from around Keshan's waist and pulled his hand from Keshan's thigh. Keshan didn't bother to lift his head from Jandu's shoulder.

Baram and Yudar appeared at the entrance of the alleyway.

"Adaru!" Baram shouted. "Are you all right?" Jandu noticed that neither of them dared enter the alleyway. Baram was concerned for Keshan, but even he would not let an untouchable shadow fall upon him.

"I'm just tired," Keshan said.

Yudar frowned at Jandu. "If people see you like that, they will say something. You shouldn't be touching him. No offense, Adaru."

Jandu extricated himself from under Keshan's head. He grabbed Yudar by his cotton shirt and shoved him up against the dusty alley wall.

"You will change him back," Jandu spat.

Yudar looked frightened. "What—"

"You will give me your oath now to resurrect Keshan as a Triya once you have the throne." Jandu slammed Yudar against the brick wall harder. "That is the only reason I'm not gutting you right now, you bastard."

Yudar held his hands up. "Of course! Of course I'll change Keshan back! I swear it on the prophets!"

Jandu dropped Yudar, wiping his hands on his dejaru. It disgusted him to touch Yudar more than Keshan's filthy clothes.

"I realize, Jandu, that you can't forgive me, not after what's happened." Yudar's voice shook. "But I just want you to know, I'm so sorry! I will kill myself if you ask it. Please forget this incident and live on!"

"Don't kill yourself." Jandu didn't look at him. "I need you alive to elevate Keshan back to Triya status."

"I never meant to harm you," Yudar started.

Jandu's rage flared and he glared at his brother. "You *staked* me, like a prostitute!"

"No!" Yudar fell to his knees in front of Jandu.

"You led them to my room," Jandu said lowly. "You snuck them past the guards. You opened the door for them. You *brought* them to my room to rape me." Jandu's throat locked in horror. Every time he said the word, he wanted to die. "It would have been far kinder if you had just killed me, brother."

Yudar began to cry. "I've taken a holy oath. I will never touch a set of dice again. I will never gamble again. I will not even set foot in a gaming room again. That is my promise to you."

Jandu said nothing, and Yudar continued, crawling on the street towards Jandu's feet. "I am in a trance when I am playing! I didn't think. I didn't mean to harm you. I honestly thought…" he paused, choking on his tears.

"You thought what?" Jandu said coldly.

"I thought… I could win." Yudar covered his eyes with his hands and sobbed.

Jandu stared down at his brother. There had been a time when he had loved Yudar more than anyone on this earth. This was his brother, his king. The man had practically raised him. He had been Jandu's hero.

Jandu tried to find a flicker of compassion in his heart. But now he felt nothing.

Yudar reached for Jandu's feet, but Jandu pulled them away.

"Don't touch me." Jandu backed away from Yudar. "I will come with you to Prasta. I will protect you from harm and I will fight for your throne if need be. But until you give Keshan back what was stolen, I will not forgive you." Jandu moved to Keshan's side protectively. Jandu glared at Yudar, daring him to say something about the unhygienic contact.

Yudar nodded. "I'm sorry, Jandu." He stood shakily. He turned to Baram, wiping his eyes. "We should prepare for the journey to Prasta."

Baram nodded, but he hesitated in the alleyway after Yudar left. "Your sacrifice will never be forgotten by me, Adaru."

Keshan smiled weakly and waved as Baram left. When they were gone, Keshan dropped his head on Jandu's shoulder once more.

Jandu kissed the top of his head. "Listen to me."

Keshan yawned. "All right."

"Whatever happens in Prasta, I want you by my side," Jandu said. "I don't care if you're disgraced. I don't care what people say."

"Well, I'm certainly not staying in this alley." Keshan smiled with a hint of his old assurance. "You may need me. I doubt Darvad will just give up half of Marhavad without a fight."

Jandu nodded. After the last three years he'd endured, he looked forward to the fight.

CHAPTER 44

THE ROYAL JUDGE'S PROCESSION LEFT THE CITY OF AFADI amidst the local populace's fanfare. The long, dusty snake of chariots, soldiers, cavalry, oxen, carts, and servants stretched ahead of Keshan in a long procession. The only people behind Keshan were the other Jegora, clustered together at the rear, eyes staunchly cast downward. But even among them there were whispers of Jandu Paran's triumph over the Chandamar cavalry. The story had begun with Abiyar and then steadily passed down through the ranks of servants and soldiers. Now even Jegora stole furtive, worshipful glances at Jandu as if he were a prophet of old.

Jandu started at the front of the procession, traveling with Tarek, his brothers, Indarel, and Indarel's sons. He was the hero of the city. A young man next to Keshan described how Jandu had ripped a chariot apart with his bare hands and killed hundreds of men with a single word. Keshan just nodded and smiled. Stories describing Jandu's effort to save Afadi were repeated everywhere Keshan went.

As they neared the river, Keshan saw Jandu walking counter to the procession, coming to join him at the rear. A fist tightened around Keshan's heart at the thought of Jandu's loyalty.

The monsoon rains still hadn't fallen and the earth was dry, begging for water. The skies bloated with moisture, and yet none fell. Dirt puffed around Jandu's feet as he walked.

The heavy sun glinted off of Zandi, strapped to Jandu's back, and the bow seemed like a streak of light piercing Jandu's silver armor. Layers of dust covered Jandu's armor and skin.

He had taken off his heavy helmet in the morning, and now his hair was gray with dirt. All around him, Suya and Chaya stooped to take dust from Jandu's feet.

Jandu smiled at Keshan. He didn't cower from the other Jegora, a testament to how much Jandu had matured, that he could walk alongside the untouchables without flinching.

"Keshan." He reached out and touched Keshan's bare shoulder affectionately.

Keshan smiled back, loving the way Jandu's low voice rumbled his name, the soft, yet fierce way Jandu always spoke to him. Even the quick touch they shared gave Keshan strength. He was a tactile person, and not being able to touch people hurt his pride more than he wanted to admit. He was truly beginning to feel the impact of the sacrifice he had made.

"How do you feel?" Jandu asked, falling in place alongside Keshan. The procession marched forward slowly. Those at the beginning crossed the bridge over the Patari River.

"I'd feel better if you didn't ask me that every hour," Keshan teased. "What's happening up at the front of the line?"

Jandu shrugged. "Politics. Nothing of interest." He flashed Keshan a wicked grin.

"Oh come on, tell me," Keshan said, laughing.

"Yudar is attempting to woo Tarek to his side. Indarel has attached himself to our family like glue. And messenger pigeons were sent to Prasta, alerting them to our pending arrival." Jandu reached into the quiver strapped to his back and pulled out a roll and a wedge of cheese bundled in cloth. He slipped these into Keshan's hands.

The softness of the bread brought tears to Keshan's eyes. For the last two days, as the Parans had prepared to journey east, Keshan had discovered the brutal truth of how unpleasant untouchable food was. The quality of the ingredients was poor and the choices few. Keshan immediately sank his teeth into the bread, luxuriating in the crisp, toasty outer layer contrasting with the buttery insides of the bread, melting in his mouth.

"Thank you," Keshan whispered, as soon as he was done with his roll and cheese. Jandu said nothing. He just walked alongside his friend, squinting off into the distance.

As the long procession crossed the river, their pace slowed. Soldiers took in the scarred earth, charred ground and scraps of decaying carrion remaining from Jandu's battle with the Chandamar raiders. Even with the dead men and horses cremated, a stench of decay permeated the air. Keshan felt the leftovers of shartas in the atmosphere like scars. The very air seemed thinner, fragile, as if stretched to breaking.

Jandu grew silent as they walked by the sight of his carnage. He adjusted his sword belt self-consciously.

Keshan furtively touched Jandu's fingers. "You did a good thing here."

"Ah. Well…" Jandu blushed, and looked towards the summer retreat. "There was no alternative."

Keshan watched Jandu's cheeks grow flush with a combination of pride and shyness, yet another sign of how different he was from when Keshan had first met him. The Jandu he had known years ago would have bragged about this victory to every man he met. Now Jandu looked pensive, keeping his eyes focused on the retreat.

Women poured from the summer house, and the procession halted. Baram already stood beside the gate with Suraya at his side. They scanned the crowd, obviously looking for Jandu.

As soon as she spotted him, Suraya ran towards Jandu, throwing her arms around him.

"How are you?" she asked, pulling back to look into Jandu's eyes.

"Fine." He smiled and touched her head. "You?"

"Ready to return to Prasta." Suraya turned to Keshan with an equally large smile. "It's wonderful to see you again, Keshan." She reached out to hug him, but Baram suddenly jerked her back.

"Wait, Suraya," Baram said quietly.

Suraya froze, staring in shock at Keshan's hands. He self-consciously looked down himself at the blackened, charred marks. The pain had subsided greatly since Jandu had used the Yashva cure, but every time he flexed his hands the skin cracked and broke the scabs, causing a sharp sting.

Suraya stood like a statue, her arms still outstretched to embrace him, her glance glued to his hands.

"Hello, Suraya," Keshan said amiably, trying his best to act like nothing unusual had occurred. "You look ravishing as always."

Jandu smirked. "Don't listen to Keshan. You look like shit, Suraya. Did you stop eating or something? Why are you so skinny and pale?"

Jandu rubbed her back affectionately, which seemed to break Suraya out of her stunned immobility. She shook her head as if to clear it, dropping her arms to her sides.

"I was worried about you, you fool." She frowned at the Jegora all around them. "Keshan? What are you going to do now?"

Keshan shrugged. "I'm taking it one day at a time."

Jandu put his hand on Keshan's shoulder. Keshan didn't miss the small gasp of surprise from Suraya.

"When we get to the capital, I'll help him find lodgings," Jandu said.

"I can manage on my own, Jandu," Keshan said.

Jandu's blue eyes burned brightly. "I'm coming with you, like it or not."

Keshan sighed. He was going to become a burden to those who loved him.

"I packed our things from the summer house," Suraya said. "Some of the belongings are yours, Keshan. What should I do with them?"

"Keep them," Jandu spoke for Keshan. "He'll want them back when he's Triya again."

Suraya bit her lip as she looked at Jandu sympathetically. She turned away.

"Suraya?" Keshan called out.

"Yes?"

"Can you fetch my saddle bag for me? There's something I want Jandu to have."

Suraya smiled, and then left.

The procession began its way forward once more, moving slowly past the retreat. A few minutes later, Baram returned, carrying Keshan's bag.

"Here you go," Baram said, handing the bag to Jandu so he wouldn't have to touch Keshan. Keshan knew better than to be offended, but he felt it all the same. "I should join Yudar and Suraya up at the front." Baram looked to Jandu. "Are you coming?"

"No. I'll walk with Keshan a while."

Baram grimaced at the Jegora around him. "Are you sure?"

"Yes." Jandu's expression was hard.

"I'll see you later, then." Baram returned to his proper place as a Triya, at the front of the line.

Jandu opened the saddle bag. "What's the present?" He pulled out the small tin of rose oil that they had used when making love. A rich blush covered his cheeks. "Is this it, you pervert?"

Keshan laughed. "No." He took the bag from Jandu and searched through it. He handed Firdaus' dice to Jandu.

Jandu scowled at the dice. "What are these for? To remind me of all the terrible things that have happened?"

"They're Firdaus' dice," Keshan said. Jandu immediately looked sick at the very mention of his name. Keshan's voice softened. "They're enchanted."

Jandu narrowed his eyes. "What do you mean? They're Yashva dice?"

"It's a simple Yashva curse. He must have used them at both the dice games in Prasta, and with your brother in Afadi. He can use a spell to select the side that is rolled."

Jandu clenched them in his hands. "That bastard."

"Give them to Yudar," Keshan told him. "If there are any problems with his ascension, use them as evidence."

Jandu sighed angrily, and then pocketed the dice. He walked in stony silence for a few more minutes. When he spoke again, he kept his gaze up ahead toward his brothers.

"Thank you," he said softly.

"What for?" Keshan asked.

"For everything." Jandu sighed. "For saving me. For staying by me while I went to pieces. For finding these. For all that you've given up. Thank you."

The other untouchables around them watched with interest, and so Keshan could not give in to his desire to kiss Jandu then and there. But he did furtively squeeze his fingers once more.

"You know, when you agreed to fight beside me if there is a war, I never asked if you wanted to," Jandu said. He kept his glance up ahead at the cavalry. "After all, you are allied with Darvad. I shouldn't have assumed anything."

"Darvad will not let me fight, ally or no." Keshan held up his hand. "I'm dead to him now. I'm dead to everyone."

"That's to my advantage then," Jandu said, smiling. "Besides, we've never had a chance to try Mendraz's chariot."

"That's true," Keshan said.

"But changing your allegiances…"

"You are fighting to free me from being Jegora," Keshan interrupted. "And I'm fighting to free you from Darvad's endless obsession with seeing you dead. It's a fair trade as far as I can see."

"If you think so," Jandu said.

"I do. Now you should probably go back up to the front," Keshan said, although he feared being abandoned, forgotten, at the end of the line. The Jegora who he traveled with had been very kind and accommodating, giving him a place to sleep and sandals from a man who had only recently been killed—perhaps even one of the lives that Jandu himself had claimed on the battlefield. But they were strangers, and Keshan felt a desperate loneliness with them.

"I don't want to," Jandu said. "I'll take my place in the chariot once we enter Prasta, but until then I'll stay with you."

"People will talk."

"Let them. All that matters from this point forward is what my heart dictates. And it is very clear on the issue of you." Jandu smiled, and touched Keshan's shoulder once more, lending Keshan his strength.

Keshan blinked. He reminded himself that he once thought Jandu shallow and stupid. *And now look at him*, Keshan thought. *He's turned into my hero.*

"What?" Jandu looked at Keshan quizzically. "You're looking at me funny."

"Can you get me another one of those rolls for dinner?" Keshan asked, changing the subject.

"Anything you desire." Jandu noticed that one of the untouchables nearby stared at them openly. "What about you? You want a roll?"

"M...My lord..." the man shrank back in line, as if he could step away from Jandu's piercing gaze.

"I'll bring enough for two," Jandu whispered to Keshan.

Keshan just shook his head.

"What?" Jandu asked.

"You are not the same Jandu I fell in love with," Keshan said.

Jandu's mouth quirked up. "Is that a bad thing?"

"You are better. Wiser." Keshan squeezed Jandu's fingers softly. "And I love you more for it."

CHAPTER 45

Jandu had nearly forgotten how beautiful Prasta was.

The city opened to his eyes like a fanciful childhood memory, the low stone walls and large marble temples, and in the center of it all, the sprawling red island of the palace. The monsoon had blessed Prasta where it had ignored Afadi, and now all the trees bloomed in brilliant color, their foliage thick, their bows laden with fruit. The fragrance of blossoms filled the air, and the ground was fresh and clean with the last of the rainfall behind them.

Jandu was home.

And it was a joyous homecoming, as thousands of citizens poured into the streets to greet their long lost Crown Prince. Jandu and his brothers feared what sort of support they could expect after the dice game. But it was clear that many were still loyal to the Paran family, and now flowers and silk cloths rained down upon their procession as wild cheers chanted Yudar's name through the streets.

Yudar looked like a king once more. He was far skinnier than when he left, his hair streaked with gray, his eyes sunk, and still bruised from Baram's rage, but he stood erect and proud, smiling and waving to the crowds serenely. Their progress to the palace slowed to a crawl as Triya lords in their chariots joined the procession, allies of Yudar riding alongside him and offering their blessings.

Jandu yearned to return to the back of the line. He wondered what Keshan was doing now. He wouldn't be allowed into the palace. On Jandu's insistence, they arranged a meeting location for later that night, so that Jandu could help him find lodgings. But Keshan's absence now made the homecoming less sweet.

At the palace gates, former servants and courtiers for the Parans greeted them affectionately. Jandu smiled as men bowed before him and touched his feet. The attention flustered him. In the crowd, Jandu made out the silver hair of his Mazar, and pushed his way towards him. Mazar saw him at the same time and the two hugged.

Jandu dropped and touched Mazar's feet, emotion welling deep inside of him. "Blessings upon you, Master," he said.

Mazar looked too choked up to speak. He shook his head and lifted Jandu up.

"My dear boy! How I've missed you." They hugged once more, and then Mazar greeted Baram and Yudar. He offered the sign of peace to Suraya and she touched his feet.

Jandu followed Mazar, his brothers and Suraya through the palace. Faces he had all but forgotten appeared. He was stunned by the opulence. They passed a chair studded with rubies, a statue of pure gold, miles of silks draped casually around the airy interiors. It was obscene. Jandu realized he could have fed the entire village in Pagdesh with one foot stool from this one corridor in the palace.

Darvad and his courtiers awaited the Parans in the reception hall. Jandu steeled his expression as he looked upon his rival.

Darvad purposefully wore the crown of Marhavad and sat in the throne. "Brothers. Welcome home."

"Greetings, Darvad." Yudar brought his hands together in the sign of peace. "We are pleased to return, after having served our three years of penance."

Darvad smiled thinly. "Please, take a seat. Mazar, will you join us?"

Baram, Suraya, and Mazar joined Darvad on the dais. The room quickly filled with lords and courtiers. Jandu stood behind his brothers, leaning against the wall. They were all tired and dirty from their travels, but it was obvious that no respite would be had now that they returned. It was straight to business.

Mazar fawned over the Parans and had servants bring tea. Indarel and his sons took seats in the hall, along with the other lords of Marhavad who were in the capital. Jandu caught Abiyar's eye as he sat nervously beside his brothers. Jandu winked at him. Abiyar grinned back happily. Soon the room was filled to capacity, everyone expectant.

Mazar cleared his throat, and held out his arms to bring the room to silence.

"Great lords of Marhavad," he began, "let me welcome King Shandarvan's sons back from their penance. Their dedication to righting the wrongs of three years ago has served as a great example to the entire nation, and I look forward to a peaceful future with both Yudar and Darvad leading our country to peace and prosperity."

Darvad coughed.

Mazar looked to him, annoyed. "Yes, King?"

"We have some issues which must be addressed before we divide the kingdom." Darvad turned slightly to face Jandu. "But before we go into details, I must ask for a report from my Royal Judge."

Tarek stepped forward. He looked weary. He embraced Darvad, and Darvad offered him a seat beside him. "Are the rumors I've heard true? Was Firdaus killed by Keshan for raping Jandu?"

Jandu wanted to sink into the floor and disappear as everyone in the room looked to him. Their snickers and heated whispers rankled. When he saw Darvad smile, he realized Darvad had said it for just that purpose.

Baram stood up in fury. "Leave Jandu out of this!"

"It is true," Tarek said. He frowned at Jandu. For a moment, Jandu thought he saw sympathy in his eyes. But then Tarek turned to face Darvad once more. "Keshan assisted the Parans during their exile, and has been branded an outcaste and stripped of his Triya status."

The noise in the room grew.

Darvad frowned. "That is very unfortunate. But it is the law."

"However, no one else aided the Parans, and they have served out their three years in anonymity," Tarek added.

Darvad gave Tarek a sharp look. "That isn't for you to decide."

"The terms of the dice game stated that my family and I would spend three years in exile as penance, as set forth in the example of the great Prophet Sadeshar," Yudar interrupted. "We have done as we promised. And now we return to Prasta to fulfill the wishes of Regent Mazar, and claim our half of the kingdom." Yudar stared hard at Darvad. "As you promised."

Darvad shook his head. "I would love to honor your request, Yudar, but you broke the terms of the penance."

"No we did not." Yudar's face flushed with emotion. "We have suffered greatly, and deserve forgiveness for my sins."

"They have fulfilled the terms of the game," Mazar repeated.

Darvad smiled. He nodded to a servant who came forward and handed Darvad an arrow. The tip bent awkwardly and the fletching was stained with blood. But Jandu still recognized it as one of his own arrows. He felt suddenly sick.

"Recognize this, Jandu?" Darvad said, holding out the arrow. "It was pulled from the throat of Druv Majeo, lord of Pagdesh. He found you on the mountain, and rather than start your exile over, you murdered him."

Yudar and Baram turned and gaped at Jandu, the shock clear.

Jandu crossed his arms over his chest. "That is a lie. That arrow could have been collected anywhere, from any of the Chandamarian soldiers I killed. Or from an animal carcass."

"I saw Druv's body with my own eyes!" Darvad cried, the vein in his forehead pulsing. "You killed him!"

"It is your word against mine."

"I have witnesses!" Darvad screeched, his voice rising in his anger.

Yudar had been staring at Jandu with a look of pain on his face. He looked betrayed. Jandu thought he deserved it. But then Yudar reached into his pocket and pulled out Firdaus' dice. "Whether or not that arrow was taken from Druv does not matter. The cheating began long before Druv met his end." Yudar handed the dice to Mazar.

Mazar frowned. "What are these?"

"Enchanted Yashva dice," Yudar said calmly. "Keshan Adaru took them from Firdaus. They were used at the dice game."

Jandu was grateful his brother at least had the tact not to mention the other game they were used at.

"What nonsense!" Darvad said. "Those could be taken from anyone as well! Keshan himself may have enchanted them!"

Mazar shook his head. "So much deception. What hope has Marhavad, when its noblest sons cannot be honest?"

As the voices began to rise again, Yudar stood. "We have served three years, Darvad. I demand my half of the kingdom, as is my right."

Darvad's face was red with rage. "I will not give you Prasta!" Darvad shouted. "I will not give you anything! Not a fucking village! Do you understand me? Go back into exile!"

"No." Yudar took a deep breath. His expression was resolute. "You force my hand in this, half-brother. But as we have fulfilled our end of the agreement, it is up to you to fulfill yours. Either I am given back my half of the kingdom or we declare war."

There was a dangerous silence. The men in the room watched Darvad closely for reaction. The vein in his forehead bulged angrily.

"I will give you *nothing*." Darvad hissed.

"Then it is war," Yudar said, his voice shaking slightly now. He raised an eyebrow towards Mazar. "Master?"

Mazar had tears in his eyes, and was shaking his head. "Yudar... I swore an oath when Darvad became King to fight at his side. It is my fate!"

Jandu could no longer stay silent. "Has it ever occurred to you, oh great Master, that fate can be changed, if only strong men are willing to question it?"

"What are you saying?" Mazar asked.

"That you should follow your heart."

"My heart and my vow are on different paths." Mazar closed his eyes. "I cannot retract a holy oath. You know better than to ask me to do so."

"You'll fight me?" Jandu asked softly. "Fight us all?"

Mazar didn't answer. He covered his face with his hands.

Darvad suddenly stood. "We should set a date at the end of the monsoons. You will rally your allies, and I mine."

"Two months time, then," Yudar stated. "Astrologers will identify an auspicious day. We shall bring our forces to Terashu Field."

Darvad nodded. "Two months time, I will see you on the battlefield."

CHAPTER 46

NIGHTS WERE CHILLY IN PRASTA AND WITHOUT A VEST OR
even a harafa to keep him warm, Keshan shivered in the
darkness.

He looked east, to the section of the city where his townhouse was, warm and full of comfort. Iyestar would be there,
no doubt already into his second jug of wine. He wondered
if Iyestar would let him stay there, if the servants would hide
him.

A pair of Triya caste women passed by the alleyway Keshan
stood in, and when they saw his dejaru and his brands, they
scowled and crossed the street. Keshan withdrew deeper into
the shadows. Night time was easier for the Jegora, and Keshan
didn't worry about his shadow crossing the upper castes, but it
was still rife with potential insult that could get him killed.

The sound of a temple bell ringing out in prayer came
from nearby, and Keshan wondered if he could find other
Jegora outside, begging for food. He needed more clothing,
badly, and they could help him. But he was supposed to meet
Jandu here.

It took all of Keshan's will power not to pick at his scabs, or
focus on the filth around him, or think too much about being
locked out of the Yashva kingdom. The future had become
nightmarishly bleak for him, and the only way Keshan succeeded at his pretense of unconcern was by not thinking about
it. But now, alone for the first time in days, huddling in the
dark with no place to live and no prospects for dinner, Keshan
was smothered in self-pity.

"Hey."

Keshan turned, and restrained himself from running to embrace Jandu. The hours apart had dragged endlessly, and the fact that Keshan had no idea what was going on inside the palace rankled him.

Jandu looked tired. He carried a large pack on his back. "You're shivering."

Keshan wrapped his arms around himself. "I'm just cold. How did it go?"

Jandu gave him a hard look. "Two months, Terashu Field."

Terashu Field was the traditional battleground of the great Triya kings of old, a large, grassy field about fifteen miles from the capital and hedged in by the Ashari Forest. "I suppose it was inevitable," Keshan said.

Jandu shrugged. "What's done is done. Come on, let's find some place to sleep tonight."

Keshan offered to take some of Jandu's belongings. Jandu handed Keshan bowls of rice and fried vegetables, and another full of fruit. "These are for you."

"Did you raid the palace pantries?" Keshan asked.

"They're from my admirers," Jandu said with a smile. "I was on my way here and women kept thrusting hot meals into my arms."

"Little did they know they would be used to feed an untouchable scoundrel," Keshan said, sniffing the warm food appreciatively. "I don't suppose you brought any wine, did you?"

Jandu pointed to his pack and Keshan smiled.

Jandu started down the road and Keshan followed a step behind him. "Should we try the market district first?"

Keshan shook his head. "They barely tolerate having Chaya nearby. I'll definitely be run out. Let's go further south."

Jandu's expression hardened, but he led the way nevertheless. They walked together for over an hour, searching for lodgings. The first half a dozen places they tried greeted Jandu with obsequious obeisance and then rejected Keshan on sight, more afraid of harboring a Jegora than they were of offending a Triya. They moved even deeper into the city, to the parts where the lower castes resided, but even the Chaya would not give lodgings to a Jegora. At last they found a seedy-looking hostel on the fringe of the city. It wasn't clean or convenient, but the owner was willing to provide Keshan a room, as long as Jandu paid in advance and Keshan didn't enter through the front of the building.

Keshan's heart sank with every passing minute, but he tried to make light of his new environment. He didn't want Jandu to feel bad for him. The room was narrow and dark, with a mud floor. It was next to the building's outhouse and the smell wafted in through the small slit window near the low ceiling.

"At least the smell outside overwhelms the smell inside." Keshan held up a stone water pitcher, and noticed the pitcher was cracked.

Jandu unrolled the bed mats on the floor, and shuddered as fleas and bed lice jumped from the blankets. "This is worse than the forest."

Keshan yawned. He sat down on the mud floor, ignoring the bugs. "As long as it's soft, it will do."

Jandu unpacked his gifts. He laid out a cloth and put before Keshan a basket of fruits, bread, and cheese. He pulled two stone cups from his bag and decanted a large jug of wine. Jandu held his cup up to Keshan, a smile lighting his face. "To our success in the war."

Keshan raised his cup as well, and then quickly drained it. The wine was sweet. He closed his eyes and savored the taste in gratitude.

Keshan noticed that Jandu had bathed, and his skin had a slight red flush, suggesting that he had been drinking back at the palace as well. His short hair curled slightly at the edges from the humidity, and his clothes smelled like cardamom.

He looked stunning in the light of the butter lamp, his skin a golden hue, his eyes striking blue and bright.

A year's worth of longing flooded him, and a need to have someone touch him, treat him like he was used to. Keshan lunged, pinning Jandu to the bedroll. Jandu's wine slipped from his hand.

Jandu smirked up at him. "Feeling a little frisky, are we?"

Keshan didn't bother to answer. He kissed Jandu's throat slowly, his tongue lingering along his skin.

"Aren't you hungry?" Jandu whispered, his voice shaking. He leaned back further to expose more of his throat.

"The food isn't going anywhere," Keshan said. He held Jandu down by the shoulders and pushed his mouth forcefully on Jandu's. Keshan moved carefully, afraid of bumping Jandu's nose. But Jandu's fingers dug into his flesh, his teeth fiercely, carelessly, grazing and nipping at Keshan's face, and all gentleness fled from Keshan's mind. He wanted to claim Jandu as his own again, scrape his initials on Jandu's body.

Keshan kissed Jandu deeper. As his weight settled over Jandu, Keshan noticed Jandu suddenly squeeze his eyes shut.

Keshan paused, staring down at Jandu's face. "Jandu?" He pulled back and shifted his weight so he laid alongside Jandu, not on top of him.

Jandu opened his eyes. "It's nothing." But Keshan could see fear there, lurking in his expression.

Keshan cursed his own selfishness, and slid further away from his lover. "We don't have to do this."

"I want to." Jandu took a deep breath and reached for Keshan again. Keshan kissed him more tenderly this time, letting his tongue play loosely along Jandu's mouth, caressing his lips. Keshan could feel the tension in Jandu's grasp, but the sensation of Jandu's heated skin against his own was too good, he couldn't stop. He laid down on Jandu to feel every part of his body, and thrust his erection into Jandu's thigh.

Jandu bolted upright.

"I'm sorry!" Keshan froze.

"I—"

"It's my fault, Jandu. I'm sorry." Keshan crawled off the bed roll.

Jandu threw himself back down on the bed and draped an arm over his eyes. Keshan shook with unspent sexual desire. That bastard Firdaus was ruining their lives even from beyond the grave. Jandu slammed his fist against the bedroom wall.

"We're going too fast," Keshan said. "We have time. Besides, I'm hungry." He smiled weakly.

A small band of light from the fires of an open kitchen across the street filtered through the slit near the ceiling. The two butter lamps in the room flickered unevenly and filled the corners with foreboding shadows. Jandu rose and pulled linens from his pack. He covered Keshan's bedroll with his own sheets. Keshan watched him, a smile on his face.

"I didn't know you knew how to make a bed."

"I had to as Janali." Jandu smoothed out the finely woven cotton with the palm of his hand. "My roommate Rani showed me how after she saw what a mess I made of my first attempt."

"Do you think she ever suspected the truth about you?" Keshan scraped the bottom of the clay bowl greedily. He moved on to the basket of fruits.

Jandu shook his head. "No. I wasn't a good woman, but I was consistent. I think that's all that mattered." Jandu sat down on the freshly made bed. "I tried to see her before we left, but she wouldn't talk to me. Maybe she's embarrassed that I saw her naked." Jandu shrugged. "I'll send her a letter. I don't want Rani thinking I'm her enemy."

Keshan's fingers were sticky with mango juice. He dampened a cloth and wiped his hands carefully.

Jandu smiled at him sweetly. "Keshan, how can you be so fastidious when you're sleeping in this shit hole?"

Keshan laughed, but continued with his ritualistic cleansing. He could see Jandu's eyes take on his piercing gaze of arousal. Keshan sat beside Jandu on the bed.

Jandu leaned in, holding Keshan's head in his hands. "Help me erase the bad memories with good ones." He kissed Keshan, pushing his tongue into Keshan's mouth.

Keshan relaxed in Jandu's embrace. Jandu moved slowly, gently lowering Keshan onto the bed. Keshan's body absorbed Jandu's heat. He worried when the first stirrings of his arousal rubbed against Jandu's thigh, but Jandu didn't seem to mind as much when he was on top. Jandu ground his hips down to meet Keshan's, and Keshan's entire body slackened, melting back into the sheets. Keshan opened his lips wider.

Jandu kissed him again, and Keshan tasted Jandu's hot mouth, hoping the warmth of his own desire could thaw the chills that had racked Jandu's body at their first embrace. Jandu fumbled with Keshan's waist sash, and then slid his hands around to Keshan's backside to pull down his dejaru.

Jandu placed feather-light kisses down Keshan's torso, and Keshan moaned. Every brush of Jandu's skin against Keshan's caused shivers of pleasure. It had been so long since he had luxuriated in the smell and taste of Jandu's flesh, so long since he was able to witness how his own touch made Jandu shake with anticipation. Jandu's body had perfected into manhood after his transformation, each muscle defined, tense with unspent power, his skin flush with desire.

Jandu gently traced the outer edge of Keshan's nipples with his thumbs, and Keshan arched up to meet him, moaning with the delicious contact.

Keshan's hands groped at Jandu's dejaru. Jandu quickly undressed, and then straddled Keshan, their shafts alongside each other. Keshan saw the pulse of Jandu's heart beating wildly in his chest.

Keshan took a deep breath, smelling and taking in the sight of Jandu's body, his mind lingering on the erotic curve of his cock, the firmness of his thighs, the small slopes of Jandu's hip bones, the tautness of his chest.

Jandu leaned down and brushed his face along Keshan's cock. Arousal rushed through Keshan's senses like liquid fire. His cock twitched towards Jandu. Jandu pulled him into his mouth.

It was that simple, really. He realized that, regardless of Firdaus' crimes, this was the two of them. Nothing aggressive could live in the soft embrace of these caresses. Jandu swallowed Keshan into the back of his throat. Keshan moaned like he was slowly dying. Jandu's hand flirted along Keshan's backside, gently kneading his muscles, slipping a finger inside.

Keshan reached blindly towards his saddlebag on the floor, and extracted the small jar of rose oil that they had used years ago. Keshan handed it to him breathlessly.

Jandu opened the jar and looked inside. "There's less here than I remember." He smirked down at Keshan.

Keshan laughed. "Oh, shut up. It hasn't been used since you left Tiwari."

Jandu held the jar up to the candlelight and squinted one eye to examine the volume more closely. Keshan poked at Jandu's ribs impatiently.

"Come on, come on," Keshan said. "Don't stop now."

Jandu dipped his fingers in the oil and circled a finger inside Keshan, moving slowly, and then with more urgency as Keshan bucked against him. Keshan wanted to return this favor, get his hands on Jandu and please him, but Jandu resisted his touches. Keshan realized that Jandu needed to be in control of this moment, reinstate his dominance, and this was more important than Keshan's own desires to stake claim to him. Keshan's vision blurred as tremors shook his body.

Keshan shifted to roll over, but Jandu stopped him, holding Keshan down on the bed by gently pressing his shoulders. "No," Jandu whispered. "I want to see your face."

Jandu lifted Keshan's legs onto his shoulders. He stared at Keshan intensely. "All right?"

Keshan nodded, anticipation fluttering through him.

Jandu opened Keshan wider and then slowly, carefully, pushed the tip of his cock inside of him.

Keshan gasped. Jandu immediately froze, a look of concern on his face.

"Does it hurt?"

"No! God no… do it some more," Keshan whispered. He put his hands under him to tilt himself higher, to take more of Jandu into him.

Jandu grabbed the small pillow from the bed and put it under Keshan to open him wider. He sank deeper, moving slowly, watching Keshan's face carefully.

Keshan's body stretched and tightened, filled with Jandu's thick heat. The feeling was so good Keshan thought he would ignite from pleasure. Jandu stretched his body along Keshan's, his body trembling, his breathing rapid, desire flushed across his face.

Jandu moved rhythmically within Keshan, and Keshan's body constricted around him, clenching tight. Jandu buried his nose in Keshan's hair, and began to make the small, inarticulate whimpers that Keshan longed to hear. Jandu sank deeper, and Keshan's cock rubbed tightly between their stomachs, engorged with the pressure.

Jandu thrust powerfully now, matching the thrusts with kisses, his tongue deep inside Keshan's mouth, and it was all Keshan could do to hold back the mounting orgasm flushing through his body. He wanted to extend this feeling forever. He had waited a long time for this. He had suffered for this. This was everything to him now.

Keshan's fingers dug into Jandu's back. He came in an explosive gasp, his eyes closed, his whole body tensing, clenching down on Jandu. The warmth of his orgasm poured between their bellies.

Jandu reached down to push Keshan's legs further apart and then thrust impossibly deep into him, until he came in one long, sweet moment, his body arching with ecstasy. He lay on Keshan, eyes closed, and stayed inside of his lover.

They held each other silently, panting, and the rest of the world seemed to grow silent. The noises of the street disappeared, all of the bird calls died, the neighbors moved away, the flies landed. Even the smells faded. The only world left was theirs, their chests rising and falling in the aftermath of their romance. Jandu slowly slipped from inside of Keshan, and rolled onto his back.

Keshan rose and used a cloth to clean Jandu and himself. He shook out his dejaru, wishing it were cleaner. He ran his hands through his hair to bring it to order, wincing as the motion caused a shock of pain on the backs of his hands.

Jandu sighed and stood as well, returning once more to his pile of supplies. As he walked across the room naked, Keshan admired his tight backside, the loose hang of his genitals.

Jandu tied his dark green dejaru loose, like a long skirt. He wrapped a green and gold sash around his waist, and pulled on a white silk vest. He strapped on his sandals and then smiled shyly at Keshan. Jandu looked so beautiful, strong and sleek.

Once Jandu was fully dressed, he reached back into his sack and pulled out a black cotton shirt. It was long and looked like it belonged to a Marshavi tradesman. The fringe frayed slightly, but it otherwise looked and smelled clean.

Jandu handed it to Keshan.

"I can't wear that if it isn't from a dead body," Keshan said.

"So tell people it's from a dead body. People won't really notice unless it looks nice, and this looks old." Jandu raised an eyebrow at him. "Don't tell me after a lifetime of lying you have suddenly chosen a path of honesty?"

Keshan pulled it on, relieved by its cleanliness and the warmth. It had been weeks since the top of his body was covered; he hadn't realized how vulnerable he had felt since he had been stripped back in Afadi.

"Thank you. For everything," Keshan added. "For the food, the clothing… bringing clean sheets, for God's sake." Keshan looked down at his tunic. "I don't know what I would do without you."

Jandu hugged him. "You're suffering this because of me. But I swear I will fix this. I will make it right for you once more." He tenderly stroked Keshan's face.

"I have to go see Iyestar." Keshan steadied his resolve. "I have to tell him what happened."

"Do you want me to come with you?" Jandu asked.

Keshan shook his head. "I think this will be less horrible if it's just my brother and I." He pulled from Jandu's embrace.

"What do you think he's going to do?"

"I don't know." Keshan took a deep breath, and then opened the door.

"Be careful. I'll be here when you return."

"I'll be back soon." Keshan hesitated in the doorway. In here, despite the gloomy atmosphere and smell, he was safe. Outside, he was hated once more. But waiting would not make Iyestar any less angry.

Keshan slipped outside, and made his way home.

◆◆◆

The news of impending war already passed from house to house, and as Keshan walked down his old street, he saw more neighbors than usual outside, discussing the impending battle with their fellow lords.

Keshan cursed his own popularity. As he slunk from shadow to shadow, he tried to go unnoticed, but his face was too recognizable, and too many lords and ladies caught sight of him and whispered.

At the Adaru townhouse, activity filled the brick courtyard. Chezek was there, obviously just back from some task for Keshan's brother. He lounged against the chariot, chewing betel leaves, and barking orders to the stable hands. When he turned and saw Keshan at the gate, his face broke into a smile and he ran to open the gate for Keshan.

"My lord! Welcome home!" Chezek leaned down to touch Keshan's feet.

He quickly stepped back, so Chezek would not touch him.

Chezek straightened, looking hurt. "My lord?"

Keshan straightened his arms. Chezek grabbed his lantern and hovered the light over the backs of Keshan hands. Even in the dim lamplight, Keshan saw Chezek pale.

"My lord! I can't believe... So it's true."

"Would you fetch my brother for me?" Keshan asked anxiously.

Chezek closed his eyes and shivered. When he looked back at Keshan, he had tears in his eyes. "I'm so sorry, my lord."

"You have to stop calling me that," Keshan said quietly. God, he was going to have to go through this painful moment a hundred times or more. "Call me Keshan. I'm not a lord anymore."

Chezek licked his lips. "Keshan." He seemed uncomfortable with the word. "I'll fetch Lord Iyestar for you."

"Thank you."

As soon as Chezek left, Keshan moved to the front of the chariot and stroked his horse's face. The horse snorted and nuzzled Keshan's palm affectionately. His other stallion bent his neck and gave Keshan big soft eyes, begging for attention.

"Oh fine, hello to you too," Keshan cooed to them. As soon as he heard the front door open, he stepped back quickly. He wasn't sure if Iyestar would forbid him from touching their animals.

Iyestar stormed out of the building, his hair wet from his ablutions, his eyes blurry with alcohol. When he saw Keshan at the gate he smiled widely.

"About time!" Iyestar scolded him, hands on his hips.

"There's going to be a war between the Parans and Darvad," Keshan said.

Iyestar stopped smiling. "So I've heard. Will you fight with Darvad?"

"No. I won't be fighting at all." Keshan took a deep breath and held his hands out for Iyestar to see them.

At first, Iyestar didn't believe it. He kept shaking his head. "This is one of your sick jokes."

"I wish it was."

"It's impossible!" Iyestar suddenly exploded. "Keshan! You fucking idiot! What have you done?"

The stable hands all froze in place, watching the confrontation.

"I think we should discuss this somewhere more private," Keshan said quietly.

Iyestar stormed towards the house. Keshan reached out to touch him, and then stopped.

"Wait, Iyestar." Keshan sighed in annoyance. "I can't go in there."

"Damn you! God damn you!" Iyestar had tears in his eyes. He raised his fist as if to strike Keshan, thought twice about it, and instead reached down and took off his sandal. He threw it at Keshan's head. It glanced off of Keshan's arm. "You fucking idiot!"

Keshan made his way back behind the stables. It was one of the few places where the Jegora were allowed to come and go freely. Several other Jegora were there working and they cowered as Keshan rounded the corner. Iyestar followed him, cursing the entire time, and then finally took off his other shoe and hurled it at Keshan.

Keshan leaned against the wall behind the stable and slid to a crouch on the ground.

Iyestar looked around, broke a low branch off the nearby banyan, and swung it at Keshan. Keshan blocked the blow, but Iyestar was fast at hand-to-hand combat, and whacked Keshan a second time in the face.

"Are you done?" Keshan snapped at him.

"No!" Iyestar was crying now. He beat at Keshan. Keshan huddled into a ball and curled his arms around himself protectively. "You are such a bastard! What are we going to do now? What are we going to do?" Iyestar's voice broke with a sob. He dropped the branch and went to pieces, collapsing to the ground and sobbing into his hands. Keshan watched him cry, his body stinging from his brother's blows.

Iyestar's performance attracted all of the nearby servants. "Go away!" Keshan hissed at them. They scattered immediately, leaving the back entrance to the two brothers alone.

Iyestar's whole body shook. Keshan wanted to hug him. But he couldn't. The fact that Iyestar was actually abiding the rules of his brother's casteless state knifed through him. He had hoped for more loyalty. He had hoped Iyestar would embrace him and offer him his old room back. It was the ultimate irony, Keshan thought, that of all people, only Jandu ignored Keshan's brands.

Everything was over for him. He knew it was vain to care about how people thought of him, but that was just the way he was. And now the people whose respect he wanted the most were staring at him like he was trash. It was too much to see. Keshan lowered his gaze to the ground, grateful that his hair hung over his face, obscuring it from sight.

Iyestar finally wiped his eyes and stared at Keshan. "I'd heard rumors, but I truly thought it was some joke of yours. Tell me what happened."

Keshan explained about Firdaus, Jandu, and the curse. Iyestar seemed to calm down slightly as Keshan finished the story.

"Jandu has asked me to be his charioteer in the war, and I accepted. Until then, I will live in rented lodgings," Keshan said. "If Yudar becomes king, he will elevate me to Triya once more."

Iyestar's eyes were red. "If there's a war, I have to fight on Darvad's side. I'm his ally."

"I know."

"We'll be fighting on opposite sides."

"I know." Keshan swallowed.

Iyestar shook his head. "I can't believe Darvad let this happen. He can change you back right now. I'll beg him to change you back."

"It won't matter what you say. It was part of his conditions, he has to stand by them." Keshan sighed.

"So you would fight for that bastard Yudar?" Iyestar asked.

"No." Keshan needed his brother to understand. "I would fight for Jandu."

"And what of your mission, Keshan?" Iyestar sneered. "I thought that was all that mattered! Our entire life, you have risked everything for your cause. You have driven us all mad with your singular purpose. And now you have forgotten everything? You will go and fight for a man who opposes the very equality you have fought so hard for?"

"My powers are gone," Keshan said. "I can do little now, in the state I am in. Everything is gone. All I have left is Jandu."

Iyestar grimaced. "And what about us? Ajani, and mother and I? Your family?"

"Will you let me inside?" Keshan asked.

Iyestar closed his eyes. "Don't ask me to do that."

"Will you?" Keshan's fear and sadness gave way to his sense of betrayal. "I am still your brother, am I not? Will you open your door to an untouchable, and let the world see that the Tiwari household continues to love his noble son?"

"We'll be ostracized," Iyestar said quietly. "We'll be disgraced."

Keshan's heart felt pulverized. "So it doesn't matter, does it? I'm dead to you anyway."

Iyestar shook his head. He wiped his eyes once more and then motioned towards Keshan's brands. "I hope Jandu is worth it."

Keshan nodded. "He is."

CHAPTER 47

TAREK AWOKE TO WARMTH.

The smell of almonds, warm hair, sun-burned flesh. Dark and musky smells, masculine smells. Tarek looked at Anant's sleeping face, and something light and joyful ignited in his heart. It wasn't fire—this was not like his all-consuming, bone-shattering passion for Darvad—this was weaker, quieter. It didn't glow, but it was present, persistent, safe.

It was enough.

Since Tarek's return to Prasta, he had spent most of his time working with Darvad to prepare Darvad's allies for the impending war. But the little time he had to himself, he saved for Anant. There had been no need for apologies with him, no need to prove his worth. Even when Tarek did something as disgraceful as brand a friend for acting honorably, Anant forgave him. Anant accepted Tarek wholly. Knowing that someone loved him, unconditionally and truthfully, gave Tarek the strength he needed to sit through the countless meetings and strategy sessions with Darvad and his commanders.

Of the eleven states of Marhavad, six would fight in support of King Darvad. Only five states allied with the Parans, giving Darvad the advantage, especially since some of the Paran allies had little or no military experience at all.

Priests in Prasta identified an auspicious date to begin the war. As if knowing that time was short, the monsoon finally arrived. The skies burst and rains drenched the north of Marhavad with endless torrents of fresh water. Streets turned into rivers. Splashes of mud appeared in the driest of places. The world seemed to weep for the fates of the 100,000 men who would fight and die to decide, once and for all, the king of Marhavad.

The numbers overwhelmed Tarek. There had never been a war this large in all of Marhavad's history. Even Tarek's warrior's blood chilled at the thought of so many men, in such a small arena of combat.

Tarek had tried to impart upon Darvad the importance of changing those last few laws regarding caste, now, before the war. With the laws as they currently stood, the Suya and Chaya would only be able to fight men of their own castes. But the Triya would have uncontrolled reign to slaughter the lower-caste men at will. It was as tradition as old as the Triya. But after Tarek's own humiliation with Lord Sahdin, when he stood practically defenseless before the man's attacks, his will to change the law was paramount.

Darvad nodded and agreed that the rules should be changed for the war, but when it came down to actually making it into law, Darvad never had time. No matter how hard Tarek pressed him, Darvad found other preparations to take precedence. Not for the first time, Tarek thought of Keshan Adaru, and how he used to hound Darvad. The thought made Tarek try harder. He had to pass these laws, if only to help assuage his guilt over ruining Keshan's life.

As the first harvests came after the swelling monsoon, Tarek refocused his energies into organizing the Dragewan soldiers to assist with the harvest. Even he took part, traveling to Dragewan to confirm enough food could be collected to feed the massive beast that was becoming Darvad's army. Grains and hay were loaded onto hundreds of carts to be taken to the battlefield. Horses began their journey to Terashu early, to set an easy pace that would not exhaust the animals before the battle had begun. The armory worked day and night forging shields, swords, and helmets.

And in the evenings, after an exhausting, endless routine of tense preparation, Tarek would return to find Anant waiting for him, eager, eyes wide and bright, ready to take Tarek's mind off the future, and what predicaments awaited within it.

Now, on the morning of his departure, Tarek roused to the smells and sights of his lover, and found that he was pleased with his decision. Anant had been the right choice. Anant did not instill in Tarek the kind of dangerous obsession Darvad did, but Anant reciprocated. He understood.

Tarek rarely had the luxury of addressing his morning desires. But now he could. He reached his hands down, under the sheets, and watched Anant wake up slowly, his eyes shooting open in surprise when Anant realized what Tarek was doing.

They smiled at each other. Quiet, safe, sweetness.

Tarek rolled Anant over, stroked his back tenderly, his powerful thighs, the musky darkness between. Tarek started their lovemaking tenderly enough, but he was always consumed with a desire to ravish Anant by the end of it, take him forcefully, almost violently. There was something about Anant's passivity that brought brutish desire to the forefront of Tarek's mind. He bit at Anant's skin, his hands groping him fiercely in the morning light, and Anant became still, his eyes dilated, his own member heavy and demanding attention.

Tarek tried to remember the delicacy of Keshan and Jandu's secret kiss. The sweetness of their embrace. But when his hands touched Anant's flesh, his senses enflamed, and tenderness fled from his mind. He forced himself upon Anant, taking what he needed greedily, slamming his body into Anant as Anant responded with utter acquiescence. When Tarek came, he flushed with immediate guilt, and sought to pacify his lover by gently returning the favor.

But Anant's eyes burned with a fiery, injured intensity, and Anant pushed himself into Tarek's mouth savagely, encouraging Tarek to continue with his frenzied assault. Anant liked it rough. He wanted Tarek to treat him wildly. Tarek's fingers clawed into Anant's thighs, he used teeth, he attacked Anant with all of his fury until Anant wept and cried out and came at the same time, his whole body shuddering.

Tarek panted, ashamed at what he had done to such a quiet, beautiful morning.

But, amazingly, Anant reached down and gathered Tarek up into a tender embrace. Tarek almost wept for joy. That he could be so brutish, and get such love and understanding in return—it was more than he had ever dreamed of. Anant accepted him, in all his berserk misery. Anant understood him. This potent embrace was the greatest gift Tarek had ever received, and that included his title, his Triya caste from Darvad. Nothing had made Tarek feel so safe, so wanted.

"I'm not lonely," Tarek said to himself, amazed with the realization. Like the slow easing of a chronic pain, his mind was whole. Tarek laughed and held Anant to him.

Anant wore a puzzled grin. "You have me, my lord," he said finally.

"Tarek."

Anant blushed. "Tarek." He kissed Tarek's neck slowly, his tongue gently darting out to touch Tarek's skin. Even though he had just finished, Tarek felt his body stir once more. "Tarek," Anant whispered, as if testing out the word, his lips traveling downwards, his tongue quick and searching, and Tarek closed his eyes and listened to Anant whisper his name as he kissed Tarek in places he never imagined to be kissed, as he showed a gentle trust and openness that Tarek had only dreamed of.

"Any man who kisses me there gets to call me Tarek," Tarek said, smiling. Anant snickered.

"That's the first funny thing I've ever heard you say," Anant told him. He grinned seductively and leaned down to continue his kiss.

Tarek smiled to himself, proud to have been funny for once. Life was so sweet and sexy and hilarious and comforting and beautiful, in the arms of this man. He laughed himself, and opened his body up to his lover, and realized, that no matter what happened from this point forward, with the war or with Dragewan or with Darvad, Tarek had, at the very least, this one perfect, happy moment.

CHAPTER 48

KESHAN CARRIED A BUCKET OF WASTE FROM THE KARVAZI Bazaar outhouse into a waiting cart, to be hauled away by Tamarus Arundan's son Lazro. He kept his grip on the bucket's handle light but firm. He didn't want to drop it in the crush of busy people. He slopped the filth into the stinking cart and turned to go for another. He dodged shoppers and the other Jegora who also worked this job. That he had adapted to his job surprised him. He'd never thought the stench of human feces would ever be bearable.

Of course, the knowledge that he would only be hauling shit for a very short time helped his attitude. The battle for the throne of Marhavad was only a week away and after that he would be a Triya or he would be dead. It was a comfort that he was lucky to have. His fellow Jegora had nothing but a lifetime of such drudgery to look forward to.

Lazro looked over his shoulder as Keshan banged his bucket on the edge of the cart to knock a recalcitrant lump free.

"Don't you know some magic that will make outhouses clean themselves?" he asked.

"I prefer not to use shartas unless I have to," Keshan replied. Only Jandu and Iyestar knew about Firdaus' curse, and Keshan preferred to keep it that way, knowing that fear of his Yashva powers kept him safe.

Lazro owned the cart and was popularly known in the impoverished district of Prasta as the "vanishing man." He made things disappear, whether broken axles, burned coal, or excrement. Jegora from all over the city adored him, because he owned his own mule, dumped their refuse, and treated them decently.

Keshan liked Lazro because he was a prolific conversationalist, and a young man fascinated with the world outside his own Chaya caste. As Keshan struggled with the other three Jegora responsible for keeping the outhouse clean, Lazro leaned against his cart and chatted with Keshan, seemingly undisturbed by the stench, the filth, or their untouchable status, as long as they never physically touched him.

"Are you really going to be Jandu Paran's charioteer and fight King Darvad?" Lazro asked him.

"I'll be charioteer, but it's against the rules of war for me to fight Darvad."

"So what happens if two Chaya meet on the battlefield?" Lazro asked.

Keshan dumped another bucket into the cart and wiped his brow.

"All the rules are established in the Book of Taivo," Keshan told him. He smirked. "Didn't your father make you read them?"

Lazro scuffed his bare foot on the ground. "I don't read much."

"I'm surprised he didn't read them to you, then." Keshan picked up his bucket. "Your father has a love of reading long passages to anyone in his company for longer than five minutes."

Lazro laughed. Keshan smiled back, and then turned once more to make the trek through the alleyway to the back of the public market.

The main streets swarmed with shoppers. With the battle to begin in less than a month, people desperately purchased essentials in fear that the war would lead to shortages. Keshan remained out of sight of the Chaya and Suya caste citizens, sticking to the narrow alley with the rest of the Jegora as he completed his filthy task.

At the outhouses, an older man handed Keshan two more buckets. Keshan nodded and then trekked back once more to Lazro's cart.

"But I don't understand how Chaya are supposed to fight if they can't fight the warriors." Lazro picked up the discussion as if Keshan had never left. He liked Lazro's conversational style. Lengthy pauses meant nothing to him.

"According to the rules, no Chaya warrior can fight against a Suya or a Triya, which means they will be relegated to foot soldiers," Keshan explained. "They can fight other Chaya foot soldiers only."

"But a Triya can fire upon them?" Lazro asked.

"Yes." Keshan dumped his buckets. "The Triya can shoot you with arrows, and cut you down with swords, or club you with maces. And you can do nothing to them, on pain of death."

"But that's madness!" Lazro spat the betel leaf he was chewing on the ground. "Why even have Chaya and Suya soldiers?"

"To create larger forces, and to provide physical barriers against the other Triya."

"So Chaya and Suya are just human shields."

"Essentially. It's just a reinforcement of the same pecking order you've always known, Lazro." Keshan looked at his hands, and shivered in revulsion. Even though he had been meticulously careful about not sloshing the contents of his buckets, a trickle of sticky urine dribbled down his palm. He crouched and scrubbed it off in the dust at his feet.

"You're too fastidious to be good at being a Jegora," Lazro teased him. "Or even a Chaya."

"I've improved greatly over the last month." Keshan smiled mirthlessly.

"But this war could change everything, couldn't it?" Lazro asked.

"Yes." Keshan retrieved his buckets and headed back to the latrines.

Lazro's curiosity bothered him. As he made several round trips to the cart, Keshan realized that Lazro must be considering joining the battle. He would have to talk him out of it.

Most of the lower caste soldiers were conscripts, forced into service by the lords of their state as part of their servitude. But the Chaya and Suya of Prasta were exempt, as they served no lord other than the king. It was one of the few benefits for the lower castes living in the crowded capital.

By the time dusk approached, Keshan was exhausted, both with his job and with Lazro's conversation. He never thought he'd grow tired of explaining things to anyone, but the last month had been hard on him, and he was a different person now. Bitterness crept into his soul, only amplified by the suspicion that, despite everything he told Lazro this day, the boy would probably join the soldiers anyway. There was glory to be had in war, and enough money to last a poor Chaya a lifetime. If he survived, Lazro could look forward to more respect in his community, and enough wealth to support his father and all of his sisters.

But the risk was monumental, and Keshan feared for him. He worried what Tamarus would do, if his only son went to war. Tamarus' wife had died a few months after Keshan last saw her, and now his old friend lived alone, supported only by Lazro and his garbage-hauling business.

"Do you want a ride home with me?" Lazro asked Keshan. Keshan used the precious gourd of water he had with him to wash his hands. He looked at the heaping wet refuse in the back of Lazro's cart and grimaced.

"After I dump this, of course!" Lazro laughed.

Keshan smiled. "No, but thank you. I'll walk."

Lazro waved and then moved to the front of his cart. He sat in the high seat and cracked his whip, forcing the old mule forward.

Keshan watched him go. His body ached. He stank. He couldn't wait to get back to Tamarus' house and take a bath. His friend's unexpected generosity had given Keshan the little comfort he needed to endure this month of hardship, and his friendly, light-hearted conversations had helped ease Keshan's loneliness. But what Keshan appreciated most of all about staying with Tamarus was the bath. The bath was everything to him now, now that he spent every day feeling so unclean.

Keshan mostly walked alleyways to return to Tamarus' house, but there were a few public streets that he had to cross. He slunk in the long shadows, hoping to remain as inconspicuous as possible.

A man dumped a bucket of waste water out into the street and nearly splashed Keshan. He turned to rebuke Keshan, but then saw the small blue ribbon sewn on Keshan's shirt, and quickly looked away. Keshan darted across the street, smiling to himself.

Everyone in town new what that ribbon meant.

Four weeks ago, after Keshan had been assaulted by Draya children on the street in front of Tamarus' house, Jandu had made a city-wide proclamation that anyone harming his cousin would be cut down like a dog. To assure there would be no confusion, Jandu personally stitched the symbol of his arrow onto Keshan's shirt, warning the public that Keshan was protected by the prince himself.

Keshan thought the gesture was sweet but pointless. He never imagined anyone would abide by it. And yet here was more proof that the declaration worked. People feared Jandu's wrath, and stayed as far away from Keshan as he tried to stay from them.

As Keshan headed down the muddy alley of Tamarus' house, he saw men fleeing the road rapidly, and heard whispers so frantic they echoed like shouts. He looked up and saw Jandu himself, arms crossed and glaring, as he waited outside Tamarus' door.

"Jandu!" Keshan called and hurried to him.

Jandu's mouth curled up in a smile. "There you are. I've been waiting here ten minutes. Why is the door locked?"

"Tamarus is helping a family move," Keshan said. He quickly fumbled for Tamarus' large iron key. "Sorry to keep you waiting, but I wasn't expecting you."

"I suppose if I said I was just in the neighborhood, you wouldn't believe me."

Keshan laughed. "No." The keyhole was rusted, and Keshan struggled with the lock. When he finally got the door open, he waited for Jandu to enter, but Jandu didn't follow him. Instead, he scowled at a group of Jegora across the road.

"What's wrong?" Keshan asked.

Jandu jerked his thumb towards the Jegora. "They're wearing my symbol."

Keshan swallowed. "I know. Are you angry?"

Jandu frowned. "Just puzzled." He stepped inside, and Keshan closed the door quickly.

"Once word got out that you were protecting me from assault, other Jegora began to make counterfeit symbols and wear them as well, in the hopes that they too would not be beaten." Keshan watched Jandu for a reaction.

Jandu continued to frown in silence.

"I don't think I can stop them," Keshan continued. "But if you want, I could—"

"—No." Jandu shrugged. "Let it be. If something as simple as a fake badge can keep them from harm, let them have it. No one else is doing anything to protect them. I might as well."

Keshan felt stunned. Jandu stood there in Tamarus' courtyard, as he had all those years ago, and look at him now. He was willing to let the untouchables wear his personal symbol, to keep them safe.

Keshan bathed in the courtyard, filling Tamarus' narrow iron basin with water heated from the fire. As he lathered and washed his hair, Jandu leaned against the courtyard wall, filling Keshan in on all the details of the war preparation that was taking place in the palace.

Before, Keshan had felt a great sense of loss whenever Jandu discussed politics. It was once Keshan's world, a world he was no longer part of, and he missed his old life like a phantom limb. But now, as Jandu leisurely chatted, and as Keshan bathed,

Keshan felt a soft, easy contentment he didn't think he could find in such a situation. He felt at home.

And Keshan came to the truth. He had thought that his mission was to change all of Marhavad society. But really, he only ended up changing one man.

But at moments like this, when Jandu yawned and gossiped and told rambling stories, absent-mindedly weaving strands of long grass from Tamarus' garden into some form of dinner plate, leaning against the wall and smiling at Keshan in the bath, Keshan realized, yes, it might all be all right. This one man might be enough.

CHAPTER 49

TERASHU FIELD WAS A LARGE BASIN, FLAT AND UNREMARKABLE save for the way the dry grassland sloped upwards to meet the edge of the Ashari Forest. The forest formed the western boundary of the field and curved north, following the path of the river. The northern portion of the forest remained blackened with soot, a reminder of the great fire that Jandu and Keshan had started years ago for Mendraz. But even in three short years, vegetation sprang forth from the ashes, and saplings burst from the forest floor, lining the edge of the battlefield.

The Uru camp claimed the northern boundary of the field. The Parans and their allies staked the south. Far to the east, the fallow grazing lands stretched out in a seemingly endless view of wildflowers and grasses. Yudar ordered a trench dug across the eastern edge of the battleground to protect the grasslands from the spread of fires any shartas might cause.

The battlefield itself burst with delphiniums, blue poppies, and dozens of other wildflowers. The blooms waved enthusiastically to the camping armies, their colors as varied as the many brilliant standards and banners of the gathered Triya noblemen.

But the machinations of men quickly thwarted the rejuvenation. Within two days the flowers were ripped from the earth, and all traces of foliage vanished, leaving a dusty bowl as teams of oxen flattened the ground and prepared the field for chariots.

In the Paran camp dirt roads were leveled, dividing the sections and creating an instant city, almost one hundred thousand people and animals gathered together to watch, participate in, and facilitate this war. Infantry, cavalry and charioted officers were housed closest to the battleground, while the edge of the camp housed the numerous kitchens, medical tents, bathhouses, storage carts, animal stables, blacksmiths, carpenters, servants, and others who now tied their fortunes to the Paran princes.

Yudar's tent marked the center of the camp, and was a large, circular structure of white wool suspended on nine poles, with a separate smaller tent attached for Yudar's private chamber. Inside, furniture from neighboring allied states and thick carpets damped down the dust. The room became the central planning office for the war. It was comfortable, despite the slightly off-putting, wet wool smell.

Jandu chose a tent near the charioteers and archers. There were five units in the Paran army. Jandu assumed he would lead one of them, and was surprised instead by Yudar's decision to appoint him general.

"You know more shartas than any man on this battlefield," Yudar said proudly. "And you have proven yourself numerous times against insurmountable odds. I want you to lead our army to victory."

Jandu's emotions had flickered at Yudar's compliments, a moment of love and gratitude breaking through the wall that Yudar's betrayals had forged.

He worried that Baram would be insulted, having been passed as second eldest for the position. But Baram had merely hugged Jandu fiercely and told him it was the wisest decision.

In his new position, Jandu was kept busy and for days he had seen little of Keshan. The Jegora part of camp was behind the latrines, and they had little access to the rest of the makeshift city. Every attempt Jandu made to visit Keshan was quickly thwarted by a not-so-subtle request from Yudar, for Jandu to oversee the archers in their practice, the distribution of provisions, or the repair of chariots. All it would take was Jandu to look to the far southeast corner of camp, and Yudar would immediately grab his arm and throw Jandu at some problem.

On the eve of battle, both Paran and Uru armies met in the middle of the field to take the oath of honorable combat.

The beat of a thousand drums vibrated the blood in Jandu's veins. Enormous energy radiated from Terashu field in sound waves. One hundred thousand men, bound by promises and fealty, gathered to swear themselves to the laws of war. Jandu scanned the crowd for a sign of Keshan, but it was impossible to spot him. There were over fifty thousand soldiers fighting for the Parans and past them, in the sea of faces, Jandu could not make out any individual.

Jandu stood beside Baram on a raised dais and watched Yudar and Darvad ceremonially greet the priest Onshu, who would officiate the battle.

Onshu made the sign of peace to both Darvad and Yudar. The priest's purple robes fluttered in the light wind. His hair was thick with red sandalwood paste.

Onshu sang a brief prayer. Yudar and Darvad closed their eyes and brought their hands together to pray. Yudar was adorned in his golden armor, his forehead smeared with holy paste, his hair oiled and slicked back under his golden helmet. Jandu stared at him, a now-familiar sensation of disgust and pride washing through him.

Jandu felt a heavy hand on his shoulder, and looked up to see Baram, smiling down at him with tears in his eyes.

"I have been waiting for this moment since the first time that bastard Firdaus rolled the dice," Baram whispered hotly. Jandu nodded in response.

Onshu finished his prayer and unrolled a large scroll. He began to recite the traditional Triya rules of war.

"Two warriors may engage in personal combat only if they carry the same weapons and they are on the same mount," Onshu said. His words echoed back to the edges of the crowd in repeated whispers.

"No warrior may kill or injure any warrior who is unarmed, unconscious, or whose back is turned away, as this is dishonorable in the eyes of God. None may raise a weapon against a warrior of higher caste than himself lest he offend God."

Jandu's eyes narrowed. The professional armies of each of their allied states were Triya, but the rest of the soldiers, almost half of them, were Suya and Chaya caste. That meant they could only fight their own equivalents on the battlefield. But they would be sitting ducks for the Triya in chariots and on horseback.

Jandu shook his head. "They'll be slaughtered."

Baram merely shrugged. "What did you expect? It's the traditional rules of war."

"Yudar should change them," Jandu stated.

"Yudar isn't going to change anything set down in the Book of Taivo," Baram told Jandu. "Besides, look at Darvad. He's the one who is supposed to be the champion of the lower castes, and he isn't challenging the rules either."

It was true. Darvad simply nodded with the ruling. Jandu noted, however, that Tarek Amia, who stood by Darvad's side, looked ready to kill Darvad. Tarek had obviously expected Darvad to treat his Suya and Chaya warriors more humanely.

"No battle may continue beyond the light of day for this is the time the Lord has allotted for war. No harm may be done to a man, ally or enemy, who comes to pay respect at the funeral pyres of the fallen," Onshu intoned. "Any man who uses a sharta to endanger the lives of civilians outside this battlefield will be put to death."

"But at least we're allowed to use them," Baram said. He slapped Jandu on the shoulder. "You know more than anyone. It will definitely be to our advantage."

"Mazar knows more than me, I assure you," Jandu whispered, looking across the dais at his weapons master.

Jandu had spoken to Mazar several times in the weeks leading up to the battle, hoping to convince his old master to fight with the Paran forces. But while Mazar did not hesitate to express his remorse at having to fight against Jandu, he refused to break the holy oath he had made to King Darvad.

At first, Jandu was hurt, but his resolve had hardened over the weeks. Keshan was right. Holy oaths and vows that made no sense, when they justified actions that went against a person's own moral standings, were pointless and dangerous. If there was one aspect of Triya culture that Jandu could change, it would be this slavish adherence to illogical oaths.

Onshu finished his litany of rules and then led Yudar and Darvad in a second prayer. As the priest blessed the two sides of the war, and prayed to God for justice, both armies joined in the prayer and the ground itself seemed to shudder with the thunderous timbre of so many voices. The drummers resumed their beat, and then the horns and conches joined in, a cacophony of battle cries and prayers and music and cheers and insults, and Jandu could feel their words in his scalp, tingling across his flesh. He spoke in unison with the soldiers, his body bombinating with excitement and adrenalin, to be here, at this moment, in history, with all these men.

Jandu's prayers grew more fervent. He added a prayer to Mendraz, king of the Yashvas, hoping the demon would favor Jandu's side of the war. Jandu knelt and supplicated himself and the men around him followed. Like a great wave, the entire Paran army prostrated itself on the battlefield, laying their heads to the ground and praying as if they all knew that this ground would also cradle their heads in death.

Onshu lit incense and poured butter onto the ground, and the ceremony concluded. Darvad and his advisors left the ceremony in one direction. Yudar touched Mazar's feet in respect, and then led his own men to the Paran camp without a glance back.

◆◆◆

That evening, in darkness, Jandu bathed and then wound his way toward the latrines. He traveled an already well-trod dirt path behind the outhouses. He carried a butter lamp, as this part of the camp did not have lamps strung along the roads.

The Jegora camp consisted of ramshackle tents made of cotton fabric. Most of the men and women slept out in the open, on thin bed rolls gathered around open fires. As Jandu searched the faces in shadow for Keshan, most of the Jegora drew back, frightened of Jandu's attention. A few who wore his blue ribbon offered him tentative, shy smiles.

"Keshan?" Jandu cried, looking upon the bleak faces around him. What used to disgust him now simply filled him with sympathy. He watched a woman wash her pan out with the one gourd of water she had, her hands clawed with age. She was beautiful once, Jandu realized, staring into her eyes. She had lovely hair, but her face was wearied with age and the elements, and she shied from Jandu's glance quickly.

"Keshan!" Jandu called again.

"I'm here." Keshan rushed to his side, looking out of breath. His hands were covered in soil and his black tunic was dirty, but his face lit with a smile when he saw Jandu.

Jandu raised an eyebrow. "Where have you been?"

"Digging." Keshan patted dirt from his tunic. "One of the oxen died. I'm helping bury him."

"I have something more important for you to do." Jandu took Keshan by the elbow and led him past the latrines, toward the soldier's section of the camp. Although many people were out, it was dark enough between the lamps that few noticed Keshan's clothing or brands.

When they reached an open area of the charioteer's section of camp, Jandu turned to Keshan.

"You still want to be my charioteer?" Jandu asked nervously.

Keshan smiled brightly. "Of course I will be."

"Can you summon Mendraz's chariot now? I'd like to have it ready for tomorrow," Jandu said.

"I don't know if it will work," Keshan said. "Since Firdaus' curse, my shartas haven't been what they used to be."

"That's why I think you should try it now, when it's quiet."

Keshan nodded. He knelt to the ground and closed his eyes. His lips moved slightly as he whispered the prayer Mendraz had taught him all those years ago in this very forest. Jandu watched anxiously. Keshan finished and nothing happened. There was a flicker of light, but that was all. Keshan tried again. Sweat beaded his forehead.

Mendraz's celestial chariot finally appeared soundlessly. Only the thump of one of the long reins against the ground made any noise. Jandu and Keshan both stared, wondering at Mendraz's magnificent vehicle.

The wood was lacquered yellow and red, and then gilded in sweeping patterns of vines, the gold trailing up the sides of the car and forming a golden banister all around the edge of the car. In the center of the chariot, a thick mast provided balance, and Tiwari's own peacock standard flapped above the yellow silk canopy stretched atop the vehicle. Even the seats were magnificent, crafted from silk and stuffed with feathers. It was the vehicle of the gods. And now it would be Jandu's in battle.

"I had forgotten how beautiful it was." Keshan admired the chariot, a soft smile on his face. Jandu stepped forward and ran his hand along the warm gold of the chariot lip.

"With you and this chariot and Zandi, we will be invincible." He turned and smiled at Keshan who grinned back.

"Not without horses we won't," Keshan replied. "Nadaru has promised you horses, yes? Let me pick out the best for you."

"All right." Jandu nodded. "I have to talk to Yudar, but I'll meet you back here within the hour."

"I'll see you then," Keshan agreed. He looked radiant with his success at summoning the chariot and when he walked away he moved with the graceful pride that had seemed lost since his branding.

Jandu threaded his way through the evening crowds of soldiers and servants. The night before the battle, the entire camp burst with revelry. Yudar distributed wine to keep morale high. Women visited their husbands and sons, and Jandu felt an overpowering affection for all these people, gathered so bravely at the edge of an abyss, risking their lives for the fate of his family. As he passed through the crowds, people bowed to him or touched his feet. Here, he was a prince again, a royal Triya, fourth in line for Marhavad's throne, and the years of servitude and starvation on the mountain seemed like they happened to another person, in another life.

Jandu reached up and touched the break in his nose. He would not let himself forget anything of the last three years. He needed that anger to fuel his strength tomorrow, on the battlefield.

Yudar's tent was guarded by soldiers loyal to the Parans for many years. Jandu couldn't remember the names of the two men who stood on duty now, but their faces were very familiar. They had protected Yudar since he had been a teenager growing up in the palace. Jandu remembered them crying when the Parans left for the forest. And now here they were once more, straight and proud at Yudar's door, and Jandu couldn't help but reach out and touch them both affectionately on the shoulders. The men looked shocked, that a Triya would do such a thing, but then they smiled and stood straighter.

"My Prince," one of the guards said. "Shall I announce you?"

"No. I'll just join the crowd." Jandu made his way into Yudar's tent.

It was filled beyond capacity. The space that had seemed too large to Jandu when they first erected the tent now looked laughably small, filled with so many commanders, advisors, sages and priests. Yudar sat in one of the gilded chairs they had brought from Afadi, and men gathered around him, talking at once and listening as Yudar issued order after order. Jandu crossed his arms over his breastplate and stood against the wall of the tent, watching his brother. Yudar responded to each person individually, as if they were the only person in attendance. Yudar made eye contact, nodded somberly, listened to sides and then made a decision without hesitation. His self-assurance and born leadership was what had brought all these people to their side in the first place. Once again, Jandu struggled with combating emotions of pride and fury.

"Prince Jandu?"

Jandu turned, and saw one of Yudar's guards eyeing him nervously. Jandu walked over to the man and leaned his head down, to hear him better in the throb of voices in the room.

"The untouchable is outside, wanting to speak with you."

Jandu's hands involuntarily clenched into fists. He excused himself and followed the guards outside. It was infuriating that Keshan had to be addressed as such. Everyone here knew who Keshan was. They knew he was a lord in his own state, a hero they all would have bragged about meeting only a few months ago. Now he was not even allowed the dignity of his own name.

At the tent entrance, Keshan stood, looking uncharacteristically nervous in the torchlight. His expression was a mixture of annoyance and shame.

"They won't let me touch the horses," he said quickly.

Jandu squeezed Keshan's shoulder, ignoring the gasps from the guards. He and Keshan marched together towards the stables.

"You found horses for us?" Jandu asked.

"I think so." Keshan scowled ahead of him. "But I can't tell much without being able to longe them, or at least see them move." Keshan ground his teeth. "It's very frustrating."

It was the first time Keshan had admitted his dissatisfaction with his new status. As they walked towards the stables, Jandu looked around for a quiet corner, but none could be found. On the eve of the battle, everyone was out and about, with friends, family, comrades-in-arms. Finally Jandu made do with a narrow, dark space between two pitched officer's tents and dragged Keshan into the shadows. He said nothing; he just hugged Keshan to him in silence.

Keshan was tense in Jandu's arms, his whole body quivering with anxiety. But within moments he seemed to melt, slumping into Jandu's embrace and resting his head on Jandu's shoulder.

As soon as Jandu felt Keshan let go of his tension, he leaned forward and kissed Keshan. It was meant to be nothing more than a brief, reassuring kiss, but a flair of heat coursed through Jandu's body as Keshan hungrily returned it, throwing his arms around Jandu's neck and pressing his body close.

"The stable hands will leave soon," Jandu whispered. "We have to pick our horses."

Keshan immediately pulled back, and shot Jandu a look of utter disappointment. "I know. I know." The two of them returned to the main road.

At the stable, Jandu used Keshan's advice to select four stallions, all of them muscular with large heads. Three of them were brothers. They were more temperamental than Jandu would have chosen for himself, but he knew that Keshan had a way with strong-willed horses and therefore didn't worry. He patted the dappled gray and almost lost his fingers for the gesture.

It was nearly midnight by the time the camp celebrations settled down. Fires were extinguished, and across the acres of tents, lamps blinked out like dying fireflies. Jandu and Keshan reviewed their own weapons, the chariot, and battle plans. They made their way back toward Yudar's tent.

The guards were still outside, but the rest of the visitors had left. Jandu stepped past the guards. They moved as if to stop Keshan from following. Jandu shot them a dangerous look and they both backed away.

Inside, Yudar still conferred with Lord Indarel, the two of them leaning over a large side-table with a map and small stones representing the units. Yudar smiled when Jandu entered the tent. But as soon as he saw Keshan, the smile slipped from his face.

"I need to speak with my brother alone," Yudar told Indarel. Indarel nodded and left quickly, avoiding looking at Keshan altogether.

Jandu moved forward, as did Keshan. Yudar scowled at Keshan. "I said, alone." Yudar grabbed Jandu's arm and led him into the small private chamber of his tent. Inside, the space was warmly lit with a dozen butter lamps and incense burned on the floor. The bed was a thick stack of mats and cotton sheets, and looked invitingly comfortable. But Yudar would not be sleeping in his bed tonight. As was tradition, Yudar and Darvad would both sleep in their chariots, at the edge of the battlefield, until their armies joined them at sunrise.

"What is he doing here?" Yudar whispered.

Jandu frowned. "Who? Keshan?"

Yudar sighed. "Jandu, he is outcaste."

Jandu squared his shoulders. "Not to me. I will not treat him as such."

"I appreciate your loyalty to our cousin," Yudar spoke carefully, choosing his words as if expecting Jandu to punch him. "And I stand by my promise to restore his caste once I'm king. But until then, I must ask you to not be seen with him in public."

"I don't particularly care what you think I should do." Jandu crossed his arms.

Yudar glared. "What do you think this war is about? How are we going to fight for and maintain the honor of our family if you are flaunting your disregard of the status of caste?"

Jandu clenched his jaw tightly to keep from saying all the curses he wanted to spew at his brother.

"You are going to ruin the reputation of the Paran household at the very moment we need to blaze as representatives of morality and tradition," Yudar continued. "You *must* keep your distance."

"Keshan is going to be my charioteer," Jandu told him.

Yudar's eyes widened. "You can't be serious."

"Of course I am." Jandu walked away from him. He angrily pushed through the cloth flap and entered the main tent.

"Jandu, wait!" Yudar followed him. "Think with your head, not with your heart!"

Baram and Suraya suddenly entered the main tent, laughing, flushed from their evening exertions. War or no war, they were enraptured with their renewed marital state. But one look at Jandu's expression had them both frozen in place.

"What's going on?" Baram demanded. He let go of Suraya's hand.

"Keshan has volunteered to be my charioteer." Jandu stood beside Keshan defiantly. "And I have accepted."

Yudar sank in his gilded chair. "That is unacceptable. The charioteers have pride, Jandu. They will be offended if we allow a Jegora to act as one of them."

"I can give Jandu an advantage no one else can." Keshan spoke so softly that Jandu could barely hear him. "I have the boon to summon the chariot of Mendraz, King of the Yashvas. And only a Yashva can drive it."

"I'm sorry, Adaru." Yudar spoke lowly, like he did when he was Royal Judge, passing an unfavorable judgment. "But we cannot sully our family's name, not now when so much hangs in the balance. We must regain the Prasta throne first. Until I am king, you are Jegora and must remain in the Jegora part of the camp. We are all grateful for the sacrifices you have made. But if you love Jandu as much as we do, you will keep your distance from him, and allow him to find an honorable charioteer."

Keshan bowed his head again. His lips had gone white. "I want nothing that will hurt Jandu or sully his name. "

Keshan moved to leave. To see Keshan accept defeat so easily sparked deep anger in Jandu. Yudar would, for the sake of honor, turn his back on a man who'd lost everything for helping their family. He grabbed Keshan by the wrist.

"You aren't going anywhere." Jandu was surprised by the calmness in his own voice. His heart hammered in his chest, but his words came out smoothly, almost dully. He looked his brother Yudar in the eye. "Keshan and I will not be separated."

"You need to leave Adaru alone!" Yudar shouted. "He will disgrace us all!"

A ringing filled Jandu's ears. "No, I will not leave him."

Yudar slammed his fist against the arm rest of his chair. "How dare you—"

"Keshan is my lover."

It was as if the world stopped spinning.

The eyes of his family turned toward him. The tent, the camp, the music and the chanting all seemed to fade. In the maddening quiet, Jandu heard the grunts of horses over twenty meters away.

"What?" Yudar stammered.

Jandu spoke without emotion, spoke as if stating the weather. "Keshan and I are lovers. We have been lovers for years. Nothing will separate us."

The terrible silence continued.

And then Baram roared. He exploded towards Keshan, grabbing him by the throat. "How dare you!"

Automatically Jandu's hand went to his sword and in one fluid motion he had the blade pressed against Baram's neck.

"—Let him go, Baram," Jandu said. "It's not his fault."

"He's corrupted you!" Baram hissed.

"It was my choice as much as his." Jandu watched revulsion wash across Baram's face.

Baram released Keshan and Keshan came to Jandu's side.

Jandu lowered his sword. Keshan, usually so self-assured, looked frightened. Jandu nodded to him. Whatever happened next, they would endure together.

Yudar had gone white at the first mention of the word "lover." Now color was coming back to his face, bright red and angry. Jandu watched the flush creep up his face, watched his eyes bulge.

"What have you done?" Yudar hissed. He stared at Jandu as if he were a stranger. "What have you done!"

"It doesn't matter what Keshan and I do in private," Jandu said. "What does matter is this war. Together, Keshan and I are the most powerful weapon in your arsenal. I need him beside me to win."

"You have been lying to me all this time?" Yudar demanded.

Keshan stepped forward. Baram and Yudar looked at him with sheer disgust. "We have never lied, Yudar. We have never spoken falsely of our friendship."

Yudar shook with rage. "There is a difference, Adaru, with saying you are friends and saying you are fucking each other!"

Silence filled the tent. Jandu was shocked by the hatred in Yudar's voice. He had never heard Yudar swear before.

"Do not pretend for one moment that you bear no stains on your conscience, Yudar," Jandu said lowly. "You gambled your family into exile. You staked me like a whore in a game of dice." Jandu felt a sudden, nauseous wave of hatred, and had to focus on Yudar's face. "Your crimes have been against *us*. Keshan and I have never hurt anyone with our relationship."

"*Relationship*? You are talking about an act that is so sinful, I cannot even speak of it." Yudar curled his lip in disgust.

"You need us to win this war," Jandu said. "If Darvad takes the throne the entire nation will suffer. And you well know that Suraya and Baram will both be killed, which means you must swallow your pride and allow us to fight for greater morals today."

"Don't you *dare* speak of morality." Yudar's voice was low and dark. "I have dedicated my *life* to morality. And the fates have seen to test my dedication and fortitude by taking the brother that I love and turning him into a faggot."

In three strides Jandu reached his brother's throne. He grabbed Yudar by the breastplate and slammed his fist into his brother's face, all reason gone, all fear and shame superceded by rage. Yudar's hands flew to Jandu's throat and he dragged Jandu down onto the ground with him. The two scuffled and kicked at each other until Baram pulled them apart.

Yudar coughed and stood shakily. The left side of his face was red and blood trickled from his nose. He wiped his hands on his dejaru, as if they were stained.

"It chills my skin to touch you," he hissed. "I swear, I will not have your depravity sully the reputation of our army."

"Without me you have no army!" Jandu struggled against Baram's grip. "Mazar's shartas will destroy them in a day!"

Yudar glared at Jandu, no love left in his eyes. "I never want to see you again," he said hoarsely. "You are banished from my sight."

At Yudar's declaration, Keshan let out a small gasp and stepped back to the edge of the tent.

Jandu stared at his brother in shock. He knew Yudar would be appalled and angry. But he never imagined his brother to be so stupid that he would throw away Jandu's fighting skills to prove his point.

Suraya suddenly knelt at Yudar's feet. "Please don't do this to him!"

"Shut up, Suraya," Yudar snapped. He rubbed at his eyes as if a great pain were lodged there.

Baram broke the silence by punching a clay statue of the prophet Tarhandi on Yudar's side table, smashing it to pieces. "Jandu! I can't believe you did this to us!"

Yudar turned away. "Get out of here. Both of you. Before I do something more drastic."

"You cannot win this war without me!" Jandu shouted.

A tremor ran down Yudar's throat. He turned and looked over to where Jandu stood, blocking Keshan from Yudar's wrath.

Yudar spoke quietly. "I would rather lose this war, my pride, and my kingdom, than ever accept the disgusting deed you have committed behind my back. You have killed us all today, Jandu. And if we lose, it is on your head, not mine. Think about that while you rut like an animal." Yudar turned and left the tent.

CHAPTER 50

JANDU STOOD STILL AS A STATUE, TOO SHOCKED TO MOVE. Suddenly, Suraya ran to him, gripping him fiercely, sobbing onto his breastplate.

"It's all right," Jandu said, rubbing her back, although he didn't know why he said it, because it wasn't true. "It's over."

Suraya's reaction seemed almost strange to him. A deep, icy coldness welled up inside him. Yudar's words were too cruel to ever be forgiven. If Jandu felt anything at all, it was almost relief, relief that Yudar could no longer break his heart, because he had no love left for his brother.

But he still loved Suraya, so he comforted her as if the insult was hers.

Baram's eyes filled with tears, but he squeezed them constantly, as if letting tears fall would be an admission to something unacceptable. Baram said nothing to Jandu, but he spat on the ground by Keshan.

"You have taken my brother from me," he growled. And then he left the tent.

Jandu wanted to go to Keshan. Keshan looked more fragile than he had ever seen him, standing by the tent flap, eyes dark with pain. Jandu disentangled Suraya's arms from around him. He wiped her face and tried to give her a reassuring smile.

"At least he didn't have us executed," Jandu said. "Not that we would have stayed around for that."

Suraya shook her head. "I can't believe you told him! I just can't believe it!" She wiped her eyes. "What will you do now?"

Jandu picked up his helmet, which had fallen off in his tussle with Yudar, and brushed off the sand. "We'll go to the forest outside the camp. I'm not leaving the battlefield, regardless of what Yudar says. If there's a way I can help from the sidelines, then I will do it."

Suraya nodded, as if making a decision herself. "Give me a few minutes. I'll pack you some provisions."

Jandu kissed the top of her head. "What would I do without you, Suraya?"

"I will speak with Baram," Suraya said. "Maybe he will see reason." She left the tent.

Jandu wanted to pull Keshan to him, but something about Keshan's expression stopped him.

"We should go quickly before word spreads," Keshan said.

Jandu nodded. It would only be a matter of time before everyone in camp knew what happened. Yudar would be required to give some explanation as to why his brother, the general of his army and fourth in line for the throne, was suddenly banished. Jandu doubted that Yudar would tell the whole truth, but he also knew Yudar well enough to know he wouldn't lie outright. So as Jandu numbly made his way towards his tent, he began to imagine what all these people would think when they saw him again. Right now, he was a respected leader of men, a hero about to begin a war for his family's honor. By tomorrow, he would be, at best, an exile shunned by his family, and at worst, a sexual deviant.

Inside Jandu's tent, he and Keshan worked quickly. They packed anything that could be eaten or that could kill. He stuffed his bedding and his clothes in a trunk. As he reached for his quiver, his hand hesitated, and he stared at the arrows inside with a sudden, absolute, sense of loss.

He wasn't going to fight tomorrow.

He wasn't going to kill Darvad, or get his revenge on Chandamar. He would have to watch his family fight Darvad, Mazar, and Tarek without him. All his expectations of sweet justice, revenge, victory, it had all, in one moment, been taken from him.

Jandu's sank to his knees. Yudar had stolen Jandu's freedom, gambled away Jandu's body, and now had robbed Jandu of his right to justice. Jandu choked on this bitter, last betrayal of a man who he had once loved.

"Jandu?"

He quickly stood back up and took a breath. He had to remain calm, for Keshan's sake.

Keshan hesitated at the flap of his tent. "Are you ready?"

Jandu nodded. The two of them silently pried loose the tent stakes and folded the large fabric, leaving the furniture inside exposed to the dust and wind. Jandu rolled up the carpets and stacked them on his trunk. The few men still awake gathered around, watching by torchlight and asking questions which neither of them answered.

It was an awkward trek, the two of them carrying their belongings through the warm, breezy darkness of the camp. Suraya met them at the western gate and lighted their way into the thick forest with a torch. Jandu picked a soft clearing in the woods near the stream for camp, and Suraya started a fire as Jandu and Keshan pitched the tent and laid down the carpets. Suraya helped them unpack bed rolls and left them a large basket of food, several lamps, and wine.

Suraya fretted over the campsite like a mother hen, smoothing down the fabric of the flap, double checking the thickness of the bed rolls, and adding more branches to the fire before finally allowing Jandu to steer her home.

"Baram will worry if you're gone too long," Jandu said, urging her through the woods back to the bright safety of the camp.

Suraya stepped carefully over the uneven surface of the dark forest. Jandu recalled the awful night she had tripped on just such a thick forest floor. The memory was like a physical pain.

At the gate, Suraya cried again. The guards watched the two of them as they embraced. Finally Jandu kissed Suraya's cheek and told her to go. He watched her small frame until it disappeared behind the tents of the infantry.

In the darkness, Jandu made his way back to Keshan.

◆◆◆

By the time Jandu returned, Keshan had finished setting up camp. He had a pot of tea on the fire, and as soon as Jandu sat on one of the logs near the flames, Keshan handed him a cup. The tea was overly sweet, one of Keshan's bad habits whenever he prepared something, but Jandu decided now was not the time to tease Keshan about his sweet tooth. Keshan sipped at his tea, and then placed the ceramic cup on the ground. He covered his face with his hands and hunched over.

"Oh, Jandu, how can you bear to be with me?"

The question was so unexpected Jandu choked on his response. He crossed his arms and stared at Keshan.

"What the hell are you talking about?"

Keshan's voice was muffled by his hands. "I've ruined you! I've destroyed your life!"

"Listen to me." Jandu crouched beside Keshan, and put his hand on Keshan's knee. "I'm fine, I'm alive. Nothing has been destroyed, other than my tolerance for Yudar's hypocrisy."

Keshan shook his head. "I thought I was here to make a difference. To change our society. It turns out I am nothing, Jandu. I'm a fool with delusions of grandeur." Keshan stood and stared at the distant lights of the Uru camp. "I had such unshakeable faith that my vision of the future would come true. And now, look at us! My brother is over there. And I cannot touch him. And here you are, living off leftovers with an untouchable lover, hiding from your own family." Keshan's expression broke, and the tears finally fell.

Keshan sat on the forest floor and sobbed into his hands. Jandu watched, unsure what comfort he could offer. There was nothing he could say that would alter the truth. They had sacrificed everything to be together.

Jandu sat beside him and let him cry. When Keshan's breathing finally slowed and his tears stopped, Jandu placed his hand on Keshan's lower back.

When Keshan didn't respond, Jandu continued. "Nothing that has happened changes the truth of your words. You told me once that it would take the death of the entire Triya class to bring about this new era. We cannot change these people. We may not have imagined the cost we would pay to fulfill your vision. But we will make it happen, I swear to you."

Keshan lifted his head from his hands, his eyes red-rimmed, his breathing ragged. "What if... What if I am wrong?"

"You're not."

"How can you know this?" Keshan cried. "How? When I don't even know myself? I've ruined your life for nothing!"

Jandu moved his hand upwards to cup the back of Keshan's neck. He forced Keshan to face him. "You're not wrong."

"Why not?" Keshan cried.

"Because... you're Keshan."

A flicker of annoyance flashed across Keshan's eyes, and Jandu felt relief. Annoyance was a great improvement over fear. It was much more like the Keshan he knew.

"I believe in you," Jandu said emphatically. "I believe you. That's all that matters."

Keshan pulled his knees up to his chest and wrapped his arms around them. Jandu left his hand on the back of Keshan's neck, massaging the tense muscles there.

"I don't feel like a man with a mission from God," Keshan said quietly. "I don't even feel like a man. I feel dead inside. Heartbroken."

"What you feel right now will pass," Jandu assured him. "It can't change who you really are."

"But if I am truly doing God's work, then why does this hurt so badly? Why couldn't I have protected you better?"

Jandu leaned forward and kissed Keshan's cold lips. "You have saved my life, and my honor," Jandu said with conviction. "You and I are destined to be together."

Keshan leaned into Jandu's shoulder. Their shadows flickered against the tree limbs. Jandu waited for Keshan to find his inspiration again.

For a moment, Jandu thought Keshan had fallen asleep. There was no sound from him, no movement. His face was buried into Jandu's neck. Jandu's arm muscles strained in such an extended position, and there was a twig or a rock cutting into his thigh, making him want to move. But he stayed there, waiting.

Finally, Keshan sniffed. "Remember when we were last in this forest?"

Jandu smiled. "That was the most exciting night of my life."

"I was a different person then." Keshan sounded sad.

"Me too." Jandu sighed. "But that doesn't change what we set out to do back then. You wanted justice. I wanted vengeance against my cousin. And here, at Terashu Field, we will have both."

Keshan looked up then. Lines of exhaustion creased his face. "I'm so sorry, Jandu. For everything."

"Don't be."

Keshan sighed. "What will we do now?"

Jandu was silent for a long time before answering.

"My whole life, I've been told to do one thing—to support my king, my brother, and I have done that." Jandu poked at the fire with a stick. "I've been through too much in the last three years to let anyone, even Yudar, stray me from my path. Yudar will be king and he will fulfill his oath to restore your caste or I will kill him myself."

A flicker of light suddenly appeared behind Keshan. Jandu jumped up, unsheathing his sword.

In silence, the ethereal glow moved closer. The light surrounded their camp, coming in from all sides, small pinpricks at first, growing larger.

For one irrational moment, Jandu thought Yudar had told the army that Jandu was an invert and they had formed a mob to kill him. But as the eerie blue light expanded, it took on the vague shape of men and women, marching towards them, surrounding their camp and standing still, as if on guard.

"What's going on?" Jandu whispered to Keshan.

Keshan stood as well. He narrowed his eyes. "Yashvas."

Suddenly, one of the lights burst into their world, so brightly that Jandu had to shield his eyes with his hand. He heard Keshan drop to his knees beside him.

"King Mendraz!" Keshan said.

Jandu dropped to his knees as well, peeking through his fingers at the demon as his glow lessened. In the human world, he was still painfully bright, especially in the heavy darkness of the forest.

"King Mendraz," Jandu mumbled, lowering his head further. "You honor us with your presence."

"Rise, Jandu and Keshan," Mendraz spoke, his voice heavy and accented, filling Jandu's ears painfully. Jandu stood once more. He helped Keshan stand beside him.

Mendraz offered them the sign of peace. "I have not forgotten your assistance, friends of the Yashva, and I am here now to honor that friendship. Our Yashva army will fight beside you in the war."

Jandu felt stunned with the honor. In a thousand years of Marhavad history, no human army had ever been supported by the demons. To have Mendraz' support now was the greatest tribute Jandu could ever have hoped for.

"My lord," Jandu said, his voice heavy with emotion. "While you have honored me greatly with your allegiance, it is my sad duty to inform you that neither Keshan nor I will not be fighting tomorrow."

Mendraz's face seemed to frown, although it was always hard to tell with him, his eyes spinning, his blue-colored flesh flickering like phosphorescence.

"What has happened?" Mendraz demanded.

Jandu bowed his head. "My lord, I have been banished from Prince Yudar's army after informing my brother that Keshan Adaru and I are lovers."

Mendraz and the rest of the body-shaped lights in the forest flickered in silence for a long, agonizing minute. Then he said, "Does he not find Keshan's Yashva blood suitable to your station as a prince? He is of very good lineage." A note of affronted Yashva pride sounded in Mendraz' voice.

Jandu sighed. "My lord, I have every intention of staying in this forest and protecting the Paran army as best I can. But I will not be able to fight with you on the battlefield."

"Then we will not be on the battlefield either," Mendraz stated. "We are allied with you, not your brother. My personal guards will stay here in the forest and protect you, and should you join the battle, they will be with you."

Keshan bowed low. "Thank you, my lord, for your support in our time of need."

Jandu wondered why the other Yashva did not materialize. They remained shrouded figures of light, hovering between the human and Yashva worlds. Jandu realized that half of them would probably be fighting in this war, against their will. Mazar's knowledge of shartas alone could call all of them into action.

Mendraz made the sign of peace once more. "Be well, brave Jandu. Come here, Keshan."

Keshan approached Mendraz, head down. Mendraz reached out and pulled Keshan into his arms. Jandu stepped back as light blazed through the Yashva's body and into Keshan's. Thunderous words crashed through the air around them as Mendraz and Keshan burned in the darkness. Jandu clamped his hands over his ears. Alarm filled Jandu.

"You are forgiven for your offence against Firdaus," Mendraz said.

And then Mendraz let go, and stepped backwards, his light fading as he shrank back into the Yashva kingdom. He joined the hundreds of other lights surrounding them. They did not disappear, however. Their camp remained washed in a bluish light as they stood guard around Jandu and Keshan's tent.

"Are you all right?" Jandu asked, gripping Keshan's shoulders.

Keshan look startled, his eyes wide. But then he smiled. "Wait a moment."

"For what?"

Keshan closed his eyes, raised his arms up, and then faded from sight. Jandu squinted in the darkness, but could only see a glimmer of light where Keshan had stood. A moment later, Keshan returned, laughing.

"I'm back!" Keshan cried.

"What do you mean?"

"I can enter the Yashva kingdom again!" Keshan laughed, and curled his arm around Jandu's waist, pulling him close.

Jandu embraced Keshan, nuzzling his sweet-smelling hair. "A celestial army! Immortal Yashva! We would have been invincible."

Keshan finally smiled, looking like the self-assured man Jandu fell in love with on his wedding day. "We still will be."

CHAPTER 51

THERE WAS NO HORIZON—ONLY AN OCEAN OF MEN.

Tarek took in the sheer size of the Paran forces. Over fifty thousand soldiers stretched in formation from one end of the battlefield to the other. Their troops clustered in the center, tapering to flanks that ended at the edge of the forest and the eastern trench. Tense, warriors shifted from foot to foot, their armor glinting as the rising sun reflected off highly polished metal. Tarek felt the army in his bones. Hundreds of glittering chariots, thousands of cavalry, and an endless array of faces, framed by gold, silver, and bronze helmets, weapons raised, ready for the first conch shell to signal the beginning of the battle.

But for all the size and grandeur of the Paran army, the Uru forces were greater. Tarek looked east at the line of Darvad's troops, awed by the magnitude of their own numbers. Behind him stood the Dragewan army, under his command and in tight formation. Seven charioted archers led each unit of infantry under Dragewan banners. Anant bowed slightly to Tarek as they made eye contact.

The night before, Mazar had assigned Tarek and his army to the right flank. Tarek would lead an offensive against the Paran left flank, and clear a path for Mazar to capture Yudar. Once Yudar was theirs, the war would be over.

Tarek turned to confirm Darvad was safely protected. He stood in his chariot, fiercely guarded on all sides by Bandari soldiers. Chandamar, under their black banners, made up the center column along with the Tiwari army, united under Mazar and his white standard. Penemar and Pagdesh took position at the left flank. Tarek had to trust they were in proper formation—the straight line of soldiers prevented a clear line of sight to the edge of the battlefield.

As the last of the soldiers, cavalry, and chariots established their positions, Tarek faced the Paran forces once more. They were too far away to make out individual faces, but Tarek could see the colored banners that separated the five units on the Paran side. The Jagu Mali troops were dead center. The left flank was made up of the Karuna army, under Suraya's father. The right flank consisted of the small armies of Jezza and Marshav, being led by Baram since Tarek had killed both their lords. And Afadi's soldiers, under Lord Indarel, protected Yudar from behind the central forces.

Tarek strained to see who led the Paran army. Last night, spies reported that Jandu had been banished for his relationship with Keshan Adaru, and would not be fighting. While spontaneous celebrations broke out across the Uru camp, and Darvad had wept for joy, Tarek felt sick and disappointed—sick that Jandu was more loyal to Keshan than Keshan's former allies, and disappointed that Tarek would not be fighting Jandu as an equal, as he had always wished.

But the loss was surely more terrible for the Paran troops, who now lacked their greatest shartic warrior. The Uru spies had been unable to discern who took Jandu's place at the head of the Paran forces. But Tarek could now see Rishak Paria's standard flying where Jandu's would have been.

The first conch shell pierced the morning silence. A tidal wave of sound surged forth as every warrior in a chariot raised their conch shells and blew. Tarek pushed his helmet low on his head, reached for his own shell, adding to the resonant whole. As the drums joined in, goose bumps jumped up on Tarek's flesh.

Tarek uttered a prayer to his bow, and then raised his arm in signal to his men.

"Forward Dragewan!"

The horses whinnied and rushed forward. Dust rose on the battlefield as hundreds of horses and chariots and men turned up the recently ploughed soil. Tarek's charioteer, Satish, whipped the horses forward. Through the dim gray cloud of dust, Tarek could barely make out the moving line of the advancing army.

The Paran foot soldiers crashed against the Uru army first. Immediately, skirmishes broke out as both forces fought to punch through the center line. Tarek blew his conch, signaling his men around the fray and into the Paran's left flank.

Enemy foot soldiers threw themselves out of the way of his chariot, and Tarek shot down anyone close to his car. His seven commanders and their cavalry stayed tight behind him. Their speed outmatched the foot soldiers, who fell back to hold an escape route for the Dragewan cavalry and chariots. Tarek blew his conch once more and shouted to Satish for more speed. The horses broke into a frenzied gallop. The chariot bounced and jerked over the ground and great plumes of dust rose in its wake.

Tarek braced his feet against the edges of his chariot as they surged upon the orange banners of the Karuna army. Arrows rained down upon Tarek's chariot canopy and clattered against his armor. Their whistles were lost under the first shrieks of horses and dying men as Tarek cut through the foot soldiers and returned a storm of arrows of his own.

He drove a wedge into the center of the Karuna flank. Through the dust and chaos he caught sight of Lord Nadaru. Tarek drew his bowstring taut, steadied his mind, and then loosed his arrow. It sang as it flew from him, and sank deep into Lord Nadaru's throat.

With Lord Nadaru dead, Tarek and his commanders savaged the Karuna army, slaughtering the commanders to a man. The clash of weapons and screams of men and beasts deafened him. Chaya infantry fell beneath Tarek's chariot; a mulch of blood, filth, and flesh caked the wheels. The Karuna cavalry splintered before Tarek's assault. Tarek's blood pounded in his ears. He led his army deeper into the enemy line. All around his chariot, bodies writhed as his own foot soldiers clashed with Karuna infantry.

Tarek caught a brief glimpse of the red banner of Yudar's chariot. A heady excitement rushed through him.

Now was Mazar's moment to charge through the gap and claim Yudar. Tarek scanned the gray horizon for Mazar's white standard.

But the general was nowhere to be seen. Something had gone wrong. None of the other Uru forces were there to take advantage of the gap Tarek had won. He and his cavalry would have to take Yudar themselves.

The sound of Mazar's conch broke Tarek's concentration. Mazar blew a short succession of notes, followed by a long wail; a call for retreat.

Mazar blew the notes again. Tarek swore under his breath and turned his own forces back to the Uru line. He looked yearningly one last time at Yudar's banner, before cutting through the remains of the Karuna defense and racing to Mazar.

When Tarek finally caught sight of his general, Mazar looked like a prophet, with his flowing white beard, his sparkling silver armor, his enormous helmet, and his blazing white chariot. He was very far from where he was supposed to have been in the morning's plans. He looked furious. He pointed across the lines of battling troops and Tarek saw why he had been recalled. A Paran banner blazed in the midst of the Uru defensive lines.

"Support Penemar's army! They're collapsing! The Parans are going to capture Darvad!"

A pure, absolute fear shot through Tarek's body. "East!" he ordered Satish.

His chariot plunged into carnage and his men followed him. They cut down any obstacle, Suya and Triya alike, without challenge or bravado. He surged into the whirling madness where the Parans had broken through the Uru's defenses in pursuit of Darvad.

Arrows fell like rain upon Tarek's car, nicking his flesh and hammering his armor. One arrow sank deep into his thigh. He swore and tore it free. Suddenly Tarek jolted forward as a Paran chariot rammed his own. Fear coursed through Tarek as he fell with the chariot. The horses screamed.

Tarek rolled to avoid being smashed by the standard mast. The ground trembled with foot beats. He scrambled to his feet. His horses screamed to be cut loose from the tipped chariot. Satish, bloody but alive, chopped through the horses' harness.

Men surged upon Tarek and he fought through the sea of soldiers. He was drenched in sweat and blood. Weariness crept to the edges of his senses but he pushed it back.

At the center of the melee Tarek saw the large, golden figure of Baram Paran. Baram was war incarnated. Penemar infantry lunged at him, only to be crushed under the weight of his mace. Even amongst the screeches of horses, Tarek could hear the revolting crack of their bones breaking beneath Baram's blows.

Baram looked up and saw Tarek, and a sneer crossed his face.

"Suya whore!" Baram cried. He leapt from his chariot car and charged Tarek.

Tarek raised his sword, blocking the blow that Baram hammered down.

The impact shattered through Tarek's arm, vibrating his joints. Tarek dodged and swung but Baram blocked his blow effortlessly. Baram looked filthy but he didn't seem to carry even half of the exhaustion that burdened Tarek.

A loose horse galloped past them but they only shifted slightly. Baram snarled in feral rage, roaring as he swung his blade at Tarek. Tarek blocked the blow again but nearly buckled beneath the force.

Suddenly thunder cracked the sky and a vibrating hum sang through the air. The world seemed to darken. And then light burst to the right of them. A storm of small, shimmering particles fell down upon them all, a fine white powder that glinted like glass, but when it touched him, nausea infiltrated his body.

Tarek hunched over and threw up explosively. The sudden sickness was so violent he nearly dropped his sword. He gagged and wiped his mouth.

To his relief, Baram, too, hunched over, gagging loudly and horribly. He desperately clung to his sword and tried to swing it at Tarek, but then he leaned over again and vomited.

Tarek tried to summon the sharta Firdaus once taught him, to fend off the effects of other magical weapons, but the nausea continued to pulse through him and was too strong for him to focus on anything else. Tarek saw that every man within one hundred paces crumpled to the ground, retching uncontrollably.

This was not a sharta Mazar had planned to use today. It had to be the Parans. Fear washed through Tarek's senses. He had to get his army to their feet, they had to hold.

The ground shook as the Paran cavalry stormed over the prone bodies of the afflicted. Within seconds, Paran troops were upon them, slaughtering the sick Uru who wallowed on the ground. Tarek forced himself to stand and gasped out to his men.

"Stand and fight!"

The Penemar once again failed to hold the line, but Tarek's own troops rallied, fighting through their sickness. And the Paran cavalry began to fall back. Tarek's stomach calmed. He turned, searching for Baram, but he was too late. Baram had taken a loose horse and escaped with the Paran troops. Tarek's victory against Baram would not come today.

But even so, Tarek took a moment to breathe deeply and feel satisfied. Despite the fact that the Parans had used a celestial weapon, the Dragewan army had defended Darvad and held the flank. The Penemar now fell in alongside Tarek's own men, killing the stragglers of the retreating Paran forces.

Tarek slipped in vomit and blood. He barely caught his balance, and only then realized how bone-weary he was.

"My lord!" Anant appeared, leaping from his chariot to Tarek's side. He steadied Tarek with a firm grip. "Let me take you to camp and see to your leg, my lord."

Tarek looked down. His right trouser leg was red from blood loss.

"I will, after I secure this breech—"

"It is secured, my lord," Anant interrupted him. Dirt caked Anant's face and armor. Tarek could only clearly see Anant's white teeth. "Commander Hadiv will ensure that our men support the Penemar infantry."

Tarek didn't have enough energy to argue. He stepped into Anant's chariot. As they made their way north, around the army to the Uru camp, Penemar's men chanted Tarek's name.

It echoed across the flank like a religious cry. Dragewan soldiers pounded their shields and shouted his name, and conch shells blew out victory to alert the rest of the Uru army that the breech had been secured.

Tarek basked in the glory. His pride felt like it would burst through his armor. He smiled and shook his fist in victory towards the men of Dragewan and blew his conch as well, a triumphant note that he knew Darvad could hear even deep in the center of the battlefield.

◆◆◆

That evening, Tarek limped from the medical camp to his own tent to change out of his blood-stained and torn clothing. His leg was numb, stitches and a liniment bandage mingling to create a stiff, tingling sensation where the arrowhead had been removed.

As Tarek made his way in the fading sunset, he watched dozens of women and medics file out of camp to stack the Uru dead for funeral pyres. The sounds of wailing already echoed through the blustery evening breeze.

Out in the forest, an eerie glow illuminated the trees and cast unnatural shadows on the ground. The same light had been seen the night before. Tarek overheard soldiers whispering that the lights were from the prophets, watching over the Urus. Others feared that the forest was inhabited by Yashvas, and they would all die for disturbing them. Spies scouting the area had found nothing other than what seemed like a ring of illumination, surrounded by foreboding darkness.

Back in his tent, Tarek changed into a loose dark dejaru and threw a yellow harafa over his shoulders. His tent flap suddenly opened and Anant walked in, beaming a smile.

Anant clearly had not been back long. His face was still blackened with dirt and dried blood, and his hair was pressed damply to his scalp, dark with sweat.

Tarek didn't care. He hooked his hand around the back of Anant's neck, kissing him with fierce joy. Anant's body responded immediately, grinding into Tarek's groin.

"You were magnificent today," Tarek said.

A smile lit Anant's face. "And you, my lord. The entire Uru army is talking about your skills. You have made Dragewan legendary."

"We would have been heroes if we had just been left to capture Yudar." Tarek shook his head. "He was in my sights! I could have had him!"

"Yes, but at what cost?" Anant smiled ruefully. "It was masterful. But we paid a heavy price for that maneuver."

Tarek frowned. "How many died?"

"Almost all of our Dragewan lower caste infantry were killed by the Karuna Triya."

Tarek's mood darkened. The only way he could bear his rage towards Darvad for not challenging the rules of battle was by not thinking about it. Now the anger bubbled to the surface, choking him with regret.

"I should have forced him," Tarek said to himself. "I should have been adamant."

"He doesn't care," Anant said, placing his hand on Tarek's arm.

"Yes, he does! Darvad wants the laws changed."

Anant narrowed his eyes. "I find that hard to believe. Otherwise he would have done it."

"He had many things to think about, he didn't have time," Tarek said. "If it is anyone's fault, it is mine. I should have pressed him."

Anant shook his head. "You'll take the blame for him for anything, won't you?"

A rush of outrage made Tarek's hands curl into fists. He breathed slowly to still his temper. "I'd do anything for him."

Anant looked pained, but he nodded. "Don't shoulder more burden than is yours, my lord."

A soldier entered the tent and announced the arrival of the king. Anant quickly stood at attention, his expression blank as Darvad entered the tent.

Tarek turned to face Darvad, who greeted him with a grand smile. When he saw Anant, Darvad's smile faded.

Anant bowed low. "Your Royal Highness."

Tarek sighed. "You can go, commander."

"Yes, my lord." Anant walked stiffly past Darvad, but at the entrance, he turned and gave Tarek a small smile before he left.

"Who is he?" Darvad asked. Uninvited, he plopped onto Tarek's bed. He looked weary, despite the fact that he hadn't fought that day, protected within his shield of Bandari soldiers.

"One of my commanders," Tarek said. He poured a glass of wine for Darvad and one for himself. "He just reported that our Suya and Chaya soldiers suffered heavy losses today. He wanted to know if the rules can be challenged."

"For God's sake. Let's not start on that again." Darvad collapsed backwards on the bed and rubbed his eyes. "I came here for a respite, not a lecture."

"But Darvad," Tarek pressed, "if we ask for the rules to change, we are at an advantage. We have more men than the Parans."

"—Stop it. Just stop it!" Darvad shouted, standing up suddenly. He looked furious. "You have become as annoying as Keshan!"

Tarek took a step back. "I apologize."

Darvad grimaced. "Once my throne is secure, I will do whatever the hell it is you want me to do. That's my promise. Do you accept it?"

"I accept."

"Perfect." Darvad smiled then, a tired smile, and Tarek wondered why it no longer mattered if he himself was happy, it only mattered that Darvad was. He sat down beside Darvad, and listened to his jokes, and ignored the churning ache of his own conscience.

It was something Tarek was getting very good at.

CHAPTER 52

In the daylight, Jandu's Yashva guardians faded, but they did not disappear.

They remained vigilant, barely perceptible as transparent shifts of light. If he concentrated, he could make out vague faces on some. Others were mere hints, existing as pockets of warped landscape.

Keshan told Jandu that their ability to appear in the human world depended on their own strengths. Some could materialize in the human world at will. Others were limited to the human world by their shartic forms alone, watching humanity pass by, summoned only by the dangerous words which would transform them into reckless energy.

On the first day of the war, Keshan left Jandu and spoke with their Yashva allies from their own kingdom. He returned with a look of triumph.

"We have almost all of the weapons here," Keshan told Jandu.

Jandu peered at their ghostly faces in interest. "Really? I always wondered what the guy who turned into the Manarisharta looked like."

Keshan laughed. "Manari is female. And, like Zandi, she looks better in her shartic form."

Jandu brimmed with curiosity about his new allies, but the battle quickly drew his attention.

Directly above their campsite, Keshan had found a thick horizontal branch on a massive banyan tree that provided a sweeping view of the battlefield while keeping them hidden from sight. They had both watched the battle unfold on day one, as Dragewan nearly took Yudar's position. Jandu sagged in relief when Tarek was forced to retreat to defend Darvad.

On the morning of the second day, Jandu awoke to find Keshan already perched in the tree, surveying the early formations of the armies as he played absentmindedly with one of Jandu's arrows. Keshan was a dexterous tree climber, moving like a monkey between the branches as it suited him. But Jandu had no natural skill. He climbed slowly, cursing under his breath as he scratched his arms on branches and struggled to keep his balance.

Jandu swung his legs over the branch to sit beside Keshan, but clung to the tree trunk for support.

"Did you eat the cheese I left you?" Keshan asked. He focused on the battlefield.

"No."

Keshan frowned, but Jandu just smiled. "I have no appetite. If I eat anything, I'm going to be sick and fall out of this hazardous perch."

Keshan grinned. "Balance is part of being a good warrior. Didn't Mazar teach you that?"

Jandu shoved Keshan playfully, but Keshan was far too comfortable sitting in tree branches to be disturbed by a little movement. He made as if to shake Jandu from the tree, but then both Jandu and he turned towards the battlefield as the first conch of the morning bellowed out.

The sight of the armies filled Jandu with longing. He wanted to be out there so badly it hurt like a physical wound.

"There's Mazar's chariot." Jandu pointed to the silver car at the center of the Uru line.

Keshan watched Jandu with a frown.

"What?" Jandu asked.

"The only way to win this war is to defeat your weapons master," Keshan said. "Jandu, he is your enemy now."

"I know." Jandu watched the white banners of Mazar's chariot flutter in the wind.

"You know it in your mind. But your love for him lingers in your heart."

"Of course it does." Jandu sighed. "The man has been like a father to me. I will always have compassion for him, even if he is now my enemy."

"You must kill your compassion," Keshan said.

Their conversation was cut off by the sudden roar of a thousand conches, blasting through the air to call the start of the day's battle.

Yudar had appointed Suraya's brother, Rishak Paria, to be the general of his army after Jandu's banishment. Although young, Rishak was an experienced warrior. Still, Jandu worried that Nadaru's death the day before would affect Rishak's judgment. No doubt Suraya was devastated by the loss of her father. But now Jandu watched his brother-in-law lead the Paran army proudly, his chariot bursting into the center of the battlefield with confident speed.

Jandu monitored the Paran flank and was relieved to see that Rishak had refortified the line to prevent a repeat of yesterday's breach. Far across the battlefield, Jandu noted that Mazar placed a majority of his cavalry to the right flank and was once again attempting to split the Paran forces into two.

As the battle progressed, Mazar's forces pushed into the Parans with a great thrust. The full strength of the Uru force charged past the forest edge to hammer into the Paran left flank. Chaya and Suya infantry fell in huge numbers. And far from the forest edge, Rishak led the Paran offensive, carving deep into the center of the Uru line.

Amongst the Paran warriors, Jandu caught sight of Afadi's banner on one of the chariots and expected to see Indarel. Instead, he spied the lanky figure of Abiyar, struggling to take aim as the vehicle jostled over the rutted field.

Horror rushed through Jandu, and it must have shown, for Keshan reached over and touched the side of his face.

"What's wrong?"

"Abiyar is out there!" Jandu couldn't believe Indarel's carelessness, allowing the boy his own chariot. The idea of someone so inexperienced amongst all the battle-hardened warriors sickened Jandu. "He's too young."

"He's a Triya warrior," Keshan said. "He would be offended to hear you speak of him this way."

"I have no doubt that one day he will grow into a great warrior," Jandu countered. "But not now. For God's sake, he's just a boy!"

"And how old were you when you first fought for Mazar?"

"Eighteen."

"Seventeen." Keshan smiled. "I remember hearing about it. What makes you think Abiyar feels differently at his age than you did?"

Jandu shook his head. "I've always been talented. But Abi needs so much work."

Keshan looked out at Abiyar's chariot and nodded. "Well, inexperienced or not, he seems to be holding his own."

Jandu watched Abiyar's chariot follow behind Rishak as they cut through the enemy flanks, heading towards Darvad. Only his anxiety for Abiyar's well-being tempered Jandu's growing excitement over the mounting successes of his army.

As more Uru cavalry galloped along the edge of the forest, Jandu realized they were in range of his arrows. Jandu wondered if he could jump down to fetch Zandi without hurting himself.

As he looked down, gauging the distance, Jandu caught one of the shimmering figures beneath him burst into light and then disappear.

"What was that?" Jandu asked.

Keshan's eyes narrowed. "More importantly, *who* was that? Someone recited a sharta."

The sky charged and wreathed. A loud crack of thunder

boomed overhead. The air surrounding Mazar caught afire and blew outwards, covering dozens of soldiers in flames. The air reeked of scorched flesh.

To Jandu's amazement, Mazar summoned the sharta again, pushing his advantage to divide the Paran line. The flames spread outwards, blackening the air and creating a wind that sucked towards the conflagration, pulling soldiers to their deaths. The air grayed with ash.

Jandu started the counter-curse, but Keshan stopped him with a hand on his arm.

"Save your strength, it's too late. He's firing another one!"

Jandu concentrated on Mazar's moving chariot, hoping to feel the sharta. Goosebumps raised on his skin. He recited the sharta backwards, the counter-curse flowing into his consciousness after years of training.

Keshan watched his fellow Yashva, and saw another disappear. "That was Tarhi. It's the Tarhisharta."

Jandu closed his eyes and focused on the words of the Tarhisharta. His mouth filled with blood. His head pulsed with pressure. He spat the final word out and watched as nothing happened on the battlefield.

"I did it!" Jandu cried happily. He spat blood.

"Jandu! Another one is coming!"

Jandu gripped the tree trunk and uttered the counter-curse again. His head ached with the effort.

He broke the sharta and immediately, the Yashva Tarhi reappeared beneath him. Tarhi looked up at Jandu and smiled. Jandu smiled in return.

"Got you back," Jandu said affectionately.

Tarhi uttered something incomprehensible in the Yashva tongue and Keshan burst into laughter.

Tarhi turned and pointed to another Yashva.

"It's Barunaz," Keshan said. Keshan closed his eyes and began uttering the Barunazsharta counter-curse.

The air felt brittle and snapped like sparks crackling from dry wood. Jandu could not stop. His guardians flickered into shartic weapons at a disheartening pace.

All day Jandu spoke with a bloody mouth, a pounding headache, and trembling muscles as he and Keshan countered every sharta that Mazar released. Jandu had never appreciated the value of such a role. Away from the chaos and threat of the battlefield he could concentrate on just the shartas and defend the Paran troops far more successfully than if he had been among them.

Beside him Keshan broke shartas quietly, his expression rapt with concentration. To anyone who didn't know him, it looked as though Keshan meditated. But the beads of sweat on his forehead and the slow trickle of blood from Keshan's nose told a different story.

Jandu passed into a trance, breaking sharta after sharta, oblivious to the world around him. At one point, he opened his eyes, and watched several Paran soldiers run underneath their tree, fleeing the battle through the forest. Loose horses charged through their camp, and later, Uru soldiers carried an injured comrade through the forest and deposited him among the leaves. Jandu's Yashva guard turned to eye the soldiers warily.

Keshan seemed oblivious to everything below them. Suspended, mouth unceasingly moving, he countered shartas until his voice grew ragged. At sunset, three shartas manifested at once. Keshan wiped blood from his nose, flicked it upon the arrow in his hands, and threw it into the air with a hoarse curse.

The world burst into light, startling the animals. Soldiers shielded their eyes. A vortex opened the sky. The wind howled, pulling the shartas away from the field as the last sliver of sun vanished. The Draya priests sounded their conches, declaring the end of the day's battle.

Jandu watched, stunned. He never knew a person could dismantle several shartas at once. But the toll was clear. Keshan leaned forward and almost pitched out of the tree. Jandu shot a hand out to steady him.

"Keshan?"

Keshan's face was white. "Need to rest."

Keshan climbed down and Jandu practically fell after him. Once on the ground he lay panting in the leaves, too tired to move. Keshan draped his arm over Jandu's chest.

Jandu fell asleep immediately. It was dark by the time they roused enough energy to wash in the river. They fell on their cold leftovers of cheese and rice like starving animals. Even after bathing and eating, Jandu's body felt stretched and weak. His chest felt bruised. He barely formed grunts in response to Keshan's questions.

As the cry of mourners permeated the darkness, and the creak of the carts loading the dead for funeral pyres rolled by their camp, Jandu and Keshan made tea and sat close together, staring at the flames and saying nothing.

Jandu heard the rustling of branches as someone approached. He recognized the three Uru men he had observed earlier that afternoon.

The glow around Jandu and Keshan's camp surged to a blazing ring, and three Yashva slipped through the barrier into the human world. These Yashva weren't beautiful like Mendraz, or Umia. They were feral things, ugly, covered in teeth and with unnaturally extended jaw lines. They had the size and bulk of Zandi, but without any of her female charm. They pounced upon the terrified Uru soldiers and gripped them by their throats.

"Wait!" Jandu jumped to his feet. He held out his hand to the demons.

The Yashvas' spinning eyes whirled rapidly in their excitement. "What shall we do with them, my lord?" one of the Yashvas asked.

The Uru men wept and writhed in the demons' grasp.

Jandu unsheathed his sword. "What do you want?" he demanded of the Uru men.

A tall, gaunt Chaya brought his shaking hands together in the sign of peace.

"Please do not kill us, Prince Jandu! We mean you no harm! We have fled the Uru army."

Keshan stood as well. He spoke in Yashva. The demons released the men and then faded back into glowing lights as the humans prostrated themselves before Jandu and Keshan.

"Forgive us!" another soldier said. His face was dark with dirt and blood. "I have a family, my lord…there is no one to care for them if I die. We heard you were here in the forest with Keshan."

Suddenly Jandu realized he was looking at Lazro, Tamarus Arundan's son. It seemed Keshan, too, had just recognized Lazro, because he started forward but Jandu held Keshan back. Such an action would be an easy way for Darvad to place spies in their camp.

Jandu frowned at Lazro, trying to radiate Triya regality. "Are you such a coward that you would desert your army? Where is your pride?"

The tall man next to Lazro lifted his head and glared. "We are not cowards!"

"Keshan, please believe me. You told me yourself about the rules of battle but I didn't understand." Lazro held his shoulder tighter and Jandu could see blood seeping out between his fingers. "Bravery is foolishness in the face of a sharta. I am an honorable man, but I am not a fool. I will return to my family in one piece. There is no honor in dying like a dog on that field and leaving my father alone."

Jandu stared down at the men with a sinking sensation in his gut. He felt ashamed for his own family's role in determining the rules of war. He resheathed his sword and brought his hands together in the sign of peace.

"Join us at the fire," he offered, making room for the men. "Lord Keshan can see to your wound, Lazro."

The men prostrated themselves low, and then approached the fire, thanking Jandu profusely. Jandu caught Keshan's eye briefly, and Keshan raised an eyebrow at him.

Jandu served the men the leftovers of their rice and tea while Keshan rummaged in their tent for his herbs.

"What are your friend's names, Lazro?" Jandu asked.

"I am Warash, Lord Jandu," the man's tall companion said.

"I am Ohendru, my lord," the third man spoke.

Jandu nodded. Keshan emerged from the tent and then sat beside Lazro. He stared at the young man's wound, but did not touch him.

Jandu watched Keshan nervously hesitate on the edge of action. He clearly waited for permission, but Lazro was obviously in too much pain to realize he needed to give it. Finally, Jandu spoke.

"If Keshan is to tend to your arm, he needs to touch you."

Lazro nodded.

"Do you understand what you are doing by allowing him to touch you? Are you willing to become tainted?"

Lazro nodded again. "My lord, I think my wound will hurt me more than Lord Keshan's tainted caste."

Jandu and Keshan both laughed. Jandu's tension subsided. He leaned back against his log as Keshan whispered shartic prayers and rubbed herbs into Lazro's wounds. Jandu asked the men about the war, about the Uru camp, and about Darvad, and they honestly responded, enthusiastically revealing details about the layout of the camp.

The three soldiers helped Jandu and Keshan wash their pots and tend to the fire, so it seemed natural for Jandu to offer them a place to stay in the camp.

"I cannot guarantee anything about the future," Jandu warned. "But as long as you are in my camp, I will protect you, deserter or no. Caste means nothing to me now, so you will be respected here for your own merits." As he said the words, Jandu couldn't help but smile. Five years ago, he would have laughed out loud if someone had predicted he would have said such a thing. Jandu went to his tent, and returned with a single blanket. He gave it to Lazro.

"You may use this blanket if you would like," he offered. He watched the soldiers carefully. "Keshan and I sleep together."

The soldiers looked at each other immediately. Lazro blanched, but then nodded his acceptance. The other two soldiers seemed to follow his lead. They busied themselves with cleaning the campsite, but didn't raise a word of objection.

"Good night," Jandu offered, letting out the breath he was holding.

"Good night, Prince," Warash responded. Lazro and Ohendru also bid them a good night.

Keshan entered the tent quietly after Jandu, lighting his way with a butter lamp. After Jandu and Keshan settled themselves under their remaining blanket, Jandu turned to Keshan, and found him grinning.

"What?" Jandu whispered.

Keshan buried his face against Jandu's shoulder to muffle his laughter.

"What's so funny?" Jandu demanded.

Keshan's eyes danced with joy. "That was a very subtle speech."

"I was testing their loyalty."

"Good decision. Testing the loyalty of enemy deserters we just met by declaring we're sexual deviants." Keshan laughed again.

"What would you have me do? Turn them away? If the Urus find them, they'll be executed. If the Parans find them, they'll become slaves. I'm willing to give them a blanket and my protection. But in exchange, they have to accept that we're together, and that you are not beneath them. That's all I ask."

Keshan kissed Jandu. His tongue flirted briefly in Jandu's mouth, and then pulled away as he grinned once more.

"Remember when I told you that the world would change?"

Jandu nodded. "Yes. I'm glad to see you are back to remembering and believing it as well."

"What you did out there, Jandu, was light the pyre on this era. The death of this age just officially begun. The Triya are over, starting with you, me, and those three frightened men."

Jandu snorted. "What a pitiful beginning to the new age."

"Wait until you see what we can become."

"I believe in you." Jandu pulled Keshan closer, relishing the heat of Keshan's body.

"Believe in us. You are the one who has begun it now."

◆◆◆

"Jandu!"

Jandu groggily awoke from his slumber. For a moment, he thought he was back in the mountains of Pagdesh again. But then he opened his eyes and saw Keshan asleep beside him, curled up in a ball and hogging all of the blanket. Jandu gently tucked a lock of hair behind Keshan's ear, and then fumbled in the darkness for his sandals.

"Jandu!"

Jandu recognized Baram's voice. He rushed out of the tent to see his massive brother struggling against half a dozen Yashva who had him pinned him to the ground. The three Uru deserters stood over Baram's prone body, spears leveled. Their loyalty warmed Jandu's heart, and calmed his nerves about this impromptu visit from his brother.

"He's all right," he assured the men. Warash and the others immediately lowered their weapons. The Yashva, however, held on.

"Jandu!" Baram cried, sounding almost frightened.

"Let him go," Jandu said in broken Yashva. He had learned that much from Keshan, at least.

The Yashva immediately released Baram, and bowed to Jandu before slipping back into their world.

Baram jumped up angrily, his expression black with rage and fear.

"What the fuck was that!" He swung his fist at the ghostly bodies, but his arm simply passed through their light.

Jandu yawned, trying to pretend that his heart wasn't hammering in his chest. "Mendraz, King of the Yashvas, has offered his allegiance to me. They are my bodyguard."

Baram's eyed widened. Jandu could see his excitement. But then Baram turned and glared at the deserters. "And who are these people?"

"My men," Jandu said.

"They look like deserters," Baram said, scowling at them.

"They're mine now." Jandu crossed his arms. "Have a seat."

He and Baram moved towards the low embers of the fire. Warash, Lazro and Ohendru watched warily.

"Would you give my brother and I five minutes alone?" Jandu asked them. The three soldiers bowed, then sidled off into the darkness.

Jandu fed branches onto the coals of the fire as Baram took a seat. Baram sniffed at the empty cup beside the log, and then tossed it aside.

"What are you eating?" Baram asked gruffly.

Jandu shook his head. Of course Baram's first question would be about food. "Rice and cheese that Suraya gave us when we left. We're almost out."

Baram didn't look at him. "Here." He stuck out his hand, in which miraculously had appeared a roll stuffed with meat and yogurt. Jandu took the roll without a word. He tore it in two and set one half aside for Keshan. Baram fed twigs into the embers of the fire and little flames leapt up. As the light increased, Jandu noticed the bandage wrapped around Baram's left bicep.

"How's Suraya?" Jandu asked.

"Mad at me," Baram said. "She called me an asshole. I guess I have you to blame for encouraging such foul language."

Jandu didn't respond.

Baram picked at the log beneath him. "She's also refusing any sexual favors until I apologize to you."

Jandu snorted. "I've been your loving brother for twenty-nine years, and you repudiate me, but Suraya refuses to sleep with you for twenty four hours, and you are suddenly contrite."

Baram smiled slightly. "Well, she's hotter than you."

Jandu sighed. "Baram, what do you want to say? It's late, and I'm tired."

Baram moved closer to him, then crushed him in a hug.

Jandu's roll leaked yogurt down the front of his cotton shirt. He was annoyed by this. And then, realizing what his brother was doing, forgave him.

"I'm sorry I shouted at you," Baram said.

Jandu leaned back and wiped the yogurt off his shirt "It's all right."

"I spoke out of shock, not out of anger," Baram said.

"It's fine."

"I love you, Jandu."

Jandu stopped wiping his chest and studied his brother's expression. He saw honest regret in Baram's eyes. Jandu hadn't considered how much Baram's rejection had hurt him, but now, seeing him genuinely penitent, affection flooded Jandu and he forgave his prior callousness. He smiled. "I love you too."

"Even if you are a big faggot."

Jandu continued to smile. "Thanks. So much."

"But you have lost all your Suraya privileges, understand?"

"I wasn't really using them, you know," Jandu replied.

Baram added extra kindling to the fire. "Suraya's pregnant again."

Jandu shook his head. "God, you two work fast. Congratulations."

Baram grinned back.

Keshan emerged from the tent, looking sleepy, with crease-lines on one cheek. Jandu couldn't help but smile.

Keshan tensed as soon as he saw Baram. "What's going on?"

"Baram is sharing his leftovers with us," Jandu said. He handed Keshan his half of the roll.

"Is it poisoned?" Keshan smirked.

Baram stiffened at Keshan's words. Baram may have made peace with Jandu, but it was obvious that it would take more time before he was ready to exchange banter with Keshan.

"I assume you two are responsible for so many of Mazar's shartas failing today," Baram said. He turned back to face Jandu, obviously ignoring Keshan's remarks.

Jandu nodded. "We tried to get them all."

"Our spies report that Mazar is furious," Baram said. "They are planning a massive assault tomorrow, using all the celestial weapons they know."

"You need to kill Mazar," Keshan stated. He stared into the fire, his expression grave. "There is only one way you will win this war, and that is by removing the general of the Uru army."

Baram shook his head. "Every time someone gets near him, he spits out a sharta. And he is well-guarded."

"Have you tried the Tunufisharta?" Keshan asked.

Baram scowled. "Only Jandu knows it."

"That's a pity." Keshan leaned back with a smirk on his face.

Jandu touched his brother's knee. "I could speak it from here but it won't do any good unless Mazar is in range."

"I could drive him close to your position," Baram said.

"He doesn't know we're still here in the forest?" Jandu asked.

Baram shrugged. "I'm not sure. The rumors are all over the place. Some soldiers believe you are fighting in the guise of another."

"If Jandu was fighting, everyone would know exactly who he was," Keshan said.

Baram threw his stick into the fire. "Look, if I can get Mazar to drive by the edge of the battlefield, can you use your sharta?"

"If he goes slowly enough," Jandu said.

"It would be better if he stopped completely," Keshan said. He continued to stare into the fire with a bemused grin on his face.

Jandu narrowed his eyes. "What do you mean?"

"If Baram can push him into the forest, I will be able to stop Mazar long enough for you to shoot him," Keshan told Jandu.

Jandu turned to his brother. "Can you do it?"

Baram thought for a moment, and then nodded. "I will get him to you tomorrow."

"Good." Keshan yawned and stretched. "Then I'm going back to bed." He smiled at Jandu, and then withdrew back into their tent.

Jandu touched his brother's arm. "Do you think you can bring us some more food tomorrow?"

Baram frowned at the tent, but when he turned to Jandu his expression softened. "Certainly."

"I need enough to provision my men," Jandu said. It felt good to say the words, to point out that he had supporters. "What will you tell Yudar?"

"As little as possible. Rishak is our general now and he's all but said he'd take you back if it weren't for Yudar." Baram nodded to himself. "Just be ready for Mazar."

"I will."

Jandu walked with Baram back to the Paran camp, feeling a reassuring burst of pleasure, striding alongside his brother once more. Two nights ago, Jandu had thought he had lost his family. Now Baram was beside him, brusquely slapping him on the shoulder. Things would never be the same between them again, Jandu knew, but now, at least there was honesty between them and it gave Jandu hope.

"Baram. Thank you." Jandu bent down and touched his brother's feet in respect. In response, Baram ruffled his hair.

"You will always be my little brother, Jandu," Baram replied with a smile. Then he turned and strode into the Paran camp.

CHAPTER 53

AT DAYBREAK, MAZAR LED HALF OF THE URU ARMY IN ONE direction, and Tarek Amia and his allied states led their troops in the other, creating a pincer around Yudar's location. Keshan watched the battle transpire, breathing deeply, preparing himself for another grueling day of battling shartas.

But he was more worried about Jandu, and whether he would actually kill Mazar.

Jandu had said little that morning, rising and completing his ablutions without a word. Jandu greeted the half a dozen new faces who had joined the other deserters in the dead of night. He spoke with them briefly, and offered them a little food and learned their names. Most were Chaya, though they came from both Paran and Uru forces. Jandu assigned them duties: building shelters, foraging for food and collecting water from the nearby stream.

Now, perched beside Keshan on the tree limb, Jandu was silent once more, Zandi held loosely in his hands.

"As soon as Mazar is within range, I will hold him," Keshan told Jandu. "I'm not sure how long I will be able to maintain the curse, so you must act fast."

"I'll be ready." Jandu showed no outward hesitation.

Keshan heard someone say his name, and looked down to see more deserters, pointing up at Jandu and Keshan with an expression of hope in their eyes. Several were burned from the previous days' shartas. Keshan knew some would die before the end of the night. But for now, they looked to Jandu to save them and to treat them with respect.

The Yashva kept constant vigil in the surrounding forest, monitoring the humans, their devotion to Jandu and Keshan unwavering.

Jandu pulled an arrow from his quiver. He nocked it into place and practiced his aim. Keshan realized he'd seen this moment in time before, in a premonition when he was still just a child and then later, time after time. But in his premonition the man's face had always been obscured, like the face of a Yashva blurred in the human world. And so he hadn't recognized it until that small motion, when the man beside him took aim.

It was him. *Jandu.* This was the moment which would change history, that Keshan had spent his entire life striving for. This was where he was meant to be. His changed world, it wouldn't have come from Darvad after all. Keshan had been wrong.

It was Jandu, all along. The savior of Marhavad sat beside him. Keshan's branding, his abandonment of the Uru side of the war, it was all intended, and now, having given up his vision, Keshan's destiny would come true after all.

Keshan had waited for this moment since he was six years old. Now, he couldn't contain the tears of gratitude and love that filled his eyes.

"What's wrong?" Jandu asked, his hard expression softening for a moment.

"Nothing," Keshan said, smiling and wiping his eyes.

Jandu glanced down at the growing crowd of deserters. "By the time the day is over, we may have more infantry than Darvad."

Keshan smiled down at the men. "One of them told me he joined us because of a rumor that you are forming a revolutionary army in the forest to challenge both armies and remove the distinction of caste from society altogether. The rumor even mentions demons on your side."

"Close enough." Jandu leaned over and kissed Keshan briefly on the lips, then surveyed his surprised troops with a smirk, issuing his own challenge. Many of the men shifted or averted their eyes, but none of them left.

Keshan turned his attention back to the battlefield before him.

The earth was dark with gore. Mazar's shartic rampage left a trail of severed heads, limbless corpses, and great spills of blood. Horses slipped on the remains of gutted humans, and trampled over charred bodies. Cratered ground, littered with corpses, marked where a minor sharta had been used to clear the path of foot soldiers. Bodies were scorched beyond recognition. Melted metal helmets and armor glittered amid the ash.

Almost worse than the carnage on the battlefield was the fact that the Triya did not pay the gruesome display any heed. Chariots rolled over limbs and men not even dead as they charged forth towards their targets, no longer bothering to steer clear of the wounded.

Unlike many of the warriors, who appeared weary from three days of battle, Baram still charged in top form. He abandoned his chariot and now galloped the battlefield on horseback. At first, his tactics confused Keshan. If he was trying to steer Mazar towards the forest, he was failing. But as noon came, Keshan saw logic in Baram's frantic movements. He turned the Paran forces perpendicular to their initial line, separating the Uru army into halves.

The noise from the field and plumes of dust wafted towards the forest, and for minutes at a time, Keshan could barely make out the shapes of men and beasts in the melee. And then, at last, as Baram galloped by the forest edge, shouting insults, Keshan caught sight of Mazar riding in pursuit.

In the afternoon sunlight, Mazar's silver armor refracted the sunlight and made him shine like a star. His silver chariot negotiated the obstacles of the field with agility and speed. Mazar's arm constantly pulled back and released an assault of arrows in a steady, even rhythm.

"Be ready," Keshan told Jandu. He stood on the branch, using the central trunk to keep his balance.

Jandu nodded. He turned his arrow anxiously in his hand.

Keshan looked down, just in time to see his brother Iyestar gallop past the forest edge. Homesickness filled Keshan. But then Mazar's white banners drew close.

Baram and his troops circled back to push Mazar's chariot into the trees. As if sensing a trap, Mazar's charioteer whipped the horses faster. They galloped ahead, leaving the rest of the Uru forces in the dust.

Keshan signaled to Hafed, the Yashva he was about to transform into a weapon. Still in the Yashva kingdom, Hafed closed his eyes, bringing his hands together in meditation.

The very moment that Mazar's chariot came within firing range of the tree, Keshan shouted the Hafedsharta and thrust his arms out, his palms facing outwards, his elbows locked.

Hafed's shining form disappeared and then reappeared as a shimmering wave of air, shooting from Keshan's palms, rolling like steam around Mazar's chariot. The shimmer expanded and swallowed the chariot.

Mazar's horses slammed into the invisible wall. They topped forward, shrieking, but stopped mid-fall, frozen.

The chariot axle broke and the car flew forward, suspended over the backs of the horses, hanging mid-air. Everyone around the chariot stared in shock.

The battle almost ceased completely around them. Warriors looked in horror at the hanging chariot. The charioteer dangled by the reins, until he let go with a cry and crashed to the ground. The horses whinnied and rolled their eyes in panic, but remained frozen.

All of Mazar's weapons and his shield tumbled out of the upturned car. Mazar desperately clung to the central pole, hanging there by both arms, his legs kicking as they grappled for the sides of the car to steady him.

"Now!" Keshan hissed through clenched teeth. His arms shook as he held them out, and his face broke out in sweat. He felt as though he were holding the chariot aloft with his own arms.

For one frightening moment, Keshan feared the worst. Jandu would not go through with it. He loved Mazar too much to kill him.

But then Jandu aimed and loosed his string. The arrow whistled through the air and sank deep into Mazar's throat. He shot three more arrows into his chest, to the lungs and heart. Blood bubbled from Mazar's mouth.

Mazar finally let go as he died, and his body dropped to the ground. It hit the hard soil with a thump and crumpled.

Keshan let out his breath and lowered his arms. Mazar's chariot slammed down atop the war master.

Arrows whizzed by his face and arms. The Uru had spotted them. Jandu didn't seem to care.

"We have to get out of this tree," Keshan said. "Now, Jandu!"

Then Keshan heard the Uru army sounding a retreat, and the archers fell back from the forest edge. Jandu followed Keshan down, dropping the last few feet to the ground. He looked sad but resolute.

"Prince Jandu!" Warash, the unofficial leader of Jandu's troops, bowed before Jandu and Keshan. "Lord Baram has sent supplies. What would you like to do with them?"

Jandu's expression remained stony. "Please see that every man who needs food gets it. Keshan will attend the injured as soon as he is able." Jandu looked Keshan over. "Assuming you are strong enough."

"I am." Keshan smiled at Warash. "Lead the way."

Keshan followed Warash through the camp, turning only to see Jandu look up at the fading afternoon light. He stared at the sky in silence, sighed, and then stepped into their tent.

◆◆◆

As darkness closed over the woods, the ethereal light of the demon guards formed a ring of illumination in which the humans gathered, talking amiably over their fires. The mood was pleasant, as Baram's load of supplies included wine, and the men shared stories and got to know each other under the flashing vigil of the Yashvas.

Keshan used all the magic he knew to help the injured, but there were several men who would die regardless, and one who had already passed away. When Keshan asked for volunteers to help build the man a pyre, he was shocked when one of the most recent soldiers to join them, a Tiwari Triya, volunteered. Keshan did not know the man personally, but the man respected Keshan enough that he decided to join him in the forest rather than fight any longer for the Uru.

Now Jandu approached from the river, wearing his mourning attire. His white dejaru and white shirt seemed to glow in the Yashva light. He had removed all his jewelry, and his cropped hair was wet from his evening ablutions.

As he walked, a dozen different men offered him refreshment or their help. Jandu asked for a torch, and as soon as one of the men brought him one, he bowed politely and said he would return.

Keshan caught him at the edge of the clearing and matched his stride. "Where are you going?"

Jandu frowned. "My master's funeral pyre. I want to pay my respects." Jandu spoke as though the answer was obvious and Keshan should have known. "Is there some problem with that?"

"No." Keshan hurried to catch up to Jandu's long steps. "I just don't want you to be hurt."

"It's against the rules of the war to injure someone attending a funeral pyre."

"I meant with words, not with weapons."

"Insults mean nothing to me now," Jandu said.

"Can I come with you?"

"If you want to." Jandu kept walking toward the distant firelight.

Keshan noticed that Jandu's torchlight seemed dim and saw the bluish glow of the Yashva, taking flight and gathering around him like massive, whirling fireflies.

The relatives of soldiers, physicians, and Jegora scavengers filled the dark battlefield, wielding hundreds of torches as they loaded corpses onto carts.

Keshan had seen the carnage from above. But here, on the battlefield itself, the smell overpowered his senses. Flies buzzed incessantly, and carrion birds gathered on exposed flesh in great clusters. As he and Jandu walked by, the birds took flight carrying chunks of their prizes.

The worst smell came from the Chaya and Suya funeral pyres up ahead. Hundreds of bodies were burned each night. Wailing widows and friends gathered around the great mountain of fire and filled the night with their cries. Looking south, Keshan saw a similar scene on the Paran side as they burned their own dead.

Mazar's pyre was outside the gates of the Uru camp, presumably since Darvad knew the Parans would want to attend. The gates behind the pyre were doubly fortified with soldiers, as if Darvad feared any Parans meandering over under the excuse of paying respects to Mazar and slipping inside.

A large crowd had gathered around Mazar's pyre. The Uru commanders stood on the outside, hands pressed together to pay respects to their leader. Inside an area cordoned off with holy icons, Mazar's immediate friends gathered, dressed in white, bowed low to Mazar's corpse, which lay on a bed of straw and branches. The wood glinted in the torchlight, wet with oil. Onshu, the officiating priest, stood beside the pyre with his torch ready. He led a series of prayers.

On one side of the pyre, Darvad stood, weeping loudly as he leaned on Tarek Amia for support. On the other side stood Jandu's brothers, shrouded in white, heads bowed respectfully. Indarel and Rishak had also come to pay their respects.

Keshan stopped just outside the first holy icon, and remained in the shadows. Jandu touched his hand briefly, and then marched into the center of the gathering.

The moment Jandu stepped into the group, the prayers ceased, and all eyes turned to him.

He looked magnificent, Keshan thought. The Yashvas who guarded him turned into pricks of light, which danced around him, protecting him in tight arcs of illumination. Many of the men brought their hands together in hasty prayer. Jandu looked like an ancient prophet, and they treated him like one as he approached Mazar's broken body. Onshu stepped back, watching the Yashvas with awe.

Yudar looked at Jandu with disgust. The fact that he did so made Keshan want to kill him, then and there.

"What are you doing here?" Yudar growled at Jandu.

Jandu stared down at Mazar's face. "Paying respects to my weapons master."

"Master Mazar would be ashamed to have you here after what you've done!" Yudar told him.

Jandu took a handful of marigolds from a golden bowl beside the pyre and placed them lovingly on Mazar's chest. He whispered something to the corpse that Keshan could not hear.

"Get out of here!" Yudar hissed.

"This is a pyre for family." Darvad's expression twisted in a sneer. Keshan had never known Darvad to look so cruel. The fact that Keshan once thought Darvad would save them all mocked him. How could he have been so wrong?

"I have allowed my half-brothers here out of respect for Master Mazar. But the casteless do not belong." Darvad pointed at Keshan. And then he made eye contact with Jandu. "Nor do filthy sodomites."

Keshan almost had to smile. Yudar couldn't lie, even when the truth was so shameful.

"Shut the fuck up!" Baram howled in rage and started forward, but Onshu quickly stepped between the families.

"Respect! Respect!" Onshu chanted, ushering Baram and Darvad into their corners.

Jandu bowed his head and prayed, the Yashvas speeding up as they circled him, their anger palpable to Keshan.

"That's enough." Darvad's voice was dark and angry. "Time for all disgraced to leave this holy pyre. Even your own brothers don't want you here. All Triya are dirtied by your presence."

"Be quiet, Darvad." Tarek suddenly said. "It is his right to be here."

Keshan could not believe it. Tarek spoke in a low voice, his expression icy.

"That's enough gloating for one day," Tarek told Darvad.

Darvad's forehead bulged with anger, the vein in his head rising up like an angry 'V'. He seemed to hesitate, looking between Tarek and Jandu. Then he suddenly grabbed a mace from one of the Triya at his side and lunged forward.

At once, the Yashvas surrounding Jandu took form. An explosive wind blew the mace from Darvad's hand and caused Jandu's hair to fly around his head, his eyes cold and angry. Dust shot out from around him into the aghast crowd. The Yashvas' faces transformed into those of beasts, spiraling eyes and gaping mouths. As one, the entire crowd around Mazar's pyre stepped back, many of them crying out in fear as the Yashva surged.

Jandu turned to leave. As he did so, he made brief eye contact with Baram and winked.

At the last icon, Jandu reached out for Keshan and purposefully put his arm around him. "Let's go." Jandu's voice was rough with suppressed emotion.

As they walked silently back towards the forest, the Yashvas dissipated into a less threatening presence of light once more. Many of the Triya must have made tributes to Mazar, for it was several hours by the time Keshan saw smoke rise from Mazar's pyre.

Jandu stayed up late, checking on the men in his camp, and consulting with the Tiwari Triya man to make sure all of the deserters were armed and armored in case of any retaliation from either Uru or Paran camp. It was near midnight by the time Jandu crawled into their tent. Keshan watched him enter, his long, sleek frame revealed slowly in the moonlight as he peeled his mourning clothes from his body. Jandu crawled under the blanket with Keshan and pressed his naked body close, spooning against Keshan's back. The feeling was as close to heaven as Keshan could ever imagine.

CHAPTER 54

"*NEVER INSULT ME LIKE THAT AGAIN!*"

Darvad's face contorted in his fury. He spat at Tarek. "How *dare* you defend my enemy in front of our own forces! I am your king, you treasonous bastard!"

Tarek took a step back, sinking further into the small congregation of soldiers. Mazar's body incinerated in the distance, filling the air with the stench of burning hair.

"I'm sorry." Tarek bowed his head.

Darvad's hands clenched into fists. "That cock-sucking bitch isn't worthy of any compassion, and I will not stand by while a perverted faggot sullies my master's funeral!"

Darvad's words sliced through Tarek like blades. He felt the blood drain from his face.

Darvad pointed at Tarek. "What were you thinking, defending a fucking queer?"

Tarek's throat was too dry to speak. But Darvad did not wait for a response.

"If you *ever* censor my commentary again, I swear I will turn you back into a Suya without a moment's hesitation." Darvad stormed into the enveloping darkness. Tarek stood still, too shocked to move.

"To your posts!" Anant cried suddenly, scattering the stunned audience of soldiers. As one they fled the scene, heading to watch towers or their tents. Only Anant remained by Tarek's side.

Tarek ignored him. He walked towards his own tent in a daze. He had never seen Darvad so angry, or ever imagined such vengeful words would be directed at him.

Once inside his tent, Tarek reached for his jug of wine. He drank straight from the jug itself, seeking numbness.

"My lord?" Anant said softly from the tent flap.

Tarek didn't respond. He swallowed, wiped his mouth, and then took another long gulp.

"Tarek?" Anant asked again, stepping inside.

Tarek put the jug down and nodded to Anant.

"What is it?" he said, colder than he intended. His body felt icy.

"Do I have permission to speak freely, my lord?" Anant asked. His face was tight with anger.

"Do as you please. I'm not going to cast you down to the Suya for something as small as stating your opinion." Tarek snorted mirthlessly.

Anant removed his helmet. His dark hair lay flat against his scalp. "How can you stand by him after what he just said? The man is a devil!"

Tarek clenched his eyes shut. "He didn't mean it."

"Tarek, don't be blind!" Anant cried. "The man hates our kind. He would hate you if he knew what you were. It makes me sick to think of fighting for him!"

Tarek glared at him. "You would desert him? Where's your honor?"

"Honor! Ha!" Anant spat. "How about Darvad's honor? What about the rule not to attack anyone at a funeral pyre? He just broke the rules of war, an offense that would have any of the men under my command hanged as traitors!"

Tarek knew Anant spoke the truth. The attack was inexcusable. Peace at a memorial was one of the most sacred tenets of the Book of Taivo. For a moment, he wanted to agree with Anant.

But he couldn't. He couldn't. "I took an oath," Tarek said weakly. "Do you understand? An oath! To defend the man at all costs, even at the cost of my life! I cannot abandon him, even if he hates me, even if he is a hypocrite!"

Anant grimaced. "You once told me you agreed with Lord Keshan, that the old ways should change."

"I never said that," Tarek snapped. "That was Keshan, not me."

"But you want change, don't you? How can you change this world if you remain so stuck in your own religious dogma?"

"It isn't that simple!" Tarek shouted. He lowered his voice, fearful others would hear them. "You don't understand, Anant."

Anant narrowed his eyes. "Yes I do. You love him."

Tarek closed his eyes.

"But you love a man who would kill you if he knew your true nature. A man who is breaking all of his promises of change, who has broken the rules. If he defiles his promises, why can't you?"

Tarek opened his eyes, and saw Anant's desperation. But Tarek felt nothing anymore, not for anyone. Even Anant wasn't enough to change the man Tarek had become.

"It's pointless," Tarek said. "This is who I am. I owe Darvad my allegiance, and it's too late to alter my path now."

"It is *never* too late to follow your conscience," Anant urged.

"He made me a Triya, Anant!" Tarek shouted. "A Triya! Do you realize how much power this man has given me?"

"And he just demonstrated he will take it away at a moment's notice!" Anant shouted back. He made as if to say something else, but clenched his jaw instead. He straightened. "So you will not leave him."

"No."

"Despite everything he has said, everything he has done."

"No."

Anant breathed heavily in the silence. "Fine then. I'm leaving." Anant put his helmet back on and turned towards the tent flap.

Panic swelled through Tarek. "Wait!" He grabbed Anant by the arm. "Where are you going?"

"To the forest," Anant said. "To Keshan and Jandu. I won't fight for a king who deserves no allegiance."

"You are deserting?" Tarek gasped, unbelieving. "You would give up your honor as a Triya and shame your family for the sake of Jandu Paran?"

"Not for Jandu Paran. For myself and for the future," Anant said. "Come with me. Please. Put aside your old loyalties, and your old hatreds. Fight for the noble cause you claim you believe in. Come, and be with me. Openly. We can stop hiding like criminals."

Anant's lips were so close, Tarek could kiss him easily. He smelled intoxicating, he looked gorgeous. He wanted nothing more than to make love to Anant and forget this horrible night ever happened. But Anant's eyes pleaded, demanding a response.

"I can't," Tarek said, regret breaking his heart even as he said the words.

Anant's eyes filled with tears. He leaned over and kissed Tarek once, tenderly, on the lips.

"I love you." Anant sighed. "But I'm leaving."

Anant left the tent.

Tarek stood there, staring at the closed tent flaps a moment longer. He grabbed the nearest object, a quiver of arrows, and he threw them at the tent post. He ripped through his room, tearing through objects, breaking everything in his hands. His anger boiled through him and out of him, but nothing stopped it, nothing slowed his heart, he was so full it burst out of him, great waves of rage. He slashed at his tent with his sword, he smashed his wine jug to pieces, and then standing there, in the midst of his destruction, Tarek realized he had descended into the person he hated the most, the hypocrite, the blind follower, useless, unloved, and worthless.

He burst from the shreds of his tent in blind wrath. He ran towards the gates of the camp, hoping to catch Anant before he left. But at the late hour, the only men still standing were the guards, who watched Tarek's madness in fear.

Anant was gone. Tarek had lost everything.

CHAPTER 54

ANOTHER TRIYA WARRIOR HAD JOINED JANDU'S CAMP IN THE
night. Keshan made an effort to greet each one. Partly it was
because he knew what these men sacrificed by joining them.
Partly it was an affinity for men like him, who had grown up
in similar circumstances.

But mostly it was because he and Jandu needed their battle
training. Since they had begun amassing troops in the forest and
dispelling shartas, they worried that either Yudar or Darvad would
send a unit into the forest to kill their deserters. Keshan knew the
Yashvas were loyal to Jandu, but he doubted they would extend
much effort to a scraggly collection of other human beings.

The newest Triya arrival was a young, handsome man with
dark eyes and heavy shadows from not shaving the night before.
He seemed familiar, but Keshan couldn't place him. His armor
gleamed in the morning light as he stood stiff at attention. A
dozen or so soldiers followed him, all of them wore the insignia
of the 8th unit of the Dragewan army. These were Tarek's men.
The thought of Tarek, combined with the insignia brought it
back. This commander had accompanied Tarek to Afadi, and
he'd been present at Keshan's trial.

"Lord Keshan!" the warrior greeted him. He reached down
and touched Keshan's feet, an action which so shocked Keshan
that he had to take a step back.

"You don't have to do that," Keshan said. "I'm Jegora now,
as you well know."

"Yes, my lord," the commander said, his eyes glinting.

Keshan smiled back. He liked the man already. "You and
your men are welcome. What is your name?"

"Anant, my lord," the soldier said, returning to stiff attention. "I was commander of the 8th unit of Dragewan's army, and these are soldiers loyal to me. We have come to fight alongside you."

"You realize that those loyal to us will almost certainly lose their caste," Keshan said. "If you would prefer to return to your homes, Prince Jandu and I will not stop you."

Anant's eyes blazed fiercely. "I have come to fight with you, my lord."

"Please call me Keshan." Keshan looked out to the nearly one hundred men that sprawled through the makeshift camp. "Most of the soldiers here are Suya and Chaya, with little or no battle training. We need men like you to lead the others if we have to fight."

Anant nodded. "I will help in any way I can, my lord. Only…"

"Yes?"

Anant drew close so that only Keshan would hear his voice.

"My lord, I humbly beg your forgiveness, but I cannot fight Lord Tarek Amia. I will do anything else, but I will not harm him."

Keshan raised an eyebrow. "Why not?"

Anant swallowed. He kept his eyes focused just to the right of Keshan's head. "We were close."

"Close?"

Anant's voice dropped to a whisper. "We were lovers. I asked him to join me here, but he would not break his oath to King Darvad."

Keshan's surprise made him momentarily speechless.

"Tarek knew you were deserting and he let you go?" Keshan had never imagined Tarek was like him. No wonder Tarek couldn't stand by and listen to Darvad insulting Jandu. Sudden sadness filled Keshan. He and Tarek could have been so much closer as friends if they had known they had this in common.

"I won't ask you to do anything against your conscience," Keshan finally said. "But if the Uru forces attack us, you may have to reconsider your decision."

Anant let out his breath. "Thank you for your understanding."

Keshan looked up at the predawn sky. Gold colored the few clouds. Any moment, the sounds of conches would fill the air and the fourth day of the war would begin.

Anant's gaze followed Keshan's, and he frowned as he looked at the battlefield, his grief plain.

Keshan steadied him, a hand on his shoulder. "I'm sorry," he said quietly. "About Tarek, I mean."

Anant nodded, swallowing. "Thank you, my lord."

"You should go to Warash, and he will help assign you and your men supplies and duties in the camp. He's the Chaya over there in the gray uniform." Keshan raised an eyebrow. "Unless you object to taking orders from a Chaya?"

Anant's initial look of surprise was quickly smothered by a look of weird excitement. "Your army truly is making a new future."

Anant bowed low, and then signaled his men to follow him.

Keshan smiled after them. As he made his way to his banyan tree perch, he wondered what Jandu would make of Anant, and the news of Tarek's nature. And then he realized that it no longer mattered. Tarek had made his choice.

CHAPTER 55

MORNING LIGHT DID NOT DIFFUSE TAREK'S ANGER. AND THE news that Anant had taken twelve soldiers of the Dragewan army with him into the forest only exacerbated his rage. He never knew he could hold so much fury inside of him. He trembled with violence. He stared at the morning formation of the Paran army, wanting to slaughter them all.

Darvad smiled at Tarek that morning, and mumbled an apology for his harsh words. He then asked Tarek to take Mazar's place as general of the Uru forces. Tarek barely looked at him. He could not let Darvad too close to him, when he was so full of rancor.

"Take position behind the Bandari," Tarek said curtly. "I'll lead the charge." Without another word, Tarek jumped into his chariot and took his place at the front of the line. The stench overwhelmed all other senses. Body parts were identifiable in the mud only by the swarms of flies and the carrion birds.

The battle opened with the shrill of conches, and Tarek's charioteer Satish charged recklessly towards the Parans. Mazar's death inspired the Parans, and they pushed into the Uru line ferociously, chariots storming through and dispatching Uru foot soldiers in great numbers. Tarek drove them back. He shot arrow after arrow, striking his targets with cold precision.

A sharta rocked his chariot, earth exploding and burning all around him. Tarek wiped a spray of dirt from his eyes. He screamed at the Dragewan soldiers to follow the charge against the Paran line. The Parans held fast, and Tarek advanced slowly, hacking through the tight Paran formation, crushing men and spearing horses with his arrows.

Tarek bellowed for Satish to push through a gap in the Paran defense, leading one of two main thrusts into the line. Ishad, Firdaus' son, led the other charge.

Up ahead, Tarek heard the Paran troops cheering Baram as his chariot rushed forward to meet Tarek's. Tarek glared at Baram's golden armor. Tarek wanted to kill Baram, for helping capture Mazar, for being Jandu's brother. Baram became the focus of Tarek's hatred. He felt almost cheated when a spear felled one of Baram's horses. Baram leapt from his chariot as it flipped over. He raised his mace and continued to fight on the ground. He swung his mace, his stance wide, his face ferocious.

The Suya and Chaya foot soldiers who could not fight back against the bulk and rage of Baram's attack broke before him. He plunged deep into the Uru line. It was clear that Baram had no idea of how isolated he had become from the rest of the Paran force. Dust and smoke from a sharta cast a haze over everything.

Without hesitating, Tarek closed his eyes and whispered the Korazsharta that Darvad had taught him long ago, words to conjure the magical Yashva spear that never missed its target. Darvad had given it to Tarek to kill Jandu, but Tarek needed to expel his rage now, and Baram was here.

The spear appeared in his hand, the shimmering bluish metal hot to the touch. It shone like a bolt of lightening in his hand.

Tossing the spear felt like nothing, like air, but the spear sang as it flew, a high-pitched wail that sounded like a newborn. It flew with tremendous speed, and struck Baram in the gut, tearing through his armor.

Baram howled in rage as he stumbled backwards. But he did not fall. He dropped his mace and used both hands to pull the long spear from his body. The moment he dropped it, the spear disappeared.

Baram screamed and gripped his wound, his face clenched in rage. He reached down and grabbed his mace.

"Coward! Who attacked me?" Baram shouted.

Blood poured from his wound, but he lifted his mace.

Tarek notched an arrow and took aim. It was against the rules of war to shoot Baram when he was armed only with a mace, but Tarek no longer cared. Fuck the rules of war. He loosed his string and the arrow shot straight through Baram's arm. Baram howled, dropping his mace.

Tarek charged him. He shot Baram once more in the neck as his chariot swept past. Then Tarek leapt from the chariot and took up Baram's fallen mace. His first blow sent Baram's helmet flying. He swung again and Baram collapsed to the ground.

The blood rushed in Tarek's ears, and the battlefield receded. He beat Baram on the ground with his own mace.

Baram moved slowly, trying to deflect the blows.

Tarek smashed Baram's right knee cap. Baram cried out, an animal scream, wild with hatred and panic.

A part of Tarek told him to stop, to just kill him, end it, but his rage was still unsated, he needed Baram to suffer, and as Baram continued to weakly resist, his right fist clenched and waving, Tarek swung back the mace and smashed it down into Baram's face.

The Uru soldiers around Tarek cheered. Tarek pulverized Baram's face, crushing his large features to a pulp. His head caved in with sickening softness. Blood and brains sprayed the dismembered torso. Tarek struck again, and again, until nothing resembling a head was left, until his arm cramped. He dropped the mace, breathless.

There was no way Baram's corpse could be properly burned now. It seemed as though hours had passed since the battle began, but the sun had barely moved in the sky. It was as if time had frozen for everyone else. Only this beating had lasted forever.

With Baram's death, the Paran army's morale crumbled. Tarek watched as his troops rallied to press their advantage. They cheered Tarek and pushed the Parans into retreat.

Conch shells blasted Tarek's victory across the battlefield, but he remained where he was, coursing with adrenalin. He stepped from Baram's body, sick with himself.

"My lord!" Satish stopped the horses beside him. "You must return to the chariot quickly! We are moving forward!"

Tarek forced his body to move. Satish clucked the horses into a canter even before Tarek was fully in the chariot. Tarek followed his units as they curved eastward, joining up with Ishad's men to crush the remnants of the Paran line.

Tarek gripped the central pole of his chariot. He wished someone would shoot him. He begged God to let someone kill him, now, before he fell any lower.

But, despite his prayers, Satish successfully navigated Tarek back into the center of the Uru line. The real battle was only beginning. Tarek heard Darvad's conch and looked over to see Darvad's chariot rush towards him.

With the Bandari shielding them both, Darvad leapt from his chariot and into Tarek's, talking quickly, laughing and hugging Tarek, celebrating Tarek's gory triumph. All cruel words were apparently forgotten in the face of Tarek's foul deed. *This is what it was to be Darvad's friend*, Tarek thought. Rewards for those who rent their souls apart. Grace for only his sins.

The soldiers cried out Tarek's name in triumph. But it brought no pride to Tarek anymore. All it brought was regret.

And now, with Anant gone, there was nothing Tarek could do to rein it in, so he let it thrive. Regret was all he had left.

CHAPTER 56

JANDU SPENT THE MORNING CAPTURING A PAIR OF TERRIFIED horses who had escaped the battle and now rampaged through their camp, kicking over tents and smashing water jugs. By the time the horses were calmly in Warash's care, the day's conflict was well underway.

The wild triumphant blare of Uru horns sent a shiver through him, and he made his way quickly to the banyan tree, looking up to Keshan for some sign of what happened.

Keshan looked nearly green. He leaned over as if he were going to be sick.

"What is it?" Jandu felt his throat tighten. "Is it Yudar? Did they capture him?"

Keshan didn't say anything. He made his way down from the tree morosely. When he reached the forest floor, he looked Jandu in the eye, his expression grave.

Jandu's heart beat faster. "Tell me!"

"I'm so sorry, Jandu," Keshan said. "Baram is dead."

The words fluttered through Jandu's consciousness, like moths in darkness.

"It can't be true." Jandu felt small tears, black and aching, where the words had fluttered through him. Pain began to build inside him, small at first, blossoming outwards, filling his mind, his ears. He shook his head. "It can't be true," he said again, willing the words away.

Jandu scrambled up the banyan tree. Smoke obscured the battlefield, but he could see chariots circling off the left flank, and could hear Urus cheering. The Paran line folded inwards as the Urus pressed their advantage.

Paran soldiers wept as they gathered around a bloody mass on the battlefield. It took a long moment for Jandu to realize it was a body, and even longer to realize it was his brother.

Jandu climbed down the tree. His throat felt as though it would close against the black ache pooling inside him. The men of the forest gathered around him, sympathy radiating off them as word quickly spread. Jandu shut everything, all of them, the blackness inside him, out. He couldn't think or feel. That would happen later. For now, he had to act.

"Who did this?" he asked Keshan, his voice breaking.

Keshan hesitated. Jandu grabbed Keshan's harafa and pulled him closer. "Who was it!"

"Tarek," Keshan whispered.

White hot rage filled Jandu. He pushed past Keshan and marched into his tent. He strapped on his silver armor. He pulled on his finger guards and strung Zandi. He attached his quiver and his sword, and then grabbed his shield and helmet as he darted from the tent.

Keshan stood mutely outside, eyes wide. Men and Yashva all watched Jandu, waiting for some signal.

Jandu pulled on his helmet, then turned to Keshan.

"Get armor."

There were half a dozen charioteers in the forest, and all of them helped Keshan harness the two horses they had just calmed to King Mendraz's chariot. Jandu heard the men whistle at the sight of the celestial vehicle, but he couldn't take pleasure in it. He needed to be doing something right now, or any moment, the reality that Baram was dead would fill him and he would suffocate with grief.

Jandu felt the presence of the Yashva swarm around him like fireflies. Behind him, the men of his camp watched warily, armed and ready to follow him.

"Stay here," Jandu instructed. "Stay protected."

He tapped Keshan on the shoulder and they charged out onto the battlefield.

If Jandu thought about Baram, he would be sick. He focused on the unnatural smoothness of Keshan's celestial chariot, the way it gleamed in the light, and the rhythm of the horses' gallop. Keshan whispered soothing words to calm them and pull them together.

As soon as they entered the melee, they were surrounded by Uru soldiers. They were like fish swimming upstream, fighting against the current of so many bodies.

Jandu burned with frustration. "We must go faster!" he bellowed.

And then, from behind him, he heard a call.

"Prince Jandu!"

A hundred men charged around the chariot, shouting his name and flinging themselves upon the infantry in his path. The men of the forest attacked Paran and Uru forces without regard.

Jandu's men. They were back in the melee for him, cutting a swathe through the two armies. Jandu briefly caught the eye of the new young commander, Anant, and Anant waved to him and then ran, charging into a cluster of soldiers.

Keshan shouted out a string of words and the Yashva took form. The air shimmered around their chariot and bodies of light sprang forth and pulled the infantry apart. The sky rained body parts as invisible hands rended the Urus into corpses. Soldiers around them fled in terror.

As the Yashva and Jandu's men cleared a path, Keshan urged the horses ahead. They broke into long, graceful movements, as if they, too, were relieved to be free of the congestion. Keshan drove them towards Tarek's chariot.

Arrows fired at Jandu's chariot fell from the air as if batted aside by invisible hands. Flashes of light burst over the field, emanating from his chariot, as Jandu's Yashva guardians protected him from assault. Jandu returned fire on any who opposed his advance. Lord Ishad, Firdaus' son, appeared alongside them. Jandu took aim and shot him in the eye. Firdaus' line was extinguished from the earth. The thought did little to warm his cold heart.

"Lord Jandu!"

Keshan swerved the chariot to meet the Paran messenger who rode up alongside their chariot. Jandu lost his balance momentarily, and glared down at Keshan. But then he readied his bow once more, and pointed the arrow at the messenger.

The messenger wore the colors of Jezza's army. He looked frightened.

"Prince Yudar demands that you leave the battlefield at once!" the messenger cried. He was out of breath, legs squeezing his horse desperately as he tried to keep pace with Keshan's horses.

"You are not fighting for the Parans," the messenger continued. "And you will be fired upon as an enemy of the Paran army if you do not leave the battlefield at once!"

Keshan turned the chariot suddenly, causing the messenger to veer off in the wrong direction. When he returned to their side, Jandu stopped shooting at soldiers long enough to shoot an arrow at the ground in front of the messenger, in warning.

"Tell Yudar that I am not here for him," Jandu growled lowly. "I am here to avenge Baram. Until I kill Tarek Amia, no one, including Yudar, will get me off this battlefield."

The messenger turned his mount aside, riding back for the Paran line.

Keshan whipped the horses forward. In the distance, Jandu could see Tarek's chariot. They were close.

Tarek shouted orders at his surrounding troops as Jandu approached. Jandu closed his eyes and began one of the worst curses he knew, the Fazsharta, over his notched arrow. He could feel his skin burn hot, his face darken, the words themselves shivering through him. The words formed letters like bursts of soot.

His grief over Baram churned within his belly like poison, and fed the curse, giving it power. Blood pooled in his mouth.

Keshan stopped within bowshot of Tarek's chariot. One of the Yashva burst into the human world and tore into Tarek's charioteer like he was made of paper. Tarek nocked an arrow.

"Jandu Paran," he bellowed. "Beware!"

CHAPTER 57

AT LONG LAST, THE FULFILLMENT OF A LIFELONG DESIRE WAS upon him. Tarek had an arrow nocked and aimed at Jandu Paran's face.

But he felt nothing. No pride. No victory. His own rage was spent.

Anant had been right. All that mattered was following your heart. Anant had chosen the right side. Tarek, blind with lust, desperate to become a different person, had given up all that had made him who he was.

And now everything had collapsed. Tarek shared more with his enemy than his best friend. Even this war twisted upon itself, devolving into a desecration.

Tarek tried to build rage in his mind. Only heavy, oily, grief remained.

"This is for Baram," Jandu shouted. His eyes brimmed with tears.

Tarek released his arrow first. Despite the accuracy of his aim, bursts of light interceded and the arrow shattered mid-air.

Jandu's arrow streaked a black trail as it flew through the air. Tarek barely noticed. The arrow shot through his armor, straight through his chest. An excruciating burn blossomed in his lungs, radiating outwards, and Tarek's legs crumpled. He tumbled out of the chariot, landing hard against his right arm. All he could feel was the agonizing fire of the celestial weapon, blackness spreading through him, consuming him.

So this is how I die, Tarek thought. He looked over and saw horse manure. *How unattractive.* Tarek closed his eyes.

CHAPTER 58

A CIRCLE OF DECAY OOZED FROM TAREK'S CORPSE AS POISONS from the blackened body rose into the air. The world smelled rank and defiled. It created a gap in the center of the battlefield, and so now armies clashed around Jandu in tight confines.

Blood from a nick above Keshan's ear trickled down his face, mixing with the dust to form a sickly dark paste. Keshan's lips were cracked and dried, and his voice had gone rough from shouting at the horses.

Jandu wanted to give him reassurance, but his heart wasn't in it. His heart had frozen at the sight of Baram's ruined corpse. He felt locked in the same, endless, moment.

A dozen warriors attacked Jandu at once. He dispatched his enemies silently. He could not have stopped even if he had wanted to. Uru warriors hounded him. Jandu took their lives as if they could buy back Baram's.

The shadows stretched, and it became harder to determine the color of banners, the identification of armies. Keshan turned the chariot to face every Uru army commander who challenged them. Jandu slaughtered them, one by one, with shartas and arrows. Only once did Keshan turn away from a chariot. Jandu saw Iyestar inside. Keshan's brother frowned at the them as they rushed past, but he did not pursue them.

Jandu's muscles trembled as he fired his arrows. His body felt stretched to breaking point. The Fazsharta had hurt him, internally he felt like he was bleeding. But he wasn't sure how much of his pain was physical, and how much was grief.

Through the dust and twilight shadows, Jandu caught sight of Darvad.

"You bastard!" Darvad's face was streaked with dirt and tears. He had vomit on his breastplate, he had obviously been uttering magical weapons. "You will pay for Tarek's death!"

The long notes of conches filled the air, signaling the end of the day's battle. Jandu glanced behind him, and saw Lord Indarel, looking exhausted. The sun was below the horizon, and only the dim red glow of its aftermath provided the light to see. Jandu's own men were fewer than fifty now, but they still kept pace with his chariot. Many were bleeding badly, their armor cracked and their weapons caked with gore.

"Anant!" Jandu called to the young commander. "Get our men back to camp!"

"Yes, sir!" Anant replied, signaling the men to retreat.

As he saw them leave the battlefield, Jandu allowed himself a moment to feel relief. His body and his heart ached, and he wanted to stop, to grieve and hold Keshan.

The Uru and Paran armies also turned to return to their respective camps. But instead of blowing his conch, Darvad growled out another sharta.

Jandu dropped to the floor of his chariot and began to recite the counter-curse. Words filled his mind, along with unwanted images of death and destruction. This was one of Mazar's darkest weapons. What was Darvad doing, uttering this at the close of the day's battle?

Jandu spat out the end of the counter just as Darvad finished as well. There was a noticeable silence. Every soldier seemed frozen for a moment.

"Continue fighting!" Darvad shouted across the battlefield. His nose bled, his eyes bled, he looked half-dead as he pointed at Jandu in his rage. "This war ends tonight!"

Uru warriors charged forward and Paran troops were forced to turn back and defend themselves.

"This is madness!" Keshan cried out. He whispered to the horses. They were lathered in sweat, but they dutifully took off after Darvad's chariot.

Through the clashing masses of Uru and Paran warriors, another of Yudar's messengers appeared on horseback. Jandu hardly glanced at the man. His Uru enemies commanded all his attention as he fired arrows through the waning light. The messenger screeched commands. Keshan answered for both of them by turning the horses around and charging the messenger. The messenger fled.

As darkness fell upon the battlefield, torches were lit. But it was becoming impossible to make out targets. The armies clashed in close confines once more, and Jandu had to slow down his assaults to check the colors of each banner before firing. Urus and Parans mingled in the blackness.

"I don't know where to shoot!" he yelled.

Keshan said something quick and dark in Yashva. Jandu's Yashva guards appeared as men once more, glowing and ethereal, and tracked Jandu's enemies, providing him the light he needed to take aim. Men fled from Jandu in panic. They turned away the moment one of the Yashvas' ghostly forms came close; Jandu's arrow would inevitably follow.

Keshan pulled the horses to a halt as another chariot almost rammed them. They turned once more and got within sight of Darvad. Jandu readied Zandi. But the second he nocked an arrow, Darvad collapsed to the floor of his chariot.

For a moment, Jandu paused, stunned. Was Darvad actually *hiding*? Was he truly that much of a coward?

But then his skin tingled, and a bluish hue radiated from the chariot car.

A burst of green light shone from Darvad's chariot. Jandu stared at it, desperate to determine which sharta produced such a beautiful, startling effect. As he tried to recall his lessons with Mazar, an icy, sinking fear began to fill him. He clutched Keshan's bicep tightly, but the panic did not subside.

"Oh God!"

Jandu froze, fear creeping through his bones. He couldn't speak, he couldn't move. Icy fingers gripped a hold of his heart.

He tried to scream out, but terror crippled his voice, left him motionless. Zandi slipped from his hand.

Fear spread through the soldiers surrounding Darvad's chariot like a gust of wind. Foot soldiers dropped their weapons. Cavalrymen cried out as their horses bolted. His own team reared, broke free of the harness and galloped into the shadows. Jandu leapt from the chariot as it lurched forward. He crouched on the ground, too terrified to do anything else.

Keshan climbed free of the chariot and knelt beside him. He lifted Jandu's head.

"Darvad released a fear sharta!" Keshan shouted. "Fight it!"

"I can't!" Jandu cried. He collapsed on the battlefield, head in his hands. Around him, hundreds of men fled the field. Only the wreckage of their chariot sheltered Jandu and Keshan from the stampede. Jandu heard Lord Indarel cry out as hundreds of his own men trampled over him. There was a riot now, pure chaos. Fright had turned the Paran army against itself. They ran screaming, senseless, stepping over each other in the darkness.

Keshan grabbed Jandu by his armor and pulled him up. "Jandu! I need your help! You have to protect me while I recite the counter-curse!"

Jandu fought off the heavy, drugged panic in his mind. He drew his sword and stood in front of Keshan as Keshan bowed in supplication on the muddy battlefield.

Keshan chanted under his breath, his body breaking out in a sweat, strain plain across his face.

"Hurry!" Jandu drove aside Paran and Uru soldiers alike. Some sobbed like children. Others shrieked as they fled. The men closest to Darvad's chariot tore at their eyes and ripped the hair from their heads. Some killed themselves in their fright. The horror radiated outwards, and those out of range of the sharta fled in fear of the terrorized armies that ran screaming towards them in the darkness.

Keshan took an arrow from Jandu's quiver. He whispered to it and then flung it into the earth, arrowhead first. A soft, green light shot from the shaft and spread over the battlefield like smoke.

Jandu felt the icy fingers that had gripped his heart let go. His mind cleared. Sheer exhaustion was the only sensation that remained. Jandu sheathed his sword and saw Keshan sway on his feet. Jandu lunged out to catch Keshan as he collapsed.

Keshan was limp in Jandu's arms.

"Keshan!" Jandu shouted.

"I'm fine…" Keshan swallowed painfully, his lips and mouth parched. "…I'm just tired."

"You broke Darvad's sharta," Jandu said. "It's time for us to go home."

Keshan sat up weakly. "I'll drive the chariot."

Jandu shook his head. "The horses are gone."

"I'll get them."

"You can barely stand up."

"We need the chariot to get out of here any time soon. Just let me rest a moment." Keshan leaned against the toppled chariot.

An eerie silence filled the darkness as the counter-curse made its way across the field. As their panic lifted men stilled. The screaming ceased, but quiet realizations of pain rose in their place.

"My brother," one man whispered, tears streaming from his eyes as he cradled a limp body in his arms. "I killed my own brother!"

Jandu felt bones break beneath his foot. He looked down and, seeing Lord Indarel, cried out in horror. Nearby, Indarel's eldest son, his pride and joy, Ramad, lay dead, his neck twisted and broken. Jandu leaned down and closed what was left of Indarel's eyes. His body was flat in terrible places. Jandu tried to drag his corpse to their chariot, to save it from further desecration, but as he pulled on Indarel's arm, the limbs separated, so beaten that Jandu was afraid his arm would rip off. Jandu fought back vomit. Abiyar would be devastated.

Jandu stepped away, unsure he could bear any more of this.

Keshan whistled in the dark, and to Jandu's surprise, their two stallions came towards them. The steeds had calmed, although their coats were white with sweat. Keshan moved like he were half-dead as he reharnessed them, using his harafa as a strap to replace the one that had broken.

Jandu jumped into the car while Keshan again took the reins.

Jandu tried to conjure a light sharta to see by, but his tongue was so swollen and cut from the dozens of shartas he had uttered, he could no longer make it form the sentence he needed. At least the darkness was no longer complete—fires from fallen torches lit the landscape. Keshan called the Yashva back and their luminous bodies cast a blue glow.

Keshan pointed east. "Darvad."

In the thin light, Jandu recognized Darvad's banner as well as his brother Yudar's. Darvad's chariot approached Yudar with alarming speed. Few soldiers blocked his path.

"The war is about to end," Keshan said. "Do you care who wins anymore?"

"It can't be Darvad, not after what he's done to his own people tonight."

Keshan nodded. He cooed to the horses and they snorted back at him, moving into an exhausted trot. A few more soothing words helped them collect themselves. They picked up speed. The battlefield was a sea of bodies now, but the horses no longer paid heed. They trampled over soil and flesh alike. Keshan drove them towards Yudar.

Jandu's weariness made even holding Zandi unbearable. He remembered when he had first changed into a woman, how his bow had grown into a bulky, unwieldy thing, beyond his ability to lift. He felt the same way now.

They sped across the battlefield unchallenged. Of Darvad's eight commanders, only Iyestar remained, his chariot surrounded by the poor remains of Tiwari's army.

Up ahead, Darvad's horses collapsed. Darvad bounded from his chariot, armed with his sword and bow, and raced towards Jandu's brother.

Yudar sat in his chariot. His guards lay dead around him.

Although the rules of war had been broken over and over again, Yudar stepped from his chariot, so as to fight Darvad on even ground. Even now, the rules of the Triya were killing him.

A thin soldier rushed to Yudar's side and unsheathed his sword. It took Jandu only a moment to recognize the boy's armor. Abiyar stood beside Yudar, the last protection of their side of the war.

Jandu felt sick to his stomach. It was all for nothing. They were going to lose. Baram had died, and they were still going to lose. Yudar must have been thinking the same thing, for his expression suddenly faltered. He froze, watching Darvad's approach. Abiyar rushed ahead of him, charging Darvad, his sword aloft.

"No! Abiyar!" Jandu leapt from the car of chariot and sprinted forward. The Yashva rushed alongside him like an army of ghosts.

But Darvad only had eyes for Yudar. He pushed Abiyar out of the way without a second thought. Abiyar tumbled to the mud and Darvad pressed onward, screaming and charging Yudar with his sword ready.

Yudar made no move to draw his sword or raise his shield. Instead, his eyes closed and mumbled under his breath.

Jandu couldn't hear what Yudar said from this distance. But suddenly his Yashva guard flashed and then disappeared, one by one. They looked shocked as they turned to Jandu and then vanished. Only one sharta called down so many Yashva at once.

"Yudar! No!" Jandu shouted. He watched his brother's lips move as if in a trance. The words clashed together in Jandu's mind, and he could feel his heart break open. His brother was uttering the Pezarisharta. But there was no way Yudar would be able to control it. It was too big for him. It wouldn't just kill Darvad. It would destroy the entire battlefield, and then spread across the countryside.

"Stop him!" Keshan screamed from behind Jandu. Even Darvad seemed stunned. He stopped running.

Yudar finished speaking, breathless. The sky turned dark red. The ground shook under Jandu's feet.

And then the weapon set the sky on fire.

CHAPTER 59

AN EXPLOSION OF NOISE AND LIGHT SENT JANDU SPRAWLING
to the earth. He gasped for air as the sky roiled and burned.
Keshan rushed to Jandu's side, arms raised, speaking lowly.

Wind surged around Keshan's palms, driving the flames
back. Jandu, Abiyar, Darvad, they all watched flames roll out
around them as the Pezarisharta engulfed the battlefield. The
trees at the edge of the forest exploded like kindling.

Overhead, the air churned into a firestorm, spiraling like a
cyclone. Keshan trembled, hands stretched out. High-pitched wails
screamed in the sky, sounding as if all the Yashvas fuelling the
weapon were begging for the curse to stop. The sharta continued
outwards, setting fire to the Uru camp. The fence and tents ignited.
People trapped inside the camp shrieked and burned.

Yudar stood in the epicenter of the burning cyclone, his
face convulsed with wonder and horror.

"Jandu!" Keshan gasped. His body shook. "You have to
stop this! I don't have the strength."

Jandu knew he was right, but the only way he could save
them would be to kill the man who uttered the sharta, to kill his
brother.

Jandu crawled on the ground towards Yudar. The air
howled around them. Keshan followed behind him, shielding
Jandu from the fire.

Yudar trembled as he stared at the expanding cyclone of
fire. "What have I done?" Yudar whispered.

Jandu stood and locked his arm around his brother's neck,
clasping him close. Dry, scorching wind whipped around the
two of them. Dust flew in Jandu's eyes, making them water.

Yudar leaned into Jandu's embrace. His bottom lip quivered.
"I'm sorry."

Jandu's tears blurred his vision. He pulled his brother's head back. Yudar didn't struggle.

"Forgive me," Yudar choked out.

"I forgive you," Jandu said, his voice hoarse.

Jandu jerked Yudar's neck sideways and back, and felt it snap. Yudar's head lolled forward as he slumped to the ground, his body dropping like a sack of millet.

Keshan seized Jandu by the shoulders and yanked him down onto the ground. The frenzied air swept down upon Yudar's body. Jandu sank his fingers into the soil and gripped the mud. Wind screamed and flames seared down into Yudar's body, as the sharta retracted back to its source, burning it to ash. And then the sharta stamped itself out.

All that remained was the silence of death.

Jandu rose to his knees, surveying the field. Everything within a half mile radius had been scorched to charcoal. Jandu knelt by the smoking remains of his eldest brother, gripping his stomach. He didn't cry. He wasn't even sure if he was sad. All he felt an icy emptiness, leaving him cold and vacant.

Survivors stumbled at the edge the blackened battlefield. Jandu watched them distantly.

"Jandu stay down!" Keshan shoved him forward and then collapsed to the ground.

Jandu heard a low-pitched whistle and felt the thump of the arrow scratch across the back of his armor. He spun around, placing himself between his attacker and Keshan.

Darvad glared at him, his face wild, his eyes bloodshot. Blood ran down both arms. He looked as ferocious and demented as a demon of revenge.

"Jandu Paran!" Darvad screamed. His voice sent a shiver through Jandu's soul. It was inhuman. Darvad lifted his bow, aimed his arrow at Jandu's face.

Then Darvad grunted, his bow suddenly slack in his hand, the arrow dropping into the ground. Darvad crumpled to the earth. His face smacked into to the mud, an arrow buried deep into the back of his neck.

Behind Darvad, Abiyar stood, breathing heavily, holding his bow, face streaked with ash and tears.

"Good boy," Jandu said hoarsely.

Despite his tears, Abiyar smiled at him. "Thank you, King Jandu."

Jandu covered his face with his hands and wept.

CHAPTER SIXTY

FEW BODIES REMAINED TO BE CREMATED AFTER THE PEZARISHARTA.
Onshu and the other priests who oversaw the battle held a coronation ceremony at the edge of the field. Darvad was dead, killed by a Paran, therefore the Parans had won. And since Yudar and Baram died in battle, Jandu inherited the throne. Marhavad was his.

The priests poured holy water onto Jandu's hair, and they wrapped his neck in a garland representing all the lands of Prasta. Jandu endured the ceremonies silently. His body hurt in so many places, it all came together as one deep pain. Keshan stood by him, looking half-dead with exhaustion himself.

Of the eleven lords who had brought armies to Terashu Field, only three survived. Jandu's brother-in-law Rishak, Keshan's brother Iyestar, and Olan, the lord of Bandari, joined other hastily-appointed representatives from the other states to pay homage to their new king. They swore fealty and offered tokens—diamonds, rubies, gold armor, and horses—to show their allegiance. They did so somberly, most still stunned by the horrific end.

Soldiers, attendants and servants cheered loudly, exulting in both their own survival and Jandu's ascension to the throne.

After the ceremony, Iyestar hesitated before Keshan.

Jandu closed his eyes. "Keshan is no longer Jegora." He turned with a sigh to Onshu and nodded. "Preform the ceremony now."

Onshu stepped forward and chanted prayers over Keshan. It seemed interminable. Once Onshu declared Keshan's Triya status restored, Iyestar rushed forward and embraced Keshan, weeping loudly. All around them nobles, servants and soldiers renewed their cheer.

Jandu called his men to him. Anant, Lazro and Warash led them. They were ragged, most beaten and filthy, but they marched with pride. Jandu appointed them as his personal guard and distributed gold tokens and new weapons to them. They bowed before him, joy and relief illuminating their dirty faces.

Onshu chanted a prayer of peace and blessing for the new king. And the gathered throngs of Paran and Uru survivors joined him.

At the close of the ceremony, Jandu limped off with Keshan to the Paran camp. At once he was thronged by physicians. He let them rub salves into his wounds. He took a bath and threw up blood. He noted absentmindedly that the entire left side of his stomach was purple and bruised, injured internally from uttering so many shartas. He left Keshan in the physician's care.

When he found Baram's tent, white mourning flags hung from it. Inside, Suraya knelt in prayer. The moment she saw Jandu, she rushed to him. The two of them collapsed together on the rugs. With Suraya's tears egging him on, Jandu wept for Baram. He even wept for Yudar. He wept for everything the two of them lost, for all the sacrifices that had been made, to make a man who did not want the kingdom king.

"I miss Baram," Suraya cried. Jandu pulled her to him so tightly, he suddenly worried that he was hurting her. But Suraya clung with equal strength.

"Me too," Jandu said. He wiped his eyes. "But we have survived—you, me, Keshan…" Jandu touched her belly affectionately. "And Baram's son will be king one day."

Suraya smiled. "Or queen."

Jandu nodded. "It doesn't matter. Boy or girl, I'll love them."

He helped Suraya pack her belongings for the journey back to Prasta. He didn't know what else to do, or say. She had lost two husbands and her father in this war. He was relieved when her brother Rishak arrived, dressed in white mourning clothes, and took Suraya in his arms. For all that she had lost, Jandu was grateful that she still had family.

Outside, Jandu found Keshan, tending to the two stolen horses that had served them through the previous night. Keshan spoke to them tenderly as he washed their legs with a sponge. Keshan looked clean and refreshed, and wore Triya clothes once more. He smiled as Jandu approached.

Jandu did not smile back, but he brought his hands together in the sign of peace.

"Has anyone given you trouble?" Jandu asked. His own voice sounded distant, even to himself.

Keshan shook his head. Jandu reached out and placed his hand on the top of Keshan's head. Keshan's hair smelled like coconut; it was warm and clean.

Keshan closed his eyes and leaned towards Jandu. He swayed slightly on his feet, showing his exhaustion.

"Lie down with me," Jandu said softly.

"Of course."

Jandu led Keshan into Yudar's tent, back into the inner chamber. He fell asleep immediately, Keshan curled hotly in his arms.

In the morning, Jandu was awakened by Anant, who informed him that the armies were preparing to depart, but needed his orders. Jandu dressed and let Keshan sleep a little longer. He met briefly with the ministers and lords, officially releasing them from their duty to the battlefield. Jandu told them to return to their families, and then congregate in Prasta. They had a lot of work ahead of them, rebuilding the nation after so much strife.

By noon, the roads away from Terashu were crowded with caravans of carts, chariots, riders and people on foot. Jandu took one look at the lines of soldiers, merchants, craftsmen, servants, and priests heading back to Prasta, and made a decision.

"I do not want to return home in this procession."

The priests and surviving lords were surprised, but did not object.

"I will meet you all in Prasta," Jandu informed his lords and generals.

This was beyond all conventions, but Jandu had no doubt that by now they all knew he was unconventional. Already there were men who called him a prophet and to Jandu's surprise, several Draya priests were among them. Jandu left with Keshan and a small party of his bodyguards. For the most part, the guards gave them space, scouting ahead through the meadow and fields or riding far behind, keeping their distance. They seemed to understand that Jandu wanted time alone with Keshan.

They passed through fields overgrown with flowers and followed small roads that wove along the streams that fed the river. The farther they rode from Terashu field, the more lush, more fragrant the land grew. Vibrant green pastures and explosions of colorful wild flowers spilled out between groves of fruiting trees.

Jandu did not speak as they rode. He still felt a crippling numbness. He had wondered how a person stayed whole after a night like the close of battle. And now he feared that one did not remain whole. One was forever tainted. Even the beauty of the surrounding landscape did not soothe him.

As the sun hung heavy and hot above the horizon, they stopped to rest beside a tranquil, isolated lake. White cranes and small swallows watched them water their horses, and secure them under the shade of a nearby willow tree.

Keshan jauntily walked to the water's edge and unbuckled his sandals with the enthusiasm of a teenaged boy.
"Come on, let's bathe."

Jandu felt ancient. His feet dragged, his heart ached.

Keshan's warm, dry hand encircled his wrist. Keshan's eyes shone as he led Jandu to the water.

"You'll feel better when you're clean," Keshan said assuredly.

Jandu swallowed. "I feel like I'll kill anything I touch. The fish are doomed."

Keshan's mouth quirked into a smile, but his eyes stared at him, large and serious. "You have touched me more than anyone, Jandu. Am I dead?"

"No."

"Then trust me and get into the water." Keshan began to strip.

Jandu reluctantly removed his sandals and helmet. His arms felt leaden, his fingers clumsily untied the leather strings of his armor. As soon as his breastplate was off, every part of him felt lighter. He took off his shirt and unwound his dejaru. Its blood red color chilled him.

Keshan waited for him in the water. He stood, up to his waist in the lake, his dark skin glittering with droplets. He held out his hand, and Jandu walked towards him. He stepped slowly, sucking in his breath at the frigid crispness of the water. After the initial shock of cold, the water felt marvelous, refreshing in the late afternoon breezes that were still warm and hot on his dry skin.

Jandu's nerves revitalized in the deliciously cool water. Standing beside Keshan, he let the aches and knots of his muscles unwind.

Keshan plunged down under the water. A few seconds later he dramatically reemerged, sputtering and splashing and hooting, pushing his wet hair back from his forehead, grinning from ear to ear.

Keshan reached under the water and jerked Jandu's ankle. Jandu fell backwards into the water. He was engulfed in crisp renewal. He stayed submerged, blowing out air to sink further, letting the cool purity of the lake cover his battle-worn body.

He felt alive.

And that was all that mattered now. Life, in its chilling, surprising, glorious fullness. Jandu had survived. His body screamed it out with each second he held his breath. He was alive, and out of danger. He was free.

Finally, out of breath, Jandu shot out of the water and gasped for air. He had gotten turned around, and couldn't see Keshan.

Keshan snaked his long arms around Jandu's waist from behind. His hands rested protectively on Jandu's chest.

Jandu leaned back into the burning warmth of Keshan's body. Keshan rested his chin on Jandu's shoulder. They stood together, watching long reeds blowing in the hot wind.

"Feel better?" Keshan whispered.

Jandu's back vibrated with Keshan's words. Jandu turned slowly and wrapped his arms around Keshan as well. They held each other, their bodies pressed tightly together, cool water lapping at their waists.

"Yes." Jandu reached out and wiped a rivulet of water from Keshan's cheek.

Keshan smiled and squeezed Jandu tighter. Keshan leaned in and kissed Jandu with exquisite sweetness. When he pulled away, Jandu's body pressed forward, drawn for more.

"I am here, more alive and more whole than I have ever been, and all because of you, Jandu," Keshan whispered.

Jandu's mouth sought Keshan's once more, thrusting into the sweet, drunk warmth of Keshan's heat. Jandu's body thrummed as he felt Keshan's immediate arousal. It was so easy to see the signs of Keshan's love. Keshan's body loosened like warm butter, melting into Jandu's arms, gripping Jandu to him with a desperate desire.

"Never leave me," Keshan said huskily. His lips caressed Jandu's lips, his hips grinding Jandu's with mounting urgency.

"I won't." Jandu's voice was choked with emotion. He needed Keshan's heat enveloping him now, completely. "I love you. I will be with you forever."

"Forever," Keshan repeated solemnly. He pulled Jandu downwards, and then they were spiraling in the water, swimming, clinging to each other and laughing, sheer joy radiating from them. As they swam towards shore, Keshan's hands wandered over Jandu's naked body, stroking him and feeling inside of him, and every nerve tingled and screamed out for Jandu to let Keshan consume him now, whole, take him once and claim him forever.

Jandu pulled Keshan onto the soft, wet grasses of the bank and pulled Keshan on top of him. He cradled Keshan's head in his hands and kissed him, mouth open, spreading his legs wider in invitation. Keshan settled his weight between them, their cocks rubbing together, hot, delirious pulses of desire radiating upwards through Jandu's chest and arms.

Keshan ran his hand on Jandu's backside, cupping his bottom, and then fingered him, Jandu's skin slick and wet with the lake's water, easing Jandu's passage. Jandu arched upwards.

Keshan leaned down and slowly kissed Jandu's chest as he fingered him, his lips teasing Jandu's nipples, his stomach. He kissed Jandu's bruised side tenderly. Jandu lifted his legs higher. Keshan's fingers scissored inside of Jandu, and Jandu shivered. Keshan slowly pushed his engorged cock into him, kissing Jandu's sensitive neck at the same moment.

Jandu's skin stretched, the delicious sting of being filled so completely causing him to gasp. He was immobilized by the high heat of Keshan's cock. Jandu's senses swallowed in the smell and feel of him, the glorious intimacy of their connection. His scrotum and cock pressed against Keshan's hard stomach.

As Keshan slowly moved within him, Jandu rocked his hips, pulling Keshan deeper. Jandu lost his sense of time and place, drowned with the electric current of this warmth and affection, his body responding to Keshan's mounting thrusts.

Keshan pulled Jandu's legs onto his shoulders and pushed deeper. He reached forward with his hand and pumped Jandu's cock in time with his thrusts. A mounting explosion of ecstasy shattered through Jandu, it coursed out of his body in great, shuddering pulses.

Keshan didn't bother to be quiet. He moaned as he came, his climax throbbing inside of Jandu hotly. Keshan shook, his skin flush and hot to the touch. The water from their swim seemed to have evaporated in their heated lovemaking.

Keshan rested his head on Jandu's shoulder. Jandu liked the feeling of Keshan's cock retreating from within him. It was slow, soothing, and quiet.

"I love you," Keshan whispered.

"Good," Jandu said. "Because I think I'm going to be sore tomorrow, and it better have been worth it."

Keshan smiled lazily, his eyes closed. "We'll just have to do that more often. Then you won't be sore."

Jandu looked up at the sky. It was perfect, blue, not a cloud in sight. The silence, the sweet smell of berries and sex and Keshan filled his senses. "Where shall we do this more often? Prasta, or Tiwari?"

Keshan laughed. "So many choices. So many places to do it."

"Do you have a preference?" Jandu asked.

"No, Prasta is fine. I just want to be where you are." Keshan finally slipped from Jandu completely, and he rolled over, lying alongside him.

"Good," Jandu said. "Because I want you to be my Royal Judge."

"I know."

"You do, do you?" Jandu felt relieved to see such a smug expression on Keshan's face.

"Yes, last night I saw our futures, the elevation of Jegora, the public hospitals and schools, our many impressive nights of passion…" Keshan grinned. "You'll bring it all about."

Jandu stretched against the soft grasses. "Not just me. I'm going to rely on you. I want your vision of a new Marhavad, but you're going to have to help me. I can't do this alone."

"You won't be alone."

A warm wind blew over them, rustling the reeds.

"Am I still attractive in this future vision of me?" Jandu asked with a grin.

Keshan's eyes remained closed, but his mouth curved into a lazy smile. "Very. Although you are going to go gray prematurely."

Jandu sighed. "Well, at least I'll still have hair. What about you?"

Keshan laughed. "I still look magnificent."

"It wouldn't matter you know. I'd still love you even if you were bald and fat and wrinkled."

"I'll hold you to that."

The two of them lay on the bank of the lake and stared upwards. A smile played across Keshan's mouth, and he lazily closed his eyes and nuzzled his face into Jandu's neck.

Just then, a large sarus crane flew overhead. He blocked out the sun with his massive white wings, his red and black head looking down at Jandu and Keshan with vague interest. And with sudden, resounding volume, the crane sang out. From a distance, other cranes called back and the air was filled with music.

Jandu stroked Keshan's face, and the beauty of this moment, it became eternal. Death and life, the dejection of the spirit and the courage to triumph—all these timeless experiences and emotions, like pigment in oil, were encapsulated, preserved forever, in this one second of a life.

He was alive. Keshan was alive. And now they could begin.

CHARACTERS

Abiyar Lokesh: Third and youngest son of Indarel Lokesh, Lord of Afadi.

Ajani Alamar: Wife of Keshan Adaru

Anant Sarkumar: Commander in the Dragewan army

Azari: Pseudonym of Suraya Paria while hiding in Afadi

Baldur Tanaraf: Lord of the State of Penemar

Bandruban: Prophet of the Shentari faith

Baram Param: Second son of King Shandarvan by his first wife Kari; brother of Yudar and Jandu; husband of Suraya Paria

Bir Soridashen: Lord of the State of Jagu Mali

Bodan: Pseudonym of Baram Paran while hiding in Afadi

Chezek: Keshan Adaru's charioteer and servant

Darvad Uru: Son of King Shandarvan by his second wife Farashi; half-brother of Yudar, Baram, and Jandu

Druv Majeo: Lord of the State of Pagdesh

Esalas: Pseudonym of Yudar Paran while hiding in Afadi

Eshau: Abiyar Lokesh's weapons master

Farashi Uru: Second wife of King Shandarvan; mother of Darvad Uru

Firdaus Trinat: Lord of the State of Chandamar; brother of Hanu; father of Ishad

Hanu Trinat: Chandamar Ambassador in the State of Afadi; brother of Firdaus

Harami: Prophet of the Shentari faith

Indarel Lokesh: Lord of the State of Afadi; husband of Shali Amain; father of Ramad, Parik, Vaisha, and Abiyar

Inaud Adaru: Uncle of Iyestar and Keshan Adaru

Ishad Trinat: Lord of the State of Chandamar; son of Firdaus

Iyestar Adaru: Lord of the State of Tiwari; brother of Keshan Adaru

Janali: Pseudonym of Jandu Paran while hiding in Afadi

Jandu Paran: Third son of King Shandarvan by his first wide Kari; youngest brother of Yudar and Baram; husband of Suraya Paria

Kadal Kardef: Lord of the State of Marshav

Kari Paran: First wife of King Shandarvan; mother of Yudar, Baram, and Jandu

Keshan Adaru: Younger brother of Iyestar Adaru, Lord of Tiwari; husband of Ajani Alamar; cousin of the Parans

CHARACTERS

Koraz: Yashva demon of the forest

Laiu: Tarek Amia's servant

Lazro Arundan: Son of Tamarus Arundan; friend of Keshan Adaru

Linaz: Mother of Lord Iyestar and Keshan Adaru

Mazar Hamdi: Regent of Marhavad; weapons master to the princes of Marhavad

Mendraz: King of the Yashvas

Nadaru Paria: Lord of the State of Karuna; father of Rishak and Suraya

Ohendru: Chaya soldier in the Uru army

Olan Osasu: Lord of the State of Bandari

Onshu: High priest of Marhavad

Parik Lokesh: Second son of Indarel Lokesh, Lord of Afadi

Ramad Lokesh: Eldest son of Indarel Lokesh, Lord of Afadi

Rani: Servant in the Afadi palace; Janali's roommate

Rishak Paria: Son of Nadaru Paria, Lord of Karuna; brother of Suraya; brother-in-law of the Parans

Sadeshar: Prophet of the Shentari faith

Sahdin Ori: Lord of the State of Jezza

Satish: Tarek Amia's charioteer

Shali Amain: Wife of Indarel Lokesh, Lord of Afadi; mother of Ramad, Parik, Vaisha and Abiyar

Shandarvan: Former King of Marhavad; father of Darvad Uru, and Yudar, Baram, and Jandu Paran

Suraya Paria: Daughter of Nadaru Paria, Lord of Karuna; sister of Rishak; wife of Yudar, Baram, and Jandu Paran

Taivo: Prophet of the Shentari faith

Tamarus Arundan: Chaya spiritual leader and friend of Keshan Adaru

Tarek Amia: Lord of the State of Dragewan

Tarhandi: Prophet of the Shentari faith

Umia: Yashva demon consort of Mendraz, King of the Yashvas; aunt of Iyestar and Keshan Adaru

Vaisha Lokesh: Daughter of Indarel, Lord of Afadi

Warash: Chaya soldier in the Uru army

Yudar Paran: First son of King Shandarvan by his first wife Kari; brother of Jandu and Baram; husband of Suraya Paria; Royal Judge

Zandi: Yashva demon and Jandu's bow

GLOSSARY OF TERMS

Adri Mountain: Mountain in Pagdesh: location of holy retreat

Ajadusharta: Magical weapon; repels other weapons

Alazsharta: Magical weapon; knocks enemy unconscious

Ashari Forest: Forest outside Prasta; home to Yashva demon Koraz

Barunazsharta: Magical weapon; brilliant light

Chaya: Unskilled labor and servant caste of Marhavad; lowest caste

Dejaru: Long piece of cloth worn by men, either secured under a belt and sash and made into loose trousers, or tucked loosely and left long like a sarong

Draya: Priestly caste of Marhavad; second-highest caste

Fazsharta: Magical weapon; arrow with endless range

Hafedsharta: Magical weapon; freezes opponent

Harafa: Long piece of cloth worn either as a scarf or wrapped across the upper torso

Hedravan tree: Magical Yashva tree that grows in the Ashari Forest

Jegora: Untouchable caste of Marhavad; casteless

Korazsharta: Magical weapon; spear of unfailing accuracy

Manarisharta: Magical weapon; burst of electricity

Pezarisharta: Magical weapon; sets fire to the sky

Prasta: Capitol city of Marhavad

Rajiwasharta: Magical weapon; creates a sucking vortex

Rebo: Three stringed musical instrument

Sharta: Magical weapon; form of a Yashva demon in the human world

Shentari: Primary religion of Marhavad

Suya: Merchant and skilled labor caste of Marhavad; third-highest caste

Tarhisharta: Magical weapon; explosive wall of force

Terashu Field: Traditional battleground of Marvad kings

Triya: Warrior and king caste of Marhavad; highest caste

Tunufisharta: Magical weapon; burns any individual to ash

Yashva: Immortal demon from the Yashva Kingdom

Zahari: a blouse and long piece of fabric wrapped around the body to form a woman's dress

Zandisharta: Magical weapon; any instrument or tool of metal

ACKNOWLEDGMENTS

First I would like to thank Nicole and Dawn Kimberling for their constant encouragement, plot-storming, editing, and endless patience as I rewrote this story a dozen times.

I would also like to thank Maxx for letting me ignore him for weeks on end. Lastly, I want to thank my parents, who always believed I could write an epic novel. It's just too bad I'll never let them read this one.